WETZEL

Richard Fleming

Wetzel

This novel is a work of fiction. However, several names, descriptions, entities, and incidents included in the story are based on the lives of real people.

The opinions expressed by the author are not necessarily those of Tate Publishing, LLC.

Published by Tate Publishing & Enterprises, LLC
127 E. Trade Center Terrace | Mustang, Oklahoma 73064 USA
1.888.361.9473 | www.tatepublishing.com

Tate Publishing is committed to excellence in the publishing industry. The company reflects the philosophy established by the founders, based on Psalm 68:11,
"The Lord gave the word and great was the company of those who published it."

Cover design by Bill Francis Peralta
Interior design by Shieldon Alcasid

Published in the United States of America

ISBN: 978-1-68164-217-8
1. Fiction / Native American & Aboriginal
2. Fiction / Historical
15.09.04

To my late brother, Loren (Mike) Fleming, 1931–78, of Sibley, Iowa. He introduced Lewis Wetzel to me. He would have loved this book and could have written it himself, probably much better than I.

ACKNOWLEDGMENTS

I'VE HAD A great deal of help along the way in completing this work. There are too many names to mention, especially since some have been lost to me. I will mention a number of institutions, which provided invaluable assistance: Clarke Historical Library at Central Michigan University, Mt. Pleasant, Michigan; Central Michigan University Library; William L. Clements Library at the University of Michigan, Ann Arbor, Michigan; Columbus Metropolitan Library, Columbus, Ohio; Greene County Public Library, Xenia Branch, Xenia, Ohio; Lowe-Volk Park, Crestline, Ohio (Bill Fisher, director); Manuscripts Room at the National Library of Congress, Washington, DC; Morgan County Library, Waverly Branch, Waverly, Indiana; Public Library of Cincinnati and Hamilton County, Cincinnati, Ohio; Seaport Museum and Archives, Philadelphia, Pennsylvania; Shelby County Library, Shelbyville, Indiana; Dr. Earl Sloan Library, Zanesfield, Ohio; Toledo-Lucas County Library, Maumee Branch, Maumee, Ohio; West Virginia Archives and History Library, Charleston, West Virginia; Wheeling Room, Ohio County Public Library, Wheeling, West Virginia; Wisconsin State Historical Society Library and Archives, Madison, Wisconsin; WTNS Radio, Coshocton, Ohio (Ken Smailes, news director).

There are some names I must mention. The late Clark Wullenweber of Moundsville, West Virginia, was of great help to me. Clark drove me all over Marshall County in West Virginia, the county of the Wetzel homestead. He was a descendent of related families and his knowledge was unsurpassed. William (Bill) Hintzen is generally regarded as the foremost expert in Wetzel lore. An accomplished author and editor of the long-running periodical, *The True Wetzelian*, Bill endured many hours of telephone conversation with me and more than fifty letters. My brother-in-law, Arthur Lambart, of Grosse Ile, Michigan, read every chapter shortly after it was completed and offered comments and encouragement. The same is true of my daughter, Margaret Fleming, of Lancaster, California. Finally, I owe so much to my beautiful wife, Diane, who edited the manuscript and continued to provide excellent advice and much-needed encouragement.

The basic outline for some of the maps comes from: http://d-maps.com/carte.php?num_car=1700&lang=en

The maps were created by Dr. Robert Chaffer of Mount Pleasant, Michigan

CONTENTS

Foreword.......... 11
Preface.......... 17
Cast of Characters.......... 21
Prologue.......... 27

1 Captivity.......... 29
2 The Siege.......... 66
3 Transition.......... 116
4 Inauguration.......... 160
5 Militia.......... 201
6 Waging War.......... 234
7 A Bloody Year.......... 290
8 The Wedding.......... 338
9 Rescue.......... 364
10 Hunted.......... 399
11 Father.......... 432
12 Kentucky.......... 473
13 Logan.......... 517
14 Rewards.......... 558
15 Adventures.......... 603
16 George Washington.......... 635
17 Beaver Blockhouse.......... 683
18 New Orleans.......... 715
19 Prison.......... 747
20 Only in Heaven.......... 787

Epilogue.......... 837
Appendix.......... 841
Underbook.......... 841
Bibliography.......... 939

FOREWORD

WHAT REMAINS IN memory through life has a logic, although that logic is often so deep in a personality as to be a mystery as well as the source of identity. Why does a Professor of Mathematics return, in retirement, to a passage from a Zane Gray novel encountered in childhood? The story of Lew Wetzel that his brother read to Richard Fleming in childhood was the story of a frontier hero. There was enough of courage, strength and adventure to catch the imagination of a boy, and Fleming remembered the story, as many boys might. What is unusual is that he returned to it in later life with an unusual amount of intensity, seven years of research and writing. *Wetzel* is the result of that return, and it is a historical novel whose fiction rings truer than much academic history of the encounters between European settlers and the aboriginal inhabitants of North America.

Lew Wetzel was born in 1763 in Lancaster, Pennsylvania and moved near what is now Wheeling, West Virginia when he was about seven years old. The settlements on the Virginia side of the Ohio River were, in that period, the frontier of white settlement. During Wetzel's youth and early adulthood, the ground was contested. British forces and their Indian allies carried on low intensity war during the American Revolution; after 1783, British influence was reduced, the population of settlers increased, and the conflict continued as Indian tribes still attempted to defend their territories and white settlers, who had become Americans, sought to take them. Daniel Boone is famous as an explorer and guide for these settlers. Wetzel was a contemporary of Boone's, knew him, and apparently was as well-known as Boone in their time. Although he has not disappeared from the historical record, he is not well-known today, perhaps because of what he was famous for: he was famous for killing Indians.

That fact makes the work Fleming has done in recreating Wetzel's life significant. It is the most balanced portrait of frontier violence that I have ever encountered. Mid-twentieth century portrayals of Indians as obstacles to white happiness who often presented themselves as targets for John Wayne and his troops have been followed more recently by portraits in film, fiction, and academic work that portray the tribes as nicer than the whites who victimized them. In this version of American history, the political structure created by the United States Constitution did not derive from James Harrington's *Oceana* (1656): it was borrowed from the Iroquois. A student reading Lewis's account of scalps hanging from a lodge pole in a Mandan village announces that Lewis must have been mistaken; the Indians didn't take scalps. Lewis's account of the fight that he and three of his men had with four Blackfeet who tried to steal their guns and horses becomes a crime in which cruel and violent whites murdered two Indian teenagers. The shot that nearly killed Lewis is not mentioned. Custer's charge into Jeb Stuart's cavalry on the Third day of Gettysburg is subsumed in the broad range of genocidal actions by whites who attempted to destroy the cultures of aboriginal peoples in the United States. Custer deserved to die. By this revision of the national history, Lew Wetzel would have deserved to die at the hands of the Indians he attacked as well; certainly he is not a suitable model for a young boy who wishes to be a hero.

Wetzel will not be many people's hero after they read *Wetzel.* He killed many people, was sought out to do so, did so willingly, and did so with calm efficiency. He was jailed repeatedly during his life, but Wetzel is part of a complex history. Some of the people he killed were also, by all of the evidence available to deal with the question, cruel and brutal men. One of his shootings, although not fatal, was indefensible in his own day. Yet his story belongs in our history in as close to a factually accurate telling as is possible because his behavior and the behavior of the people around him, aboriginal and white, mirrors human reality and the role of violence in that reality. Not bad Indians, good whites. Not good Indians, bad whites, but mixtures of good and evil in the people who faced off on both sides of the frontier conflicts. For fundamental anthropological reasons, the Indians were bound to lose the contest for their territories. One of the important causes was disease. But social organization, technology, and demographics were absolute. The outcome was, at least until recently, continuing and tragic loss for the tribes, but they defended their lands with courage and skill and, because they were people engaging in what is now called asymmetrical warfare, often with ruthless violence. Thus the center of Wetzel's life was fighting, and *Wetzel* the book about his life, is a history of the decades of warfare between Indians and whites who fought for control of what is now the state of Ohio.

That Fleming is not an historian, is not attached to a university history department, strikes me as a strength of his book. A biography, as non-fiction, would not have the formal structure of *Wetzel* which is based on a fictional stalking of Wetzel by an Indian seeking revenge for an earlier injury. Several episodes created by Fleming to enlarge our sense of Wetzel's character would have to disappear. But Fleming is a serious and careful researcher and equally careful and transparent in his handling of his sources. In an appendix that he calls the "Underbook," he describes very concisely what the sources available to him are and how he has used them. Some are primary, documents available in various archives and libraries. Some are secondary, local histories of towns and counties that collect accounts from individuals. These range from first to third hand reports about what happened in various places and incidents. Fleming is careful to assess the plausibility of these accounts and, where they differ, to explain his decisions. This is historical fiction, but it is an admirable effort to make clear what really happened in cases where there is enough evidence to do so.

The repeated accounts of ambush and slaughter can, in most cases, be substantiated with good evidence. Indians and whites lived alongside or near each other. Accidental encounters produced death. Typically, a party, Indian or white, would surprise and attack a party of the enemy, Indian or white, if they saw them first, were not detected themselves, and could surprise and overwhelm their victims. Wetzel was himself kidnapped in such an attack as a child. He escaped. As an adult he lost a brother and his father in such ambushes. Most of the Indians he killed fell in similar attacks by him and his parties. This was guerilla warfare that is reminiscent of turf warfare in big city gangs or of tribal conflicts in the Middle East. It was brutal. The description of the three day ceremony by which the Shawnee burned to death the first prisoner they captured each year stands alongside the hacking to death of more than a dozen captives by white militia. It was bloody stuff.

That Wetzel was successful at killing and managed to stay alive while doing so made him famous. Fleming's character is a good shot, knows how to navigate in the woods, can run and walk very fast, understands the tactics and values of his enemy, is calm in the face of combat, even combat that is not going well, and has a rigid sense of personal honor. This portrait is plausible on the facts that Fleming is able to assemble in his research; he is not as nice as Cooper's Chingachgook. He is as a literary type, more like Homer's Odysseus. If you are his enemy, he kills you. As a human type in contemporary culture, we would not live next door to him because he would be in jail.

Reading this history, thinking about the violence that is its defining feature, I come back to Richard Fleming's dedication of the book to his brother, who died young. I don't think that it was a fascination with violence that led Fleming to remember this story that his brother read to him when he was seven. I think it is the memory of his brother reading to him that took him back to the story that his brother, whom he loved, read to him. In seeking out the story of Lew Wetzel, a skilled killer, and, incidentally, an important chunk of American history, he remembers and honors his brother.

Peter Koper, Professor of English Language and Literature (Emeritus), Central Michigan University, Mount Pleasant, Michigan

PREFACE

> With loud yells of triumph, the band jumped upon him. There was a convulsive, heaving motion of the struggling mass, one frightful cry of agony, and then hoarse commands. Three of the braves ran to their packs, from which they took cords of buckskin. So exceedingly powerful was the hunter that six Indians were required to hold him while the others tied his hands and feet. Then with grunts and chuckles of satisfaction, they threw him into a corner of the cabin. Two of the braves had been hurt in the brief struggle, one having a badly wrenched shoulder and the other a broken arm. So much for the hunter's power in that single moment of action.

THESE WORDS, WRITTEN by Zane Grey in his novel *The Spirit of the Border*, brought wonder and excitement to me as a young boy. My older brother, Mike, called me into our shared bedroom one evening when I was about seven and read that passage to me. When he told me that the hero in this story, Lewis Wetzel, was a real person, it struck a chord in me that has persisted to this day. The desire to know more about this man has been with me, though on a back burner, for most of my life.

When I retired seven years ago from my position as a professor of mathematics, I began the work, which has culminated in this novel. Lewis Wetzel, who was first thought of as a hero and defender of his people, as famous as Daniel Boone according to some, evolved as the years passed into a person regarded by modern historians as, at best, a rogue and, at worst, a murderer. The hero of Zane Grey's novel was magnificent and mysterious, referred to by the Indians as *le Vent de la Mort*, "the Wind of Death," or *Atelang*, "Deathwind."

Although I wanted to very much, I could never find convincing evidence that Wetzel was known to the Indians by this name. A driving force in Wetzel's life was to kill Indians—not an admirable quality. Yet it must be remembered that he was a man of his times. For twenty years, from 1774 to 1794, a vicious war raged between the woodland Indians living mostly in the modern state of Ohio and the settlers in western Pennsylvania, western Virginia, and Kentucky. There were plenty of atrocities on both sides. The Native Americans were fighting to preserve their lands and their way of life. The whites were looking for places to build homes and provide a livelihood for themselves and their families.

Although they did win some major battles against white armies, the Indians were outnumbered and outgunned, which led them to adopt fighting tactics that infuriated their enemies. Most families that built cabins in the border regions suffered attacks that resulted in deaths and captivity, and victims included men, women, and children. Here is what their neighbors had to say about the Wetzels in a petition addressed to the Virginia legislature: "Your petitioners further state, that it is well-known to the whole country where they live, that their father and his sons during the period of Indian warfare aforesaid, rendered more service and protection of the frontier than any family that ever lived on it and more to their private detriment."

My goal was to tell the story of a part of Lew Wetzel's life, beginning when he was almost fourteen and ending twenty-four years later. Finding the truth about such a life is not easy. There is very little in the official records and so we depend on the words of early—mostly amateur—historians, on legends, on family stories, and on recollections of people who may have been speaking forty or fifty years after the events they are trying to describe. My effort must thus be described as historical fiction, and although I have tried to remain as close to the truth as possible, I have also inserted pure fiction in order to help move the story along.

At the end, you will find what I am calling an underbook. Here I try to tell you what is true and what is fiction, and you will find a discussion of some of the events and my reasons for telling the story a certain way. There are references to a fairly extensive bibliography for those interested in finding out more of the story. I have tried to be accurate with my accounts of actual historical events, but I realize the difficulty in this. My recommendation would be to read the novel in its entirety before consulting the underbook, but that is a matter of personal taste.

I want to say a few words about the language in the text. I have included some bad grammar and light profanity in order to remind the reader that the characters are mostly rough and uneducated. I realize that their actual language was no doubt much worse and much more profane. In my opinion, this becomes annoying to the modern reader, so I have tamed it down considerably. When the Native Americans speak, I assume they are speaking correctly in their own languages.

Cast of Characters

Wetzel Family

Lewis Wetzel		
Captain John Wetzel	Father	(Killed in 1786)
Mary Bonnett Wetzel	Mother	
Martin Wetzel	Older brother	
Christiana Wetzel Wolf	Older sister	
George Wetzel	Older brother	(Killed in 1782)
Jacob Wetzel	Younger brother	
Susannah Wetzel Goodrich	Younger sister	
John Wetzel, Jr.	Younger brother	

Bonnett Family

Lewis Bonnett	Father and brother of Mary Wetzel
Elizabeth Bonnett	Mother
Lewis Bonnett, Jr.	Son and later source of information
Four others not featured	

Grandstaff Family

Adam Grandstaff	Father	(Killed in 1787)
Catherine Wetzel Grandstaff	Mother	Niece of John Wetzel)
Lewis Grandstaff	Oldest son	
Jacob Grandstaff	Son	(Killed in 1777)
Four others not featured		

Zane Family

Ebenezer Zane	Founder of Wheeling	
Elizabeth McColloch Zane	Wife	
Noah Zane	Son	
Jonathan Zane	Brother	
Andrew Zane	Brother	
Isaac Zane	Brother	(Lived with Wyandots)
Betty Zane	Sister and heroine of Ft. Henry	

Pioneers of Historical Prominence

David Bradford	Involved in Whiskey Rebellion
Samuel Brady	Virginia Ranger
Daniel Boone	Kentucky leader
Lydia Boggs Shepherd Cruger	Wife of Moses Shepherd
Simon Kenton	Leader in settlement of Kentucky
David Shepherd	Ohio County Lieutenant and legislator
Moses Shepherd	David's son and later political leader

Other Pioneers

Henry Baker	Friend of Lew Wetzel
Billy Boggs	Friend of Lew Wetzel, brother of Lydia
John Boggs	Settler and Commander at Ft. Henry
Josh Davis	Companion and chronicler of Wetzel
Veach Dickerson	Frequent companion of Lew Wetzel

Henry Jolly	Neighbor and chronicler of Wetzel
Hamilton Kerr	Friend of Wetzel family
Henry Lee	Lieutenant of Mason County Kentucky
John Leith	Indian trader
Jacob Link	Neighbor of the Wetzels
John McColloch	Settler and militia leader
Sam McColloch	Made a famous leap to safety
James McMechen	Physician and Ohio County leader
John Madison	Cousin of President James Madison
Sam Mason	Militia leader and outlaw
Jacob Miller	Frequent companion of Lewis Wetzel
Isaac Williams	Settler and friend to the Wetzels

Prominent Military Leaders

Colonel Daniel Brodhead	Commander at Fort Pitt
Major Ebenezer Denny	Aide to General Harmar
General Josiah Harmar	Commander of first federal army
General Benjamin Logan	Kentucky militia commander
General Anthony Wayne	Commander, Battle of Fallen Timbers

Prominent Native American Leaders

Little Turtle	Miami war chief
Blue Jacket	Shawnee war chief
Half-King	Wyandot war chief
Moluntha	Shawnee chief, murdered by McGary
(Captain) Pipe	Delaware chief
Wingenund	Delaware chief

Buckongehelas	Delaware chief
Black Fish (Little King)	Wyandot leader, captured L. Wetzel

Fictional Characters

Little Fox	Chippewa warrior
White Eagle	Delaware warrior
Red Storm	Delaware warrior
Fire Heart	Shawnee warrior
Pierre Le Clerk	French trader

Overall view

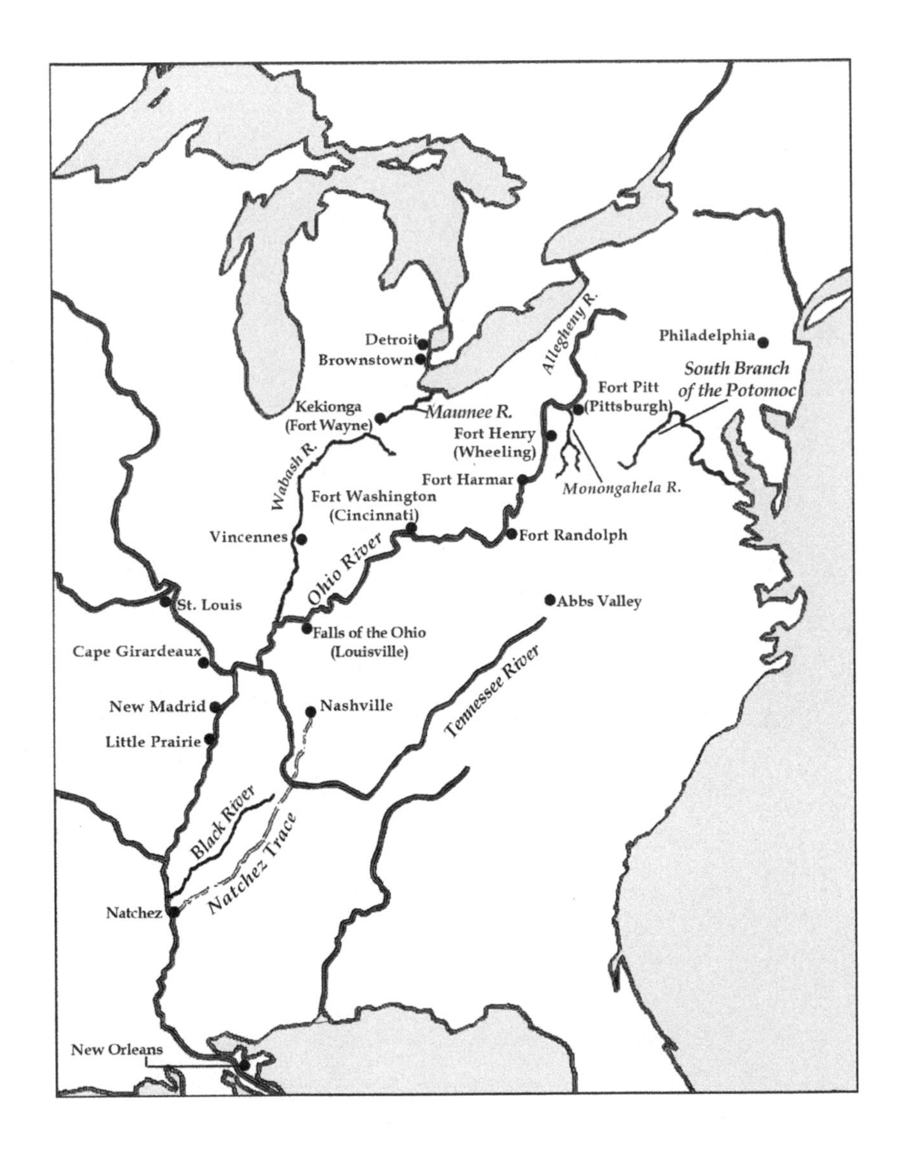

PROLOGUE

August 15, 1804

THE TWO MEN sat quietly on the front porch, each lost in his own thoughts. The younger of the two was feeling quite proud of himself for having located the cabin where the famous hunter was living. It was a long trip from the upper Ohio to this spot on the Black River some distance up from Natchez. Even more gratifying was the reception he had received when he had finally arrived. He had been warned about coming up too quickly and unannounced. "Halloo," he had offered cautiously. "I am Benjamin Wells."

"Ah," said Wetzel, stepping from behind a tree several feet from the front of the porch. "I thought you looked like a Wells."

Wells stood where he was, struck by the suddenness at which Wetzel had appeared, but also speechless in the presence of this man of whom he had heard so much. He couldn't help but stare at the hunter's long black hair, whose ends stretched below his waist. "Your daddy is Absalom?"

"Yeah, that's right."

"A good friend," Wetzel had declared. "What brings you out here?"

"I had some business down this way."

"There ain't much business out here, I reckon."

"I was comin' back from New Orleans, and I was told you were out here somewhere. You're a famous man, Mr. Wetzel."

"Ugh," grunted Wetzel. "You've wasted your time, but it is good to see somebody from home. And the name is Lew."

Wetzel came forward now and put his left hand on young Wells's shoulder then shook hands with his right. "I bet you could use somethin' to eat. Let's go inside." And so the two had settled in comfortably, and Wells had stayed for several days. Now as they sat together, Wells thought about the wonderful stories he had managed to get out of Wetzel. He had heard some of them before, of course, but to hear them from the actual source, well, that was exciting.

His reverie was interrupted by a quick movement beside him. "Stay here," was the command. Wetzel bounded down the porch steps and grabbed his long rifle that was leaning against the rail. He disappeared among the trees between the cabin and the river. Wells strained to see what was happening. He thought he could see a flash of Wetzel's back as he slipped down toward the river, but there was no sound. Far to the left, through a small gap in the tree line, he caught sight of something on the river. It appeared to be a small canoe with two occupants. Then it slid out of sight again. He moved to the corner of the porch, not sure what he should do.

Obviously, Wetzel had sensed some danger. The sharp report of the rifle from the shore of the river reinforced the young man's fear. He moved to the steps and down into the edge of the woods. He could barely see the canoe spinning slowly in the river's current, the body of an Indian slumped over the side. In the river, the dead man's companion was holding on to the back end of the canoe, trying to pull it closer to the far bank. He tried to keep his head out of sight, but the current caused the canoe to twist just enough to expose him. The rifleman was ready, and the second shot also found its mark. The second Indian's hand released its hold, and its owner slipped lifelessly into the stream. Still at the edge of the woods trying to see, Wells finally saw the canoe drifting downstream with its lifeless cargo.

In a few minutes, Wetzel came up from the riverbank and stepped into the clearing. He had not attempted to recover the bodies nor to scalp them, which Wells knew to be his custom. "It will be best if you don't tell nobody about this," said Wetzel. "Times ain't quite the same as they used to be."

1

CAPTIVITY

August 8, 1777

OLD JOHN WETZEL leaned on his hoe, brushing the sweat from his forehead with the back of his hand. It was only midmorning but already hot. In the distance, he could see the smoke curling toward the sky above his family's cabin, although the cabin itself was obscured by the lay of the land and the tall stalks of corn in the intervening fields. His sixteen-year-old son, George, toiled only a short distance away, and the older man rested with a warm glow of satisfaction.

Life is good, he thought, *God is in His heaven.* The thought of God brought a brief feeling of guilt. He knew that he did little in this life to show any kind of reverence for God. Still he considered himself a Christian, a Lutheran, he supposed. There was an old family Bible someplace. He was sure the family had one when he was a boy. Wetzel's parents had emigrated from Germany in 1731, only two years prior to his own birth in Pennsylvania. They had moved to Maryland and then to Virginia with the Bonnett family and there, in 1756, John had married Mary Bonnett. In the next year, their first child, Martin, joined the family. There followed, like clockwork, Christiana, George, Lewis, Jacob, and Susannah, each born two years apart, until after a couple of family moves, a son John was born in 1770 on a tributary of the Monongahela called Dunkard Creek.

Not long after that, Wetzel, along with Lewis Bonnett and nine other men, had come west to Wheeling Creek. The Zanes had preceded them, however, and Ebenezer Zane, with brothers Jonathan and Silas, had claimed the land along the creek from its mouth at the Ohio to the forks about six miles above. When the Bonnett and Wetzel party had arrived, the men had to make their claims above the forks. With first choice, Bonnett had settled a short ways up the main creek, and Wetzel had eventually chosen a spot some seven miles above the forks. In the next year, they brought their families out to the new lands.

Mary Wetzel, when she first saw the Wetzel claim, had asked if it was wise to be at the far end of the line of settlers. But her husband had assured her that the Indians wouldn't come up that far but would come to the other cabins first. He admitted to himself now that his assurance to her wasn't quite true, but so far there had been no hostile raiding along this part of Wheeling Creek. Indeed, there had been mostly peace along the entire border country, except for the brief interlude of Dunmore's War in which both he and his oldest son, Martin, had served. Until the last few months, of course. Indian raids had become more numerous, and the settlers knew why. Ever since the colonies had become rebellious, the British had been urging the tribes to take action against the Americans.

Back in April, a family had been attacked with the husband killed and the wife and three children burned up on the Ohio across from Yellow Creek. A man, whose name he thought was McBride, had been murdered and mutilated very close to the fort at Wheeling. Then he had heard of an attack up the Allegheny above Fort Pitt where the Indians had left a letter addressed to the inhabitants, threatening them unless they remained loyal. The letter, he was pretty sure, had been signed by the British devil, Hamilton, in Detroit, and it confirmed the suspicions of all the border men that the Indian aggravations were being incited by the English. A new round of attacks had broken out, not only along the Ohio but over on Dunkard Creek, which was on the other side of his place.

When his neighbor David Shepherd, the newly appointed county lieutenant and the owner of a blockhouse at the forks of the Wheeling, which everybody called Shepherd's Fort, told him of warnings that had come to the authorities at Fort Pitt, he decided it was time to take his family to safety. By that time, some of his neighbors had fled to Shepherd's Fort: his brother-in-law Lewis Bonnett and his family, for one, and, he thought, the Grandstaffs, Messers, and Stroups had gone as well. He had resisted forting up, as it was called, because it meant taking animals and possessions into a crowded enclosure that wasn't really big enough to hold everybody. It had rankled him to have to put up with the assault on his senses that came with being bottled up so closely with so many relatives and friends.

Yet, as his wife, Mary, had quickly pointed out, such discomfort was much preferable to being murdered in his bed by the red savages. He had given some thought to taking refuge at Wheeling since the fort there was much larger, but in the end, they had stopped at Shepherd's Fort since it was closer to the homestead. Just two days earlier, he had come back to the home cabin with three of his boys, intent on planting a small patch of turnips. They had brought the three plow horses with them to break up the hard ground. It wasn't quite the right time to be planting turnips really, but the year had been a hard one, and he thought they might at least be able to grow enough to have some greens to feed the livestock, if nothing else.

Early this morning, he had been lucky enough to shoot a small buck, and after skinning it, he had cut it into strips for jerking and hung it to dry over a small fire in the fireplace. After working for awhile in the turnip field, he thought it necessary to check on the fire, partly because there was an old dog at the cabin with some new pups, and he was worried that she might take a liking to the hanging venison strips. So he sent Lewis and Jacob back to the cabin to check. As an afterthought, he suggested that they should bring his and George's rifles back with them.

"Crack!" The sharp retort of a rifle from the direction of the cabin jolted his consciousness and sent a tremor of fear through his body. "Oh God, George!" he cried. "The boys, the boys."

Lewis Wetzel had welcomed his father's instructions to go back to the cabin, not just because it relieved him from very hard and disagreeable work, but because it meant a few minutes of freedom to run through the grass with his little brother Jacob on a hot but beautiful day. Plus, he was looking forward to carrying the big guns back out to the field, for he loved the feel of a gun in his arms. He and Jacob, who was just a month shy of his twelfth birthday, were good buddies, and they enjoyed being together.

Lewis, who, himself, was nearing his fourteenth year, led his brother down toward the creek bank. "Let's go along the creek, Jake," he said. "It'll be cooler." Of course this was not the most direct way back, and he half expected to hear a shout from his father commanding them to quit playing around and do what he told them. But the old man was talking to George and did not seem to notice their detour along the water. It was tempting to go into the water, but Lew knew better than to get his father's unwanted attention. So they sauntered along, stopping to skip a few rocks into the shallow stream. After finally making it to the cabin, they both went inside to check the fire.

"It's kind of low, Lew," observed Jacob.

"Yeah. There's some sticks just outside the door."

"Wait. Did you hear something?"

"Yeah," said Lewis. "I think it's Injuns! They might grab you!"

With that, Lewis jumped and caught hold of Jacob, wrapping him up in a tight bear hug.

"Stop it, Lew. What are you trying to do?"

"Just to scare you a little, Jake. Besides, we saw no sign of nothin' as we came up. Don't be so skittish."

Still, as he let Jacob go and started out the door, Lew felt himself being cautious. As he came out on the step, something caused him to turn sideways. The sound of the shot was almost simultaneous with the searing pain in his chest as the bullet tore through the front of his shirt and shaved splinters from the breastbone. Wetzel could not breathe nor think, and he dropped to the ground. Somehow he managed to struggle to his feet. A low moan escaped his lips. He had no idea from where the shot had come, but the thought of grabbing his father's gun, which leaned against the cabin wall on the far side of the door, did briefly surface in his mind.

As the confusion began to clear, he gave up that idea and began to run back toward the little milkshed to the south and west of the house. When two Indian warriors stepped out from the corner of the shed, Wetzel turned back to the southeast where a cornfield lay in the flatland next to the creek. If he could get across the creek, he might be able to get away. Another large brave appeared at the other corner of the house, and as he started to reach for Lewis, Jacob came charging out of the door that was behind Lewis now, and the distraction allowed him to slip past and head for the corn. Jacob screamed and tried to run, but the three braves were immediately upon him and held him fast. Lewis heard Jacob's scream, but he couldn't look back, and he was aware that the Indians were in hot pursuit. Lewis Wetzel was a fast runner, but he was only a boy and had no real chance against a strong adult Indian warrior. Still he managed to reach the edge of the corn when he slipped and fell headlong into the little valley between the rows. His wound was bleeding profusely and he felt faint, but he tried to struggle to his feet.

It was then that he felt the strong arm curl around his waist and pull him upright. He was caught. The Indian grunted in triumph, and Lewis stifled a cry. In spite of his pain and his fright, he had heard enough talk from the old hunters to know that how the warriors viewed his behavior might mean the difference between life and death. He was now dragged, not gently, by his captor and a companion back toward the main cabin. He looked for his brother and saw him backed against the wall of the house with a large brave next to him. Jacob was fighting back the tears for he also knew the danger in appearing too frightened. There were seven braves in all, Wyandots, as Wetzel was to learn later.

Although he was to eventually become expert in discriminating between members of different tribes, he was currently ignorant of such things. Even though the presence of hostile Indians was a constant with the border families, Lewis had never really been around one before this. There was an excited chatter among the Indians, and though he could understand none of the words, it was easy to spot the leader. The others called him by a name, but Wetzel could not really make it out. The Indian leader was rather small in stature, but the manner in which he carried himself indicated that he expected the others to do what he said. There was a lot of pointing and gesturing, and both Lewis and Jacob came to understand that they were not in immediate danger of being killed. There was clear approval of the way in which Lewis was handling the pain of his wound, and the leader made the boys understand that they were to be taken along as captives. It was common for the Indians to take prisoners for possible adoption, especially if they thought the captives had potential to make good warriors.

After a search inside the cabin, three of the braves came out with blankets and other assorted items. Another had gathered the three plow horses. Still another, whose name sounded something like Kilarni to the boys, had removed some bark from a pouch and, after chewing it for a bit, made from it a poultice, which he applied to the bleeding wound on Lewis's chest. It wasn't long until the bleeding subsided, and the braves seemed to be satisfied that the boy was not too seriously injured. The Indians seemed to be uninterested in the venison strips curing above the fire. The group now lined up in preparation for leaving, putting the boys in single file with a warrior in front of them and one behind. Just then, a tall Indian came around the corner of the cabin with a small puppy in his hand and a big smile on his face. He came to Jacob and handed him the dog, but Jacob threw it down. When this was repeated a second time, the brave slapped Jacob hard on the side of his face and handed him the dog again. Lewis whispered something quickly to Jacob, and as a result, Jacob accepted the pup with a look of heavy disgust. He was determined to get rid of the dog at the earliest opportunity.

Out in the field, filled with grief, John and George Wetzel cursed themselves for having left their guns at the cabin.

"Let's cross the creek, George," said John Wetzel. "If we climb the hill on the other side, we may be able to see what's happening."

Scrambling up the hill through the trees and bushes, and now on the south side of the river, the two of them felt relieved when they saw that the boys were still alive. They watched silently as the Indians, with the boys, horses, guns, and other booty, moved out toward the west and south, on opposite side of the fields from where they stood. Without weapons of any kind, the two men were completely helpless.

"Let's try to get back to Shepherd's."

"Yes, Pa," replied George. "Do you think they saw us?"

"I doubt it. Otherwise they'd 'uv come after us, since there were so many of 'em."

As they began to move down the hill, the elder Wetzel was trying to decide how best to get back to Shepherd's Fort. They couldn't go along the creek, as that would put them on the wrong side of the war party. They would have to swing around to the north and go through the woods and hills.

"'Course, if they've been watching the house for a time, they would know we was somewhere close. They might not know whether we had guns with us."

"Yeah, I was thinking they may have been watching us. How many do you think there was?"

"I counted seven."

"Maybe there are more. Maybe they are out here with us," suggested George with a tremor of fear in his voice.

"I don't think so. We can't worry about it. We've got to get to the fort as fast as we can. Let's stay up here for a bit and cross the creek farther to the north." John Wetzel realized, though, that no matter what they did, it was unlikely to help his two young boys.

"I'm afraid they are lost to us," he couldn't help uttering aloud.

"I know," said George.

The Indians moved out in a single line with the obvious man in charge leading the way and riding one of the horses. The Wetzel boys, who liked to have names for everything, soon began to refer to him as Little King. Behind him was another horseman, then two more on foot, then came Jacob Wetzel carrying the puppy, a fifth Indian, followed by Lewis and Kilarni, who continued to stay close to the wounded Lewis. The seventh brave brought up the rear, riding the third horse.

They kept the pastures and fields of the Wetzel farm on their left and moved along the low side of the hill, which bordered the farm on the upper side. After a half mile or so, the hill began to curve in toward the creek as it turned sharply to the south before beginning a wide curve back toward the north and up toward the forks where lay Shepherd's little fort. They moved quickly, and as they came to the sharp turn in Wheeling Creek, they angled across the neck of the loop and down to the bank of the creek on the other side, where they prepared to cross.

Little King, still mounted on the plow horse, stood aside as the others crossed the shallow creek in line. Jacob Wetzel was still holding fast to the tiny dog, which he realized now was not moving. In his fear and tension, he saw that he had held the dog's head so tightly against his body and under his arm that he had smothered it, and the puppy was dead. He felt bad, but he tossed the body into the stream as he crossed. The brave behind him, the one who had brought the puppy out in the first place, jumped aside and retrieved the lifeless form from the water.

Upon understanding now that the pup was dead, he gave a shout and lunged at Jacob, giving him a savage push. Jacob fell headlong into the stream, but struggled quickly to his feet, moving ahead in a hurry. No one else seemed to pay much attention. Lewis had seen his brother pushed down, and although his first impulse was to strike out at the brave ahead of him, he felt the hand of Kilarni grasp his arm. Coupled with the pain and weakness he was enduring, it was enough to prevent him from some foolish act. The far bank of the stream opened into a grassy clearing, and the party stopped there for a brief rest. The Wetzel brothers fell to the ground and managed to get close enough to each other for a few whispered words between them.

"Lew, can you make it?" inquired Jacob.

"It hurts bad, Jake, but I can't let them see."

At this point, the Indian Kilarni, who had paid so much attention to Lewis, kneeled in front of them and indicated that he wanted Lewis to remove his hunting shirt. The wounded breast had begun to bleed again, and Kilarni again produced the bark from which he had first dressed the wound. He handed a piece of it to Jacob and urged him to put it in his mouth and chew it. Jacob at first refused, but the Indian insisted, and finally Jacob plopped it in his mouth and began to chew. He now recognized what it was; the bark of the tree the settlers called slippery elm.

After a short time, he spit it out into the hands of Kilarni, who loosened the rawhide band he had fastened around Lewis's chest to hold the original poultice in place. The newly chewed bark was added, and the band put back. As Jacob helped Lew to put the shirt back on, he leaned over and said, "It's slippery elm bark, Lew. It don't taste too good."

The hint of a smile graced the pain-stricken face of the older brother. "We'll call him Slippery Elm," he said, indicating their benefactor. Lewis noticed the tall Indian who had pushed Jacob, watching them with a look of fierce disapproval. As the warrior rose and took a step toward them, Lewis spoke quietly to Jacob without looking at him. "We've got to be careful about talking too much. They don't like it."

As a punctuation to that timely remark, the tall brave moved between them and pushed the brothers roughly apart. Though his words were not understandable, there was no question about their meaning.

"You'd better watch out, Dog Man," muttered Lewis under his breath, though he knew there was nothing he could do to back up such a threat. Slippery Elm appeared again, speaking sharply to the Dog Man. Then he offered the boys a drink of water, which they drank greedily. The brothers wondered about the reason for the kindness being shown to them by Slippery Elm. They noticed that he was now in an earnest discussion with Little King, and there were frequent looks over to where Lewis Wetzel was reclining. Shortly, Slippery Elm led one of the horses back to where Lewis, who had regained his feet, was waiting. He indicated that Lewis was to get on the horse's back, and with the help of the disgruntled Dog Man, this was done, and Slippery Elm was helped up to sit behind Wetzel. Lewis leaned low over the horse's neck and held on tight. He would have never asked for this great favor.

However, he was extremely grateful to this Indian captor for relieving him from what might have been an impossible trek through the woods and hills that lay between them and the Ohio River. The group moved out again, this time with Little King leading on foot, since he had given up his ride to Wetzel and

Slippery Elm. They moved in a southwesterly direction along a little path that led into the woods ahead of them. There were high wooded hills to be crossed now, and the going was difficult. Even in his low state of alertness, Lewis noticed that braves had moved out some distance on either side of the trail. Little King was taking no chances of being surprised on the flank by some white hunter or hunters who might be out in this area.

The horse carrying Lewis and Slippery Elm followed directly behind Little King, then another horseman, Jacob, Dog Man, and the final rider at the back. By midafternoon, they had reached the edge of another small creek, flowing to the west toward the Ohio. Lewis was sore from the jostling he was taking from the horse but still glad he was not so exhausted from the hard walking. It was clear to him that some of the Wyandots did not think he should be riding. He supposed that was why Little King had given up his own mount. He expected one of them to knock him off his perch at any moment.

Of course they would have had to deal with Slippery Elm first. It was dawning on Wetzel that Slippery Elm meant to adopt him, provided that he continued to remain in his favor. He knew that Indians did one of two things with their prisoners, and adoption was the choice he favored. But before that, it was likely that the boys would have to endure a torture of some kind. He looked back at Jacob, trudging along with Dog Man poking him with his tomahawk whenever he stumbled or held back. Their eyes met briefly and knowingly. Escape was never far from their thoughts, but they knew it would have to be done together if in the unlikely event it could be done at all.

Little King did not stop at the creek side but moved out into the stream, and the entire party followed. The purpose was to conceal their trail, but Wetzel figured that anybody following would have no trouble guessing their intentions. They hoped to cross the big river to relative safety as soon as possible. The ground on the other side of the Ohio from Virginia and Pennsylvania was supposedly off-limits to the white settlers, and though hunters did venture across, it was known to be extremely dangerous.

Two more hours slid by when the leader moved to the north bank and motioned for the followers to do the same. A broad grassy area came down to the creek at this point, and an open trail extended for some distance ahead. It was much easier going now, for the rocky creek bed was not easy on the feet. It was also clear that not far ahead, the gurgling creek would reach its destination at the banks of the mighty Ohio. After a short time, the party came to a halt. Every change in procedure brought new anxieties to the Wetzel brothers, who knew that their lives might be snuffed out in a flash if the red men sensed some danger. In this instance, their fears were quickly assuaged when they saw the two scouts from the flanks who had come in and were now working at a clump of bushes and fallen branches to retrieve two canoes they had obviously hidden there earlier.

It was only a few yards from here to the mouth of the creek. Preparations were made to cross the big river. Lewis Wetzel and his adopted bodyguard were helped from the horse and put into one of the canoes while Jacob and Dog Man were placed in the second. The two canoes, with four occupants each, were taken out into the Ohio, and the seventh brave, still mounted and leading the other two horses, followed along behind. Lewis was unsure about where they were when they began to cross but knew it was some distance below Wheeling. It might have been Little Grave Creek that they had come down, and if so, the Tomlinson settlement and fort were just a little farther south. His captors remained tense and alert, but the crossing was carried out with no interference, and Wetzel's brief hopes of possible rescue were soon dashed.

It was sometime past noon when John and George Wetzel arrived at the front gate of Shepherd's Fort. John was sure that they had been observed from inside the fort, but as yet, no one had appeared to open the gate.

"Hey, in the fort. Open the gate! It's John Wetzel."

In a short time, the gate swung open, and young Lewis Grandstaff stood there. "Uncle John!" exclaimed Lewis. "Hello, George. What's happened?"

"Injuns got my boys," reported John Wetzel as he pushed past the astonished Grandstaff and into the fort itself.

"They got Lew and Jacob," echoed George. "We think they might have been Wyandots. They was seven of 'um."

Several people had begun gathering in the open area, curious about the commotion, and beginning to realize that something tragic had happened. A woman rushed from the blockhouse, and the cluster of onlookers stepped aside for her. Mary Bonnett Wetzel ran toward her husband who had stopped and watched as she saw him for the first time. A look of curious anguish filled her face.

"John, John," she cried as she collapsed in his arms. "Where are my boys?"

"They're gone, Mary," said her husband, stifling a sob of his own. "The Wyandots have got 'em, but they are alive. They're alive!"

They were joined by a young woman who had followed Mary Wetzel from the cabin. It was their eighteen-year-old daughter, Christiana, who put her arms around her mother, helping to hold her upright.

"What is it, Pa? What has happened?"

"It's those red niggers, Christiana. They've carried off Lew and Jake."

Mary Wetzel let out a cry and began sobbing, no longer trying to hold back.

"Oh, Mother," cried Christiana, beginning to tear up herself. She pulled her mother close and tried to comfort her.

Through her tears, Mary managed a fearful question.

"Will they kill them, John?"

"They might, but I doubt it," answered John more truthfully than diplomatically. "They maybe intend on adoption."

"No, John. They will kill them! Oh God!"

"Now, Mary, if they wanted to kill them, they'd have done it on the spot. Get hold of yourself, my love. This has happened to lots of families. There's a good chance we'll get them back."

This last statement was made with much more confidence than John Wetzel actually felt.

"Why, all the Zane boys were captured once, and they all came back," he continued.

"All except Isaac," Mary managed to get out between sobs.

"Well, that was mostly his own choice."

The collection of people surrounding this scene now opened again, and a good-looking, dignified, but somewhat portly man walked through. This was Colonel David Shepherd, the owner of the land and the stockade where they now stood. Just this past June, Shepherd had been appointed as the Ohio County lieutenant, which meant he was the chief administrative officer of the county and in charge of its military operations. In that capacity, his headquarters were at Fort Henry in Wheeling. He was taking a few days away, however, and had left Captain Samuel Mason in temporary charge there.

"Here's Colonel Shepherd," said one of the bystanders.

"Hello, David," was the greeting from John Wetzel.

"John, they told me about Lewis and Jacob. How did it happen?"

Shepherd was well aware of the increase in Indian incidents along the border, as he was in frequent correspondence with authorities at Fort Pitt. There had been some rumors of a major Indian push against Fort Henry itself, and he wondered if this raid was somehow part of something bigger.

"George and me were out in the field. I sent Lew and Jake in to check on the venison strips curing over the fire. We heard a shot, and by the time we got to where we could see the house, the devils had the boys, the horses, and my guns and were ready to head home. Damn, if we only had our guns with us!"

"Could you see how many there were? Was it just a small war party?"

"I counted seven of them, David. I think it was just a hit-and-run war party. We hadn't seen no Indian sign at all before. I don't know if they had been watchin' us, or if they just happened on the place while the boys was there."

"Could you tell anything about 'em. What tribe?"

"I ain't sure, but I think they was Wyandots."

"Which way did they go?"

"They was headed to the Ohio, no question about that. We came around to the north to get here. David, give me some men, and we'll go after 'em."

"I can't let you take anybody from here, John. The only militia we've got is at Fort Henry."

Adam Grandstaff, who had been listening to the talk between Shepherd and Wetzel, stepped forward.

"We can come with you, John," he offered. "Lewis and I can come along, and we can get a couple more."

"No!" said Shepherd forcefully. "I won't allow it. We may need all of you to defend this place before all this is over."

"I'll go to Fort Henry and get help from there," said John. "But I've got to hurry. They've already got a big head start."

"John, by the time you got back to your house to pick up the trail, it would be hopeless to ever catch up," argued Shepherd.

"I won't do that. Maybe we can pick up the trail at the place where they cross the Ohio. They're bound to do it somewhere below Wheeling. I'm going to Wheeling now. Take care of my family, David, will you? And thanks for the offer, Adam."

"I'll get you a horse," said Grandstaff.

After a quick farewell to his wife and daughter, John spoke quickly to his son.

"George, take care of your mother 'til I get back."

With that, John Wetzel mounted the horse that had been quickly brought up and galloped out the front gate.

Safely across the Ohio, the war party with the Wetzel boys in tow, had sunk the canoes in a shallow pool near the mouth of another small creek and struck off on a narrow trail toward the west. There was a certain urgency to their movements, and they seemed eager to get away quickly from the Ohio River shore.

Lewis Wetzel was no longer riding but, along with Jacob, was being prodded to move with some speed. The pain from his injured breast had subsided a little during the canoe trip across the river but now had returned with more vigorous activity. He wanted to cry out against it but continued to keep silent, not only because he feared the response of his captors, but because of his own belief in how a man should handle his difficulties. He tried to remember some of his father's efforts to teach him to be a good woodsman, and in particular, the constant admonition to be alert to the conditions around him.

A feeling of dread came over him as he realized they were now on Indian grounds. There were no white settlements in the Ohio country, as it was referred to on the border. French and British traders came there certainly, and on some occasions, groups of white men in hot pursuit of an Indian raiding party such as this one. It was for this reason, no doubt, that Little King was eager to get his small band deep into the Ohio lands as soon as possible. Wetzel began to wonder which of the seven braves had shot him. His natural desire for revenge flared up, and he thought he should try to find out in case an opportunity for reprisal came up. Not all of the warriors had guns. Little King carried one, and perhaps it was he who had fired the shot.

When they had taken his shirt off, Lewis had noticed a second hole near the armpit, which meant there might have been a second shooter. The big brave who had caught Lewis in the cornfield also carried a rifle, and Lewis thought there was another gun or two among them. And, of course, they now also had the guns that belonged to John and George Wetzel. There was no way he would ever be sure which one was responsible for his agony, Lewis concluded. And what difference did it make anyway. They were all enemies, and if the chance came to do them harm, he would take it. As young as he was, his body was beginning to develop into the strong, powerful form it would soon become, and he truly felt that if the opportunity came, he was capable of making good use of it.

The sun was dropping behind the western hills in a burst of glowing red when Little King finally called a halt. The path was a bit wider here, and Wetzel could see signs that this place had been used as a campsite before. He guessed that they were several miles inland from the Ohio. The boys were made to stand against a tall maple at the edge of the small open area, and Dog Man was assigned to keep watch while the others went about setting up camp. No fire was built.

As they found places to sit, Slippery Elm slipped into the woods on the far side and returned, carrying a deerskin pouch, which he held in front of each of his companions. There were grunts of satisfaction and a quiet chatter as he made his rounds. Finally he came to where the boys sat, slumped against the tree. Jacob, in spite of the uneasy feeling he couldn't shake, realized that he was quite hungry. Slippery Elm pushed the pouch toward him and smiled. "Eat," he commanded with one of the few English words he apparently knew. The pouch contained cracklings, strips of venison from which the tallow had been fried out. As Jacob began to reach in, something caught his eye. Something was moving among the strips.

"Maggots!" was Jacob's cry, and he jerked his hand back.

On their way into the settlements, the Indians had left the pouch hanging high on a tree limb, out of the reach of animals, and available for their use on the return trip. In the hot weather, the contents had become infested. Slippery Elm persisted.

"Eat," he said again, offering the cracklings once more.

"No! No! No!" shouted Jacob vigorously, and he slumped back against the tree.

This outburst provided great amusement to the Indians, who laughed and pointed at Jacob. Nothing they said, however, was understandable to the brothers. Lewis was also offered this sustenance, but in his misery he felt no hunger, and it was of no difficulty for him to decline the offer. Slippery Elm turned away with a shrug, but in a few minutes he returned with some wild lettuce, which Jacob received and found to be tastier than he expected. It was sweeter than the lettuce he had eaten at home. He ate it with increasing gusto and finally reached over to give some to his brother.

"Squaw salad," he said. "Eat some, it ain't bad."

Refusing at first, Lewis finally put a few of the leaves in his mouth, determined not to like it. Surprisingly, it was somewhat refreshing to his dry mouth, and he ate. "Yeah, squaw salad," he agreed.

It was past the midway point in the afternoon when John Wetzel came within sight of Fort Henry, perched on the bluff, overlooking the big river. He had traveled along the well-beaten trail that followed along the Wheeling Creek (and that would, in the next century, be part of what was called the National Road.) The trail, hugging the creek for a ways, made its way up the hill, which overlooked a sharp U-turn in the creek, before descending gently onto the plateau just to the east of the fort. It was here that several settlers' cabins had been built, and below them to the east and south, fields of corn stretched down to the creek bank. The creek itself, coming out of the sharp turn, flowed south before turning to the west and emptying into the Ohio.

Wetzel pushed his mount past the cabins and up to the main gate on the east side. A militiaman, posted on the corner bastion on the northeast, had alerted the people inside that a white man was approaching, and another, who was in charge of the gate, swung it open. As Wetzel rode inside, someone shouted, "It's John Wetzel."

That announcement brought activity in one of the barracks built along the stockade wall. A young frontiersman bolted out the door and ran toward Wetzel, who had slipped down from the sweaty horse's back.

"Pa," exclaimed Martin Wetzel as he ran toward his father. "What are you doing here?"

Martin was the oldest of John Wetzel's seven children and was posted at Fort Henry with a volunteer company of militia. Now twenty years old, he had served with his father three years earlier in Lord Dunmore's War. He was noticeably shorter than his father but possessed the same husky body shape that promised strength and endurance. He got along well with his father, and the two men now hugged affectionately as they came together.

"The Wyandots has got Lewis and Jacob, Martin, and they're headed across the Ohio," explained John. "I want to go after the rascals right now. Who's in charge here?"

"God!" exclaimed Martin. "When did this happen?" he continued, ignoring his father's question.

"Martin!" came the explosion from the father. "Who's in charge?"

"It's Sam Mason, Pa. He's in the commander's house."

Without another word, the two men strode swiftly toward the headquarters cabin, although the elder Wetzel was muttering bitterly to himself. He was not fond of Mason, who was rumored to have had difficulties staying out of jail before he had come to the frontier. In spite of his reputation, Mason had exhibited enough leadership qualities to have been chosen to be a captain of a militia company. The two Wetzels found him seated at a small desk facing the door.

Captain Mason was a good-sized man, rugged, but not handsome. He had a crude manner and was not generally friendly.

"So it's you, Wetzel," he said without smiling. "I heard the commotion when you rode in. What do you want?"

"The Injuns carried off my two boys, Lewis and Jacob."

He could not bring himself to address Mason by his formal title.

"I want some men to go with me to chase the bastards."

"Tell me how it happened," demanded Mason.

John Wetzel felt the rage rising within him, and he struggled to give an answer in an even tone. All the way from Shepherd's Fort, a seething anger had built up in him until he was ready to strike out uncontrollably. The fact that he felt himself responsible for leaving his boys vulnerable made it worse. Once again he recounted the events at the farm, and he knew that his voice had an edge to it that showed his irritation. His son Martin was also hearing this for the first time. When he had finished the account, he once more made his urgent request.

"Let me have some men to go after them."

"No, I can't do that, John. We don't have people to spare to go on some wild-goose chase."

"The hell, you don't!" shouted Wetzel, who could no longer contain himself. "You son of a bitch!"

Mason jumped from his chair, and his right hand felt for the knife handle at his belt. "Watch out who you're calling a son of a bitch, John Wetzel!"

Wetzel stepped back a bit, and Martin, who had watched this scene unfold with increasing anxiety, tentatively reached out to grab his father's arm. He knew this could get very ugly. He didn't want to act against his own father, but he knew what kind of wicked temper Mason had and that there was no way to know what he might do. But the momentary wild look on Mason's face suddenly softened, and he sat down again in the chair.

"I'll overlook this," he said quietly. "I'd be the same as you if it was my kids in the hands of them savages. But it would be a useless chase, Wetzel. By the time you could get back to pick up the trail, you would be a day behind."

"We won't go back to the farm. We know they got to cross the Ohio somewhere below here. We'll pick up the trail at the crossing point."

"I think that would be impossible," said the captain. "Besides, we've been warned of a possible attack on the fort here, and this may be the beginning of that. I'm responsible for all these people here."

Martin Wetzel thought that Mason made a lot of sense, but he didn't feel he could argue with his father while he was in such a state.

Unnoticed by the three of them, another person had entered the room. He was a slender man, taller than the average, with wide shoulders and big arms and hands. His face was long and narrow but exuded strength. His blue eyes showed a softer side and hinted at wisdom and good humor. It was Jonathan Zane, the younger brother of Ebenezer, considered the founder of Wheeling. Jonathan had accompanied his brother when they first came to the area. He was well respected by all who knew him, including John Wetzel.

"He's right, John," interjected Zane, throwing a knowing glance at Martin Wetzel. "There are many places they might have crossed, and we would never be able to find it in time to do any good."

"Damn it to hell," said John Wetzel. "How can I sit here and do nothing?"

"They'll not kill them, John," continued Zane. "They're good boys, and the reds will want to adopt them."

"They'd be better off dead," declared John, but he turned away with resignation. "It's all my fault. If only George and me had taken our rifles with us. Oh God!"

"It's not your fault, Pa," said Martin as he put his arm around his father's shoulder. "You did all you could."

"Martin's right," offered Jonathan Zane.

"What will I tell Mother?" asked the elder Wetzel.

The meal had ended in the Indian camp, and as darkness had surrounded them, preparations were made for sleeping. The Wetzel boys were made to take off their shoes, which were taken away and out of their sight. The warrior they were calling Dog Man appeared with a pair of rawhide cords. Pushing the boys down to a prone position, he wrapped a cord around each boy's wrists, then around the waist, and through the belt loops of the pants. Lying down between them, Dog Man attached a cord to each of his own wrists so that any sudden movement on the part of one of them would instantly arouse him from sleep.

The friendly Slippery Elm situated himself next to Lewis on the opposite side from Dog Man while a third brave was lying on the other side of Jacob. The cautious captors were making sure there would be no escape, and they were also guarding against any surprise from possible pursuers. As they all settled in, one man was assigned to stay awake and on guard. He sat with his back against the big maple on the edge of the camp.

Lewis lay as still as he could, filled with the realization that he would find it difficult to sleep. The pain in his chest was sharp. Nothing more had been done to dress it, and in the darkness and stillness that now enveloped them, it was hard for Lewis to think of any thing else. There had been little opportunity to talk with Jacob, and now there was none at all. Escape was clearly impossible on this night. He wanted desperately to be able to move, to roll over on his side, or to move in any way possible to relieve the pain. Just the idea that he couldn't move at all was itself enough to unsettle him until he was impelled to just cry out as loud as he could. But he must not! He had to hold it within.

The night was clear, and in his agony he could see the stars shining through the openings among the leafy branches above him. He searched for the moon but could not see any sign of it from his limited vantage point. The sounds of sleeping men were around him everywhere. Both Slippery Elm and Dog Man were soundly asleep, and he allowed himself a quiet whisper.

"Jake, are you awake?"

There was no answer and he assumed now that his little brother had been able to do what he could not. In the darkness, he could barely make out the guard at the tree, and he could see that the man was slumped forward. They were all asleep. If only he could get free of these bonds. But the cord was tight, and Lewis had no strength. He slumped back against the hard ground. Would this night ever end?

Wetzel came awake suddenly as he was being shaken by Dog Man. He was surprised to find that the little glade was alive with light and even more surprised to realize that he had actually been asleep. Dog Man had brought him to a sitting position and was looking steadily into his eyes. Now the Indian tilted his head and looked closely at the side of Wetzel's face.

"Ugh," he grunted and pointed at the smallpox scars, as if he had not noticed them before. He said something to one of his comrades who came over to look for himself. Lewis could see that this brave had apparently suffered the same fate as he, since the warrior's own face was well pocked. Smallpox was a major scourge on the border, and it had hit the Indian tribes even harder than the whites. Wetzel had survived his bout with the disease when he was much younger.

Now the second brave turned away, and Dog Man continued to untie the cords so that both Lewis and Jacob could get to their feet. He pointed to a clump of bushes behind them, obviously believing they would need to relieve themselves. As they moved off, Lewis felt again the sharp pains along his breastbone, but he also noted that the Indian guard, standing now by the tree, was watching them closely. When they returned, the boys were met by Slippery Elm, who had some water for them along with a handful of the wild lettuce. They both drank and ate eagerly, glad for even such a paltry meal as the squaw salad. It wasn't long before the group was ready to move out.

Dog Man had returned with their shoes and demanded that they put them on quickly. Soon they were all on the move again with the morning sun at their backs. One warrior stayed well behind and off the trail, making sure they were not being followed. Lewis and Jacob had no time to talk to each other, and although their fear of being killed had abated, they remained tense. The travel was hard, the day passed by uneventfully, and late in the afternoon, as the sun was dropping ahead of them, the leader, Little King, called a halt at the banks of yet another creek.

Lewis Wetzel had no idea where they were, but he noted that the unknown creek was flowing in—what seemed to him, anyway—a northerly direction. In fact, it was the stream later called Wills Creek by the white men, and it emptied into the Muskingum River not too many miles farther along. There was a much lighter mood around the camp on this evening as the Indians no longer feared being surprised by a search party. They soon set about building a fire and in a short time, two of the braves returned from downstream with three small fish. They were soon cooked but none was offered to the prisoners, whose mouths had been watering at the smell of this delightful dish coming from the fire. Instead, they again ate the "squaw salad" and wondered what was to come.

Slippery Elm came to them after supper and was gesturing excitedly toward the northwest. He was trying to tell them something, pointing to the sky behind them and then in the opposite direction. Lewis understood the word *Goshackgunk*, which he knew was an important Indian village on the Muskingum River, which the white settlers referred to as Coshocton. The English word *Delaware* was also mentioned. Lewis surmised that Slippery Elm was trying to tell him that sometime tomorrow morning they would reach one of the principal Delaware towns. A stab of fear went through him, for he knew that when prisoners were brought into a significant town, they would be forced to run the gauntlet. He had heard this activity described in detail in discussions at Shepherd's Fort by a French trader who had witnessed more than one.

Wetzel knew that there were three possible results from running the gauntlet, and two of them were very bad. In the first place, the gauntlet runner could be killed by blows received as he ran. Even if the runner were to reach the end safely, if he did so in a way judged to be cowardly, he might still be put to death. The third outcome was to get through the lines successfully and be adopted by a tribesman.

The Wyandots would be proud of their captives and might try to ease the painful encounter to some extent, but they would also be bragging about the bravery of these two boys and would be quick to turn if the conduct was less than brave. The pain in his chest was forever with him, and he tried to imagine what would happen as he tried to run between two lines of screaming savages swinging clubs at him. They must try to escape this very night. The captors were paying much less attention to the boys as they prepared for the night's slumber, and Lewis was able to edge close enough to Jacob for a short conversation.

"Jake, we've got to get away tonight. They're not watching us as much as before."

"But Lew, how can we do it?"

"Watch it," said Lewis suddenly. "Dog Man is looking at us."

Holding a hand over his wound, Lewis lay back on the ground and whispered quietly, "I ain't sure, but we've got to do it somehow."

The other braves were sitting around the campfire, laughing and telling stories as darkness settled in. Dog Man came over to the boys, again carrying the cords to bind them. As on the previous night, their shoes had been removed and hidden, and Dog Man tied them in the same way as before, though not quite as tightly, Lewis noticed. Also, he had not bothered to tie their hands.

Before long, the Indians had found places to lie down, with one left on guard near the fire. Lewis noted that the firearms had been stacked near the fire, including the two taken from his parents' cabin. He and Jacob were wedged between three braves in the same way as the night before. Though he tried to shut it out, his wound seemed to hurt even more on this evening, and it was beginning to fester. He felt sick and weak, and he began to think it might be better to just accept things the way they were. He was probably going to die anyway.

The night was clear, and the stars seemed even brighter than ever, he thought. Lewis was anxious, and it seemed that his captors would never get to sleep. He began to shake his earlier defeatist thoughts and tried to anticipate the action that it would take to get free. He wanted to move now, but he knew he must be patient. Patience was hard, and though in later life it would be one of his trademarks, it was not easy for him now. He looked over the sleeping Dog Man next to him and tried to make out whether Jacob was awake. Poor Jake, still a month away from his twelfth birthday. *How can he help with this?* wondered Lewis. *Hell, I'm not quite fourteen yet myself*, he thought. *There's no way this will work.*

In spite of his mood and the discomfort he felt, Wetzel had a tenacity and confidence in himself that won out now in this internal argument. He thought again of what might await them, and he returned to his vigil, waiting for everyone to fall asleep. Finally, the one on guard dipped his head against his chest and his heavy breathing satisfied Wetzel that it was safe to try to talk to Jacob.

"Jake," he whispered softly, hoping not to disturb the sleeping Dog Man. "Are you awake?"

"Yes," came the soft reply. "I ain't tied too tight, Lew, but I can't see how to get loose."

Dog Man stirred briefly, and both boys held their breath. When he settled back again, Lewis offered a suggestion. "See if you can slip out of your pants."

The cords passed around their waists and through the belt loops of their pants, with the ends tied beneath the sleeping braves on either side. As Jacob began trying to squirm out of his pants, he jerked the cord enough to awaken the guard on his side. The warrior awoke with a start, and he cried out loudly enough to awaken the others. He grabbed Jacob, who had raised himself to a sitting position. Somehow, in his terrible fright, Jacob managed to calm himself and with gestures, conveyed to his captor that he was thirsty and needed some water.

"No!" shouted the angry brave. Pushing Jacob back to the ground, he tightened the cords and lay down again.

After another interminable wait, all were asleep once more, and the boys resumed their attempts to free themselves. Jacob's bonds were now too tight, and he could do nothing. With extreme care, however, Lewis managed to loosen his pants enough that he could wriggle out of them. Urging Jacob to lie quietly, he saw that Dog Man's knife was in a position that was accessible, and he slipped it carefully from its sheath. Immediately he was filled with the urge to drive the blade home into the chest of the man he had come to despise. Instead, he moved around behind Jacob's head, and reaching forward over his body, he managed to slide the knife between Jacob and the Indian next to him, cutting the cord as close to Jacob's side as he could. It wasn't easy, and it took more time than either boy thought could be endured, but eventually it was done.

As Jacob eased himself up and out, Lewis returned to free his own pants from the tether. Clutching them to him, he quickly moved to the edge of the camp and into the trees with Jacob close behind. They were free and their spirits soared.

"Let's get out of here fast," whispered Jacob. He took several quick steps toward the trail they had followed the day before. Lewis followed but then stopped.

"Lew, what are you doing? Let's run."

"Wait a minute, Jake," cautioned Lew. "We ain't got no shoes. We need something on our feet."

Lewis moved back to the edge of the camp and watched for a moment. There was no sign of any movement, but his eye caught sight of the moccasins that had been hung up to dry over the fire. "We need to get those moccasins," said Lewis. "You wait here behind one of these trees. If you hear anything, you take off running and don't ever look back."

"No, Lew," pleaded Jacob. "Let's just go. We can go barefoot."

"Do as I say." With that, Lewis crept away around the tree past the sleeping guard and to the campfire.

In the dim light, he could see each of the sleeping braves, and satisfied that they were out, he quickly grabbed two pairs of the drying moccasins and bounded away. Jacob, thinking he had heard some movement, had run deeper into the woods, but now he saw that it was his brother coming with the treasured moccasins. The moccasins were stiff, however, and they could not get them on.

"We'll need to dip them in the stream," said Lew. "But we'd better go a ways first."

Finally, thought Jacob to himself. But now he saw that Lewis was looking back at the camp again.

"What is it Lew? Are they coming?"

"Wait here again," said Lewis. "I want those guns."

"What guns?" asked Jacob. "We don't need no guns."

"They've got Pa's gun and George's. I think I can get them."

"Lew, forget it. I'm scared, and I want to go now."

"Go on a ways and wait. I'll be there in a minute."

Again the older Wetzel brother moved back to the camp and eased himself up to where the guns had been placed. He recognized George's gun immediately and lifted it away from the stack. Then he saw that his father's rifle had slipped down and was lying next to a slumbering Indian, with the stock almost under his head. As he tried to slide the gun away, the sleeping brave stirred. Lewis looked around in a quick panic, cursing himself for having insisted on getting the damned guns. But the sleeper actually turned a bit, freeing up the gunstock, and Lewis snatched it up swiftly, bounding away with a gun in each hand. The guns were heavy, and he had to avoid snagging them on anything as he rushed out of the clearing and into some safety behind the trees. Now he turned and hurried up the trail where his brother waited breathlessly.

"You got 'em!" exclaimed Jacob. "You got 'em."

"Yes," said Lewis with pride. "Now let's make tracks!"

Hurrying down the trail for some distance, they slowed and made their way to the creek bank, where Lewis directed Jacob to soak the stiff moccasins briefly in the cool water.

"Let's see if we can get 'em on now," said Lewis.

After a bit of struggle, both boys were shod, and they again ran back along the trail they had traveled the previous day. They stopped again and listened carefully, straining to hear any movement or sign from the Indian camp that their escape had been discovered. Hearing nothing, they began to move again, when suddenly they heard a sharp yell coming from the camp. A stab of fear shot through both boys, and they looked anxiously at each other. "We best get off this trail," said Lewis. "I think they'll wait until light to follow us, but we can't take no chances."

He thought it might be an hour or two yet before dawn, and he led Jacob off to the left of the trail into the dense woods and brambles. It was very hard going, and by the time the first rays of light were filtering through the branches, both of them were exhausted. Lewis felt particularly weak, and his chest felt like it was on fire. He flopped down with his back against a small tree. "I've got to rest a minute, Jake," he uttered in a low voice.

"Yeah," agreed Jacob. "Me too."

They were silent for a few minutes, breathing heavily, too tired to even think.

"How far are we from the trail do you think, Lew?" asked Jacob finally.

"I don't know," said Lewis after another moment. "Prob'ly not far enough."

"It's so hard trying to walk through here, though, Lew. Maybe we should go back to the trail."

"It's too dangerous. They'll come along there, and they can move lots faster than we can."

"But I don't think we can make it through this brush. And we don't even know where we are going." Jacob was near to breaking out in tears in spite of himself.

"Well, you're right about that," agreed Lewis. "I ain't feeling so good, and it would be easier for me."

They were silent for a bit longer, and then Lewis struggled to his feet.

"All right," he said. "Well, swing back toward the trail and see if there is any sign of 'em."

It took a while, but eventually, after following a long arc back to what Lewis figured was the southeast, they again approached the well-worn trail.

"Stop!" ordered Lewis. "Do you hear anything?"

They listened for several seconds, but no sound came to them. Now they approached the trail slowly.

"Look!" said Lewis quietly and suddenly. He pointed to a clear horse footprint in some soft ground at the edge of the path.

"It's shod," continued the older brother. "It's one of Pa's horses." Shortly they found other prints and quickly assessed the situation.

"There's two of 'em on horseback already past here and headed toward the Ohio," observed Lewis, now excited. "We've got to get away from here. They could come back along here any minute."

"Let's go!" said Jacob, who needed no convincing.

Once again they scrambled off toward the north and east, anxious to get as far into the brushy woodland as possible. Their only thought now was to put as much distance between them and possible pursuit as they could. Forgotten for a while was the difficulty of the terrain, exhaustion, pain, and hunger. They continued for more than an hour before giving out and falling to the ground, completely used up.

They were lying in a clump of trees near the base of a high hill.

"God, I'm hungry," said Jacob, whose breathing had at last returned to normal.

"Me, too." Lewis was battling a dizziness that prevented him from sitting up. *Food would surely help this dizzy feeling*, he thought. But they had absolutely nothing.

"Even some of that squaw salad would taste mighty good," continued Jacob, who searched his pockets.

He felt something and realized it was one last piece of the slippery elm bark that their Indian friend had provided. He remembered now his brother's injury and how it must be hurting him something awful.

"I've got a piece of the slippery elm," he said now to Lewis. "Do you want me to chew it up and put it on your wound?"

"No, but keep it. I might need it tonight. Are there any berry bushes around here?"

Jacob spent several minutes looking around the area before coming back to where his brother was lying. "Nothing," he said dejectedly. "I don't see nothing to eat anywhere. What are we going to do?"

"Help me up, Jake," requested Lewis. Standing somewhat unsteadily, he pointed to the sun, shining brightly through an opening in the leafy canopy above them. "I reckon it's about noon. We've got to keep moving to the east. If we do that, were bound to hit the big river somewhere."

"Yeah," said Jacob, "and we got to climb that big hill to do it."

They moved out again, climbing the hill and struggling on beyond. By nightfall, they had found a large hollow standing tree, and they decided to spend the night lying in its base. Though fear of pursuit had subsided, both boys were overcome with exhaustion and hunger. Lewis was in more pain than at any time previously, and Jacob chewed the last piece of bark, placing it on his brother's angry, festering wound. Eventually, both had drifted off into sleep, obtaining much-needed relief at last.

August 10, 1777

Jacob was the first to come awake the next morning, awakened by a splash of sunshine that found its way to the base of the tree where he lay. Confused at first, his mind then grasped their predicament. He remembered that they were free and then that he was ravenously hungry. The sound of his brother's labored breathing came to him, and he worried now if Lewis would be able to go on.

Jacob had no idea of where they were, although Lewis had seemed to think that the distance to the Ohio River could not be great. He thought about looking around for something they could eat, but he did not want to go far. The realization that they were still on the Indian grounds was a sudden and unwelcome thought. Even in Lewis's weakened condition, Jacob felt some comfort in his presence, for he had great respect for his brother's strength and ability. He moved cautiously out from the shelter of the hollow tree.

Looking around in all directions, Jacob had a brief hope that he might find some of the wild lettuce that they had eaten while in captivity. He saw nothing at first, but then he saw some tiny shoots at the base of a small bush. He broke two of them off and put them gingerly into his mouth. There was a bitter taste, but the coolness felt good on his parched tongue. He found a few more, and he bought them back to where Lewis continued to slumber. "Lew," he whispered as he gently shook his brother's shoulder. "Lew," he repeated. "It's morning."

The older boy began to stir and gave out a low moan.

"Sshh," cautioned Jacob. "We need to get going."

The chance that their former captors would find their trail and give pursuit remained high enough to spur them to action. Even with a night's rest, Lewis was not getting stronger and was feeling worse than he had at any time. Still he knew that Jacob was right. He tried to eat the bitter roots that Jacob had given him, for the lack of nourishment was contributing to his sickness and weakness. He stood now, and stretched. Reaching back inside the tree, he retrieved his father's gun from where he had placed it.

"Get George's gun, Jake," he said finally. "We'll go now."

They trudged along slowly, stopping frequently for Lewis to rest. Jacob found himself worrying more and more about being recaptured. "Do you think they might still be after us, Lew?" he eventually asked.

"I think they prob'ly gave up. Otherwise, they would have caught up by now. I don't think our trail would have been too hard to follow."

This was not reassuring to Jacob.

"I hope you're right, Lew."

"We still have to be careful, though," observed Lewis. "There could be other parties traveling through here."

By midmorning, the terrain changed slightly, and they came out of the tall trees into a more open area covered with smaller bushes and scrub trees. Jacob veered off to the left a ways and then became excited. He started to yell but caught himself and ran back to where Lewis had stopped.

"Lew, there's a creek over there not far," he said quietly but with a controlled excitement. "We can get a drink." He quickly turned to go back. Thirst had been stalking them throughout their flight, and this was great news.

"Be careful, though, Jake. If there are any reds about, they might be watching the creek."

"I didn't see nobody, but I'll be careful."

Soon both boys stood on the banks of the creek. Lewis noticed that it was flowing to the east.

"She's flowing toward the Ohio, Jake. We can follow her home."

Jake had thrown himself to the ground and crawled to the edge of the low bank.

"I'll watch while you get a drink," said Lewis. "Then you can watch for me."

After both of them had drunk their fill, they moved off along the bank, their steps quickened with a purpose and a much surer hope that they would soon reach the Ohio. Not much more than an hour had passed when Jacob gave a shout.

"It's Zane's Island!"

"Shut up, Jake. We ain't safe yet," reasoned Lewis. But he wanted to shout as well. It was Zane' s Island, which stood in the Ohio River just opposite Wheeling and Fort Henry itself. "We've been following Indian Wheeling Creek."

Indeed, it was Indian Wheeling Creek they had found, so named because its mouth was on the Indian side of the Ohio River. They hurried to where it emptied into the Ohio and then moved a little way to the south along the Ohio's shore. Faced now with the problem of crossing the big river, their excitement waned a little and exhaustion replaced it. They sat for awhile, staring at the channel that flowed by in front of them on the west side of the island. Although this channel was narrow, compared to the one on the other side, it was still a formidable obstacle.

"There's no way I can swim across there," said Lewis sadly. "You'll have to go on yourself, Jake. You can bring back help for me."

"Lew, I couldn't do that," protested his younger brother. "I can't leave you here. What if the Injuns find you."

"In that case, what difference would it make for you to be here?" asked Lewis. "Then they'd just get us both."

"Well, we've got guns," remembered Jacob. "And I know how to shoot."

"We've got no powder and no balls, you silly fool."

Although he was trying to sound brave and concerned about his brother, the fact was that Jacob was frightened out of his wits about going on alone. "Don't call me no fool! I ain't leavin' you," he blustered.

Tired and miserable, Lewis argued no more. He sat quietly as Jacob turned away, his feelings hurt. Realizing that his brother was not going to do what he wanted, Lewis offered an alternative.

"Well, find some driftwood then. Get a couple of pieces big enough to keep us afloat. We can try to paddle across holdin' on to the driftwood."

Without a word, Jacob went down along the shoreline and back into the edge of the forest that stretched away to the west. Shortly he returned with a large piece of wood.

"Will this do?" he asked his brother hopefully.

"Yeah, I think so."

"Good. I think I saw another piece just about like it."

"See if you can find some vines to use as ties," Lewis called after him as he went back into the woods.

After Jacob had returned with a second piece of wood and some wild grapevines, the boys fastened the rifles to the wood chunks as best they could. They looked at each other with a look filled both with hope and apprehension and plunged into the current with the chunks of wood held out in front of them. Fortunately, the current was not strong here and they made progress. As weak as he was, it was all Lewis could do to hang on to the wood and the gun, which tended to roll under the water. But they reached the other bank on the island before too long. Jacob was able to scramble out of the water, and then he helped his brother up onto the dry ground, where they both lay without a word or further movement for several minutes.

Finally Jacob sat up. "Are you all right, Lew?" he asked with considerable tenderness for an eleven-year-old boy. "Are you all right?"

Although Lewis heard the question, he had no strength to answer. A moment later, both boys were startled to hear sounds coming from somewhere a little off to the east of them but still on the island.

"Oh God, what is that," wondered Jacob, his voice filled with fear. "Could it be Injuns?"

It was well-known that war parties frequently came to this island to observe the whites across the river. Could it be their bad luck to have landed on the island only to be recaptured by such a party? Lewis had managed to rouse himself enough to sit up, and he listened for a moment. Even in his misery, a slight smile came to his lips.

"That ain't Injuns, Jake," he managed to say. "I think that's kids, white kids."

The sound of laughter came to them now, and then a shout.

"Cut it out, Jim," came the cry, followed by more laughter and shouting.

"Yell at them, Jake," said Lew. "Yell as loud as you can."

Giving his brother a quizzical look, Jacob took his advice.

"Hey!" he shouted at the top of his voice. "Help us! Help us!"

Suddenly there was quiet in the place of the shouting and laughter.

"Whoever it is might be scared of us," suggested Jacob.

"Yell again."

It wasn't long until they saw the source of the sounds they had heard. A young boy, near to them in age, followed by three other boys came into view along a grassy trail leading directly to where the Wetzel boys sat. Lewis recognized the leader.

"That's James Ryan. I've seen him before when we've been at Wheeling."

"Who is it?" asked young Ryan, who came to a stop several feet away.

"I'm Jacob Wetzel," was the answer. "And this is my brother Lew."

"It's the Wetzel boys," exclaimed one of the others.

"We thought you was dead," said James Ryan.

"Well, we ain't," replied Jacob. "We're sure glad to see you. My brother is in a bad way. He got shot, and the Injuns grabbed us both and..." The words tumbled out of Jacob's mouth in a rush.

Seeing Lewis, who had sunk back into the grass, Ryan ran over to him. "God, you look awful. We need to get you back to the fort. We've got a canoe. Let's get them back to the other side and get them in the canoe.

"We thought you was Injuns," said Jacob who, in his relief at finally being saved, could not stop talking.

"We were over here picking wild grapes," explained Ryan. "We sure ain't no red devils."

Thirty minutes later, James Ryan and another of the grape pickers had the Wetzel boys in the canoe and were halfway across the wide eastern channel of the Ohio River, having left the other two on the island to be picked up later. They could see Fort Henry high on the bluff above.

James began shouting in the direction of the fort. "It's the Wetzel brothers! They're alive! They're alive!" Ryan continued to shout this message until he had attracted the attention of one of the soldiers posted at the wall of the fort. By the time the canoe had reached the shore just below, a delegation had come down the trail from the bluff above. Colonel Zane was one of them, along with his wife Elizabeth. But the one out in front was Martin Wetzel. He helped to pull the canoe from the water, and then he helped Jacob step out where he swept the boy up in his arms.

"Jake, Jake, are you all right?"

"Yeah, Martin, but Lew ain't so good."

The two boys were helping Lewis to his feet, and Martin now reached over to lift him out of the canoe. In his hand, Lewis was holding tight to old John Wetzel's rifle. "I've got Pa's gun, Martin," said Lew. "But I'm afraid it got wet."

Martin hugged Lewis to him and helped him to sit on a log that was lying there at the landing. Elizabeth Zane pushed in and pulled the shirt away from the wound on Lewis's chest.

"Send for Dr. McMechen," said Elizabeth. "This is a very sick boy."

2

The Siege

August 28, 1777

Fort Henry was built in 1774 during Dunmore's War, and its original name, Fort Fincastle, was changed at the beginning of the American Revolution to honor the name of Patrick Henry, the new governor of Virginia. It was one of five main government forts in the region: Redstone Old Fort, Fort Pitt, Fort Kittanning, and Fort Randolph being the others.

However, there was no regular garrison at Fort Henry, only militiamen who were gathered when danger was imminent. The fort enclosed something more than half an acre, bounded by a fence made of squared white oak timbers and extending more than twelve feet in height. There were blockhouses on each corner, built so that the second story was extended past the lower level, allowing riflemen on the second floor to see the wall at the base of the first. There were cabins along the inside walls to provide temporary quarters for soldiers or for families taking refuge there. There was a powder magazine, a corral for livestock, and a commandant's cabin.

It was here that David Shepherd sat now, looking over a message he had just written for General Hand at Fort Pitt. The settlers on the border had been heartened by the appointment of General Edward Hand as the commander of the western department with headquarters at Fort Pitt. Hand had served in the east with General Washington at the battles at Trenton and

Princeton. He was steady, decisive, and well-respected. Shepherd had been in frequent correspondence; indeed, the general had directed him to move his family from his own fort at the forks of Wheeling Creek to take command at Fort Henry.

Shepherd, as the county lieutenant, was the ranking officer of the county, and in this position he now took over command at the fort in place of Captain Sam Mason, who remained in command of a militia company. He had written only a few days earlier to inform the general of the arrival of three companies of militia under Shannon, Leach, and Marchant. He had also mentioned that a promised contingent of one hundred men under Colonel Zack Morgan from the Monongahela had not arrived. Just now, he had written that since there had been no recent Indian sightings, he had sent the three companies of militia home, leaving only the two commanded by Mason and Captain Joseph Ogle. He worried a little about what the general might think of that, especially since earlier in the message, he had complained that Morgan had still not appeared.

"Those damned soldiers were eating way too much of our food," he said aloud to himself. "And they did nothing but complain." He wondered if he should tell the general about the capture and escape of the Wetzel brothers. It should have been mentioned in his earlier letter, but he had forgotten to put it in. Of course they were safe now, so maybe it was of little importance to the general. He thought, *Too late anyway. It's old news.* He signed the letter, wrote the date as August 28, 1777, folded it, sealed it, and called for a rider to take it to Fort Pitt. When the man appeared, Shepherd handed the note to him. "Get this to General Hand at Fort Pitt. Be careful and on watch between here and Catfish Camp," he warned. "We ain't seen any Indians around lately, but that don't mean they aren't there."

Colonel Shepherd sat quietly for a few moments after the courier had left. He couldn't quite shake the feeling that General Hand was going to be displeased with his decision to send away the extra militiamen that had been sent to him. Just then,

Ebenezer Zane entered the room. "David, you look disturbed. Some bad news?"

"Hello, Eb," Shepherd sighed. "No, I just finished a note to General Hand, and I don't know what he'll think of it."

"Yeah, well, I wouldn't worry about it too much," offered Colonel Zane. "I've had to write a few of them myself."

Although Ebenezer Zane held no official position, his status as the founder of the Wheeling settlement, and the general respect with which he was regarded, afforded him a kind of unoffcial authority. He did carry the title of colonel, having served as an officer in Dunmore's War. Shepherd recognized that he would make a good sounding board. Zane pulled up a chair and sat down near the corner of Shepherd's desk.

"Do you think I should have kept Shannon and his men here, Eb?"

"Is that what you're worried about, David? I was kind of glad to see 'em go, if you wanta know the truth."

"Well, all those extra men can be a lot of trouble. Hell, they practically ate everything in sight."

"Still," Shepherd continued after a moment, "we might wish they was here if the Indians show up."

"How likely do you think that is, David?"

"Well, you know about the message from Reverend Zeisburger at the Moravian towns. He sent word with Chief White Eyes to tell the general that there was a large bunch of Wyandots and some Ottawa, Chippewa, and Mingoes that'd come to the Delaware villages on the Muskingum and were set to attack the whites on the Ohio, especially here at Wheeling."

"Well, we know the British have whipped those far Injuns into a frenzy. What about the Delawares and the Shawnees?"

"White Eyes told General Hand that the Wyandots are trying to get the Delawares to help them, but so far, them and the Shawnees are mostly stickin' to the treaty they signed a couple of years ago at Fort Pitt. But who knows what they might do."

Zane pulled a pipe from his pocket and stuck it in his mouth. There was no clear way to light it just then, and he removed it again. Both men sat quietly for a moment.

"Any fresh Injun sign," Zane asked finally.

"Nothin' much lately. Ogle and his company are up north at Beech Bottom. He's to report back in a couple of days."

Captain Ogle had thirty-eight men in his company, but Shepherd had suggested that he might want to leave some of them at Beech Bottom in case the Indians attacked the settlements up there. Now he wondered if that had been wise. Being in charge, he was realizing, wasn't always such a great thing.

"You've still got Sam Mason's company. How many men has he got? Twenty five or so, don't he," said Zane, answering his own question.

Shepherd nodded in agreement. "I think so, but you know how it is with them volunteers. Sometimes they're here and sometimes not."

"John Wetzel is here, and his son Lew is healed up some now. And there are people up here from Grave Creek and Tomlinson's settlement. I think we'll be all right, David." Zane got up now and made his way to the fireplace, where a few coals remained hot, ready for the evening meal to be cooked. He lifted the tongs to pick up a live coal, using it to light his pipe. Shepherd watched him intently, waiting for the puff of smoke that rose up from the bowl and then from the smoker's mouth. "You're a good man, Eb. I hope you're right."

August 31, 1777

It was the last day of August and toward evening when Captain Joseph Ogle and twelve men rode into Fort Henry, returning as ordered after a scouting trip up to Beech Bottom. Colonel Shepherd stood outside the door of his quarters watching as the men rode in and dismounted.

The leader, Captain Ogle, nodded at Shepherd and, after asking one of his men to take care of his horse, began walking quickly toward his commanding officer. Three others, Abraham Rogers, Joseph Biggs, and Robert Lemon, followed closely behind him. Shepherd had turned and entered the building, where he now sat down behind his desk and waited for the militiamen to come in.

"Come in, Joseph," beckoned the colonel as the figure of Captain Ogle appeared in the doorway. "Have a seat and tell me what you know."

"I think I'll stand if ya don't mind, Colonel," said Ogle. "I've been ridin' that damned horse awhile, and it feels good to just be on my feet."

The three other men crowded in behind with no word of apology or greeting; it having never occurred to them that they might be intruding on an intended private conversation between two commanders. After all, they knew each other well and were neighbors and friends in quieter times. Showing any special respect to officers was not a high priority among these rough men, and a position of command was more form than fact.

"Suit yourself," answered Shepherd, after eyeing the other three men with some hint of annoyance. "Hello, men," he finally said to the three. "What can you tell me?" he now asked of Ogle. "Did you see any Injun sign?"

Ogle, who was not a tall man, stood as straight as he could. He had removed his hat, and his heavy black hair was matted with sweat along the top of his forehead. He shook his head sideways now as he spoke to Shepherd.

"We didn't see nothin', Colonel," he said. "There's no sign of the bastards anywhere between here and Beech Bottom."

Although he had stopped talking, Ogle seemed to be contemplating something more but not sure whether to bring it up.

Abraham Rogers, who had been standing back, now stepped forward.

"Tell him about the smoke, Joe," he urged.

"Smoke? What smoke?" The colonel was now agitated.

"Well," said Ogle, drawing out the word. "There seemed to be kind of a smoky haze down south of here a ways."

"We think the devils might've burned the blockhouse down at Grave Creek," interjected Rogers again.

"Is that what you think, Captain?" asked the colonel, thinking now that a little more formality might be good.

"It seems likely. Don't know what else it could be, Colonel."

"Damn!" exclaimed Shepherd. "If I 'd knowed that, I would have insisted on Shannon staying here with his men. Still it don't prove nothin' about a big attack, even if it's true."

Joseph Biggs, who had been listening to this exchange, spoke up suddenly. "Do ya' want a couple of us to go down there and check it out?"

"No," answered Shepherd a bit peevishly. "And don't say nothin' about this just yet. Besides, you boys have been ridin' a lot and need some rest. Go on now and get somethin' to eat," he urged as he nodded toward the door.

The three men turned and walked out. As Ogle started to follow, Shepherd called out to him. "Joe, wait a minute. Maybe we ought to see if somethin's goin' on down at Grave Creek. Tell Mason to send me a couple of his men that can handle a canoe and know their way around down there. Oh, and Joe, thanks for the report."

Mary Wetzel stood in front of the fireplace in the little cabin built against the west wall of the fort. It was one of several such huts designed for the use of families staying there temporarily. It was small, not more than ten feet in length, and maybe seven feet in width. A bed was built in to one corner, anchored on three corners to walls of the cabin, and the fourth corner was a post going from floor to ceiling. Crosspieces at the head and foot completed a frame on which several flat boards were laid and then covered with ticking and blankets. There was a second level, which could be used for storage, although right now it served as a bed for young Lewis. The fireplace was at the other end, and a door and window were cut out of the inward side.

Mrs. Wetzel tended a pot hanging over the fire. A single chair was placed under the window, and a small low table stood next to it. John Wetzel sat in the chair quietly smoking his pipe, watching his wife preparing their supper. When word had reached them shortly after that Lewis and Jacob had returned to Fort Henry after their (miraculous, it seemed to their mother) escape, John and Mary had hurried to Wheeling to be with them. The rest of the family was still at Shepherd's Fort, and Jacob had also been sent there after a couple of days.

Mary's time had been entirely devoted to nursing Lewis back to health. The first few days after his return had been difficult, and she was so grateful for the care that Dr. James McMechen had provided. She knew that he had come from somewhere in the East, Baltimore, perhaps, and he had tried to secure land in the area. He and a brother, William, had established a settlement some half-dozen miles below Wheeling. Lately they had come to Fort Henry for safety, and the word was that James was sick of the frontier life and had decided to return to his original home in the East.

Mary stopped stirring for a moment and looked intently at her husband. "John," she began, "a lot of the folks are leaving here and going back east. They say there is too much trouble with the Indians. I think we ought to go back too."

This was the first time John Wetzel had heard this kind of talk from his wife, and it surprised him a bit.

"Back to where?" he asked finally. "Back to Dunkard Creek?"

"Farther than that, John. Away from these Indian raids."

"You mean you want to go all the way back to South Branch? Leave our home here? Damn, Mary, I don't much want to do that."

"Don't swear, John," she admonished him mildly. "I know you don't want to do it, but I'm tired, and I'm scared. We almost lost our boys, John."

John said nothing.

"My brother is talking about it," she said.

"When did he say that? I never heard him say nothin' about leaving his land."

"The day the boys were captured. After you rode off to Wheeling."

"Well, everybody was excited then. I bet he isn't thinking about that anymore."

Mary Wetzel usually didn't win these arguments with her stubborn-minded husband, and she didn't figure she would win this one either. She decided to change tactics. "John, can we at least go back to Shepherd's? We need to get the family back together."

"But it's..." John began but then caught himself just in time.

It would not do to tell Mary that they would be safer here in Fort Henry than at Shepherd's smaller less well-defended fort because five of their children were there. In fact, he realized there was no good reason not to do what Mary was asking.

"What?" she asked.

"You're right, Mary. It's time to go back to Shepherd's. And I can go out from there to see what's happened at our farm. We'll go tomorrow."

"Good," said Mary, feeling some satisfaction. "Go and find Lewis and tell him supper is ready."

It was quite dark out now as James Harris and Philip Finn strode swiftly toward the commandant's quarters, wondering what was in store for them. Captain Mason had come to them just a few minutes ago and asked them to go to see Colonel Shepherd right away. They found the door closed, and after looking at each other with some confusion, Finn finally rapped timidly against the rough wood. When there was no answer, he knocked again much louder this time.

"Hold on," came the voice from inside. "I'll be right there."

After a short wait, the door opened, and Colonel Shepherd stood there.

Behind him, the men could see his wife, Rachel, and their twelve-year-old son, Moses. Shepherd stepped outside and pulled the two men away from the building.

"Are you the men from Mason?" he asked as he continued to move down the path a ways.

"Yeh," allowed Finn while Harris nodded agreement.

"Good," said Shepherd. "I've got an important job for you."

He knew the men, although not well, and he knew that they both lived in the Grave Creek settlements.

"Ogle and his men saw some smoke coming from down toward Grave Creek," explained the colonel. "They think the reds might have burned the blockhouse there, and we need to know what's happened. I want you to take a canoe and go down the Ohio and check on it."

"You want us to go at first light?" asked Harris.

"No, I want you to go tonight and get back as soon as you can."

"In the dark?" Finn clearly questioned the wisdom of that idea.

"Yes, in the dark. It may be safer that way, especially if there are Indians still in the area." The colonel, who had been skeptical at first of the need for this mission, was now very sure of himself and of this decision. "You fellas know your way around down there," he continued. "And you can find out what we need to know even in the dark."

Both men were quiet, staring intently at the ground, not wanting to look Shepherd in the face. The chance for an adventure sounded good, but the obvious danger in this mission was leaving them wishing they had been someplace else when Mason came calling. However, they could see no way out now.

"I want you to find out what has been burned, if anything, and if it was a large raiding party or a small one. Of course you need to find out first if there are any Indians still around."

Shepherd eyed the men closely in the dim light coming from the open door a few feet away. "Are you willing to do this?" he asked in a kindly tone. He could force them, he supposed. He had the authority, but this was not his way of operating, and he knew that any information they might bring back would be worthless if they were not committed to the mission.

"Yeh, we'll do it, Colonel. You can count on us."

"Good," said Shepherd with a feeling of relief. "Be sure you stay close to the east bank of the Ohio, and be extra careful when you get down there."

"Don't worry, Colonel, we'll be careful," exclaimed Finn with a nervous laugh.

Within the hour, the two men had pushed a canoe out into Wheeling Creek a short distance above the mouth and were soon out into the big river. The canoe moved swiftly with the current, and they stayed as close to the Virginia shore as they could. It was not long before they had passed the McMechen settlement a few miles below Wheeling. There was nothing but darkness there for the inhabitants were at Fort Henry. The two men did not talk, fearing that any Indians that might be on the shore would hear them. The smell of smoke was becoming much stronger as they came closer to Grave Creek.

Harris leaned close to Finn and whispered softly. "We can't see a thing. If there are any of those red bastards there, they'll see us before we see them."

"Yeh," agreed Finn in a voice that Harris thought was much too loud.

"We'd better pull in to shore well short and sneak in there on foot."

"I think we'd better do it pretty soon. It sure smells like they've burnt the place."

"Not yet," said Finn. "I ain't lookin' to walk too far neither."

They spoke no more and after a few more minutes, Finn touched Harris on the arm and pointed to the shore.

The nearly full moon had peeked out from behind a cloud, and gave out a pale light as they pushed the canoe onto the shore. By luck they had found a reasonable landing spot. They pulled the little watercraft out of the water and pushed it into some bushes so that it could not be seen from the river. Finn pointed to a tall birch tree several yards ahead of them.

"See that tree, James," whispered Finn, more quietly this time. "That will help us find our canoe when we head back."

They moved cautiously along the bank but far enough back to be among the trees and bushes. They decided to split up and stay apart far enough that if one of them were suddenly attacked, the other might be able to get away. They continued in this way until they got into the cabins at the settlement. There was no sign of any human life anywhere, but they now saw the burnt ruins of a couple of outlying cabins. They came together again behind one of the little huts that had been left untouched. They remained there for a long time, saying nothing and listening for any sound that might betray an intruder.

As the moon again slid out from a wispy cloud, they were able to see the remains of the blockhouse that had once stood close to the creek. It was flattened, except for a part of the stone chimney, and it was still smoldering. The smell was strong—the sour and stale odor of wood ash after it had been dampened. More time passed while they waited tense and uneasy, startled at every sound.

"Nobody's here," whispered Harris. "I think we should go."

"Looks that way. No way to tell when they was here and how many of 'em there might 'uv been. Mebbe we ought to poke around a mite more."

"Let's don't. We got enough to report. I ain't for pushing our luck."

"I guess you're right," agreed Finn. "But let's take it slow and easy."

Harris had already turned and was moving back along the path they had followed. He slowed to allow Finn to catch up.

"Do you think we need to split up again?" he asked his partner.

"No, let's just go, but keep quiet."

Their return was uneventful. They found the canoe and got it in the river without mishap and began the struggle against the current. Both men relaxed as they moved further north, and by the time they had passed the McMechen settlements again, they were conversing quietly, able to laugh. Dawn had not yet broken as they reached the mouth of Wheeling Creek, and they glided the canoe into the creek and up to the landing from which they had embarked several hours earlier. After stowing the canoe, they started up the path toward the fort.

"I don't mind telling you I'm glad to be back here, Philip," said Harris, with a sigh of relief.

"Me too," answered Finn. "Wha—"

His voice was cut off as a stealthy figure arose from the weeds along the path and swung his tomahawk into the back of Finn's head. Finn dropped lifelessly to the ground, and as Harris turned at the sound, a second warrior ended his life with a knife thrust into his belly. Each warrior retrieved the scalp of his victim and melted away into the nearby cornfield.

September 1, 1777

Dr. James McMechen had decided to return to Baltimore. He and his brother William had been discussing the wisdom of getting back from the frontier, spooked by the looming Indian troubles. William had proposed moving back to the Redstone area for awhile, then returning to their property in the settlements a few miles below Wheeling. James, however, had enough of the rough life here on the border and was going all the way back to

Maryland where he hoped he could rebuild the practice he once had in Baltimore.

Once the decision had been made, the good doctor could see no reason to delay, and he had gotten up early to leave. His Negro servant, a man named Loudon, was overjoyed with the prospects of returning to an easier life, and he was only too happy now to embark on the task of retrieving the horses. They had been turned loose to forage in the hills east of the fort, and acting upon instructions from Dr. McMechen, Loudon had hired a man named Boyd to help him. Bridles in hand, the two slid aside the bar that secured the main gate and slipped out. They started to follow the road that led to the north and east and over the big hill that rose up to that side of the fort. Shafts of light from the rising sun made their way above the ridge, but it remained rather dark along the road. A figure appeared from the direction of the outlying cabins.

"What are you men up to?"

Startled, the two men stopped and peered at the form in the shadows, trying to make out who it was.

"Oh, it's you Mr. Drennon," said the slave, Loudon. "We'se going out to get the doctor's horses. He's goin' back to Balt'more."

"Kinda early, aren't you?" offered Jacob Drennon.

"Do you want to help us?" asked Loudon. "You'd git a dollar from the doctor."

"Not me," objected Drennon. "You ain't gittin' me up in the hills with them red devils about."

"Ain't no red devils here now, Mr. Drennon. The doctor said so."

"How's he know?"

With that, Drennon moved quickly to the fort's gate and went in.

"Humph," exclaimed Loudon, whose excitement about going home overshadowed all else. "Don't scare me."

Boyd said nothing, and the two hurried on up toward the top of the hill. They expected the horses to be on the other side, maybe down toward the creek bottom. While they were still some distance from the crest, several shadowy figures emerged from among the trees. It was Boyd who first realized what they were facing.

"Injuns!" he screamed. He backed up a couple of steps, then turned and began running back down the trail toward the fort. Loudon stood still, his face frozen in fright as three of the warriors rushed past him in pursuit of his partner. They overtook him after a few strides and hacked him to death with their tomahawks. The other three braves now advanced toward Loudon who had watched Boyd's killing with breathless terror.

He took off now back toward the fort, rushing past the three red men who stood over their victim in the weeds just off the path. They made no effort to stop the fleeing Loudon. Plunging down the slope at full speed, Loudon dared not look back until he had gone some distance. Slowing now, he risked a furtive look back and was surprised to see no sign of any pursuers. It was a small comfort, but he picked up his pace again and did not slow until he could see the east gate of the fort. It was much brighter now, and he could see the cabins off to his left. He wondered who might be hiding among them, and he began to scream toward the fort at the top of his voice.

"Injuns! Injuns! Open the gate. Open the gate."

The oppressive fear welled up inside of him until it was hard for him to speak.

"It's me, Loudon," he yelled as loud as he could muster. "Please, please, let me in."

At last, the gate swung open, and Loudon charged in past Jacob Drennon, who had opened it for him.

"Where's Boyd?" shouted the astonished Drennon at the back of the speeding Loudon who was headed toward the commandant's quarters as fast as he could go.

"Injuns! Injuns!" shouted Loudon as he ran. Men began to gather around the walkway to Shepherd's quarters where the screaming slave now stopped. The door opened to reveal the commander still in his nightclothes. Shepherd said nothing, however, as Dr. McMechen arrived to question his servant.

"Loudon," he cautioned. "Calm down and tell us what has happened. Where are my horses?"

"Don't know, Doctor, sir," exclaimed Loudon, wide-eyed with fright. Naturally he had forgotten all about the horses, and that seemed now to be another problem. How could he explain to his master that he had failed in his mission. "We didn't see them 'cuz when we got up the hill, they came runnin' right at us."

"Who was runnin' at you?" asked the doctor.

"Injuns!" repeated Loudon, still breathing heavily.

"What happened to Boyd?" broke in one of the other men standing near. It was Andrew Zane, the second youngest of the five Zane brothers.

"They was chasing him, but I couldn't see cause I was runnin' back here," explained Loudon. He thought it best not to mention everything he had seen.

"How many of them was there?" asked Zane.

The slave did not answer immediately, trying to think as he struggled to control himself. It was not unusual for observers among the frontiersmen to grossly overestimate the number of Indian foes, but Loudon did not succumb to that temptation.

"I saw five or six of 'em," he offered at last.

"Sounds like a small raiding party," said Sam Tomlinson, who had joined the group a bit earlier. Tomlinson was a lieutenant in Mason's militia company.

"I think we should go out and try to find Boyd," said Zane, who liked the young Irishman in spite of the fact that he was but a laborer and not highly-thought-of around the settlement. This suggestion was met at first by total silence, and then Tomlinson suggested that they should check with Colonel Shepherd. Shepherd had closed his door and could be heard inside shouting something to his wife.

"There's no time," said Zane. "Who knows what the devils have done with Boyd or whether they've even caught him. We might be able to save him, and even if they've kilt him, we might be able to get his body before they mutilate it."

This speech continued to be met with silence as the men mostly stared at their feet and avoided looking at Zane.

"Come on Sam, let's get our rifles and go have a look."

Tomlinson was not lacking in bravery, and he nodded his approval.

"We'll need more than the two of us."

"Well, we can take the darky with us," offered Zane.

"Hell, he won't help us none," protested Tomlinson.

Loudon was interested in this conversation, for he had no intention of going back out there. He looked at Dr. McMechen, hoping for his intervention.

"You go with them," said the doctor, nodding his head toward the young black man. "You can show them where to go."

"They don't need me for that," Loudon was quick to point out.

"Take him," said McMechen, now speaking to Andrew Zane. "But you need more than three men."

"Oh, hell. I'll go." The speaker was a huge man who had been standing on the edge of the crowd. It was Jacob Greathouse, one of the Greathouse brothers, a family well-known on the frontier for their rough and cruel manners. It was generally known that they were responsible for the killing of the Mingo chief Logan's family, the act primarily responsible for setting off Dunmore's War.

Zane was not an admirer of Greathouse, but he was glad to have him along for this particular mission.

"Good," he said now. "Make sure your rifles are loaded, and let's go. There ain't no time to waste."

With that, the three men and the reluctant slave moved quickly to the gate and out onto the trail. The door of the commander's quarters opened again, and Colonel Shepherd stood there, fully dressed.

"What's goin' on?" he wanted to know.

"Indians chased Loudon and Boyd, and we think they may have killed Boyd," explained McMechen. "Andrew Zane and some others have gone out to see if they can find him."

"I don't think that's wise," said Shepherd. "Wait, wait," he called.

It was much too late, the big gate having swung shut behind the departing rescue party. Zane and his companions moved up the trail, with the young black slave pushed into leading the way. Each of them felt the increasing tension as they moved toward the top, searching for some sign as to where Boyd, or more likely, his body, might be found. It was Greathouse who made the first discovery.

"Here!" he shouted, pointing to a bush that was partly trampled, just to the left of the path. Tomlinson and Loudon pushed in behind him, but Zane had turned the other way, thinking he had heard something. They pushed on among the bushes when they saw the body of Boyd lying face down in the grass. The back of his head was split open where a blow from a tomahawk had swiftly ended his life. He had been scalped, but they saw no other obvious mutilations.

"Let's get him back to the fort," said Tomlinson. "Get his shoulders, Jacob, and I'll take his feet."

"Wait a minute."

Greathouse walked a few feet toward a nearby tree, stooping to pick up a long stick of some thickness.

"We can use this," he said. They used Boyd's clothes to tie hands and feet to the pole. Handing the rifles to Loudon, who had watched the proceedings with nervous impatience, the two big men each grabbed one end of the pole and began to carry the dead man back to the main trail. As they descended the path to the fort, Loudon, looking back, suddenly shouted with alarm. Three Indian warriors appeared just above the area where the three men had turned aside to recover the body. With tomahawks raised, they gave a yell and started forward. Loudon screamed again and rushed past the other two, still holding on to the two guns. Greathouse and Tomlinson were unsure what to do.

"You damned nigger, bring back our guns," shouted Greathouse.

Loudon, however, was already at least fifteen yards below them.

"It's no use," said Lieutenant Tomlinson. "There's no stopping him. Let's just go as fast as we can."

Greathouse started to put down his end of the pole.

"Let's leave him then and git going."

Tomlinson, who was below Greathouse and could see what was happening above them, noted that the warriors had stopped.

"No, Jacob. They aren't following us. But I don't see Andrew. I wonder what's happened to him."

"Never mind him. Let's git back," cried Greathouse, picking up his end of the pole again. "Go! Go!"

Tomlinson turned around now, and hoisting his end of the pole to his shoulder, he began to move down the path again. The Indians did not follow but turned their attention to Zane, who had wandered off the path in the other direction. Hearing the commotion, he started back down the hill when he was cut off by another pair of braves who were in the woods below him. His first thought was to kneel and aim his rifle at one of those two, but he quickly realized that after one shot his gun would be useless.

More than one foe was converging on him, so he opted to move in the opposite direction, up toward the top of the ridge above him. Zane was in a wooded area off the main trail and a good distance from where it passed over the crest of the hill. The big hill itself continued to the south from the crest, gradually descending down as it curled back to the southeast until it settled into a flat area along Wheeling Creek. The creek flowed in a southerly direction here until it made a sharp bend to the west and to its final destination into the Ohio.

There was a strip of land just below the top of the ridge that was more sparsely covered with growth and which extended all the way down to the creek bottom. If he could get to that strip, Zane thought he could possibly outrun his pursuers and reach safety across the creek. He scrambled upward until he reached the sparsely covered area. As he turned toward the south, he saw still another Indian directly in his intended path. He started to bring the rifle to bear on that target, but the sounds of the two warriors coming up behind him propelled him in the only direction possible, straight up to the top of the ridge. He knew that there was nothing but a steep cliff on the other side of the ridge, but there was no alternative.

In sheer panic now, he made his way to the top, where he stopped momentarily. He looked over the edge in front of him—a sheer, deep drop. He looked behind where two of the red men were closing fast. Neither had a gun, but both had raised their hatchets and appeared to be determined to use them.

As Zane watched, one of them suddenly hurled his tomahawk in his direction. He quickly turned and threw himself over the edge, immediately losing his balance and tumbling down over the jagged rocks and through the brambles, which tore at his clothing. He lost his grip on the rifle, which preceded him down the steep incline, landing with a thud near the bottom. Zane tried in vain to grab something that would stop his fall. Finally he stopped, wedged against the main stem of a small tree growing up from the bottom of the cliff.

Andrew Zane was surprised to be alive and relatively unhurt. He twisted his body in order to look back up the hill to see if his pursuers were still coming, but he could see no sign of them. He struggled to stand up, his knee paining him now where it had banged against the tree trunk. He moved down a few steps until he was on the narrow strip of flatland along the bank of the creek. He saw his broken gun lying not far away, and he picked it up. It could not be fired, but he thought it might be possible to repair it if he ever got out of this mess.

The Indians had obviously decided not to try to follow him in his desperate plunge down the cliff. However, he worried that they might try to shoot him if he showed himself along the creek. He stayed on the cliffside of it and made his way under the lee of the steep side, as he followed the creek bank moving upstream. After several minutes of careful travel, he was satisfied that the Indians had given up on him, and he moved out onto the wide trail that led to Shepherd's Fort at the forks.

Lewis Wetzel, hearing the commotion outside, had slipped out of his upper bunk and quickly dressed, concluding with the moccasins he had taken from the Wyandots a couple of weeks earlier. The steady breathing and light snoring told him that is mother and father were still asleep, and he quietly moved past the end of the bed and out the door.

It was light, and he relished the coolness that enveloped him; such a contrast to the hot cabin. He could see people gathering over toward the east gate, and after a brief visit to the outhouse built against the west wall of the enclosure, he went over to join the crowd and find out what was going on. He arrived just in time to see the black slave Loudon holding the big gate open while Greathouse and Tomlinson carried the body of the Irishman Boyd inside and laid him down, still attached to the makeshift pole.

Colonel Shepherd was there to meet them, and he saw Dr. McMechen as well.

"What did you see, Lieutenant?" asked Shepherd, addressing Tomlinson.

"We saw Injuns, that's for sure. They kilt Boyd."

"How many?" the colonel wanted to know. He was acutely aware of the warning about a big attack, yet all the evidence so far suggested just a small war party.

"I saw three myself, but there coulda been more," answered the lieutenant.

"What about you?" Shepherd nodded at Greathouse.

"They was mostly behind me, but there were more than three I'd bet. Some were after Zane."

"Zane? Where is he? Why didn't he come back with you?" The colonel's tone had become accusatory.

"We don't know, Colonel," said Tomlinson. "The bastards quit chasing us is all we know. Andrew went off the trail on the other side just as we discovered Boyd's body. We never saw him again."

Young Wetzel felt someone move up next to him and realized it was his father.

"What's goin' on Lew," asked John Wetzel.

"Injuns kilt the man Boyd," responded Lewis.

"What was he doin' out there?"

"Don't know for sure, but somebody said he'd gone out to git some horses."

John Wetzel heard the name Zane being discussed.

"Who're they talkin' about? What Zane?"

"Andrew, I think. Mebbe the reds got him too."

Most of the militiamen had come out of their quarters and joined the group gathered around Colonel Shepherd, who was shouting now.

"Sam! Sam Mason, where are you?"

"Here," said Mason. "I'm right here, Colonel."

"We've got to find out what we're up against, Captain Mason," said Shepherd. "I want you to take a dozen men and go up the trail to see what you can find. See if you can find out what happened to Andrew and try to find these damned warriors. We know there are five or six of them for sure."

Mason immediately began calling out names of men in his militia company.

"Take Lieutenant Tomlinson. He knows where to start lookin' anyway."

Shepherd wasn't always so formal with the military titles, but this seemed like serious business.

There was an excited murmur going through the crowd, yet no one seemed to feel there was any terrible danger.

Mason soon had his men chosen, and they marched out the eastern gate, the third group of men to do that already this morning. Shepherd gave orders to make sure there were men posted in each corner blockhouse to keep watch in all directions. Mason set two men, Thomas Glenn and Sam Tomlinson, to lead along either side of the trail. He followed behind them and then placed five men in single file behind him and at a distance of several yards off the main path on either side. They soon came to the place where Tomlinson and Greathouse had turned aside to find the body of Boyd.

There was plenty of sign of the Indian presence both here and farther along. After conferring with Tomlinson for a moment, Mason indicated that they should move on. In a short time, they came to the slightly open area that Andrew Zane had tried to reach earlier. There were obvious indications that the Indian warriors had been here as well, and in fact, the signs showed that they had gone along this open area toward the south.

"Looks like they're headed on down the ridge to the bottomland," observed Mason. "Sergeant Steele, I want you to take the lead, along with Glenn. Sam, you go to the back of the western line. Make sure none of the bastards gets in behind us. Everybody! Keep a careful eye."

As they continued to move south and east, the militiamen encountered no resistance, although they continued to find plenty of signs that the Indians had preceded them along this trail. Mason did wonder a bit at the fact that they had made no attempt to conceal their presence. The hill was now much lower, and they were very close to the flat plain through which Wheeling Creek flowed in a westerly direction toward its mouth. There was a cornfield to their right that extended up to the bluff just below the fort, and on the left, tall grasses and bushes that lined the bank of the creek.

The two lines of men behind Mason and the two leaders had moved closer together, and almost the entire body of men was down into the flat. It was foggy here and difficult to see. Suddenly Thomas Glenn, who was at the front, raised his rifle and fired. An Indian brave tumbled out of the tall grass on the creek side, and then there were Indian braves on all sides of them at once. Mason had moved up next to Sergeant Steele who shot at two warriors just ahead and to the right. The Indians fired their guns at the same time. One of the Indians fell wounded, as did Steele while a bullet had hit Mason's gun, tearing off the lock and injuring his hand.

Warriors were boiling out of the weeds and the corn ahead of him, and as he turned back, he could not really see any more of his men in the melee. It struck him that the shot by Glenn had sprung an Indian trap just a little earlier than the red men had hoped. His own position was precarious, and he reached down now to take hold of his sergeant's arm, trying to pull him up.

"Don't bother, Captain," said Steele with great difficulty. "I'm done fer. Take my rifle and git!"

Mason was torn, but only briefly, and he grabbed the gun and began to run back toward the creek. Two braves were closing in on him, intent on dispatching him with their tomahawks. Strangely, other Indians nearby seemed to ignore him and his pursuers, and he managed to pass through and into the tall grass. The heavy fog was hanging over the low ground near the creek, and he realized that he was not visible to his foes for a moment. He felt a hand grabbing at his arm, which he pulled away and then tripped over a root, tumbling hard to the ground.

Fear shot through him as the angry painted face appeared above him, but he managed to roll away and, miraculously, Sergeant Steele's rifle was in his hand and free to aim. He pulled the trigger just as the warrior jumped on him, intending to pin him to the ground. The speeding ball tore into the belly of the attacker, who fell on top of Mason, no longer a threat. Savagely pushing the dying Indian off him, Mason scrambled to his feet, surprised that he was suddenly alone. He saw a large tree that had fallen close to the creek bank. Noting that it had many leafy branches still intact, Mason climbed into the tangle and burrowed deeply under several of the heaviest limbs. His heart was beating so fast he was afraid it might be heard, but he lay still, hoping to remain undiscovered.

The remaining men who had marched out with Captain Mason were not so fortunate as he. All but two others were killed by the braves who had waited in ambush. In the confusion, however, John Caldwell had managed to get back up the hill a short way where he pushed in among the trees just below the ridge. A warrior with a sharp eye had seen him and immediately gave chase. Caldwell was soon aware of his pursuer, and he decided to turn straight up trying to get over the top and along the creek valley below. When he tripped and fell headlong, wedged between two small trees growing close together, he thought all was lost. The Indian saw him fall just a short distance ahead, and as Caldwell struggled to free himself, the warrior stopped, and giving a hideous yell, he drew his tomahawk. He let it fly with all his force, but at the last possible instant, the frightened white man jerked himself free, and the weapon stuck harmlessly into the ground. The disappointed brave ran to retrieve the wayward axe, but when he had done so, he stopped to watch his quarry racing down the slope. With a shrug, he turned away, thinking that somehow the Great Spirit was protecting the man. Caldwell continued along the stream and later that day, he too arrived safely at Shepherd's Fort.

Sam Tomlinson had been at the rear of the squad of militiamen, and for some reason, unknown to himself, he had hung back up the hill a ways, unable to see the men just ahead, who had been swallowed up in the fog. When he heard the shooting and the screaming, he stopped, straining his eyes to see what might be happening. He detected some movement ahead and below him and could make out a number of shadowy forms moving into the trees. The Indians were moving up to prevent any escape from the men who were under attack below.

"God," exclaimed Tomlinson aloud to himself. "There's way more than five or six of them devils."

Thinking first of self-preservation, he turned back and began to move up to the shelter of the woods above him. He stopped again, beset with the notion that he should go down and try to help his comrades. He continued to see movement, but he realized that he had not been discovered. The thought came to him that he should get back and report what had happened. Yes, yes, that was his duty, and if he tried to go back down the hill he would be seen and killed.

In spite of a feeling that his action might be seen as cowardly, he moved again with haste, keeping the trees between him and the action below. The fort was less than a quarter mile away if he went in a direct line, but he couldn't tell how far the line of Indians might extend below him. He continued along the edge of the trees for another fifty yards where he stopped and listened. The sounds were some distance to the southeast of his location, and he began to run now in a westerly direction, hoping to arrive at the hillside above the settlers' cabins just east of the fort.

He came into the open, then into a second stand of trees on the lower slope of the hill. He fought his way through, determined to continue on this line even if there were Indians in sight. Suddenly, he was in the clear, and the cabins just in front of him. He ran through them, yelling at the top of his voice. "Indians! Indians! Lots of 'em!"

He passed through the cabins and neared the east gate. Only now did he believe he was safe.

Inside Fort Henry, the yard had filled with people. The sound of shots coming from Wheeling Creek had roused everyone who had spent the night inside the walls. Mary Wetzel stood next to her husband and son, watching as Lieutenant Tomlinson rushed through the big gate, which had been opened just wide enough this time to let him slip through. Mary was thinking about her other son.

"Where's Martin?" she asked. "John, is he out there with those men?"

"No, Mary. I saw him over there by Joe Ogle just awhile ago."

"Are you sure? What's happening?"

"Martin's still here, Ma," said Lewis. He took hold of her arm and turned her toward himself slightly. "Don't worry. He's fine."

Someone shouted at the sentry on the bastion in the southeast corner.

"What do you see? Can you see our men?"

"I don't see nuthin'," shouted the sentry. "There's too much fog."

Tomlinson had collapsed to the ground, breathing heavily, and he looked up now to see Colonel Shepherd and Captain Ogle making their way to him with quizzical looks on their faces. He wondered for a moment if they would accuse him of deserting his comrades, but he could think of nothing to say that would sound good. He struggled to his feet. If he could report what he knew first, maybe there would be no questions about how he managed to escape.

"Colonel," he began.

"Take it easy, Sam," interrupted Shepherd with a soft look of compassion on his face. "Are you hurt?"

"No," said Tomlinson. "Just winded."

"Bring a cup of water over here," commanded Captain Ogle, and one of the bystanders ran back to the commandant's cabin.

"We ran into a hornet's nest, Colonel," continued Tomlinson, still fighting for breath. "They set a trap for us. There's a bunch of 'em."

In fact, as they were to learn later, there were over two hundred braves, mostly Wyandots and Mingoes, with a few Delawares and Shawnees mixed in. In the hours shortly after midnight, this little army had crossed the Ohio at what was later known as Boggs Island, a few miles below Wheeling Island. Arriving at the mouth of Wheeling Creek sometime after Colonel Shepherd's two-man scouting party had left for Grave Creek, the warriors had formed up in a narrow crescent with its extremities at the foot of the hill and its far end at the creek. A decoy group of six braves had been sent to the top of Wheeling Hill whose job was to entice a body of soldiers to follow them down the hill, which served to funnel them into the jaws of the trap.

"What happened, Sam? What happened to Mason and the rest of the men?"

"Colonel, I don't know for sure. There was too much fog, and I was at the back of our line. When I saw a bunch of them, red devils, coming into the trees below, I ran back up into the woods above and made my way back here."

"You don't know if the others were fighting?"

"Oh, they was fighting all right. I could hear plenty of shots and lots of screaming. We've got to send more men! We've got to help them!" Tomlinson had become excited again, and he wanted to do something to help relieve the sick feeling he had about having run away from the fight.

Colonel Shepherd seemed to read some of this in the lieutenant's face.

"Sam, you did the right thing. We needed your report." He turned to Ogle now, as his son William walked up with a cup of water for Tomlinson.

"Joe, what do you think? Did you hear what Sam had to say?"

"Let me take some of my company and go after 'em, Colonel."

"I don't know, Joe. We still don't know what we're up against."

"Let me take a few men, Colonel. We've got to do somethin' to help Mason."

"All right," said the colonel against his better judgment. He could see that it was going to be impossible to refuse to at least try to send a relief party. "No more than a dozen men, Joe. We may have to defend the fort itself before this is over."

"Good," replied the captain, who began picking out men to go with him.

"Be extra careful, Joe. If you come under attack, retreat to the fort as soon as you can."

Several men formed up around Captain Ogle, including Hugh McConnell, Martin Wetzel, Jacob Ogle, the captain's younger brother, and to the colonel's dismay, his nineteen-year-old son, William.

He immediately moved to intervene. "William!" he shouted, but the look on the young man's face, as well as that of Captain Ogle, brought him up short. He turned away, distressed that he could not protect his own son, and walked slowly back toward his quarters. As Ogle led his men out the gate, he was joined by Lieutenant Tomlinson, who was entering harm's way for the third time in a little more than an hour. This time, the party did not ascend Wheeling Hill but turned to the right to take a direct path to the creek and in the direction of the sounds of the earlier fighting.

Colonel Shepherd had stopped to watch the men filing out the east gate once more. As the gate swung shut, he began to shout orders. "We need to alert the folks in the outlying cabins. They need to come inside the fort until this blows over."

"I'll go," said Jacob Drennon. "My wife's out there."

Drennon had been planning to leave with Dr. McMechen this morning to take his family back east and away from the dangers of the border. He was actually of mixed feelings about the revolution itself, having been educated in England and commissioned in the

British army. He was careful to keep his feelings to himself, since Tories were not tolerated in this border community. He went out now to bring in the cabin dwellers.

"I want men in each of the corner blockhouses and someone to be in charge at both the east and south gates," directed Colonel Shepherd. "The rest of you men get your rifles and plenty of ammunition and man the portholes around all the walls except the west."

John Wetzel began moving back to their cabin when he noticed the worried look on his wife's face. She reached out and grabbed his arm.

"Martin's out there, John. He's sure to be killed."

"Mary, I know he's out there, but Martin knows how to handle himself. He'll be back." He pulled her to him and hugged her tightly against his body. She was sobbing openly now, and he felt helpless. Still holding her firmly, he turned to his son.

"Lewis, go and get my rifle along with my pouch and horn."

"Yes, Pa," said Lewis. "Pa, do you think I could man the south gate?"

"Sure, that's a good place for you. I'll tell David. Now go."

He held his wife a bit longer, then released her.

"Mary, we can't dwell on this. Lots of mother's sons are out there. Go back to the cabin but be ready. You and the other women are going to be needed if this gets worse."

As Lewis returned from the cabin with his father's rifle, he met his mother, who stopped him and grabbed his arm.

"You be careful, Lewis. I don't want to lose both you and Martin today."

"I will, Ma," said Lewis, pulling away, wanting to get to his post at the gate before someone else did. She let him go and continued on toward the cabin door.

As he hurried toward the small south gate, Lewis was met by his father, carrying a firearm himself. He took his rifle from Lewis and gave him the one he was carrying.

"It's a musket, Lew," he pointed out. "It ain't accurate and won't shoot very far, but if one of the devils gets over the wall, you can blast him with it."

Lewis knew about the smoothbore musket. It was the gun that soldiers in most armies carried and was easier to load than the long rifle that the border men used. He knew how to load and fire it and was pleased that his father had brought it for him.

"Here's some powder and a few balls. Load it and be ready, but don't fire it unless you have to."

"Yes, Pa,"

"I spoke to David, and he agrees for you to man the south gate. Don't open it for nobody unless you're damned sure who it is." John Wetzel looked hard at his son and nodded.

Without another word he moved off to the blockhouse on the southeast corner, just a short distance to the east of the south gate. Lewis had gone to the gate and was looking through the small peephole. As soon as his father had disappeared inside the blockhouse, Lewis moved over and ascended the ladder to the small platform against the wall just to the west side of the gate latch. From there he could look over the top of the wall.

Captain Ogle and his men had moved swiftly down the path where it went into a cornfield. They began to slow as they realized there could be danger lurking among those corn rows. The men continued to move, but the wild enthusiasm to come to the aid of their fellow soldiers had diminished, replaced with caution, and then fear.

Sam Tomlinson, so eager to assuage the feelings of guilt that had accompanied his earlier flight back to the fort, had come to the sure realization that this was a suicide mission. He looked for Captain Ogle, hoping that he could reason with him and convince him to take the men back before it was too late. As he began to shout, his voice was punctuated with the sharp retort of a rifle, and then the Indians appeared ahead of them and in the cornstalks on either side. More shots rang out, and the line of militiamen crumpled under the assault. The sounds of renewed battle soon reached the fort, and three men of Ogle's company, Rogers, Biggs, and Lemon, came running from their quarters toward the south gate. Lewis Wetzel stood in front of the latch, determined not to open the gate unless ordered to do so.

"Get out of the way, you young whelp," shouted Rogers. "We're goin' out."

"My pa said not to open for anybody," retorted Lewis. He shrank back a bit, however, in spite of himself.

"Hold on," yelled David Shepherd who, while talking with Ebenezer Zane, had observed the action near the gate. "Where do you men think you are going?"

"Our friends are out there, and we mean to help them," answered Rogers.

His tone indicated that he expected no opposition, even from the commander.

"We've sent too many out there already," said Shepherd.

Rogers turned back to young Wetzel. "Open that gate!"

Lewis looked at Shepherd, who nodded his head in agreement.

"You're fools, Rogers, but I won't stop you." Lewis threw the latch upward and pulled the gate open, holding it as the three men rushed out.

Colonel Shepherd and Ebenezer Zane moved into the opening and looked out. The sounds of battle came to them, but the action was still out of sight. The sounds had also reached the settlers who remained in the outlying cabins, and they increased the urgency with which they began their retreat to the safety of the stockade. Some brought personal items and food with them, others ran with thought of nothing but reaching the fort. The east gate was held open as they streamed in. Jacob Drennon had helped his wife and daughter in from their little house, but now

Mrs. Drennon grabbed her husband's hand, looking up at him with terror in her eyes.

"Little William is still out there," she screamed. "I forgot all about him. He was asleep in the back."

She tore herself away and began to run toward the gate.

"Martha, Martha," yelled Drennon to his departing wife. "Come back!"

He started after her, but she was out the gate before he could stop her.

He knew he should follow her, but he stopped for a moment. He was filled with fear. How could this have happened, he wondered. Were people watching him?

"Someone, give me a gun," he finally shouted. "A gun, I need a gun."

Out in the cornfields, Ogle's men were in full retreat. There had been no time for any orders, and it swiftly became a matter of every man trying to save himself. The main thrust of the Indian ambush had come in just behind the captain, and he was quickly separated from the rest. He had dashed off to his left into the standing corn, where he began to run back up toward the settlement. To his surprise, he was not being closely followed, although he could tell that there were far more warriors than his little group could handle, and he could hear the screams of some of his comrades who were being cut down.

Ahead of him, he saw some movement among the stalks and then it stopped. He assumed that one of the savages had stopped and was waiting to attack him as he came near. He slowed and moved over a couple of rows and then advanced along between the rows so that he did not cause any visible movement in the stalks. He could not see anyone standing or kneeling, but he half-expected to be shot at any instant. Then he saw a figure lying on the ground, and he could hear a low moan. It was one of his own men, and he hurried forward to see that it was Matthew Hedges.

The man had been shot in the upper right chest, just below the shoulder, and he was bleeding profusely.

Ogle helped him to his feet, and half dragging him, the two men made their way to the edge of the cornfield and to the corner of some fencing that separated the field from the area where the cabins stood. There was a heavy stand of horse weeds and briars along the fence row, and Ogle burrowed under the entanglement, pulling the wounded Hedges in behind him. The effort brought a grunt of objection from the injured man, and then a loud moan.

"Be quiet, man," urged Ogle. "If they hear us, we're dead."

He couldn't tell if Hedges could hear him or understand their predicament, but he became quiet.

"We're goin' to have to lay here until things calm down," said the captain mainly to himself.

Rogers, Lemon, and Biggs had not advanced very far before they saw some of their comrades emerging from the cornfield on the dead run. They could make out Martin Wetzel and Hugh McConnell as two of the runners who were coming fast and under fire. Biggs immediately turned back toward the fort and began yelling at Lewis Wetzel, who was standing behind the gate, which was still slightly ajar.

"Open the gate, open the gate," shouted Biggs. "Men are comin' in! We're coming in."

John Wetzel kneeled at a firing port on the second level of the southeast bastion. He saw another figure emerge from the path in the cornfield and into the open, followed closely by a half-dozen screaming warriors. It was William Shepherd, the son of the commander, and as he watched in horror, John saw the young man trip on a vine and fall headlong. The braves were on him immediately, flailing at him with their tomahawks. Wetzel aimed his rifle and fired, but the distance, though within range of the long rifle, was too great for accuracy. The bullet hit the ground in front of the nearest Indian and chewed up a cloud of dust. Other riflemen along the south wall also fired but were equally ineffective.

One dusky brave grabbed young Shepherd's head and, with a quick swipe, lifted the scalp and held it high, shouting defiance at the white men in the fort. A line of Indians had now appeared at the edge of the cornfield where they stopped, and those with guns fired with a ragged volley toward the fort. The south gate had been flung open, and six men came in, none having been hit by the rain of bullets coming from the Indian line.

"Shut the gate!" shouted someone in the corner blockhouse. "Nobody else is comin'."

Lewis Wetzel, with help from Biggs, pushed the gate shut and dropped the latch. A crowd of both men and women had come to the south wall, and many were pushing their way up against it, trying to see out the various firing holes. In the confusion, men with rifles were having difficulty getting in position to shoot.

"Get back, you women," cried one of the men. "You are in the way."

Colonel Shepherd was talking with Hugh McConnell.

"Where is Rebecca?" asked McConnell. "I've got bad news for her and you too, David." Rebecca was McConnell's sister and her husband was William Shepherd.

The colonel's shoulders sagged. "William?" He had not been at the gate to see what had happened to his son, but he had feared the worst when he saw the look on McConnell's face.

"I'm sorry, David. He was right behind us, but the bastards caught him."

McConnell couldn't think of anything else to say, and he went off looking for his sister, dreading even more having to tell her. Lewis Wetzel, who was overjoyed to see his brother Martin safe, watched sadly as Colonel Shepherd walked slowly back to his quarters. A flurry of firing came from riflemen along the south wall.

"They're comin," came a shout from the blockhouse.

A long line of Indian braves had emerged from the cornfield and was advancing toward the fort. It appeared to some observers along the wall that the Indians were actually holding hands. The volley from the fort's wall began to have an effect.

Two warriors fell wounded, and the line stopped and scattered. The wounded were dragged back among some stumps that stood on the south slope under the bluff where the fort was located. Many of the Indians took cover there and were pinned down by the constant firing from the fort. Others moved off to the east and came up toward the outlying cabins, which were now empty of occupants.

The east gate was still open, held by Jacob Drennon, who was shouting at his wife to hurry. She emerged running from the row of cabins nearest the fort, carrying a child wrapped in a feather mattress. Musket balls whistled past her, as warriors who had come in among the cabins caught sight of her and began shouting their frightening war cries. Drennon released the gate and dropped to one knee to better aim the musket he had been leaning on.

Some sharpshooters from both corner bastions on that side also began to fire at targets that had moved out of the shelter of the wooden huts. Mrs. Drennon swiftly crossed the open field with her precious cargo and made it to safety. Her husband came quickly behind her and closed the gate. Exhausted from fear and exertion, she slumped to the ground, and one of the women who rushed to her aid unfolded the mattress, retrieving the screaming child who was unhurt.

"He's all right," she exclaimed. "But there are bullets in this mattress."

It was midmorning, and the fighting had subsided to sporadic shooting, mainly from the walls of the fort.

The Indians who had taken shelter among the stumps on the underside of the bluff on the south were unable to change position because of the riflemen who kept firing at any sign of movement.

The raiders had infested the settlement cabins and were moving up to the north until they had surrounded the walls on three sides. The west side was inaccessible since it stood so close to the edge of the bluff. Inside, the defenders were trapped, but in the short run they were in no real danger. There were at least twenty militiamen left, plus another group of men from Grave Creek, the Wheeling settlement, and other nearby areas who had taken refuge in the fort. Most of them knew how to handle a rifle.

In addition, there were many women and children who could help by molding bullets, cutting patches, reloading guns, providing water, and running various errands necessary to keep the riflemen going. The magazine held plenty of powder and extra muskets. A major fear was that the Indians would try to set fire to the fort, and several pots were gathered to fill with water for fighting fires.

The Indians on the other hand had lost their momentum and were in a situation that did not fit best with what made them formidable enemies. They had been successful in drawing out a good number of the soldiers, and they had inflicted major damage. A clever ambush had been set, and the hated white men fell into it. The fort was surrounded, but there were more riflemen left inside the walls than had been expected.

Many of the braves were pleased with what had been done and were ready to return to their villages across the big river. But the leader, the Wyandot chief Half-King, had intended to destroy the fort and its inhabitants. He wanted to take captives to Detroit; in fact, he carried several written proclamations from Henry Hamilton promising safety to all who would proclaim their loyalty to the king. There was still a chance to take the fort if it could be set on fire, but it would have to wait for nightfall since it was too dangerous to appear out in the open and close to the walls.

About noon, a horseman appeared to the north on the road that led to Fort Van Meter and the Beech Bottom settlements. It was Francis Duke, the deputy commissar for Ohio County and the husband of David Shepherd's daughter Sarah. He had been at Beech Bottom when a rider from Shepherd's Fort brought the news of the attack at Fort Henry.

When Andrew Zane had appeared at Shepherd's, the nature of the Indian attack at Wheeling was not yet clear. However, when John Caldwell showed up a half hour later, there was no question that a large party of red men was involved. Lewis Bonnett, who was temporarily in charge of the small garrison at Shepherd's Fort, had immediately sent a rider to report to Van Meter's, Beech Bottom, and several miles further north, to Hollidays Cove. Duke, naturally anxious about his wife, was impatient to go to the rescue. Part of Joseph Ogle's company was left at Beech Bottom, but the lieutenant in command had orders to stay there and was reluctant to send any of his men into what might well be a disaster. Six of his men agreed to go with Duke, at least to see what the situation was. As they came within sight of the fort at Wheeling, they could hear the irregular gunfire, and they could see a number of Indians milling about between them and the fort.

"It's no use," pointed out one of them to Francis Duke. "We ain't goin' to be able to get in there. We'd better go back."

"No," said Duke. "I'm goin' in."

The others all argued with him, making it clear that they thought it foolish to ride into certain death.

"To hell with you, then," shouted Duke, and he spurred his mount forward. He came in on the trail close to the riverbank, and the suddenness of his arrival took the first line of Indians by surprise. He was by them before they could react and then into the open just north of the fort itself. Now he swung over to the east, trying to reach the main road that led into the east gate.

"Look," screamed one of the men on the northeast bastion. "It's young Duke!"

By now, the rider was in clear view of the warriors gathered on the north and east of the fort, and they opened with a withering fire. Riflemen in the fort tried to suppress the Indian gunners with shots of their own, but as he came close to the road off the northeast corner of the fort, Francis Duke tumbled from his horse and fell to the ground. He was dead, and his body lay where it fell for neither side could retrieve it without coming under killing fire. This incident brought great depression to the fort's defenders, who could barely tolerate having to see the body lying so close and yet totally helpless to do anything about it.

It was the second major blow to their commander, who had lost both a son and a son-in-law to this savage army. Shepherd had gone into his quarters to console his grief-stricken wife, Rachel, and his daughter Sarah as well. Ebenezer Zane had watched his friend's sorrowful walk, and shaking his head sadly, he turned toward the blockhouse on the southeast corner. Carrying his long rifle, he made his way to the second floor and moved next to where John Wetzel was kneeling, looking out through the rifle port.

'What can you see, John? Are the devils in my cabin?"

"'Fraid so, Eb. They've taken shelter all through the cabins."

"Can you see to shoot the varlets?"

"They're keepin' outta sight, Eb. They know our rifles can pick 'em off at that range."

"Who're we up against, John? Do you recognize any of 'em?"

"Hell, Eb, I don't know one Injun from another. Somebody said he thought they was mostly Wyandots."

"Well, they're the ones who've been raisin' the most hell. The reverends up at the Moravian villages sent word to General Hand that a big bunch of Wyandots had shown up there with Half-King. I'd recognize him if I wuz to see him."

Ebenezer thought of his brother, Isaac, just then, who lived among the Wyandots. Ebenezer's father, William, and all four of his brothers had been captured by the Indians from their home on the South Branch of the Potomac. Ebenezer was fifteen at the time, and they had been carried back to the Indian towns until two years later when they were all ransomed in Detroit. All of them, that is, except eleven-year-old Isaac, whom the Indians refused to give up. Young Isaac had been fancied by the young princess Myeerah, daughter of the Wyandot chieftan, Tarhe, the Crane.

Although he had escaped for a brief time when he was nineteen, Isaac had been recaptured and remained among the Wyandots, living on the Mad River. He eventually became the husband of Myeerah. It pained Ebenezer to think of all this, but he was confident that Isaac was not out there among the besiegers. Isaac, although living peacefully among the Indians, had never converted to the Indian ways and fought against his race as some white captives did. In fact, Isaac was known to warn the settlers of impending danger whenever he could.

A shout came suddenly from the north wall. "Riders!"

Once again, men on horseback appeared on the north road. This time it was Sam McColloch along with his brother John and Peter Hanks. The McColloch brothers lived on Short Creek, and Sam was in command at Fort Van Meter. Their sister Elizabeth, the wife of Ebenezer Zane, was inside Fort Henry and her brothers were determined to join her. Hoping to break through the line of Indians in front of them and reach the fort by surprising the warriors, they put their horses at full gallop and headed for the northeast corner of the wall, in much the same way as the unfortunate Francis Duke had tried a short time earlier.

There were excited yells from among the Indians, who saw a chance to capture these riders. Sam McColloch was out in front by a few yards, and a cluster of warriors focused on trying to drag him from his mount. Somehow, Sam managed to fight them off, and urging his horse to greater effort, he was soon in the clear.

To get away, he had turned the horse away from the fort and toward the road that led to the crest of Wheeling Hill. In the meantime, his two companions, taking advantage of the attention being given to Sam, raced past the corner and were approaching the east gate.

"Open the gate!" came the cry from the wall. "They're coming in."

The warriors on the eastside were intent on stopping the two riders. As shots came from the edge of the woods and from the abandoned cabins, several bold braves rushed out to intercept them. Return fire came from the east wall of the fort, and the warrior in the front of the onrushing group staggered and fell. This brought the entire party to a halt, and they returned to the safety of the cabins, dragging their wounded comrade with them.

The two riders took advantage of this confusion, coming through the gate, which was pushed shut behind them. Sam McColloch was not faring so well. There seemed to be Indians everywhere, and as he reached the road that led over the hill, he dug his heels into his horse's flanks, pleading for even more speed. He was aware that for some reason, the red men behind him and on his right were pursuing but not shooting. They wanted to capture him, and he knew, suddenly, the reason. They wanted to torture him and provide a spectacle within the sight and sound of the people in the fort. This realization shook him, and he was even more determined to get over the top of the hill ahead.

The trail went over the crest at the northernmost end of the long Wheeling Hill, where it pushed up against another higher hill, which met it at almost a right angle. This hill now loomed up on his left and if he could get over the crest, he would be able to outrun the braves easily and make it down to the creek bottom and safety. To his dismay, however, he now saw another party of Indians, which appeared immediately in front of him.

"Where did they come from?" he said aloud to himself. He pulled in his horse, stopping momentarily. The Indians were closing in from both behind and in front. He could not go to the left because of the steep hill. To his right was a shear cliff, which dropped some two hundred feet to the creek below. He pulled on the reins, turning the horse to the right.

"Come on, ole hoss," he shouted. "Don't fail me now."

Believing he was plunging to certain death, Sam much preferred that outcome to the alternative. The horse leaped off the edge, and they began an uncontrolled descent, with the horse sliding on its haunches, struggling to his feet and falling again. McColloch managed to stay in the saddle, slapped with tree branches and brambles, expecting any moment to slide off and fall to his death. A great shout had erupted from those at the fort who had been able to see McColloch and his mount disappear over the side of the cliff. But they could see no more.

The Indians, disappointed at having their sure victim escape their grasp, rushed to the edge to watch what they assumed would be his death. After a short time there was silence, and then to their utter shock, the horse emerged along the bank of the creek with its rider still in the saddle. A scream of admiration arose along the line of Indians, and far below, Sam McColloch turned back, waving his hat in derision. Hardly believing his good fortune, he rode on until he could turn safely northward for the return to Van Meter's.

Captain Ogle was in a bad way. He had been lying with the wounded Private Hedges under the tangle of weeds by the fence corner for several hours. He was in constant fear that Hedges, who drifted in and out of consciousness, would cry out in a moment of painful wakefulness. Any Indian who was determined to follow the bloody trail could easily discover them in their flimsy hiding place. Yet nothing had happened until now.

Ogle had no real injury, although he had several gashes and scratches incurred when he dove into cover. It was warm, and he was thirsty, but when he contemplated his suffering companion, he felt guilty. But a short moment ago, two Indians had appeared and were sitting on the fence just above him. He could have reached up and touched the nearest one who was injured. The other warrior was trying to comfort him, but he moaned and cried, and Ogle could see his blood dripping into the weeds just inches from his own leg. His rifle lay next to him, and he carefully felt along the stock for the hammer, which he slowly pulled back until it was fully cocked. He was determined to make a scrap of it when he was discovered.

Now a new horror presented itself. Hearing a slight rustling in the weeds, he twisted his head enough to see its source, the dark shape of a snake crawling along the base of the log pile not more than four feet away. It was moving toward him when it stopped, raising its head slightly as if surveying and measuring the distance to an intended prey. The captain could barely contain himself, having been born with a dreadful fear of snakes. Yet he knew that anything he did now was likely to mean death for both him and Private Hedges. There was nothing he could do to prevent a strike from the snake, which was likely to attract the attention of the braves on the fence anyway. The fact that it was a rattlesnake did not really matter. The snake, however, had other ideas, and to Ogle's utter relief, it turned back and slithered away.

After what seemed to be a lifetime of minutes, the two Indians slipped down from the fence rails and made their way up toward the cabins. Captain Ogle prayed for night to come quickly.

Inside the fort, the people were feeling a bit better. Clearly their predicament was known in the neighboring communities so that there was reasonable hope that a rescue party of sufficient size might yet come to their aid. No one inside the fort had been hurt, and the besiegers had not yet mounted any kind of serious threat. The biggest worry was fire, and there could be an attack under the cover of darkness.

In the meantime, the defenders could relax a bit. The women and young girls were making the rounds of the walls to provide drinks of water and some bread to the riflemen. Lewis Wetzel watched as his mother and a young girl about his own age came toward him with some refreshment. He didn't know the girl's name, but he was glad she was there, and a feeling of pleasure came over him.

"Are you all right, Lewis?" asked his mother as she handed him a cup.

"Sure, Ma," he said proudly. "I'm fine." His eyes went to the girl, who smiled and then looked away. Lewis was normally very shy around the female sex, but just now he felt important, like a man, and he liked the thought that this pretty girl might be regarding him as a hero. He smiled wide when she gave him a piece of bread.

"Thanks," was all he could say.

"You be careful, Lewis," warned his mother, and then they were gone.

Darkness had fallen, and the overcast sky shut out any light from the moon. The Indians who had taken shelter among the stumps on the south slope now began to move around, no longer having to fear that a sharpshooter might have them in his sights. Most of them moved around to the east and up into the settlement where the action seemed to be.

Captain Ogle could hear them moving, and he waited until it was silent around him. He thought he was within a hundred yards of the south gate of the fort, and it was his intention to make a dash for it at the first opportunity. It would not be easy because Hedges was weak from loss of blood, but Ogle was hoping he would be able to walk a little of the way.

Easing himself up out of the weeds, the captain crouched low against the fence and looked about in all directions. He could see very little, but the glow of light from within the walls of the fort was a welcome sight. He could also see the glow of flames among the settlers' cabins, and he realized that the Indians were setting fire to them. There was no one nearby that he could detect, and he decided that this was the time to try his run to safety. He leaned down and put his arm under the head and shoulders of Private Hedges.

"Matt," he whispered. "I think they're gone. We have to make a run for it now!"

"You go on," muttered Hedges. "I'm a goner."

"Nonsense, Private. You're goin' in with me."

Pulling the reluctant man to his feet, Ogle began to move, dragging Hedges along.

"Try to walk, man," he pleaded. "Help me a little. We'll make it."

They made progress, although it seemed agonizingly slow to Captain Ogle. He had already made the decision that if they were discovered and attacked, he would have to abandon the private and try to save himself. Fortunately, it did not come to that, and at last, they approached the south gate. Lewis Wetzel could hear the commotion outside, but he could not see who it was. *It could be the damned redskins*—he thought—*trying to get me to open the gate.*

"Who's out there?" he shouted.

"Captain Ogle. Open the gate. Hurry!"

"How do I know it's Captain Ogle?" came the reply.

"Goddamn it! Who do you think it is? Pocahontas? Open this gate."

"I guess you ain't no Injun. I'm openin' it."

Wetzel raised the latch and gave the gate a pull. He saw Ogle standing there with Hedges lying at his feet.

"Give me a hand," said Ogle. "I'm worn out."

September 2, 1777

The Indians had looted the cabins and then began setting them afire. They had also slaughtered all the livestock, killing hogs and cattle, and rounding up the horses they could find. A halfhearted attempt was made to bring fire to the walls of the fort, but a warrior carrying a torch was an excellent target, and they soon gave up that idea.

There was really no good way to reduce a well-defended fort without artillery, and after a while, Half-King and his army decided that they had done as much damage as possible. They realized also that the escape of McColloch insured that the alarm was now well spread in the entire area. This could bring enough men against them to take something away from what was clearly a good victory for them.

Sometime after midnight, the entire Indian army melted away and went back across the Ohio. That the attack had ended was, of course, unknown to the fort's defenders, and they continued to make preparations to defend against an assault. Some of the women had gone out the north sally port beneath the northwest bastion and down to the river, bringing back water to fill the big pots. These were kept in readiness to be used on roofs and walls to put out fires. One man, who had prayed all day for rain, had his prayers answered when a shower came up in the late evening. Shortly after dawn, a loud knock was heard at the north sally port.

"Who is out there?" came the cry from Jonathan Zane, who was on the top level of the northwest bastion.

"Colonel Andrew Swearingen, from Hollidays Cove. I've got some men with me."

"Just a minute," said Zane, who came down to open the gate.

Colonel Swearingen, along with Charles Bilderbeck and William Boshears, stepped inside. Swearingen, along with thirteen others, after hearing of the attack on Fort Henry had climbed into a large continental canoe at Hollidays Cove and floated downriver.

It had not been easy in the fog and the dark, and toward morning, seeing the glow of fires from the bluffs ahead of them, they had come ashore some distance to the north above the fort. Not knowing what to expect, the three men had volunteered to scout ahead to make sure they were not falling into some ambush.

Thinking it may well be Fort Henry that was afire and that they had seen burning from the river, the three men were delighted to have found their way to the fort itself, which appeared to be untouched.

Zane led the three men to David Shepherd's quarters, finding him on the walkway in front speaking with Ebenezer Zane, John McColloch, and James McMechen.

"What's this?" asked Shepherd as the four men came in sight.

"Hello, David. It's Andrew Swearingen."

"Good lord, Andrew," exclaimed Shepherd, offering his hand. "How did you get here?"

"We came in a canoe down the river. I've got eleven more men waiting upriver for us to signal them in."

"Did you see any Indians? They had us pretty much surrounded last night."

"We didn't see a single one, David."

"Well, that don't mean they ain't there. I don't think it's safe to send a signal. That just might get your men killed."

"I think he's right," interjected Jonathan Zane. "Why don't the two of you go back and lead the others in. But keep your eyes open."

Swearingen turned to Bilderbeck and Boshears. "Do what he says. For God's sake, be careful."

The two men left on their errand, and Swearingen turned to Shepherd again.

"What happened here, David?"

"They showed up here yesterday morning. At first, just a small party attacked a couple of men sent out to get some horses. When we sent out a group of men to investigate, they was ambushed. Eventually, the whole bunch came up around the fort."

"How many?"

"We don' know for sure. Maybe two or three hundred."

"God!"

John Wetzel came walking up, having just left his post in the southeast corner blockhouse.

"David, we ain't seen any of those damned red men this morning. They may be gone."

"That's interesting. Swearingen here and some of his men came in from the north side, and they didn't see any sign of them either."

"But," noted Dr. McMechen, "they could have just moved back into the woods or into the corn. That's where they were in the beginning."

"The doctor is right," said Ebenezer Zane. "Why don't you send a couple of men out to make a search?"

"I suppose we should," agreed Shepherd. "But let's wait until the rest of Andrew's men get in. If the bastards are still out there, they will surely try to stop them."

Shepherd turned away with a dejected look and went into his quarters. Swearingen watched him with some dismay.

Ebenezer Zane, seeing the look on Swearingen's face, spoke up. "He's had a tough time, Andrew. He lost both his son and his son-in-law yesterday."

"My God," said Swearingen. "No wonder he is down."

"Well, it's been tough for a lot of us. My brother Andrew is missing and probably dead."

"Andrew? Andrew Zane ain't dead. He's at Shepherd's Fort."

"How do you know that?" asked Ebenezer, suddenly filled with hope.

"A runner came to us from Shepherd's. He told us that Andrew Zane had come in, and also John Caldwell. That's how we knew about the attack."

Swearingen felt good at being able to provide such good news.

"Well, ain't that somethin'," said Ebenezer Zane with a broad smile. "Some good news in the midst of all this misery."

A short time later, the remainder of Swearingen's men came in. Jonathan Zane and John McColloch volunteered to scout the areas nearby the fort. When they returned having seen no sign of the enemy, the fort's defenders began to believe that the Indians were really gone.

Another shout came from the northeast corner bastion. "Riders, lots of 'em. Comin' in over Wheeling Hill."

It was two companies of militia from Catfish Camp under John Boggs and Reasin Virgin. A great cheer arose from all over the grounds.

David Shepherd came out of his quarters. "What's happened?"

"It's over, Colonel!" came the answer. "It's over."

"Yeah, we whipped them," someone said.

"I don't know," said Shepherd cautiously. "We've got fifteen or twenty men killed."

"But we killed at least fifty of them," was the reply.

"Hell, I bet we killed a hundred of the bastards," offered another bystander.

"I doubt it," said Jonathan Zane. "We didn't see any bodies."

The siege of Fort Henry was over.

Eastern Theater West

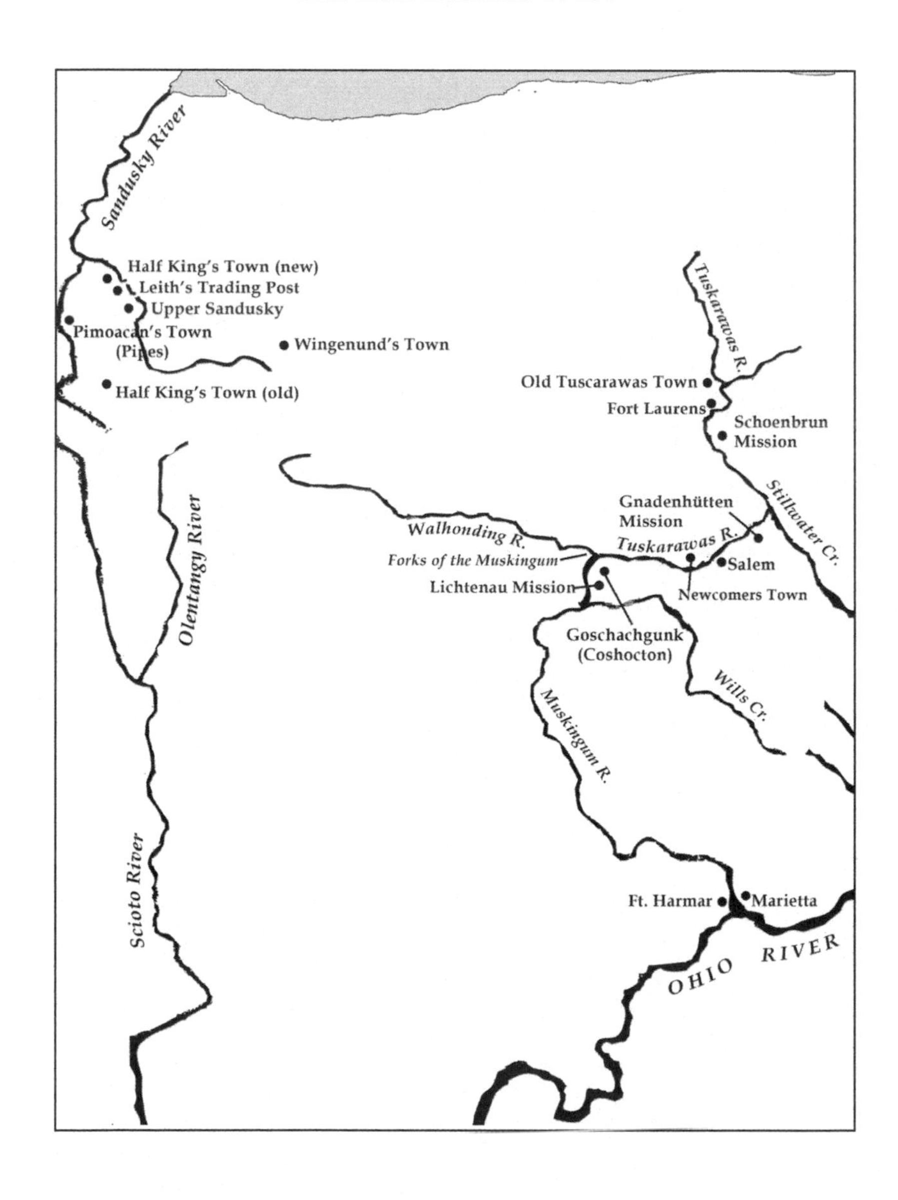

Eastern Theater East

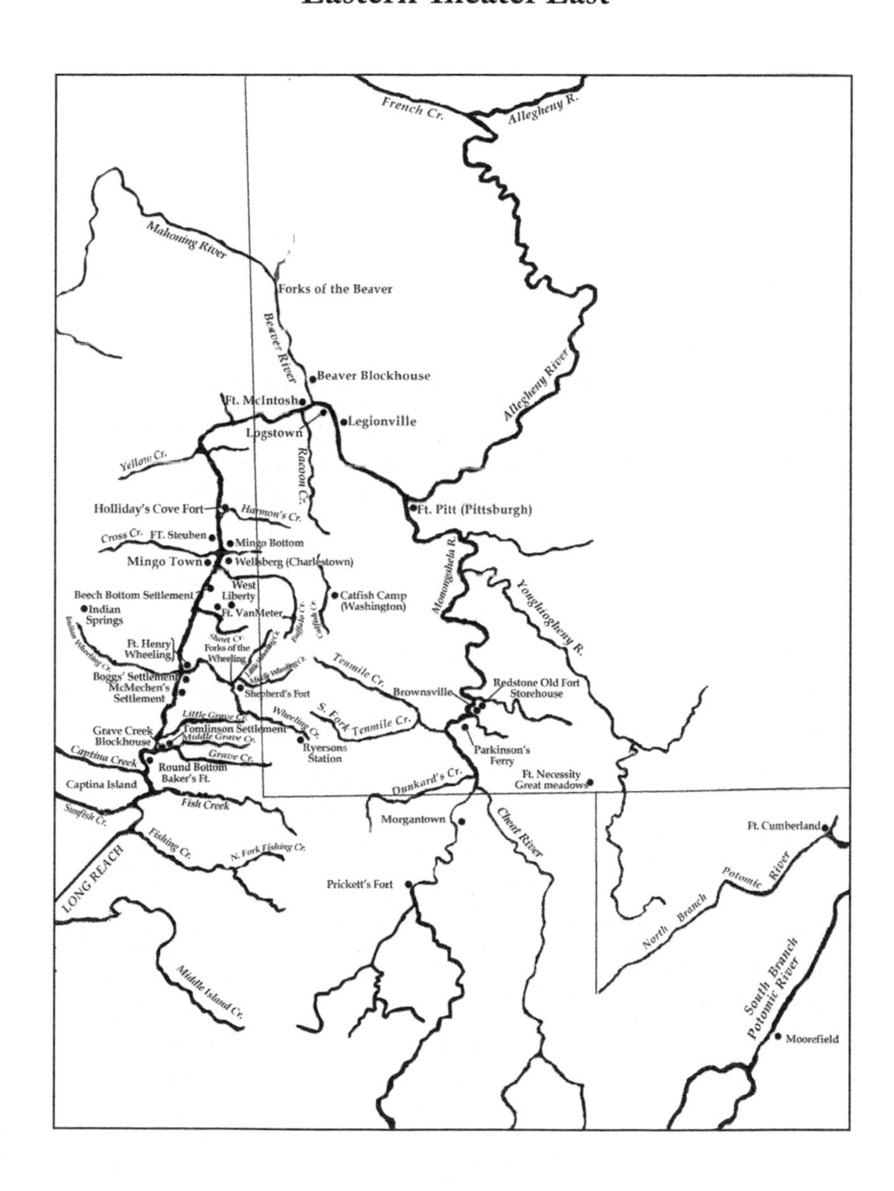

3

TRANSITION

September 30, 1777

LEWIS WETZEL STOOD with his back against the wall. They were in the big room of the house at Shepherd's Fort. The men at the table were in earnest discussion, and because his father was one of them, Lewis listened intently. Following the attack on Fort Henry, many of the settlers in the Wheeling area had left for safer regions to the east. A lack of horses was slowing the departure of others, but the most recent events at the McMechen Narrows had spurred even the most reluctant to consider a prudent flight.

Just two days ago on Sunday morning, William Linn had appeared at the fort, carrying a militiaman named John Collins. Collins had been shot in the leg and was in bad shape.

"Good God, man, what happened?" Lewis Bonnett, who was in temporary command at Shepherd's Fort, had asked.

Linn had then regaled them with the gory details of another Indian ambush that was already being referred to as the Foreman massacre. Forty-six men under the command of Captain William Foreman, an inexperienced but strong-willed man, had set out from Wheeling on the previous Friday morning, September 26, to scout for Indian activity at Grave Creek and possibly on down to Captina Island. Having found the blockhouse at the Tomlinson settlement on Grave Creek had been burned, they decided to return to Fort Henry the next day.

There had been a lively disagreement between Captain Foreman and Linn about the route to follow on the way back. Linn was worried about an ambush at one of the narrow spots on the trail that went along the river and advised that they take the high ground above the main trail.

Foreman would not hear of it, saying he thought there were no Indians within thirty miles. Unable to win the argument, Linn took a few men with him and followed along just below the top of the hill above on the east. A few miles up from Grave Creek, the men on the lower trail struck the Indian ambush, set by the Wyandot chief Half-King and forty of his warriors. Many of the militiamen were slaughtered, including Foreman, his son Hamilton, and Joseph Ogle's brother Jacob. Hearing the shooting, Linn and the few with him on the upper trail came down shouting and firing. Their sudden appearance disrupted the Indian attack, and the Wyandots left the scene.

Linn came upon Collins, who had been shot in the leg while scrambling up the hill from the ambush site. After hiding Collins among some fallen tree branches, Linn promised to return to bring him to safety after dark. Being one of the first of the survivors to make it to Fort Henry, Linn, true to his word, had returned with a horse to bring Collins in. Thinking it unsafe to proceed directly to Fort Henry, Linn had brought the injured man all the way to Shepherd's Fort. Dr. McMechen, who was at Shepherd's at the time, had examined Collins's leg and determined that it should be amputated. Collins protested so hard that the doctor gave up and dressed the wound as best he could.

The Wetzels had been relieved when Linn assured them that their son Martin was safe. The Grandstaffs on the other hand had not been so fortunate. Jacob Grandstaff, a sixteen-year-old boy, had joined the militia shortly after the early September attack on Fort Henry. Catherine Grandstaff, a niece of John Wetzel, had rushed up to Linn, inquiring about her son. Linn could not tell her anything except that he had not seen the boy. The Grandstaff family had immediately gathered some things and set out on foot for Fort Henry.

The discussion around the table was focused on plans for the proposed move to the east.

"I think we ought to leave tomorrow," said Jacob Drennon. "It surely isn't safe around here anymore. 'Course we could take up Hamilton on his offer. Might be best for everybody."

The rest of the people in the room were stunned at such a remark. That anyone would be brave enough to say anything nice about the British, and especially the man Hamilton—who was regarded as somewhat worse than the devil himself—was unthinkable. They knew that Drennon had been educated in England though he was Virginia born and commissioned in the British army.

When word of the Declaration of Independence had reached the frontier, the inhabitants had celebrated with great joy and were quick to provide support and men for the new revolutionary army. Plenty of the men had served in militia that had fought with the English; but now they considered themselves American, and any loyalty to the king and his subjects had been cast off like a tattered coat.

There was little sympathy or patience for anyone who was not with them.

"You a Tory, Jacob?" asked John Wetzel as a murmur now rose around the room.

Lewis had heard his father speak highly of Drennon in the past. He knew that the man had been in Dunmore's War and that he traveled frequently to the Kentucky country. He could feel the tension around him, and he wondered what his father intended to do.

Drennon stood now, realizing he had said a dangerous thing. "I'm not a Tory," he declared. "But I am worried about our safety. Even if we go in a group, we could be attacked. Look what happened to Foreman's men. They had forty-six with them all armed fighters, and they were attacked with fifteen or twenty of them killed."

There was no response, and Drennon could not restrain himself although he realized as he spoke that he was sinking deeper into trouble. "Well, you've got to admit, we're not any better off under King Washington than under King George."

Lewis Wetzel could not believe his ears. George Washington was extremely popular on the frontier, having been present at Braddock's defeat near Fort Pitt, and then later taking a surveying trip down the Ohio. How could anyone refer to him as a king? He saw the anger on his father's face as Drennon's wife tugged at his arm, trying to get him to sit down. Lewis Bonnett jumped to his feet.

"Shut your damned mouth, Jacob. We're not gonna listen to that kind of talk. What's wrong with you?"

"There's nothing wrong with me," answered Drennon as he pulled his arm away from the hand of his worried wife. "I'm just trying to get you people to think about what you're doing."

William Linn was standing near the door, listening to the proceedings but having determined not to participate. He was planning to return to Fort Henry that very day. He had stayed longer at Shepherd's than intended, but he felt interest and responsibility in the welfare of John Collins. He had expended considerable effort to save the man's life, and when he became aware of the settlers' intent to go back to the east, he prevailed upon them to take Collins as far as Catfish Camp. He had been surprised and glad to find Dr. McMechen at the Fort, and the doctor had agreed to go with Collins to Catfish. Linn, currently a captain in the militia, was one of the more highly respected men on the border.

People still talked of his daring mission in the previous year to obtain much-needed powder for the rebellious colonists. The British were confident that a lack of powder would doom the rebellion, particularly in the west. Linn, a lieutenant at the time, went with George Gibson to New Orleans in September of 1776 to buy powder from the Spanish authorities. The Spanish were willing, but the British consul was suspicious, so a plan was hatched that resulted in Gibson being thrown into a Spanish jail. This lulled the British into complacency, and with the aid of an American sympathizer residing in the area, Linn was able to secure the powder.

Accompanied by forty-three men, he started up the Mississippi River with several barges loaded with ninety-eight barrels of powder. Suffering severe hardship, illness, and attempts by Indians to intercept them, Linn delivered the powder to Fort Henry in May of 1777. David Shepherd, heading the commissary at that time, signed an affidavit recording the receipt of ten thousand pounds of black powder.

Now stung by the language of Jacob Drennon, Captain Linn could not hold back. He stepped forward, standing over the table of seated men, glowering at Drennon. The two men were well acquainted, having served together in Dunmore's War.

"You damned fool, Drennon," he shouted. "You've been warped with all that British learning 'til you can't understand what's clear to the rest of us. We're fightin' for something worthwhile here. I'm ready, and so are my friends, to give my last drop of blood in defense of my country, especially when we are fighting for that blessed enjoyment called liberty."

The room fell deathly quiet. No one there had heard the rebellion defended with such vigor, and each of the men was wondering if he really felt that strongly. Drennon was looking down, unable to face the angry Linn. He was not a coward, and he certainly was not a Tory. On the other hand, he had not been able to embrace the cause with any enthusiasm, and he could not foresee that life for his family was going to be good anytime soon. He also realized that it was up to him to defuse this current situation. He looked up at Captain Linn, whose anger had not abated, and saw that the wrong word said just now could lead to violence. Still he was an independent, full-grown male, a frontiersman, and such a person was not expected to be called a fool to his face without reacting. And, as he thought about it, he felt his own anger rising.

"I'm not a damned fool. I've signed the oath of allegiance. Have you?"

The male citizens of Ohio County had recently been asked to sign an oath of allegiance to the commonwealth of Virginia before a justice of the peace. The oath also contained language including a pledge to report treason against Virginia or any of the United States of America. It was quite likely that no one else in the room had yet signed the document.

"I ain't seen such an oath. But I've signed one already in my blood and that of my friends."

Somehow this exchange had taken the fire out of him, and Captain Linn turned away.

Lewis Bonnett spoke up now. "Jacob, will you take back what you said about General Washington?"

"Well, I didn't mean anything against him," said Drennon quickly. He knew that his outburst had been foolish, and he was searching now for a way to get things settled down. "I just wanted to get people thinking about getting our families to safety."

"Do you take it back?" asked Bonnett again. His voice continued to carry a sharpness and a threat.

"Yes! Yes! I take it back!" shouted Drennon.

"All right, then," said Bonnett. "Let's get back to deciding what we're goin' to do."

Jacob Wetzel had moved next to his brother.

"God, Lew," he whispered. "I thought there was gonna' be a fight."

"There almost was," agreed Lewis.

"Do you think we hafta move?" wondered Jacob.

"Yeah," said Lewis. "But I don't want to!" he added with disgust.

"Where to?"

"That's what they're arguin' about."

The tension in the room had ebbed, and the conversation at the table had become chaotic with every one talking at once. Catfish Camp was the most likely immediate destination. Some were suggesting the region around Redstone Old Fort on the Monongahela.

John Wetzel managed to get his voice above the din, and the others quieted to hear what he had to say. "I'm thinkin' we'll go back to Dunkard. There was lots of space there when we left a few years ago." He nodded at Bonnett and Abraham Messer. "Lewis, you, and Abraham may want to go there too, and maybe Kellers and Stroups."

"I'm not goin' any place just yet," spoke up Conrad Stroup. "I've got some business back at Zanes' that I got to take care of. But then after that, we might go back to Dunkard."

"I think it would be too dangerous to split up," said Dr. McMechen. He had been quiet through most of the talk. His own brother, William, had gone back to Redstone several weeks earlier, and he had intended to go all the way back to the east coast himself. It was a month later now since he had first decided to go on the fateful morning of the Indian attack at Fort Henry. Since then he had been afraid to go far from the safety of that place, although he had proceeded the five miles down to the fort at the forks of Wheeling Creek.

It wasn't just fear either, he realized, for he was having second thoughts about whether it might be best for him to stay in the area. After all, he was a county official, and he felt a responsibility to the people there. But now that there were enough people gathered so that a departure to Catfish Camp would be safe, it seemed like a good idea to at least join his brother for a time. "Let's all go to Catfish first, and then we can go separate ways from there."

Although Catfish Camp was well within range of Indian excursions, it had not been hit by Indian attack itself and was regarded as a safe haven by most of the settlers who had advanced to the west beyond it. It was not clear to any of the settlers what they would do once they arrived there.

"Well, in any case, we can all go toward Catfish and beyond the head of Little Wheeling. Then those goin' to Dunkard may want to go down the valley of Tenmile." John Wetzel had made his own decision. What he had said was a major speech for him.

"Are we agreed then?" asked Bonnett. "We'll go together to Catfish Camp, at least as far as the head of the valley of Tenmile Creek."

There was no disagreement, and Bonnett quickly suggested that they leave on the following morning.

"We can take only what can be packed on the horses," he said.

"What about the animals?" someone asked.

"Well, we take all the livestock with us," answered Bonnett.

Captain Linn, who had stepped outside for a time, reentered the room. "If you don't mind a bit of advice, Lewis," said Linn, "I'd suggest you form a small party of horsemen to follow after the main group at some distance. That could be handy in case there are some reds in the area who aim to molest your train."

This idea was met with enthusiastic agreement. The vulnerability of a body of people and animals strung out along a trail was well understood. Bonnett quickly let it be known that he would head up this party. A man named Parker volunteered, as did Abraham Messer.

"How about your boy George?" asked Bonnett, addressing himself to John Wetzel. "He can shoot."

"Yeah," agreed Wetzel. "I reckon he'll do."

"Thanks, John. You can be the leader of the main group then." Bonnett turned now and addressed the entire room.

"It's settled. We'll leave at full light in the morning. It is getting late now, so everybody needs to see to your belongin's. We'll need four horses for the guard party and one for Collins to ride. The rest will be used as packhorses."

"What about Grandstaffs?" asked Mary Wetzel. "They might want to go with us."

Word had reached them just that day that young Jacob Grandstaff had been killed in the Foreman affair.

"They might," agreed John Wetzel. "But we don't know when they'll be ready."

"Yes," said Lewis Bonnett. "It's a shame, but we just can't wait for them."

As people began to leave the room, a man named John Grice approached Lewis Bonnett and John Wetzel as they stood talking. Grice had a farm on Peters Run, whose mouth on Little Wheeling Creek was only a mile or so up from the forks.

"I'm taking my family up to our cabin to get a few things. We'll meet you at the mouth of the run in the morning."

"That's a bad idea," said Bonnett immediately. "It ain't safe to go up there alone."

"He's right," chimed in John Wetzel, who was usually very reluctant to butt into someone else's business.

"It'll be all right," said Grice. "I've talked it over with my wife and my daughter Nancy. There's some stuff we'd really like to get."

"Nothing's that important," said Bonnett. "Forget it, John."

But Grice was adamant. Bonnett and Wetzel did talk him into taking a horse and scouting a bit before taking his family. The afternoon was well along when Grice returned, still determined to go.

"I didn't see no sign of any Injuns," he reported to Lewis Bonnett.

"I still say it is not wise to go up there tonight," cautioned Bonnett. "At least leave the women and children here."

"No, I need them all to help carry things."

There was nothing more that could be said. Frontiersmen were independent, and no one was inclined to try to argue too much. Grice soon left with his family and no more was made of it. Lewis and Jacob Wetzel went to find their brother George.

"Wish I was goin' with Uncle Lewis instead of him," said Lew. "I'm a better shot than he is."

"Yeah, but you ain't old enough," Jacob reminded him.

"So they think. At least we know now where we're goin'."

"You mean to Catfish?"

"No, to Dunkard."

They saw George out near the stockade gate.

"Hey, George," hollered Jacob. "Did you hear what you're gonna do?"

Lewis followed along sadly.

October 1, 1777

It was approaching midmorning before the large company of settlers had begun to move away from Shepherd's Fort and toward Catfish Camp up the road, which followed along the banks of Little Wheeling Creek. When the movers reached the mouth of Peters Run, they stopped, expecting to find the Grice family waiting for them.

Lewis Bonnett, who intended to hang back with his small party of horsemen, had nevertheless stayed close to the main group in this first mile. He rode up to where John Wetzel stood at the front of the column, holding the bridle of the packhorse he had been leading.

"They ain't here, eh," observed Bonnett.

"Don't see no sign of 'em," said John.

"Guess I'd best go see what is keepin' 'em."

"Better take the other three with you."

"I will, but we've heard no shootin' or no commotion."

"Could still be trouble."

With a nod of understanding toward Wetzel, Bonnett turned his horse back to where his three mounted companions waited. He waved for them to follow, and he turned up the west bank of Peters Run.

"Better have a look," he explained to the others. "The Grice farm is not far up the way here."

Nothing more was said. The trail led along the creek bank where trees and a tangle of bushes grew near the path. In less than a half mile, the woods curved back and the open meadow of the farm appeared. Bonnett stopped here, holding up his hand, gesturing for the other riders to be quiet. They looked out over the open field. Nothing was moving. In the far distance, they could see the cabin nestled against the low hill at its back.

"This ain't right," said Bonnett. "I don't see any sign of life."

"Could they still be in the cabin?" wondered Abraham Messer.

"Don't seem like it," answered Bonnett. "They can't all be in there this late in the morning."

All four riders stood together now on high alert. Something had happened, and it wasn't likely to be good.

"Abraham, take George and ride along the creek. Keep your eyes open for I reckon there has been trouble here, and the redskins are behind it. Parker and I will go along the other side of the meadow. Give a shout if you see anythin'." With that, Bonnett turned his horse to the left along the trees at the edge of the field.

They hadn't gone far when Messer gave a shout. "Here! There's a body in the grass."

Half expecting a shot from the unseen foe, Bonnett and Parker rode across the open field to where Messer, who had dismounted, stood over the body of ten-year-old James Grice. His head was caved in where it had been struck by a war club.

"There's another body," cried George Wetzel, pointing to a crumpled form not more than twenty feet away.

All four men were on foot now, leading the horses and trying to keep themselves shielded from any would-be shooters hiding in the woods on either side. Bonnett was the first to reach the newly discovered victim, and he kneeled down for a closer look.

"It's little Rachel" he said. "She's been tomahawked and scalped, and not long ago." He bent down further and placed his ear against her chest.

"My God! he exclaimed. "She's still alive!"

"Are you sure?" asked Messer. "How can that be? She sure looks dead."

"That's what the Injuns thought, I guess," answered Bonnett. "But she ain't. Her little heart is still beating." He motioned now to young George Wetzel.

"George, bring your horse over here. Abraham, you, and Parker keep a lookout. We don't want no unexpected visitors."

Messer and Parker led their horses a few yards away closer to the cabin. Wetzel brought his mount over next to where Rachel lay. "Get on your horse, George, and I'll hand her up to you. Then get her to your pa and the rest. Tell him to go ahead and start for Catfish. We'll take care of things here and then follow along behind."

Lifting the young girl's body carefully, Bonnett raised her and slid her up in front of George, gently resting her head against the front of his left shoulder.

"Try not to bounce her too much, George, but you need to hurry as much as you can." Bonnett turned to walk away, then looked back.

"And, George," he cautioned, "tell your pa to keep a sharp eye out. Them, red bastards, may be out there watching for a chance to cause some more trouble."

With a nod, George Wetzel and his bloodied passenger turned back and rode along Peters Run up the path toward Little Wheeling. The three men spread out in a line and walked with the horses, searching for more victims. They found the body of Nancy, John Grice's married daughter, felled by a tomahawk blow. She was pregnant, and as Messer turned her body over gently, he fell back in shock. "Them damned devils!" he exclaimed. "They killed the baby too."

Nancy's abdomen had been ripped open, and the fetus torn out. Messer turned his head away and put his hand up to shield his eyes. "Damn them," he said again.

"It's their custom," said Bonnett, who put his hand on Messer's shoulder.

He saw the body of the tiny fetus lying on the tall grass a few feet away, but said nothing. Farther along lay the lifeless forms of John Grice and his wife, both shot with arrows. Bonnett bent down to examine the arrow protruding from the back of John Grist.

"Can you tell what tribe it is?" asked Parker.

"I ain't sure. I think it's Mingo or maybe Wyandot. It was a silent attack."

The woodland Indians on the border had mostly abandoned the use of bow and arrow when attacking the whites, much preferring the gun.

"Mebbe they were afraid we could hear shots, even at the fort. It ain't that far," offered Messer, trying to get himself under control after witnessing the gruesome sight of the slain mother-to-be.

"Could be," said Bonnett. "I think we scared 'em off. They didn't scalp anybody, 'cept Rachel."

A number of household items were scattered near the bodies. The right hand of Mrs. Grice still grasped the edge of a bag that had been fashioned from a bed sheet. It was torn and its contents—several pieces of delft tableware—lay broken in the grass. Bonnett stirred them with his feet, then reached down to pick up an item that caught his eye. The possession of dishes made from china, delft, or silver was almost unheard of amongst the pioneers on the frontier. It was apparent that the Grice family had some special heirlooms, and there was no doubt it was one of the reasons they had insisted on returning to their home against all adverse advice.

Bonnett held a silver cup high above his head.

"A pretty expensive piece, I reckon," he said. "Cost 'em their lives."

"Wasn't there another boy?" asked Parker.

"Yes," answered Bonnett. "John Jr. He was about fourteen, I think."

"They took him along with 'em, I guess," said Messer.

"Damn, I wish Grice would have listened to us. This is bad!" Bonnett stuffed the silver cup inside his hunting shirt and looked all around. "We got to bury these bodies if we can."

"We don't have anything to dig with," noted Messer.

"I'll check in the shed to see if there's a spade to use." Parker mounted his horse and rode off toward the buildings.

"Should we try to track 'em, Lewis? I don't think they've gone too far yet," said Messer.

"We don't know how many there was, and we've got to get on to following after the other folks like we promised. No, let's get this job done and get on back to the others."

George Wetzel was worried. He was afraid that Rachel Grist, her body leaning against his with her bloody head resting on his shoulder, might die right there on the horse's back. He wanted to hurry the horse along faster, but he was aware of every jolt and trying hard to keep himself straight up and as stiff as possible. Suddenly he was aware that her eyes were open. She was trying to twist enough to see who was carrying her. "You're awake," was all he could think of to say to her. She said nothing but relaxed back against him, satisfied, perhaps, that he wasn't an Indian.

How could she be awake? George wondered to himself. He'd heard of people surviving a scalping, but he'd never expected to see it himself. He could see ahead to the mouth of Peters Run and where it emptied into Little Wheeling Creek. As he came closer, he could see that the people in the caravan had crossed the run and were waiting along the road that led to Catfish Camp. He splashed down into the shallow water and emerged on the other side where people had finally noticed him riding in.

"Here's George Wetzel," someone shouted. "And he's carryin' somebody."

"I've got Rachel," hollered George. "Where's my pa?"

"He's in the front," was the answer.

George had stopped for a moment, and one of the women walked up and put her hand on Rachel's leg.

"Oh my!" she exclaimed. "She's hurt bad. Dr. McMechen is up there with your father."

"Best get her down," said Jacob Drennon, who had come quickly to see what was happening. He and the woman helped to lift Rachel off the horse and laid her gently on a grassy spot just off the trail. George Wetzel felt very tired and relieved. He slid down from the horse when he saw his brother, Lewis, walking toward him.

"Lew, go and get Pa real quick." And as Lew turned to run, George added, "And bring the doctor too."

Mrs. Drennon had joined them.

"Her eyes are open," she observed as she knelt beside Rachel. "What happened, honey? Can you tell us?"

"I don't think she can talk none," said George. "Injuns killed the rest of the family."

"Oh lord. Where is the doctor?" Mrs. Drennon took her shawl, folded it, and put it under Rachel's head.

"Where are the other men you were with?" she asked George.

"Uncle Lewis said they would take care of things there. I guess he meant to bury the others."

In a few minutes, John Wetzel and James McMechen arrived. Lewis Wetzel was with them. Dr. McMechen went immediately to tend to Rachel. John had questions for his son.

"What happened, George, and where are your uncle and the others?"

"They're burying the dead, Pa," said George. "All the rest of the family, as far's I know."

"Did you see any of the red devils?" his father wanted to know.

"They was gone as near as we could tell. Uncle Lewis said to tell you to start movin' everybody to Catfish, but he's thinkin' the Injuns might be watchin' us too."

"Well, I think there's too many of us for them to attack unless there's a big bunch of'em. Did your uncle say how many they was?"

"No, but we didn't try to track 'em. They sent me back with Rachel as soon as we found her."

"John," came the call from Dr. McMechen. "Rachel's alive, but I don't know for how much longer. I can't do much for her. We need to get her to Catfish Camp as quick as we can. Dr. Moore is there, and he might be able to help her."

"Why don't you take her, James? We'll give you a horse, and you can ride with her as fast as possible."

"But what about the Indians? A single rider wouldn't be safe."

"We'll send somebody with you. Where's Collins? He needs to see the doctor too."

"But Collins is hurt," argued McMechen.

"Yeah, but he can shoot."

The doctor was much distressed, but he didn't see a way out. The girl needed help and quickly. And he would get to Catfish Camp much faster this way. Still there was the danger from the Indians.

"John, I don't think it's wise to send Collins." Jacob Drennon had entered the discussion. "They might need to dismount, and they couldn't without some help."

"But we can't spare another horse," responded Wetzel.

"We can figure some other way to carry Collins," persisted Drennon.

"I agree," said McMechen. "If I'm going to make that ride, I want someone along who is fully able."

A man named Joseph Alexander stepped forward. He had lived in the Grave Creek settlement and had volunteered to serve in the militia. He was a good friend of the McMechen brothers and was along because he intended to join William McMechen, who had already gone back to the Redstone region.

"I'll go with you James," he said in a confident tone. "We'll be fine. I don't think the Injuns will bother us if we're moving fast on horseback."

"Good, good," said John Wetzel, glad to have this settled. "Somebody bring Collins and his horse over here."

In something less than a half hour, eleven-year-old Rachel Grice had been secured on a horse in front of Dr. McMechen, and together with Joe Alexander, they had ridden off in the direction of Catfish Camp. A crude-carrying device, something like what would later be called a travois, was put together for John Collins, and the main body of settlers began to move in the same direction.

After posting his two sons, George and Lewis, to move through the trees at the edge of the caravan, and asking Martin Keller to act as a rear guard, John Wetzel took the lead. Progress was slow since a good number of hogs, milk cows, and a few sheep were kept in the middle of the group, at least as much as that was possible. Though it was trouble and added greatly to the time needed for this migration, the livestock would be crucial for survival during the coming winter. Lewis Wetzel was delighted with the job he had been given.

"Stay hidden among the trees as best you can," his father had commanded, "But keep your eyes open. I'm countin' on you, boys, to keep us from bein' surprised by any stray warriors on that side. The creek will help protect us on the other."

"We will, Pa, you can trust us," said Lew.

"If we come to a wide open spot, then come in with us," said John. "I don't want you out too far. Understand?"

"Yes, Pa," said George. "Don't worry about us."

The caravan of settlers bound for Catfish Camp had proceeded for several miles without incident. Lewis Wetzel was slipping through the forest along the left flank. The line of trees had begun to flare out from the trail, creating a greater distance between Lewis and the other travelers. He stopped for a moment and glanced behind, searching for a glimpse of his brother George, who was in the rear by some one hundred yards.

He remembered his father's admonition about getting out too far, but after a careful search to his left and to the front, he decided to keep going. He felt important and confident. It was the first time he had been given a job with this much responsibility, and in his own mind, it was something at which he was quite good. He was carrying the musket that had come from the stores at Fort Henry, and his father had mentioned that sometime soon he should have his own long rifle. But the old musket felt fine, and he was secretly hoping for a chance to use it.

The open space continued to widen, although a bit farther ahead Lewis could see the land sloping upward to a heavily wooded ridge, both to the north and to the east. Looking deeper into the woods to the northeast, he thought he detected some movement. Moving behind a stout maple tree, he dropped to one knee and continued to watch. After a moment, young Wetzel was amazed to see three painted warriors making their way cautiously toward the open field before them. They stopped and gestured to each other, pointing toward the crowd of settlers moving slowly along the side of Little Wheeling Creek, and then to the hillside that overlooked the trail a bit farther along.

Each of the Indians had a gun, and it was obvious to Lewis that they intended to mount some kind of attack. Without thinking about what might well be his own perilous situation, he quickly brought the gunstock to his shoulder and took aim. He had loaded and primed his weapon at the very beginning, and it responded with a loud roar when he squeezed the trigger. He fully expected to see one of the braves tumble to the ground, but he was disappointed when he realized that the shot had missed. The Indians had jumped at the report of Wetzel's gun and instinctively moved to take cover behind the trees. One of them shouted and pointed in Lewis's direction, whose activity in frantically trying to reload his musket had exposed him to view.

Two of the braves emerged, thinking to close the distance to their adversary before he was ready to shoot again. The third warrior hung back, waiting to see if it was a lone attacker. The attacker who, even at his young age had practiced the loading of a muzzle-loader many times, had succeeded in tamping the main charge and the lead ball in place. Using a tactic taught to him by his father, he turned the gun on its side and tapped it to shake some of the black powder from the main charge into the priming pan. Satisfied that he was ready, he pulled the hammer back and prepared to fire again at the two targets rapidly closing on him.

Suddenly, however, they stopped and began running back from where they had come.

"Lew!" came the shout from behind him. It was his brother George who was crashing through the underbrush and screaming at the top of his voice. "Lew, are you there?"

At the same time, there was a volley of shouts coming from the caravan, and Lewis could see his father and some other men rushing toward the edge of the clearing. One of them stopped, dropped to one knee, and raising his rifle, fired off a shot into the woods at the movement he saw through the trees. The three Indians were running at top speed back up the little ravine just below the main slope. By this time, George Wetzel had arrived at his little brother's side.

"What were you shooting at?" he wanted to know. He had not been able to see the warriors as he ran. "Are you hurt?"

"They was three of them devils, George," said Lew with excitement. "But I missed."

"Lew, George, where are you?" It was their father who, with the others, had reached the edge of the stand of trees.

"Over here, Pa," called George. "Lew took a shot at 'em."

"How many was there?" asked John Wetzel, somewhat out of breath.

"There was three, Pa," said Lew. "I had a good shot, but I missed."

"Well it's hard to hit anything with that old musket," said John.

"Shall we go after them, John?" asked Martin Keller, who had come up from the rear of the expedition.

"I don't think that's such a good idea," offered Jacob Drennon, who had followed along just behind John Wetzel. "We need to stay together, especially since we don't really know how many we're up against."

"I think he's right, Martin," said John.

"Pa, George and me can go after 'em," said Lewis. "It's a shame to let em git away. Let us, Pa, please let us!"

George said nothing.

"No, Lew, that's probably just what they're waitin' for. We best let 'em go this time." John looked proudly at his son. "You did a fine job, Lew. If you hadn't stopped 'em, likely they'd have picked off two or three of us." John Wetzel turned to the other men. "There's a stream ahead, and I reckon they hoped to catch us while we were crossin'."

"No doubt," agreed Drennon. "Thanks to you, Lew, that plan was foiled."

Lewis was happy to hear such words of praise, which didn't come that often from his father. He felt good about what he'd done, though he figured it would have been better if he'd killed one of the Indians.

The sound of riders coming in from the west now caught their attention. The horses were at full gallop in single file but close together. Lewis Bonnett was in the lead, and he reined in his mount, sliding to a stop just short of where the Wetzels stood watching.

"What's happened?" Bonnett wanted to know as he dismounted. "We could hear shooting."

"There was three warriors stalking us," answered John Wetzel. "Lew took a shot at them."

"Probably part of the bunch that hit the Grice's."

"Any idea how many Injuns we're talking about?" John Wetzel wanted to know.

"No, but there had to be seven or eight of 'em at least. They took young John with 'em, so at least some would be heading back over the Ohio."

"The rest of the family all dead?"

"Yeah, except for Rachel. Was she still alive when George got to you?"

"She was. We sent her off to Catfish with James McMechen and Joe Alexander."

"I think we scared the Injuns off, John. They didn't have time to scalp anybody but Rachel."

The two brothers-in-law stood and looked at each other for a moment. Lewis Bonnett shook his head and looked back in the direction from which he had come.

"I sure wish Grice had listened to us. Damn it!" he said.

"Well, there's nothin' we can do about it. We best worry about what's happenin' here right now," cautioned John Wetzel.

"If there was only three, I don't think they'll bother us anymore," observed Bonnett after another short silence.

"But we don't know," said Messer, who had been listening carefully, looking for an opportunity to join the conversation. "There could be more of 'em out there just waiting for everybody to get strung out on the move."

"We could camp right here," suggested Jacob Drennon. "We could defend ourselves well if we're pulled in tight."

"I was hopin' to get as far as the Dutch Fork for the night," said John Wetzel. "I think we'd be safer over there too."

"I agree," said Bonnett.

"Lewis, if you and your mounted men stay up close to us, ready to make a rush against any attackers, I think we'll be safe. The worst will be crossing the creek just ahead."

"We can do that, John. You can set up some shooters to help guard the crossing." Bonnett turned to Messer. "Do you agree with us, Abraham?"

"I reckon," said Messer, although he wasn't so sure.

"What about you, Jacob?" Bonnett thought it best to get Drennon's approval as well.

"I still think we ought to camp right here."

"The closer we git to Catfish, the safer we are," said Parker, who was still astride his horse. "I'd say let's git movin."

Drennon shook his head and walked away.

"Can't please everybody." Bonnett watched Drennon talking to his wife. He reached now inside his hunting shirt and retrieved the silver cup he had stowed there. He held it up and spoke to Wetzel. "This belongs to Rachel I guess."

John Wetzel stared at the cup, and its significance dawned on him. He didn't speak but shook his head in disgust.

"Take us to Dutch Fork, John," said Bonnett.

October 7, 1777

The Wetzel party was camped along a little creek called Meadow Run. The party included the families of Lewis Bonnett, Martin Keller, and Abraham Messer. It was three days since they had separated from the rest of the people who had left Shepherd's Fort headed for Catfish Camp.

After camping together on the first night near the Dutch Fork of Buffalo Creek, the Wetzel party had turned to the south at the east fork of Buffalo, found the head of Tenmile Creek and followed it down until it turned east toward the Monongahela. After continuing in a southeasterly direction for another ten miles, they had come to this expanse of grassland on Meadow Run where they had had rested for a couple of days.

There was talk of settling in this area. Dunkard Creek was not much farther to the south. There had been no further incidents with the Indians, although one of the main Indian trails had crossed their path. Lewis Bonnett, along with Abraham Messer and George Wetzel, had resumed their role as a rear guard, keeping a good distance from the main body and watching closely for any pursuit behind them.

Just this morning, the camp was visited by John Syckes, who was married to still another sister of Lewis Bonnett and Mary Wetzel. Syckes lived at the mouth of Dunkard Creek and had received word about his relatives having arrived along Meadow Run. After he had ridden into the main part of the camp, the first person he saw was Anna Elizabeth Bonnett. He dismounted and moved toward where she stood in amazement at seeing this brother-in-law.

"Elizabeth," shouted Syckes, reaching out to hold her by the shoulders. "We heard you folks were down here on Meadow Run."

"Well, yes, John, we didn't expect to see you."

"Where's Lewis?" Syckes wanted to know.

"He's back a ways," she answered. "Watchin' out to see if any Indians are following."

"Well that's good. It ain't safe here, Elizabeth. You folks can't stay here."

"I don't know, John. The Wetzels kinda like it here and are talkin' about building a cabin."

"It ain't safe, I tell you. Where is John Wetzel right now?"

"He's close by some place. Oh, there he is, and Mary too."

"John Syckes!" exclaimed John Wetzel who was striding quickly toward them, his wife, Mary, almost running to keep up with her husband. "You're lucky somebody didn't shoot you, John. What are you doing here?"

"You're right, I did almost get shot. Lucky for me, it was young Lew had a bead on me, and he recognized me afore he pulled the trigger." When he had seen the gun barrel raised from behind a tree off to the side, Syckes had realized how silly he had been to approach the camp as he had. Fortunately it had lowered again, and Lewis Wetzel had stepped out with a grin.

"It was a good thing it was Lew. He's young, but he's got a lot of sense. That's why we put him out there as a guard." The elder Wetzel found himself feeling considerable pride in his young son.

"I came to get you people to move out of here. It ain't safe, John."

"Well, we been watching close for Injuns all the way down here, John," pointed out Wetzel, "But we've seen none lately."

"They're raisin' a ruckus on upper Dunkard Creek, and there's all kinds of sign all over this area, John," said Syckes. He turned now to face his sister-in-law. "Hello, Mary. Marguerite says to come in a hurry down to our place. She's worried about you."

Mary Wetzel knew that her husband was not keen on moving back to the old settlements at the mouth of Dunkard, but she felt the urgency in her brother-in-law's words.

"John," she said somewhat timidly. "Maybe we should do as he says."

"I agree with Mary," said Elizabeth Bonnett forcefully.

John Wetzel felt the intensity of the forces building up against what was expected to be his opposition to moving on. It had seemed good to him to claim the land here, but he had been having second thoughts about all the work required to erect a cabin of some kind to live in for the winter. He knew there were probably some vacant huts back at the old settlements enough for the entire party even. It made sense to go there, and now he had a good reason for changing his mind. Still it was distasteful to have to give in to a fear of the Indians and to pressure from others.

"I don't know," he said finally. "Let's see what the others think."

It did seem reasonable to Wetzel to get input from the other families. Of course, Bonnett and Messer weren't in the camp, but Keller was, plus all the wives.

"Well, don't take too long with this," admonished Syckes. "I'd like to get you over to our place by nightfall."

"Jacob, run and get Martin Keller. Tell him to get over here quick."

Jacob Wetzel had followed his parents over to meet his uncle and was now given this urgent errand. He knew where to find him, and it was not long until the two of them returned along with Mrs. Messer and Mrs. Keller.

"What is it, John?" asked Keller, nodding to Syckes whom he knew well. "What has happened?"

"John here has come to warn us that we need to move and real soon. He says there's lots of red men about, and we aren't safe."

"Where to, Syckes?" asked Keller. "Where is it safe?"

"Down at the mouth of Dunkard. The Injuns haven't bothered us there."

"Is there room for all of us? There are four families here."

"Yes," said Sykes, "and it will be easier than trying to build up protection here."

Keller looked at John Wetzel, who shrugged.

Syckes became more insistent. "Come on! There's no time to lose."

"I know what my Lewis would say," chimed in Elizabeth Bonnett. "He'd say go!"

"John?" Mary Wetzel looked at her husband expectantly.

"Looks like I'm outnumbered," said Wetzel. "Let's pack up and go."

The packing up had not taken long, and the entire company was on the move well before noon, with John Syckes leading the way. They had not gone more than a mile when they noted a clearing on the far side of the little creek. A small cabin had been built there as well as a small milking shed, and as the Wetzel party was passing, a man named Stephen Spicer and his wife shouted and waved at them.

"What is the news, and where are you going?" asked Stephen Spicer.

"We've come from Wheeling Creek," answered John Wetzel. "We're headed to the mouth of Dunkard."

The caravan had stopped, and the people were straining to listen to the conversation.

"What brought that on?" Spicer wanted to know.

"Injun trouble," said Wetzel. "The murderin' bastards are everywhere."

"No trouble around here that I know of," asserted Spicer.

"Well, there soon will be," said John Syckes. "It's not safe here at all. You'd better come with us."

Two boys of about twelve years of age had come from behind the shed and moved up near the Spicer couple. One was William

Spicer and the other was a visitor named Francis McClure. They looked at the elder Spicer with a quizzical expression.

"We've never had no trouble with the reds here," he insisted. "I don't think they even know about our little place."

"The hell they don't. Besides, they're on the warpath all around here. They hit some folks on upper Dunkard just a couple of days ago, and it's likely they will get here before long." Syckes couldn't believe how anybody could be so ignorant. "You'd better come. We got safety in numbers, but you'll be easy prey out here by yourselves."

"Well I reckon we'll just stay right here. We're not scared of no Injuns, are we boys?" He gestured toward William and Francis, who did not reply.

"Damn!" exclaimed Syckes, and before he could continue, John Wetzel reached out and took hold of his arm.

"Folks have to do what they have to do, John. We've warned them, and that's all we can do. Let's get movin' again."

"But, John, if they stay here, they're as good as dead."

He shook his head and stared at Spicer. Wetzel threw up his hands in exasperation. "You might be right, but Spicer's a stubborn man, John. Let's get on with it."

So the four families with their packhorses and small contingent of farm animals, waved good-bye and moved on down toward Dunkard Creek. They had not gone more than another mile when they heard gunshots coming from back toward the Spicer settlement. John Wetzel and John Syckes exchanged worried glances and urged their people to hurry on.

"We can't save them," Wetzel said to Syckes. "Let's save our families."

Lewis Bonnett kneeled along the bank on the south side of the South Fork of Tenmile Creek. With his fingers, he traced around the imprint of a moccasin track formed perfectly in the soft mud.

"It's an Injun track all right," he said, looking up at his two companions. "I don't know how you happened to see it, George, but I'm glad you did. Let's look around and see if there are more." He pointed to a clump of trees not far away.

"Abraham, you, and George take a peek over there. I'll keep watch from here." A few minutes passed, and then there was a shout from young George Wetzel.

"Over here, over here. I think they camped here."

Both men soon joined him, searching through the ashes of a campfire and examining other prints and signs of occupation by several humans.

"There are five or six of them, I would think," offered Abraham Messer.

"Yep, and not that long ago," said Bonnett. "They're trailing our travelers, sure enough."

The three of them had been deliberately hanging back a great distance from the Wetzel party for just this reason. They had been crossing through an area of a main Indian trail that came from the Indian towns in the Ohio country across to the Monongahela River, and they knew that it was a likely spot for Indians to be found. It was pure luck that George Wetzel had happened to find the track, since the passing of the four families left a broad trail and made it impossible to discern white travelers from red ones. The Indians would not worry about covering their own tracks.

"We need to get moving and fast," said Bonnett.

"But, Lewis," said Messer, "what if they are just waiting to take us as we come along?"

"I doubt they know we're here, Abraham," answered Bonnett. "They're following a clear trail and in a hurry, I figure."

"I think we ought to take a different trail, one that's in the same direction but not directly behind." Messer was thinking about what had happened to the Foreman company.

"Trouble is there is no clear trail like you want. We'd have to cross that ridge over to the east, and then we would be too far away."

"I still think that would be best."

Neither one thought to ask George Wetzel what he thought. In their minds he was still a boy. George knew better than to speak out of turn, but he was thinking they needed to be moving and not talking.

Lewis Bonnett was getting annoyed. "If you want to stay back a ways, you could do that, so if they do attack George and me, you might be able to drive them off."

Messer thought for a moment. "No," he said finally. "Let's stay together."

"Let's go then," said Bonnett, and the three of them rode off.

They traveled quickly and without difficulty, and it was not yet noon when they came to the spot along Meadow Run where the families had camped. They dismounted and looked around for a bit, when they heard the shots from further down the run.

"God," shouted Bonnett. "They're hittin' our people." He swung up on his horse and began a gallop in the direction of the sounds. Messer and Wetzel were immediately behind him. There were two more shots, then silence.

It wasn't long until the Spicer farm came into view. The buildings were on fire although not burning with much ferocity. There was no sign of any life. Before Messer could stop him, Bonnett splashed across the little creek and rode toward the burning buildings. With a look of exasperation, Messer followed across the creek, as did George Wetzel. When they reached Bonnett, they found him standing near the front stoop of the cabin, shaking his head. The bodies of a man and woman lay at his feet, not far apart. "They're both dead. Shot and scalped." Bonnett now looked up at Messer. "Do you know em?"

"I think the name is Spicer," said Messer. "They used to live down on Dunkard, but I'd heard they'd moved. There was a boy too, I think."

"They shot a couple hogs," yelled George Wetzel, who had gone around behind the shed.

"Probably ran off the other livestock," observed Messer. "Should we try to put out these fires?"

"No," said Bonnett emphatically. "Let's get after our own people and make sure they're safe."

"Do you think the red bastards have gone after them too, Lewis?"

"I doubt it. This was a much easier job for them. But we better not wait around here. Those warriors could still be close by, even watchin' us."

"I agree," said Messer. "But what about these bodies?"

"We have to leave 'em be," said Bonnett. "There's no time."

"Right. Come on, George. We're goin' to catch up with your pa."

There was no hesitation now, and the three men quickly crossed the creek and set off at a fast trot to catch up with the Wetzel party. It was not long until they caught sight of them, and they began to shout.

"Hey, hey, we're comin' in."

John Wetzel, who was following along at the rear of the caravan, saw them riding now at a gallop, and he yelled to the others to stop.

Martin Keller was quickly by his side. "What is it?"

Wetzel pointed back up the trail. "It's Lewis, Abraham, and George, and they're in a big hurry."

"I hope they ain't bein' chased," said Keller.

"I don't think so. They must have come by Spicer's."

Lewis Bonnett was soon upon them, and he reined in, talking as he dismounted.

"Have you had any trouble?" he wanted to know.

"We're fine, Lew, but we heard shootin' not too long after we left the Spicer place." John Wetzel was glad to see that his son George had arrived and was unhurt.

"Yeah, the damned rascals hit the farm, killed both Spicer and his wife."

"What about the boys? There was two boys there with them."

"No sign of them. They must have taken them as captives. They killed a couple of hogs and set fire to the buildings."

"Did you run 'em off?"

"No, they was gone by the time we got there."

Bonnett turned now to George Wetzel and handed him the reins of his horse.

"Let the horses get a drink, George, but not too much. They've been runnin' hard." Turning back to John Wetzel, he asked, "Where are you headed?"

"We was camped back a mile above Spicer's when John Syckes found us. He said it wasn't safe, and I guess he was right."

"Those reds were on your trail, all right," said Bonnett. "But Spicer was an easier target."

"John is leading us back to the mouth of Dunkard where he is living."

"That sounds good to me. It's been quite a trip so far, John."

April 25, 1778

"What a beautiful spring morning," said Martin Wetzel to himself as he rode along the bank of the Dunkard Fork of Wheeling Creek.

The morning chill had left the air, and the sun was climbing high, bringing the warmth that fostered a feeling of well-being. It was the second day of a trip to the settlements at the mouth of Dunkard Creek that had begun at Fort Henry. Martin was accompanied by John Wolf, a young married man with a wife and two children who lived on Dunkard. Martin did not know Wolf all that well, but he knew that John's brother Jacob had become enamored of his sister Christiana, and the word was that they might marry before too much longer.

The purpose of the trip was twofold. On the one hand, they were bearing messages from Colonel Shepherd at Fort Henry to the settlements on Dunkard Creek. For Martin, the more important reason for the trip was to become part of the new company of militia that had been raised by his father, now Captain John Wetzel. Officially, it was a company of rangers under the overall command of Colonel Daniel McFarland, and its duty was to scout in Monongahela and Ohio counties.

Martin was looking forward to soldiering again with his father, having done so earlier during Lord Dunmore's War in 1774 when he was only seventeen. His uncles, Lewis Bonnett and John Syckes, were also in the company, as was his cousin, another John Syckes. Wolf was returning to his family. They had come from Fort Henry to the forks where Shepherd's Fort had once stood, and then followed along Big Wheeling Creek. The previous night had been spent at the abandoned Wetzel cabin, which, strangely, had so far escaped being burned by the marauding Indians.

An early start had enabled them to progress far up the creek and onto the Dunkard Fork, passing from the state of Virginia into Pennsylvania, although the travelers would not have been thinking of that. They had come to a place where the creek made a big loop to the north and east before turning back to a southeasterly direction. To save time, they had crossed from the north side to the south of the creek and were cutting across the neck of land formed by the loop.

The trees along the bank had quickly thinned, and they were now facing into an open grassland that extended for some distance. Instinctively, Martin had stopped his horse and was observing what lay before them before going out into the open. He thought he had seen something flash among the trees off to his left, but after staring for a moment, he decided he had been mistaken.

John Wolf pulled up beside him. "Somethin' wrong, Martin?" he wanted to know.

"No, nothin's wrong. Just bein' careful before ridin' out into the open."

"You think there might be Injuns out here?" asked Wolf, suddenly fearful.

"Hell, John," said Wetzel. "There can be Injuns anywhere. We just have to be alert." He sat watching awhile longer, noting how the line of trees revealed the course of the creek as it came back to the south. Some distance ahead, he could make out another line of trees coming in from the southwest, indicating what he figured was a small stream entering the main creek from that direction. "Well, we can't wait here forever, I reckon." With that, Wetzel rode out into the sunlight, putting his horse into a fast trot.

Wolf followed, trying hard to catch up so they could ride side by side. Before he could get there, he heard two shots and saw Wetzel tumble off his horse. Martin had felt a sharp sting on his left side, just above the hip, and his instinctive jerk had caused him to fall back just as the horse gave a jump and began racing away. He hit the ground with a thump but quickly realized that he was not badly hurt. He jumped to his feet, looking back to where John Wolf was stopped, sitting still on his horse as if paralyzed.

Wolf was staring back toward the creek bank not far above where the two of them had emerged just a short while ago, watching as a group of some half-dozen Indian braves came storming out of the trees, yelling and brandishing their weapons.

Wetzel tried to decide what to do next, realizing that he could expect no help from his confused companion. He looked remorsefully toward his own horse which was racing away at a full gallop, still carrying his rifle. He felt at his belt and was relieved to find that he still had his hunting knife. The screaming braves were still some forty yards away but headed directly for him. Clearly they were intent upon capture rather than killing.

Wetzel looked back once more to where Wolf still sat upon his horse, wondering if he could climb up, and the two ride off to safety. He couldn't understand why the man was still there.

"Ride!" he yelled to Wolf. "Save yourself! Go!" With that last exclamation, Wetzel turned back and began to run through the tall grass. He thought of trying to reach the far off juncture of the creek with the small stream he had surmised came in from the southwest. But it was too far, and he instead headed directly toward the main creek to the east, hoping he might escape in the woods on the far bank. He was a fast runner, and he managed to stay ahead of the pursuers who had swerved to try to cut him off. There was no time to think anymore; all of his energy was focused on reaching that creek bank. The five warriors who were now chasing him had not been fast enough to cut off his line of flight, and were behind him. He began to have some hope of getting away.

After running for several minutes, Martin was near his objective. He was out of breath, his sides hurting from the exertion. He chanced a quick look behind, noting that the Indians were strung out, but two of them had managed to close the gap. He plunged ahead and was suddenly in a tangle of bushes along the edge of the creek. His shirt caught the edge of a branch and slowed him, but he grabbed at it, and it broke loose. Now he splashed into the creek, which was shallow here and not very wide. Still, the banks were a little high, and he angled toward a low spot on the other side, just past a small, scraggly tree.

Unfortunately, one of its branches was bent down into the water, and as he went past, his left foot caught the branch, and he fell headlong into the stream. He heard splashing behind him, and as he tried to scramble to his feet, he felt a strong hand grab his right leg and pull him back. Though he struggled with all his might, he could not break free. He was trying to reach for his knife, when a second Indian, screaming at the top of his voice, leaped on him, forcing his shoulders and head down into the water. He was held fast, and the fight went out of him.

Half expecting a life-ending blow from a war club, he allowed them to pull him upright out of the water and onto the grassy bank. The first Indian pulled his arms behind his back and quickly wrapped them with a rawhide thong. The two of them pulled him along between them as their friends arrived. They were pleased and chattered excitedly to each other. They waited there near a small stand of birch trees until another brave came up leading Martin's horse.

A short time later, two more arrived with John Wolf in tow, tied in the same way as Martin and leading Wolf's horse. There were eight warriors in all, and Shawnees, as Martin was soon to learn. Martin could see the fear on John Wolf's face, and he shook his own head when he caught Wolf's eye. He was trying to convey to Wolf the danger in showing weakness and fright in front of these braves. But when he tried to speak, he was jabbed in the ribs with the tomahawk handle of one of his captors. The reason for the Indians being so intent on capturing them began to dawn on Wetzel.

He recalled hearing Jonathan Zane talk about this one time at Fort Henry. It was a custom of the Shawnees Zane had pointed out, and believed to bring good luck, that the first captive of the spring should be burned at the stake. Whether they considered him or Wolf to be the first captive, Wetzel was not sure. Probably they would just burn them both.

The Shawnees were quite happy to have the horses, maybe even more than the two men, and they quickly gathered up their rifles and other belongings and began the long trip back to their home village. They moved to the south along the Dunkard Fork of Wheeling Creek until they came to where it split into a north and south branch. They continued along the south branch, and Martin figured that they would shortly angle across on the ridges until they reached the well-traveled Indian trail that ended up on Fish Creek and went down to the Ohio across from Captina.

He noted that they paid more attention to him than to Wolf, and his conclusion was that he would be the one selected to burn at the stake. Wolf was despondent and nearly in tears. Wetzel was determined not to give in to his own fears. He tried to keep a smile on his face, as if he considered it a real privilege to be a captive of such fine warriors. Also he watched for a chance to speak to Wolf.

They camped for the night at the base of a high ridge and near a spring that bubbled merrily from a crevice a few feet up from the base. The water flowed into a small stream that Martin thought might be the head of Fish Creek. It was a cold camp; no fires were lit, and the captives were offered a drink but no food. No one spoke directly to them, although Wolf's hands had been released and tied in front, and he was directed to make sure the horses had some water to drink.

There was an air of expectation in the camp, when three more Shawnee warriors arrived just after dark with a string of six horses. From observing the captors' behavior, Martin decided that the horses had been stolen sometime earlier, probably along Dunkard Creek somewhere, and that the three newcomers had been holding them while the rest of the raiding party made mischief elsewhere. He wondered why they were treating Wolf differently from him, and he decided that his earlier conclusion was valid. He was the prize to be burned and Wolf was being treated more like a slave.

The warriors now began to settle in for the night. Wetzel and Wolf were tied in a sitting position to the opposite sides of a sturdy birch tree and in such a way that they could not move their arms. It was a very uncomfortable position for both of them; their captors were unconcerned. Eventually it became quiet.

May 3, 1778

The eleven Shawnees, with the eight horses and two white captives, had moved out quickly the next morning, following the well-worn Indian trail down Fish Creek and across the Ohio near Captina Island. The second night was spent near the head of Captina Creek, and on the next day, instead of following the usual path up to the Delaware towns, they turned west and south.

"They're goin' toward the main Shawnee towns," Martin managed to whisper to John Wolf when he finally had an opportunity. "That's not good for us, I'm thinkin'." He could see that Wolf did not comprehend his meaning; the look on his face a mixture of fright, confusion, and dejection. It did register with Wolf that Martin had spoken to him, but he did not want to look at Martin. Finally he managed a reply. "What?" he muttered.

"Never mind," said Wetzel, noting a stare from one of the captors. He looked at the warrior with a smile on his face. Then suddenly a Shawnee word came to his mind that he had learned years earlier when he had served in the militia against the Shawnees. He nodded toward the man. "Ne-kah-noh," he said. He thought it meant something like "my friend."

The Indian was startled to hear this word in his own language. "Ne-kah-noh?" Then a small grin came to his lips. "Ha-ha. Yes."

Well we are hardly friends, thought Martin, though he was hoping he could find one of the warriors who might speak up for him.

It was not a good time to be in the hands of the Shawnees, especially after what had happened in early November of the preceding year. The Shawnees had signed a peace treaty in Pittsburgh in 1775 with commissioners from Virginia and the Continental Congress. They had remained mostly at peace with the Americans in spite of pressure from the British and the tribes, such as the Wyandots, who had sided with the British.

However, in the fall of 1777, they had made a tribal decision to go to war with the colonists against the wishes of their principal chief, the one called Hokolesqua or Cornstalk. The chief had gone to Fort Randolph at Point Pleasant to inform Captain Matthew Arbuckle, in command there, about the Shawnee intentions. He thought it only fair, since the Indians would be abrogating the treaty signed earlier.

Arbuckle had felt it wise to take Cornstalk into custody, including two of his companions. When the chief did not return quickly, his son Elinipisco came into the fort inquiring about his father, and he too was detained. The next day, two of the militiamen stationed at Fort Randolph decided, against orders, to go deer hunting. Crossing over the Kanahwa River, they passed a place where several young Shawnees were waiting, and the Indians fired at them, killing one. The other escaped and returned to his company, which had only recently arrived from the east.

The men of this company were outraged and marched to the fort. Although Arbuckle and an aide tried to stop them, the men were not to be denied. They burst into the room containing the four Indians and killed them all. When the details of the action were eventually learned in the white settlements, the authorities were disturbed and worried about the effect on the Shawnees. Even hardened bordermen felt regret when hearing what had happened.

Martin himself remembered feeling sorry for the old Shawnee chieftan whose last noble act had resulted in such a death. With all that in mind, Martin knew they could expect little mercy in their current predicament. He decided to try his best to keep a positive attitude in front of the Shawnees and to cultivate a relationship with the brave to whom he had spoken. He knew that Wolf's demeanor could prove fatal to them both.

Hunger was another problem nagging at the captives. They had been fed some dried venison strips the previous evening and again this morning, but it wasn't enough. Martin knew it was pointless to complain about that, but his mind kept wandering to thoughts about his mother's johnnycake or a meal of mush and milk.

Martin noticed that the pace of travel had slowed considerably, and the braves took turns riding on the horses. Even Wetzel and Wolf had been allowed to ride on two occasions. On the third evening, the big Indian to whom Martin had spoken earlier came to where he was sitting. "*Scoote*," he said, pointing at the fire. "*Scoote*," he said again, now pointing at himself. Then he placed his hand on his chest to the left side. Pounding his heart, he said "*Kitehe*."

Martin pointed at him. "Your name is Kitehe?"

"*Mattah*!" said the brave. Pointing at himself now, he said "*Scoote kitehe*."

Puzzled, Wetzel tried to piece it together when he suddenly comprehended. The man's name was Scoote-kitehe, and it meant fire heart.

"Fire Heart!" exclaimed Martin, pointing back at the warrior but unable to repeat the name in the Shawnee tongue. Poking himself in the chest, he smiled and said, "Martin."

The Indian, Fire Heart, nodded and walked away. After two more days, they came to the large Shawnee town called Chalahgawtha, which stood on the Little Miami River. Women and children ran out toward them, cheering and shouting. Martin and Wolf were put up on horses so that they could be seen more easily. Some of the young boys picked up small stones and threw them at the white men, who crowded their horses together and tried to avoid the stinging missiles.

"Will they make us run the gauntlet?" asked Wolf, looking at Martin.

"It's likely," answered Wetzel quickly, although it occurred to him that they might not risk the death of a captive in that way when they were determined to have a burning.

"God, Martin, I don't think I can take it."

"I ain't lookin forward to it either," said Martin, "but I'm tellin' you, you're better off not to let 'em know it."

Some warriors from the village had joined them now and were in earnest discussion with the members of the war party. Martin heard the word *cutta-ho-tha*, and he knew what that meant. It meant someone condemned to death, and more particularly, death by burning at the stake. Noting that they had begun pointing at him, his earlier fears were confirmed. He was regarded as their first captive, and according to the custom, they were planning to burn him at the stake. He saw Fire Heart come from out of the crowd and step up beside the horse. He nodded his head sadly toward Martin and repeated the dreaded word.

"*Cutta-ho-tha.*" He shrugged, pointing at the sun, now low in the west and swung his arm around to the east, nodding his head again. Martin understood that the death sentence would be carried out the next morning. The big Shawnee village stood on the eastern side of the Little Miami River, nestled between two creeks that flowed into the river from the southeast. The southernmost and smaller creek was called Shawnee Creek, and the northernmost, which was bordered on its southern bank by a marsh, was called Massies Creek by the whites.

A wooden council house stood in the center of the village. Martin Wetzel was led to a bare spot on the edge of the marsh where his clothes were stripped from him, and his entire body was painted black. This, he knew, was the method of marking the condemned prisoner. He could not help noticing the small sapling standing in a cleared area that had been stripped of limbs and its top cut off some ten to twelve feet above the ground. Leaves and branches were piled around it in a large circle, with the closest part of the circle a good six feet from the post.

He knew that he would become intimately acquainted with that area on the next morning because it was the burn site. Two braves led Martin to a large tree not far away and secured him in a sitting position at the base. Women and children stood around and jeered at him. He felt embarrassed at being naked in front of them, and the fear that was rising up in him threatened to defeat his resolve to maintain a brave front. One of the braves brought him a small wooden bowl in which he supposed was some kind of corn mush. In spite of everything, he was extremely hungry, and he ate the food with relish. Although the jeering by the women continued, he was being watched closely and silently by several warriors. He wondered what had happened to Wolf but could see him nowhere.

May 4, 1778

The night was long and miserable. Fatigued as he was, Wetzel could not fall asleep. He could only think of what awaited him when it grew light in the morning. He tried to think of his family. He wondered if they would ever learn of his fate, for he knew of many settlers who had been taken by Indians and never heard from or about again.

If word of his death reached the Wyandot towns, then Isaac Zane might hear of it and get word back to his family. His mother would take it hard for he was her first, and her favorite. He thought of his brothers and sisters, and especially of Lewis and Jacob, who had escaped their own imprisonment. How overjoyed he had been when they showed up at Fort Henry on that August day. It was strange, he thought now, that those two little boys had managed to escape while he, a grown and experienced hunter and member of the militia, had failed and would now pay for it with his life.

The sun streaming in above the trees brought Wetzel awake. He had dozed off just before dawn in spite of all that was on his mind. The first thing he saw was the burn site waiting only a few yards away from where he sat. He felt again the churning in his stomach as the anticipation of this horrible ordeal came to his consciousness. He wanted to scream out in protest, but he knew it was hopeless, and he did not want to give the captors any satisfaction. He wondered if they would offer him a last meal. He didn't think he would be able to eat anything.

Again he thought about John Wolf, but there was no sign of him. He sat now, fighting back tears. The camp was coming to life, and Martin figured they would see to their breakfast before coming to him. Indeed, he was alone with his fearful anxiety, but he could hear the activity. After a short time, he was surprised to see Fire Heart, followed by two others, striding toward him. Fire Heart came directly to him and bent down to unfasten the ties holding him to the tree.

Wetzel thought it odd that Fire Heart would be the one to tie him to the deadly stake. Now came a second surprise. The three Indians led him to the east of the campsite to a small stream that came from a spring and ran up along the back of the camp and northward to Massies Creek. Fire Heart pointed to the water and then brushed himself with a washing motion. Wetzel stood dumbfounded. Fire Heart repeated the motion, and his companions grabbed Martin and pushed him into the stream. Still Martin stood, looking at Fire Heart with a questioning look on his face. The big Indian nodded his head and pointed again at the water.

Wetzel's heart jumped with relief and joy as he finally accepted what was clearly indicated by Fire Heart—he was being told to wash off the black paint. Immediately he bent down and began splashing himself with the cold water. It made him shiver, but that was unimportant as the full impact of what was happening sank in. He laid down in the water and then sat up in the shallow stream. The paint was coming off, and he began rubbing himself vigorously, suddenly ferocious with desire to remove it all.

When he finally came out of the stream, he noticed for the first time that Fire Heart was holding something for him. It was a piece of cloth and a rawhide thong to be used as a belt. The cloth was pulled up between the legs and secured with the belt while the ends flopped down over the belt to form the classic Indian breechclout. He felt so much better to be clothed again, however briefly, and the relief at having his life returned to him continued to wash over him.

What had caused this change? he wondered.

The three braves led him back toward the camp. As they neared the burn site, Martin could see a crowd pushing in, and then he comprehended what had brought his own salvation. In the midst of the people was John Wolf, painted black, trying to resist being carried toward the stake. They had obviously decided to substitute Wolf for Wetzel as the burning victim. Martin knew the reason: it was their behavior, and eventually the Shawnees had decided that Wolf deserved to die and Wetzel deserved to live.

Wetzel was directed to stand where he could easily view what was to take place. They tied Wolf securely to the stake and brought torches to light the materials that had been placed around the stake. Soon the fire circle became complete, and as it blazed, Wolf began to scream. The fire was not close enough to burn him, but the heat was difficult to bear.

The ordeal, once begun, lasted for three days. Except for the few hours each night when the Indians slept, there was a constant line of braves dancing and singing while the women and children devised various ways to annoy and torture the victim. On the second day, the fire was pushed closer, and the victim was prodded with spears whose tips were heated in the fire. Wolf screamed and cried, and then was silent for periods.

Martin was forced to watch it all, but he could not tell if Wolf could see him. Several times, Wolf cried out for someone to shoot him, and Wetzel wished he had some way to oblige. On that second day, another event occurred that was to have a future impact on the life of Martin Wetzel. In midafternoon, a large cry went up among the Indians crowding around the fire. After further commotion and shouting, the edge of the crowd opened to provide an aisle into which strode a dignified, graceful warrior upon which an air of authority hung like a cloak. He wore leggings and breechclout of deer hide and moccasins adorned by beads. A necklace of bear claws, separated by silver bars, adorned his neck, and his shoulder-length black hair sported a band with a single eagle feather protruding from the back.

This had to be an important chief, mused Martin to himself. Even more surprising was the short slender man who walked beside him. He was white! The crowd had quieted, watching the two men closely as they walked toward the fire. An English word had escaped the lips of some, and it came to the ear of Wetzel.

"Boone."

Martin strained to get a better look. Could this be Daniel Boone? Word had reached the Wheeling area a month ago indicating that Daniel Boone had been captured at a salt lick in Kentucky. No one knew if he was still alive, but here he was; it had to be him. When the suffering John Wolf saw the white man standing in front of him, he began to shout, "Save me, save me. You're a white man, can't you save me?"

Immediately several of the old women standing to the side began poking at him with sharpened sticks. He screamed and then hunched back against the post. The chief, whose name was Black Fish, and who was the successor to Cornstalk, said nothing. Boone turned away. It was then that Boone caught sight of Martin Wetzel. He looked at Black Fish and then at Wetzel, turning back to Black Fish as if asking permission to speak to Martin. Black Fish nodded, and Boone walked over to where Martin stood at the edge of the crowd.

"Who are you?" asked Boone.

"Martin Wetzel," was the reply. "You're Daniel Boone, I reckon."

"Yes," said Boone quickly. "Who is that at the stake?"

"His name is John Wolf. Can you do anything to save him?"

"Afraid not," answered Boone. "I escaped that fate myself a couple of months ago."

"But you are with the chief," insisted Wetzel. "That ought to mean something."

"Well, officially, I am adopted into old Black Fish's family. But they still watch me like a hawk, and I have no influence."

Boone looked at Martin in silence for a minute. "I'm sorry for your friend. What about you? What do they intend? Do you know?"

"I was painted black until yesterday. Then they substituted John for me."

"Lucky for you," said Boone. "I reckon they'll adopt you now if you don't rile 'em."

The chief had come to where they stood and took Boone by the elbow, scowling at Wetzel. Boone shook his head, and the two of them walked away. The crowd filled back in and resumed their taunting of the prisoner.

On the third day, the burning branches were pushed in close to the post, and the heat brought blisters to Wolf's bare skin. His life was finally ended by an old woman, who stuck the red hot end of a rifle barrel into Wolf's belly. Shortly after, his body was enveloped by the flames. Martin Wetzel bowed his head and looked down, a tear falling to his cheek. It could have been him, and he was intensely grateful that he had escaped. Yet there was a sickening sadness at the thought that his own good fortune had come at the expense of his unfortunate companion.

As he turned to walk away beside the Shawnee assigned to guard him, he sensed that someone was watching him. He looked up to see an older woman staring at him with great interest. He learned later that the interested woman was Cornstalk's widow.

4

INAUGURATION

June 14, 1780

THE FLIES WERE bad. They buzzed around the rear haunches of the sweating horse, whose tail flicked at them constantly, and in the eyes of young Lewis Wetzel, who batted at them with futility.

He held the reins tightly and gripped the handles of the simple plow as he guided it between the rows of corn. The stalks were flimsy and not yet very tall, and it was a hard task to keep from plowing them out or covering them with the turning soil. He hated this job of cultivating corn, but then, as he often admitted to himself, he hated most of the jobs associated with farming. He reckoned that the horse hitched to the infernal plow didn't like the job any better than he did. The horse was his father's favorite mare, although he didn't know why she was favored. One horse was the same as another as far as he was concerned. Old John called the horse Susannah, after Lew's youngest sister, who was now about thirteen years old.

"She's rambunctious, and she's also sweet," his pa had said. "Just like our Susannah."

Lewis and his brothers teased the girl endlessly about being named after a horse. "Maybe someday, you'll be just as smart," they would say to her.

"Well at least I ain't named after a mule," she had said once. "Every mule in the country must be called Lewis or Jacob."

These thoughts brought a smile to his face, as did the sight of the rifle barrel protruding from the sling on the mare's front shoulder that Lewis had devised as a carrying case. It was a dictum now in the Wetzel family, learned from hard experience, that one never went to the field without a gun. This rifle belonged to Lewis and had been a gift from his father at his last birthday. It was a Pennsylvania long rifle, the kind carried by the frontier sharpshooters, and it was his prized possession. He had spent many hours with it, practicing both shooting and loading, and he believed that the special skill he had with the gun was a gift from God. It brought him pleasure now just thinking of it.

As it often did, his mind turned toward his brother Martin, who had been missing for over two years. The family knew very little about his disappearance, except that he and John Wolf had been sent to the Dunkard Creek settlements, where the Wetzels were living at the time, and they had never arrived. It was several days before anyone knew they were missing.

John Wetzel, who was the captain of a militia company in which Martin Wetzel was enrolled, knew that Martin was coming from Fort Henry with a message. Taking a small group of men, he went back along the trail he expected Martin to use. They found no conclusive evidence of what had happened, but they assumed that Indians had either killed or captured the two messengers. When he returned to the family residence, Captain John tried to comfort his wife by pointing out that they had found no bodies. Of course, there was nothing conclusive about that, and Mary Wetzel wasn't fooled.

The Wetzels had asked Colonel Ebenezer Zane to find out what he could, since Zane's brother Isaac lived among the Wyandots. No solid information came back, however, although it was pretty clear that Martin and Wolf were not captives nor victims of the Wyandots. The word was that there were a number of whites in captivity among the tribes, and there had been some burnings. News of Boone's capture and subsequent escape had reached the Wheeling area, but Boone was in Kentucky, and no one had talked with him.

Zane had said that from what he knew, it was most likely Martin was with the Shawnees if he still lived. Lewis was unwilling to think that his big brother was dead, and he had come to think of Martin as living in some Shawnee village, maybe even as an adopted son or brother. Nor could he imagine that Martin would adopt the Indian ways as some whites did. No—in his mind—Martin was as he always had been and would be just waiting for his chance to escape and join his family again.

The family didn't discuss the matter because Lewis's mother would burst into tears at any mention of Martin. The horse, Susannah, had reached the end of the row, and Lewis turned her back in the opposite direction, heading back somewhat parallel to the creek, which flowed gently in its course off to his right. The rows ended in the flat area between the house and the stream.

The Wetzels had returned from Dunkard Creek in the late fall of 1778 when the Indian summer was past, and the Indian forays suspended for the winter. They had built a much sturdier cabin, what could really be called a blockhouse and was even referred to by some as Wetzel's Fort. The cornfield was in the same location as the one in which young Lewis had been captured nearly three years earlier. The thought of that fearful day came to him, and Lewis contemplated it with mixed emotions. He had been terrified, of course, but in the end, the escape by him and his brother Jacob had brought them some satisfying appreciation and kind words from their neighbors.

Young Wetzel was staring intently at the corn rows moving slowly past him when there was a sudden change in the mare's demeanor. Her ears had perked up, and she stopped momentarily. Lewis stepped from behind the plow and moved to retrieve the rifle from its sheath when he saw what had disturbed the horse. A party of seven or eight riders was splashing across the creek and heading up the path that led toward the Wetzel house. He was relieved to see that the riders were white men. They rode up toward the house, and the one in the lead began shouting. "John, Captain John Wetzel. Are you there?"

"Over here," called one of the others. "Young Lewis is in the field."

Lewis had urged the mare forward, anxious to see who the riders were and what was happening to bring them here with such urgency. The riders had turned now toward the cornfield, and the leader, who Lewis recognized as Jacob Link, started to ride into the field. Just before the horse he was riding had begun to trample the small shoots, Link reined him in, and all the riders stopped to wait for Lewis to come to the end of the row. Lewis forced himself to keep the mare in check for there was danger in plowing out the corn if he let her go too fast. It wasn't far, however, and he continued the plowing until he had reached the end.

"Whoa, Susannah," he called to the horse. Dropping the reins over the plow handles, he walked out from behind the plow and up to where Link sat watching him.

"Hello, Mr. Link," said Lewis cheerfully.

"Good mornin', Lewis. Where is your pa?"

"They've all gone down to the mill at Shepherd's," answered Lewis. "What do you need?"

"The red bastards have been stealin' horses up our way. We're chasin' 'em to get the horses back. We wanted your pa to go with us."

"Well, you can go with us, Lew," said Jacob Rigger, who had dismounted and walked up close to where Lewis was standing.

He was known to Lewis because he was one of the men who had come out to Wheeling Creek with John Wetzel ten years earlier. Lewis looked at the other men. He recognized Thomas McCreary and Robert Rigger, Jacob's seventeen-year-old son.

"I don't reckon I better, Mr. Link," said Lewis. "Pa said I wasn't to leave the place. I got to finish cultivatin' this corn."

"This is more important," argued Rigger. "That corn will be here tomorrow or the next day."

"That's right," added young Robert Rigger. "Come on, Lew, it'll be fun."

"We'd really like to have you, Lew," said Jacob Link, as Lewis stood shaking his head and looking at the ground. "We know you're a good shot, and you know how to track."

The words of praise added to Lewis's discomfort for he wanted very much to go, but he also feared his father's wrath. He looked up at Link.

"I just can't do it, Mr. Link. Besides, they took all the horses."

"What do you mean? What about the horse you're plowin' with?"

"Oh, I couldn't ride her," protested Lewis. "She's Pa's favorite mare. I could never ride her."

"Your pa rides her, don't he?"

"Yeah, but he's never let me ride."

"You ain't afraid to go with us, are you, Lew?" challenged Robert Rigger.

There was complete silence from all the men, who were shocked at such a remark, especially aimed at someone in the Wetzel family. Lewis felt the anger flare, and his first thought was to pull Rigger from the horse and beat some sense into him. He took a step in that direction, but Jacob Rigger stepped in front of him.

"Pay him no mind, Lew, he didn't mean nothing. Sometimes he ain't too smart."

"I'm not afraid," said Lewis quietly.

"We know that," said Link. "That's why we want you to come."

One of the other men spoke now, a man Lewis didn't know. His name was Andrew Robinson.

"Come with us, Lewis," he pleaded. "We need you to help us. We'll get you and your pa's mare back here by tomorrow."

"Why did you come this way?" asked Lewis.

"We tracked them to the bottom of the hill over there." Link pointed back across the creek where a narrow trail led up a steep incline.

"I don't see how that could be," said Lewis. "We didn't hear anything last night."

"We can show you the tracks," said Rigger.

After a bit more persuasion, Lew Wetzel gave in and agreed to go with them. He knew it was a mistake, especially since he didn't know when his father and the other family members would be back. If they came back that night and found him gone, what would they think? Not only would his father be furious, but his mother would be frightened and sure that he was dead.

He went to the mare and removed the collar and harness, which he placed very carefully on top of the plow. This, he hoped, would show Captain John that he had left deliberately and under control. It wouldn't prevent the furious anger, but it should show that he hadn't been carried off by the Indians. He retied the sling that carried his rifle, checked the halter and bit, shortened the reins, and climbed onto the mare's back. The rest of the men had ridden back across the creek and started up the trail where the Indians and their captured horses had gone.

Lewis urged the mare forward, hurrying to catch up. Jacob Link had taken the lead, and the others followed single file up the hill and along the ridge at the top. They continued to follow the ridge, eventually swinging back toward the Ohio River, whose shoreline was reached sometime after noon.

"Looks like they crossed up there at the little island," said Jacob Rigger.

The little island, later called Boggs Island, was a short distance below the bigger Zane's Island, and a favorite Indian crossing point.

"So it seems," agreed Link. "Let's watch a bit. They could still be there."

The men had dismounted and were spread out in the tall grass along the shore. Lewis Wetzel moved upstream a good distance, looking intently at the island. Soon he stood and began walking quickly back toward the rest of the party.

"There's nobody there," he said as he came near to Jacob Link, who was crouching near the bank.

"I think you're right," said Link. He turned to the others. "Let's get mounted and get across."

The river was high at this time of the year, but the eight riders had no difficulty getting across. They stopped only momentarily at the island and then moved quickly across the narrow channel that flowed by the island on the west side. An examination of the tracks soon found on the western shore of the river convinced them that the Indian party had swung to the north.

"They must intend to go along Indian Wheeling," observed Wetzel.

"I reckon they're headed toward the Moravian villages," said Link.

"Maybe they're Delawares," speculated Jacob Rigger. "I'd figured they was Wyandots before."

"Could be either one," noted Link. "All the tribes use those damned missions as a stopping point. Sometimes I think we'd be better off without those so-called Christian Indians."

"Well, they've helped us before," interjected Tom McCreary. "They warned us about the attack on Wheeling a few years ago."

The little party of white men followed the Indians' trail until they came to Indian Wheeling Creek. There they halted two to three miles inland from the Ohio River. Dismounted, the men began to converse in a low chatter that began to build in volume. They were admonished to hush by Link.

"Boys, we best be quiet. Those devils may not be far off for there is a hint of smoke in the air."

It was decided to send a pair of scouts ahead to find the Indian camp, for it was believed they might have stopped for the evening. Lewis Wetzel and Andrew Robinson were given this duty, and they crossed the shallow stream and proceeded on foot along the north bank. Within an hour, they were back and reported that the Indian camp was another two miles upstream. There were six Indians and ten horses.

Immediately, the men climbed aboard their horses and began a quiet ride toward the camp, with Wetzel and Robinson leading the way. The plan was to come in on the site from a low hill to the north, provided they could do so in complete surprise. The sun was in the west but still fairly high when the whites found themselves in position and still undiscovered.

The Indian warriors, feeling secure on their side of the Ohio, had taken few precautions to prevent an attack, although they had hobbled the horses in an open grassy field to the far side of the camp. They had built a small fire and were sitting around it enjoying a meal when they heard the sounds of shouting riders coming down at them from the hill above. The attack was so sudden and unexpected that the Indians gave no thought of fighting back.

Instead, they grabbed what weapons they could and rushed to the creek, splashing across and disappearing into the stand of trees on the other side. The attacking white men pulled up when they reached the campsite, astonished and relieved that their red foes had simply fled. Not a shot had been fired, but the Indians were gone, and the stolen horses stood but a short distance away, hobbled and easy to recover. The men were feeling quite proud of themselves.

"I knew they'd run," said Jacob Rigger. "Just like that bunch we ran off up on Buffalo Creek a while back."

No one else said anything to that, as the men who knew Rigger understood him to stretch the truth when he could. Not that he ever told a falsehood when it hurt anybody, for that was his reputation, but they were pretty much convinced that he had never run off any Indians on Buffalo Creek or anywhere else.

"Let's get those horses and get back across the Ohio before dark," suggested Thomas McCreary.

"I agree," said another man, Robert McCoy. "They might come back after us if we are still on this side. We can easily get over to Fort Henry for the night."

Everyone was in agreement with this notion, but there was the problem that the horses they had been riding needed rest.

"I think we should leave our current mounts here to blow for an hour or so," said Link. Turning to Rigger, he said, "Jacob, you and your boy Robert can stay here with them, and you too, Ed." This last remark was aimed at a tall man named Ed McGuire. "The rest of us will take the stolen horses down to the river and wait for you there. After about an hour, bring our mounts down and we'll cross over the Ohio together."

"Damn, I ain't too fond of that plan," objected Rigger. "What if them devils is waitin' over there in them trees?"

"I think they're long gone, Jacob," said Link. "They left some of their weapons right here, and we'll take them with us. You'll be fine."

"But what if you're wrong," persisted Rigger.

"We'll send our spies over to see if they're gone. Would that make you happy?"

Wetzel and Robinson were again dispatched to do the scouting, and in a very short time they returned.

"There's no Injuns anywhere close near as we can tell," reported Robinson.

"Hell, that still don't mean they ain't," protested Rigger. Now he tried a new argument. "Why don't we all stay here while our mounts are resting, then go down to the river together?" This argument sounded altogether reasonable to Wetzel, who was uneasy about leaving his father's mare anyplace without being there himself. But Link was not willing to bend from his original plan.

"I think we ought to get as many horses and men ready to cross as we can, so as soon as we know you are coming, we can get started." What he didn't emphasize was his thought that if the Indians did come back, most of the horses and men would be safe.

"That still don't make much sense to me," responded Rigger.

"Do you want someone else to take your place, Jacob?" asked Link.

"I'll do it," said Lewis Wetzel quickly.

"No, I'll stay," said Rigger. "I ain't afraid."

Rigger did not want it being told around the settlements that he had acted like a coward.

"Then it is settled. Let's get moving, men."

The hobbles were removed from the ten stolen horses. Link and the four going with him each rode one horse while leading another. The two Riggers and McGuire stood watching them go. McGuire had said nothing, but he had hoped that Rigger would win the argument. He was a big man and noted for his strength, but he didn't consider himself much of an Indian fighter. "Let's us and these horses move to the other side of the creek," he suggested. "I'd feel better waiting among them trees."

"Good idea," agreed Jacob Rigger, and they quickly acted on the suggestion. They brought the horses to the other side and left them standing in the open, just at the edge of the trees while the three of them moved inside.

"Should we hobble them horses?" asked young Robert Rigger.

"No, we won't be here that long," said his father. "They'll be okay. Besides, it will make it easier if we have to leave in a hurry."

The grove of trees and heavy grasses was nearly fifty yards in length and twenty yards wide. There were open areas at each end and a sparsely wooded hill rising at the edge opposite from the creek. McGuire took his rifle and moved farther into the trees.

"I don't want the bastards sneakin' up on us from the other end," he said.

Lewis Wetzel and his companions had stopped at the mouth of Indian Wheeling Creek, where they tied the horses to nearby trees and sat on the trunk of an old birch that was lying along the bank. They were just opposite the big island, and they could see Fort Henry perched on the bluff in the distance. Nothing was said for a time, but then Jacob Link, who had been stewing about it for awhile, finally spoke out. "I might have been a little hasty, runnin' off and leaving those men back there," he offered.

"They'll be okay, Jacob," said Andrew Robinson in a kindly tone. "As soon as we hear them coming, we should start across. I don't much want to do it in the dark."

Thomas McCreary thought it would be best to go ahead and start crossing right away, but it was decided that they must wait for the others. While discussing the matter, they heard the sound of men running and when they looked back, they saw the two Riggers and Ed McGuire rushing through the grass on the other side of the creek. When they caught sight of their companions, the three men slowed down and angled across the stream.

"What happened?" asked Link, running to meet them.

"They got between us and the horses," said Jacob Rigger. "They ran the horses across the creek, and we took that chance to get away."

"Did you shoot at them?" Link wanted to know.

"There wasn't no time," answered Rigger. "There was nothin' to do but run."

"They got the horses?" Lewis Wetzel was suddenly animated. "They got Pa's mare?"

"'Fraid so," said Rigger.

"Damn!" exclaimed Wetzel. "How did they do it?"

"They came from the other side, opposite to the direction they ran off in. We were watching the other way."

"There's such a thing as circling around you know." Wetzel was very angry.

"What's done is done," said Link. "There's nothin' to be done about it now."

"The hell there isn't," fumed Wetzel. "We can go after them. There's still plenty of light."

"They'll be long gone by now," said Rigger. He wanted no more to do with the Indians. "There's as many of them as there's us, and they'd by watchin' for us this time." In fact, he had seen no more than three warriors, but this was no time to mention that.

"They probably figure we've gone across the river by now," argued Lewis Wetzel. "I say let's finish what we started and go home with all the horses."

Not a single man spoke up to agree with Wetzel. The men were ready to return home. Finally, Link spoke again.

"I think we best go home. At least we got the horses that was stolen. We could end up fighting them in the dark, and that gives them the advantage."

All but Wetzel spoke in agreement.

Lewis was furious. "You cowards. Everyone of you. What's the matter with you? Why did you even come after them and insist on me comin' too? Did you think the bastards would just give the horses back to you without a fight?"

Link was stung by these words from such a young man.

"Watch who you're callin' cowards, young Lew. We're just usin' our common sense."

"Don't make no sense to me," said Lewis, who was shouting. "I ain't goin' home. I'm goin' after Pa's mare. Will any of you go with me?"

No one spoke, nor would any of the men even look at the fuming Wetzel. He looked at each man but none would look him in the eye. He stopped in front of Robert Rigger. "What's the matter with you, Robert? Are you scared?" Robert continued to look down until Wetzel turned away with disgust. "Well, I'll go by myself then. I'd rather come back with the mare without my hair than come back with my hair and without the mare."

He grabbed his rifle, which he had fortunately brought with him when he left his horse behind, and began walking swiftly back upstream.

"Wait a minute," said Andrew Robinson. "I reckon I'll go with you, since I was the one that urged you to come with us."

"I'll come too," said Robert Rigger, pulling away from his father's grasp.

The three of them advanced at a quick pace with Wetzel in the lead. They covered the five miles to the Indian camp in less than an hour, but the sun was beginning to sink low in the western sky. They crossed to the other side of the creek where the tall grass, vines, and occasional tree provided more cover. To their surprise, the Indians were still in the same location as before.

"They're still there!" exclaimed Robert Rigger.

"Hush," cautioned Wetzel as he surveyed the scene. The horses were across the creek, again hobbled and grazing in an open field. The Indians, three in number, were on the opposite side sitting at the edge of the heavy stand of woods, eating their evening meal. Lewis searched widely for sight of any further warriors.

"Robert, how many warriors did you see when they ran you off before?" he asked Rigger. "It's important to know how many we're up against."

"I think we should go back, Lew. It ain't worth us gettin' killed here."

"I didn't ask for advice. I want to know how many Injuns you saw before."

"His pa said there was six," said Robinson. "That's too many. I agree with Robert. Let's give it up."

"But I only see three," insisted Wetzel. "How many, Robert?"

"Well, I saw only three," admitted Rigger. "But I wasn't really countin'. Mostly, I was runnin'."

"That's what I thought. My guess is that only three came back 'cuz that's all the guns they had left."

Lewis stepped forward and down into the creek's edge, peering intently through the tangle of saw grass along the bank. After a few minutes, he crept back to where Rigger and Robinson crouched motionless in the grass. "There's three birch trees strung out just ahead of us," he said. "We'll go up in single file along the edge of the water. Mr. Robinson, you get behind the first tree, and Robert, you fall in behind the second. When I get to the third tree, we'll step out and fire our guns."

Without waiting for affirmation from his companions, Wetzel began moving along the creek as he had indicated. When he stepped up behind the third tree, he was disappointed to see that the Indians had scattered into the trees behind them. Of even greater dismay to Wetzel was the sight of both Robinson and Rigger running at top speed back toward the Ohio River.

Lewis was in a tight spot. The Indians could no doubt see that they now faced only one foe. He could run for it himself, but there was still the stubborn fact that his father's mare was standing there across the creek, and he simply could not return home without her. He kneeled down behind the tree and some weeds that stood on either side. He slipped off his hat, placed it on the end of his gun barrel, and lifted it slowly to the left of the tree and above the weeds. His enemy took the bait, and all three warriors raised their rifles, firing almost simultaneously. At least one of the balls struck the hat, and Lewis quickly dropped it to the ground, making it appear that the wearer was hit and down.

The three Indians, believing Wetzel to be dead or, at least, badly wounded, sprang from behind the trees and began advancing, eager to finish the job and secure the scalp. Lewis, however, stepped calmly from behind his tree, brought the loaded weapon to his shoulder, and squeezed the trigger. The leading warrior took the screaming ball in the middle of his chest and tumbled into the grass. The other two, knowing that Lewis had no loaded gun, increased their speed, drawing their tomahawks and shouting a war cry.

Wetzel turned and began to run as fast as he could. He was nearly full grown by now, having reached a height over five feet ten inches. He was slender, with wide shoulders, and blessed with excellent running speed. He began to gain on his pursuers. Now he was going to find out if the endless hours of practice with his rifle would pay off. As he ran, he pulled the powder horn from off his shoulder and poured a charge of black powder down the end of the rifle barrel. Without losing a single stride, he fished a ball from the pouch at his waist and dropped it into the barrel of the gun, which he was careful to keep upright.

Suddenly he stopped, wheeled around and dropped to one knee. Quickly he sprinkled some powder in the priming pan, pulled back the hammer, and aimed at the brave closest to him. The shot hit the surprised Indian in the midsection, and he fell dead. The third warrior stopped for an instant, trying to comprehend how his friend had been shot with an empty rifle. Then he began the race again, sure that there could be no more shooting. Lewis Wetzel, however, was already in flight, and as before, in the act of reloading.

The pursuer had closed the gap while Wetzel had stopped to shoot. Lewis's speed allowed him to maintain his lead and maybe increase it just a bit. Once again, when the powder and ball were in place, he turned, kneeled and primed the pan. Just as the warrior hurled his hatchet, the rifle spoke, the ball emerging in a long string of flame coming from the unburned powder in the barrel. It too struck home, and Wetzel let out a cry of both relief and triumph. He knew how easily he could have been killed if his reloading on the run had resulted in a misfire. But the Indian foes were dead, all three of them.

He stood for a moment, contemplating what he had done. It occurred to him that the sounds of shooting might have brought other Indians to the scene. He decided it would be wise to reload his rifle, and he went about the deliberate processes required. With time to do it properly, he took the wiping stick and cleaned out some of the powder residue in the barrel. He leaned over the end and blew down the barrel, hoping that might clear any obstructions in the touchhole. Next he poured a measure of powder down the barrel, and removing a patch and ball from the carrying pouch, he placed the patch, then the ball, at the end of the rifle bore.

He pushed them into the barrel as far as he could, then took the wiping stick and jammed it down until he felt the patch and ball seat against the powder. Removing the stick, he placed it in its slot under the barrel and carefully poured a small bit of powder into the pan. He closed the pan by pulling the mizzen back and then pulled the hammer to the half-cocked position. The gun was properly loaded and ready to cock and fire when needed.

He reflected on the number of steps just completed and wondered how he had been able to do this while running for his life. Of course the patch and the action with the wiping stick had been deleted. He was thankful that all the practice had served him well. Just next to where he stood, the Indian's tomahawk lay half buried in the grass. He picked it up and examined it for a moment. The handle was made of maple and was brightly painted while the head was iron with a sharp cutting edge.

No doubt this weapon had been obtained in trade with the English or French. Many frontiersmen carried such a hatchet, along with a knife and a rifle, but Wetzel had never owned one. He stuck this one under the belt at his waist and began to walk toward the spot where the tomahawk's previous owner was lying face down. Lewis had killed many animals and had never felt any compassion for his victims. He remembered one time when his little brother Jacob had expressed some sorrow over a rabbit they had killed.

"His ma and pa will be sad," Jacob had said.

"Hell, Jake," Lewis had answered, "Rabbits don't feel sad. They're just dumb animals." He had laughed then, and Jacob said no more.

As he looked at the body lying lifeless at his feet, it struck him that this was the first time he had ever taken human life. He felt no more remorse, however, than he had felt about the rabbit or any other animal he had killed. Was it because it was just an Indian? Certainly the killing of Indians by whites and the killing of whites by Indians was a natural event on the border. Still the thought crossed Lewis's mind: *Would I feel the same if the man lying there was white?* He shrugged it off. *No, I killed these men to save my own life. It is as simple as that.*

Another thought now surfaced. What about the scalp? Should I take his scalp? Obviously Lewis had never taken a scalp, nor had he observed it being done. It was always done by the Indians when they had time, he knew that, and he also knew that the frontiersmen did it frequently as well. He had never thought about why it was done, although he figured the whites did it in retaliation and thinking it was an insult to the red men. One thing it did accomplish, however, was to establish the victory of the scalper over his victim.

If he took the scalps of the three warriors he had killed, it would verify his story when he told it to the other men. He took out his knife and squatted down over the body. He was not sure what to do, but he grasped the hair at the crown of the Indian's head, and he began cutting along the edge of the hairline. It wasn't easy, and he started again, cutting now at the top of the forehead. The scalp began to come loose at the front and as he pulled, it began to come off. He placed his knee in the middle of the man's back to gain leverage, and he completed a circle cut around the head and just below the crown. With one more jerk, the topknot tore loose, and he held the scalp in his left hand, with blood dripping profusely.

At first, he experienced a feeling of disgust, then one of some satisfaction that he had been successful. He shook the scalp vigorously, freeing it from excess blood. Next he began looking for some way to carry it. He found a vine growing on a nearby tree, and tearing a piece of it loose, he threaded it through a hole he pierced in the scalp with his knife, an inch from the edge. Picking up his rifle, he began the walk back toward the other bodies, carrying the bloody scalp, dangling from the vine, in his right hand.

Darkness was falling rapidly now, and Wetzel felt the urgency in gathering up the horses and trying to catch up with the rest of the party. He figured that they had already crossed the big river. In spite of his need for haste, he took time to retrieve the other scalps, and after crossing the creek, he found his father's mare among the horses standing hobbled as the Indians had left them. He placed his rifle in the sling and next to it, he tied the vine with the three scalps. "It's all right, Susie," he said to the mare, soothing her as best he could, for the smell of blood had spooked her a bit. "We're goin' home now."

Tying together the short pieces of cord that had been used for hobbles, Lewis fashioned a line to tie the horses together. Once this was done, he climbed on the back of Susannah and started back downstream, with the remaining seven horses following behind. It was totally dark by this time, and after a few minutes, Lewis dismounted and led the mare the remaining distance.

As he approached to within a quarter of a mile of the Ohio, he saw the flicker of a campfire and could hear the faint sounds of men talking. Apparently, the men had camped on this side of the river, and Wetzel was surprised. Knowing that his companions might have heard the shooting and would be anxious, he prepared to announce his presence from far enough away to avoid the danger of friendly fire. After traveling another two hundred yards, he began to shout. "Hey, hey. It's Lew Wetzel. I'm coming in, don't shoot. Don't shoot." Lewis shouted again after a few minutes, "Hey, I'm comin' in with the horses."

He stopped, able to see the campfire, but unable to see any human figures.

"It sounds like Lew," someone said.

Probably Jacob Rigger, thought Wetzel.

"It can't be no Indian."

A figure appeared suddenly out of a clump of bushes off to Wetzel's right.

"It is Lew, by God. It's him," exclaimed Tom McCreary.

"Hello, Mr. McCreary," said Lewis, impressed that the men had apparently posted a guard at the edge of the camp.

"My God, Lew. We figured you was dead." McCreary grabbed Lew's right hand and shook it vigorously.

The other men soon appeared, and there was an excited chatter as they gathered around to express their joy and congratulations. The last two to approach were Robert Rigger and Andrew Robinson, unsure of their reception by Wetzel after having deserted him.

"Lew, we thought you had been shot, and we ran for our lives." Robert Rigger thought it best to get in the first words. In the darkness, he could not see the look of incredulity that came to Wetzel's face.

Lewis was well aware that the two of them had run long before any shots were fired. It had angered him at the time, but now, as things had turned out, he had no more hard feelings. He nodded but said nothing.

"We sure thought you was a goner," said Jacob Link. "How did you get the horses away from them?"

"I killed all three of 'em," said Lewis simply.

"You killed all three? Are you sure?"

Wetzel unfastened the string of scalps from the mare's neck and handed it to Link. "I'm sure," he said.

"Son of a bitch!" exclaimed Link. "He's got three scalps." The men crowded in again, trying to get a look at the bloody trophies.

"Tell us about it, son," urged Ed McGuire.

Lewis recounted the events, trying as best he could to keep the pride out of his voice. He never liked to hear men bragging, and he didn't want to sound that way himself. When he had finished, the men sat quietly, amazed at this incredible story. No one could think of having heard of anything like it before.

"By God, you're a hero," said Thomas McCreary. "Wait'll they hear about this at Fort Henry."

January 7, 1781

The tomahawk was stuck firmly into the post, and Martin Wetzel stood in the council house, admiring his handiwork. It was hard to imagine that he could have done such a thing, and he wondered now if it was a bad idea. According to Shawnee custom, it meant that the owner of a war club stuck into the war post was ready to lead a raiding party.

Others were invited to join by putting their own tomahawks in the post. That thought staggered him. Martin Wetzel leading a party of hostile braves against a target in the white settlements? There had been no war parties out against other Indian tribes in a long time, so the meaning was clear. It was more than two and a half years since Martin had been taken captive on Wheeling Creek, and the changes in his life, as a result, were massive.

Having barely escaped a burning at the stake, he had instead been adopted as a son by an Indian widow. And not just any widow, it was the wife of the murdered Shawnee chief, Cornstalk, who had taken him in. Her son had died with his father, and she regarded Martin as a replacement. Her name was Wandering Bird, and to say she was an interesting woman was putting it mildly.

Martin was amazed at the fitness of her name for she did love to travel. No more than a month after Martin's arrival, she had embarked on a shopping expedition to the trading post at Vincennes, taking Martin with her. Two strong braves, including Fire Heart, had accompanied them, taking several horses loaded with trading goods. On this trip, Wandering Bird had shown a startling affinity for liquor and had become quite drunk. The Shawnees had kept close watch on Martin at first, but gradually they allowed him more freedom.

After a couple of months, they let him accompany a hunting party and gave him a gun with one load. When he was fortunate enough to shoot a deer, his captors were impressed. The next trip, they gave him a loaded gun and one extra load. Martin had seen no more of Daniel Boone and in mid-June, Boone had slipped away, returning to Kentucky. In the next month, George Rogers Clark had completed his famous conquest of Kaskaskia and, later learning that there were no British troops at Vincennes, had sent a platoon of soldiers to occupy that post.

Word had reached the Shawnee town in time to frustrate another visit to Vincennes by Wandering Bird. Instead, she had taken Martin and a young Indian boy of fifteen years, who also lived with her, to the east to visit the previous home village of Cornstalk on the Scioto River. At first, Martin thought that no one else would accompany them, and he thought of trying to escape. However, the ever-present Fire Heart and another warrior had joined them.

The trip proved interesting when they visited the town of Wandering Bird's famous sister-in-law, Nonhelema, the so-called Grenadier Squaw. Wetzel had heard of her, of course, but the sight of her six-foot-six-inch frame was still a shock to him. She was very friendly with the Americans and served as a messenger between the Indian and white leaders. She had come to Martin to find out who he was. It was pleasing to be able to speak English with someone, and Wetzel asked her to get word to his family that he was still alive. She would not promise that, however, saying she owed allegiance to her brother's widow.

In September of that year, Black Fish had led an Indian army of 450 warriors into Kentucky and all the way to Boonesborough. They had returned nearly two weeks later in a foul mood, having achieved little success. At the same time the Shawnees stood at the gates of Boonesborough, three white men had come to the Chillicothe village on a spying mission. After stealing some horses the three had returned to the Ohio River, and while they were delayed by high water, a group of Indians in pursuit caught up with them, killing one and capturing another, a frontiersman going by the name of Simon Butler. The third spy had managed to escape across the river, but the Shawnees were overjoyed by the capture of Butler, a well-known foe.

Martin had not been in Chillicothe when Butler was brought in. By the time he did return to the village with his adoptive mother, the white captive had been taken on to the important Indian town of Wapatomica further north where he was to be burned at the stake. The name Butler was still being repeated by the inhabitants of Chillicothe, who were disappointed that the execution was not to be carried out in their village. Martin knew of Butler, for the man had been a prominent scout and courier during Dunmore's War.

After a considerable amount of time—several months, Martin figured—word had come that Governor Henry Hamilton had ventured out of his fortress in Detroit and, with a hundred British troops and five hundred Indian allies, had retaken the lightly held post at Vincennes. Wetzel had lost track of any method of keeping time and date, and so did not know that this event occurred in December of 1778.

Wandering Bird was overjoyed at this news, and she quickly organized an expedition to the trading post. This time she had taken only Martin and the young Indian lad, whom Martin called Bird Watcher. As usual, they also had a string of packhorses with them. He had seriously considered making his escape since he would have had no trouble overpowering the two Birds. The weather, however, was miserable and the thought of trying to make it to safety by himself through hostile territory in such adverse conditions was more than he wanted to risk. Thus he had gone along, in the blustery weather, moving west from Chillicothe, aiming for the White River, which angled down toward Vincennes.

He had attempted to dissuade Wandering Bird from making the trip, trying to make her understand that the weather would make things too difficult. His ability to communicate in the Shawnee tongue was quite limited, however, and he could not make a reasonable argument. It would not have mattered anyway, he reckoned. The trip itself was as wretched as Martin had imagined it would be. Temperatures hovered around freezing, and there were intermittent snow showers. At night, they were able to fashion an open-ended tent out of some hides they had, and by taking refuge in heavily wooded areas, they had some protection. Still Martin could not remember being so miserably cold.

It was several days before they finally crossed the White River and made their way a dozen miles west and south to the trading post on the Wabash. The White River eventually flowed into the Wabash, but that occurred several miles below Vincennes. Winter rains had led to some flooding around Vincennes, and it was to get even worse. The trading of goods had been accomplished fairly quick when Wandering Bird disappeared. Martin knew that she had found a place to do some drinking, so he and Bird Watcher found accommodations in one of the vacant huts nearby and settled in for the night.

In the morning, there was still no sign of the woman, but they went about the chores of loading the goods on the packhorses and preparing for the return trip. The weather had warmed up a little, and they were anxious to leave. After a while, Martin sent Bird Watcher to find Wandering Bird. He came back shaking his head, and Martin understood that their mother was passed out drunk. They unpacked the horses and settled in for another night.

The next morning, Wandering Bird showed up, seriously hungover and with a sheepish grin on her face. The two young men immediately readied the horses, and they set off for the home village. As he thought of it now, Martin smiled. He felt a tenderness toward Wandering Bird that surprised him. She had treated him well.

That trip to Vincennes and its fort, called Fort Sackville, was to be their last for George Rogers Clark later brought an army against it and, overcoming severe hardships because of the intense flooding, retook the post. Also Clark had captured the English governor, Hamilton. It was a blow to the Shawnees when they learned of it. Worse things had followed. The Shawnee tribe had divided, and a large portion, numbered in the thousands, had decided to move west across the Mississippi. Martin had marveled at the sight of so many Indians from Chillicothe and surrounding villages following the French trader, Louis Lorimer, who was leading them to some lands set aside for them in the Missouri country.

Not more than one hundred warriors were left in the once populous capital village on the Little Miami. Not many months after that, an army of Kentuckians, led by the man the Indians knew as Bowman, appeared outside the town. The warriors had evacuated the little huts and taken refuge in the main council house, but not before making sure that the women, children, and elderly men, along with others such as Martin Wetzel, had been sent to safety into the woods far to the north. For some unexplained reason, only one wing of the colonial army had made much of an attack, and then, after setting fires to some of the huts, all had retreated. The warriors had followed the retreat and harassed the militia as it fell back.

What could have been a disaster had been averted because of leadership deficiencies among the whites. Unfortunately for the Shawnees, their chief, Black Fish, had been wounded, and after several days in agony, he died. His successor was Catehecassa or Black Hoof. It was shortly after this that Martin met Joseph Rogers.

Normally the Shawnees kept their white captives apart from each other, trying to prevent, Martin supposed, any attempted escapes. The Indians had returned to the partially burned-out village and began restoring some of the log huts, called wigewa, that had not been completely destroyed. Martin was employed in this carpenter work and was enjoying it. One day, as he knelt at his task, he noticed a white man struggling to carry a log some distance away. A quick glance around revealed no one watching, and Martin jumped up and ran over to provide some help. Catching hold of one end of the log that was dragging on the ground, he introduced himself. "I'm Martin Wetzel. Looks like you can use some help."

"Joseph Rogers," answered the man, looking furtively from side to side. "They won't like it if they see us talkin'."

"Well I don't suppose they'll do too much to us," said Wetzel. "It's nice to have a chance to talk to a white man for a change."

"I ain't so sure about that," cautioned Rogers. "But I agree, it's good to be able to talk with a friend. I saw you a couple of times across the camp and wondered who you was."

They tossed the log down at the base of a nearby cabin.

"How long have you been a captive?" asked Wetzel.

"Since sometime in '76," was the answer. "I was captured in the Limestone area down in Kentucky. We was after some buried powder. What about you?"

"In the spring of '78. I've been through one big winter, so it must be '79 now. And winter ain't too far away."

"I guess I don't remember when they brought you in. Maybe I was at one of the other villages then." Rogers stared at Wetzel as he spoke, puzzled that he couldn't recall that day.

"They brought me in with another fellow, John Wolf. They burned him."

Wetzel figured that Rogers would have surely remembered that.

"Oh God, that was awful. I was up on the Mad River when it happened, but I sure heard about it."

"Boone was here then too."

"I know. I never got a chance to talk to him, but I was surprised when he got away."

Martin saw that two Shawnee braves were coming toward them, clearly disapproving of the two captives having a conversation. Rogers saw it too.

"We'd better move on," he said. "I'm hopin' George will come before too long and set us free."

"George who?" Wetzel had asked, chancing another moment of conversation.

"Why, George Rogers Clark," exclaimed Rogers. "He's my cousin."

"Good-bye, Rogers," Martin had said. "And good luck to you."

Now as he recalled this conversation, Martin was saddened when he thought of how things had ended for Rogers. It had been in the following summer, he thought. After a large Indian army, led by the British officer Bird, who had some British troops and a couple of cannon, had captured two Kentucky forts, the Kentuckians had been determined to retaliate.

George Rogers Clark had led an army of nearly one thousand men straight up the Little Miami toward the Chillicothe town. The Shawnees, when they discovered who was coming, had evacuated the village, taking as much with them as they could manage and took refuge at Piqua town, a dozen miles north, and on the Mad River. Clark had burned Chillicothe, destroyed the crops, and moved on to confront the Indians at Piqua.

Although outnumbered three to one, the Shawnees put up a brisk fight but were eventually overwhelmed. Clark had brought a cannon with him, and with it he smashed the principal building in the town. The Indians took to the woods and tried to mount a counterattack, but they were driven back even farther. Martin had watched this battle, thankful that his captors had not forced him to fight against the Kentuckians. During the battle, Joseph Rogers had made a dash for freedom but had been riddled with bullets from both sides. Having witnessed this tragic affair, Martin had turned and ran deeper into the woods, feeling sick.

Clark's men had destroyed the Piqua village and more of the precious crops before returning to Kentucky. The Shawnees had been stunned by this reversal, and the loss of the corn and vegetable crops had brought hunger to their villages. Some had tried to move back to Chillicothe, but the town was a shell of its former self, and Wandering Bird, after a short stay there, took Martin and Bird Watcher with her to one of the villages to the north on the Great Miami River near Louis Lorimer's trading post. There was great anger among the warriors, and Martin had often felt their hostile stares. He knew there was talk of putting together another strike against the Kentuckians.

Just a few days ago, Fire Heart had come to find Martin, pleading with him to follow him to the old Piqua village on the Mad River. Although Martin was unsure of what was planned, he felt compelled to go. Even Wandering Bird seemed to be encouraging him to go, and when he finally prepared to leave that morning, she had bid him an affectionate farewell. Quite beyond his control, tears had filled his eyes, and he hugged the old woman as if she were his own mother. Bird Watcher had also watched and nodded to Martin with a look of both sadness and respect. Their manner seemed to indicate that they did not expect to see Martin again, and he wondered what they knew.

His mind returned now to the present, and after looking at the tomahawk for a few more minutes, Wetzel walked to the door of the council house, which had been partially repaired after Clark's attack. Pausing to look back at the war post, he turned and went outside. He searched out a spot off to the side, which gave a clear view of the doorway where he squatted and sat cross-legged on the hard ground. His breath was visible in the frosty air, and he suddenly felt the cold, wanting very much to return to the fire in the little hut he was sharing with Fire Heart. He needed to see, however, who was going to respond to his challenge. Wetzel had decided on this course of action shortly after they had arrived in this village.

The young men talked of nothing but revenge against the hated whites. Their ferocity was highest against the Kentuckians who occupied their sacred hunting grounds. Although always on the edge of the circle of conversations, Martin had occasionally offered some advice. It was clear that Fire Heart had convinced most of the warriors that Martin was now one of them, and they were willing to listen. Steal the settler's horses was what he had told them. Without horses these farmers would be unable to plant and grow their crops. Eventually they would be compelled to go back across the mountains from where they had come.

This sounded reasonable to the young braves, although they also thought it would help to kill a good number of the settlers as well. Considerable commotion was about the camp as different Indian leaders came through as well as some of the renegade whites. The day before, Jim Girty had been in the town. Fire Heart had kept Martin out of Girty's sight, explaining to Martin as best he could that Girty was especially mean and could cause trouble for him. It was then that Martin was sure that he needed to take bold action before it was too late.

If he were to lead a small raiding party to one of the Kentucky settlements intent on stealing horses, perhaps he could slip away when they were close enough to one of the forts. He remembered that Joseph Rogers had tried to slip away as well, and it resulted in disaster. Still he had to try something. Today he had acted, sinking his tomahawk in the post. Now he waited to see who would add their war axes to his in the post. It was not what Martin had expected. Sitting there in the cold for at least two hours, he saw no one come near the council house. Finally a group of braves came by, appearing to give no notice to Martin, and went inside.

When they left a few moments later, Martin rushed in, only to be greatly disappointed. There were no new tomahawks in the war post. He wondered now if his plan might fail. Perhaps he wasn't as well accepted and trusted as he thought. When he returned to his hut, he found that Fire Heart was there, sitting close to the little fire built in the center. It was smoky inside, although most of the smoke was going out through the hole in the roof above it. Martin crowded up close to the fire, trying to stop the shivering that had overtaken him. He wished that his ability to speak in the Shawnee language was better for he wanted to discuss his feelings with Fire Heart.

The dusky Shawnee had looked up when Martin entered, but said nothing, returning his stare to the flames. Martin tried to put together some words and start a conversation, but he couldn't seem to do it in a way that would make sense, so he sat down without speaking. Fire Heart had explained the significance of the tomahawk in the war post to Martin one day, and Martin was sure that Fire Heart knew why he had gone to the council house that morning. He would just wait now for his response.

The warmth from the fire brought on a sense of drowsiness, and soon Martin had fallen asleep. Fire Heart got up and went out. After an hour had passed, Wetzel awakened, feeling hungry. He noted the absence of his companion, and he supposed he should see about something for the two of them to eat. The effort seemed too great, and he stayed next to the fire, reclining on one elbow. Fire Heart suddenly appeared inside with a wide grin on his face. He raised his right hand and made two chopping motions.

"Two," he said in English, holding up two fingers.

"Yes?" asked Wetzel, jumping to his feet.

"Yes," repeated the Shawnee, shaking his head. They both fully understood the significance.

"Eat now," said Fire Heart.

Though Martin wanted desperately to go to the council house and look for himself, he thought better of it and nodded his agreement. Wetzel watched as the Indian added a small chunk of wood to the fire and then began putting some ingredients into an iron pot sitting near the fire. Some kind of corn meal along with a little water was dumped in, then some pieces of turnip and squash, and finally several bits of dried venison. Setting the pot on the fire, Fire Heart looked at Martin with a smile of satisfaction.

For his part, Martin was glad to let Fire Heart do the cooking. He was a bit ashamed that he tended to let the Shawnee do most of the necessary chores but not enough to volunteer for too much. He knew that Fire Heart had a woman, but she was in the larger safer town of Wapatomica, farther north near the source of the Mad River. He was still not sure why Fire Heart had insisted on Martin coming with him to the Piqua village. Was it that his friend had wished him to do the very thing that he had determined to do on his own? Perhaps he would find out before much longer.

January 16, 1781

It took three days for seven tomahawks to be added to Wetzel's on the war post. A flurry of activity followed as the raiding party made its preparations for the expedition. Although Wetzel's tomahawk had precipitated this activity and indicated him as the leader, it was clear that Fire Heart would be the actual person in command. Still, Martin realized that the response by seven warriors showed their trust in him as one of them. He felt a pang of remorse about the fact that he intended to reward their trust with a betrayal. On the other hand, he comforted himself with the thought that he truly hoped that none of them, and in particular, Fire Heart, would come to any harm.

There was a discussion, in which Wetzel had little input, as to whether they should ride horses or make the trip on foot. Although it seemed desirable to be able to ride on such a long trip, there was the problem of getting the horses across the icy cold Ohio River. Riding and swimming them across was not palatable, and in the end, the decision was to make the trip on foot. If they were successful in stealing horses, they would have to face the same problem on the return, but that would be dealt with at the time.

Each man was responsible for his own provisions, which generally included a heavy robe or blanket for sleeping, some mostly dried foodstuffs, and a line of some kind for securing the captured horses. The little raiding party set out on a cold but clear morning, heading for the old Chillicothe town, and on down the

Little Miami River. Although Wetzel had no way of knowing it at the time, the date was January of 1781.

In the afternoon of the second day, they came to the Ohio shore. Leaving the Little Miami a mile or so above its mouth, they had angled in a southwesterly direction to a point on the shore directly opposite the mouth of the Licking River on the Kentucky side. Here in a dense thicket up a small ravine, they found two canoes that had been hidden for just such a purpose as they now had. The skies were overcast and spitting some scattered snowflakes. All agreed that they should rest and spend the night on the Ohio side, saving the crossing of the big river for the next morning.

As darkness fell, they built a good fire, and spirits among the warriors were high. They laughed and sparred with each other, and every one of them had made sure to pound Martin on the back to show approval. He felt himself taken in a bit with the genial comradeship, and for the first time, he began to understand how some white men could decide to stay with the Indians and even fight with them against their own race.

These white renegades were thought of as the most evil of men among the settlers, and Martin had always thought of them in that way himself. He drifted into sleep, struggling with these thoughts. The morning was clear but cold. There was a light blanket of snow on everything, but the rising sun would soon erase it. They pushed the two canoes into the river's edge and Martin jumped into the bow of one while Fire Heart took the other.

Two warriors in each canoe did the paddling, and they were soon out into the middle of the chilly river. They fought against the current and aimed at the west side of the mouth of the Licking River, which came up from the interior of the Kentucky country. Upon landing, they stowed the little boats into some cover near the shore for use on the return or for the use of some other party that might come along. The good spirits of the warriors continued, and they set off on the path along the bank of the Licking with little attention to the surroundings.

The white settlements were still miles away, and they did not expect discovery by an enemy any time soon. On the second day after leaving the Ohio, the little party of seven Shawnee braves and one nervous white man left the stream and moved off on an old buffalo trail toward the southwest. They skirted the burned-out ruins at Ruddell's station and at Martin's station a bit farther along. Both of these places had been destroyed by the Indian army under the British Colonel Bird the previous summer.

By nightfall, they neared the settlement called Bryan's Station, which was still inhabited by the whites. Most of the cabins in the settlement were inside a rectangular area enclosed by a log wall. It sat recessed a short distance from the south bank of a creek known as the Elkhorn by the settlers. The horse and cattle herds attached to the station were quickly located, but the decision was made to camp for the night and carry out the intended raid in the next morning.

It was to be a cold camp since they could not risk a premature discovery. Fortunately, the weather had turned a bit warmer, and they settled in comfortably under the blankets and robes that they had carried with them. Martin Wetzel was unable to sleep. His mind continued to return to the plan that had been put together for the morning's actions and for the scheme he had devised for his own flight. It was simple enough, he thought, but he couldn't keep from seeing, in his mind's eye, the scene at the Piqua town, when Joseph Rogers had tried the same kind of escape.

He was struck by the quietness of the winter night, and he felt the chill in spite of the heavy robe that covered him. He pulled it tighter around his shoulders and thought again of the Indian woman who had adopted him, and who had made the robe for him. Although Martin had eventually drifted into a light sleep, he was wide awake when the first rays of daylight appeared and his companions began to stir. Soon all were awake and after a short council in which the plans were reviewed again, they ate a light breakfast of corn cakes and dried venison. Then they began to scatter to carry out the assigned duties.

The seven braves were to gather as many of the horses as they could while Martin was to serve as a guard against possible discovery. He moved to the edge of the clearing nearest the main gate of the stockade. Fire Heart had come with him at first but now moved off to help with the captured ponies. The second part of the plan was to secure the horses some distance away and return to set up an ambush for any of the residents of the station who came out to check on the livestock, gather wood, or perform some other chore. Martin had argued vigorously against that part of the plan, but it had no effect. He had abandoned his opposition when he could see that the warriors were beginning to suspect him of something. He was sure that was the reason that Fire Heart had stayed close to him and likely was still keeping an eye on him.

One of the braves had suggested that if someone were to come out of the gate of the fort, Martin was to shoot him and then rejoin the rest of them. Fire Heart, knowing that this might be impossible for Martin to do, had overruled that idea and insisted that Martin simply run to them with a warning as quickly and quietly as possible. Wetzel waited now as his Shawnee companions quietly moved in among the horses. The sun had risen enough above the trees to dispel the darkness, and he could see the walls of the stockade clearly. He could not see anyone along the walls, and the gate, which was on the north wall, remained securely closed. There were a few log huts on the east side of the fort, and the livestock was beyond those to the east and south.

He could no longer see any of the warriors, nor could he see Fire Heart. The time for him to run was now, but he continued to wait. It was at least a hundred yards to the gate, and he had to get there without being seen by Fire Heart or one of the others. The thought flashed through his mind—would Fire Heart actually shoot him? It was likely, he figured. An even greater problem lurked on the other end. What if no one came to open the gate, or worse yet, what if they simply fired on him from inside without asking any questions? He looked at himself and realized how much he resembled an Indian brave.

The people inside the stockade would not be able to recognize him as a white man. He had deliberately not scraped off his whiskers that morning, but the stubble would not be enough to show that he was a white man. Suddenly Martin burst from his cover and ran at full speed across the clearing toward the gate. As he neared the wall, he began to scream. "Don't shoot, I am a white man. Don't shoot, don't shoot."

He lifted his gun in both hands and held it high above his head.

"Open the gate!" he yelled again. "My name is Wetzel."

A man appeared above the wall, aiming his rifle.

"Stop you red devil, afore I shoot," he hollered down.

"What is it?" came a voice from inside.

"It's an Injun," answered the man on the wall. "Claims he's a white man."

"Maybe he's a spy," came a cry from inside. "Let's take him."

The gate swung open, and a group of five men came out.

"Let's rush him and kill the bastard," urged the man in front.

"I ain't no Injun," shouted Wetzel. "Look, I'm throwin' down my gun."

With that, Martin threw the old musket to the ground in the direction of the gate, which was only a few yards in front of him. Making sure that the men could see him, he jerked the tomahawk from his belt, throwing it to the ground and followed by doing the same with his knife. "See, there's my tomahawk and knife too. I'm harmless."

Without another word, the men rushed forward, with the first two each grabbing an arm and jerking Martin toward the open gate. One of the others had his rifle pointed at Wetzel, and the remaining men threatened him with raised tomahawks. It was not clear to Martin that he would ever make it inside.

"Get him inside and shut the gate," said the man with the gun. "He's prob'ly got friends out there. Keep an eye out up there, Silas." This last aimed at the guard on the wall.

Pushing and pulling him roughly, the men brought Martin inside the stockade, and the gate was quickly pulled shut.

"I say let's kill him now and get it over with," said one of the men whose name was John Cook. "He ain't no white man, that's fer sure."

Martin feared for his life more than he ever had among the Shawnees. His temper flared, and he wished for an instant that he had his tomahawk. He would do some damage to these fools, maybe even escape and go back to the Indians. The men appeared to be Irish, and that irritated him too. The moment passed, and he struggled to stay calm.

"I am a white man, I tell you," insisted Martin again. "My name is Martin Wetzel from Virginia, up on Wheeling Creek."

"Anybody know any Martin Wetzel?" asked Joseph Bryan, a member of the family that had founded the settlement.

"I do," came the reply of a man who had just walked up. It was Daniel Boone himself who had heard the commotion and hurried over from another part of the station. He looked directly at Martin, still being held firmly between the two men.

"Hello, Wetzel," he said. Turning now to Bryan, who was his son-in-law, Boone said, "Joseph, I saw Wetzel up in Chillicothe when we were both captives of the Shawnees."

The men holding on to Wetzel were not easily convinced, and they grasped him even tighter. The one named Cook spoke again.

"He could still be a spy. How do you know he ain't, Boone?"

"What is he spying on, do you think?" questioned Boone.

"Findin' out how many of us are defendin' this place for starters," said Cook. "There could be a big bunch of them bastards out there just waitin' for some signal."

"Is that right, Wetzel?" Boone asked of Martin.

"There's seven Shawnee braves that came with me. They're after horses."

"And there's no attack planned on this station?"

"No, Boone, not at this time."

"But there might be one coming later?"

"I don't know. The Shawnees are damned mad about the destruction of their villages on the Little Miami by you Kentuckians. It was Clark, I guess."

Martin had heard Clark's name spoken with respect, fear, and hate by the Indians.

"So was this little raiding party sent to spy on us?" Even Boone could see that this could be possible and that the captive Wetzel might prove to be of use to the Shawnees.

"No!" said Wetzel emphatically. "I organized this raid myself as part of my plan to escape. I convinced them it was better to steal horses than try to kill a few white men."

"Hell, I don't believe that," interjected Cook.

"Well it's true," insisted Martin. "Old Fire Heart and his braves are long gone by now, I reckon."

"Let's go after 'em, then," said Cook, looking at Boone.

"Not this time," answered Boone, perhaps remembering other occasions when hasty pursuit had met with disaster. "Let him go, men. Wetzel has made a good escape, and we need to treat him better."

Looking at Bryan who nodded agreement with his father-in-law, Cook and his colleague reluctantly released their hold on Wetzel. Shaking his arms to free himself, and after giving a hard look to his two captors, Martin extended his right hand to Boone.

"Thank you, Daniel," he said simply.

"You're welcome," said Boone. "I hope you'll forgive our rudeness, but we're a little jumpy here about Indian visitors even in the winter. Now come with me, and we'll get you some clothes and something to eat."

Across Elkhorn Creek, Fire Heart and his six companions with ten horses were moving quickly back toward safety, sure that there would be pursuit. Fire Heart looked back toward the fort, the sadness in his eyes revealing the bitterness of this betrayal. He had, after all, taken a real liking to the young white man and had convinced himself that Martin was becoming a true Shawnee. Now, filled with both anger and regret, he made a silent promise to himself, and then he slipped up on to the back of the horse he was holding and rode off to catch up with the others.

January 21, 1781

The young Chippewa warrior stood quietly and stared at the older man, his father, sitting cross-legged before the fire. The young man was awaiting a reply to the announcement he had just made, and as he waited, his face showed the admiration and respect he held for his father, whose name was Maw-kawte-we Maw-in-gawn, Black Wolf.

Well-known among the Chippewas, Black Wolf was a fierce fighter who had been with the French commander Montcalm in the big war between their French brothers and the English. In a big fight far away toward the rising sun, he had taken many scalps at the foot of the lake the English called Lake George. This had happened after the foolish French had let the British soldiers march out of the fort that had been taken by the combined forces of Indians and French.

This had occurred before the young man was born, but he knew well the story of what had happened when Black Wolf did come home. He had brought with him the dreaded white man's disease, which had killed the older brother he never knew and had nearly taken his mother as well. Fortunately, she had recovered from that ordeal, though her face bore the awful pockmarks.

She had still mourned her lost child well after her second child was old enough to understand, and it fueled his own hatred of the whites. When he was older, he did occasionally have to deal with the thought that maybe some of the blame should be placed on Black Wolf himself, for he could have stayed home on the Chippewa lands and avoided all contact with the whites. But this thought was easy to put down for a return to the simple hatred that he nurtured.

His father had gone again to aid Pontiac, the chief of their brothers, the Ottawa, in his war against the English. Now, however, Black Wolf had renounced the war path. The young warrior's name was Waw-goosh-ons, Little Fox. It was a name he wasn't entirely happy with, for his childhood playmates often made fun of the *little* part. Even when he was a man, his friends sometimes chided him about being little. His father had insisted on the name, however, because on the day of the naming, he had encountered a very small fox at the edge of the woods, and the fox had looked him in the eye. Convinced that it was a good omen, Black Wolf had run home to say that the boy's name would be Little Fox.

The hut in which Little Fox stood was a part of a small Chippewa village situated along the Saginaw River, a few miles from where it emptied into the Saginaw Bay. The framework consisted of poles cut from small saplings and placed in a circle of some fifteen feet in diameter, bent over, and tied together at the top. These were covered with large mats made with strips of reeds or, as in this case, birchbark, and a hole was left in the top for the smoke to escape. One of the mats was left loose, and it could be easily lifted and dropped to serve as a door. The fire was built in the center, and mats, made of reeds and corn husks and used for sitting and sleeping, were placed around it.

It was warm and dry, and on this particular morning, a welcome respite from the wind and snow howling around them on the outside. He watched his father who remained seated in silence, and he knew that the older man was carefully processing the thoughts that were racing through his mind as a result of his son's startling announcement. Little Fox felt a moment of tenderness, knowing how his words had been disturbing. Black Wolf, whose back was toward his son, came to his feet and turned slowly to face the young man, who was suddenly uneasy.

"My son," began Black Wolf. "You are a grown man and ready to be a fine warrior. I know this." He looked intently at the fire for a moment. Little Fox said nothing. "It is natural that you should want to take your place as a warrior against our enemies," he continued. "As you say, our brothers to the south are fighting against the Long Knives and with the English who are now our friends. It is not our fight. I fought many battles on behalf of the Great Father far away in France. Now there is a new Great Father of the English. I do not know him."

"The Long Knives are the enemy, Father," said Little Fox. "They are trying to take the lands of all our people."

A Chippewa named Red Bird had come to their village a few days ago, filled with stories of battles with the white settlers. His words had enflamed Little Fox and filled him with resolve. He intended to attach himself to one of the tribes below the big lakes and help in this fight for honor and for life.

"What do you know of the white man?" his father wanted to know.

Little Fox did not answer quickly. He had experienced almost no contact with whites, except for some French traders who came to their villages and, more recently, British traders. He knew there were settlements at Mackinac, where the two big lakes came together, and also at Detroit, where there were many French as well as English. The English were mostly soldiers stationed at the fort there and although he had never been there himself, he had heard much talk of the place since many Indians from a variety of tribes spent time there.

Red Bird, however, had spent several years among the Wyandots and Delawares who lived below the lakes on the Sandusky River. Red Bird had fought the Long Knives, and

Little Fox was satisfied that Red Bird could teach him all he needed to know.

"Red Bird has told me much," was the son's eventual answer to his father's question.

"And who is this Red Bird?" asked Black Wolf. "I do not know him."

"He is of our village, Father. He has been fighting with the Wyandot and the Delaware. His father is Wild Buffalo."

"Ah, Wild Buffalo," exclaimed Black Wolf. "I might have known it would be a son of his to fill you with such foolishness."

"It is not foolishness, Father. Do you not think we should fight to save our lands."

"They are not our lands. The lands belong to no one."

"A noble thought, my father. But the white man does not believe it. They believe the lands are theirs to take."

"Have white men told you this?"

"No, but Red Bird has."

"Yes, Red Bird. Such a wise man is he." Black Wolf took a step forward and raised his hand, pointing a finger at his son. "I do not give my approval for this. If your mother were alive, she would want me to forbid you."

"Father, you cannot forbid me!" Little Fox had shouted these words and regretted them immediately.

His mother had died two winters ago miserable with a ferocious fever. He knew that his absence would increase his father's loneliness that had been so obvious after his mother's death. Still he could not reverse the decision he had made with such internal firmness.

"No, I cannot forbid you," said Black Wolf quietly. "You are a grown man, and you must take your own place in this world." He turned away, but Little Fox did not fail to see the tears that had formed in the corner of the old man's eyes. "Once you leave, I will not see you again, my son."

"That is not true, Father," said Little Fox earnestly. "I will return to our village often to see you."

"I have had my say, and you have had yours. We will speak of it no more." Black Wolf sat down again. "When will you leave? Will you wait for the spring?"

"I must leave now, Father." Little Fox was relieved that there was to be no more argument. He realized then how wise his father really was and how much he loved him.

"Then we must get you ready for your journey."

5

MILITIA

April 8, 1781

GEORGE WETZEL LOOKED over and smiled at his younger brother Lewis, who rode beside him. They were slightly behind their father, Captain John Wetzel, and all three kept their mounts at a slow trot, no one speaking.

It was a cool April Sunday morning, exactly one week before Easter. They were responding to a call for volunteers from Colonel David Shepherd for men to form an expedition to the Delaware towns on the Muskingum. The Delaware tribe had recently ended its troublesome neutrality and allied itself with the British in the conflict the Delaware chiefs later explained was considered a fight between father and son.

Colonel Daniel Brodhead, in command at Fort Pitt, had determined to punish them and so had ordered the formation of this expedition. He would command the effort himself and, in that connection, had left Fort Pitt the previous day with 150 regular troops headed for Fort Henry. Lewis and George were pleased that their father had brought them along, and they were looking forward to what they expected to be a great adventure. As they rounded a slight curve in the road, Lewis could see off to his left the back side of Wheeling Hill while a half mile or so to the front and right, he could see the smoke rising from the chimney of a rough log cabin set off the road a bit and nestled against the bottom of a low ridge. This cabin was a bit larger than the average family home. George eased his horse close to Lewis and pointed at the cabin. He spoke in a voice low enough that their father could not hear.

"That's Sam Mason's tavern. What d'ya bet we stop in there?"

"I reckon you're right although I don't know. It is Sunday, ain't it?"

"Yeah, but Ma ain't here. I figure the old man will make a stop."

"Do you think he'll let us drink a little whiskey?" wondered Lewis. When they had returned last summer from recovering the stolen horses, Jacob Link had given Lewis a drink when they had stopped at the fort. "Anybody that can kill three of them red bastards can surely have some whiskey to drink," he had said at the time.

Lewis remembered now that he had more than just a little drink, and it had been enough to make him feel kind of strange and not in complete control. He hadn't liked the lack of control, but the feeling-strange part was kind of pleasant, and he looked forward to repeating that mood. Unfortunately, his mother had found out somehow, and had been quite upset. His father had made light of it, but the opportunity had not presented itself again.

"What are you two jabberin' about?" asked Captain John, who had stopped and let the boys catch up.

"Nothin'," said George. "Are we goin' to stop at Mason's?"

"Now why would you boys want to stop in there? There's nothin' good in there for you two whelps." John said this gruffly, but there was a slight smile on his face. "Besides, it's a Sunday. Your ma wouldn't approve." With that, he turned his horse forward, and they started again along the dusty road. George and Lewis urged their horses forward, and George nodded his head as he whispered to Lewis,

"We're gonna stop."

It wasn't long before George's prediction was verified. When they came to the lane that led up to the front of the tavern, John Wetzel abruptly turned onto it, the boys following behind, filled with anticipation. Three horses were already there, tied loosely to the crude hitching rail. John slid off his horse and threw the reins over the rail, tying them with a quick twist.

"Maybe we can get a bite of dinner here. It'll be better than what they'll have at the fort," he said quietly.

There was no more talk of what Mary Wetzel might think. George and Lewis dismounted and tied their reins to the rail just as their father had done. They followed him through the door, which was covered with nothing more than an old deer skin hanging loosely over the opening. It was very dark inside with the only light provided by a fire in the fireplace at the end of the room to the left as they entered, and a small window opening at the far end to the right. Two men stood at the bar, which was formed by a crude plank supported by thin posts and covered on the back side by some thin wooden strips. To the back and right of the bar was a dark green curtain, which provided a divider for a separate room. Sam Mason stood behind the bar talking quietly with the two men, pausing only briefly to acknowledge the new patrons.

"Hello, Wetzel," he said. "What can we do fer you?"

One of the two men turned to see who had come in and while nodding at Captain John, his eye fell on Lewis, and his face broke into a smile.

"Why, it's young Lew, the Injun killer. Come up here young man and let me shake your hand and buy you a drink. Jacob Link told me all about what you done last summer."

Lewis recognized the man, whose name was Hamilton Kerr, but he was distracted by the antics of a man and woman seated at a table in the corner of the room near the fireplace. The woman was sitting on the man's lap, laughing and giggling while he had torn open her blouse and was fondling her naked breasts. Having never seen such a thing before, Lewis could not keep his eyes off the pair, and he could see that George was watching intently as well. Their father seemed not to have noticed. Sam Mason, however, had followed Lewis's gaze, and his reaction was swift.

"Rufe," he bellowed. "Get the hell out of here with that stuff. This ain't no brothel down here."

This was news to Rufe, who began to protest until he saw the look in Mason's eyes. He knew better than to challenge Mason, whose temper and inclination to violence were well-known, so he jumped up and pulled the young woman after him.

"Come on, sweet thing," he said. "We'll go upstairs." He pushed her toward the ladder that led to the loft while she struggled to cover herself, although she flashed a shy grin toward the two boys who stood watching with open mouths. George Wetzel leaned over and whispered to his brother.

"She's that whore I've heard men talkin' about."

Lewis knew what a whore was, but he hadn't expected to see one. The thought excited him somewhat, and he tried to imagine what it would be like to be the one climbing up into the loft behind this naughty girl. He said nothing to George. Captain John had ignored all of this and now gave an answer to the question from Mason that had preceded all the commotion.

"What's to eat in that pot?" he asked, gesturing toward the kettle hanging over the fire.

"Beef stew," responded Mason. "A dollar a bowl."

"My God, that's robbery," exclaimed the elder Wetzel, giving Mason an unbelieving stare.

"Well, that's the price. Take it or leave it, it don't make me no—nevermind." Mason returned to his conversation with the two others.

"We'll take three bowls," said Captain John as he placed three paper bills on the counter.

Mason eyed the bills. "Hell, I don't want them continentals. Ain't you got no gold?"

"That's all I got. If you don't want it, I reckon I can take my business elsewhere."

"Ha," laughed Mason. "Where you goin to take it, Fort Henry?"

John Wetzel picked up the money and began to walk back toward the door.

"Wait," said Mason. He turned and called to someone behind the curtain. "Hey, Belle, come and get some stew for these hungry customers."

A woman appeared from behind the curtain and took down three bowls from a shelf on the wall. She was not an old woman, but Lewis thought she looked like she'd had a hard life. She was not like his own mother, whom he thought of as soft and sweet. He wondered if she was Mason's wife or was she just a whore like the other girl. He watched her spoon some of the stew into a bowl and hand it to John Wetzel, who moved to a table and sat down with the bowl in front of him. He motioned to the boys to join him.

"Pa didn't seem to even notice that girl," Lewis suggested to George.

"He noticed," said George. "Let's eat."

Belle had filled two other bowls and set them on the table. George and Lewis went to sit down with their father and began to eat the stew with the spoons that Belle had placed next to the bowls. Hamilton Kerr decided to have some of the stew for himself, and he sat down at the table with the three Wetzels.

"How is this stuff?" asked Kerr. "Is there any beef in it?"

"Knowin' Sam Mason, it's more likely to be horsemeat," grumbled John.

"I reckon you're right," laughed Kerr.

"God," exclaimed Lewis. "I don't want to eat horsemeat."

The others laughed, and Lewis finally tried a bite. "It ain't too bad," he said.

April 13, 1781

Captain Daniel Brodhead had come down the Ohio River with 10 boats loaded with regular soldiers, some 150 in all. They had arrived three days ago, on April 10, coming ashore on the Wheeling side and camping on the flat plain along Wheeling Creek below Fort Henry. On that same day, Lewis Wetzel, along with his father and his brother George, had signed on to a militia company commanded by Captain Joseph Ogle. The pay for one month for a private in the militia was sixteen dollars and sixty ninetieths, although the extent of duty was due to be something less than a month. This was more money than Lewis had ever had at one time, and the idea excited him.

When Captain Ogle had explained the pay to him, Lewis had given a loud whoop of joy, which had caused George, who was behind him in the line and embarrassed, to punch him in the back.

"You fool," George had said with disgust. "You're actin' like a little kid."

Lewis's high spirits were not dampened, however, and he was pleased to see a number of men that he knew. One was a friend who lived on Buffalo Creek. His name was William Boggs Jr., but people called him Billy. He had a young sister named Lydia that Lewis had noticed with interest. She was the prettiest girl around as far as he knew, but he had barely spoken to her.

Billy was in Ogle's company along with Lewis, as was Hamilton Kerr. Conrad Stroup, who was one of the settlers that had come to the Wheeling Creek region at the same time as the Wetzels, was one of Ogle's lieutenants. Another of the officers that Lewis knew was Hugh McConnell, who had served in the militia at the time of the Fort Henry siege. McConnell's sister Rebecca had lost her husband, William Shepherd, in that battle. Even Ebenezer Zane was enrolled as a private.

Lewis thought this unusual, but then his own father had been captain of a militia company himself a few years ago, so maybe it wasn't so strange after all. Another friend of his, Jacob Miller, was a private in Jacob Lefler's company while his uncle Lewis Bonnet and cousin Lewis Grandstaff had arrived with Captain William Crawford's company from over on the Monongahela. Another man who had come in with Crawford's company was Jacob Riffle, who had served in Captain John Wetzel's company in 1778. Riffle had recently returned from Kentucky, and he had joyous news for the Wetzels. He had deliberately searched out John Wetzel upon arriving at Wheeling.

"Captain John," he said urgently when he had found him. "Have you heard about Martin?"

"No, we've heard nothin'. We figured he was dead."

"Well, he ain't dead," said Riffle triumphantly. "I saw him down at Bryan's Station."

"You saw him? What was he doin'? How is he?" John hardly knew what to say.

"He came in escaped from the Shawnees. It's been a couple of months now, I reckon, that he came in. He was there when I arrived."

"God, ain't that just the best news ever," exclaimed John. "What else can you tell me?"

"Not much," admitted Riffle. "We didn't have much time to talk, but he wanted me to tell you he was alive and well. And that he would be home, but he was goin' back to the South Branch first."

"The South Branch?" asked Lewis Wetzel when he heard the news. "Why the hell is he goin' back there?"

"A woman, I reckon," said George Wetzel with a wide grin on his face. "He's always been sweet on that Mary Coffield."

"I never knew that," said Lew.

Lewis Bonnett had brought the same news about Martin, having talked with Riffle as Crawford's company had come to Fort Henry from the Monongahela. He told John Wetzel that he had arranged for the news to be sent to Mary Wetzel as soon as he had heard it.

"Won't that make her real happy," observed Captain John. "I wish I could have been there when that news arrived."

Colonel David Shepherd was the overall commander of the militia, which included 134 men in four companies, with Major Sam McColloch serving as the second in command. Jonathan

Zane was the spy, an appointment that met with great approval from the Wetzels and the others in the militia. There were also five friendly Indians along as guides, including the Delaware chief Pekillon, and the two known as Captain John Montour and Captain Wilson.

"I don't much like havin' them redskins along with us," Billy Boggs had observed once it was realized among the militiamen that these Indians were a part of the expedition.

"Me neither," agreed Lewis Wetzel, although his opinion was greatly affected by what the others were saying. The Indians were sworn enemies, and he thought it confusing to have to deal with some who were supposed to be on his side.

"They might be just waitin' to lead us into some trap," continued Billy. "Someone ought to knock 'em in the head while we got the chance."

Lewis thought that was a bit extreme, but maybe Billy was right. He saw his father talking with Ebenezer Zane, and he joined them. "Colonel Zane," interjected Lewis after listening to the two men for a few moments. "What do you think of having them Injuns along?"

"Why, Lewis, I think they might be real helpful," said Zane. "Colonel Brodhead is very happy to have them with us."

Lewis had seen Brodhead on several occasions, and he was impressed with the colonel. He admired Brodhead's confident and decisive manner, but he knew that many of the settlers had a different opinion.

"I ain't never met an Injun who was helpful," said Lewis, not ready to give up on the original concern even if the big colonel thought it was good.

"Well I guess the ones you met ain't had much chance to be helpful," laughed Zane.

"That's right," chimed in John Wetzel. "You ain't the best judge of a good Injun."

Although they were laughing at him, Lewis was pleased because he knew they were just acknowledging his reputation as an Indian fighter. He decided to change the subject.

"When are we goin' to get moving to the towns do you think, Colonel Zane? We're gettin' tired of waitin'."

This was another of the big complaints heard in the camps. Three days had been spent getting everyone across the big river.

"Anxious for some action, are ye, young Lew?" asked Zane. "We'll be off first thing in the morning, I'm thinkin'."

April 19, 1781

Six days had passed since the Brodhead expedition had left the Ohio River and moved out toward the Delaware towns at the forks of the Muskingum. It had taken longer than Lew Wetzel thought was necessary, but he had to admit that not everyone was mounted. The regular troops from Fort Pitt were on foot, and even though nearly all of the militia troops were on horseback, their mounts were workhorses not accustomed to being ridden into combat. Most riders had no saddles and sat on blankets or sacks of meal.

Colonel Brodhead seemed to be satisfied with the progress, however, and had ordered a halt the night before along the south and east side of the Tuscarawas River not far from the Moravian town of Salem. This town stood on the other side of the river and was home to the missionary, John Heckewelder. Colonel Brodhead had dispatched an Indian runner to ask Heckewelder to visit his camp and provide a few provisions. The missionary had appeared that morning and was shown to the commander's tent.

"Come in, Reverend Heckewelder," invited Brodhead, rising to shake the visitor's hand. "Thank you for coming."

"Thank you, Colonel," said Heckewelder, sitting carefully on the top of a barrel of gunpowder that had been placed just inside the tent.

"Here, we can do better than that for you to sit on," apologized the colonel. "There is another chair here someplace."

"This is fine," insisted the reverend. "You have quite a large number of soldiers with you, Colonel. What are you planning to do?"

"We are marching against the hostile Delaware towns on the Muskingum," answered Brodhead. "Are any of your Christian Indians likely to be in the line of march? We do not want to harm them if we can avoid it."

"Why, that's very thoughtful of you, Colonel Brodhead. I suppose there could be a few of them about. They will offer you no resistance, I'm sure."

"We greatly admire your work among the red men, and we think you and your colleagues along with your Indians have behaved very well in these troubled times. It would bring me great pain to hear that we had harmed any of them."

"We have tried very hard, Colonel."

"Yes, and I think you and your people are to be praised for the fact that the Delaware tribe has remained neutral for as long as it has. But now they have decided to throw in with the British and already they have been carrying out raids against the settlements in Virginia and Pennsylvania. Were you aware of that Mr. Heckewelder?"

"Yes, of course, but it does not change our purpose or our work." Heckewelder was becoming uncomfortable with this conversation. He wondered what else this restless army might be contemplating. Outside the tent, a number of shouts could be heard and then the sound of a galloping horse as Isaac Meeks, the adjutant, came riding up, dismounted, and screamed at Brodhead.

"Colonel, Colonel, we've got big trouble!"

"What is it, Isaac?" asked Brodhead, who had run quickly out to discover what was causing such a disturbance.

"It's the militia, Colonel. A bunch of 'em are heading out to kill the Indians in the Christian towns. It's mostly Crawford's company, but he couldn't stop 'em."

"That won't do. What gave them that idea?"

"They're worked up over some of the recent raids, especially the ones up near Buffalo Creek. Some kin of Jesse Van Meter's was killed, and Jesse is wantin' revenge. He got some of the fellows riled up, and well, it don't take much to get the men a goin'. It'll be easy pickins' they was a sayin'."

"Where is Sam McColloch? They'd listen to him." McColloch, well-known and respected among the militia, was Shepherd's second-in-command.

"Sam's off with Jonathan Zane. They're scoutin' up ahead."

"Damn. What about Shepherd? Where is he?"

"I sent word to him too. He is on his way over there to try and stop them. I think you'd better get there quick. You can take my horse."

John Heckewelder had come out and was listening to the two officers.

"What is happening?" he interjected, grabbing Brodhead by the arm. "Are my people in danger?"

Turning to the missionary, Brodhead answered quickly, "Yes, Mr. Heckewelder, I'm afraid they are, and I must put a stop to it. Mr. Meeks will stay with you and explain. I have no time to waste." With that, he swung up on the back of Meeks's horse and started to ride away.

"I must get back to Salem and warn the people," exclaimed Heckewelder.

Brodhead reined in the horse and yelled back. "No, No. You must not leave until we get this stopped. You would not be safe if some of these angry men thought you were going to warn the Indians. We'll handle it. You must stay here. Isaac, you see to it."

The colonel rode hard toward the eastern end of the camp, and he could see now a group of some forty to fifty men mounted and ready to ride out. David Shepherd had managed to get ahead of them and had turned his horse to face them with his right hand held high.

Brodhead skirted the group to the left and came up abreast of Shepherd, who was trying his best to reason with the restless riders. There were men from all four militia companies, and the leader seemed to be Captain Jacob Lefler, the commander of one of the companies. Lewis Bonnet, the three Wetzels, Billy Boggs, and Jacob Miller were all there.

"Men, this ain't no good," Shepherd was saying. "We came out here to kill hostile Indians, not peaceful ones."

"One Injun's the same as another," said one of the men. "Kill 'em all, I say."

There was a murmur of agreement from the others.

"They been killin' our folks," said another of the riders.

"We have no reason to think it was any of the Christian Indians," protested Shepherd.

"Hell, all the raids across the Ohio came from these villages," said Jesse Van Meter. "They killed Martha Van Meter and two of her daughters just the other day, and I think we should clean out all of those Moravian villages."

"It's more likely we'll find the ones guilty of that hideous crime at Coshocton," argued Shepherd. "Here's Colonel Brodhead. He's ready to lead us there."

"Men, I know how you feel," began the colonel. "I know you want to fight Indians. One of the main towns is at the forks of the Muskingum, only a few miles from here. We are marching immediately to destroy that town. I need every one of you right now."

"There's plenty of the bastards a lot closer and a lot easier to kill," came a cry from the crowd. "Let's start with them."

"Men, that wouldn't be smart," answered Brodhead. "It would spoil our surprise and make it much tougher to take the more important village where the Delaware warriors are. That is our target, and we need to get moving."

Brodhead turned his mount back toward the main camp, making it plain that he expected to be obeyed. "Colonel

Shepherd," he said as he passed between Shepherd and the rest of the rebellious militiamen, "please get your four companies ready to march within the hour." He slapped the horse on the side and rode off at a gallop.

"You heard the colonel, men. Captain Lefler, get your men ready to ride. Those of you from the other companies, rejoin your captains. Anyone who doesn't join us will forfeit his pay. You signed on to follow me and Colonel Brodhead."

"Wait a minute, David," said Lefler. "I ain't leadin' my company anywhere they don't want to go. We signed on to kill Injuns, not to follow that Colonel Brodhead."

"Jacob, you signed on to lead a company of militia under my command. You know we can't just have people doing what they want. You're a good leader or else you wouldn't be one of my captains. Killin' the Moravian Indians would be no different than killin' a bunch of women and children. We're not barbarians."

"We ain't barbarians, but they are." Lefler wasn't ready to give up. From the corner of his eye, he noticed that several of the men had started riding back toward the camp. Lewis Bonnet and John Wetzel, unable to hear all of the conversation between the officers, had concluded that the incident was over and began riding away.

"I reckon that David is right," observed Bonnet. "I ain't got much stomach for killin' them Moravians."

Captain Lefler watched the men disperse with a look of disgust. "Well, it looks like they're votin' to go along with you, David. I still think you're wrong about them so-called Christian Injuns." He rode away sadly as Captain William Crawford came up.

"Thank you, David," he said to Shepherd. "You've avoided a bad mistake. I couldn't get them to listen to me at all. Maybe you need a new captain."

"Forget it, William. They'd probably cooled off a bit by the time I got here. Let's get organized and get off to Coshocton."

Colonel Brodhead had pushed his army hard for the past few hours, and by a little past midafternoon they had reached a spot just a few miles from the Coshocton village. At this point, Johnathan Zane and his advanced party had joined them with a captive in tow. This frightened Indian had assured the colonel that their approach had not been discovered. He had provided information about a party of some forty warriors who had been celebrating successful raids on the Virginians and had crossed the river with some captives and some scalps. These warriors were quite drunk, and Brodhead detached a party of militia to cross the river and attack them. This detachment consisted of fifty-one men and included Crawford's, Lefler's, and Benjamin Royse's companies under Sam McColloch's command.

It was raining heavily as the remaining troops moved on toward Coshocton, the village nestled along the east bank of the Muskingum right where it forked: one branch, the Walhonding, going to the west and north while the other, the Tuscarawas, meandered off to the east. Zane and his fellow scouts flushed out two other hostiles who both escaped, though one was wounded.

Brodhead was now sure that his surprise would be ruined, and so he decided to continue the attack in spite of the foul weather. He divided his army into three divisions. Captain Ogle was ordered to take his company of some seventy-two men and veer to the left so as to come upon Coshocton from downstream. On the way, Ogle was to go through the little village of Lichtenau, which stood on the east bank of the Muskingum, a couple of miles below Coshocton and was thought to be abandoned. Colonel Shepherd, with fifty of the regulars, was to go to the right and descend on Coshocton from upstream. Colonel Brodhead, with the remaining troops, would approach the town directly from the east.

Although the information he had indicated that there were not many warriors in the town, the colonel was taking no chances, and he urged his commanders to move quickly, for he was sure that the advantage of surprise was lost by now. Lewis Wetzel rode next to his father, shivering in the coolness of the April evening, which was sharpened by the driving rain. He, as well as most of the men in Ogle's command, understood little of the overall strategy, but it was good to be moving with real conviction and focus.

Lewis had felt envious earlier when he had seen Jonathan Zane come in, for he felt that he could serve best in a scouting capacity. His only experience involving combat with a group of men had not gone so well, and he had functioned much more efficiently on his own. He had learned that you could not put your trust in how other men might behave under stress. Of course, he was with his father and brother. Surely they could be trusted. It wasn't long until they approached a small village, which Lewis assumed was the one called Lichtenau. The company was strung out and not riding in any particular formation. The Wetzels were near the front just behind Ebenezer Zane and Hugh McConnell.

"It looks deserted," observed Lewis in a low voice.

"It's likely," said Zane quietly, looking back at Lewis and putting a finger to his lips to indicate a need to be quiet. "At one time, there was lots of Christians here," he continued in a whisper.

"What happened to them?" asked George Wetzel, taking pains to keep his voice down.

"They moved back closer to the other Christian villages, I reckon. There's been a lot of movement, and the other Indians have tried to get them to leave this area completely. I—"

Zane broke off the conversation when some loud shouting broke out ahead of them. That was followed by a gunshot. The visibility was poor as they rode toward the sounds before them. Several of Ogle's men had ridden ahead from on their right and were now surrounding five young Indian men, standing with obvious fright in front of a small hut. Captain Ogle had arrived and was trying to talk with the captives while many of the militia scattered among the other huts, searching for more inhabitants.

Ogle was gesturing and pointing off toward the north and east. He motioned to several of the men near him who came and began to lead the Indians away. Ogle, who had dismounted, now climbed back upon his horse and rode back to where Ebenezer Zane and the Wetzels were stopped, shielding their faces from the pelting rain.

"Those five claim to be Christians," he explained to Zane. "I've sent some men to take them to Brodhead. We need to see if there are any others and then get on to Coshocton."

A search of the village produced no other human life, although a couple of beef cows and a few chickens were found.

"Kill them," commanded Captain Ogle. "We've got to be moving on and quickly."

This seemed to be an awful waste to Lewis Wetzel, and he mentioned it to his father, who just shrugged.

"We're supposed to destroy the Indian towns," he said finally. "That includes the animals."

He rode ahead quickly, ending any further conversation. Lewis could think of lots of ways to make use of such livestock, but he didn't know much about how armies should operate. His distaste for army life continued to grow.

The rain was letting up slightly as Ogle's troops reached the southern outskirts of the main village of Coshocton. It had been a large town at one time, and there were many of the small lodges standing empty as the white men rode through. They could hear some scattered shooting and yelling ahead, and soon four warriors were seen running toward them, trying to escape the assault of Brodhead's troops in the center of town. When they realized that the escape route was cut off by Ogle's militia coming up from the south, the Indians stopped and stood defiantly, awaiting their fate.

After a couple of shots were fired by the militia, Captain Ogle was able to stop all action, and the four braves were disarmed and led captive back toward the center of town. The shooting and fighting was over in only a few minutes. Lewis Wetzel was a bit disappointed.

He had not fired a single shot; and by the time he had seen any hostiles, they were already taken as prisoners. Once all the soldiers and captives were gathered in the town center near the council house, darkness had fallen and the rain had stopped. Someone had found some dry wood in one of the huts and started a fire.

A total of fifteen warriors had been taken along with about twenty old men, women, and children. These people were put inside the council house, and a guard placed at the door. In spite of all the shooting, no one on either side had been injured; the only casualty being Sergeant Major James Lemon's horse. Colonel Brodhead had decided to spend the night in the town since his men could find shelter in the Indian lodges in case the rains returned. He gathered his officers and interested men near the campfire to discuss the plans for the next day.

The first order of business was to determine the fate of the captives. Brodhead preferred to take the entire group back to Fort Pitt to be used for future exchanges. The troops were calling for their execution. Earlier, he had sent the five Christians who had been found at Lichtenau back to their people at Salem and Gnadenhutten. This had met with opposition from some of the militia who knew what Brodhead had decided. He cautioned the five to avoid contact with any white men until they had reached the safety of their village.

During the discussion, the Delaware chief Pekillon, who had accompanied the soldiers from Wheeling, stood up and began to talk. He spoke in the Delaware tongue, and most of the listeners were puzzled at what he was saying, assuming he was pleading for the lives of the captives. Abruptly he stopped and sat down.

Colonel Brodhead whispered something to John Montour, who stood and addressed the assembly. "Here is what the great chief, Pekillon, had to say," said Montour. "These fifteen warriors are bad birds. They have flown over the big river to the lands of the Long Knives and taken many scalps. They have boasted of their feats. They are not your friends."

These words brought an uproar from the militiamen who were able to hear. "Kill them, burn them!" was the shout. "Let's kill them now."

A stirring began, and several of the men started toward the council house.

"Stop, men," shouted the colonel. "We do not just kill our captives. Let us discuss this further."

Lewis Wetzel was surprised when the men stopped and returned to the fireside. Next to him, his friend Billy Boggs, took up the cry again. "Kill them," shouted Billy. "I say kill them."

Others took up this cry, and Brodhead realized that further discussion was not likely to change the mood. "Let's have a vote of the officers here," he said quickly. "Quiet men, let me hear from your leaders."

One by one, Brodhead asked his officers for their vote. It was unanimous. Each man voted for execution of the fifteen warriors. The other prisoners would be spared.

"All right," agreed Brodhead. "The fifteen warriors will be put to death in the morning. After that, we will destroy the village and march back up the Tuscarawas."

As they walked away, Billy Boggs grabbed Lewis Wetzel and pulled him into the shadows. "The five Injuns we caught back in Lichtenau, they're out there somewhere headin' back for their town. Let's go get 'em tonight. Them officers can't stop us from doin' that."

"But they're Christians, Billy," protested Lewis. "No need to kill them."

"Hell, they just said they were Christians. They don't look no different than them redskins we got shut up in that council house. They need killin'!"

"I ain't so sure, Billy. You heard the colonel. We could get in some trouble."

"Nobody will know 'til it's too late. Go get your horse. I'm goin' to see if Tom Mills will go with us."

Lewis was not convinced that it was a good idea, but Billy was insistent, and he did have to agree that there was no real reason to think that those so-called Christian Indians were any different than the others. He found his horse and led him off to the east side of the town, where he stopped to wait for Billy. He had been careful to avoid either George or his father, for he knew they would stop him. He remembered the thrill of his victory over the Indians the previous summer, and he began to think that maybe he would be considered a hero again if he came in with some more scalps.

In a few minutes, Billy Boggs found him, but Billy was alone. "I couldn't find Tom," he said, "but it don't matter. You and me are enough to handle any five Injuns."

"Well, since they ain't armed, I suppose you're right. But I ain't so sure we can find them."

"Hell, Lew, you can track anything."

"It's mighty dark, and there's hundreds of tracks. I don't reckon we'll find their tracks."

"They're sure to go back along the same trail we came in on," argued Billy. "If we just ride back that way, we're bound to find them. They ain't tryin' to hide." With that, Boggs rode off in a rush.

Wetzel mounted his horse and followed after but soon came to the conclusion that this was a futile chase. It took him awhile to catch up with Boggs who had slowed his own pace on the muddy path. They had come nearly a mile when Billy finally stopped and Wetzel rode up beside him.

"I guess you was right, Lew," admitted Billy. "I can't see a damn thing."

Lewis Wetzel intensely hated not finishing something he had started, but since this venture had seemed unwise to him at the beginning, he was willing to end it here. "I hate to give up, Billy," he said, "but I think we'd better."

Not another word was said between them, and they rode back to the camp in silence.

April 20, 1781

The clouds had been chased from the sky during the night, and the sun was streaming into the occupied Delaware town along with a brisk breeze coming across the Muskingum. The soldiers had stirred early but were forced to eat a cold breakfast since dry wood was hard to find.

Colonel Brodhead was anxious to move out quickly, but first it was necessary to carry out the decision of the previous night. The fifteen Delaware braves who had been sentenced to death were removed from the council house and led out to a grove of trees on the lower side of the town. The militia had been put in charge of this duty, and Colonel Shepherd had given Captain Ogle the order to get it done. Ogle, who still remembered the death of his brother at the hand of the Indians during the Foreman massacre over three years earlier, was quite willing to see this justice done. Most of the men in his company were ready to help.

The condemned braves were handled roughly, and each one was tied to a tree. Knowing what was coming, none of the warriors begged for mercy but stared straight ahead with their heads up. Lewis Wetzel had moved close enough to watch the action. He was impressed with the manner of the prisoners, although he thought he could see the fear in their eyes in spite of their determination to hide it.

The men were jeering at them, and Wetzel joined in, but he didn't feel as good about it as he expected. He noticed that his father and George had stayed back and were standing with their rifles cradled in their arms. Lewis wondered if they were planning to be part of a firing squad.

"All right, men," shouted Ogle. "Let's get this over with. I need fifteen men, and each one pick out a target."

"No, Captain," said a man named George Tate. "Let's waste no lead on these bastards. Let's give a tomahawk to the head."

Scattered agreements grew into a full chorus. "Bash 'em in the head!" was the cry.

Ogle started to protest then shrugged. "It's all right with me," he said. "Just get it done."

The men in the front immediately rushed forward with their tomahawks held high and began swinging at the bound Indians who, though resigned to their fate, still tried to avoid the blows as best they could. Wetzel saw his friend Billy Boggs rush up to one of the captives and swing at his head with his tomahawk. Another man had swung from the other side but had missed the head, his axe slicing into the shoulder. Boggs aim was better, and the red man slumped in death against the rawhide thong binding him to the tree. Lewis figured that the red men deserved to die, but he was a bit uneasy as he watched.

Young Boggs ran back to where Wetzel was standing, grinning and holding up his bloody weapon.

"Come on, Lew," he shouted. "Help me kill another of those bastards."

"I don't think they need us," observed Wetzel, for he could see that by this time each of the condemned warriors had been struck dead. "I like to kill Injuns," Lewis continued. "But I don't much want to do it while they're tied to a tree."

"Oh hell," exclaimed Billy. "I forgot to get a scalp."

It was clearly too late as several of the militiamen had crowded in to take care of that chore. Lewis mounted his horse and rode back up through the town where the army was busily destroying as much of it as they could. Because of the drenching rain of the previous day, it was not possible to burn anything, so the soldiers were smashing the little huts and slaughtering the cattle and chickens that they found. Lewis had no stomach for this and continued on out toward the trail at the east where he found Jonathan Zane sitting on a stump with an old saddle blanket thrown over it.

"Hello young Lew," said Zane. "Come and set a spell. I figured you'd be back there bashin' and killin' since you're the big Injun killer, or so I've heard tell." These last words were accompanied by a wide grin.

"They got plenty of men for that job," said Wetzel as he slid down from his horse. "It's a helluva sight."

Zane said nothing, and Lewis felt he had to explain himself. "Injuns deserve to be killed, that's for sure, but I ain't much for doin' it that way."

"What way? How was they doin' it?"

"Tied 'em to trees and hacked 'em with tomahawks."

"I'll be damned. You'd rather shoot 'em with that big rifle of your'n, I reckon." Zane was smiling again.

Wetzel had found a small piece of a log nearby and sat down on it. He had forgotten how wet it might be, and he could feel the moisture soaking through his pants, but he didn't want to look foolish in front of this great woodsman, so he sat still.

"I guess I ain't much of a soldier," he said finally. "I'd rather be what you are."

"Ah, so you figure I ain't much of a soldier either."

Lewis started to protest, but Zane cut him off. "I know what you meant. You'd like to by a spy. Well, maybe I can help arrange that. You'd be a good one fer sure."

The two men fell silent, watching as the soldiers began to gather for the purpose of beginning the return march. Colonel Brodhead, Colonel Shepherd, and the other officers appeared, as did a group of militia, escorting the remaining prisoners. A cry went up calling for their deaths as well, and when one of the old men tried to pull away form his escort, he was struck down on the spot. Other soldiers began to crowd in, and Colonel Shepherd, seeing what was about to happen, rode quickly into their midst. "Stop it, men. These prisoners are harmless. Let them be."

Shepherd was well respected but it was not clear that even he would be heeded at this point. Conrad Stroup, one of Ogle's lieutenants, rode up beside Shepherd, shouting at the men to listen. Colonel Brodhead came up as well, followed by eight or ten of the regular troops. "No more killing!" shouted Brodhead. "These prisoners will be taken to Fort Pitt and used for exchange. Any further action against them will be dealt with by me." He had wanted to say that anyone threatening these helpless Indians would be shot, but he doubted that anyone would obey that order. He nodded to Colonel Shepherd and rode back out of town. The old Indian had not been killed, but the blow had broken his shoulder. One of the women had knelt beside him, and she looked up at Shepherd with a pleading look.

"Form up, men," commanded Shepherd. "We're marching back upstream." He pointed at the wounded man. "Someone bind up that wound and get the prisoners moving."

Within an hour, the army was on the march along the south bank of the Tuscarawas. There was a considerable amount of grumbling among the troops, especially the militia, but they were marching in the direction of home, and that suddenly seemed like a wonderful idea. Lewis Wetzel was back with his father and brother among the men of Ogle's company. He wondered if Jonathan Zane had meant what he had said. The thought of riding with Zane was quite appealing although it was already in Lewis's mind that he would decline any further opportunities to be part of an army.

The troops were brought to a halt, and from all the shouting ahead, Lewis assumed that they had reunited with McColloch's detachment. This turned out to be the case. McColloch explained to Colonel Brodhead that he and his men had been unable to cross the river because of the high water. The Indians they were after had gone away in the night, and so the disappointed militia had stayed put, waiting for the rest of the army to rejoin them.

Once again, there had been agitation to march against Salem or Gnadenhutten, but the rain and the dark had suppressed the enthusiasm for that idea. Colonel Brodhead proposed that the army march to one of the Moravian towns and obtain canoes from the Christian Indians to ferry the army across the river. From there, they would commence operations against the Delawares who had escaped. There was no interest in this proposal from anyone, and the officers, sensing the mood of the soldiers that their campaign had already been a success and it was time to go home, advised Brodhead against going ahead with his plan. Realizing that it would be futile to try to lead so many volunteers into a battle against their will, the colonel acquiesced and ordered a march a few miles further upstream, where camp was made across from the village of Newcomerstown.

The Indians at this town were mostly friendly, especially those led by a chief known as Killbuck, who was a well-known friend of the whites. Killbuck came across the river to talk with Brodhead, bringing him a scalp taken from one of the Delawares that had escaped from McColloch's men. Broadhead sent runners to the Moravian towns asking for provisions to help his army in returning to Fort Pitt, and also requesting that the missionaries meet with him. John Heckewelder came from Salem, the second time for him; William Edwards came from Gnadenhutten; and David Zeisberger, the director of all the missions, also joined his colleagues.

The colonel received them at noon on a warm April day, just two days after having sacked the town at Coshocton. They sat in the sunshine at the edge of a small grove of birch trees.

"We appreciate your concern for our Christian brethren, Colonel," said Zeisberger. "The five young men that you found at Lichtenau made it safely to Gnadenhutten, although they were pursued for a time by some of your militia."

"I warned them to avoid any white men. I'm afraid that some of our men have trouble distinguishing between good and bad Indians." Brodhead tried to make his voice sound sympathetic.

"Yes," said Zeisberger. "Were it not so."

Zeisberger's tone was annoying to the colonel, and he could not resist defending his men a little. "They've had some provocation, Reverend. There have been some nasty raids on our side of the Ohio."

Reverend Zeisberger nodded and looked sadly toward his colleagues.

"Colonel Brodhead and Colonel Shepherd worked hard to avoid an ugly incident a few days ago," interjected Heckewelder.

"Yes, I know that, John," said Zeisberger quickly. "Anyway, we are not here to argue about such things. Why are we here, Colonel. It was you who sent for us."

"You are right," answered Brodhead. "We are very appreciative of all you do for us."

"Careful what you give us credit for," said Zeisberger with a hint of mirth in his eyes. "The Half-King, Pipe, Wingenund, and other chiefs accuse us of that very thing. But our intent is to be neutral."

"I know," agreed Brodhead. "We've been told of threats against you by the Wyandots and the hostile Delawares. You should return with us to Fort Pitt."

"We can't do that!" exclaimed Heckewelder, who had jumped to his feet.

"No," said Edwards, who was also standing now. "What would become of our Christians? We cannot abandon them."

"Do you see, Colonel, how important our work is to us." Zeisberger nodded to his two colleagues, indicating that they should be seated. "We are not afraid."

"Bring your converts with you. We can all go to Fort Pitt. Killbuck is bringing his followers with us." Colonel Brodhead had risen now, and he came close to where the missionaries were seated. "You are caught between two fires, and you are bound to be burned."

All three missionaries stood once again, and Zeisberger grasped both of Brodhead's hands and held them tight. "We appreciate your concern, Colonel, but our place is at our mission stations with our dear people who love us. God will protect us if it is His will. We must return now. Our prayers go with you as you complete your own journey."

"I cannot stop you, of course," said the colonel as the three men prepared to leave. "But I believe you are making a terrible mistake."

"Godspeed," said Zeisberger.

Brodhead watched sadly as they walked away. "Terrible mistake," he repeated, looking at Shepherd who was sitting nearby, smoking his pipe.

"I'm afraid you're right, Colonel."

April 25, 1781

Little Fox had gone south. The trip had been long, hard, and cold. But after more than ten days, he had arrived in the Delaware village called Wingenund's town. It lay a number of miles to the east on the Sandusky, and Little Fox had been told to go up a tiny creek named Sugar Run, which flowed into the Sandusky River just a short distance below the principal Wyandot village known as Half-King's Town.

Sugar Run had dwindled to nothing, and he had kept on across the rolling hills until he came again to the Sandusky itself. He followed it upstream and finally reached the town. In reaching this destination, he had passed through several Delaware and Wyandot villages in the upper Sandusky region. And in each case, the villagers had been happy to give him the directions he needed. He had been tempted to stop at the first such village he encountered, but his Chippewa friend, Red Bird, had been insistent that he should seek out Wingenund's town.

The final miles had left him very uncertain, for he had expected to find the village on Sugar Run. Now he was thankful for Red Bird's wise counsel, for he had been welcomed into the house of a young Delaware warrior called White Eagle. The house was a small one, built for an individual family rather than the long houses, which were common in the Delaware towns; and White Eagle lived there with his pregnant wife, Bright Moon. When word had reached

White Eagle of the arrival of the young Chippewa who was a friend of Red Bird, he had sent a message inviting Little Fox to share his hut. Red Bird had spoken of many of his friends to Little Fox, and although White Eagle was a name he recognized, Little Fox had not expected such an invitation. He had approached the door of the little house with hesitancy, not sure how to introduce himself.

"Come in, friend," said White Eagle, who had heard the approach. "Come in and share my home."

Little Fox raised the door flap and entered. The warmth in the room struck him in a pleasant way, as did the gentle smile of the warrior standing near the fire. He could not hide, however, his surprise at the sight of the young woman, obviously with child, who stood beside White Eagle. "This is my wife, Bright Moon," the young husband said quickly. "As you can see, we will soon have a little one."

"It is not good that I should intrude," protested Little Fox. Although the Chippewa language and the Delaware were different dialects, they were close enough that communication between the two was possible.

"It is not an intrusion," replied White Eagle. "You will be a help to us."

Bright Moon smiled and nodded her agreement.

Although Little Fox had been uneasy at first, he had protested no more; and in a short time, the three of them settled into a comfortable relationship. He watched with interest the interplay between husband and wife. It seemed closer and warmer than he remembered between his own father and mother, but then he had paid little attention to that as he grew up. His focus had always been on becoming a warrior of whom his revered father would be proud.

He had been embarrassed at being present during the lovemaking between White Eagle and his wife. Both were often naked inside the house. Nudity, in itself, was not uncommon, for Indian men were often naked in the summer, both inside their homes and outside. The practice had become less common in public in more recent times, and they more frequently wore shirts and leggings made of linen and wool obtained from the white traders. Little Fox learned to lie on his mat next to the outside wall, turning his face to the wall and trying to block out the sounds.

Bright Moon was often uncomfortable in her pregnancy and complained a lot, it seemed to Little Fox. He was often surprised at how much White Eagle gave in to her. The culmination of this behavior had come in less than a month after Little Fox had joined them. Bright Moon had developed a craving for cranberries, and it was a practice of the tribes to dry them for winter consumption. White Eagle had asked around, but no one in the village had cranberries. A trip to Leith's trading post and to Half-King's Town turned up none of the desired fruit. One morning, White Eagle had come to Little Fox to inform him that he had learned that a trader at Lower Sandusky had dried cranberries, and he meant to go there to get them.

"That is a long trip just for cranberries," Little Fox had noted.

"Yes, but it is something my wife wants very much. I want to get them for her."

"Do you want me to go in your place?"

"Your job is to go hunting," White Eagle had explained. "We need meat."

He had mounted his horse, and with a small pouch of provisions slung over his shoulder, he rode out to complete his errand. Little Fox had gone that very morning, and after spending most of the day, managed to kill a rabbit, which he brought to Bright Moon who took it gratefully and began to prepare it for their supper. After they had eaten, Little Fox had sat back feeling very proud of himself, watching Bright Moon as she cleaned up. She was a nice-looking woman, he thought, and he found himself wondering what it would be like to lie next to her. Even in her condition, she looked appealing, and her husband was absent.

Little Fox was ashamed of the thoughts he was having, and it occurred to him that he should go outside. When Bright Moon looked at him and smiled, he wondered if it was an invitation. He was not without some experience with women. There had been a Chippewa maiden in his home village that he had thought seriously of taking as a wife, but he had rejected the idea, believing it would interfere with his plans for fighting the Long Knives.

Little Fox contemplated his own appearance, thinking, as he had many times over the years, that he might look good to a woman. He was taller than average for his tribe, and his slender frame was covered with tight muscles. He had the usual tattoos on his body, circles of beads hanging from his ears, and the hairstyle was that of the Ottawas: standing upright and straight at the front and then tapering off until it was very short at the back. This was to prevent an enemy from grabbing it.

Little Fox was most proud of the ornamented stone, which dangled from under his nose. He had tried to copy this from what he knew was the style preferred by the great Ottawa chief, Pontiac. He had seen Pontiac once when he was very young, but the image had stayed with him so that when he was grown, he had determined to wear a similar adornment.

Bright Moon had retreated to the far side of the room where she slept and slowly removed the light robe she had been wearing. Little Fox could not keep his eyes off of her, and the sight of her full breasts brought him great pleasure. She turned her head and smiled again, her eyes seeming to beckon him to her side. He could not believe that she really meant anything, and the thought of White Eagle riding through the cold brought him to his senses. He smiled back; and drawing his bearskin robe tighter around him, he stepped out through the door and walked away.

White Eagle had returned five days later, carrying a bag of dried cranberries but without his horse. Little Fox was standing outside the hut when White Eagle appeared.

"Where is your horse?" Little Fox asked, noting how tired the traveler looked.

"I traded him for the cranberries," was the reply.

Little Fox shook his head in wonder as White Eagle went into the hut to enjoy the reunion with his wife. In spite of the pleasant life he had enjoyed so far, Little Fox was anxious to go to war. There was much talk of war in the village and especially among the Wyandots at Half-King's Town. He had been surprised at the amount of anger directed toward the Moravian Indians. Being ignorant of that nation, he had asked White Eagle about it.

"It is not a nation," explained his friend. "They are mostly Delawares who have turned to the white man's religion. They live in towns on the Tuscarawas."

"Why is there such anger against them?" Little Fox knew nothing of the Tuscarawas but decided not to pursue that.

"Our chiefs think that messages are sent from their towns to warn the Long Knives of our raids. The Wyandots want them removed and brought here. The white men who lead them are not to be trusted."

This morning the two friends had made the long journey to Half-King's Town to find it in something of an uproar. A large party of Delawares, including women and children as well as warriors, had arrived the previous day from their former home at Coshocton on the Muskingum. They told of fleeing before an army of Long Knives, and this news brought cries for vengeance. White Eagle and Little Fox had worked their way to the center of the town, and they could see several chiefs and a single white man talking earnestly inside a circle of braves.

"Who is the white man?" Little Fox wanted to know.

"That is Simon Girty," said White Eagle. "He fights with the British and has much influence. The chiefs are Half-King, Pipe, and Wingenund."

"Why do they listen to a white man?" Little Fox had no concept of a good white man. White Eagle smiled.

"You have no love for a white man?" he asked, amused at his friend.

"I came to kill white men," said Little Fox with some ferocity.

"Girty has renounced the Long Knives," said White Eagle. "He fights on our side."

Little Fox was not convinced, but he said no more. It was decided that a party of warriors should go to Coshocton to determine what had happened there. As warriors were being selected for this task, Little Fox tugged at White Eagle's arm.

"Let us go with them," he urged. "I want to see this place."

"I think it is the Wyandots who will go," said White Eagle.

"But it was a Delaware town that was attacked. They should let us go along."

White Eagle approached Walk-in-the-Water, a village chief among the Wyandots and the man who would lead the expedition to Coshocton, suggesting that he and his friend Little Fox would like to go along. This was acceptable to the chief, and Little Fox was overjoyed when he learned of it.

White Eagle was concerned about leaving his wife, and he decided to go back to see her. "I'll join you on the trail," he said to Little Fox.

The scouting party led by Walk-in-the-Water consisted of twenty Wyandot warriors, plus White Eagle and Little Fox. It was quickly organized, and enough provisions gathered to suffice for the journey, which would be done without benefit of horses. There was a fairly well-established route between the Upper Sandusky towns and the one at Coshocton, and the more than eighty-mile trip was accomplished in three days. White Eagle, after detouring through Wingenund's town, caught up with the others in camp at the end of the first day. He was fully committed now to this mission, having learned that his father's brother, Spotted Elk, who lived in Coschocton, was not among the refugees who had come to the Upper Sandusky.

Little Fox was overjoyed to see that his friend had come after all, and especially pleased that White Eagle shared his own enthusiasm for the trip. When the group, traveling along White Womans Creek, arrived at the junction of that creek with the Tuscarawas, where the two formed the river called the Muskingum, they saw that the abandoned settlement on the west side of the Musingum had been untouched. The water was still high in both the Muskingum and the Tuscarawas, and no canoes were found along the bank for use in crossing.

It was decided that they would ascend the north bank of the Tuscarawas to Newcomerstown, where they might learn something from the inhabitants of that town and obtain canoes to take them back to Coshocton. In Newcomerstown, there were many who were eager to tell what they knew. Colonel Brodhead had come with an army of more than five hundred men, they explained; and he had destroyed the village at Coshocton, killing many warriors. He had released a few of them and took as prisoners the old men, women, and children. These he had taken with him back to Fort Pitt.

Also, they informed Walk-in-the-Water that the chief Killbuck had befriended the whites and, along with his followers, had accompanied the white soldiers back to Fort Pitt.

"We will deal with this Killbuck," promised Walk-in-the-Water.

Enough canoes were procured to take the party back downstream to Coshocton, where they came ashore on the east bank amidst the ruins of the town. The weather at the end of April had turned warm, and the stench of the decaying animal bodies in the devastated town was dreadful. The anger among the Wyandot warriors was growing, and when the bodies of the Delaware warriors were found tied to the trees, the demand for revenge became furious. White Eagle moved among the bodies with great trepidation, and then his worst fear was realized.

"Ahh!" he cried in a loud voice. "It is my father's brother." He reached out and touched the body, noting the great gash in the side of his head, and also the one in the right shoulder.

He looked at Little Fox, who was standing beside him, fighting back tears that he could never allow himself to shed.

Then he drew his knife and sliced through the thongs, binding the body to the tree. It slid to the ground, still slumped against the tree. White Eagle placed his hands under the armpits of the corpse and tenderly laid it flat. He stood, staring off toward the river, shaking with anger and grief.

"We must bury him here," said Little Fox quietly. He had noted that others were beginning this task as the bodies were cut down from the trees. When it was possible, the Indians liked to remove the bodies from a battlefield, and even return them home. In this instance, since decay had already set in, burial seemed the best option. Some digging tools were found, and the graves dug. After Spotted Elk had been placed in the shallow grave and covered with dirt and leaves, White Eagle stood over the spot for a long time.

"I swear to seek revenge for you, my uncle," he said to the grave. Turning to Little Fox, he spoke with quiet conviction. "I will find the white man who did this, and I will cut out his heart."

Although Little Fox doubted that White Eagle would ever find the real killer, he expressed his wholehearted support. "I will help you, my friend. It will be my purpose in life to kill him and all other white men who cross my path."

6

WAGING WAR

August 25, 1781

THE DEER HAD led him much farther from his camp than he had intended. Wetzel had come upon the tracks more than a mile back along the east bank of Stillwater Creek and had first sighted the young buck when it bounded out from among the trees and into a small clearing. The animal had stopped then and struck a magnificent pose, lifting its head high before looking back in the direction of the hunter, as if challenging him to a duel. Next the deer darted away, now angling for a spot in the woods along the creek, which came back to the northeast after a wide bend to the west.

Wetzel was forced to enter the clearing himself, and he kept to the east, hoping to avoid being seen but also not wanting to lose contact with his prey. He quickly reached the woods on the far side and then moved back upstream until he could see through a slight opening in the trees that the buck had stopped on a low beach down at the level of the creek. Wetzel checked his rifle once more, making sure it was ready to fire, and then eased forward through some low bushes, where he was well hidden but able to maintain a clear line of sight to the target.

The thrill of the tracking process was still upon him, and Wetzel had been in full concentration on the task at hand. He lifted his rifle and took careful aim. Now, however, as he watched the buck lower his head to drink the cool water, he began to have second thoughts. He and Jonathan Zane had left Fort Henry three days ago under orders to discover any unusual Indian activity that might pose a threat to the fort and the Virginia settlements. Word had come from the Moravian missionaries, via Fort Pitt, that a large body of hostile Indians was on its way to the towns on the Tuscarawas.

The two scouts had come up Indian Wheeling Creek and then crossed the ridges into the valley of the Stillwater. They had made a camp in a heavy grove at the base of a small hill on the east side of the creek. Having decided to leave their horses here, they split up for some individual exploring, with Zane going up over the high ridge to the west of the creek, and Wetzel traveling north along the Stillwater.

It must be at least half-dozen miles to their camp from here, Wetzel reckoned, certainly much farther than he had any desire to haul a deer carcass. He lowered the rifle barrel. To his amazement, Wetzel's thoughts were interrupted by the loud report of a gun and, as he watched, the deer took a short jump and fell dead at the edge of the water. Wetzel dropped silently to a prone position, hoping his rifle barrel had not been seen poking through the branches.

He watched as a young Indian brave stepped into the open on the opposite bank and, after looking both up and downstream, slid down the bank and into the stream. His scalp lock was unlike any that Wetzel had seen, and the stone hanging from under his nose caught the white hunter's eye as well. Wetzel's first instinct was to raise his rifle and shoot the brave where he stood in midstream, but he thought better of this when he saw movement in the trees, and two more warriors appeared. He also remembered the last caution given him by Zane. "Remember, Lew, we're out here to find out what the Injuns are up to, not to kill 'em," Zane had said.

The first Indian had reached the body of the deer and leaned down to make sure it was dead. Two more braves appeared, carrying a strong tree branch about six feet long. Wetzel's position had suddenly become precarious, and he began to ponder his options as he watched the Indians tying the legs of the deer to the branch in preparation for transporting the carcass back to their camp. All thoughts of an attack were gone, and the question was one of extracting himself from what was now a clear danger. The five Indians gave no indication that they knew of his presence, but there could be others about who might have happened upon his trail.

He glanced back behind him and noted the heavy cover of bushes and trees along his side of the creek that would shield him if he wished to escape in that direction. What was his duty here, he wondered. The party of Indians had departed back through the trees in the direction from which they had come, carrying the dead deer hanging upside down from the branch, which was held by an Indian on each end. The behavior of the Indians indicated to Wetzel that it was a hunting party rather than a group intending to raid the white settlements across the river. The fact that they were carrying the entire body of the deer was evidence that there were other Indians not too far away.

Wetzel stayed motionless for a long time, waiting patiently to see if there were other warriors nearby. The question in his mind was whether he should try to follow the hunting party or return to base camp. He and Zane had agreed to return to the camp that night. It was well past midafternoon, and it would take more than two hours to get there. Still he knew that Zane had gone over toward Coshocton, and he didn't think the scout would get back that night. The agreement was that if either did not return, the other would wait for one more day. Wetzel thought he may as well see where this small hunting party was going.

Having reached a decision, Wetzel waited for another thirty minutes before leaving his hiding place. He figured that the Indians could not move very fast, and he would easily find their trail. When he finally arose, he moved cautiously farther downstream, staying in the woods. Eventually, he crossed the stream into cover on the opposite side, and then moved back upstream until he reached the spot where the Indian braves had appeared. He stopped and remained still for several minutes, and then confident that he was alone, he pushed forward along the clear trail left by the five Indians and their bloody burden.

Little Fox and his companions had made good progress trading off in carrying the deer carcass and moving away from the creek. They had begun a gradual ascent up a rough trail and had reached the top of a ridge, which extended in a westerly direction toward the Tuscarawas Valley. His spirits had soared with his successful shot, which brought down the young buck, and he was still buoyed with this joyous feeling. He was in for considerable praise, he expected, when the little hunting party returned to camp with fresh meat.

The Delawares had warmed up to him, and he was beginning to feel at home with them. This small triumph should raise his standing even more. White Eagle had been especially pleased. One of the young Delaware warriors called Red Storm had expressed some concern, stating that he thought he had seen what could have been a rifle barrel showing through the trees on the far side of the creek when the deer had been shot. The others had derided this idea, thinking there could be no enemy near them at that point. Hence, they had made no effort to hide their trail.

"If there is some white man behind us, let him come," Little Fox had said boastfully. "There are enough of us to stop him."

"Yes," was Red Storm's reply. "After he has shot one or two of us."

Nothing of the kind had happened, and now, from their position on the northern slope just below the ridgetop, Little Fox could see the large Indian camp spread below them, encircling the Moravian village of Gnaddenhutten, which lay along the eastern bank of the Tuscarawas River. He knew that there were over three hundred braves gathered here, including Wyandots under Half-King, Delawares under Pipe and Wingenund, as well as a scattering of Monseys, Shawnees, Ottawa, and even a few of his own Chippewa tribesmen.

The principal purpose of this assembly of warriors seemed to be convincing the Moravian Christians to accompany them to a new home in the upper Sandusky area. Little Fox had heard some of the speeches, mostly from Half-King; and although they had been gentle and kind at the beginning, the rhetoric in recent days had grown more frightening and blustery, filled with threats.

The Christians had continually refused the offers, and the British agent, Mathew Elliott, had pushed Pipe and Half-King to be even more belligerent in their demands. Matters had become very tense when it was discovered that two of the Christians in the village were missing and assumed to have gone to warn the whites at Fort Pitt. The general belief that the Moravians were regularly guilty of sending warnings to the whites about impending raids was the reason that the bands hostile to the Long Knives were anxious to remove the Moravians to a place where they could be watched.

Little Fox had difficulty following the discussions, although White Eagle tried to patiently explain what was happening. However, he shared in the disgust with the Christian Indians and was not disturbed when things began to turn ugly. Threats were being made toward the white missionaries, who were blamed for the intransigence of the Christians, and the hostiles began shooting the fowls and hogs in the village and even some of the cattle.

Little Fox took the lead as they descended the slope into the camp, and the two men carrying the deer took it to a place where it could be dressed.

Red Storm had insisted upon staying up on the ridge, and he had returned along the trail a short distance where he set up watch among some bushes on the opposite side. The others had thought him foolish, but they did not try to argue with him.

A large fire was burning in the center of the camp, and many of the warriors had crowded around it. Little Fox had urged White Eagle to come with him to see what was happening. As they moved in closer, they could see two of the missionaries and several of the Christian Indian leaders huddled in a small clearing near the fire, and one of the chiefs was speaking to them in a fiery tone. The English agent Elliott stood nearby, nodding his head in agreement with the chief. The Wyandot chief, Half-King, was speaking, and Little Fox strained to hear what was being said.

"You cannot escape the danger that awaits you," said the chief. "No one wants you to stay here. The Six Nations will not let you stay. The Chippewas and Ottawas will fall upon us and destroy us all."

Half-King stood for a moment to let his words sink in and then he continued in a more sinister vein. "Even if these tribes were to let us alone, the Long Knives will certainly fall upon us and kill us all. And when we try to raid them in order to protect you, your teachers send warnings to them." The chief pointed accusingly at the missionaries.

"Who are the white men?" whispered Little Fox to White Eagle, who had pushed up next to him.

White Eagle, who had visited relatives in the Moravian villages in the past, knew David Zeisberger, but was a bit unsure about the other of the two missionaries. "The taller one is Zeisberger. He is the chief among the teachers. The second man may be the one called Heckewelder, or it might be Edwards." White Eagle pointed toward the other white man who was standing near Half-King. "That one is Elliott. He is English and our friend."

Elliott was known to Little Fox, who had heard the English agent talking several days earlier with several of the chiefs, urging a strike against the American settlers across the Ohio. Now the young Chippewa watched intently as one of the Moravians stepped up to reply to Half-King.

"You push too hard on us,'" he said quietly. "We know you mean well and are our friends, but it would be too hard on us to go now. We are at peace with all mankind and are not part of this war. We cannot leave our harvest here, for there is much corn and vegetables. We will not have enough for the winter if we leave all these."

Half-King was sympathetic to this answer, but Elliott now came forward and spoke to the Wyandot with intense animation. The Delaware chiefs, Pipe and Wingenund, were also part of this conversation. Little Fox and White Eagle could not hear all the words, but it was clear that Elliott was threatening them in some way. Now the Wyandot chief spoke again, and it was not difficult to hear him.

"Eliott, you are our friend, as is our father in Detroit. Our brothers, the Delaware, have many friends and relatives among the Christians." He pointed to Pipe and Wingenund. "These chiefs and I do not want bloodshed here. You must be patient."

"It is their fault," shouted Elliott, pointing at the missionaries. "If they are removed, the others will do what you ask."

"Our friend Elliott speaks truth," said Half-King with a nod of his head. "Still the Christians love their teachers and will not suffer them to be harmed."

Elliott stomped away in disgust, and some of the rowdier Wyandot warriors took this as a cue to advance menacingly toward the frightened ministers. One of them fired his gun in the air while a second drew his tomahawk and shook it in the face of Zeisberger.

Little Fox looked quickly to Half-King to see what he would do, but the famed chief simply stood still with a deep scowl on his face. As suddenly as they had risen, the threatening warriors lowered their weapons and walked away. Half-King raised his hands and waved them outward, signaling that the council was ended and all should return to their huts. Little Fox felt unsettled and somewhat disappointed by what he had seen and heard.

"I think Half-King is much too easy on the Moravians, and especially on those white men," he said to White Eagle as they headed toward their hut. "They should be killed."

"You are harsh, my brother," laughed White Eagle. Then, in a serious tone, he added, "Half-King does not want to spill the blood of our brothers, the Moravians, which might be necessary if we were to kill their teachers."

"Hah! They are not my brothers who listen to white men."

"Perhaps it is not good to hate so much," observed White Eagle.

"Do you forget what they did to your uncle?"

"No, and the time will come to right that wrong," said White Eagle with firm determination. "But now let us go and enjoy some of the fine meat you have provided."

As they walked, they were met in the path by Pekillon, another chief among the Delawares. Pekillon was regarded with some contempt by many of his tribesmen and certainly by the Wyandots. He had formerly been a friend of the whites, and it was known that he had been with Brodhead at Coshocton not many months before. In recent days, however, he had been pushing for a raid against the Virginia settlements, and he had been chosen to lead in that endeavor. Both Little Fox and White Eagle had eagerly volunteered to be part of the raiding party.

"Have you seen my nephew, Red Storm?" asked Pekillon.

"He was with us when we went to hunt the deer," replied White Eagle. "But he stayed back on the trail. He had the mistaken idea that we were being followed."

"How do you know he was mistaken?" wondered the chief.

"There was no sign of any one near us, and no reason for it anyway," said White Eagle.

"All of us agreed he was being foolish," added Little Fox.

"And you are all so wise, I assume." Pekillon was becoming annoyed and could not hide it. "The Long Knives know that there are many of us here. They may have sent spies."

White Eagle and Little Fox looked at each other and shrugged.

"He may be in danger," said Pekillon. "Take some men with you and bring him back."

The urgency in Pekillon's voice and manner moved the two young braves to action. They hurried to their hut where they retrieved their weapons.

Finding several of their friends seated near the campfire where the recently dressed carcass of Little Fox's kill was being roasted, they informed them of Pekillon's command. Within a few minutes, a party of nine warriors led by Little Fox began ascending the trail to the top of the ridge.

The sound of a distant rifle shot had startled Wetzel, and from sheer instinct, he stepped immediately off the trail and crouched down behind the trunk of a large willow oak that stood just a few feet from the path. He realized that in the last mile or two, he had been hurrying and had relaxed his usual alertness to detail. The shot had come from a considerable distance away, and whether it meant danger for him, Wetzel could not say. He remembered the warning Zane had given him about following a trail.

"The reds like to waylay a trail, Lew, so don't let your self get caught by that old trick," Zane had said to him as they parted.

It occurred to him now that he may have left himself in just such a pickle. He kept still for several minutes before striking off at an angle and straight up the ridge above him. He was possessed of an urgent desire to see what was on the other side of the ridge, and he scrambled up through the brush and trees at a rapid rate.

He did not think that a foe watching the back trail would have set up on this side, and so he was confident in being able to reach the top without being seen. When he reached the crest, the amount of foliage prevented him from seeing anything, and so he continued directly over and down the far side. After a short distance, he found a small clearing; and from here, he could see the smoke coming from a multitude of fires down in the river valley to the west. He knew that the Moravian village of Gnadenhutten was there, but this was a much larger camp than he would have expected.

"God," exclaimed Lewis aloud. "That's a big camp. I reckon there must be more than two hundred warriors down there."

He knew that he needed to get a better look, but there was still the problem of a possible Indian on his back trail. Although he had seen no sign of that, he knew better than to ignore it. He went to his right across the clearing, and after twenty rods or so through some dense forest, he turned again to go back over the ridge to the south. His plan was to make a big half square, crossing the original path somewhere below where he had left it, and then come up through the woods on the other side. He had a feeling that if someone were watching the trail, that was where he would be.

The falling darkness forced Wetzel to hurry more than he might have wished. Having intersected the old trail and moved a good distance to the west, Wetzel turned back to the north, toward the top of the ridge. The original path followed by the Indian hunting party now angled across like the hypotenuse of a right triangle, and Wetzel was moving slowly up the left leg. Although he could not have given a good reason, he seemed sure that anyone waylaying the old trail would be somewhere in this vicinity. Lewis had learned how to move stealthily through a wooded area, and he used every bit of that talent now.

Lewis had come more than one hundred yards up the slope when he stopped suddenly, as he had done frequently during the ascent. His keen eyes had detected what he thought was some slight movement. He dropped down until he was lying on his stomach, and he continued to stare at the base of a big maple tree several yards to his front. Gradually he was able to make out the form of an Indian seated at the base of the tree.

In the dim light, he could see the three eagle feathers in the topknot, flopping at odd angles off the back of the head. It almost looked like a giant bird waiting to pounce on an unsuspecting prey. He remembered the same headdress of one of the members of the hunting party back on Stillwater Creek. Silently he thanked Jonathan Zane for reminding him to be alert for just such a tactic.

Wetzel could feel his heart pounding under him, as his body readied itself for action. But what should he do? His rifle was lying next to him, but to use it would alert the Indians in the big town below, and they could mount a search party much too big for him to handle. He could just turn back here and return to his base camp without being seen. He would still be able to report on the size of the Indian encampment, which surely meant trouble for the Virginians across the Ohio. However, he really wanted a closer look at the camp, and that would be impossible unless he disposed of the warrior guarding the trail.

Filled with purpose, Wetzel stashed his gun in a clump of bushes just behind him, taking careful notice of the surroundings so that he could easily find it later. He pulled his tomahawk from its place on his belt and eased forward again toward the target. He moved a bit to his left so that he was more directly behind the young Delaware warrior, and without making any sound, he crept to within a few feet. Now he sprang at his target; and though it was not a conscious act, a loud screech escaped his lips. He brought the axe head down with the intention of splitting the skull; but at the very last instant, the Indian, who had turned to face his screaming adversary, jerked his head sideways just enough that the blow missed its intended target, and sheared off the red man's ear. His momentum and the brave's uplifted leg had caused Wetzel to tumble hard to the ground, and the tomahawk had flown from his hand and hit the ground well out of reach.

The Indian brave, Red Storm, had gathered himself and was rushing straight at Wetzel, holding a knife in his right hand. Lewis had managed to get to his feet, and now he lowered his shoulder and drove with all his force straight into Red Storm's midsection, knocking the wind out of him. In spite of this, the warrior had managed an underhanded thrust with the knife, which had cut through Wetzel's hunting shirt and grazed his side, bringing blood but no real damage.

Shouts from farther up the trail brought awareness of a new danger for Wetzel. Help was coming for his enemy, and it would be on the scene very soon. The shouts were repeated several times; obviously the relief party was calling out the name of Wetzel's foe. There was no indecision on his part now. He must get away from there and as far away as possible. He raced back down the slope, quickly locating the bushes where he had hidden his gun and continuing almost directly to the south. It would be much easier traveling if he went back to the route he had followed before, but the Indians could easily find him along that trail.

The darkness that was his enemy was also his friend, for the Indians would be unable to actually find his trail until morning. He thought that at some point they would stop for the night and take up the search when it was daylight. By then, he hoped to be back to Stillwater, although it would not be so easy to find in the dark. Thorny brambles and fallen limbs provided annoying obstacles to Wetzel's progress and led to several falls. The worst happened when he slipped at the head of a small ravine and fell in a hard slide to the bottom. After coming to a stop, he pulled himself to a sitting position and rested. He had managed to keep his rifle from digging into the dirt, and he was glad to realize that it was still in good condition to fire if needed.

Wetzel listened for a moment and thought he could still hear sounds of his pursuers above him, and as best he could tell, they seemed to have spread out somewhat. Wetzel knew that he needed to get back toward the old trail again and beyond it. Surely his foes would know that, and some of them were likely following that path. It seemed best to continue in the direction he had been going, but the problem was that he knew nothing of the nature of the terrain and could easily become lost. He scrambled to his feet and began running again, following the same line as before.

The foliage opened up a bit and there seemed to be a natural trail, which was easier to follow. He could not see very much, and though this easier path had veered off to the right, he continued to stay on it. Distance from his pursuers was more important to him now, he thought, than any worry about getting lost.

After a few minutes, Wetzel came to a small creek flowing to his left. The night was warm, and the water inviting. He stepped off the low bank into the stream and walked for a short distance downstream before climbing out and moving on to the south. He had been tempted to follow the creek to where he assumed that it ran into the Stillwater. As he came down Stillwater Creek the day before he had been aware of a couple of streams coming in from the west—although he had not crossed one while on the trail of the hunting party—he decided that he would continue in the current direction. If he encountered a second creek flowing to his left, he might follow that one. He began to think that perhaps he had evaded pursuit. He stopped at the top of a small hill to listen. He could hear nothing other than the normal night sounds of the forest.

"Mebbe they stopped if they came to that creek," he said aloud. "They sure ain't goin' to find no trail in the dark."

Satisfied, he continued on over the hill, moving more deliberately now.

"I sure hope I ain't lost."

Little Fox and White Eagle—leading the rescue party, including seven other Delaware warriors—had reached the top of the ridge when they heard the scream. Aware now, and surprised, that their colleague Red Storm was in danger, they had begun to shout his name. Having urged the others to spread out as they moved down the hill, White Eagle and Little Fox had moved directly toward the sound of the scream they had heard. It wasn't long until they had reached the spot where Red Storm was sitting, holding one hand against his injured ear. The blood was still oozing through his fingers and dripping off the side of his face.

"White man?" asked Little Fox, helping the wounded man to sit back against the tree trunk.

White Eagle had pulled a soft piece of cloth taken from an old blanket and was holding it against the bleeding ear, most of which had been sheared off.

Red Storm had nodded in assent to Little Fox's query, and the look on his face conveyed the message "I told you so" although the words remained unspoken.

"Did you see which way he ran?" questioned Little Fox, anxious to organize a pursuit.

Red Storm did not speak but indicated with his head the direction in which Wetzel had fled.

"What did he look like?"

"What difference does that make?" snapped White Eagle. "Just find him, then you'll know what he looks like."

Red Storm, whose head was on fire, did not feel much like talking, but he tried to answer Little Fox's question.

"Big man, dark hair, long," he managed to say.

"You lead the others and go after him," White Eagle said to Little Fox. "I will take care of Red Storm." As he said this, he took some sassafras leaves from his pouch and began to chew them. They would form a poultice to put on the wound. As four others came up, Little Fox pointed to the south and waved for them to move on. The remaining members of the party were coming in from the left when Little Fox stopped them and indicated that they should continue to search in a spread out to that side.

"Go down the old trail," he shouted to them.

Little Fox had given up the chase when they reached the creek that Wetzel had crossed only a few minutes earlier. His companions had lost interest when it was clear that they could find no trail in the dark, and there was no way to guess where their prey might have crossed the creek.

"We can stay here for the night and find his trail when it is light," said Little Fox, but he received no encouragement from the others. In fact, they had all wanted to go back to the village, and Little Fox had finally given in. By the time they got back to where White Eagle was tending to Red Storm, they discovered that the other three warriors who had been out to the left side had also returned.

One of the warriors reached down into the grass near the tree where Red Storm was sitting. "Look," he exclaimed, holding the tomahawk up for the others to see.

Not much could be seen in the dark, but the warrior, first holding the blade up close to his face, grasped the head in his left hand, and with the fingers of his right hand, traced out the *W* carved into the handle just below where it was attached to the head. He handed it to White Eagle, showing him the carving.

"It is a mark in the white man's language. It probably indicates his name. Someone at camp will know what it is. Now we must go."

Red Storm, while holding the poultice against his ear, indicated that he could walk; and so the braves moved in single file out to the trail and back up over the ridge.

Little Fox, walking at the end of the column, reflected on the great knowledge that White Eagle seemed to have. Once again, he was thankful that he happened into White Eagle's lodge.

When they reached the Indian Camp, Pekillon was waiting for them. "What happened?" he wanted to know.

"Red Storm fought with a white man who was spying on our trail," explained White Eagle. He reached up and took Red Storm's hand, removing it and the bandage to show Pekillon the torn ear, of which only a small piece remained attached at the bottom.

Pekillon placed a hand on each of Red Storm's shoulders. "Did you hurt him?"

Red Storm put his hand to his belt and removed the knife from its sheath. He held it up for Pekillon to see. In the dim light,

Pekillon was able to make out a small smear of blood. He grunted in approval.

"The white man escaped," interjected White Eagle, responding before Pekillon could ask. "Little Fox and the others went after him but couldn't find him in the dark."

"Not good," expressed Pekillon with a shake of his head. "Soon we will attack the Long Knives across the big river. Maybe we will find this man and kill him there." He strode off without looking back, and the tired warriors scattered away to their own huts. Red Storm, dejected and in pain, was helped back to the hut White Eagle shared with Little Fox.

September 1, 1781

Mary Wetzel placed the wooden plate down and looked lovingly at her son Lewis, who sat on the low bench with his elbows resting on the tabletop. The plate was covered with a generous serving of johnnycake, and Lewis broke off a piece and ate it eagerly.

"Thanks, Ma, it's good," he said, looking up with a smile.

"Do you want some hominy with that?" she asked. "The milk's all gone, I'm afraid."

"Some hominy would be good."

"I'm sorry about the milk," Mary said with a quiet laugh. "You've got to get up early to get any milk around here."

"I know, Ma, but I needed the sleep." He watched as she retrieved a bowl from the ledge at the front of the fireplace and brought it to him.

She spooned out a clump of the hulled corn, soaked in a liquid he assumed included some of the missing milk. "It's nice to have you home, Lewis," she said, rubbing the top of his head.

Lewis laughed. "Yeah, my scalp is still there, Ma. Them redskins didn't get it this time."

"You worry me, Lewis," she said, walking away a few steps. She turned and watched as he ate, her face serious, and her brow wrinkled. She had been a pretty woman in her youth, but the hard work and difficulties of everyday living had taken their toll. "You should stay here more, your Pa could use the help."

"I ain't much of a farmer, Ma. But I am pretty good in the woods, and that's what I really like."

"Hah! You're a growed-up man now, Lewis. You can't spend your whole life in the woods, you got to do somethin' useful and earn your keep. Besides, you're gonna lose that beautiful scalp to them Injuns. That's what I'm afraid of."

"It is useful, Ma. Me and Jack Zane did a good thing out there. We brought back some good information on this last trip."

It bothered Lewis that his mother did not appreciate the things that had already made him a hero to the frontiersmen. It was not surprising though, he supposed, for she had never approved of violence, loud talking, and boasting. Yet he still felt warm inside when he thought of the recent scouting trip with Jonathan Zane.

He did have to admit to himself that he had been concerned for a time about his own safety. After crossing the first creek, he had continued on in the dark until he had come to a second stream. It was shallow, and he had entered it and walked along the edge downstream, trusting that the little creek would empty into the Stillwater. He had been right about that, although it had taken much longer than he had expected, and the creek had been joined by another coming in from his left. This, he realized, was probably the first one he had crossed.

When he finally reached the Stillwater, he had rested there for a time, actually falling asleep. He awakened in full light and not sure whether he was still being followed; he had hurried off again toward the camp where he expected to find Jonathan Zane. The ground was familiar; and after crossing the stream, he saw that he was near the place that he had begun following the deer. On approaching the camp, he had decided to see if he could reach it without being detected by Zane. Accordingly he had ascended the hill behind it and moved down, careful to avoid making any noise. He was good at this, and he stopped to congratulate himself on his success up to this point. He could see the remains of a small fire, which suddenly reminded him that he was ravenously hungry. He could not see Zane, however, and it dawned on him that the horses weren't there either.

Had the wizened old scout already left? That hadn't been their agreement. Maybe Zane had heard him coming and was watching from some hiding place to see whether it was friend or foe. He had waited a bit longer before stepping into the open, when his eye caught a movement among the trees over near the creek bank at least fifty or sixty yards away. When he saw it again, he smiled for it was the swishing of a horse's tail, and he was relieved because it meant that Zane was still around. As he started to step out, he felt something poke him in the back near his left side.

"If I was an Injun, you'd be a dead man," said Jonathan Zane, holding his rifle hard against young Wetzel's back.

"I guess I would," Lewis had answered, embarrassed that he had been fooled and taken so easily.

"It ain't smart to sneak up on a friend. You can end up dead real easy."

"I'm sorry," Lew had said, determined that such a thing would never ever happen to him again.

Zane had pulled his gun back and walked away heading down toward the creek. Wetzel couldn't let the subject drop so easily.

"Did you hear me walking up above? I don't know how you could have."

"No," said Zane. "I was downstream a piece, and I saw you when you started up the hill there. I figured you meant to slip up behind and surprise me."

"So you surprised me instead."

"Appears so. Don't take it too hard, but learn the lesson."

They had walked a ways in silence.

"Is there anything to eat?" Wetzel asked. "I'm starved."

"There's some dried venison in my saddlebags. We need to get back to the fort, I think. Did you see any Injun sign?"

Wetzel had recounted his encounter with the hunting party and that he had seen a very large camp of Indians near Gnaddenhutten.

"Sounds like trouble is coming," noted Zane. "Let's get back with this news."

They had retrieved the horses and pushed hard to get back to Fort Henry late that evening. Captain John Boggs was in command of Fort Henry, and the two scouts had met with him the next morning. He wasn't surprised at the news, but it confirmed the reports that had come from Fort Pitt and strengthened his resolve to advise the residents to look for safety.

"I can't pay you anything just now," he had said to Lew, "but I sure do appreciate what you did."

"That's all right," said Lew, although he had been disappointed. He had almost suggested that Boggs should let him call on his sweet daughter, Lydia, but he didn't say anything. He laughed to himself now as he thought of it. He had noticed young Lydia although he had never spoken to her, and now her family had moved into Fort Henry from their old place on Buffalo Creek. He'd heard that they had bought a place just a few miles below Fort Henry, so he hoped to see more of her.

Captain John Wetzel, along with Lew's brothers George and Jacob, had gone hunting early this morning. Lew had declined the opportunity to go along, since he had arrived at the cabin late the night before and wanted to catch up on sleep that had been lost on his latest adventure. He had told his father of the Indian threat and relayed the advice from John Boggs that they should come in to Fort Henry until the threat was over.

"I ain't thinkin' they'll come out here this time," was Captain John's reply to what Lew had to say. "I think the four of us could defend this place all right."

"What about Ma and the others? I could take them back to the fort today."

Lew's sister Susannah, who was fourteen, and little brother John, now eleven, were both at home. Surprising to Lew, however, his mother had thought it unnecessary, and hadn't argued with her husband at all. It was late afternoon when Wetzel, who had been dozing under a shade tree near the cabin, was awakened by the sound of a horse and rider coming down the steep hill across Wheeling Creek from the Wetzel farm. Grabbing his rifle from where it stood against the tree trunk, he hollered to his mother who was inside the cabin.

"Ma, somebody's comin'. Where are Susannah and John?"

Mary Wetzel appeared at the door. "Susannah's here with me, but Johnny's out there somewhere. Do you think it is Indians?"

"I doubt it, Ma, but I don't know yet." He didn't think Indians would be coming by horseback from that direction. "John, John! Get in the house right now."

His little brother appeared from behind the milkshed.

"There you are. Get in with Ma until I find out who is coming."

The look on his brother's face was enough to stifle an argument, and John ran past Lewis and into the cabin. After checking his rifle, Lewis walked around the corner of the cabin and stopped where he could get a clear view of the hillside. He could see now that the rider was not an Indian and that he was hunched low over the horse's back, clearly in some kind of distress. Satisfied there was no danger, Lewis ventured out to meet the visitor. As he came closer, Lewis could see that it was a man named George Blackburn who had a cabin up on the ridge at least two miles away. Upon seeing Wetzel, Blackburn raised himself slightly in the saddle.

"Lew, help me. Help me! A rattler bit me, and I think I'm goin' to die."

Wetzel helped the man down from the horse, supporting him under both arms.

"Can you walk?" Wetzel wanted to know.

"I think so," whimpered Blackburn. "But it hurts like hell!"

Mary Wetzel had come to open the door, and she stepped aside as Lewis helped the snake-bitten man into the cabin, where young John was staring, wide-eyed and mouth open.

"I'll put him on my pallet," said Lew as he helped Blackburn lie down. "Let's see your leg."

His mother had joined them. "Pull his boot off first, Lewis," she advised. As Lewis pulled the boot off his right foot, Blackburn twisted in agony.

"God, it hurts!" he cried.

Wetzel tried to push his pant leg up, but the swelling caused it to bind. Taking his knife from its sheath, Wetzel slit the buckskin legging several inches and pushed it up out of the way. The wound was just above the ankle, and it was an angry red and swollen, with two fang marks plainly visible. Lewis didn't really know what should be done next, although he knew that such a wound was often cut open, and an attempt to suck out the blood was made.

"Should I cut it open, Ma?" he asked.

The look on Blackburn's face indicated that the victim was not going to be of much help in suggesting treatment.

"Yes, and see if you can suck some of the poison out. Then put some salt and a little gunpowder in the cuts. I'll boil up some chestnut leaves, and we'll make a poultice of them. I've heard that will help."

The two of them went about their tasks and did what they could for the suffering Blackburn. Eventually the poultice was in place, and a cool wet cloth placed on his brow for he had become feverish. To his credit, he had composed himself and was suffering mostly in silence.

Just before dark, John Wetzel and his two sons returned, bringing a small rabbit they had killed. Mary Wetzel met him just outside the door.

"We've got company," she said quickly, not sure how Captain John might react.

"I see that," said John. "That looks like George Blackburn's horse," he added, pointing to the horse still standing patiently where Lewis had tied him to the hitching rail at the end of the cabin.

"It is, John," agreed Mary. "George is in a bad way. He was bit by a rattlesnake. We've got him inside."

"Good Lord," exclaimed her husband. "Jake, take care of that horse. I don't know why Lewis hasn't done that already."

He turned and held up the dead rabbit for his wife to see. "We got us a little rabbit, Mary. Do you want to cook it for supper?"

"I will if you skin it," was the reply.

Captain John handed the rabbit to George Wetzel, who was standing just behind him. "Here, George, skin this thing and give it to your mother. I better go in and see how Blackburn is doing."

Once inside, he went to the bed where Blackburn was sleeping fitfully. He lifted the poultice up carefully, and after a brief examination of the wound, he replaced the poultice and looked up at his wife, who had followed him in shaking his head.

"It don't look good," said John after a moment. "We should get him to the doctor over at Catfish Camp."

"It's too late now," said Mary. "It's already dark."

"We'll have Lewis take him there first thing in the morning. Where is Lewis?"

"Out at the shed, I think."

"What did he do all day?" John wanted to know.

"Just laid around mostly," answered Mary.

"That's what I figured. Ain't much of a farmer, is he?"

"Didn't notice you doin' much farming today either," taunted his wife with a slight smile.

John chuckled. "Guess you're right about that."

Later after they had eaten, Lewis grabbed a blanket and strode to the door.

"Where you goin'?" asked Captain John.

"Well," said Lewis, "I reckon since Blackburn is sleepin' on my bed, I'll just sleep outside."

"I'd rather you stayed in here," said John.

"Pa, it's too damned hot in here. I'd rather sleep outside where it's cooler."

"You'll think it's cooler if some rovin' Delaware lifts that hair off your head. And watch your mouth. Your ma don't like that cussin'."

Lew looked at his mother. "Sorry, Ma. But I'll be all right. Goodnight everyone." With that, he was out the door.

September 2, 1781

Shortly after breakfast the next morning, Lewis saddled Blackburn's horse and one of his father's mares, and then went into the cabin to help Blackburn outside. The man had spent the night with a series of chills and sweats, and as Lewis helped him hobble out and get up in the saddle, he was still complaining about how poorly he felt.

"Maybe you should just let me die," he grumped. "That would be an improvement."

Lewis said nothing, but he was thinking that the man was not very appreciative of what had been done for him. Blackburn did manage to wave good-bye and express a simple thank you to John and Mary Wetzel, who had come outside to watch the two men ride away. They followed Wheeling Creek downstream until they came to the forks, where Shepherd's Fort once stood.

The fort had been burned back in October of 1777, after the Shepherd family had left, along with the other people in the area, and it had not yet been rebuilt. The old mill was still standing, as well as a small cabin, where one of the Shepherds sometimes stayed when working at the farm. Colonel Shepherd had not yet brought his family back to live there again. As they approached the site, Moses Shepherd came out to the trail to meet them.

"Hello, Lew," shouted Shepherd in greeting. He was about the same age as Lewis. "Who's that with you?"

"It's George Blackburn. He's been snakebit and is in a bad way. I'm takin' him over to Catfish to see a doctor."

Shepherd looked hard at Blackburn who was slumped down against the horse's neck saying nothing.

"I'm headed back there myself," he said. "I'll go along with you. Just let me get my horse."

"Suit yourself," agreed Wetzel. "But hurry up. We need to get this man over there." They headed up Little Wheeling Creek to the point where it was joined by Middle Wheeling. Wetzel turned up that stream, which seemed to surprise Shepherd.

"Why you goin' this way?" he asked.

"Pa wanted me to drop somethin' off at Link's place. It ain't really any farther, may even be faster this way."

"Don't seem that way to me," protested Shepherd.

Wetzel was annoyed at that remark, but he only shrugged.

"Don't matter none to me though," continued Shepherd. "Might be fun to see the Links."

The three riders continued along the banks of Middle Wheeling Creek. There was not always a clear trail, and they had to fight their way through low-hanging branches and prickly bushes. A few times they went into the edge of the creek itself and crossed it once or twice to cancel out some sharp bends. Blackburn was in agony and several times had pleaded with Wetzel to stop and let them rest. After doing that once, Wetzel had refused future pleas, thinking the difficulties in dismounting and mounting again were worse for the injured man than the continuous jostling of uninterrupted riding. "We'll stop and give you a good rest when we get to Link's," he said finally after the latest request. "It ain't much farther."

They had reached a spot where the ground had flattened out and a wide expanse of grassland spread out from the edge of the stream. Suddenly a shot rang out, and then a second. Shouting could be heard. Moses Shepherd rushed up beside where Wetzel had halted his horse. "That was rifle shots!" he exclaimed. "Do you think they're under attack? What should we do?"

Wetzel knew that just ahead, where the creek made a slight turn to the right, they would be able to see Link's fortified cabin. "I don't know, but it didn't sound like Injuns yellin'. Let's cross the creek here and come up among the trees on the back side of the buildings."

He motioned to Shepherd to take hold of the reins on Blackburn's horse and lead it behind them. They splashed through the creek, which was shallow, and rode through the trees on the far side until they could see Link's blockhouse. More shots and shouting had occurred; and when Wetzel could see what was happening, he burst into laughter.

"They're havin' a shootin' match, Moses," he yelled at Shepherd, who was more than ten yards behind him. "Maybe we can get in on it."

With that, he urged his mount quickly back across the creek and into the open. Shepherd followed with Blackburn in tow. Three men were out in the clearing in front of the Link cabin, shooting at an old whiskey barrel set up some fifty yards away. A woman and small child stood near the door of the cabin, watching. Wetzel recognized one of the men as Jacob Link and a second as a man named William Hawkins, who had a cabin over on the Dutch Fork of Buffalo Creek. He didn't know the third man, learning later that his name was William Burnett. As he observed the man, it did occur to Wetzel that he might have seen Burnett when out with Brodhead. Upon recognizing the first of the incoming riders, Link shouted with delight.

"It's Lewis Wetzel. We can have a real shootin' match now!"

Wetzel reined in his horse near where the men were standing and slid to the ground. He pointed back to the other two riders.

"It's Moses Shepherd and George Blackburn. Blackburn's been bitten by a rattler, and we're takin him to Catfish to see a doctor."

"Well, you can rest here a spell or even spend the night if you like."

"We heard the shootin' and thought the Injuns was after you," said Wetzel, as Shepherd and Blackburn rode up.

"We was just doin' a little shootin' for fun. This here's William Burnett, and I think you know Hawkins." Link moved over to help Blackburn down from the saddle and eased him to a sitting position on the ground. He turned and motioned to his wife.

"Get these men somethin' to drink," he told her. Then he turned back to Blackburn. "You don't look so good, Blackburn."

"I'm in a bad way, all right," he agreed. "Ridin' that horse is a bitch."

"Beats walkin' though, I reckon," said Link. "But you can rest here as long as you like. We'll get you something to drink." He remembered now that Shepherd was also standing there. "Hello, Moses. Want to shoot with us?"

"I guess," said Moses. "What are you shootin' for?"

"We're shootin' at that old barrel. Closest to the center wins." Link watched as his wife walked up to the men, carrying a small jug and a couple of wooden cups.

"Thank you, Mrs. Link," he said to his wife with a smile. "We won't need the cups," he added as he handed the jug to Lew Wetzel.

Wetzel nodded without speaking and lifted the jug to his lips. He couldn't suppress a small grimace as the fiery liquid passed his tongue and down his throat. He felt the warmth almost immediately in his stomach and was tempted to take a second drink but thought better of it and handed it to Shepherd. The jug made the rounds except for Blackburn, who entered a protest. "What about me? Don't I get some of that?"

"Whiskey ain't the best thing for rattlesnake bites, George," said Link.

"Hell, I'm prob'ly a goner anyway," whined Blackburn. "Might as well be drunk when I go."

"You'll live, George, but I reckon you can stand one drink." Link handed him the jug and spoke to Wetzel. "What about it, Lew, are you up to a little contest?"

"I don't think we have time, Jacob. We need to get Blackburn to a doctor."

"He can use a little rest while we shoot. Besides, if he ain't dead by now, I doubt it will happen."

"What's the prize for winnin' this contest?" Moses Shepherd wanted to know.

"Winner gets to keep that jug," put in William Hawkins. "How 'bout that Jacob?"

"What's in it for Jacob, then?" asked Wetzel. "It's already his jug."

"Well, he gets to keep it if he wins. Otherwise we might take it away from him anyway," said Hawkins with a laugh.

"Suits me," said Link. "It's worth it to me to watch you shoot, Lewis."

With that settled, Link stepped off fifty paces from the barrel and marked a line in the grass. "We'll shoot from here," he said.

It was agreed that each man would have three shots, and the closest to the center would be the winner. Of course, the problem was that the target might be destroyed before the third shots were completed. They began by having each man shoot once. Burnett was first, and his ball hit the end of the barrel near the outer rim on the upper right. Moses Shepherd was next, and he missed the barrel altogether, stirring up the dirt to the right. Hawkins followed with a shot to the left side near the rim. Wetzel's turn came; and from a kneeling position, he took careful aim and watched his ball tear a hole in the bottom just a couple of inches from the center to the right. The men watching gave out a cheer.

"That'll be tough to beat," noted Link. "But I guess I'll give it a try."

Link's shot hit low just above the ground but inside the rim.

"Well, Lew's beatin' us pretty bad so far," observed Link. "Let's go again."

Burnett took more time with his second shot, and it paid off. His shot hit the target just three inches above the center but well-placed from right to left.

"That's a good one, Burnett. But now we'll see how a real man can shoot," laughed Hawkins.

"Wait," said Link. "It's Moses's turn."

Shepherd shot again but just nicked the rim. "Aw, I can't shoot worth a damn today," he said, shaking his head.

"You still got one more chance, son," said Link. "Now, Hawkins, let's see if you can shoot as good as you talk."

Hawkins's effort made no new hole in the barrel. "Ha!" he exclaimed. "Must have gone right through the hole that Lew made."

This remark brought a host of guffaws from the others. Wetzel's second shot hit left of center and a bit high, but it was still better than any of the others. Link's second try hit low on the right.

"Well, it all comes down to this last round," said he. "Lew's still got the lead. Who's gonna beat him?"

"I'll give it my best try," announced Burnett, and he took careful aim, snapping off a shot that was below and just to the right of his previous mark.

It splintered a good portion of the barrel bottom, tearing a big hole up to and including the one previously made by Wetzel.

"I can't beat that. I'll give up my last try," said Moses, who replaced his rifle against the small sapling nearby.

"Hell, I'll put a ball right through that big hole," boasted Hawkins, but his attempt hit in the upper left, which brought him plenty of verbal abuse from the bystanders.

"It's your turn, Lew," remarked Link. "But I don't see how we can tell if you beat Burnett's last shot."

"Do you see that little splinter just up and left of Burnett's hole?" asked Lew. A small piece of the wood about the size of a thumb extended into the hole like a peninsula in a lake. The other men all agreed that they could see it, although Burnett and Hawkins had walked up a few steps closer before acknowledging it.

"If I hit that with my third shot, will you say I'm the winner?"

"I have a shot left, you know," Link reminded them. "But I could never make that shot from this distance, so yeah, I guess that would make you the winner. What about you, Burnett? Do you agree?"

"I do," said Burnett quickly. "But what if you miss?" he asked Wetzel.

"If I miss, then you win the jug," asserted Wetzel. "But I don't aim for that to happen."

Wetzel took particular care in cleaning the barrel and loading his gun.

He was a little bit ashamed at having been so boastful. His father would have never approved of such an attitude. Still he felt confident, and he guessed he had let that show a little too much. Now he had to perform, and he got ready, kneeling and taking aim. As he looked down the sight, he felt a tremor in the fingers of his left hand holding the barrel. The sight was not steady, and he lowered the gun for a moment, taking a deep breath. Then he raised the barrel again, saw that it was steady, and squeezed the trigger. The recoil felt good against his shoulder, and he let out a sharp cry as he saw the target splinter disappear.

"Hurrah!" shouted Link and Shepherd at the same time. "What a shot," continued Moses. "I ain't never seen nothin' better."

"That is some shootin', son," acknowledged Burnett. "Link told me about you, and I guess I have to say he was right."

Hawkins just shook his head, and Link handed the jug to Wetzel. "It's yours, Lew, won fair and square."

Lewis sported a wide grin as he accepted the jug from Link. "Have another drink, boys. It's on me." He passed the prize to Burnett, who quickly tipped it to his lips. "That reminds me,

Jacob. Pa sent something for you." Wetzel went to where his horse stood, patiently waiting and grazing on the short grass. He retrieved something from a bag attached to the saddle and handed it to Link, who had followed him. "It's that bridle that was on that old horse you sold Pa awhile back. He meant to get it back to you before now. Said to tell you he was sorry about that."

"That's all right," said Link. "I'd forgotten all about it."

Wetzel nodded and walked over to where Blackburn was sitting. In spite of his pain and general discomfort, the man had watched the shooting match with great interest. "Didn't surprise me none that you won, Lewis," he said as Wetzel came near.

"I was lucky, I reckon," answered Wetzel. "How are you feelin'? We need to get on our way real soon."

"I ain't good, but I suppose I can travel."

Wetzel hollered for Shepherd to come and help him get Blackburn back on his horse. As they did so, Link, leading a horse, came over along with his wife and child.

"Lew," he said. "I've a favor to ask of you. My child here is sick with a fever, and I wonder if you would take her and my wife along with you to Catfish. I want them to see the doctor. Besides, if the Indian trouble we've been hearin' about comes, they would be safer there."

"Sure," replied Wetzel. "They can come along. We need to hurry though. It will be dark before long."

"You can spend the night at Presley Peak's if you need to. It's just a few miles over the ridge there. Burnett and Hawkins will be goin' along too."

"Is there room enough at Peak's?"

"He'll be glad to have the company."

"What about you? Aren't you comin' too?"

"Nah, I need to stay here and take care of the place. Be on your way now and good luck."

Wetzel resumed his journey to Catfish with the number in his party increased to seven, including the snakebit man Blackburn, and the sickly three-year-old daughter of Jacob Link.

"I reckon we'll need to stay at Peak's all right," he said to himself.

September 3, 1781

The morning sun pierced through a layer of wispy clouds, making it difficult to see. A group of warriors, which included Little Fox and White Eagle, stood near the banks of the Ohio just above the mouth of Wheeling Creek, and still others were coming up along the shore below it. There were some eighty braves altogether, consisting of Delawares and some Wyandots under the leadership of the Delaware, Pekillon.

They had left their camp at Gnadenhutten two days ago and had crossed the Ohio earlier that morning at the island that was later called Boggs Island, a few miles south of where they stood. Another small war party had left the same day and had crossed upstream at Short Creek, where they had carried out a raid in the neighborhood of Fort Van Meter

"That is Wheeling Fort up there," said White Eagle, pointing to the stockade perched on the hill a quarter of a mile upstream from them. "Pekillon hopes to burn it down, and kill everybody in there."

The chief directed ten of his men to advance along the Ohio shore and along the bluff under the west wall of the fort. The rest skirted the cornfield that was in front of them and came up among the trees on the sloping hill to the east of the fort. The only possible approaches to attack the fort were from the east and the north.

As they came closer and could get a good look at the structure, Little Fox grabbed White Eagle by the arm. "What do you think that is?" he asked, pointing at a platform seeming to rise out of the center of the enclosure with something mounted on it.

"Looks like a cannon," said White Eagle. "But there is no cannon at Wheeling Fort. At least that is what the Wyandots say."

Little Fox had seen cannon before. They had them at the fort in Detroit, but this one didn't look quite right to him. Still he could see others pointing at it, and the warriors closest to Pekillon were in an intense discussion with him. Suddenly there was a commotion off to their right, where some braves had come upon three boys playing near a spring at the base of the slope. One was quickly slain; and a second, captured. The third boy had run away and past the southernmost of the cabins that stood east of the fort.

The Indians gave chase with much shouting, spoiling any chance of surprise that Pekillon may have been planning. The boy reached the east gate when one of the Indians fired at him, the ball hitting him in the hand. The gate flew open, however, and the injured boy made his escape. The cabins were mostly abandoned, but the one shot by the Indian was answered by a volley from the southernmost cabin, the fortified home of Ebenezer Zane. The Indians were astonished to see a young woman run from the house to the southern gate of the fort, and after a few minutes, she returned carrying something. Not a single shot had been aimed at her.

The prisoner, an eleven-year-old boy named David Glenn, was brought to Pekillon, who knew enough English to question him. The boy willingly gave up the information that the settlers had been warned and had taken refuge in the fort. Young David also divulged the important information that the supposed cannon was actually a fake, made entirely of wood. Pekillon was furious. "The Moravians sent a warning to the Long Knives. It is good that they are being dealt with."

Some scattered shooting was going on, but there were no real targets. It was clear to Pekillon that there was little chance of taking the fort, and he directed the warriors to set fire to the cabins and kill the livestock. But even this, carried out halfheartedly, was not very successful. The fort's defenders were able to keep a fairly constant fire at any movements they saw; and after a few minutes,

Pekillon's forces were gathered out of range and along the trail leading up over Wheeling Hill. At least half of the warriors were dejected and ready to return home while the remainder was eager to continue the attack.

The Indian band divided here, with one part taking the prisoner and going back to Gnadenhutten. The rest, about forty in number, went with Pekillon, who led them over the big hill to Wheeling Creek below and along the trail that led toward the forks and the former site of Shepherd's Fort. Little Fox and White Eagle were with this party. Neither of them had performed even one hostile act so far and were quite disappointed.

As they tramped along moving deeper into the white man's country, their spirits lifted, and Little Fox began to feel more confident that he was finally going to get his chance to fight the hated Long Knives. Pekillon had determined to make an attack at Catfish Camp if possible; but if not, he knew there were plenty of isolated farms along the way that would make easy conquests.

Discovering no one present at Shepherd's mill, he led his followers on up Little Wheeling, and when they came to the point where Middle Wheeling joined, he stopped. One of the warriors, who had been scouting ahead, came to the chief and pointed excitedly to something along the bank of the stream. Pekillon followed him and made his own investigation.

"Ah," exclaimed the chief. "Three horses headed upstream, and they must be ridden by white men. Let us follow."

The three men had set out at midmorning from Miller's blockhouse, making their way across the Dutch Fork of Buffalo Creek and into the wooded ridges to the west. They were looking for stray horses, and while at that task, they were also alert to any Indian sign they might encounter. Jacob Miller, though the youngest of the three, had assumed leadership of this mission. After more than an hour of frustrating and difficult passage over the rough terrain, which had produced no success in either purpose, he called a halt.

"I think we ought to split up for awhile," he suggested. "Those horses have got to be out here somewhere."

"'Les the Injuns found 'em first," offered Frank Hupp.

"We ain't seen no Injun sign neither," chimed in Jacob Fisher.

"It's possible the horses strayed over the east ridge 'stead of this direction," observed Miller.

"You thinkin' we ought to go back, then?" asked Fisher, who thought that sounded better than splitting up.

"No, I reckon we'll keep lookin' around here," said Miller. "But we can cover more ground if we separate."

"Separatin' is a good plan when you're lookin' for horses but not so much when it's Injuns you're after." Hupp shared Fisher's misgivings.

They were near the top of a ridge, and Miller walked up to a slightly open area at the top. He pointed down in a southwesterly direction to a low heavily wooded region in a valley between the ridges.

"There's the head of a small run down in that valley," he said. "That'll make a good spot to meet up again. Frank, you go to the left and circle in from that way. I'll go up to the right, and Jacob, you just go straight down from here."

Hupp and Fisher looked at each other, both showing their disagreement with Miller's plan, but they said nothing.

"Well, I'm going," announced Miller. "I guess you can stay here if you want, but I'd rather we meet down there at that little stream. Keep your eyes open." With that, he adjusted his hold on his rifle and strode away.

Hupp gave a shrug. "Well, I ain't stayin' here," and he started off to the left, leaving Fisher with no alternative but to start down toward the meeting point.

An hour had passed, and Fisher had reached the designated meeting spot sometime before that. He didn't like the fact that he was by himself, and he began to worry whether something had happened to his companions. The sound of someone crashing through the brush off to his left sent him scurrying behind a big oak tree standing near.

"Hey, it's me, Frank," was the shout. "Don't shoot me now, Jacob."

Fisher stepped out, feeling a rush of relief. "Sure am glad you spoke out, Frank. I was gettin' a little skittish, waitin' here by myself."

"I figured that all right," answered Hupp. "Did you see anything?"

"Not a thing," replied Fisher. 'What about you?"

"Not much. I did see a couple of horse tracks, but they wasn't fresh. Miller'll come in with a coupla scalps I suppose."

"I don't reckon so," said Fisher. "If it was Lew Wetzel, I might."

"Ha," came the laugh, as Miller appeared walking in alongside the little ditch in which a small trickle of water was flowing. "So you don't think I'm as good a hunter as Lew, eh? You boys hurt my feelings."

He sat down on a fallen tree limb, which angled across the little run.

"Course, if I was an Injun, you two would be dead."

"We knew it was you all right," laughed Hupp. "No Injun I ever knew could make that much noise."

After resting for several minutes, the three men decided to swing to the south, venturing all the way to Little Wheeling Creek. It was past midafternoon when, as they moved slowly upstream, Frank Hupp thought he heard something.

"Did you hear that?"

"What? I didn't hear nothing," said Miller quickly.

"It was faint, but it sounded like rifle shots to me," said Hupp. "Did you hear it, Fish?"

Fisher wasn't sure. "I might have heard somethin', I don't know."

"Where was it comin' from?" Miller asked.

"Off to the south and east a bit, I think," replied Hupp. "Wait, there it is again."

"Yeah, I heard it that time," agreed Miller. "That's off toward Link's place. Do you suppose they're under attack?"

"Maybe we've found some Injun sign after all," exclaimed Hupp.

"We'd better go have a look," said Miller, and he immediately splashed across the stream and began ascending a sloping hill in the direction of the sounds they had heard. Hupp and Fisher followed quickly behind. Over the next ridge, they came to a very small stream.

"I think this one goes all the way down to Middle Wheeling," said Miller.

"Then we can follow the creek right to Link's place."

"We've heard no more shooting," noted Fisher. "Maybe we should just go back to your place."

"It'd be way past dark before we could get there. I think we'd better just stay at Link's for the night."

"What if the Injuns have taken the place," asked Hupp. "That might be what the shootin' was about."

"If so, they ain't likely to still be there," Miller pointed out. "We might need to see if anyone is left and bury the dead."

"That ain't a pretty thought," said Hupp. "But I reckon you're right. We'd better hurry, the old sun is gittin' low."

By the time they reached the clearing, Link's blockhouse was dimly illuminated in the last streams of the fading twilight. There was no sign of life at all, but neither was there any indication that a battle had taken place. The three men hesitated in the trees at the edge of the open area, but Miller ventured out a short way.

"Haloo, the house. It's Jake Miller. Anybody home?"

After a moment had passed, the door to the house opened, and Jacob Link stepped out. "I'm here, Jake. Is that good enough for you? Come on in."

The visitors, filled with relief, hurried forward grasping Link's extended hand, and all talking at once.

Miller was finally able to make himself heard. "We heard some shooting, and thought you were under attack."

"Well, you might say that. We had a shootin' match, and Lew Wetzel won the jug."

"Lew was here? Where is he now?" Miller considered Wetzel to be a good friend. They had spent many hours together while out with Brodhead.

"Him and Moses Shepherd came in with George Blackburn, who was bitten by a snake. They took him on toward Catfish to see a doctor. I sent my wife and kid with them."

"So you're here alone?" Frank Hupp had joined the conversation.

"Reckon I am, Frank. Hawkins and Burnett were here too, but they went on with Wetzel." Link eyed the three men for an instant. "The wife left me some johnnycake, and there's some jerked venison too. You fellas might as well spend the night."

"We'll take you up on that offer," said Miller. "It's too dark for us to get to my place now."

The four men enjoyed the supper and the conversation that went with it. Link was peppered with requests for details about the shooting match.

"Wish we'd got here in time for that," said Miller. "I figure I can outshoot Lew Wetzel."

"I surely doubt that," said Link confidently.

As they prepared to ascend to the loft, Link's two dogs began to put up a fierce ruckus. He let them out, as the others all picked up their rifles.

The dogs continued their barking, although they did not venture far from the cabin.

"Maybe somebody ought to take a look," proposed Miller.

"I don't think so," replied Link. "Them damned dogs will bark at anything. Probably a wolf is snoopin' around."

"Could be a red wolf, I'm thinkin'," offered Hupp.

"I sure wouldn't want to go out there right now," said Fisher. "We're better off in here."

"Let's go to bed, men," insisted Link. "I don't think there is anything to worry about. You didn't see any Injun sign did you?"

"We didn't see any sign, but I don't think that means much. It's when you don't see the bastards that they get you." Frank Hupp tended to take the pessimistic view.

The dogs had quieted, and the men went to bed. After a short time, the hoot of an owl and an answering hoot came to their ears.

"Do you think that was really an owl, or something else?" Jacob Fisher had stood up and walked toward the ladder, as if he intended to go back down to the ground floor.

"Go back to bed, Jacob," said Link. "Unless you intend to go out and look around." Fisher realized he was making a fool of himself; and while his uneasiness refused to be put down, he returned to his bed. The night passed without further incident, although the sleeping men were uncommonly restless.

Pekillon and his Indian band had worked their way carefully up Middle Wheeling Creek as carefully as was possible with nearly forty warriors. There were braves on both sides of the stream, and Little Fox thought there were too many of them to sneak up on anyone. He wasn't sure about what Pekillon was expecting to find ahead, but Little Fox was pretty well convinced that there couldn't be any large group of the enemy on this little creek.

He and White Eagle had stayed in the center of the band near to Pekillon. They could see the one-eared brave, Red Storm, just ahead. He had prevailed upon his uncle to let him come along even though his wound was certainly not yet healed. Revenge was uppermost in his mind, for he was sure that at some point in this raid, he would see the big hunter who had inflicted this damage upon him.

Some excitement had occurred shortly before dark when a scout on the left side had discovered the tracks of three more white men moving in toward the creek and turning upstream in the same direction as they were traveling. This was getting much more interesting, thought Little Fox, for there were at least six enemies not too far ahead of them. Pekillon had signaled a halt, and there was a discussion between him and three of his closest lieutenants. Little Fox sought out his friend White Eagle, who always seemed to know just what was happening.

"Why did we stop, do you think?" he asked White Eagle.

"We are not far from a cabin that the chief knows about. He does not want to arrive too soon and alert the people there. The plan is to attack in the morning. We will wait here and move into position during the night."

Little Fox laughed. "How do you know these things, my friend? Do you listen to Pekillon's thoughts?"

"Perhaps I do, Little Fox. You may laugh, but you will find that I am right."

"That, I did not doubt."

"Let us see if we can be in on this attack. Come." White Eagle beckoned to Little Fox to follow him, and they moved up beside Red Storm, who was clearly intent upon joining the circle of men around the chief.

Word was passed through the warriors that there would be no cooking fires and that silence was required of everyone. About half of them were selected to move forward quietly through the dark and completely surround the cabin, which was no more than three quarters of a mile further along. As they came to the clearing where Link's blockhouse stood, some moved to the woods on the north side of the clearing while others moved along the creek bank, hoping to get in among the buildings.

The barking of the dogs brought everything to a standstill, and when the cabin door opened to let the dogs out, the whole line shrank back. Little Fox and White Eagle, who were near the creek bank and just short of the little milkshed, froze in their tracks. If the dogs continued toward them, they would have to act, and Pekillon's plan would be foiled. Little Fox couldn't see why they didn't just attack anyway; it seemed to him that the numbers were clearly in their favor.

The dogs did not advance, however, and after a few minutes of barking, they retreated to the front step of the blockhouse and laid down. Every warrior's eyes were on the door, expecting that it might open, and an enemy appear. Although the night sky was bright with starlight, it was difficult to see, and there was no light inside to help them see if the door was opening. When an owl hooted from the trees back near the creek, a young brave near Little Fox answered with a sound that had Little Fox searching to see if there really was one of the feathered creatures in the tree behind him.

Another warrior had grasped the hooter firmly and put his hand over the young man's mouth. After a few moments, there were no more sounds other than those usual to the night. The attackers settled down to catch some sleep and await the morning's action.

The morning came with no breeze and a hanging, heavy sultriness that encompassed everything. In the branches above him, a blue jay scolded Little Fox with his loud cry. The young Chippewa warrior shrank back farther behind the trunk, sure that the jay's harsh call would give him away to the men in the cabin. Shortly the bird flew away, and it was mostly quiet but for the usual sounds of a new day awakening.

The sun had begun to peek over the hills to the east, and Little Fox wondered when Pekillon would begin the attack. The normal plan was to wait for an enemy to open the door and step out at which point shots would be fired and a rush made to get through the open door. He adjusted the grip on his gun, checking for the fifth time that it was ready to fire. He wiped the sweat from his forehead and continued to watch the front of the cabin. When the door finally opened, two men stepped out, and in spite of his keen anticipation, Little Fox remained still as they walked slowly toward the spring some fifty feet from the door.

Strangely his companions did the same. The white men were laughing, completely oblivious to the danger lurking near. Reaching the spring, one bent down and brought water to his face, and the other took a step toward the woods on the other side. It was then that a shot rang out, followed by several others. The man moving toward the woods, Jacob Fisher, dropped in his tracks while his partner, Frank Hupp, started running back toward the safety of the blockhouse.

Little Fox fired his rifle now, although he saw no effect of it. Halfway back to the house, Hupp was hit, and he tumbled to the ground. Indian attackers erupted from the woods on all sides and from behind the buildings. Hupp gathered himself and jumped to his feet, racing toward the door, managing to stumble inside just as a second shot hit him in the leg. Jacob Link, who had rushed toward the open door at the sounds of the battle outside, tried to push it shut as Hupp slipped past him. But two young braves hurled themselves against it from outside.

While this struggle went on, two other Indians brought a small log they had found at one end of the cabin and shoved it into the opening, preventing Link from shutting it even as the two braves stopped pushing and stepped away. One of the others now fired his rifle into the house through the door, making it clear what would happen to anyone who tried to remove the log. The attackers were fully aware of the danger in being the first one who tried to enter the house, however, and there was a momentary impasse.

Little Fox and White Eagle had come to the front of the house and were standing near Pekillon when a shout of triumph came from near the spring, and one of the Delaware warriors lifted his rifle aloft in one hand and the bloody scalp of the slain Jacob Fisher in the other. This brought answering war cries from all sides. Pekillon, who from his long association with the whites could speak English fairly well, addressed the inhabitants of the cabin.

"You in the cabin. Let us stop the killing now. Come out." There was no answer. "You cannot keep us out," said Pekillon after a short time. "If we come in, we kill you all."

Little Fox could hear talking from inside, and though the words were unintelligible, he could tell the men were arguing. Pekillon turned to the warriors around him and nodded his head, a clear signal to the others to make a rush through the door.

"We come now!" Pekillon shouted.

"Wait! Wait!" came the cry from within. "What is your promise if we give up?"

"We not kill," answered Pekillon. "We take you captive to our village."

"And burn us at the stake?" asked the speaker, Jacob Miller.

"Not kill," said Pekillon again. "I promise nothing more." Pekillon stepped up close to the half-open door. "Show now, with no weapons."

Miller and Link stepped cautiously in front of the opening, as Pekillon pushed the door open further.

"Where are the rest?" asked Pekillon. "We saw tracks of six."

"The others left before dark yesterday," answered Miller quickly, "along with his family." He had nodded at Link as he spoke.

Little Fox and the others moved inside, pushing past Pekillon and grabbing Miller and Link, binding their hands. Miller had hoped they might forget about Frank Hupp, who had managed to ascend to the loft to breathe his last. The trail of blood was clear, however, and Hupp's body was retrieved and dragged outside where the scalp was taken, bringing another great cheer from the bystanders.

Pekillon dispatched a party of scouts to go ahead of them, looking for targets or for possible danger. Two Wyandot warriors were given the task of watching the prisoners and bringing up the rear while the rest all moved forward upstream along Middle Wheeling. Pekillon had indicated that there were other settlers' cabins in another creek valley beyond the ridges ahead of them.

After an admonishment from the chief to quiet their celebrations, the entire group of warriors moved out at a good pace and with remarkable silence. After a trek of about three miles, they were met by the returning scouts who gestured excitedly to Pekillon, pointing back in the direction from which they had come. Little Fox and White Eagle pushed in as close as possible.

There were more cabins not far ahead, and the group thrust ahead again, anxious to repeat the success at Link's house. They halted again along a hill that bordered the valley of the creek the white men called the Dutch Fork of the Buffalo. The word was quickly passed to take cover, for the sound of horses and riders had come to the scouts.

Little Fox found a place along the ridgetop that afforded a grand view of the valley below where he could see the cabin of Presley Peak, although Little Fox had no idea about that. He noted that Red Storm had moved in beside him, and White Eagle was lying next to him on the other side. As they watched, a party of more than twenty horsemen appeared, coming down the trail from their right. This trail was the much used path that went between Catfish Camp and the settlements around Fort Henry. As the riders came by in front of them, Red Storm suddenly stiffened and looked intently at one of the riders.

"What is it?" whispered Little Fox. "What do you see?"

With his finger, Red Storm scratched out a ragged W in the dirt. "There!" replied Red Storm emphatically, pointing at one of the riders below.

"What?" asked White Eagle who had sat up when he heard Red Storm's declaration. He looked down at the riders and then back at Red Storm. "The one who cut off your ear?"

"Yes," said Red Storm, who had raised his rifle to his shoulder.

"No," hissed Little Fox. "You cannot shoot now. You will give us away."

"I do not care," snarled the angry warrior. He pushed away from Little Fox and once again raised the gun to take aim.

"Nephew!" was the sharp command. "Do not shoot!" Pekillon had appeared suddenly and now grasped the rifle and wrested it away from Red Storm. "Why do you behave so badly?"

"He thinks he saw the white man who hurt him," put in White Eagle.

"It does not matter. We cannot reveal our presence just yet. Red Storm, can I trust you now?" Pekillon had taken his nephew by the shoulders and was shaking him.

"Yes, Uncle." Red Storm felt humiliated, which sharpened even more his hatred and desire for revenge.

The white men had ridden out of sight, having paid little attention to their surroundings, clearly headed toward Fort Henry. As soon as they were clear, Pekillon gave the sign to proceed, and the warriors moved down and across the valley, completely surrounding the Peak cabin, shouting their war cry and shooting their rifles.

There were three men in the cabin, and the owner, Presley Peak, had slipped out a window in the back and tried to make his escape through a patch of hemp growing there. He was seen immediately, however, and the shower of bullets tore through the hemp but missed their target. Peak made it to some bushes just past the hemp but found it occupied by several braves who quickly made him their captive. Meanwhile, the men remaining in the cabin—the two Williams, Burnett and Hawkins—realized the hopelessness of their predicament and gave up the fight by tossing their weapons out the front door, shouting out their intentions to surrender.

The captives were quickly bound and questioned about the nearby farms, which his scouts had told Pekillon about. To the left was the farm of Edward Gaither, less than a mile downstream from Peak's place. A Delaware brave named Long Arms was given charge of fifteen warriors and sent to attack the Gaither cabin. Pekillon took another eighteen men with him to go upstream to the Hawkins farm, and the remainder were left to guard the prisoners.

September 4, 1781

Edward Gaither sat down with his family to enjoy dinner, watching as his wife finished putting the food out and helping the youngest of their two children to his place. He had been cutting a little patch of hay to add to the small stack already standing just back of the shed. He was tired from the work and looking forward to enjoying this noon meal. When the sounds of gunfire reached their ears, it upset everything.

"What is that shooting?" asked his wife immediately, the concern obvious in her tone and the dark look on her face.

"Injuns, I reckon," said her husband. "Down at Peak's."

He jumped from his place at the table and took his rifle down from its holder above the door. "Take the kids, go out the back, and get in the woods as fast as you can. Go all the way up to Miller's if you can."

"Ain't you comin' with us?" his wife asked.

"Yeah, but I want to get the cow if I can. We'll need her this winter. We'll leave everything else here, and maybe they won't follow."

When she continued to stare at him, he motioned her on. "I'll catch up to you."

Without another word, Mrs. Gaither grabbed each child and pushed them out a back window, and with a long look at her husband, she scrambled out behind them.

"Stay in the woods!" Edward shouted after her. He then dashed out the front door and angled over toward the hayfield, which lay next to the creek.

He thought he'd seen the cow there earlier that morning. He didn't see her now, but then a flutter among the stalks of corn caught his attention. "Damn," he muttered. "She's got into the cornfield."

He changed course, moving toward the spot where he had seen the movement. As he neared the edge of the cornfield, a dusky warrior suddenly stepped out, and Gaither noted the missing ear just before the tomahawk sank into his skull, ending his life.

Red Storm gave a shriek of delighted triumph and took out his scalping knife, quickly removing the farmer's scalp. Long Arms and the rest of his band had now appeared, and they moved in concert toward the cabin. It was soon discovered that the cabin was empty, and the leader entered, followed by a half dozen of his braves. They were all smiles as they saw the table laden with good things to eat. Long Arms gave a grunt of satisfaction and motioned to the warriors to sit at the table and eat. This they did with great relish, and the others joined them from outside.

There was some scuffling as the late arrivers tried to get some of the disappearing food. The warriors were in a happy mood, and when they had eaten everything they could find, they filed out. After killing what livestock was found nearby, they set fire to the cabin and set off in the direction of Peak's place to rejoin their friends. The friends had gone in the opposite direction, going upstream to the home of William Hawkins.

Hawkins, who had been captured at Peak's, when he realized that his own place was the next target, had pleaded with Pekillon to take him along. He would talk his family into surrendering, and they would all go back as captives to the Indian villages. This fell on deaf ears, and the chief directed Hawkins to be bound and kept with the other prisoners. The Hawkins' farm, like that of Gaither's, was less than a mile from Peak's, and the sound of the fighting there had alerted the inhabitants to the coming danger.

Mrs. Hawkins was there with her four children: The youngest, a babe in arms, was no more than two weeks old. The oldest was a young teen named Elizabeth, who was sick with a fever and barely able to function. Also present was George Blackburn who had stubbornly decided to travel no further, doctor in Catfish Camp notwithstanding, and demanded to be left at the Hawkins cabin by Wetzel and his party early that morning. Mrs. Hawkins knew her husband was at Peak's, and she worried about what might have happened to him. The safety of her children was more pressing, however, and her first and best instinct was to take them and run.

"Take the little ones and go over the bluff," insisted George Blackburn, who had finally stopped thinking of his own misery and was trying to take charge in this emergency. "I'll take the lass, and we'll head into the corn. You can travel much faster without us."

Mrs. Hawkins wasted no time in arguing. Taking up the infant, she commanded the other two to follow her and whisked out the door and up the steep bluff at the back, the family dog in pursuit. They had disappeared over the top and were well out of sight by the time Pekillon and his braves came into the yard in front of the cabin. The escape path taken by Blackburn and Elizabeth Hawkins was soon discovered, and since neither of them could move with any speed, they were soon overtaken.

Blackburn was quickly killed and scalped, but Elizabeth was taken captive. Too weak to even put up any resistance, she was led out of the cornfield where a great shout went up at the sight of this pretty young prisoner. White Eagle motioned to Little Fox and another warrior named Walking Deer to follow him to the bluff behind the cabin.

"There had to be others in this cabin. Let us see if we can find them." Little Fox, not satisfied with his own part in the raids so far, was eager to be part of this mission.

Nothing more was said, and the three braves quickly ascended the hill and dropped down to the stream on the other side. They made their way upstream, searching carefully the banks on both sides. After some seventy-five yards, they came to a small run flowing in from their left. Not more than ten yards up the run, where it bent slightly to the west so that it was blind to its mouth, Mrs. Hawkins squatted low in the water, holding her infant tight against her. She put her finger to her lips as she turned to look at the other two children, huddled under some bushes on the bank.

Mrs. Hawkins tapped her lips to indicate that they should be quiet. The sound of the three braves talking, where they had stopped along the big creek, brought a rush of fear to the mother, and she stuffed the bottom of her apron into the baby's mouth to prevent him from making any audible sound. Then the low growl of her little dog sitting on the edge of the stream caused her to reach out frantically, worrying that the dog might suddenly run out into the open. She could not reach him and could do nothing but stay as quiet as possible, though a quick whisper of a prayer escaped her lips. *Could they have heard that growl?* she wondered. She watched as the dog looked at her expectantly, and she felt the baby squirm. All seemed lost.

At the mouth of the run, Little Fox had stepped out into the shallow waters of the Dutch Fork.

"We should check up this tiny stream," he said. "They could easily have turned up here."

"Yes, but wait! I thought I heard something up ahead." White Eagle ran on up the main stream a few feet. "I hear a horse walking up there."

"I hear it too," said Walking Deer, who moved immediately to join White Eagle.

The sound of voices convinced Little Fox, and he followed the others. After going a short distance toward the sounds, White Eagle stopped. "It is at least two whites on a horse," he said. "And they are coming toward us."

"We saw no such tracks," noted Little Fox. "Could they have turned around?"

"It does not matter. Let us take cover. Walking Deer, you cross the stream and get behind that stand of trees just ahead. Little Fox and I will set up on this side."

White Eagle's orders were quickly executed, and it was not long before a horse with two riders appeared along the narrow trail on the side occupied by White Eagle and Little Fox. Wasting no time, Little Fox raised his rifle barrel and fired, watching with satisfaction as the man, whose name was James Walker and who was riding in front, toppled to the ground. All three Indians jumped out of hiding and caught the horse's bridle before it could turn to run away. The young girl, Walker's daughter, was taken down off the horse but not harmed.

"Get the horse," White Eagle said to Walking Deer. "We will take the girl back to our village."

He watched as Little Fox, with a loud cry of triumph, took Walker's scalp. "Let us return to the others now."

Indicating to the girl that she should walk behind him, White Eagle motioned for Little Fox to follow behind Miss Walker while Walking Deer came last with the horse.

The sound of the gun and the shouting had spurred Mrs. Hawkins to action. She had watched in unbelief but with relief when the dog, never taking its eyes from her, had settled down with its head on its paws. She had stayed put even after she came to know that the Indians had moved on upstream; but now, knowing they might well be returning after an encounter with someone, she moved out of the water and herded her children farther up along the west bank.

She could hear the Indian party coming back, and she knew they had to be still again. Finding a stand of small saplings surrounded by several low bushes, she pushed the two children in among them and followed herself. She had feared that she might have smothered the tiny boy in her arms, but there was no choice. He was still breathing, however, as she sat down beside the others. This time she managed to get the dog to lie down at her feet. There was nothing else to do but wait. As the three braves and their captives (including the horse) came again to the mouth of the small run, Little Fox thought an investigation should still be made.

"Did you see any tracks before?" asked White Eagle of his determined friend.

"No, but they could have stayed in the water and left no tracks."

"We have done enough. It is time to return before the others leave us behind." White Eagle smiled at Little Fox. "You have killed a hated white man and taken his scalp. Be happy, my friend."

Little Fox shrugged and gave a wave of his hand, indicating that he would go along. Still he took a quick look up the run, going a few feet before turning back. He patted the bloody scalp hanging from his belt and took his place in line again behind the young girl.

Jacob Miller sat on the fallen tree trunk with his hands firmly tied with rawhide. They were on a ridge to the south and west of the Peak house, and Miller was joined on the log by four other prisoners, Link, Peak, Hawkins, and Burnett.

Pekillon, who had been with warriors at the Hawkins cabin, had rejoined the others, although not all of his men had arrived. A discussion was held by Pekillon with several of the braves present, after which the chief came and confronted the prisoners. He spoke with each one, asking questions about the number of fighters the whites had in the vicinity at the time. Miller had offered the number of 150, at which Pekillon grunted and shook his head in disagreement.

Attention was paid to Hawkins, whose red hair was tousled by several of the warriors, one of which pointed at him in an accusing manner. This warrior then went to Hawkins and jerked him to his feet, pushing him along to one of the several saplings growing nearby. Others followed suit with Link and Burnett, whose heavy shock of dark hair had invited handling by several of the braves. The three unfortunate men who had been chosen were each tied to a sapling. For a few moments, the warriors danced in front of them, making menacing gestures with their tomahawks, shouting and spitting on them. Finally each was tomahawked and scalped.

"Now we be militia!" exclaimed one of the braves in broken English.

The others laughed and began making preparations to move on.

"What was that about?" Presley Peak managed to whisper to Miller. "Are we next?"

"It had to do with Brodhead, I think," answered Jacob. "The militia killed some Indians there just like that." He had nodded at the figures slumped against the trees.

"But why'd they spare us?" Peak had risked the question in spite of some angry stares from the braves standing near.

"I ain't sure," whispered Miller without looking at Peak. "I guess it's old Pekillon honorin' his promise to me."

Miller and Peak were placed in the middle of the line, and they began to move out toward the Ohio, retracing the route the Indian party had followed from Link's. They continued along the north bank of Middle Wheeling Creek, and shortly they were joined by White Eagle, Little Fox, and the others, bringing along the two female prisoners. Miss Walker and Miss Hawkins were momentarily cheered when they saw the two white men walking ahead of them.

Elizabeth Hawkins searched in vain for sight of her father; but even in her misery, she was able to mask her severe disappointment. She knew that her demeanor could mean the difference between remaining in captivity, or in being put to death as too much trouble for her captors. She looked forward to having a chance to speak with Miller, who was someone she knew and trusted. Miller was thirsty, but the prisoners had been offered nothing to eat or drink.

Eventually the leaders crossed the creek and set out upon a rough trail that led up to the top of the low-lying hills and then descended again to a tiny rivulet that Miller thought was the one called Turkey Run. If they continued in this way, they would come to Big Wheeling Creek, no more than a mile or two from the Wetzel homestead. This seemed strange to him, but then he supposed their intent was to cross the Ohio well below Wheeling.

This was not the most direct route to the Delaware towns, but perhaps Pekillon was worried about running into a militia army that might be out searching for them.

A party of white men had passed near them earlier in the day. Nightfall came upon them, and as they came to the banks of Big Wheeling Creek, a halt was called, and a camp was set up. A fire was built some distance back from the camp, and food was prepared for the Indians. Apparently a hunting detail had brought in some meat, but Miller did not know what it was or when it had been obtained. Perhaps it was something that had been confiscated from the whites. He could smell it when it was brought back from the cooking fires, and he realized that he was ravenously hungry. No one brought any food to the four captives, who were being kept well separated from each other.

Miller had caught the eye of Elizabeth Hawkins, who had looked at him inquisitively, hoping, he knew, for some word of her father and the rest of the family. Before he could convey anything to her, she was whisked away and out of sight. He knew that the other girl's name was Walker, but he had only one brief glimpse of her. He had been separated from Peak soon after they had stopped for the night. Eventually one of the warriors did appear with a bowl formed out of a gnarled tree root and filled with creek water.

He drank it with relish, assuming that his fellow prisoners would also receive at least this much. Miller could see that the Indians were tired and ready to sleep, and it was not long after full darkness that the camp was quiet as the captors had quickly settled in for the night's rest. The prisoners were tied and fettered with a thong fastened to a guard lying next to them. It was not possible for them to communicate with each other, and Miller had been thinking hard about making an escape. His hands were tied in front of him, and the rawhide cords were wrapped around his body and arms, holding them tight against his sides. The line was then looped around the waist of a big brave who had fallen asleep. His feet had also been tied together.

His plans for escape, Miller realized, were not very sophisticated. Try as he might, he could not loosen the bonds by any exertion of strength, and the only sharp weapon of any kind available to him was his own teeth. Tightly bound as he was, he discovered that he could bend his head just low enough and his wrists just high enough that he could get one of the thongs, where it left his hand, into his mouth. Having learned this was possible, he had to wait until all were asleep. The other problem was that he had to do the chewing without pulling on the tether enough to awaken his guard. He was almost afraid to even try for fear it would quickly prove impossible.

With no other hope before him, Miller began the task, despising the taste, and seeming to make no progress. He stayed at it stubbornly, but his mouth and jaw were soon aching from the effort. He stopped for a few moments and listened carefully for any sounds that might indicate someone was aware of what he was doing. Miller returned to his chewing but becoming more and more dejected, for he could detect no progress. He began to think about his fate.

The women would probably be left alive and taken to the villages to become the wives of some warriors. He could think of no reason that Peak had been spared, and he had little faith in Pekillon's promise to him, particularly after he had watched the execution of Burnett, Hawkins, and Link. Clearly Pekillon was taking retribution for what had happened at Coshocton, and Pekillon knew that Miller had been on that expedition.

Miller went back to his task with renewed vigor. Surprisingly, his tongue detected a small tear in the rawhide, and he focused his attention on that spot. His spirits began to rise as he realized that he was actually beginning to work his way through the tough cord. Forgotten now were tired jaws and a sore mouth; and it wasn't long until he felt the strap loosen against his arm, and he knew that the thong was nearly cut through.

The brave next to him turned slightly but did not awaken. Miller waited patiently for a few minutes and then began again to untangle himself from the loosened bands. At last he was free, and he eased himself to his feet. It was not easy in the dark to make his way to the edge of the camp, avoiding the sleeping bodies sprawled everywhere. He thought briefly of the other prisoners but decided he had no chance of freeing them without being discovered. He also rejected the idea of trying to secure a weapon of some kind. The best plan was to get away from there as quickly as possible.

During the ordeal of chewing on the strap, Miller had been thinking about which way to go should he manage to get free. He could follow Big Wheeling downstream, but that could lead pursuing braves directly to the Wetzel farm. He could try to backtrack and head to his own home, but that was a considerable distance away, and he could not be sure that some of the Indian party were still back along that trail.

The best choice seemed to be to strike out to the north where eventually he would hit Middle Wheeling and then go west toward Shepherd's mill. With this decided, he made his way out of the camp and, noting that the creek was to his left, circled his way around the western edge of the sleeping Indians and struck to the north.

September 5, 1781

Henry Jolly was feeling frustrated. He and his twenty companions from Washington County, Pennsylvania, had been riding back and forth for days in response to Indian threats and were yet to see a hostile.

Four days ago they had gone to Fort Van Meter, arriving after an Indian raid had ended. They returned to Catfish Camp, only to be called out again yesterday morning when word came of an attack on Fort Henry. On their way, they had met Lewis Wetzel escorting Mrs. Link and her child to Catfish, along with Moses Shepherd. When Wetzel learned of their mission, he had joined them, leaving Shepherd to take the Links on to their destination.

Now they were returning from Fort Henry, and as they neared the forks, Jolly turned to Wetzel, who rode beside him.

"Will you leave us here, Lew?"

Before he could answer, Wetzel saw his friend Jacob Miller step out from behind the mill and wave to the riders who had stopped just short of the spot where Little Wheeling Creek merged with its big brother. Wetzel, Jolly, and two others splashed their mounts across the stream and dismounted next to where Miller awaited them. Wasting no time, Miller quickly explained to his friends what had happened to him, describing what he knew of the Indian raids on the Link, Gaither, Peak, and Hawkins homesteads. After a discussion of what to do, it was decided to go immediately to those sites and take care of the dead.

"Shouldn't we see if we can find them reds?" Wetzel had asked.

"There are too many of 'em, Lew," Miller had assured them, and the rest of the men readily agreed. "They're likely well on their way to the Ohio by now, anyway," he continued.

Knowing that the mutilated bodies of Hupp and Fisher lay unburied at Link's, Miller suggested that they go by there first and then follow the trail the Indians had followed the day before. There was some discussion of splitting into two groups, but that idea was soon rejected.

One of the men, John Bradford, said he had some business to attend to up Peters Run, and that he would rejoin them when they reached the Dutch Fork. It was past midafternoon when they had completed the cleanup and burial rituals at all but the Hawkins place. Here they found Bradford waiting for them by the road. Henry Jolly was in the lead, and Bradford came up to him. "Henry, there is a woman and her children up this little run on up ahead. She needs help."

"Are they hurt?" asked Jolly, who had dismounted.

The others rode up as close as possible, trying to hear what was being said.

"I don't think so, but they're mighty scared," answered Bradford. "They are soaked. Sat out there in the rain all night. I couldn't get her to come with me, so I said I would get help."

"Do you know who she is?"

"She said her name was Hawkins."

"Well, that makes sense. This is her place."

"She said she'd seen a party of Indians about two hours after noon yesterday."

The word *Indians* spread throughout the group of men like wildfire.

"Indians here two hours ago," someone shouted and spurred his horse forward.

"Let's get out of here," came another shout, and suddenly the entire party, with three exceptions, was riding at a gallop toward Catfish Camp.

"What the hell?" was all Jolly could think to say.

"We'd better go get Mrs. Hawkins," said Lew Wetzel quietly.

"I'll show you where she is," said Bradford.

"Damn!" exclaimed Henry Jolly, shaking his head and following after Wetzel and Bradford. "If that don't beat all."

Meanwhile, George Blackburn's body lay bloody and broken in the cornfield not far away; its presence known only to a few Indians and a young lady now their prisoner. Perhaps the rattlesnake had won after all.

7

A BLOODY YEAR

May 28, 1782

THE AFTERNOON WAS warm, and the soft sliding of the canoe in the slow current was making Lewis Wetzel quite sleepy. He reached back and loosened the tie that held his long hair in place and let it fall. Behind him, Jacob Miller was amused as he occasionally paddled and helped to steer the craft along the Virginia side of the channel.

"Some young red buck's goin' to have a fine time relievin' you of all that hair, Lew," he said finally with a laugh.

"Well, he might try," said Lew. "But tryin' ain't doin."

"Hell, they could get behind you and grab that hair afore you even knew they was there."

"You want to try it yourself, Miller?" asked Lew. "See what would happen?"

"Hell, no, not me. Some brave Injun I'm talkin' about."

"You're just jealous you ain't got such a beautiful topknot yourself."

Lew shook his head vigorously and turned back to look at Miller, giving him a vicious stare. Then he burst out laughing. Miller was a dear friend and a brave fighter himself, and he had lost his father during an Indian raid on the Miller blockhouse only two months ago. Wetzel was glad to see his friend was coming out of a rather dark period of despair. Young Miller had blamed himself for not having been at home when the attack came. Still Lewis knew that Jacob, along with two other men, had come from Rice's Fort and managed to get through the Indian lines and inside the house in time to save the women and one old man who were trying to fight off the attack.

It was good, Lewis thought, that Jacob had decided to come along on this Wetzel family hunt. Captain John had decided that the time was right for a hunt down on the lower Muskingum, and that is where they were headed.

"Since Crawford's out, the Injuns should be too busy to bother us," John Wetzel had said.

Colonel William Crawford and some 480 mounted men had embarked from the Mingo Bottom with the intended purpose of destroying the Indian towns on the upper Sandusky. Most of the men were from Washington County in Pennsylvania, joined by a large number from Westmoreland County and a few from Ohio County in Virginia. None of the Wetzels had gone on this expedition, and John had reasoned that with the Indians occupied by the invading army, it would be relatively safe for a hunt on the other side of the big river.

Having restored his hair to its usual state, bunched up and tied at the shoulder line, Lewis stared with satisfaction at the broad back of the man seated just in front of him in the center of the big fifteen-foot canoe. It was his long lost brother Martin, who had appeared less than two weeks ago with his new wife, the former Mary Coffield. George had been right about their brother's whereabouts and what he might be up to when the news of Martin's escape from the Shawnees had reached them over a year ago.

Their mother had been overjoyed when Martin and Mary showed up at the Wetzel farm, although Lew had noted that she was a bit put off at first, seeing her beloved firstborn in the clutches of another woman. But that had quickly passed, and there had been nothing but happy times in the household since. It was a bit crowded now, however, and Lewis had taken to spending most of his time at Fort Henry and Fort Van Meter when he was not in the woods. This hunting trip was his father's way of celebrating Martin's return.

George Wetzel was sitting in the front of the canoe, and Captain John was seated just behind him, dropping a paddle in the water occasionally when it was needed to keep them on course. After a late start shortly after noon, they had let the current carry them lazily down past Grave Creek, Round Bottom, Cresap's Bottom, Captina Island, and Fish Creek Flats. The stretch of the Ohio River called the Long Reach was not far ahead of them.

"That's Fishing Creek up ahead, I think," shouted George.

"I reckon you're right," said his father, "but you don't need to announce it to the whole country, I guess."

"Why don't we pull in there," suggested Martin. "I need to see a man about a horse anyway."

"Hell, Martin. What is this married life doin' to you?" chided Lew. "You're as bad as any woman."

"Watch yourself, little brother," said Martin as he turned and gave Lewis a sharp shove. "What do you know about women?"

"He knows about that Lydia Boggs, I reckon," chimed in Jacob Miller.

"Shut your damned mouth, Miller," cried Lew. "You don't know nothin'!"

"If you dandies don't mind, we'll just pull in there for the night," said Captain John. "Maybe one of you great hunters can catch us some fish for supper."

The stream called Fishing Creek flowed into the Ohio from the left, less than a quarter mile ahead, and they began angling the canoe in that direction. They were all glad that John Wetzel had decided to spend the night here instead of pushing farther down the river. Lewis was happy that Martin had mentioned the need to answer nature's call. It was not the kind of thing one liked to admit to other men. Lewis had noted that Martin still liked to refer to him as a little brother even though Lewis was bigger than Martin, and George, too, for that matter.

Martin was two or three inches shorter than Lew and his father. He often said that his growth had been stunted by all the heavy packs his father made him carry when they served together in Dunmore's War. Lew figured he could best any of his brothers, and his pa too, if they ever got in a fight. Of course, that wasn't something to be mentioned, or else it might have to be demonstrated on the spot.

A good landing place was found on the upstream side of the mouth of Fishing Creek, and they pulled the canoe up out of the water and behind a couple of bushes. There was a large black willow along the bank of Fishing Creek and a small stand of yellow birches a bit closer to the mouth. It was a good place to spend the night as they could establish their camp out of sight from the Ohio.

"Lew, you might best take a look around," suggested John Wetzel. "We don't want to be joinin' somebody else's party."

George and Martin took some old fishing poles they had brought with them and went to catch something for supper. George threw his line into Fishing Creek while Martin tried his luck in the Ohio. John Wetzel and Miller set about building a fire. Lew was gone for more than an hour; and when he returned, he was pleased to see that the fishermen had already been successful, for the smell of frying fish had reached him even before he had come out of the woods.

"There's nobody around here, for sure," he said to his father. "What little sign I saw was several days old."

"Good," said Captain John, "We can enjoy an evening in peace."

"Them brothers of yours is fine fishermen, Lew" exclaimed Jacob Miller. "Maybe you could take lessons."

"Hell, I didn't catch nothin'," admitted Martin. "I guess the creek is the best place to catch them catfish."

"Pa, I hope you ain't goin' to make us catch our own supper," said Lew. "I remember one time when you did that to Jake and me."

"Well it ain't a bad idea, but I guess George has caught enough for all of us this time."

With supper and the cleanup ended, the five men sat around the glowing embers of the fire that was slowly dying. Not much was being said when Martin spoke up.

"What's all this talk I hear about some kind of massacre up on the Tuscarawas a couple of months back?"

"You must mean Williamson's attack against the Moravians," offered George.

"I wouldn't exactly call it a massacre," said John. "Williamson's men were chasing a raiding party that raised hell up in Washington County."

"Uncle Lewis said they killed a bunch of the Christians."

"Christians or not, they trailed the raiders back to that village and found Mrs. Wallace's dress," said Lewis. "At least that's what I heard. You were there, weren't you, Jacob?"

Miller nodded but said nothing.

"What's this about a dress?" asked Martin.

"What I heard was that that some bucks attacked the Wallace farm up on Raccoon Creek and carried off Mrs. Wallace and her kids," continued Lewis. "A couple of weeks later, Williamson took an army and went to kill the red bastards on the Tuscarawas. They figured the raiders came from there."

"But Uncle Lewis said the Indians killed was Moravian Christians," protested Martin.

Lew knew that his uncle Lewis Bonnett had been with Williamson on that mission, but he hadn't received his information from him. Lew wasn't sure there was any important difference from one Indian to another, and besides, there was the business about the dress.

"But they found Mrs. Wallace's dress on some squaw at the Moravian village," explained Lew.

"And didn't they find her body along the trail?" This came from John Wetzel who nodded at Jacob Miller.

They all turned to look at Miller, expecting him to take up the narrative. Miller had wanted to stay out of the discussion, but he could see that would be impossible. He shrugged and began to talk quietly.

"We crossed the river at Mingo Bottom on about the fourth of March, I guess," he said. "The river was high, and it wasn't easy. Not long after that, we found the body of Mrs. Wallace jammed down on the sharpened trunk of a small tree. She was naked and bad torn. Her little baby was close by, all ripped and mangled. The men were pretty mad."

"Wasn't her husband along?" asked John.

"He was there and screamin' for revenge."

"I reckon he had a right to that," said Lewis.

"When we got to the village, we realized that it was the Christian Injuns that was there," continued Miller. "Mostly women and kids, but some men."

"No warriors?" asked Martin.

"There was a few painted up and with hair trimmed. Williamson wanted to take them all to Fort Pitt, but then some stuff was found."

"What stuff?" asked Martin again.

"Some of it was stuff taken from Wallace's place."

"How did the Christians explain that?" Martin Wetzel knew something about Indian life, and his days among the Shawnees had affected his outlook. He no longer subscribed to the common borderman's belief that there was no such thing as a good Indian.

"They said that a small party of Wyandots had come through and traded the stuff they had stolen for food. But some of them admitted that a few of the Moravian men had gone on the raids too. When they found the dress, all hell broke loose."

"That's when they decided to kill everybody?" Martin had heard only a little of the story from Lewis Bonnett, and he had found it hard to believe.

"Williamson took a vote. Only eighteen of us voted against the death penalty, and that includes your uncle."

Jacob Miller was sickened at the thought of all this again, but he went on after a moment or two of silence.

"They killed them with mallets and hatchets. Some of the Indians sang and prayed in the little church during the night, and they were all killed in the morning. Somebody said there was ninety-six in all. It was bad."

Miller wondered a little to himself at why he had such feelings about the death of a bunch of Indians. After all, they had just killed his own father. In fact, he could not help but think there might be a connection between the two incidents.

"Sounds to me like they deserved it," said Lew. "Course, I ain't too keen on killin' women and kids."

"I reckon I agree with Lew," admitted John.

Nothing else was said.

May 29, 1782

Joseph Parkinson had built a sturdy boat, one that could travel the length of the Ohio River and beyond, even down the mighty Mississippi. When it was finished, he left his business at Parkinson's Ferry on the Monongahela and took the boat to Fort Pitt, where he hired ten hands and loaded the boat with sacks of flour. Although it had not been done before, Joseph was sure that he could sell the flour in New Orleans at a big profit, if only he could get it there. He was confident that the boat could make it, and he thought the ten strong men he had employed were adequate to complete the trip against what he knew might be formidable difficulties.

In two hard days, they had reached Wheeling where they stopped for a rest; and pushing on in the morning of the fifth day, the boat, caught in the current and closer to the right bank than intended, ran aground on a sandbar at the edge of a small island. Parkinson was furious at this calamity, and he cursed the helmsman as well as any of the others who happened to be close by. He supposed the cursing did little good, but he was paying these rascals, and he figured it gave him the right to curse them.

One of the men had noticed a canoe floating in the reeds along the shore a short ways upstream, and two men were sent to retrieve it. When this was done, Parkinson set the men to unloading the flour from the boat and into the canoe where it was transported to a safe spot on the island. Eventually the boat was lightened enough to get it off the sandbar, and the reloading process was begun. By the time this was done, night was falling, and it was decided to stay there until the morning.

"Let's stay on the boat tonight, men," said Parkinson. "We're too close to the wrong side of this river to suit me, but I think we'll be fine on here."

Feeling a bit sorry for his verbal explosion earlier, Parkinson thanked the men for their hard work in freeing the boat. Unfortunately he didn't think to set up a watch for the night. During the night, a party of thirty Shawnee warriors had arrived on the scene, tipped off by one of their scouts who had been attracted by the loud talking and shouting of the men trying to free the big boat from the sandbar.

A half dozen of the braves had crossed the narrow channel from the shore to the little island and made their way alongside and then under the bow of the vessel. There they remained awaiting the morning. The rest of the party had arranged themselves among the trees on the nearby shoreline. Shortly after dawn, one of the men on the boat had awakened and made his way to the bow, thinking to relieve himself. As he neared the edge, a shadowy figure in the water below raised his rifle and fired a shot. The man tumbled into the water, and when a second man appeared, he was shot also. Some further firing came from the shoreline, and pandemonium broke loose on the deck.

The six Indians who had been under the bow had scrambled aboard and stood ready to shoot again. One of them, who spoke

English, shouted that if the men would surrender, they could be saved. After a quick survey of their predicament, Joseph Parkinson agreed.

"Stand down, men. We've got no chance."

It was all over then, and the nine prisoners were hustled ashore. The narrow channel between the island and the shore was not deep, and they were able to walk through it. A fierce argument broke out among the Shawnees, and Parkinson realized that his fate and his men's was being decided. To his relief, the prisoners, after having their hands tied, were led off into the woods accompanied by fifteen braves. Parkinson relaxed a bit when he understood they were being taken to the nearest Shawnee town. The remaining Indians, after a leisurely breakfast, busied themselves at unloading the flour from the boat, except for a few who moved up the riverbank to keep watch.

Upriver a short distance, the Wetzels had maneuvered their canoe into the current and were floating with little effort. They had let Miller off on the Virginia side a little way back, and he was hoping to find some game to kill for their dinner later on. The idea was to put ashore a few miles down and wait for him there. A small island came up on their left favoring the Virginia shore, and they swung wide of it, coming closer to the Indian side of the big river than they would have intended. It was then that Captain John caught sight of the Parkinson boat.

"What's that," he shouted.

"Looks like that big boat that they were saying came by Wheeling the other day," suggested Lew.

"I reckon that's right," said John. "Looks like they're unloading her."

Lew, who was in the front, straightened up suddenly. "By God!" he exclaimed.

"What?" cried Martin.

"It's Injuns!" said Lew with assurance, reaching for his rifle. "And a big bunch of 'em."

"That's who it is all right," agreed John. "We'd better get away from this side of the river."

George Wetzel, who was in the stern and responsible for steering, began to turn the canoe to the left. It was then that shots rang out from the woods on the shore closest to them, and George pitched forward, struck in the back just below his right armpit. A scream had escaped his lips, but then he sat up again as if possessed with new life. Somehow he knew that his wound was fatal.

"Get down, everybody, and lie flat. I'll get us out of this. I'm a goner anyhow."

John started to argue, but Lewis pulled him down next to himself, both lying flat on the bottom of the canoe. Martin had dropped down as well but not quite soon enough. A ball had grazed him on the right shoulder, causing severe pain but no real damage. George was paddling with all his strength, which was ebbing rapidly. Still he managed to get the boat turned; and though the current carried them a little farther downstream than intended, George was able to begin angling back toward the island that would give them safety.

"I'll try to get us behind that island," he managed to choke out. Blood was coming out of his mouth, and he could say nothing more.

Shots were still flying by them, some chewing holes in the side of their craft. Fortunately, the new shots continued to miss George, and there were no holes below the waterline. Martin watched his brother's incredible effort and wanted to jump up and take over, but he knew that George was right: the wound was mortal.

By now, Lewis and John had managed to get into a position to get off a shot, and one of them managed to hit one of the Indians firing at them. Jacob Miller, hearing the shooting, had raced through the woods and reached a spot where he could see the action. He took aim with his own rifle and managed to hit one of the warriors on the island. The canoe had reached the island passed by earlier; and with a last mighty effort, George propelled it past the end and into the channel on the far side.

A stand of willows on the island provided a saving screen, and they were out of danger, at least for the moment. Martin eased George down from his seat and laid him carefully on the floor. He grabbed the paddle and continued moving them slowly upstream. Lewis was paddling now too, and they began to make better progress. Even though they were moving past the cover of the trees, the range was too far for any effective shooting by the Indians.

John was bending carefully over his dying son, wiping the blood from his face. "Should we go ashore, Pa, and tend to George?" asked Lew.

"I think we'd better just keep going upstream," replied John. "We need to get George more help than we can give."

"That's right," agreed Martin. "Besides, we ain't out of this yet. Those bastards may decide to chase us. They've got us outnumbered."

"Where's Miller, I wonder," said Lewis. "If he was with us, I'd say we'd make it pretty hot for those red buggers."

"I never did see him. That had to be him shootin' though." Martin could see the grief on his father's face. "I'm sorry, Pa," he continued. "I'm afraid George was right."

John Wetzel just shook his head but said nothing.

"I reckon Jacob will just make his way back to Fort Henry and not try to get back with us," speculated Lew. "We can't worry about him now anyway. Pa wants us to get help for George if we can."

Martin was still feeling the pain of his own wound, but he didn't want to complain. Lewis and Martin continued to row hard against the current, staying as close to the Virginia shore as possible. They had passed several islands. The Indian threat seemed to be over, and now the fight was for time, which they could tell was quickly running out for their suffering brother. His breathing had become labored, and the loss of blood was continuing.

John, sensing the end was near, took his son in his arms and held him close. Martin reached down and put his hand against George's neck. He shook his head and bit his lip.

"Pa," he choked out. "He's gone, Pa. He's gone."

"I know," cried the grief-stricken father. "My boy is dead. He never did nothin' to deserve this."

Lewis did not know what to say. Nothing had ever happened to him like this before, and he couldn't have anticipated how he would feel. George had been very close to him, and they had enjoyed many hours together. He paddled even harder and wished he could do something to ease the pain that was building up inside. Revenge against the Indians occurred to him, but he knew that really would not help. Fighting against them was a natural part of life anyway.

"I'm so sorry, Pa," said Martin after a moment.

"I know, son," replied John. "There's an island just ahead. Maybe we should just put in and bury him."

"We can take him home, Pa. Wouldn't that be best?"

"It would, but I ain't sure them reds ain't comin' after us yet. I'd hate it if they caught us, and we hadn't given George a decent burial."

It was nearly sundown when they put the canoe into the island. Making their way to the highest spot on the island, Martin and Lewis dug a shallow grave, and they laid the body carefully down into it. Martin stood holding the spade, ready to begin the dreadful final process. The thought came to him that it was good they had brought the spade along.

"What a foolish thought at a time like this," Martin chastised himself. He waited, for he could see that his father wanted to speak.

"We should say something over him," said John. "We are a Christian family after all."

Both he and Lew bowed their heads.

"Lord, we ain't much for talking, but we loved our boy, George, and we know you loved him too. Please take him to be with you now." He stepped back slightly, and Lewis was amazed to see the tears forming in his eyes and dripping softly to his cheeks. He had never before seen his father cry.

"He saved us, you know, Lord," John said as the tears began to flow freely. In a voice just above a whisper, he said again, "He saved us."

June 7, 1782

Little Fox was there in Wingenund's town when they brought in the Big Captain. He was led right by in front of Little Fox's lodge. There was another man with him, a white man's medicine man he had heard one of the captors say. He called his wife, Spotted Fawn, out to see this spectacle. Little Fox had taken a wife during the previous winter, a few months after the birth of White Eagle's son.

White Eagle had insisted that Little Fox should marry, and he had arranged for his friend to marry his cousin, the daughter of his slain uncle, Spotted Elk. Little Fox had balked at first, not finding Spotted Fawn to be as attractive as some of the other young maidens he had noticed. But White Eagle was not to be denied, and Little Fox, who was anxious to have a woman, had given in. Now he was glad for the Fawn, as he liked to call her, had proven to be everything he could have wanted. He smiled as she emerged from the little hut and came to his side. "What is it, husband?" she asked.

"It is the white chief who led the soldiers against us. He has been captured by Wingenund's warriors."

Shouts and cheers were erupting everywhere in the village as news of this great triumph spread through the village. Someone shouted in good English, "Crawford!" Others took up the chant, trying as best they could to shout the English name. Some of the young boys and women threw pebbles at the white prisoners, and the crowd hurled angry epithets, crying "Gnaddenhutten."

Little Fox and Spotted Fawn stepped out and began following the others, hoping to see what would happen next. He knew that the Indians were using the massacre of the Moravians as reason for revenge, although Little Fox also remembered how the warriors had treated those same Moravians the previous summer when they forced them to come to the upper Sandusky.

"What will they do to him?" Spotted Fawn wanted to know.

"I think they will burn him," answered Little Fox quickly.

"Here?" she asked. "Will they burn him here?"

"I don't think so," said her husband. "They will want to show him off in the other towns."

Crawford had led his army into battle at a spot just west of the Sandusky River, a few miles upstream from Half-King's Town. They had taken refuge in a large clump of trees, later to be known as Battle Island, on the fourth of June after a sharp battle. Failing in his attempt to surprise the defending Indians who had watched while his army marched from the Ohio to the Sandusky, and after scattered shooting on the second day, Crawford had intended to press the attack late that afternoon. However, the arrival of a force of 150 Shawnees to reinforce a combination of Delawares, Wyandots, and British Rangers had changed his mind.

An attempted retreat during the night of June 5 and the morning of June 6 had disintegrated into a disaster. Although about 300 of the original force of 480 managed to escape together under the command of David Williamson, the others who had not been killed in the main fighting were scattered all over the area, some in small groups and some alone, all trying desperately to get back across the Ohio River somehow. Many of these men were killed or captured by bands of Indians out searching for them.

Colonel William Crawford and Dr. John Knight had become separated from the others and were trying to escape to the east, traveling at night and hiding during the day. At one point, four other men had joined Crawford and Knight; but on the morning of June 7, they were spotted by warriors from Wingenund's town just before they had managed to find a place to spend the day. Crawford and Knight were captured without a fight, and although the others were able to run, they were hunted down and killed.

The little procession with two braves in front of the captives and four others just behind continued to the town center, followed by the villagers, continuing to shout Crawford's name. Nine other prisoners were being held there, and they brightened at the sight of their commander, for they thought he had been killed. However, Crawford and Knight were kept separate and there was no chance for the white men to converse with each other. The crowd began to thin out and little more happened, except that a party of Delawares came into the town center waving two bloody scalps.

White Eagle, along with his wife Bright Moon and their son Swift Hawk, who was nearly one year old, had joined Little Fox and Spotted Fawn; and they all stood watching. The next day, eight Chippewas came into the camp with a white prisoner and accompanied by another white man carrying a rifle. The sight of his fellow tribesmen excited Little Fox, and he hurried along behind, hoping for a chance to talk to them. It was surprising to see this many of his brethren in this part of the country, although he knew that the British had convinced a number of the lake Indians to come to the upper Sandusky region to help fight against the expected invaders.

The Delawares seemed somewhat cool to these strangers, and a group of them went up to the Chippewas where a heated argument soon broke out. There was much pointing to the white prisoner although the other white man, still holding his gun, was ignored. When Little Fox was close enough to hear the voices, he understood that the Delawares wanted the prisoner to run a gauntlet. This suggestion was firmly rejected by the Chippewas. Eventually the Delawares gave up and invited the Chippewas to rest there for awhile, providing them with some welcome food.

Little Fox used this opportunity to interrogate the visitors, who were surprised themselves to find a Chippewa living here. "Who is the other white man?" he asked one of the men who called himself Running Otter.

The man was hesitant but finally answered. "He is our prisoner too."

"What?" exclaimed Little Fox. "How can that be?"

"Are you a Chippewa or a Delaware?" asked Running Otter. It wasn't so much a question as a challenge.

"You know I am a Chippewa. Can you not tell?" Little Fox touched his scalp lock and the stone hanging under his nose.

"But where are your loyalties? You are living as a Delaware."

"But the Delaware and the Chippewa are not enemies," protested Little Fox, who was becoming annoyed with this supposed brother.

"Did you see them try to take our prisoner away from us?"

"Ah," said Little Fox, beginning to see the light. "You were afraid they would take them both away."

"Yes," was the answer as Running Otter felt some relief that he was not betraying his colleagues. "We knew we had to come through Wingenund's town, and so we made it appear there was only one prisoner."

"But the gun," insisted Little Fox. "How could you give the white enemy a gun?"

"The gun is not loaded," Running Otter pointed out. "And the prisoner knows what would happen if he tried to take advantage. Besides, we told him that if he didn't behave, we would give him to the Delaware, who always burn their captives."

Little Fox was disappointed that none of these Chippewas knew of his home village. He had hoped to hear news of his father. One of them had heard of Black Wolf, but had no information. Little

Fox watched with a touch of sadness as the Chippewas moved on that afternoon, both prisoners safely in their care. Two days later, Red Storm had turned up at Wingenund's town and sought out Little Fox and White Eagle. That very morning, Crawford, Knight, and the other nine captives were led out and started on the more than twenty-mile journey to Half-King's Town.

Little Fox knew that they would be put to death in one of the Delaware or Wyandot towns in that vicinity. He and White Eagle had determined to go along and watch the burnings, but Red Storm had other ideas. The three of them had participated in the fighting at the island of trees called Battle Island and had gone with the main group of warriors trying to catch the large body of white soldiers who had escaped under the leadership of the hated Williamson.

A battle occurred near the Olentangy River, a few miles south and a little west of Wingenund's camp. The Indians were beaten off, and for the most part gave up a serious chase of the main body of troops after that. White Eagle and Little Fox had chosen that time to go home while Red Storm went back to his village above Half-King's Town. Now he had returned and wanted the three friends to try their hand at finding one or two of the stragglers from the white army who were still trying to get home.

"We wanted to watch the Big Captain burn," argued Little Fox.

"If we wait for that, it will be too late to track the white soldiers," said Red Storm. "I think my enemy W must be out there."

Red Storm had learned how to say the letter that was scratched on the tomahawk handle. He had taken to carrying that tomahawk, hoping to use it to take an ear for an ear.

"There's no way we'll find him out there," scoffed Little Fox.

"Then stay here with your wife where it is safe. I am going." With that, Red Storm stomped off in disgust.

"Maybe we should go with him," suggested White Eagle. "He was right the last time we refused to listen to him."

Little Fox nodded his assent, and they set out to catch up with their determined friend. They left early the next morning and took the well-traveled route that led to Coshocton. There were many tracks, but they were old, and there were no stragglers to be found. Below Coshocton they turned down the valley of the Stillwater. Here they found some tracks that looked interesting. Following slowly, they went over the ridges to the head of Indian Wheeling Creek. It was there that they met a body of Wyandots and Delawares traveling back toward upper Sandusky. From them they learned about a white man's horse that had been left to graze in the woods far downstream. A bell was tied to its neck, which indicated that the owner might hope to reclaim it. Several of their party had decided to stay there in hopes of catching the white soldier if he returned.

"Let us go there," said Red Storm. "There might be several of the soldiers coming back for the horse. It is a chance for us to take a captive."

White Eagle and Little Fox looked at each other, sensing that they both felt this was a futile endeavor.

"We've come a long way," said Little Fox with a shrug. "We may as well go on."

White Eagle agreed. "But let us spend the night here, for the sun has nearly gone from the sky."

The next morning, they pushed on down toward the Ohio.

June 12, 1782

Thomas Mills was feeling much relieved as he waded into the narrow channel of the Ohio River that ran past Zane's Island on its western side. He had escaped from the Sandusky battlefield with Williamson's troops, aided in no small way by the big gelding he called Gray. He was proud of the horse, and its strength had enabled him to evade capture more than once on the way to finding relative safety with the men riding behind Williamson.

The Indians had continued to harass the retreating army for several days but had finally given up. It was at least five days, Mills thought, since they had disengaged from the main battle and having gone down the valley of the Walhonding, or White Womans Creek as Mills liked to call it, they passed by a bit north of the old Delaware village of Coshocton. They had crossed the Tuscarawas not far from the abandoned Moravian village of Salem and below Gnadenhutten. It was there that old Gray had become lame and Mills was forced to stop and let him rest.

It had been less than an hour, but he was now well behind the others, and he set out with the intent to catch them. He knew that he couldn't hurry his mount too much, but he was confident that if he kept moving steadily, he would be able to overtake them in due time. As he rode, he began to hear sounds ahead and off to his left. He knew that Stillwater Creek could not be too much farther in front of him, and the noises implied that riders were coming up that creek and would intercept his path. He pulled off to the right, dismounted, and led Gray into a thick stand of spruce at the bottom of a low hill.

It wasn't long until a small party of Indians on horseback came into view on the main trail, no more than a hundred yards from where Mills was standing. They stopped only for a moment as one of them got down to examine the ground. He pointed in the direction taken by the white soldiers, and with a shout, the Indian party galloped off in pursuit. Mills gave a sigh of relief that old Gray had not taken a notion to communicate with the Indian horses, and made a quick decision. He would no longer try to catch up with his former companions but would strike out instead up the Stillwater, where eventually he could find a trail that led to Wheeling. This he had done, but he had pushed too hard, and as he came along Indian Wheeling Creek on the south side, Gray had given out.

There was nothing to do but leave him here, Mills thought. There were too many Indians about to risk spending the night there while the horse recovered. He removed the saddle and bridle and carried them over to a brush-covered depression not far from the creek bank. Hiding them as best he could, he returned to where the exhausted horse stood, having not moved since they had stopped. Gray belonged to his father, and Thomas hated to leave him there even though convinced it was necessary. He returned to where he had stashed the saddle, retrieving from one of the bags a small bell with a rawhide string attached. He brought it back and tied it around Gray's neck.

"I'll come back for him," said Mills aloud to himself. "And this will help me find him." He slung his rifle over his shoulder; and carrying only that and his hunting pouch, he strode off down the trail in the direction of Wheeling. He heard the tinkle of the bell, and he looked back to see Gray shaking his head from side to side.

"I reckon the damned reds'll find him too," he said aloud again.

But he turned and went on. Now he had reached the island and walked across its width. There were no canoes along the shore, and he prepared to swim the wide part of the river, aiming at the foot of the high bluff just below Fort Henry. There were times when the Ohio was shallow enough to walk across, but this wasn't one of them. He stacked his rifle and his pouch behind a tree, determined to get a canoe and return for them immediately after getting across.

Mills landed at the base of the bluff directly below the fort. He was exhausted, and he rested there on the muddy bank before scrambling up the steep path that led to the fort. His homeplace was up on Short Creek, not too far from Fort Van Meter, but he had no desire to go that far on this day. The sun was well to the west and its setting was not too far away. He remembered that there was an uncle of his, James Davis, living in a cabin in the cluster to the east and north of Fort Henry. He would go there now.

When he arrived at the Davis cabin, he was met outside by his young cousin Josh Davis, who was just past fifteen years of age.

"Hello, cousin Tom," said Josh with genuine enthusiasm. He greatly admired his older cousin and especially his status as a militiaman. "We thought you might be dead."

"Oh," exclaimed Tom. "What have you heard?"

"Pa said you'd been whipped," admitted Josh. "But I never believed it."

"Well, I'm afraid it's pretty much what happened. I'm just glad to be back with my hair still in place."

Josh stepped back and looked at Mills, then peered around him on both sides. "Where's your horse…and your gun?"

"Old Gray gave out a ways back on the trail, and I left my gun and powder over on Zane's Island. I suppose I ought to git 'em, but I'm too tired right now. I had to swim the damned river."

"I'll go and get your gun and pouch, Tom. I know where to get a canoe."

"Would you?" responded Mills. "I'd really be grateful to you for that."

Young Davis was surprised by the response, but thrilled. He had expected to have to make an argument. Now he wanted to get away before someone stopped him. His folks were not at home just then, otherwise, his father would no doubt put a stop to this. "I'm on the way!" he exclaimed.

"Wait, Josh. You'd better let me tell you where the stuff is."

"Oh yeah," said Josh, who had stopped and turned to face Mills with a sheepish grin on his face. "I reckon that'd be a good idea."

After giving the explanation and watching the boy go off with joy, Mills let himself into his uncle's cabin. He just wanted to lie down and sleep, but he realized that his clothes were still damp from the swim. He curled up on the floor and was soon fast asleep.

June 13, 1782

It was a full day since Thomas Mills had returned to Wheeling, and he had remarked to Josh Davis that he really should try to go back and retrieve his father's gelding.

"I'll go back first thing in the morning," Mills announced.

"Lew Wetzel is out on a scout but should be back tomorrow," Davis pointed out. "He'd be mighty nice to have along. I'd wait for him if I was you." Josh thought of Lew Wetzel as the best person on the entire border. He was so proud that Wetzel often spent time with him when he was around the fort.

"I ain't much for waitin'," said Mills. "If I don't get him soon, them reds'll have him."

"They might have you too." Josh was surprised at himself. He was sounding wiser than his cousin. Of course, he was hoping to go on this errand himself, and he wanted Wetzel to be along.

Mills was remembering the Indian party that had surprised him on the trail just a few days ago, and he knew there was great danger in what he intended. He also knew Wetzel's reputation.

"Are ya sure he's comin' back tomorrow?" Mills asked after a bit.

"It's what he said," said Josh.

"Wal, I guess I'll wait. But not past tomorrow."

Lewis Wetzel appeared at Fort Henry sometime after noon on the next day as he had promised. Mills and Davis were there waiting for him, and Mills approached Wetzel immediately.

"Hello, Lew," began Mills. "I've got a favor to ask you."

"Hello yourself, Tom." said Lew. "You was out with Crawford. When did you git back?"

"Just a couple days ago." answered Mills. Then he launched into an account of all that had happened since the expedition began over two weeks before.

Wetzel listened with interest. He had heard there had been trouble, but he hadn't talked with any survivors. Mills finished with the description of his horse's failure and how he had left him on the trail.

"I've got to git him back, Lew. He's Pa's favorite, and I just have to git him back. Won't you go with me?" he pleaded.

Lew remembered what it was like to have left a father's horse in danger. Still he wasn't keen on this proposed rescue operation. He had been scouting across the river a ways upstream, and he had seen plenty of Indian sign.

"I understand your wantin' to git that horse, Tom," he said after a minute. "But it ain't a good time to do it. Them woods across the river is full of Injuns lookin' fer trouble."

"I didn't see any down on the trail below Indian Wheeling," observed Mills.

"You think the damned devils just stay in one place, Tom? I tell you, they're thick as ticks on a hound out there, and they've probably got that horse of yours already."

The argument continued for a while. Wetzel, who didn't mind a little adventure, finally gave in. He did not want to go home, where his mother was grieving for his brother George. It seemed like she and his sister Susannah were constantly in tears, and he found himself fighting them back as well. Maybe the chance to even the score a little for George would be just the thing. It was decided to leave early the next morning. At this point, Josh Davis began his campaign to be included.

"Josh, it ain't a good idea," said Mills. "There's no way your pa would let you go on this trip."

"My pa ain't here. If we spend the night here in the fort, he'll never know."

"The hell he won't. And he'll have my hide over it fer sure. Tell him, Lew."

"I ain't tellin' him nothin'," protested Lew. "He'll make a scout yet. He's big for his age, and he's got mettle."

"But he's too young, Lew, and I don't want nothin' to happen to him."

"I don't want nothin' to happen to him neither, nor to me or you for that matter."

"Don't worry 'bout my pa, Tom," interjected Davis. "If somethin' happens to me, you ain't likely to be around to face my pa neither."

"He's got somethin' there," said Wetzel. "Besides, he can shoot, and an extra shooter ain't a bad thing to have."

That settled it, and they prepared to go out the next morning. They left by canoe from below the fort at daybreak. After angling just below the tip of Zane's Island, they rounded the island and paddled back upstream to a spot below the mouth of Indian Wheeling Creek. Here they stowed the canoe and moved up the ridge south of the creek. At the urging of Wetzel, they moved slowly and carefully along the ridge. They stopped fairly often, and Wetzel would look around while Mills and Davis rested.

"How far up here do you think it was?" Wetzel asked Mills after one of his little scouts.

"Not much farther. There was a spring there, I think."

"I know that place. It is called Indian Springs."

The day was very hot, and it was nearly noon. Wetzel knew that they were very close to the springs. "If there are any Injuns around, they're likely to be at the springs. Let me go ahead now, then Tom you come next, and Josh behind. Be on the watch."

With that, Wetzel moved on slowly, and the other two followed as directed. Presently, Wetzel stopped and motioned to the others to stop as well. He moved back toward them. "The springs are just ahead. Did you leave that horse tied, Tom?"

"No, I left him loose," answered Mills.

"Hell, he could be miles from here then," exclaimed Wetzel. "Josh, you keep a lookout here on this ridge. Tom and me'll see if we can find that horse."

He looked at Mills and shook his head. Wetzel and Mills started down toward the little valley below them where Josh assumed the Indian Springs were located. There were lots of trees and bushes there and a gentle slope rising up to the north behind. As they reached a row of bushes, Wetzel bent down to examine something that had caught his eye.

"Tom, watch out. There's been Injuns here and not long ago."

But Tom was no longer there; having heard the tinkling of a bell, he had broken into a run out in the open, pointing toward a big tree at the base of the slope.

"There he is," Mills shouted. "We've found him."

Wetzel saw the tree and the horse standing tied to the trunk. "Wait, Tom, that horse is tied. Injuns tied him!"

It was much too late, for a shot rang out, and Mills screamed and plunged to the ground. The bullet had caught him in the ankle, breaking it and throwing him down. Wetzel threw his rifle to his shoulder and fired a shot as a group of Indians broke out of the trees, firing their guns and rushing at the stricken Mills. Wetzel's shot felled one of them, and seeing that his companion was doomed, Wetzel began running back toward where Davis waited along the ridgeline. Davis could see that Wetzel was loading his rifle as he ran, and when he saw the Indians pursuing, he fired a shot and then began running himself.

It wasn't long before Wetzel had overtaken Josh, and the pursuit was still some distance back. Wetzel was a very swift runner, and as he himself had once proclaimed, no Indian alive could outrun him. He ran with long strides at a fast trot. He encouraged Davis to trot rather than try to run at full speed. As they ran, Davis looked back, and it seemed to him that the Indians were too close.

"There's only four of 'em after us now, Josh, and they've dropped their guns. I'm going to shoot the one nearest us." With that, Wetzel stopped, dropped to one knee, and turning his rifle on its side, tapped the butt. This move was done in order to prime the pan. Now he raised the barrel and squeezed the trigger. The leading warrior fell face down. The other three were startled, not expecting the white man to have a loaded gun. They slowed for a moment, but then plunged on, certain that there was no more danger from their quarry's rifle.

Wetzel and Davis ran on at a trot, and Wetzel reloaded his gun once again. The ridge made a turn or two, and one of the Indians cut across the turn and was upon them more quickly than Wetzel had anticipated. As Wetzel brought his gun up to fire, the big brave grabbed the barrel. There was a short tug of war, and then Wetzel jumped past the Indian, which turned the muzzle against the Indian's breast; and when he pulled the trigger, the blast ended the battle. The two white men began running again, now with only two warriors in pursuit. Josh was breathing hard and unsure whether he could go any further. As they ran near a high spot on the ridge, Wetzel spoke between quick breaths.

"Josh, when we make the next turn ahead, there's a high bank and a clump of bushes right below it. Jump down there and lay quiet 'til the Injuns pass. They'll follow me. I'll meet you at the creek."

Davis did as directed, jumping down and laying in the bushes. Wetzel ran ahead, and the first of the two trailing Indians followed him. Wetzel had turned again and shot the Indian as he came out from behind a tree. As he fired, Lew had screamed with an awful roar, which was becoming a customary act of his. Upon hearing the crack of the rifle, the second brave, who had stopped and was standing just above where Davis lay, gave a shout of frustration and began running back in the direction from which he had come. Josh waited for a few moments and then made his way north to the creek, where he found Wetzel waiting for him.

"You all right?" asked the scout.

"Fine," answered Josh. "God, Lew, you killed four of 'em."

"But I couldn't save Tom."

Neither one spoke again, and they made their way down the creek toward Fort Henry.

June 15, 1782

Red Storm had tried to hurry them, but Little Fox and White Eagle had found some interesting tracks leading off to the left of their line of travel. They were sure that the prints were those of a white man.

"He could be trying to get back to where he thinks the other soldiers are going," offered White Eagle.

Red Storm had expressed doubt there would be any white man going in that direction. "I don't think so," he said. "We have a much better chance if we get to where the white man's horse was left."

"But we're too late for that," argued Little Fox. "We know there are at least twelve of our brothers there waiting to see if anyone comes for the horse."

"There will be several white men coming for the horse. I am sure of it, and we will be needed there."

White Eagle had gone off the trail and through a small stand of saplings and some bushes, which hid him from their sight, although they could still hear him.

Red Storm lost his patience. "I am going on. You two must do what you think best." He stomped off down the trail, which had taken them along the right bank of the creek, the one called Indian Wheeling.

Little Fox was annoyed with both of his companions, but he felt sympathy for Red Storm; and he had to agree what little chance for action they might have, most likely lay in the direction Red Storm was going. He plunged in after White Eagle, and after a short argument, convinced him that they should catch up with Red Storm. Enough time had passed, however, that by the time they reached the place called Indian Springs, the encounter between the Indians and the Wetzel party was over.

There were eight Delaware braves at the site. The big gray gelding was with them, and one who was holding the horse had a fresh scalp at his belt. Another warrior was talking and gesturing, pointing to the ridges downstream and to the right. They were startled at the hurried arrival of Red Storm who had rushed ahead, with Little Fox and White Eagle also running up to the group, eager to find out what had happened.

"Did the white man come for his horse?" asked Red Storm, nearly out of breath.

The one who had been talking before, a Delaware named Long Pine, turned to answer. "Three came. We killed one, the others got away."

"More than got away," exclaimed the warrior holding the horse.

"Yes," admitted Long Pine. "He killed four of us."

"Who did? What did he look like?" Red Storm was highly animated. He had no doubt who this man was, although there was no real reason for him to know that.

"We shot the first one who was coming for the horse." Long Pine was ready to give a full account. "It is his scalp you see hanging there." He pointed to the brave holding the horse.

Red Storm nodded, then asked. "And there were two others?"

"Yes," continued Long Pine. "They ran, but not until they had shot Walking Man there." He pointed to a body lying crumpled in the grass. There was no sign of the body of Thomas Mills, although Little Fox saw it later. It had been dragged behind some of the bushes and badly mutilated.

"But one of them killed three others?" asked Little Fox. He knew what Red Storm was thinking.

"White Feather, Running Beaver, and Red Otter. They came with me to chase the two men."

"But how could this happen?" Red Storm was astounded.

"The big man, his gun was always loaded," explained Long Pine.

"Big man? Tell me what he looked like?" insisted Red Storm, his interest and curiosity highly aroused.

"He was a big man with much hair. That is all I can say. The other one was young and not quite so big."

"What do you mean that his gun was always loaded?" asked Little Fox.

"Both of them shot their guns at the first, as did we. We dropped our guns and ran after them, and then after a while, the big man turned and shot White Feather dead. We did not see him stop to load his gun. Twice more this happened." Long Pine stopped talking and spread open his arms in despair. He did not know what else to say.

Red Storm looked at Little Fox. "It is him, I think. It is W!"

White Eagle started to argue, saying that that there were many big white men with much hair. He stopped himself, seeing the fierce expression on the face of Red Storm. "Perhaps so, my friend," he said finally.

"Are you sure they are all dead?" Little Fox said to Long Pine.

"All but Red Otter. I did not see him, for I decided to come back here." Long Pine was sorrowful but not apologetic.

"Then we should go and see," said Little Fox. "At least we should bring back their bodies."

"And maybe we can catch this man whose gun is always loaded," suggested Red Storm with vehemence.

Two were left with the horse, and the others moved cautiously off in search of their slain brothers.

July 26, 1782

Betty Zane and Lydia Boggs were on his mind. He found himself thinking about girls more often than he would want to admit, and those two seemed to be there most often.

Betty was the young sister of the Zane brothers, who had recently joined her father and brothers after being left in Philadelphia for schooling. She was often around the fort, and Lew Wetzel, though he didn't suppose he was an expert on such things, found her to be quite beautiful. He liked her slim form and delicate features. She was vivacious and a bit of a flirt, so much so that she even flirted with young Lewis, whose awkwardness around her she found amusing.

For his part, Lew could never think of the right thing to say to her and usually retreated into a corner where he could just watch. He thought of a dance held in the commandant's quarters not long after Betty had arrived. He was watching her with great interest when her brother Jonathan eased up next to him along the wall.

"What do you think of my sister, young Lew?" he had asked with a grin on his face and mirth in his eyes.

"She's pretty much tops near as I can tell," Lew had answered.

"Why don't you dance with her then?" questioned Jonathan with a laugh.

“Oh hell, John,” said Lew. “She wouldn’t dance with nobody like me.”

“Sure she would. I’ll go ask her.”

“Don’t you dare,” exclaimed Lew. “I can’t dance nohow.”

Jonathan had laughed heartily and walked away. Later while Wetzel hadn’t yet moved from his spot along the wall, he noticed Betty looking at him, and then she winked. He figured Jonathan had put her up to it, but it still caught him by surprise, and he was mortified. Of course, in spite of his lack of experience, he knew what it was that went on between married couples, and he felt a tingling throughout his body at the thought of holding this pretty young girl in his arms.

He tried to smile back at her now, but she had turned away, and he hurriedly left the room, hoping no one else had seen him. Lydia Boggs was another matter. He had seen more of her because he was a friend of her brother Billy. And now that her father William had bought land and moved his family to a farm just a couple of miles below the Wheeling area, he saw her often. She was not shy, and he even imagined that she might like him some. She didn’t seem as untouchable as Betty Zane, who, he had learned, was interested in Moses Shepherd.

He didn’t think Lydia was quite as pretty as Betty, yet she attracted him even more somehow. Maybe it was her earthiness, although that was not a term Lewis would have used. He couldn’t describe this quality that he observed in her, but he was well aware of her affect on him. She was shorter than Betty and not quite as slender, but her breasts were prominent, and he felt that he was a fairly good judge of women’s breasts. Thinking about Lydia’s breasts made him smile, and it almost caused him to miss the moccasin print in the soft ground just off the path. He saw it though, and as soon as he knelt to study its shape, he knew it was not made by a white man and it was fresh.

He looked around in all directions before standing again, wondering what else he might have missed. It was more than a month since his adventure with Mills and Davis. He had gone into the hills south of Indian Wheeling Creek just two days ago and had seen no Indian sign until now. He was on his way back up the river, intending to cross at Zane's Island, and here he was no more than a half mile below the island that was beginning to be called Boggs Island, since it was opposite the land recently purchased by the Boggs family. Wetzel stood finally and inspected his rifle, making sure it was ready to fire. It was early afternoon, and the day was hot.

He moved along in the direction indicated by the track he had found, and he soon found another. The Indian was moving along the path parallel to the tree line, which ended at the riverbank. Lewis knew that the Indians often used the islands such as Boggs Island to help them cross the Ohio, and he figured that this warrior was heading directly to the shore opposite the island.

"This red buck ain't doin' much to cover his trail," said Wetzel aloud to himself. "And he ain't too far ahead neither."

He came to a break in the tree line, and he could see the island in the distance. There was tall grass and some light brush in the open area, then another clump of trees. Wetzel dropped to a crawl, keeping his head below the taller grasses until he reached the trees. He looked for some sign of his quarry and eventually saw a broken twig just a few feet to the left of where he had entered. A natural path led along the base of a low-rising hill, and Lewis followed it, stopping often to listen and examine the forest floor to both sides.

It seemed to Wetzel that he should be close to what he had thought was the Indian's intended destination. He heard something that sounded like singing, a female voice. His eye then caught sight of his prey, kneeling behind a big maple and watching something intently. Wetzel dropped down behind some bushes and stared at the husky brave. What was he looking at?

Lewis backed up a bit and shifted to his right where there was a small opening in the trees through which he could see to the riverbank. What he saw nearly took his breath away. A woman stood at the edge of the stream, splashing water on herself. She was completely naked, and she was singing softly. Wetzel knew immediately that it was Lydia, and he could not take his eyes off her. When she began to turn, Lewis was so enthralled that he nearly forgot his dusky friend who was sharing this view.

Lydia stepped toward the canoe that was pulled up on the bank near where she stood and reached for the towel, slung over its side. In so doing, she exposed her front side to the two men watching her with avid attention. Lewis was conscious of the effects this sight was having on his body. Her breasts were as beautiful as he had imagined, and as his eye dropped down to the dark thatch between her legs, he could scarcely keep himself from crying out. He felt the desire well up within him, and he wanted to rush down and take her in his arms.

Lydia casually lifted the towel and began to dry herself, completely unaware of the two men watching her from so nearby. Lewis, remembering finally the danger to Lydia crouching behind the big tree, looked to see what the warrior was doing. The Indian, as if mesmerized by the erotic show in front of him, had not moved. This couldn't last much longer, and Wetzel eased back into the woods behind him and moved to a position advantageous for an attack. How should he do it without revealing to Lydia that the two of them had been peeping at her. He could not wait much longer, he knew.

He dropped down to a prone position and raised his rifle, sighting through the opening at the Indian who stood next to the tree, still watching the girl. His face was painted and a stone hung from his right ear. Wetzel aimed just in front of the dangling gem and squeezed the trigger. The ball slammed into the unsuspecting brave in the right jaw, plowing through his mouth and out just under the left eye. He dropped instantly and without making a sound. Wetzel could hear the scream from Lydia, but he waited for a short while before moving.

He was confident that the Indian was dead, but he made no move to go to the body and retrieve the scalp. He could not see Lydia now, but he figured that she was scrambling to get dressed and get the canoe out into the river. Waiting until he thought she was probably dressed, he then pushed through the trees, making as much noise as possible. Lydia was visible as Wetzel neared the edge of the woods, and he could see that she was no longer naked. She had put on the gown, but he could see that her petticoat was still in the canoe. She had crouched down by the side of the canoe that was nearest the river, and as he came into the clearing, she screamed again.

"Lyddy, it's me, Lew Wetzel," he shouted, hoping to stop her screaming.

It had just occurred to him that they might not be alone, even though he had seen no one else.

"Who?" Lydia stopped screaming but remained half hidden by the canoe.

"Lew Wetzel!" exclaimed Lew, louder this time.

Now Lydia stood up and immediately recognized the young hunter.

"Lew Wetzel, you fool. You look like an Indian. You scared me to death."

"That wasn't my intent, Lyddy," protested Lew.

"Was that you shooting?" Lydia demanded, walking around the bow of the canoe and approaching Lew. Her expression had changed from one of fright to one of fury.

"I reckon it was," admitted Wetzel.

"What were you shootin' at then?" Lydia wanted to know. "I thought somebody was shootin' at me."

"I was shootin' at a rabbit, Lyddy. I missed him."

"I thought you was supposed to be a crack shot," said Lydia, beginning to calm down.

"Suppose to bein' and bein' are two different things, mebbe," said Lew.

He had decided it was better not to mention the Indian.

"Well, everybody says you're one of the best shots on the whole border. Guess you got 'em fooled."

Another thought occurred to her, and she felt herself beginning to blush. "When did you first see me?" she asked suddenly.

Wetzel was ready for this question. "Why, just when I came out of the woods," he explained. "I saw you crouchin' there behind the canoe. Why do you want to know that?"

"None of your business, Lew Wetzel." In spite of herself, Lydia's face broke into a coquettish grin. "Maybe I wasn't dressed proper for receivin' company."

Wetzel stole a glance at the petticoat draped against the side of the canoe. "Maybe you ain't dressed quite proper even now," replied Lew, surprised that he would talk that way to a girl. He surely would never say such a thing to Betty Zane.

Lydia had seen his glance, and she blushed even more. Still she was feeling a certain excitement at this turn in the conversation. "Well, it's better than it was before I heard that shot. I was takin' a bath in the river."

"I sure wish I had seen that!" said Wetzel emphatically.

"You're bad, Lew," said Lydia. "Would you have watched me without warning me?"

Lew realized he could be on dangerous ground here, and he answered accordingly. "Of course not, Lyddy. Why, you're my friend Billy's little sister."

"What difference does that make? Does that mean if it was some other girl, like Betty Zane, you would have watched?" Lydia was not particularly fond of Betty Zane. It was rumored that she was engaged to Moses Shepherd, a young man that Lydia had in mind for herself.

"No, I wouldn't have looked at Betty Zane neither. Listen here, Lyddy, it ain't smart for you to come over here by yourself like you did. I could've been an Injun, and if I was, you'd be dead about now."

"Well, I ain't dead, and I don't like you sneakin' up on me like some Injun anyway."

"I didn't sneak up on you, Lyddy. I'll go behind these bushes and turn my back while you finish gittin' dressed. Then I'll take you back home."

Wetzel did as he promised, and Lydia finished dressing. She wanted to stay angry with him, but she supposed she didn't really have a good reason. The look on his face, though, made her wonder if maybe he had seen more than he was admitting. When she was ready, she called to him and climbed into the canoe. He laid his rifle carefully on the bottom and pushed the little craft out into the water, jumping in as the current began to carry it away from the shore. He took the paddle and began the trip back around Boggs Island and to the shore on the other side.

Two days later, Lydia sat in the commandant's room at Fort Henry when John Linn came in to talk to her father, Captain John Boggs. The two men spoke for a few moments when a remark of Linn's caught her attention.

"Funny thing, Captain," said Linn. "Across the river, in the woods across from your island, I found the body of a dead redskin. He'd been shot through the head but wasn't scalped. I don't know how long he'd been there, but he was beginnin' to stink. His gun was leanin' against the tree right where he fell. I didn't see no sign of any others around anywhere."

A puzzled look came across Boggs' face. "Weren't you over there a couple days ago, Lyddy?" he asked his daughter. "Lew Wetzel said he'd found you there. Did you hear anything that day?" Boggs had intended to address the matter with his daughter and give her a good scolding, but he hadn't got around to it yet.

"Not a thing," said Lydia immediately, wondering how much Wetzel had told her father.

The men looked at each other and shook their heads. "Let that be a lesson to you, Lyddy. You'd best not go over there again like that," said Captain Boggs.

"I won't, Pa," answered Lydia.

Some rabbit, she was thinking to herself.

September 11, 1782

They were on the same trail they had been on nearly three months ago, heading toward the Ohio River and the big island across from the Wheeling fort. It was the second time that Little Fox, White Eagle, and Red Storm had been along on an expedition whose aim was to capture Fort Henry. The first one, which had taken place a year ago, had resulted in failure to take the fort, but had led to some exciting action at several settler's cabins a bit farther along.

The three warriors were confident that the current effort would meet with much more success. This time there were over 250 of their fellow braves plus a contingent of 40 British rangers under the command of Captain Andrew Bradt. The presence of the British should have been a very important addition to the strength of the little army; but to Little Fox and most of his brethren, the British were also a problem.

The Indians did not like Captain Bradt and resented taking any kind of orders from him. Bradt, of course, considered himself above the red savages, as he thought of them, and he was unable to get them to follow his lead. Several times along the way, the Indians had threatened to simply go home. It was only the presence of the renegade, Jim Girty, that had kept them all together and moving toward their objective.

The Indians, particularly the Delawares, had been planning a strike against Fort Henry since the end of their victory over Crawford in June. At one time, 1,000 warriors and 150 rangers had been slated to move against the Virginians at Wheeling, whom the Indians held responsible for the massacre at Gnadenhutten. It was a matter of revenge, and all the tribes understood the feelings of their Delaware brethren on this score.

Little Fox was certainly sympathetic to this view, although he also remembered that there were very hard feelings against the Moravian Indians by the same ones who were now screaming for revenge. The Wyandots had been the ones pushing for the Moravians to be moved the previous year and had even threatened violence and death against them if they refused to move. Revenge was a good motive, though, and Little Fox was glad to see so many of his race focused on killing white men.

Plans had gone awry, however, when reports came of movement by George Rogers Clark, who supposedly had a large army pointed toward the Indian villages at Wapatomica and Sandusky. The Shawnees refused to move any further to the east and eventually the Shawnees, some of the Wyandots, the lake Indians, and a body of British rangers under Captain William Caldwell began to move south, headed toward the mouth of the Little Miami on the Ohio.

Before they reached there, however, word came that the reports of Clark's movements were in error. This led to humiliation of the Shawnees, especially at the hands of the lake Indians; and the Shawnees mostly went home in shame and anger. Eventually a combined party of Indians and rangers, over three hundred strong, attacked in Kentucky, winning a big victory at Blue Licks. The Shawnees, who were usually concerned about events in Kentucky, were mostly absent from this fight.

The Indians who accompanied Captain Bradt in the march to Wheeling were Wyandots and Delawares, with a smattering of Shawnees and lake Indians. Unknown to the Indians was the fact that the Revolutionary War was essentially over, and orders had been sent from Major DePeyster in Detroit to his commanders in the field to refrain from any offensive moves against the Americans.

The order to Bradt, however, had arrived after his departure from Wapatomica, so he had no idea that this expedition was unauthorized. It had begun under the understanding that there was a threatened campaign against the Sandusky villages by an

American army originating at Fort Pitt and Wheeling. Indeed, such a move was being planned, but it had been postponed, and in fact would be canceled because of the peace negotiations.

Little Fox was watching as James Girty and Captain Bradt held a spirited conversation. Girty was trying to explain something, it appeared; but the British officer was having none of it. He clearly gave some order to Girty, who turned away with disgust, but went to gather the Indian leaders together. Little Fox followed along, eager to hear what was going on. He recognized the ground they were on, for it was not far from where the white man's horse had been tied, just three moons ago.

Neither of the principal Delaware chiefs, Pipe and Wingenund, was on this mission. A chief named Peketelemund, who was perhaps the next most powerful chief among the Delawares, was there along with another war chief called Hailstone. Pekillon was along also, but his standing among the Delawares was somewhat diminished. The prominent Wyandot, Half-King, was also missing; and the principal chief among the Wyandots was a village chief named Roundhead. There were some others who were mostly unknown to Little Fox.

Girty gathered them around him at the edge of the trail. "The captain wants you to send some scouts out in front to make sure the Long Knives do not learn of our approach and give warning to the settlements," Girty began.

"We do not care what that fool captain thinks," said Hailstone. "He cares nothing for us."

"He thinks we are ignorant savages," agreed Roundhead. "Why should we listen to him?"

"He commands British soldiers," answered Girty. "You want to destroy Wheeling Fort, don't you? Those soldiers will be a big help."

"We can do it without them," said Hailstone indignantly. "Let them go away, I say."

Captain Bradt could see that the conversation between Girty and the Indian leaders was not going well. He strode into the circle, signaling to Girty that he wanted to speak directly to the chiefs. Girty and the chiefs had been seated while they conversed, and Girty motioned to Bradt that he should be seated himself. The young captain refused, spitting out some angry words, which caused Girty to flinch, and Little Fox could easily imagine that the words were not kind ones.

The arrogance of the officer was obvious to the Indians and contributed heavily to their dislike of him. Bradt talked directly to the Indians seated in front of him, with Girty providing the interpretation. The Indians did not listen, however, and talked quietly among themselves, ignoring the exasperated captain entirely. Girty, not wanting to tell Captain Bradt the truth that the Indians had no faith in him, explained that they didn't understand what he was trying to tell them. Determined to make them understand, Bradt began telling of his experiences with the Iroquois in the Mohawk Valley, explaining how he and Joseph Brant, the Mohawk war chief, had pulled off an ambush.

Even without a translation, the chiefs understood the name of Brant, which aroused their ire even more. Although the British captain could not have known it, there was no name he could have uttered that was more hated by the Ohio Indians. Brant, who had tried to command them in some earlier adventures on the Ohio River, was regarded as an arrogant blowhard, and the chiefs informed Girty that they would quickly abandon any commander who was a friend of Brant.

After a bit of hard persuasion, Girty and some of the cooler heads were able to head off this disagreement, and it was finally agreed that scouts would be sent ahead. Little Fox had observed all this with disgust, for he wanted to get on with the assault on the hated fort at Wheeling. He found Red Storm and White Eagle, and the three of them volunteered to join the scouting party. They moved out with scouts flaring out into the woods on each side of the trail.

A few of the Indians were mounted, as were several of the British Rangers. They moved to the front, not far behind the scouting party.

Ahead of them, less than an eighth of a mile, there was a rise to a small ridge that crossed the trail. Little Fox could see movement in the crotch of a big tree just to the side of the trail. To his amazement, he saw a man slide to the ground, dropping a pack near the base of the tree, and running to a horse standing nearby.

"White man," yelled Little Fox at the top of his voice, pointing up the trail as the rider and his horse disappeared over the ridge. "Catch him!"

The scouts on the flank were not far enough advanced to cut off the rider, but the mounted Indians just behind Little Fox set off in furious pursuit. Little Fox knew that their hope for surprise was lost if they didn't stop this rider. Captain Bradt and James Girty rode up just a few minutes later.

"What is it?" Girty asked Little Fox.

"A white man was watching us."

"Where is he? Did we get him?"

"No," said Little Fox sadly. "He had a horse, and we will not catch him."

"Damn!" exclaimed Girty, and it was echoed by Bradt.

It was an English word that Little Fox well understood.

September 16, 1782

The attack on Fort Henry by the combined Indian and British force began on the afternoon of September 11, 1782. Lewis Wetzel was not at the fort during this attack, but he learned about it later, having importuned Jonathan Zane to tell him everything in detail. He knew that John Linn, having been sent to scout by Ebenezer Zane, had brought enough warning that the nearby settlers had been able to get into the shelter of the fort. A pang of regret had come to him when he heard this, for it was Lewis Wetzel who should have brought such a report.

He had laughed when he heard about the fort's answer to Captain Bradt's surrender demands. The little swivel gun, which had been rescued from a watery grave at Fort Pitt, had been brought to Fort Henry and installed on a platform that was raised higher than the walls of the fort. The gun had been fired at the appearance of the British flag, a big surprise to the attackers, who remembered that the supposed cannon in the 1781 attack was actually made of wood. Captain Bradt was heard to yell, "There's nothing wood about that gun!"

Wetzel's two favorite women were both in the fort at the time, and Lew was delighted to hear about the heroic part played by Betty Zane. Earlier in the summer, Colonel Ebenezer Zane had requested a supply of gunpowder from General Irvine at Fort Pitt. Spurned at first, Zane had persisted, and although he held no official government position, his standing and reputation resulted in Irvine's approval of the request. The powder was sent, but Zane was ordered to keep it in his own blockhouse so that it would not be misused.

On the second day of the battle, the store of powder inside Fort Henry was nearly spent. A constant stream of gunfire was needed to keep the Indians back and prevent them from setting fire to the fort and to Zane's blockhouse. Inside the blockhouse, in addition to the colonel and his wife Elizabeth, were Andrew and Molly Scott, George Green, and the colonel's slave, old Daddy Sam, along with his wife, Katie. The fire from the blockhouse had been very effective in disrupting the Indian forays against the fort.

At the fort, it was clear that someone had to make a run to Zane's blockhouse to get gunpowder. Sixteen-year-old Betty Zane volunteered for the job, saying that she could most easily be spared, could run swiftly, and maybe the Indians would not bother to shoot at a woman. Her brother Silas, who was in command of the fort in the absence of John Boggs—who had gone to Catfish Camp for help—finally agreed. The south side gate was opened, and Betty ran out, quickly covering the sixty yards from the gate to the blockhouse.

"We were amazed," Jonathan Zane told Wetzel. "The Injuns didn't shoot at her at all. They just yelled 'Squaw, Squaw.' They shot at her plenty on the way back though."

Betty had carried a keg of gunpowder poured out into her apron. Shots fell all around her as she ran back to the fort, but nothing hit her.

"She's got some spunk," marveled Wetzel.

"She saved the day all right," Zane had agreed.

The other great and amusing story involved the Indians' attempt at constructing a wooden cannon. At about the same time that the Indian army had arrived at the fort, Daniel Sullivan and two other men had put in at the usual landing spot below the fort in a boat loaded with cannonballs intended for George Rogers Clark at the Falls of the Ohio. They immediately came under fire from the Indians, and they rushed up to the fort, Sullivan having been wounded in the foot just as they got through the gate.

The Indians had discovered the cannonballs, and after the setbacks of the first two days, they had decided to make use of them. They found a hollow tree trunk and managed to fashion it so that a cannonball would fit into the hole. They had wrapped chains around the trunk to strengthen it and sometime in the afternoon of the second day carried it to a position out of effective range of the defender's rifles and pointed it at the walls of the fort.

Some of the men on the fort walls could see what was happening and watched with interest. When one of the braves touched off the powder, the makeshift cannon exploded, sending splinters in every direction, killing several of the Indians close by and wounding others. After one more failed attack that day, the Indians and rangers decided to abandon the siege early the next morning. No doubt, Zane had reckoned, they were aided in that decision by the discovery of the imminent arrival of a relief party coming from Catfish Camp led by Captain Boggs.

The British and most of the Indians returned across the Ohio, but a remnant of over seventy warriors went to the east where they ultimately made an attack on Rice's Fort on the Dutch Fork of Buffalo Creek. Three defenders of the fort were killed and at least nine of the Indians. Lew knew that his friend Jacob Miller had been engaged in that affair.

Wetzel was sorry to have missed all of this action, although he had not been idle himself. His brother Martin and a man named Thomas Younkins were acting as scouts for Fort Beeler and had stopped by the Wetzel home. Lewis was there by himself, as his parents, conscious of the extra-Indian activity in the vicinity, had taken Jacob, John, and Susannah to visit the Bonnetts down on Dunkard Creek.

Lew's sister Christiana had married Jacob Wolf more than a year earlier and no longer lived at the homeplace. After a bit of persuasion, Lew had agreed to accompany the two men to Beeler's, especially since they were convinced that there might well be some Indian action against that fort. They crossed Wheeling Creek and made their way up the ridge on the farside and followed it along, swinging to the south and a little bit east toward their destination. They found some signs of Indian activity but so far had seen no warriors.

When they were within a half mile of the fort, sometimes called Beeler's station, Lew called a halt. "You two go on ahead," he suggested. "I think I'll take a look around. We may have company closer'n we think."

"That's prob'ly a good idea, little brother," agreed Martin. "Be careful though. We don't want that pretty hair of your'n hanging from some buck's belt."

"You and me both." A grin had broken out on Lew's face as he patted his brother's shoulder. "Just make sure you git that fort gate open if I come a runnin'."

With a quick wave, Lew plunged off to his right, and the other two men went on toward the fort. Lew moved easily through an open area in a shallow depression with low hills on either side.

The fort was to his left, and he knew that Grave Creek was less than a mile straight ahead of him. If there were Indians about with designs on attacking the fort, he figured that they might be coming up along the creek.

In fact, a small party of Indians, mostly Mingoes and Wyandots, had broken off from the main body headed to Wheeling and crossed the Ohio at Boggs Island. They swung down along the old trail, followed by the ill-fated soldiers under Foreman five years earlier, and skirted the old Tomlinson settlements until they struck Grave Creek. Scouting parties had roamed through the woods and ridges from Grave Creek north all the way up as far Wheeling Creek near the Wetzel homestead.

Having decided to attack the fort at Beeler's, they had regrouped and were moving toward that objective. Wetzel had not gone far when he began to hear movements in the woods below. He moved out of the open and in among the trees, stopping to listen, then moving ahead cautiously. He had reached a stand of cottonwoods when he could see three stealthy figures sliding through some low bushes just ahead. He jumped beside the larger of two trees next to him and watched. It was then that he heard a shot and the sound of a speeding ball whistling through the leaves just above his head.

Wetzel could not see his attacker, and he knew that hesitation now might mean death. He sprang from behind the trunk and began running at top speed back in the direction from which he had just come. He veered to his right, across a narrow open field and into the trees on the farside. He was running slightly uphill now, and two more shots had been fired at him, both missing. He knew that if he continued in this direction, he would eventually reach the fort. He was confident that he could outrun the three Indians who had fired at him, especially if they stopped to reload their weapons. What he didn't know was how many more there might be, or if there could be others already between him and the fort.

He crossed one ridge, descended again for a short time, then ascended another low hill fortunately covered with trees. He was slightly winded, and he stopped for a moment to listen. He could not hear any pursuer close behind, and he surmised that the Indians had given up the chase. Still he must not make any assumptions of that kind, and he continued on, though at a slower rate.

He saw that the woods thinned out straight ahead and then ended. To the left at the crest of the hill, he could see his objective. The tree line curved down to his right, and he followed until he came to a wooded ravine that extended up almost to the south end of the stockade that formed the walls of Beeler's fort. There was a spring there in the ravine and a gate into the fort just above it. Thankful that he could reach the gate without having to go into the open, he pounded on the gate.

"It's Lew Wetzel," he cried. "Let me in."

It was Martin Wetzel who opened the gate. "Thank God, Lew. We heard shooting and thought you might be done for."

"Well, they tried Martin, but they ain't very good shots, I guess."

The fort's owner, George Beeler, stood just behind Martin. He was eager to hear Lew's report.

"Your brother says we should be ready for an attack. What did you see?" he asked anxiously.

"There's a bunch of bastards coming up along the creek. I reckon they intend to attack us real soon."

"How many?"

"I don't rightly know, but enough to cause us lots of trouble, I expect."

"Well I'm glad you three men got here in time," said Beeler. "We got three other families here besides mine. That gives us seven grown men and a couple of young boys. At least we can get somebody in all four corners."

The fort was built in the same manner as most of the forts in its day. The stockade was built in an elongated rectangle, with the long side running north and south. There were small blockhouses in each corner, some small cabins along the sides, and the Beeler cabin built in the center. Portholes were built into the stockade walls to provide opportunities for shooting at attackers.

"When do you think we should expect 'em to hit us?" asked Beeler of Martin.

"Tonight, I reckon."

"What do you think, Lew?"

"Any surprise they was planning is ruined. I think they will be here very soon."

Just before dark, two of the Indian leaders appeared on horseback at the crest of the hill just north of the main gate. Their appearance was accompanied by war whoops and shrieks from the woods to the west. One of the chiefs called out in clear English. "Give up now or we will burn down your fort and kill you all."

A shot rang out from the blockhouse on the northwest corner of the stockade, and the Indian who had been speaking fell into the tall grass. The other retreated quickly as his fellow warriors stormed out of the trees, firing their weapons, and screaming as loudly as they could. Their shots were ineffective, and return fire from the walls of the fort sent them back to the edge of the woods. Sporadic firing and yelling went on until it became quite dark.

Lewis Wetzel took his brother Martin by the arm and led him toward the south gate. The very wooded ravine that had helped him earlier now posed a problem for the small group of defenders. "I don't like it much that this ravine with its wood cover is so close to the south wall," Lew explained to Martin. "They can get right up close without being seen."

"I know. But the walls are pretty high. I doubt they can climb them."

"They'll try to fire them, though, and if we don't molest 'em, they'll likely get it done."

"Maybe, but the walls are still damp."

The women had spent some time in the late afternoon using the spring water to wet down the walls of the fort, especially along the southern side. This would make it a bit more difficult for the Indians to set them on fire. Lew walked along the wall just past the gate and stopped, pointing at something.

"There's a little gully there, Martin, just under the pickets. We'd better keep an eye on that."

The attackers had appeared with firebrands and tried to throw them against the base of the walls but were unsuccessful in getting a fire started. One brave, determined to set one of the frayed pickets on fire, had stayed too long, and a rifleman in a corner blockhouse had been able to bring his gun to bear on the hapless Indian. After this, there were no more attempts of that kind.

The Wetzel brothers had stationed themselves along the south wall of Beeler's house, but in the early morning hours, both had drifted into a light sleep. Lewis was awakened by a scratching sound. It was very dark, but he detected movement along the south wall, near the low spot he had mentioned to Martin. He jumped up, awakening Martin as he did so. He began to run toward the wall, lifting his tomahawk from his belt as he ran. He could see that the little gully had been widened and deepened, and the head and shoulders of an Indian warrior appeared under the wall. The warrior was almost all the way in when he caught sight of Wetzel, looming above him. The tomahawk struck him squarely in the head just above his left ear, and he began to fall.

Strong hands caught him and finished pulling him through the opening. Martin Wetzel dragged the body off to the side as Lewis retrieved his weapon. Lewis raised his finger to his lips to quiet his brother who was about to speak. Motioning that they should sink back against the wall, Lewis pointed to the opening. Another head appeared, then the shoulders. As the hips wriggled through, Wetzel's tomahawk struck again, and the brothers pulled the body the rest of the way in as before. Now they heard voices arguing just beyond the wall, footsteps, and then silence.

"I reckon they'll change their mind about comin' in that way," said Lew, who took his knife and scalped the last victim and then threw the body against the wall and into the little passageway. He scalped the other Indian and returned to his spot along the wall of Beeler's cabin.

"I hope there's enough of us to keep 'em back," said Martin, slumping against the wall next to Lew.

"I think we can," said Lew. "If the powder holds out."

"I don't think there's too big a bunch of 'em," volunteered Lew after a while.

The besiegers stayed around most of the day, trying several rushes against the walls but had no success. During the night, they had retrieved the body of their dead chief; and by nightfall of the second day, they withdrew, although the Wetzels and their companions couldn't be sure of that until the next day.

When Lew had finished recounting this story to Jonathan Zane, the old scout smiled.

"Well young Lew, I reckon we won this round."

Neither fort was ever attacked again.

8

THE WEDDING

January 6, 1783

JOSH DAVIS WAS very much looking forward to the day. It was January 6, Old Christmas Day, sometimes called the Twelfth Day of Christmas. Josh wasn't particularly religious, but he enjoyed the celebration.

For years, it was the custom to have a big feast at the fort, which included the roasting of two big turkeys. Josh's father, James, had promised to supply the turkeys this year, and the two men had brought them in just a few minutes ago. The plump birds had already been beheaded, and were ready for the scalding pots. Josh's mother, Katy, and two other women were tending a large fire built on the bare ground inside the enclosure and not far from the commandant's quarters, where the meal would be eaten later.

The women had hung two big pots over the fire, and they were full of boiling water. There had been a snowfall two days earlier, and the weather had remained cold enough that very little had melted. It had been necessary to scrape the snow to the side to clear a spot suitable for building a fire.

Josh was surprised when Lew Wetzel suddenly appeared and asked for one of the turkeys. "Let me have one of them afore you scald it," he said to the elder Davis.

"You want one of these turkeys?" asked the startled Davis. "What in hell are you goin' to do with a turkey."

"I need some turkey feet and wings, that's all," answered Lew with a tiny grin.

"If that don't beat all. What you plannin' to do with some ole turkey feet?"

"I bet I know," interjected Josh. "Is it 'bout that gobbler Injun everybody's been talkin' about?"

For several winters, the settlement had been bothered by an Indian who would station himself on one of the surrounding hills and make a call like a turkey gobbler. Several men had lost their lives trying to hunt that turkey. Most recently, the call had been coming from one of the big ridges overlooking Indian Wheeling Creek across the big river. On the previous night, Josh had been present at the fort while Wetzel, Jonathan Zane, and some others sat around drinking from an old jug and telling stories. The subject of the Gobbler Indian came up.

"I've got me an idea about that," Lewis Wetzel had said finally. "I think I'll take care of that problem one of these days."

Now in response to Josh Davis's remark, Wetzel said with a smile, "Could be, Josh. We'll have to see."

He took his hunting knife and cut the turkey's legs off just at the point where the feathers started, then took off the wings at the first joint. He put these treasures carefully inside his hunting bag and carried it off to the little hut along the west wall of the stockade, which served as his sleeping quarters when he was at the fort.

Josh didn't understand at all what Wetzel intended, and he wanted to ask him to explain, but thought better of it. He took the mutilated bird to his mother, who put it into boiling water. What came next would be Josh's job, and it was one he thoroughly hated. Once the birds were scalded, Josh would pluck the feathers. The smell was awful, and he almost had to hold his breath while he did it. The end result was worth it, of course, but it made the job no less reprehensible. When he was finished, Josh carried the carcasses over to where his mother and the other women had made preparations for roasting the turkeys above the fire.

Cooking the turkeys on a special fire outside freed up the fireplace inside the main cabin for the cooking of other items, such as turnips and potatoes. Josh walked around the end of the building and entered through the main door. Two big tables were arranged in the center of the room, and on each were several big pans containing twelfth-day cake. Josh looked to see if any of the women at the hearth were watching, and then he broke off a small piece of the cake and plopped it into his mouth. It was delicious, another of his favorites. Although it was called a cake, it was really more like bread.

The bread was made with unleavened dough and sweetened, with cloves and cinnamon bark worked into it. The bread was baked in a Dutch oven and baked the day before so that it could be eaten cold. Other food was being brought in, but it would be several hours yet before the dinner was set. Josh grabbed another piece of the cake and ducked out the door. It was cold outside, and Josh moved over close to the fire where his mother stood, watching the turkeys roasting above the flames. His father stood not far away talking to Ebenezer Zane who had come into the fort from his cabin, which stood close by. Zane's wife, Elizabeth, who normally took charge at these events, had not yet appeared.

Josh was hoping that Wetzel would come back soon, for he wanted to ask about the hunter's strange actions earlier that morning. People continued to arrive, with the women going inside to add their food contribution to the collection on the tables. The men moved out near the fire, crowding close enough to feel some of its warmth. Elizabeth Zane appeared with little four-year-old Noah in hand. "Look who's here, Eb," she said, pointing back toward the gate where a man and woman had just entered.

"Why, it's John McColloch," exclaimed Zane, who took several quick steps toward the arriving couple. "Welcome, brother-in-law, and you too, Mary. Great to see you."

Others gathered around the fire shouted their greetings to the McCollochs.

"Sorry about your brother, John," said James Davis.

Elizabeth Zane stopped and stared at Davis. How could he still be saying something like that, she wondered, feeling very much annoyed. Her younger brother, John, seemed unflustered. Their brother, Sam, famous for the leap off Wheeling Hill, had been killed by the Indians the previous summer while he and John were on a scouting trip out from Fort Van Meter.

"John, you were with him at the time, weren't you?" asked Davis. "Tell us how it happened."

Elizabeth, standing next to John and visibly annoyed, started to rebuke Davis for his insensitivity, but John grabbed her arm, pulling her back slightly. His glance told her to stop, that he was willing to tell the story again. She turned abruptly and headed toward the cabin door.

John McColloch moved closer to the fire and began to recount the previous summer's adventure. "We was on a scout," he related. "Goin' first south toward the fort here, then back up and across Short Creek at the mouth, and then up to Girty's Point toward Van Meter's. It was around there the bastards shot poor Sam. There was nothin' to do 'cept run, and that's what I did. I did manage to shoot one of 'em afore I got away."

"I reckon you was lucky to get away without losin' your hair too." allowed Davis. "What is Girty's Point? I never heard that before."

"It's what the folks up on Short Creek has been callin' that high ground a ways in from the mouth of the Creek. That's where Simon Girty and his Injun friends went through after capturin' Stevenson last spring."

"I heard the damned reds cut out Sam's heart and ate it," exclaimed Josh.

"That's a fact," admitted John sadly.

"Damned savages," said James Davis.

"It's a sign of respect," said Lew Wetzel, who had rejoined the group just in time to hear the last few words.

'Well I'll be," exclaimed Ebenezer Zane. "Lewis Wetzel defending the Indians. Now that's a surprise."

"I ain't defendin' no damned Injuns," said Lew quickly. "But what I said is true. My brother, Martin, lived with 'em for more'n two years, and he says he saw it happen more than once. They think if they kill a brave man and eat his heart, it will make 'em bold and brave just like their enemy."

"Of course, you're right, Lewis," agreed Zane. "It shows what the red men thought of your brother, John. His name was well-known among the savages."

"It still don't make me feel too good," said John.

The call came from the cabin that the food was ready, and the hungry men, with happy shouts, made their way inside. The long table was filled with food, and a line was quickly formed as the men and boys grabbed a wooden plate from the stack and prepared to fill them.

"Hold on, you gluttons," cried Elizabeth Zane. "This is a Christmas celebration after all, and nobody gets a bite 'til we have a blessing."

The room became quiet. It didn't surprise Wetzel that Elizabeth had insisted on a prayer. It was well-known that she had become very religious. There were no established churches in the settlements yet, although an ordained minister might come through now and then. When that happened, Elizabeth made sure that a worship service was held.

"There ain't no parson here today, so, Eb, you will have to do the honors."

No doubt, Ebenezer had been apprised of this task much earlier, and he gave no protest now. His prayer was short, and the feast soon began. When everyone had finished eating, Lew Wetzel asked for one of the turkey drumsticks, and taking a piece of quill, he sat down against one of the sidewalls in the room. With his knife, he punched a hole in both ends of the drumstick, and after shaving the quill a bit, he inserted it into the big end of the bone. Then he put the other end to his lips and began to blow.

Just as was intended, the sound that came out was something like what an old turkey gobbler might make. He blew it several times and quickly drew a crowd of small children. Four-year-old Noah Zane tapped Wetzel on the shoulder. "What's that?" he asked, pointing to the makeshift turkey caller.

"Are you a turkey?" Lew asked little Noah with a laugh.

"No!" Noah was clearly offended. "What is that?" he insisted.

"That's a turkey caller, and since it called to you, I reckon you're a turkey." Lew pointed his finger at little Noah, whose face wrinkled up in disgust.

"I am not!" The tears were beginning to form, and Noah took a wild slap at Wetzel that missed the mark.

"I know, I'm just teasin' you, Noah."

"Can you play a tune?" asked one of the little girls who had pushed in beside Noah.

"I don't reckon so, not on this thing, anyway." Lew was watching Noah, who was still trying to decide if he was angry. "I can sing though. Would that be all right?"

Wetzel smiled and began humming softly, finally adding some words in German. The tune and meter were attractive to the children, and soon at least ten of them were sitting in front of Wetzel, trying to join in.

"We can't sing that song," said the little girl. "Those are funny words."

Elizabeth Zane had wandered over and stood behind the children. "Sing it in English, Lewis," she said. "The children will love it."

Wetzel nodded and began again, this time in English.

"Five fat sausages, sizzling in a pan, one went pop, the other went bang."

Lew slapped the floor hard as he said the word *bang*, and the children, startled at first, began to clap.

"Four fat sausages, sizzling in a pan, one went pop, the other went bang."

By the time Lew got down to "two fat sausages," the children were singing with him and clapping joyously. The song ended with "No fat sausages sizzling in a pan," and the youngsters immediately demanded an encore. They had been through the song three times when Lew spied Sally Burkitt, a girl of about ten years, standing in the back. He stopped for a moment and began a new tune.

"Of all the girls who are so smart," he sang. "There's none like pretty Sally. She is the darling of my heart, and she lives in our alley."

Poor Sally screamed and threw her hands up to cover her face, then turned and ran away. Josh Davis stood amazed at what was happening. Lew Wetzel, the big brave hunter and Indian killer, was singing to the children. Wanting to get into it himself, he blurted out some words without thinking about their effect. "But Lew, you should substitute Lyddy for Sally." Once the words were out, Josh could see Wetzel's face darkening, and he knew he had really put his foot in it.

Wetzel jumped to his feet. "You should watch your mouth, Josh." He stomped from the room, brushing off Elizabeth Zane's attempt to mollify him. Once outside and into the cool air, he regretted his action. Josh was a good boy, and Lew didn't want to make an enemy of him. He knew that Josh almost worshipped him as it was. The mention of Lydia Boggs, however, had returned him to his earlier bad mood. He had been hoping that Lydia would be at the dinner, especially when her father and her brother James had arrived. Her mother was quite ill, however, and Lydia had stayed at home to care for her. Besides that, the rumors were that Lydia and Moses Shepherd were pretty thick, some even said that they were engaged to be married.

Although he would never admit it to anyone else, Lew was well aware of his feelings for Lydia, and he was just plain jealous of Moses. Earlier, Moses had been linked with Betty Zane, Lew's other favorite woman; but that was apparently over with now, and Lydia had replaced her in Moses's affections.

Lew had not seen much of Lydia since that summer day when he had actually seen all of her. It was a pleasant memory, even now, but he hadn't talked to her at all since then. Some suitor I am, he thought now to himself. It was foolish, he knew, to even hope that someone like Lydia would care for him. Foolish or not, it was something he lived with. He thought of leaving immediately for the solace of the deep woods, but it was still too cold. He went to his cabin instead.

January 11, 1783

The weather had turned warm, and much of the snow had disappeared, except on the north side of hills and ridges. On the fourth day after the Twelfth Day celebration, a cold spell had returned; and during the night, a hard freeze came.

A couple of hours before dawn, Lewis Wetzel got up and dressed quickly. Taking down his rifle and his hunting bag, he hurried from the fort in the darkness and made his way down to the river's edge. He found the canoe he had tied there the previous evening and shoved it out into the cold dark river. He shivered as he began paddling out into the current, angling his way toward the upriver end of Zane's Island. After rounding the island, he swung into the channel on its western edge, beaching the canoe at the northern edge of the mouth of Indian Wheeling Creek.

The darkness was receding, and he could see the shafts of light from the rising sun coming up behind the hills across the river. There was no hesitancy in Wetzel's movements, and he made his way deliberately along the north bank of the creek, thankful for enough blackness in the early morning to make him invisible to any interested observers. He seemed to have an uncanny ability to move easily through the trees and bushes that lined the creek, avoiding any entanglements in the dim light.

He continued in this way for nearly a mile before coming to a small run tumbling down the hillside on his right. He turned here and began an ascent up toward the top of the ridge, veering off to the right at a fork in the tiny stream. He followed this fork for a ways then stopped to rest. Ahead and above him he could see a ridge that began up to his left and angled down toward the southeast, with its point terminating not far above the mouth of Indian Wheeling Creek.

"If I was a red gobbler, that's where I'd hang out," Wetzel said aloud softly.

He moved away from the little run and toward the rising sun, climbing slowly through the heavy woods until he reached the top of the ridge, coming out in a shallow saddle between the higher parts. He worked his way across, aware of the need to be careful. He looked for any sign that would confirm his theory about his prey. It was daylight by now, and as he moved along the ridge toward the river, he took the turkey feet from his hunting bag and made tracks along the edge of the snow that remained on the north and eastside of the hill.

"That damned gobbler has been mighty careful," Wetzel whispered to himself. "I ain't seen no sign of him."

Just then he saw what looked like the edge of a heel print in the mud, now frozen in place. "Ah, so he is here."

Crouching low, Wetzel listened carefully for several minutes, not moving a muscle. He was on the side of the ridge and unobservable from the top, where he assumed that the Indian was stationed.

"I reckon I ought to hide over there on the hillside under one of those little ripples."

Lewis sighted toward the intended spot along the upper edge of the snow. He now began to move in that direction, and wherever there was snow on that line, he made turkey tracks, with the toes pointed to the east. He was careful to avoid stepping in the snow himself. The cold night had rapidly given way to the warm sun, and the snow was already sticky enough that making the tracks was easy.

When he had reached a spot within twenty steps of his hiding place, there was a slight incline in the ground and a big pile of snow. He made more tracks, trying to make them appear as they would for a turkey preparing to fly to his roost. He fixed the wings and flapped them in the snow. Satisfied that he had created a scene in the snow that would appear to an observer that a big gobbler had taken flight at the spot, Wetzel now went back some distance and crossed over to the south side of the ridge, making his way down to the creek below. He walked around and climbed back up to his hiding place.

Once situated, he pulled out his homemade turkey caller and began to call like a turkey. After a while, there was an answering call, and as Wetzel remained quietly in his spot watching along the ridge above him, a large Indian came into sight, looking down intently, then walking back and forth. Wetzel called again, and the Indian answered. Shortly he came to the line of tracks, the sight of which seemed to excite him. He bent down and examined the tracks, then stood and looked up into the trees. He began to walk again with halting steps and peering even more at the trees.

Wetzel sent one more call, which was answered, and the Indian began coming directly to where Wetzel crouched. Lifting his rifle slowly, Wetzel checked the priming carefully and made sure that it was ready to fire. Meanwhile, his intended prey had reached the little rise in the ground and continued to examine the tracks, as well as looking up at the trees. He grunted and kept moving. Apparently thinking he was closing in on the phantom turkey, he lifted his gun in his left hand, turned it sideways, and struck it with his right. At this point, Wetzel raised his rifle and fired. The Indian threw up his hands, trembled for a moment, and fell backward.

"I reckon we won't be bothered with the 'gobbler' Injun anymore," said Lewis aloud with satisfaction. He gave a loud shout, and pulling his knife, he moved in to take the scalp.

March 10, 1783

The weather had warmed a bit for early March. Lewis Wetzel left the family homestead quite early in the morning and made his way downstream for a mile or two, turning up a narrow trail that climbed a high wooded hill. The creek had made a big turn to the north, and he had left it shortly after that. The trail was parallel to a tiny run that came down the hill and spilled into Wheeling Creek.

It occurred to Wetzel that he was probably following the route of his Indian captors from more than five years earlier. Reaching the top of the ridge, he turned to the west. He knew that Little Grave Creek lay not too far to the south, and that's where he thought the Indians had taken him, although he wasn't completely sure. His goal now, however, was to end up on Boggs Run, which would take him by the Boggs cabin. His friend Billy Boggs had returned from Indian captivity several weeks ago, but Lewis had not yet seen him. This was the reason for his current trip, or so he had told his family. His real reason, of course, was the chance that he would find Lydia there, for his silent and secret infatuation with her had not abated.

He took his time making his way over the ridges watching, as he always did, for any signs of their red neighbors. It was a bit early in the season yet for any large scale Indian forays, but there was always the possibility that some individual might be on the hunt. The gobbler Indian he had killed only two months before was a good example of that. He was amazed to see some early daffodils poking their heads out in places where the sun had access. He found this satisfying, similar to seeing the first robin, assurance that spring and summer were on the way.

It was nearly noon when he approached the Boggs cabin, built on a low knob of a hill rising a few feet above the small stream called Boggs Run. The home was located more than two miles in from the mouth of the run on the Ohio. The family hoped the inland location would not be as accessible for the warriors who sometimes frequented the trail along the edge of the big river. There was some low-lying land under cultivation across the run from the cabin, and a larger acreage on the rolling land behind the house.

Wetzel leaned down and dipped his hand into the fast-moving water and withdrew it quickly, reacting to the coldness. The current flowed through a ditch of some depth, but narrow enough that one could leap it in most places. Having done that, Wetzel walked slowly up the incline to where the cabin stood. Everyone was inside, eating dinner, he supposed. He knew that his timing was bad, and he wondered for a moment whether he should wait for an hour or so before actually knocking on the door.

On the other hand, he was hungry, and the smells sifting out from the interior were enticing. He knocked loudly. The conversation inside stopped, and Wetzel could hear someone approaching the door. It was pulled open, and Captain John Boggs stood there. "Well, hello, Lew," he exclaimed. "I wasn't sure who had come callin' on us. Just hopin' it wasn't some red feller."

"Reckon not, Captain John. Sorry to barge in just at dinnertime."

"That's all right, Lew. We've got plenty. Come in and join us." He motioned to Billy. "Git Lew a plate and set him up there, Billy."

"Don't mind if I do," said Lew. "Hello, Billy. I'd heard you was home."

"Hi ya, Lew. I've been back awhile already," Billy replied. "Wondered where you'd been."

Wetzel sat down at the place provided. "The whole family's here, eh?" he began to say then caught himself. "I mean all except Mrs. Boggs. I'm sorry."

Jane Boggs had died in January, just after Billy had returned. The oldest son James was there after serving in Washington's army in the east, along with eleven-year-old Martha and six-year-old Jack. The two youngest daughters, who were toddlers, were playing on the floor near the fireplace. Wetzel noted an empty chair; and at first, he thought they had left it empty in remembrance of Jane. Then he realized that Lydia wasn't there, and his countenance fell. He hoped his disappointment wasn't obvious. *Where could she be?* he wondered.

"Git Lew some of that stew, James," ordered John Boggs. "Billy killed us a deer just yesterday over by the river."

There was a commotion in the loft above them, and then two feet appeared on the ladder that led there, followed by a skirt, and then the full figure of the absent Lydia.

"Why, here's our Lyddy," said John. "We've got company, Lyddy. It's Lew Wetzel."

"I see that," said Lydia as she turned from the ladder to face them. She did not seem pleased at his presence, noted Lew; but rather, it seemed to him that she was annoyed. Nevertheless, he was very glad to see her.

"Hello, Lydia," he said quietly.

Lydia took her place, filling her plate, and eating without any further talk. Lew felt awkward but could think of nothing clever to say, and he remained silent. They concentrated on the food for a bit, but then Captain John opened the conversation again.

"What brings you out, Lew?" he asked.

"I wanted to see Billy," said Wetzel. "You must have lots to tell us about, Billy. And you, too, James. I guess you've got a few tales to tell yourself."

"They've both been tellin' us lots of stories," agreed John.

"Billy had to run the gauntlet," blurted six-year-old Jack.

"He did?" asked Lew. "Well, did he live through it?"

Little Jack was dumbfounded at such a silly statement, and he glared at the smiling Wetzel with profound disgust.

"I did," interjected Billy, "but I don't recommend it for fun."

"Was it Delawares that took you?" asked Wetzel.

"It was, but there were some Wyandots too. They took us up to the Sandusky villages. One of 'em was an old half-breed who could speak some English, and he could tell me what was goin' on. I sure was scared they was goin' to burn me. They was mighty riled about what happened with Brodhead."

"I'd sent Billy out to catch some calves when they hit us," said Captain Boggs. "Some of them took Billy. The rest came after our cabin, the one we had up on Buffalo Creek. I managed to drive 'em off, and they never came back."

"I convinced 'em that there was eight men at the cabin," noted Billy. "I guess it worked."

"Did they have any other prisoners?" wondered Lew.

"No, but after a couple of months, they brought in Presley Peak, and they took him and me to Detroit."

"Yeah, I remember when they took poor old Presley," said Lew. "Miller got away from 'em that time, you know."

"Presley told me about that," replied Billy. "They didn't treat us too bad, I guess, but the food was awful. The British was worse."

"How did you get away?"

"We was traded, I guess, Lew. Must have been exchanged for some Brits. They gave us a little food and turned us loose."

"I'm glad you made it, Billy. Not everybody does."

Lydia had remained quiet, but now she spoke up, wanting to make sure that Lew heard her special news. "I'm tired of this Indian talk. Lewis, have you heard the news about Moses and me?"

"I guess it depends on what news it is," said Lew, although he was afraid he knew what it might be.

"We are goin' to be married, Lew." Lydia had no idea of the effect this announcement might have on Wetzel.

"I reckon I heard some people speculatin' on that," answered Lew, trying to keep his face from showing his true feelings.

It seemed a bit cruel to him, but then Lydia had never given even the slightest indication that she might think of Lew as a suitor himself. Lydia saw that Lew was not thrilled by this news. Still she waited for his congratulations. Finally it came.

"I wish you the best, Lyddy. Moses is a good man." There he'd managed to get the words out.

"It won't be for a while though," said Lydia. "Moses is back east doin' some work for his father."

The conversation wound down, and Wetzel prepared to leave, intending to spend the night at Fort Henry. Lydia followed him out the door and called after him.

"Lew, wait a minute."

He stopped and turned back, not looking forward to what she might have to say but thrilled at the sound of her voice calling his name.

"Have you been shootin' any rabbits lately?"

"Not lately," said Lew, not sure where Lydia was going with this question.

"I never did thank you for savin' my life, Lewis Wetzel. You killed an Indian that day on the river, didn't you?"

Before he could answer, she rushed to him and threw her arms around him. It surprised him, but he pulled her close. She kissed him quickly on the cheek then pulled away. Lew was speechless, already trying to remember the sweetness of feeling in her embrace.

"Why didn't you tell me what you'd done?" Lydia wanted to know.

Lew was slow to answer. "I didn't want to scare you," he said finally.

"Well you did a good job of scarin' me anyway. I thought you was an Indian when you came out of those trees."

"I didn't see no other way." He looked down, shaking his head slowly.

"It don't matter none, Lew," she said. "John Linn found the body, and I heard him tell my pa." She stood looking at him for a moment, but Wetzel avoided her gaze. "You didn't tell pa, did you?" she remarked.

He looked up at her now. "No, I reckon I never did."

"I thank you for that too, Lewis. I won't forget what you done, ever!"

He relished the sound of his name on her tongue and the warm feelings of what he supposed was love welled up inside him. But he knew that this was the end of it for him. She'd forget soon enough, he figured, as soon as she was with Moses. He nodded to her and turned away.

As he started up the path alongside the stream, she called after him one more time. "Lew, you'll come to my wedding, won't you? I want you to come."

He stopped and looked back at her, a vision he would lock into his memory. "I reckon," he said softly and then shuffled off down the trail.

May 27, 1784

More than a year had passed, and Lydia was preparing for the big day. Her wedding had been set for the last Saturday in May. Moses had finally returned from his tasks in the east, and to top everything, Lydia had a new mother. Her father had come home one day last October with a widow from Washington in Pennsylvania, the town formerly called Catfish Camp. She had two young boys of her own, near to Jack's age. Lydia was shocked at first and determined not to like her new stepmother, but it had been impossible. Lydia didn't think her very pretty; in fact she was rather heavy.

"She's fat!" had been little Jack's pronouncement.

Sadie's easy smile, joyous energy, and full commitment to preparing for the upcoming wedding had quickly convinced Lydia of her father's wisdom.

Upon his return, Moses had brought her several gifts, including some black silk and blue calico. She had taken the black silk to Sadie and asked her to make it into a wedding dress.

"What?" was the surprised response. "You want a black wedding dress? What will people think?"

"I don't care what they think," exclaimed Lydia. "They'll be green with envy. Who else anywhere near Wheeling has a silk dress?"

"My goodness, child, you'll shock your pa somethin' awful, not to mention your intended. Does he know about this?"

"Moses wanted me to wear the blue calico, but he won't care. He' s hired a preacher from up at West Liberty, and that's what he's excited about."

"He's excited about a preacher?"

"Moses is very religious, I guess. I never knew how much."

"Well that ain't all bad, honey."

Lydia smiled as she remembered that conversation. Now she watched as Sadie put the finishing touches on the dress. Suddenly overcome with emotion, she rushed over and grabbed her stepmother by the shoulders and hugged her tight.

"You are a wonder," she said. "So good for pa and the children. I love you very much."

"What's come over you, child?" was Sadie's surprised response. Her beaming face revealed her pleasure at this unexpected outburst.

"It's just that I don't know what I would have done without you. You have been so good to me and made this dress out of the black silk. I know you think it is silly of me." Lydia had let go of Sadie and stepped back.

"I admit, I was taken aback a bit, but it will be stunning." Sadie took Lydia's hands in hers and squeezed. "You'll be a beautiful bride, Lydia, and I'm proud to be your new mother."

"My pa is so wise and so lucky to have found you."

"Your pa is a fine man, and he's made me very happy. Now, this weddin' is only two days away, and I ain't sure we're goin' to be ready for it. Why don't you try on this gown right now?"

The two days passed quickly, and the day dawned sunny and bright. Lydia was awake early, and the first sounds she heard were of Sadie, who had been up several hours already, rattling pots and pans preparing for the day's feast. The excitement that had led to a night of fitful sleep had now given way to anxiety, and Lydia could feel the butterflies in her stomach.

She laid down again on the bed and wondered if somehow she could put a stop to all of this. How could a day that had been anticipated for so long suddenly become a nightmare? She thought of Moses. He was handsome, and she was sure she loved him. But was she ready for this night that now loomed over her? What would he think of her? She thought she knew what to expect. Indeed, there had been several times when the two lovers had been alone, and their passions were high that they had been tempted to consummate their love. Always, however, they had stopped in time, and she would be a virgin bride. She was proud of that, and she knew it was important to Moses.

She thought about the words she and Moses would say to each other in the ceremony, words that she had thrilled to at other weddings she had attended. She wanted desperately to say them to him and to hear him repeat them to her. It was the other things that happened at weddings that bothered her. The silly pranks and customs that newlyweds were forced to endure—she had laughed at them when they were at others' expense. Now they didn't seem so harmless. She had complained about this to Moses already, but he had only grinned and assured her that it wouldn't be so bad.

Lydia contemplated calling down to say she was sick, but she knew that nobody would believe her. She closed her eyes and tried to put all thoughts out of her head. She was still for several minutes.

"You silly fool," she finally said to herself. "This is your day, you'd better git up and enjoy it."

Her natural energy and vitality could only stay suppressed for so long, and they finally jerked her out of the "weddin' day jitters," as she had heard Sadie call them. She quickly dressed and descended the ladder to the main floor below.

"Why, good mornin', Miss Lydia," called Sadie, placing a pan of bread dough in front of the open oven that would be used for baking it once it had risen. "The sun is shinin', which makes for a happy bride and a beautiful weddin' day."

"Good mornin' to you, mother Sadie. You've been up mighty early."

"All for a good cause. Your pa and your brothers is mighty busy themselves."

Lydia looked out the door where she could see the fire trench. It was filled with hot coals, and several kinds of meat were already cooking. Several rough tables had been set up in the yard, with stools and stumps arranged around them for seating. She saw her father, John, and brother Billy duck into the shed.

Sadie had come up beside her in time to see that as well. "I think your pa and Billy may be samplin' the drinks. I told 'em it was too early for that." She took Lydia's right hand in hers and gave it a squeeze. "It's goin' to be a fine day, honey. Now let's get busy. Why don't you get the girls bathed, and then it'll be time for you to have a good long bath yourself."

It was nearly noon when most everything was ready. Guests had been arriving steadily for more than an hour, all bringing some kind of food to add to what Sadie had prepared. Many of the neighbors from downriver as well as those from Wheeling were there. No one from the Shepherd family had yet arrived, for it was the custom that they would come last, accompanying the groom and his friends.

The beautiful pendulum clock on the mantle had just struck its twelve tones announcing that it was noon, when the first sounds of the approaching groom and his party were heard.

Lydia, who was fully dressed, but whose job it was to stay out of sight, heard the gunshots first, and then the shouting. She went to the tiny window on the west wall of the loft in time to see two riders coming fast on the trail that led up to the Boggs cabin from the Ohio River. One of the riders was Zeke Thornburg, a cousin of Moses and the man Moses had chosen to stand up with him. The other rider, the one slightly ahead, was Lewis

Wetzel. A smile crossed Lydia's face, and she silently cheered for Lew, never doubting that he would be the winner. This was the customary run for the bottle, the prize being a bottle of whiskey, which the winner would take back in triumph to the oncoming groom and friends.

Out in the yard, the crowd had edged out to watch the race. They shouted encouragement and cheered as Wetzel swooped up, urged his mount to leap across the stream, and rode up to the cabin door. John Boggs was at the door with the prize and handed it to the rider, who wheeled and began the return ride. Thornburg was laughing and yelling as he followed Wetzel back. Moses Shepherd was at the front of the pack of women and children accompanying him, which included all of the Shepherd family, the Wetzels, the Bonnetts, the Grandstaffs, and others.

Moses stopped and waited for Lew to reach him. Wetzel pulled up with a flourish and a yell, handing the bottle to the groom. It was passed then to Zeke, who had just ridden up, and down the line of people arranged in pairs along the trail. Each adult was allowed one small drink, and when the bottle reached the end of the line, it was given back to Wetzel, who put it away inside his hunting shirt. As the last of the Shepherd family came in, another small group of men rode up. This was the minister, James Smith from West Liberty, and the men who had been sent to escort him. When Lydia saw that Smith had arrived, she descended the ladder. The room was empty except for her father, who stood next to the door.

"I'm ready, Pa," announced Lydia.

"My God," exclaimed John Boggs. "Ain't you the pretty one? I wasn't so sure about that black dress when Sadie told me about it, but you're dazzlin'."

"Do you like it, Papa?" Lydia straightened herself, throwing her shoulders back, lifting her chest. She smoothed the tight fitting dress against the side of her thighs.

"When Moses sees you, he may not wait until after the ceremony."

"Papa, you're naughty," said the blushing bride-to-be.

"Hurry up in there," came the shout from outside. "We're gittin' hungry."

The wedding ceremony must precede the dinner, and Mr. Smith took his place near the front door, with Moses and Zeke Thornburg standing next to him. On the other side was Moses's older sister Sarah, whose own husband, Francis Duke, had been killed in the 1777 battle at Fort Henry. She was serving as Lydia's maid of honor.

The cabin door opened, and Lydia appeared on her father's arm. The sun caught the shimmering black silk, and the vision was stunning. A low sound of approval erupted from among the women, and a sharp whistle from one of the young men standing near the front. This brought a sharp look of disapproval from Preacher Smith. The crowd grew quiet, and Smith motioned for John and Lydia to come forward. When John gave Lydia's hand to Moses, the onlookers shouted their approval. The minister called for silence and began a long prayer.

May 29, 1784

Lewis Wetzel stood at the back of the crowd, only half-listening to Preacher Smith, who was taking the opportunity to preach a sermon before he got to the vows part of the ceremony. Martin Wetzel stood next to his little brother, and Martin's wife, Mary, was on the other side.

"Is this a little hard for you, Lew?" he whispered.

"Why would it be?" responded Lew.

"'Cause you're a little sweet on the bride yourself, ain't you?"

"That's what everybody says, I guess, 'ceptin' me."

"Then what are you skulkin' around back here for then?" asked Martin.

"I ain't skulkin'. I just ain't much interested in listenin' to some long-winded preacher." Lew had said this a bit louder than intended, and Mary gave Martin a hard dig with her elbow while glaring at Lew with her left index finger pressed against her lips.

They were quiet again, but Lew felt disgusted with his brother and his wife. Most of all, of course, he was disgusted with himself. When Lydia had stepped out from the cabin in her beautiful black silk dress, the pangs of jealousy had shot through Lew like a flash of lightning.

Why did Lydia prefer that Moses Shepherd?" he asked himself. *I could take him easy.* He rubbed the pockmarks on his face. But that wasn't the kind of thing that would impress Lydia, he knew. Moses was more of a gentleman, and he would be rich too. Wetzel's reputation was growing, and he was appreciated by the people who knew him. However, it was not the kind of reputation to impress a young woman like Lydia. She most likely thought of him as a rough, wild man—a killer. Useful for some things, but not the kind of man you would want as a husband.

"We are what we are, Lew," his mother had said to him once when he had complained about his lot in life. "You might as well accept that and be content with it."

The preacher had reached the part where the vows were said, and Lew listened while Lydia promised to love and cherish Moses Shepherd. He couldn't stifle the feeling of regret that trickled through him, but he determined to stop pouting and at least pretend that he was happy. There would be plenty of whiskey flowing soon, and he planned to take advantage of that. The ceremony ended with the traditional kiss, which Moses and Lydia carried out with a flair that delighted the crowd.

It was now time for the feast to begin. David Shepherd had supplied Preacher Smith with a handsome payment and now mischievously offered him a drink from the jug. Smith, known for fiery sermons—many of which were aimed at the evil of drink—refused, but with good humor.

Though he didn't approve, he knew that there would be much drinking going on with the feasting and dancing that would now transpire for the remainder of the day and well into the next one. "Thank you, David, but I must be on my way, as you well know.

I wish the best for the young couple and for you and your entire family. It was my pleasure to perform this sacred service."

Smith was also handed the reins to a packhorse, which carried a variety of foodstuffs, including a live hen. He rode off with three men hired to escort him home. It was their plan to return before the party had ended. People had scattered to find seats, as Sadie and some of the other women began to bring out the large quantities of food. There were many kinds of meat on the spits, including beef, a whole hog, and some venison. Some of the beef had been boiled with a combination of potatoes and other vegetables to make a delicious stew. There was ham, turkey, and also a variety of fish. In addition, there was an assortment of corn and beans, corn pone, mush, and johnnycake. A special treat was the raised wheat bread, a delicacy that was not often on the table of the settlers.

When the eating was finished, some of the furniture was taken out of the cabin to make room for dancing. There were at least two fiddlers present, and they would take turns keeping the music going throughout the day and well into the night. Moses and Lydia started it off, but everyone was expected to join in, including the children who mostly did their dancing outside. John Boggs, with the help of son James, rolled out a big barrel of whiskey, what the settlers referred to as Black Betty.

"Come and get it, boys," called John. "There's plenty here and more if we need it."

Plenty of trips were made to this happy fountain during the afternoon and evening. Lewis Wetzel had passed around his own jug, won in the race earlier in the day, and he visited the barrel as well. Fortified as he was, he took to the dance floor, even dancing with the beautiful but unattainable Betty Zane, who had married Ephraim McLaughlin earlier that same year. He had danced with Lydia too, although it had been his intention to avoid that. It was the custom that every man should dance at least once with the bride, and people kept asking him about it until he gave in and sought her out. "Why, yes, Lew," she had said immediately. "I'd love to dance with you."

She had continued to talk without pausing, and he was not required to say much, which suited him.

"Did you like my wedding, Lew," she had asked insistently.

He had to say something. "You are a beautiful bride, Lyddy," was his reply. "'Bout the prettiest gal this side of heaven, I reckon." He couldn't believe that all those words had spilled out.

"Why, Lew, you make me blush. That's the most wonderful thing you've ever said to me."

She kissed him quickly on the lips; but before he could say anything, Moses stepped in and whisked her away.

Not long after the dancing had begun, Zeke Thornburg raised his hand and called out. "Where is Black Betty? I want to kiss her sweet lips."

Someone brought him a cup freshly filled, and he raised it high.

"Health to the groom, not forgetting myself. And here's to the bride, thumping luck and big children."

A large cheer followed, and all drank to the health of the newly married. Such toasts were raised with regularity throughout the day, and often the bride and groom were required to respond with a drink and a kiss. The festivities continued into the night, and no one, except the children, was allowed to opt out and go to sleep.

Sometime around ten o'clock, a deputation of women surrounded Lydia and prepared to take her off to bed. The ladder to the loft was behind the open door so that as they pushed her up ahead of them, not much could be seen by the remainder of the crowd. Once in the loft, they crept past the sleeping children who had been sent up much earlier. A pair of blankets was hung to separate the far end from the rest of the room. Inside, a feather mattress borrowed from one of the neighbors had been laid over the clapboards and spread with quilts.

The women undressed Lydia, who hardly knew how to react, and helped her put on a linen bridal bedgown. They combed her hair and splashed her with perfume, the level of giggling and suggestive glances increasing as time went on. Finally they put her in the bed and covered her with the quilts, whereupon, they withdrew and climbed back down the ladder.

It was time now for the men to do their part. Lew Wetzel made sure he was not a part of this. When the women came down the ladder, a loud cheer went up, and a previously arranged group of six men grabbed Moses and pushed him toward the ladder. Lydia could hear the commotion below, and she knew what was happening. It was the part of the day she had dreaded most. She worried that the noise might awaken the children sleeping not far away, and she wondered what effect that might have on the proceedings.

She could hear some of the women below fussing at the men about the same thing. Nothing was going to impede the men from carrying out their part in this customary ceremony. They forced Moses up the ladder, though he was a bit unsteady from the amount of whiskey he had consumed as well as the anticipation of what was to come. Soon they were all standing around the bed, and one of them produced a jug from which each took a long swig, including Moses. There were some crude jokes and lots of laughter.

Lydia closed her eyes tightly at first, but she could not resist a peek to see what was happening. They were undressing Moses, of course, and soon he was standing there naked while each of them took another pull on the jug. Then one of the men—she thought it was Zeke, but she tried not to look—pulled down the covers and left her lying there exposed to all. Fortunately, she thought, *I do have on this thin gown*. Then suddenly, Moses was pushed down beside her, and the covers were thrown back over the two of them. "Have fun folks," said the men in unison, and then they were gone.

Afraid to move for several moments, Moses and Lydia finally turned together in tight embrace and forgot about everything else. Below, the dancing and frivolity continued, although some walked to the end of the room beneath where the bridal bed had been placed and tried to listen for the sound of creaking clapboards. An hour or so past midnight, Lydia and Moses heard some noise on the ladder. A tankard appeared under the hanging blankets, full of Black Betty, along with a plate that included large helpings of meat, potatoes, and bread.

"You young folks must be hungry by now," said Zeke Thornburg, poking his head and shoulders through the opening and staring at the couple. A gruff voice behind him admonished them.

"Make sure you eat it all, or we'll be up to feed it to you ourselves."

There was silence again.

"I ain't hungry, Moses," whispered Lydia. "'Least not for food."

"We'd better humor 'em," laughed Moses. "Otherwise they'll be up here again."

"I don't care," said Lydia, and they snuggled together once more. By dawn, most of the dancing had stopped, and the partiers had begun returning to their homes. Lew Wetzel and some of the other young men had settled at the edge of the woods for a few hours of sleep. By the time the sun had appeared above the ridges to the east, he had found his horse and rode back along the trail on which they had arrived the day before.

It hadn't been such a bad day after all, Lew decided. He had even enjoyed the dancing. There had been a young woman named Virginia Burns who had danced with him several times, once even when it was the ladies' choice. She had danced very close to him and kissed him on the cheek a pair of times. The look on her face had made him think that maybe she wanted more than just to dance, but then he supposed he was just imagining things.

"I just don't know nothin' about women," he said aloud.

There would be a house-raising for the newly married in the next day or two, but Lew was not looking forward to that. He didn't much care for that kind of work, and he needed to get away from Lydia anyway.

"I'll go to Fort Pitt."

9

Rescue

May 31, 1784

WETZEL LEFT HOME the day after the wedding on what he told his mother was a long hunting trip. He had spent one night at the home cabin, and after packing some provisions, he took some of the small stash of money he kept in a secret place and rode out early the next morning. He did not take his time as he usually did but kept moving steadily upstream along Wheeling Creek before angling up over the ridges toward Link's old cabin on Middle Wheeling Creek.

Eventually he made his way to the well-traveled road to Catfish Camp, which he continued to call the town now referred to as Washington. His ultimate destination was Fort Pitt; and for one of the few times in his present life, he was uninterested in hunting Indians. Fort Pitt remained the farthest western outpost for the new national government. It had served as the principal military post in the west for both the British and the Americans for the past twenty years and more. That Wetzel should be interested in seeing such a place was natural and perhaps it was surprising, thought Lew to himself, that he had never had the idea of visiting there before.

The question had flashed through his mind as to whether he would be known there. It was clearly satisfying to him that his reputation was growing so rapidly in the Wheeling area. He was aware that people talked about him and pointed him out to strangers as a skilled scout and hunter. His reason for going to Fort Pitt, however, had nothing to do with curiosity about military or governmental matters, nor as a means of widening his sphere of fame and influence.

On the contrary, he hoped to remain unknown and unnoticed. He had decided that it was time for him to have a woman, and he figured that Fort Pitt was the best place for that to happen. He had heard plenty of talk from soldiers and militiamen who had been there, and he thought he would be able to find what he was looking for, even if he had to pay for it. He had not been able to discuss it with his brothers nor any of his friends. Jonathan Zane had been his mentor in many ways, but not in the ways of women. It was a subject much too embarrassing for him to discuss with anyone he knew.

The first day was hard travel, and he reached Washington and camped for the night on Catfish Creek, just below the town. He rose early the next morning to make the last push of some twenty miles to reach the forks of the Ohio. He came to the banks of the Monongahela, just a short way above its junction with the Allegheny, which created the forks. He followed a trail that led up to a bluff overlooking the river. There was a big rock slab near the edge of the bluff and an old gnarled oak standing just past the rock. He dismounted and crawled up on the top of the slab.

The view was breathtaking. He could see the point of land formed up like an arrowhead, with the blue Allegheney framing it along the far side, and the Monongahela sliding up to the point from below him. He turned his gaze to the left where he could see the Ohio, born from the combination of the two rivers, flowing silently off to the northwest. The fort stood very near the point, with a scattering of log houses and buildings flanking it to the east and to the south along the right bank of the Monongahela. He was surprised by the width of the Monongahela here, which he judged to be close to a quarter mile, much wider than it was at the mouth of Dunkard Creek, where Wetzel knew it so well.

He was also struck by how still and dark it was. It looked deep, and he realized that this might not be a great place to cross. There was a hint of a sandbar in midstream directly across from the site of the fort. He thought he could see on the far bank, upstream a good part of a mile, a kind of platform that suggested a ferry. That would cost money he didn't want to spend. "We'll find us a better crossin' ole Jack," he said aloud to the horse as he jumped down from the rock and remounted. He went down near the edge of the river and rode back upstream for several miles.

Finally, at a place where the river was not nearly as wide nor as deep, he urged his mount into the water and made his way across. The horse was forced to swim, but there were no major difficulties. Although he would have had no way to know it, Wetzel had chosen the very spot where Braddock had crossed his army twenty-nine years earlier on the way to his disastrous defeat and untimely death. The detour had taken over three hours, and it was dusk by the time Wetzel rode into the first line of cabins that made up the settlement already being called Pittsburgh.

The trail along the right bank of the Monongahela was called Water Street, and he soon passed the site of the ferry he had seen from across the river. It sat next to a tiny stream that led inland, and his horse splashed through the water with no trouble. A single board sign with letters painted on it hung at an angle from a tall post that supported the dock for the ferryboat.

Wetzel assumed it was the owner's name, but he couldn't read the crude lettering that spelled out the name Henderson. An early morning shower had left the street muddy, and the horse plodded through it lazily. Both he and his rider were exhausted, and Wetzel felt no urgency to push the horse any faster. They passed a tavern not unlike Sam Mason's place on Wheeling Creek. He remembered the day he had gone there with his father and brother, George. He remembered too the woman at Mason's, and how she had looked at him.

He resolved to return soon to see if this Pittsburgh tavern had some of the same accommodations as Mason's. He finally reached the fort and rode up to the gate, expecting it to open for him. He soon realized that there was a big difference between Fort Pitt and Fort Henry. There were two sentries at the gate, and the bigger one snarled at him with a voice of utter contempt.

"What's your bizness here, farmer man?"

"I ain't no farmer," answered Wetzel, feeling his anger rising. "Just hopin' to spend a night or two at the fort."

This was Wetzel's common practice at Fort Henry, where he was always welcome to stay in one of the cabins that lined the inside of the stockade and to place his horse in the animal corral. He had assumed this would be the case at Fort Pitt as well. He could already see that he was wrong about that.

"This ain't no inn, it's a military post," explained the sentry, and not kindly. "The tradin' post is closed for the night, so 'less you got official business with the commander, Lieutenant Luckett, you ain't welcome."

"He don't look smart 'nuff to have no official business, Lem." The other sentry had decided to speak. Now he glared at Wetzel. "Git you, dumb ass."

This was more than Lew Wetzel was accustomed to taking, and he reached for the tomahawk at his belt, figuring these two needed to learn some manners.

The one called Lem was too quick, however, and he had his musket pointed right at Wetzel's chest.

"Watch it, Buck!" he shouted. "This is a mean one."

Wetzel let the tomahawk slide back into his belt. "I reckon I'll meet you boys again sometime," he hissed. He turned the horse and rode back in the direction from which he had come, trembling with rage as he heard the laughter from the two sentries.

The second of the day's major disappointments was about to greet him. He had noticed a place called Samuel Semple's Tavern just a short way back that he recognized as a possible place to spend the night, even though he could not read the signage. There was a building in the back that he thought could be a stable. He reined in his horse at the gate, slid off, and went inside. He was faced with a long bar that stretched away from him, with several tables beside it.

Two men stood at the bar, and another man sat at one of the tables. They paid him no attention, but the man behind the counter, Sam Semples himself, came to the end immediately to attend to this possible new patron. Wetzel's anger had not yet subsided, and the dark look on his face brought the man to a halt, not sure what to expect.

"I need a place to stay the night," said Wetzel gruffly.

"You can have a bed for two dollars, three if you want it all to yourself. And clean sheets. If ya got a horse, that's another two dollars." The man could see the surprise on Wetzel's face, although he was relieved that the hard look had softened.

Taken aback by the prices, Wetzel could only shake his head without speaking. He had never thought about what it might cost him to stay at Fort Pitt; only that it seemed a good idea to come here. He had only a few dollars with him, and it would all be gone well before he had a chance to carry out the purpose for which he had come. Sam Semples had seen this before. These hunters came in from the woods with no idea of what life was like in a settlement like this one.

"If your horse is decent, I'll buy him from you for six dollars."

Wetzel pondered this offer. It would cost him that much if he stayed for even three days, and having the cash in his pocket was enticing. If he didn't take this offer, he couldn't stay in this town at all.

"How about ten for the horse?" he asked after a bit.

"The offer is six. Take it or leave it." Sam turned to go back down the bar.

"I'll take it," said Wetzel suddenly. "And the two-dollar bed."

"Let me look at the horse first," said Sam, who lifted the plank and walked out toward the door.

"He's a damned fine horse," said Lew.

"They all are," replied John sarcastically. "But I'll see fer myself."

The deal was completed and after a light supper of soup-and-corn bread, which came with the two dollar rate, Wetzel was shown to the small room. It had one bed, with a lumpy mattress Wetzel figured was filled with corn shucks. So far, no bedmate had appeared; and if that happened, Lew had decided that one of them would sleep on the floor.

As soon as he had time to think, Wetzel was sick with regret at what he had done. He had given up a valuable horse, and now, what was he going to do when he was ready to leave? Clearly he couldn't stay here very long, and as he thought about it, he could have spent the nights out in the woods. He would have had to buy some food for himself and his horse, but he could have managed that. Now it was too late.

He tried the bed and eventually drifted off into a troubled sleep. The next morning, Wetzel waited for the owner, Sam, to appear. He had made the decision to buy back the horse and forget his entire plan. It was midmorning before Semples appeared, and when Wetzel informed him about the horse, Sam was quick to answer.

"He's yours again for fifteen dollars."

"What?" cried Wetzel. "You only gave me six."

"You were right. He's a damned fine horse." Sam saw Wetzel's face darken again as it was when he first saw him.

"That's robbery," said Wetzel. "The deal's off. I'll give you the two dollars for the night, and you give me back my six. You can't prove we ever made the deal anyway."

"Oh, we made the deal all right, friend."

"You ain't my friend, and I ain't got fifteen dollars."

"That's your problem and not mine. You can take the saddle and pouch though. I won't charge you for keepin' them overnight."

Fearing that the big hunter might take matters in his own hands, Semples had reached under the plank bar and produced a pistol, which he laid on the bar next to him.

"You're the second man that's waved a gun at me since I've been here," growled Wetzel. "I don't like it much." He had his own rifle with him, but he was not holding it in a threatening way.

Sam said nothing but remained wary.

"Well, I've got only myself to blame for this mess," Wetzel said finally. "I'll be back for my things."

With that, he stomped out, and Semples, relieved that nothing worse had happened, made no protest. Wetzel headed for the waterfront, hopeful that he could find some work and improve his financial condition. He had planned all along to try to earn some wages. The settlement was bustling with earnest businessmen, taking advantage of its position as a military post and as a jumping off place for travelers going down the Ohio.

He was able to get a job, loading provisions on one of the flatboats, and after working most of the afternoon, he was paid one dollar. He had met a man named Nat Lollar whom he liked. Lollar was a bit older than Lew and seemed well-informed. Although it was quite unlike him, Wetzel had confided in Lollar about his predicament, and the man had told him that many visitors to the town simply slept on the grounds over on the other side of the fort. "There's usually some Injuns camped over there, but there's plenty of room if you don't mind the company."

"I ain't much for sleepin' with Injuns, but don't want to be payin' for it neither."

The two men stood near the pier where they had been working, Wetzel leaning on his rifle.

"I see you don't like to be separated too much from that gun, do you?" observed Nat. "It is a beauty, I hafta say."

"It is a part of me, I reckon. I don't never plan to be without it anyways."

It had been somewhat of a problem to have the gun where he could keep an eye on it while he worked. The man who hired him had offered to store it for him, but Lew didn't trust that. "I'll keep it with me if you don't mind."

"Well, suit yourself," the man had said. "As long as it don't interfere with your workin'."

Lollar had laughed when Lew told him about the two sentries. "Yah, I know those two. They think they're pretty tough. They like to do their drinkin' over at Richard's Tavern right up this street."

Wetzel took note of the location and indicated he might like to visit the place.

"They've got good food there too," added Nat. "You can git a fine meal for a dollar." He held up the gold coin just received for the day's labor. "Course that's kind of dear when that's a whole day's wage. Sometimes you can get some bread and soup for fifty cents."

"I reckon I'll go there for some supper," said Wetzel. "You want to go too?"

"Mebbe tomorrow night," replied Lollar. "I've got somethin' else to do tonight."

Wetzel wondered if Nat's plans involved a woman. He had mentioned to Lew that there were women to be had at the Black Bear Saloon if he was of such a mind. "Watch out for that bartender though. He ain't to be trusted."

Wetzel went to Richard's Tavern first and spent his day's earnings on food and drink. There were more than ten men in the room, and he noted with interest that several contests were held, including a hotly contested arm wrestling match. He waited for some time, hoping that Lem or Buck might show up. When that didn't happen, he made his way to Semple's to pick up his bedroll and personal gear, which had been kept for him as promised.

Now it was decision time, and he made it quickly. There was never really any doubt in his mind as to what was coming next. He headed for the Black Bear Saloon, which was some five streets deep away from the waterfront. The saloon was in a large log structure with two stories. A weather-beaten sign protruded out over the door, with a faded picture of a bear displayed on both sides.

Just inside was a bar with a man sitting on a stool at the end closest to the door. The man gave Wetzel a big wave and a wide grin. He was missing several teeth, and his wide nose was flanked by a hideous scar that covered his right cheek. He had heavy eyebrows, but his head was mostly bald, with a small patch of gray just at the back. "Come in young feller," he croaked in a hoarse voice. "We've got just about anything you might want here. What will it be?"

Lewis was at a loss as to how to proceed. He knew what he wanted all right, but he didn't think he should come right out with that. There were two men at the bar, and another man was seated at a table with a bottle of whiskey in front of him. In the dim light, he could see two women standing in the back, both clad in loose fitting dresses and watching the men in the room with a certain wariness.

"A shot of whiskey," said Wetzel after a moment.

"That'll be twenty-five cents, mister," said the bartender.

His name was Bart, as Wetzel learned later when one of the other patrons addressed him. Wetzel paid him the money and sat at one of the tables. He couldn't keep his eyes off the women, and he didn't notice when Bart caught the eye of one of them and nodded toward Wetzel. The girl immediately made her way over to where Lew was sitting. The other thing that Lew had failed to notice was the look on Bart's face when he saw the coin pouch that Lew had taken from beneath his belt and opened while searching for the money to pay for the drink.

"Hello there, handsome," purred the young woman. "And what's your name."

Wetzel was embarrassed but also pleased. He thought the girl was quite pretty.

"They call me Lew," he managed to stammer. "But nobody ever called me handsome."

"My name is Eva, and I think you're mighty handsome."

She slid into the chair next to him, opposite the one on which he had piled his gear and his rifle.

"So what might you be lookin' for, Mr. Handsome Lew?" asked Eva, leaning in close to him and allowing her loose dress to fall open in the front.

This is exactly what I came lookin' for, thought Lew to himself, but he wasn't sure what he should do next. "You're mighty pretty," he said aloud, feeling very stupid.

"Why, thank you, Mr. Lew. For two little dollars, I'd be glad to show you just how pretty I am."

As desire and arousal rose up within him, Lew could barely speak. "I'd like to see that," he eventually choked out.

"Come with me then," said Eva, standing and beckoning him to follow. He picked up his belongings and his gun and stepped toward her. "You don't need all that, Lew," she said. "We ain't goin' huntin'."

"Can't leave it down here," Lew pointed out, although he could see that it didn't fit the mood of the moment to be lugging the stuff. "Suit yourself, but I'd rather you'd be thinkin' about me." She opened the top of her dress enough to expose one breast, then covered it again, and began walking quickly toward the stair at the back.

The other girl gave them a knowing smile as they passed and laughed at the sight of the lumbering hunter with a bag under one arm and the long rifle cradled in the other, climbing the stair with such determination.

Wetzel heard her laughing and knew that he was the object, but it didn't matter now. He was very close to finally realizing what he had thought about and dreamed about so much. His plan for coming here was about to be fulfilled. At the top of the stairs, they turned back into a big room, which had been divided into a hallway and several small rooms to the side, all separated by hanging curtains. The curtains were open, and in each room was a low bed with no other furniture.

Eva turned into the last of the little rooms and waited for Lew to follow her in. She pulled the curtain closed and grinned at Lew. She pulled the dress straps off her shoulders and let the top drop down. She was naked to the waist. Without taking his eyes off her, Lew began removing his hunting shirt.

"Whoa there, handsome," cautioned Eva. "You have to pay me before the dress comes all the way off."

Lew said nothing but quickly fumbled at his belt to find his money. He fished out two coins and gave them to her. She pushed the dress down to the floor and stepped out of it gracefully, standing near the head of the bed and by the curtain that separated them from the next room. Graceful he was not, but he tore off his clothes, dropping his breeches and his belt together near the bed. So focused was he on this beautiful woman that he failed to notice as she nudged his belt and pants over near the bottom of the curtain. She sank down on the bed then, and he fell into her arms.

June 1, 1784

Wetzel had fallen asleep and had to be prodded awake by the girl, who was still lying beside him. At first he could not remember where he was, but it came back to him quickly. His eye caught the sight of his pants and belt stretched out just inside the curtain, and he saw his coin pouch lying by itself. He jumped up and retrieved the pouch, turning it upside down and shaking it.

"Damn! It's empty," he shouted. "Somebody stole my money." He turned to look at the girl, but she had disappeared. "Of course," he exclaimed. "She was on it too." He grabbed his breeches and put them on, relieved to find that his knife and tomahawk were still attached to his belt. He finished dressing and raised the curtain, ducking under it into the next room, which was empty. Dashing out into the hallway, he raced to the end and down the stairs.

"What a damned fool I am. I'll kill that Bart."

Wetzel stopped at the foot of the stairs. Bart was nowhere to be found, nor were there any of the women present. A half-dozen men were quietly drinking, and all eyes were on him as he stood by the stairs. A dark-haired skinny man stood behind the bar. Wetzel wanted to blurt out that he had been robbed, but something stopped him. He wondered if he should search everyone in the room, but he knew that would be of no use. He had no doubt who the thief was, and he was long gone. "This is not the end of this," Lew told himself quietly.

Already a plan had begun to gather in his mind, and he realized that it would never work if he indulged his angry feelings just now. Even though he wanted to tear the place apart, he knew that it would not get his money back. He turned and went back up the stairs to retrieve his rifle and his other things. After leaving the Black Bear Saloon, Wetzel thought of reporting the robbery to someone, but had no idea who that would be. The only authorities in the town would be the soldiers, and he didn't expect any help from them. He continued to chastise himself for his foolishness, and he tried to stifle the guilty feelings that kept erupting. He made his way toward the camps on the Allegheny side.

What am I going to do? he thought. *I've got no money and no horse, and several men to get even with.*

In spite of all his troubles, he also felt warmth and satisfaction over his first experience with a woman. Eva had been very nice, even if she was a thief. He found a place to spend the night among some trees, a distance back from the banks of the Allegheny. Several other men were already sleeping nearby; and in the moonlight, he could see some little huts near the stockade that he knew were occupied by Indians. He pulled a blanket from his pack and spread it on the ground just under a big maple. He stretched out on the blanket, fully clothed and with his rifle partly under him. It was not long before he had drifted off.

Morning came quickly, and the sounds around him brought Wetzel awake shortly after the sun had appeared. He reached inside his hunting shirt to retrieve the last of the parched corn and jerked venison that he had brought with him. He had not had enough to eat to really satisfy him since he had left home, and he wasn't likely to have much today. It was vital that he be able to find work again—a fact that struck him even more forcefully, recalling his misfortune of the night before.

He hurried down to the waterfront. Lew had hoped that an earlier start might mean he could earn more than the one dollar of the day before. His hopes were unfulfilled, but he did manage to get a job of loading a flatboat just as on the previous day; and once again, his friend Nat joined him. At the end of the day, they made their way to Richard's Tavern. Lew had not told his friend about the previous night's tragedy for he was embarrassed. Likewise, he did not reveal his purpose in going to the tavern.

With only a dollar to his name, Lew took the fifty-cent supper, for he needed to have some coins in his pouch if he was to carry out his ultimate plan. Nat seemed to understand his companion's money problems and bought him a drink. They sat there for quite sometime, watching as a pair of men settled into an arm wrestling match. Just before Lew started to get up to get closer to the action, Nat punched him with his elbow.

"Look who just blew in," he whispered.

Lew looked quickly to see the two sentries, Lem and Buck, stride into the room, waving to some of the other customers. They looked around the room, and though they saw Nat and Lew, there was no indication of recognition. Wetzel was glad of that, although he very much would have liked to get even with them for their earlier treatment. That, however, would have disrupted his planning for the evening. His first purpose was to get his hands on some spending money. It wasn't long before Lem had challenged a man to an arm wrestling match, and he won twice in a row, winning a dollar.

A big man drinking by himself at the bar became annoyed at Lem's bragging and challenged him with a dollar bet. The rest of the crowd had gathered to watch this match and root against Lem, but he won the match. It was then that Lew Wetzel stepped up.

"I'll take ya on fer two dollars," he said quietly.

"Well, what have we here?" asked Lem. He looked Lew up and down, trying to judge whether it was someone he could easily beat. Although Wetzel was a big man, much taller than the average man and broad shouldered, he appeared to be slender with average-sized arms and hands. Lem decided that he would be an easy mark.

"Let's see your money then," said Lem. "You seem mighty anxious to part with it."

"Here's my money," exclaimed Lew, pulling his tomahawk from his belt and laying it on the table.

There was a loud gasp from the onlookers.

"That ain't money," protested Lem.

"It's better'n money," answered Lew. "Besides, there ain't much chance for you to lose anyway, is there?"

"Well, that's true," boasted Lem. "If you wanta give away your 'hawk, who am I to refuse."

Lem put down his two dollars, and the two men put their elbows together and grasped hands. Before Lem knew what was happening, Wetzel had slammed his hand to the table, pulling Lem's arm with it.

"Damn!" shouted Lem. "I wasn't ready."

"Too bad," said Lew. "That's one."

The match consisted of two out of three, so they set up for the second try. Lem was sure that he was the stronger, and he wouldn't be surprised the second time. They exerted themselves against each other for several seconds with no movement either way, when suddenly Wetzel again slammed their arms down.

A look of bewilderment came over Lem's face. "You cheated me," he shouted suddenly, rising to his feet.

His friend Buck also stood and took a step toward Lew. He stopped when he saw the knife appear in Wetzel's left hand. Lew had grabbed Lem by the front of his shirt.

"I didn't cheat, and you owe me two dollars. I ought to stick this knife right in your gizzard, you son of a bitch." Lem looked around him, his face white with fear, hoping for help from somebody. No one else moved.

"Do you remember me yet?" Lew was holding the knifepoint just under the breastbone. "I'm the so-called farmer you pointed a gun at the other day. My name is Lewis Wetzel."

Lem was unable to say anything. Wetzel pushed him back into the chair, grabbing the tomahawk and the two dollars from the table. He backed up to where Nat was standing, a look of astonishment on his face. Lew picked up his bag and his rifle. "Thanks for your help, Nat," he said, and then he was out the door.

"What do you know about him?" asked Buck, his question directed at Nat.

"Not much," said Nat. "But I think he may have killed a few Indians in his day."

Wetzel was on his way to the Black Bear, and he was wasting no time. When he arrived, he looked for a place to hide his rifle and his bag, not wanting to be bothered with it inside. He walked around to the back of the building. It was dark and there were no other buildings or houses in sight. An old rotten log lay against the base of the building, and Wetzel placed his gun and bag behind it. He looked again in all directions to make sure no one could see him. Satisfied, he returned to the front door.

He was hoping that Bart would not remember him from the previous night, but he had no choice but to go in. Another man was sitting on the stool at the end of the bar. Wetzel wasn't sure if he was the skinny man he had seen on the way out the previous night. The man welcomed him and asked what he would like.

Feeling that there was no time to waste, Lew came right to the point. "I want a woman," he said with some urgency.

"Well, I reckon we can help you with that," said the skinny man, whose name was John.

"Good," exclaimed Lew.

"It'll cost you two dollars for an hour with that beauty right over there," replied John, pointing at a dark-haired woman sitting at a table near the back wall. John motioned for her to come over. "Her name is Mary."

Lew was relieved to see that the woman was not Eva, who might spoil his plans. However, Mary was not so pretty in his view, and he was a bit uneasy since Mary was his mother's name. It didn't seem right to be making love to a girl named Mary. Still, as Mary walked provocatively toward him, Lew felt a stirring of desire.

"You can pay me 'stead of her," said John.

Lew took out his coin pouch and found the two dollars. He had two small coins left, and he made sure to let them clink together for John to hear.

"Hello, big guy," crooned Mary. "Would you like to go upstairs with me?"

"I reckon I would," said Wetzel.

They went up the stairs and back to the same room that Lew had been in the night before. Mary said nothing but began to undress. Wetzel removed his pants and carefully placed them and the belt close to the curtain wall. He climbed into the bed next to Mary, taking her in his arms, but keeping an eye on where his clothes were lying. Although it was difficult, he kept his attention there enough to notice, after a few minutes, the hand reaching under the curtain to retrieve his pants.

Immediately he rose from the bed and dove under the curtain just as his pants disappeared. He grabbed a leg and held on tightly, being dragged under the curtain. Once on the other side, he got to his feet with enough traction to cause the owner of the leg to stumble when he gave it a tug. He could see that it was his old friend Bart, just as he had hoped it would be. The man was facing Wetzel; and as he regained his feet, he produced a knife in his right hand. Lew shifted his own weight to his right foot and swung his left in a high arc that caught Bart's wrist and sent the knife flying. The cracking sound let Wetzel know that his blow was crippling.

"Owww! You damned fool, you've broke my arm," shrieked Bart.

"That ain't all I aim to break," shouted Lew as he lowered his shoulder and drove into Bart's chest with all his might.

Bart's head hit the floor first, and he was unconscious, unable to feel the broken ribs. As he hit the floor, his coin purse had come loose, coins spilling out in all directions. This was an unexpected prize. As he stooped to pick up his pants, he sensed another danger, and he turned to see Mary coming at him with his tomahawk raised high in her right hand, intent on bringing it down against his head. Wetzel was too quick for her, stepping to the side and reaching across to seize her arm before she could complete the blow.

She started to scream, and he put his left hand over her mouth. "If you scream, I might have to harm you," cautioned Lew. "I ain't never hit a woman afore, but I reckon I can do it if I have to." He removed his hand slowly.

"He'll kill me when you're gone," she whimpered. "He'll think I helped you."

"He ain't about to kill nobody for awhile," Lew assured her. He leaned down and picked up Bart's coin purse, picking out two coins. "Here's your two dollars, Mary," he said somewhat tenderly. "Take it and get out of here. Go where he can't find you."

Mary said nothing more, turning to go back to the other room. Wetzel reached out and took her arm. "Don't go down until I'm gone," he said somewhat sternly. Then he let her go.

Wetzel finished dressing, then picked up the spilled coins, put them back in Bart's purse and stuffed it safely under his belt. He hadn't counted the money, but he could easily tell it was much more than he had lost and had ever possessed at any time in his life. He restored his tomahawk to its rightful place and stuck Bart's knife under his belt as well. He checked Bart and determined that he wasn't dead, although it would be sometime before he was conscious again.

Suddenly he drew his scalping knife, and with a practiced flourish, he sliced off a small piece of the scalp at the crown, the place where the little tuft of hair grew. He dropped the bloody piece onto Bart's chest and, after admiring his work for a moment, walked out. Once down the stairs, Lew walked straight through the room, looking to neither side and acknowledging no one. He wondered what sounds had been heard by the patrons, and especially John, who he thought might try to stop him. John watched as Wetzel went out the door, but said nothing.

Once outside, Lew went to the back to pick up his pack and his rifle. He listened for a moment to see if there was to be pursuit from inside the Black Bear. Hearing nothing and seeing nothing, he moved quickly toward the small pond that he knew was not far, and then he headed down the first street he came to and walked in the direction of the waterfront. This would bring him just a short distance up Water Street from Semple's tavern, his intended destination. He held no grudge against Semple, but he needed a horse.

"Maybe old Jack is still here," he muttered to himself as he came to the stable.

He could see the lamp inside the tavern was still lit, and that there was a patron still drinking at the bar. It was late, but he knew he would have to wait until all was quiet. He wondered if Semple would come out to take a look around before he went to bed. On the back side, well out of sight of the tavern, he knew there was a big door through which the horses were taken in and out. He went there and tried the door, but it was locked. He knew it was barred from the inside. The door on the front side had a lock that opened from outside, but it was too risky to try that one.

He moved back to a log hut on the far side of the block. It was dark, and he sat down beside it to wait. This was not hard for him for it was an important part of being a successful hunter. Wetzel waited for what must have been two hours. His only fear was that Bart might have come around and organized a search of some kind. He smiled at his good fortune in getting Bart's money. What a fool Bart had been for carrying it with him.

How many fools like me has he robbed? wondered Lew. Bart hadn't appeared, and Wetzel had heard no commotion nearby to suggest that there was any kind of search for him underway. Now he moved around to the front of the stable and tried the small door. It was locked as he expected. There was a window that he had noticed on the side of the stable to his right. He went there now and looked at it carefully. It was square and uncovered, big enough that he could squeeze through it. The difficulty was that it was too high for him to reach. He must find something to stand on.

He went to the back again and placed his pack and gun on the ground next to the door. It was then that he saw a small stump near the corner of the building. It was badly scarred on its top, clearly having been used as a chopping block. To his relief, Wetzel discovered that he could lift it and managed to get it around to the side and under the window. The block was just tall enough to enable Lew to reach the window and get a good grasp on its edge. He gave a quick push up and was able to pull himself up enough to get his head and shoulders into the opening.

He rested his chest against the edge for a moment, and with a second pull, he propelled himself through and tumbled to the floor. His good luck was holding, for he fell into an open stall that contained some loose straw. He had landed on his right shoulder, and it hurt a bit, but not enough to be a worry. It was very dark, and Wetzel waited for his eyes to adjust as much as possible. Though he couldn't see much, Lew made his way down the walkway along the end of the stalls.

At the third stall he heard a soft whinny. "By God," exclaimed Lew aloud. "Is that you, Jack?" It was Jack, and Wetzel's spirits lifted immediately. His own horse was still there, and on the low wall next to Jack was his saddle and bridle. Lew wasted no time in putting them on Jack and leading him out of the stall. They went to the back door where Lew raised the latch and pulled the door open. He could not believe that he was actually free of the troubles he had been in only a few hours before.

He tied his pack on the horse, placed his rifle in its sling, and began to pull the stable door shut. Before closing it completely, he stopped and pulled out his money pouch. Counting out ten of the large coins, he walked back to the stall where Jack had been kept and placed the coins on top of a corner post.

"I reckon that's fair," Wetzel said aloud. "Gives him his price back and two night's stay." Nodding his head in satisfaction, he walked back, mounted Jack, and began riding out of the settlement. The wonderful feeling of freedom reminded him of the night he and Jake had slipped away from the Wyandot camp seven years earlier. As he neared the woods outside of the town, Wetzel turned back for a last look.

"Never did git into Fort Pitt, did we Jack!"

July 3, 1784

It was the third day of July, and Lew Wetzel was on the river trail below Beech Bottom where he had spent the previous night. He wanted to be in the Wheeling settlements before dark because he figured there would be a big party at Fort Henry tomorrow to celebrate the nation's independence.

The war with the British was officially over, although the announcement of the final treaty had not reached the frontier until late the previous year. The fighting had been stopped for nearly two years, at least with the British soldiers. The skirmishing with their Indian allies had lessened but continued to be a constant problem. That didn't bother Wetzel too much, for he expected his war with the red men to continue as long as he drew breath. He had been gone for over a month.

After leaving Pittsburgh, he had gone back down along the south bank of the Ohio and crossed to Logstown, where he had purchased some provisions. He did some hunting as he made his way on down the Ohio. When he came to the location of Baker's tavern, he spent time looking around. The old tavern, which was located on the Virginia side of the Ohio across from the mouth of Yellow Creek, had been abandoned. It was here in 1774 that members of the family of the Mingo chief, Logan, had been killed by frontiersmen led by Daniel Greathouse.

It was widely believed that these killings had led to Dunmore's War. Lew's father and brother Martin had both fought in that war. Passing by Mingo Bottom and Hollidays Cove Fort at Harmon Creek, he came to Cross Creek. Here Lewis turned to follow it eastward into Pennsylvania and then turned south, pursuing narrow trails and tiny creeks through rough country until he came to Buffalo Creek. This was more familiar ground, and he turned down the Dutch Fork until he came to the Miller farm.

He stayed several days with his friend, Jacob Miller, especially enjoying the good food that came with the visit. He was careful not to tell Miller of his Pittsburgh adventures. Instead of returning across country to his own home, he followed down the Buffalo all the way back to the Ohio and then to Beech Bottom. It was the longest trip he had ever taken, and he was beginning to think longingly about the return to Fort Henry. Now as he approached the mouth of Short Creek, something caught his eye. He dismounted and walked along the bank of the Ohio to the edge of the creek. Some bushes crowded the bank, but there was an open landing spot at water's edge.

On the opposite edge, the terrain was rocky, and it was here that Wetzel could see what had attracted his attention at first. In the water just next to a large rock was the end of a canoe, which was protruding by a couple of feet above the water level. *Tryin' to hide it for the return trip, eh, boys'?* mused Lewis. "*I reckon we got some red visitors 'round here somewheres.* An attempt had been made to sink the canoe out of sight, but it had hadn't remained completely sunk. He searched along the bank for a ways and noted several moccasin prints in some places where the ground was soft. *There's at least two and probably four of the bastards,* he speculated. *Looks like they're headed up the creek.*

He wondered if he should try to warn the people at West Liberty or at Van Meter's, but he didn't think this party was strong enough to cause trouble in either of those places. It was the individuals in the remote farms who were in danger, and he could not warn all of them. "There is one thing I can do though," he said, thinking aloud. He climbed up on Jack and splashed across Short Creek, quickly dismounting on the other side. He made his way to the partially submerged canoe and began to tug and pull on it, finally succeeding in drawing it up on the bank.

Turning it over, he drew his tomahawk and struck a hard blow in the bottom. The bark skin was tough, and it took several blows to break through. "Don't reckon this one will float too good anymore," he remarked with satisfaction. He replaced the canoe in its supposed hiding place, trying to do it in the same way as the Indians had. Once done, he swung up on Jack again and rode along the trail toward Wheeling. It was dusk by the time Wetzel had reached Fort Henry. He hadn't noted before how much the old fort had decayed. Many of the pickets along the north wall were rotten and part of the wall was leaning badly. There was no garrison stationed there now, nor even a permanent commandant. There were a couple of families staying there along with some single men.

Lew found an empty hut and placed his belongings inside. There was a fenced-in area for livestock, and Lew put Jack inside, removing the saddle and bridle. A pile of loose hay rested just outside the gate of this corral for the use of the residents. This was provided by Ebenezer Zane, who also helped keep a variety of provisions in one of the huts, which was used as a storehouse. Although John Boggs was still technically the commandant at Fort Henry, he spent little time there.

Catherine Zane, the wife of Silas, was living in the commandant's quarters with her infant son, whose name was also Silas. Her husband was away on a long trip with a trader named George Green to the Indian country with a load of goods and was not expected to return for months. A young woman named Rose Forrest was also living there. She had been busy acting as a nurse for John Frazier, who had come to Wheeling from his home near Williamsburg with a plan to go on to Kentucky. Unfortunately, he had taken ill and was only now well enough to begin thinking about resuming his journey. In the meantime, however, Frazier had fallen in love with Rose.

The fourth of July dawned in a splash of sunlight, the beginning of a beautiful day. The celebration had begun before noon, and the fiddlers had commenced playing their tunes almost immediately. Plenty of food was available, and while the dancing began inside the commandant's cabin, games and contests were underway outside. Wetzel had come early and enjoyed the fine food. While he was eating, Rose Forrest sat near him with some of her friends, to whom she announced that she and John Frazier were planning to marry. Just then, Frazier walked in and came to where they were sitting. Lewis knew Rose but had not met the young man. He remembered dancing with her a time or two at Lydia's wedding.

"Here he is now," beamed Rose. "We are going up on the Buffalo to meet my family."

She introduced Frazier to Wetzel. "John, this is Lewis Wetzel," she said with a smile.

"Pleased to meet you," offered John. "I've heard lots about you."

Lew nodded, offering his hand. "Congratulations," he said finally, and with a nod to Rose, "you, too, Rose." He had always thought Rose was quite attractive, and he felt just a small twinge of jealousy. The two lovers conversed happily with the others for a short time, then made ready to leave.

"You say you're going up to the Buffalo?" asked Wetzel of Rose.

"Yes," said Rose. "We're leavin' right now."

"I ain't sure it's a good idea," warned Lew. "I just came from up that way, and I saw some fresh Injun sign up on Short Creek."

"Oh, Lew," cried Rose. "Don't spoil our day."

Frazier, who was alarmed by the comment, did not want to disappoint his fiancé, and so he spoke with a false bravado.

"We'll be fine, Mr. Wetzel," he said. "I have a gun, and I know how to use it."

"If you must go, then you best not take the river road, for you'd be too easy to spot along there. Take the woodland trail up to West Liberty. And the name is Lew."

"Thank you for the advice," responded Frazier, extending his hand. "Lew."

"Advice is cheap, but you need to be careful." With a wide smile, Lew continued, "We've only got one Forest Rose."

Rose laughed. "He likes to call me that," she explained to Frazier. Not a large woman, Rose was slender and well proportioned. She had a fair complexion, though her hair was dark and short. Her face was round, with a touch of rosiness on each cheek, graced by a dimple on each side. Frazier gazed upon her lovingly, then took her arm, and they walked out.

Ebenezer Zane watched them go and then came to talk with Wetzel. "I heard what you told them, Lewis. Do you think I should stop them?"

"I don't reckon they'll stop for nobody, Colonel Zane. Rose seemed pretty determined."

"I'm afraid you're right," admitted Zane. "But maybe they'll listen to me."

"Prob'ly them reds'll go up north and stay away from the fort at Van Meter's. If so, they should be all right."

The midday sun dodging through the overhead branches was pleasant as it fell on the two riders. The trail was rough, and much of it uphill, but it was beautiful. The lovers enjoyed the solitude as well as the scenery. They had gone only a few miles when Frazier suddenly reined in his horse. "Look there, Rose," he whispered, pointing up the trail at the top of a small rise. A large buck stood there along with two smaller ones.

Startled, the two young ones bounded away, but the buck stood his ground for a moment, staring at the two riders. His delay cost him dearly, for Frazier had pulled his rifle from its sling and quickly slid off his mount. Kneeling, he got off a shot just as the buck turned to run away. The buck fell to the ground but struggled to his feet and ran into the woods to the right of the trail.

"I got him," shouted Frazier. "We can take some meat to your folks. That'll make a nice present."

"But he ran away, John," Rose pointed out.

"He won't go far. You stay here with the horses while I go after him."

Rose sat down on a fallen tree trunk and held the horse's bridles in her hands. "Don't go too far," she pleaded. "I don't much like being here alone."

"I'll be right back, Rose." It did occur to John that he should reload his gun, which he did before rushing off into the woods. The deer had plunged down a little ravine that fed off from the trail, and Frazier followed after him, noting the drops of blood on the leaves of some bushes at the head of the ravine.

"I hit him all right," he said to himself. "He can't go far."

In spite of his injury, the deer managed to make his way through the brush much easier than the man, and they had ventured away from the trail by some two hundred yards. Here the deer made a sharp turn and began to double back. Frazier retreated along the path he had come, planning to cut through to intercept the struggling buck. It was then he heard the loud scream. "Oh God, it's Rose!"

He began scrambling back toward the spot where he had left her. "Oh, please, God. Don't let her be hurt. What a fool I am for leaving her there for a stupid deer." When he was close enough to see what was happening, his heart nearly stopped. Two Indians had Rose, one was tying her hands together and the other held his hand over her mouth. Two other braves had secured the horses and were watching the spot where Frazier and the deer had entered the woods.

Frazier's first thought was to shoot the big Indian who was tying Rose's hands. He raised the rifle barrel but quickly lowered it. *If I shoot now, they'll kill us both*, he thought. If he stayed where he was, he would be easy to find, and he would be of no help to Rose. *I must go for help*, he concluded, and quickly turned back down the ravine. He would go back through the woods and reenter the trail toward Wheeling a mile or so from here. He realized that he wasn't that good in the woods, and if the Indians came after him, they could probably catch him. His only hope was that they would consider that too much trouble.

Trying to be as quiet as possible, Frazier made his way through the dense undergrowth, then stopped to listen. He could hear nothing, and satisfied that he was not being pursued, he made his way directly back to the trail he and Rose had so joyfully traversed just a short time ago. Once there, he began to run back toward Fort Henry. "Damn that deer," he said aloud. "He's cost me my Rose!"

July 4, 1784

Lewis Wetzel stood against the wall watching the former Betty Zane dance with her husband, Ephraim McLaughlin. Wetzel had not entered into the dancing very much for he felt inadequate in that department. He had enjoyed a brief fling with Virginia Burns, who had flirted with him so openly at Lydia's wedding.

He thought he might be better equipped to deal with her this time after his experiences in Pittsburgh; but it wasn't the same. Virginia seemed to be more interested in some of the other men, and Lew found himself shrinking into the background as was his custom. The commotion outside, and then at the door, quickly drew his attention, as it did the others.

The music and dancing stopped when John Frazier appeared, shouting frantically. "They took my Rose! I need help to get her back."

Colonel Zane was quick to take over the situation, helping Frazier to a seat near where the musicians were sitting.

"Tell us what happened, John."

"Four Indians. They took her and the horses. It was my fault."

"No one is finding fault, John," said the colonel, trying to calm the anguished Frazier.

"I left her to get the deer I shot," sobbed Frazier, tears now dropping on his cheeks. "They had her when I came back. I couldn't do nothing."

"A bunch of us will go after her," shouted McLaughlin, who pointed to others in the room. Several men stepped forward, eager to help.

"Lewis, will you lead them?" asked Colonel Zane of the silent hunter, who had not moved from his place along the wall.

"No!" said Wetzel emphatically. "I won't."

"What?" cried McLaughlin in disbelief. "What kind of man are you anyway?"

A murmur began to build among the others in the room. This was not an answer they expected from Lewis Wetzel.

"Wait," said Colonel Zane. "I know this man, and he must have a good reason for that answer. What is it, Lew?"

"If you all go, they'll be sure to kill her," Wetzel said quietly. "I'm willing to go, but only if I go by myself."

"That's crazy," offered McLaughlin, determined not to be denied. "One man against four? Crazy!"

"No, it ain't," said Lew with a bit more spirit. "It's the only way."

"Maybe he's right," said Colonel Zane. "If my brother Jonathan were here I think he'd agree with Lew."

"It's settled then," said Lew, finally stepping away from his spot along the wall. "I'll be off, for there's not time to waste."

"I'm goin' too!" spoke Frazier in a tone indicating no compromise. The tears had dried.

"I reckon not," said Wetzel.

"She's my gal, and I'm goin'. You'll have to shoot me to keep me away."

Wetzel smiled. "Well, I don't much want to shoot such a determined feller."

"Good," exclaimed Frazier.

"But you do what I say," cautioned Lew. "Or you'll go by yourself."

"Agreed," said Frazier. "Now let's go."

Wetzel took some bread and a piece of smoked ham from the food table and shoved it inside is hunting shirt, indicating that Frazier should do the same.

"I'll get my rifle," announced Lew, "and meet you at the gate."

They were soon on the trail. Lew had explained that it was best that they go on foot, and that he knew where the Indians would be heading with their victim.

"We'll take the river road cuz it's fastest. I think we can get there afore they do," he assured Frazier.

They moved at a fast pace, alternating between walking and the fast trotting that Wetzel favored. It was difficult for Frazier to keep up, but he was highly motivated, and he did not complain. It was much easier to travel along this path than the one through the hills that Frazier had taken with Rose earlier in the day. In less than two hours, they were within a mile of the mouth of Short Creek; and here Wetzel halted. He pointed to a high hill ahead and to their right.

"We'd best go up there where we can have a good view of the mouth of the creek and keep outta sight ourselves."

"Are you sure they will come to the mouth of the creek?" Frazier was anxious, and he couldn't see why Wetzel was so sure.

"They stowed a canoe right at the mouth," reasoned Wetzel. "They'll want to take your girl over that way."

"What if they're already gone?" Frazier was pessimistic.

"Then we'll swim over and follow 'em." He looked hard at Frazier. "You can swim, can't you?"

"I ain't never tried to swim a river that big," said John, pointing at the Ohio.

"Well, I reckon they won't be there just yet. The girl will slow them down, and they won't figure on anyone comin' after them this soon." Lew broke into a wide grin. "Besides, they'll have to deal with what I did to their canoe."

Wetzel moved off to the hill, which was well covered with brush and trees. They made their way up, but it took them a half hour to get to the top. Once there, they settled among some tall weeds between two big trees, where they had a clear view of the creek mouth, although it was partly obstructed by vegetation along its banks. Wetzel could see the end of the canoe just as he had found it and as he had left it. After a moment, he pointed down at a clump of willows, just above the creek mouth and growing between two fallen tree trunks.

"We are too far away up here," whispered Wetzel. "Let's get down behind that bunch of willows."

Without waiting for a reply, he started down the slope toward the stream, but stopping when he noted that Frazier was slow to follow.

"Hurry up," he hissed. "We need to get down there quick and quiet."

Frazier rose and followed, the two men staying low and using the tall grasses and multiple trees to give them cover. Wetzel reached the larger of the logs, which was behind the willow bushes, and crouched behind it, pulling Frazier down beside him.

"We'll wait here," said Lew softly. "We can see the creek mouth from here and most of the far bank."

"What if they've already been here and gone?" Frazier couldn't get that idea out of his head.

"They ain't," assured Wetzel. "Look just past those rocks and that little tree right at the mouth. That's the end of a canoe, you can just barely see it."

It was not at all clear to Frazier what Wetzel was pointing at, but it seemed easier to assent. "Yes," he said hesitantly.

"That means they ain't come yet."

They waited what seemed like hours to Frazier, but was really only a few minutes.

"Shh," warned Wetzel. "I hear 'em comin'."

Up the little stream a ways, Frazier could see some shadowy movement through the trees along both banks. Soon there appeared in an open area a large Indian, leading Rose by a cord. Her hands were tied, and a second, smaller brave walked close behind.

"God," exclaimed Frazier, his mouth quickly covered by Wetzel's big hand.

"Be quiet," said Wetzel in a coarse whisper. "You gotta be calm now or you'll get your girl killed."

They watched as the two Indians and the girl moved near the mouth of the creek. They stopped, and the larger Indian instructed the other to get the canoe. The creek was fairly deep at its mouth, although not over the warrior's head, and he crossed to where he could reach the mostly submerged canoe. With a mighty pull, he managed to pull it up and turn it upright without noticing the defect that Wetzel had introduced to its bottom. He began to pull it to the other bank.

"There are two more with the horses someplace," said Wetzel to Frazier. "So we'd better take care of these two right now." He checked his rifle quickly and raised it to sight just above the log. "Wait 'til I tell you, then shoot the smaller one. I'll shoot the one holding onto Rose."

"I'm ready," hissed Frazier.

"Don't miss," cautioned Wetzel. "Soon as we shoot, you get over there and git the girl. Take her up the hill and keep her hidden. Wait until I come."

Wetzel looked along the far bank, as far upstream as he could see, looking for the two remaining Indians and the horses. Then he saw them. They had stopped and put their guns down and were looking at something. He looked back at what was happening at the mouth in time to hear the small brave grunt and point into the canoe. He had reached the bank near where his companion and Rose were standing. The large brave stepped away from Rose in order to see what his friend was pointing at.

"Now!" yelled Wetzel, and the two white men pulled their triggers almost simultaneously. Both Indians fell dead, and Rose screamed.

Frazier plunged out of the hiding spot and into the creek, shouting at the top of his voice, "Rose, Rose, I'm coming, I'm coming." He quickly crossed the creek and climbed up the bank, taking Rose in his arms. He produced his knife and cut her bonds. "Hurry, Rose. We've got to cross the creek and get away from here."

"But there are two others," protested Rose. "They're right behind us, and they've got our horses."

"I know, darlin', but Wetzel is after them. Come on!"

Wetzel made his way quickly upstream along the bank, reloading as he went. When the gun was ready to fire again, Wetzel rushed into the stream and quickly splashed across, holding his gun high.

The two braves stood for a short time, bewildered at what was happening. They had been slow, and now it was too late. Wetzel gained the bank and brought his weapon up firing at the Indian closest to him. As he saw his ball strike home, he rushed toward the other, a Mingo he recognized as the one called Old Crossfire. This name was given him because he was left-handed, and as he reached for his gun, Wetzel crashed into him, grabbing for the left arm. Old Crossfire was strong, and the two men grappled for a moment with neither managing to gain anadvantage.

Then Wetzel, who was able to pull his knife from his belt, seized a temporary opening to push the blade deep into the Mingo's side, just under the ribs. Unable to use his stronger left arm, Old Crossfire had used his right to get a hard grip on Wetzel's head, trying to slip down to the neck and a fatal choke hold. Wetzel kept twisting the knife, and the grip on his head gradually relaxed. Lew pulled back and the Indian slumped to the ground, a look of hate taking over his face. Wetzel now drew his tomahawk, but he saw that it was unnecessary. Old Crossfire was dead. It was all over. Wetzel stood and raised both the tomahawk and the bloody knife above his head and gave a mighty roar.

Frazier, who with Rose in hand, had scrambled partway up the hill and into a heavy stand of cedars. "We'll wait here," he said to Rose, who was still shaking with fright.

She fell into his arms and began to sob. It was then that they heard Wetzel's signature yell. The two horses had fled upstream a ways, frightened by the shooting and fighting, and it took Wetzel a short time to retrieve them. When they returned to where Old Crossfire and the other brave were lying, Wetzel took their scalps. He washed the blood off in the stream, then fastened them to a rawhide string he found in one of the saddle bags. As an afterthought, he pushed the two bodies into the water. "Might as well get them other scalps too," he said aloud as he led the horses along the bank.

A feeling of satisfaction and relief filled him as he walked. It was pleasing to have been able to rescue the girl even more than the killings, which he accepted as a necessary part of the operation. He found the smaller Indian, the one shot by Frazier slumped against the bank, and the other sprawled on the ground just above him. He took the scalps and pushed the bodies into the Ohio. Again, he washed the blood from the scalps, for he knew that horses did not like the smell of blood. He strung the scalps on his line and hung them off one of the saddles. He led the horses across the stream and over to the narrow trail along the Ohio shore.

Looking up the hillside, Wetzel brought his hands to his mouth and shouted as loud as he could. "Frazier! Come on out. It's safe now."

His eyes caught the movement as John and Rose emerged from the trees and made their way quickly down to where Wetzel stood with the horses.

"By God, you did it," exclaimed Frazier, his eyes falling on the four scalps hanging from the lead horse.

"I reckon so," said Lew quietly. "One of 'em is yours." He pointed at the scalps.

"Hell, I don't want no scalp. I got what I want." He pulled Rose close to him. "My beautiful girl," he added.

"I reckon she's mighty purty, all right," agreed Lew. "You best take good care of her."

"I intend to do that!" said John with emphasis.

"I don't know how to thank you enough, Lew," said Rose, her eyes still red from crying. "And you too, my love," she added with a loving look at Frazier.

"We best get back to the fort," said Wetzel, feeling very pleased with himself.

Frazier mounted the first horse, which was his own, and Lew helped Rose to a seat behind him. He got on Rose's horse and started back toward the Wheeling settlement. It was nearly sundown as they rode through the gates of Fort Henry. The celebration was still in progress at the fort when the three of them arrived. Frazier burst through the door with Rose on his arm, and the room erupted in loud cheers.

"We rescued her, me and Wetzel," beamed Frazier, as people rushed to embrace them. Lew entered and stood near the door. "There was four of 'em," continued John. "I killed one, and Lew killed the other three."

"Who is that, Colonel Zane?" asked Pierre Le Clerk, a French trader who had arrived at the fort that afternoon. He pointed at Wetzel.

Le Clerk moved freely among the Indian tribes, a friendly trader who brought them a variety of needed goods in exchange for pelts. He was not a large man, but one who could clearly hold his own in a fight. A long scar graced his left cheek, and his pierced ears held two colorful tassels that hung to his shoulders.

"That's Lewis Wetzel," answered Zane. "He's becoming a legend around here. He's not twenty-one yet, I don't suppose, but this ain't the first time he's come back with at least three scalps."

"Impressive," said the Frenchman. "Funny thing though," he continued. "I was at Fort Pitt a few days ago, and they were tellin' about some hunter who had a big soldier backed up at a tavern. Had a knife at the man's throat, then let him go. I believe they said the hunter's name was Wetzel."

"Not likely it was Lew," said the colonel quickly. "Don't think he's ever been to Fort Pitt."

"They said the man called him a cheater," added Le Clerk.

'Well it wouldn't do to say that to Lew Wetzel," commented Zane.

"There was another man scalped in a brothel. Some think it coulda been the same hunter."

"No, that couldn't have been our boy," replied the colonel. "I'll introduce you to him," he said, waving at Wetzel to join them. "Lew, this here is Pierre Le Clerk," Zane pointed out to Lew when he had come to them. "He trades with the red men."

"Hello," was Lew's response. He was never sure what he really thought about the French traders. They weren't much different than the savages themselves, he figured.

"Quite a feat for such a young man," said Pierre.

"I'm old enough, I reckon," was Wetzel's response with some steel in his voice. Then in a softer tone, "We had to git the girl back."

"Who was they, Lew? The reds, I mean," asked Colonel Zane.

"One was Old Crossfire. I had quite a tussle with him."

"Oh, I always kind of liked him," replied Zane. "He's been here to the fort a time or two."

"I didn't have no time to pay my respects, Colonel," said Lew, a bit surprised by Zane's comments.

"I don't reckon you did," acknowledged Zane. "But we're mighty proud that you saved Rose Forrest."

"Yes, the Forest Rose," smiled Lew. "She deserves savin'!"

Le Clerk listened with great interest.

10

HUNTED

August 27, 1784

THE FRENCH TRADER, Le Clerk, stood inside the little trading post on the upper Sandusky, the one managed by John Leith. The post had been there for several years, strategically placed among the Wyandot and Delaware villages in the area. The Wyandot village called Half-King's Town was still inhabited, but the chief for whom it was named was getting old and not the tower of strength in the region that he once was.

Pipe, or Captain Pipe, as he was sometimes called, maintained his village on the Tymochtee. Wingenund also remained in the area, his summer camp still some twenty miles to the east. Little Fox had moved with his wife to Pipe's village the previous winter and had not moved back to Wingenund's camp when summer came. His friend Red Storm had taken a wife and lived in the same town. White Eagle had remained with Wingenund, and they had seen much less of their friend in the recent months.

Leith's store was a common gathering place, especially for Red Storm, who spent countless hours there, hoping to hear something of his great enemy, the man he called W. As one whose hatred of the whites was, in his own opinion, as keen as that of anyone, Little Fox was becoming annoyed with his friend's unrelenting fury toward W.

"Red Storm, you are becoming too much obsessed by this man W," Little Fox had said one day. "After all, you were waiting to attack him yourself. What did you expect him to do?"

Red Storm had scowled at him but said nothing, and Little Fox had not brought up the subject again. They both stood near a pile of blankets along one wall and listened as Le Clerk and Leith spoke to each other in English. Little Fox was not listening carefully, for even if he could have understood the language, he was thinking of other things. His wife was with child, and he was concerned about her. It was the second pregnancy; the first having ended in a premature birth and the death of the child.

Spotted Fawn had taken the loss quite hard, considering it her personal failure. She had not wanted to try again, and the strain between the two of them had nearly broken them apart. Things were better now, but as the term progressed, they both were feeling anxious. As these thoughts tumbled through his mind, a sudden stiffening by Red Storm, standing very near, brought Little Fox back to the present. Red Storm nodded toward the two white men and grabbed Little Fox by the arm.

"Listen," he hissed.

As Little Fox began to protest that he could not understand the speakers, Red Storm stopped him.

"Be quiet and listen," he said again.

Le Clerk was speaking, and Little Fox tried and could not follow. But then his friend squeezed his arm as Le Clerk uttered a word sounding like it could be a name.

"There," exclaimed Red Storm. "Did you hear that? He said the name."

"I don't know what he said," protested Little Fox. "Though it could be a name."

"It is a name. It is his name, W's name."

"How do you know?"

"I know."

Leith and LeClerk continued to talk, Leith asking the French trader to repeat the name he had mentioned.

"Lewis Wetzel," repeated Le Clerk.

Across the room, another listener took note, jumping up from a crouch at the sound of the name. Red Storm noticed and pointed in his direction.

"See?" he said to Little Fox. "That Shawnee recognizes the name."

Red Storm now walked swiftly to where the white men stood talking. He spoke loudly in his native tongue.

"Tell me about this man. What are you saying about him?"

Le Clerk was startled by this interruption, but he understood the Delaware language, and he was eager to repeat his story.

"At the fort at Wheeling, this man came in with four scalps. His name is Wetzel."

"What scalps?" demanded Red Storm.

"They were Mingoes I think. One was the Mingo the Long Knives call Old Crossfire. They had captured a young woman, and this man Wetzel took her back."

Red Storm drew his tomahawk from his belt and held it up for Le Clerk to see, pointing to the letter scratched in the top. "Would this be his name?"

When he had recovered from his reaction to having a tomahawk suddenly thrust in his face, Le Clerk examined the etching and nodded.

"It could mean his name, yes."

The Shawnee had crossed the room. "I knew a man named Wetzel," he announced in a halting mixture of Shawnee and Delaware dialect.

Red Storm ignored this announcement and pressed Le Clerk for more information. "Was he a big man? What did he look like?"

"Yes, he is big with lots of hair, and his face is scarred by the pox."

"Ah," grunted Red Storm with a satisfied glare aimed at Little Fox. "It is him."

Leith stepped forward now and spoke in perfect Delaware. "You think this is the man who took your ear, Red Storm?"

Red Storm nodded once, then turned away.

"A white man sliced off his ear," Leith explained to Le Clerk. "And he has sworn to avenge himself. This Wetzel could well be the man, I suppose. The tomahawk that Red Storm carries, it belonged to him, and it has the W engraved on the head as you saw."

The Shawnee spoke up again, addressing the Frenchman, "When you say this man was big, what do you mean? How big?"

"Taller than anyone here and wide of shoulder," answered Le Clerk.

"And you are sure of the pox?"

"Quite sure," said Le Clerk. "He's had the smallpox all right, likely as a child."

"It is not my man then," said the Shawnee.

"I do not know you," said Leith in the Shawnee dialect.

Leith had been several years among the Indians and had served as an interpreter. He was comfortable speaking in Delaware, Shawnee, and Wyandot.

"My name is Fire Heart, and I live now at Wapatomica."

"And how do you know a man named Wetzel?" asked Leith.

Red Storm and Little Fox had rejoined them, and Red Storm was keenly interested.

"Many summers ago, we captured this man across the big river, and he lived in our village at Chillicothe. He was adopted by the widow of Cornstalk, and he became my friend. His name was Martin, but he also tried to teach me this other name, which I hear spoken by the trader."

"He could be the brother of the man of whom we speak," offered Leith.

"He betrayed me," hissed Fire Heart with some venom in his voice.

"What did you expect?" said Red Storm. "He was a white man."

"How did he betray you?" inquired Leith, ignoring the comments of Red Storm.

"He led us on a raid to the Kentucky lands, then ran away to the white man's fort."

"And you blame him for this? Wanting to return to his people?"

"I befriended him and treated him like a brother. I do not forgive!"

Leith shrugged. "Well, Red Storm here and his friend Little Fox intend to hunt down this man Red Storm calls W. You can join them."

Having understood only part of this conversation, Red Storm turned to Le Clerk again. "Frenchman. Do you know where this Wetzel lives?" He had trouble saying the name.

"I do not," answered Le Clerk. "Somewhere around Wheeling. He is a hunter and lives mostly in the woods, I think. Old Zane says he has taken many scalps."

"We will find him," declared Red Storm. "You too!" he shouted, pointing at Fire Heart.

October 20, 1784

It was a cold day in the late fall, and Little Fox found himself once again at Leith's store, taking advantage of the warmth coming from the fireplace at one end of the room. He stood watching as the slender proprietor dragged a bundle of furs across the floor. The store was nearly empty of goods.

"You'll have to move, Little Fox," said Leith in the Delaware tongue. "I want to pile these pelts right where you're standing."

Annoyed at having to give up his space, Little Fox moved only a few feet. "Maybe I should add your hair to the pile," he barked suddenly to Leith, who appeared to ignore him.

Pushing the pile into place just to the side of the hearth, he patted them with satisfaction. "There, that ought to help them dry out a bit." He stood now and faced the young Chippewa warrior, a wide grin on his face. "Are you an expert now on taking a man's hair, Little Fox? I'm not too worried about it. How many scalps have you taken anyway?"

"Enough," said Little Fox quietly. He could not suppress a slight smile of his own. In spite of his incessant hatred of white men, he realized that he had grown fond of this white trader. It was disturbing, then, to learn that Leith was moving his store to a new Delaware town, the one called Buckongehelas's Town. It was located more than forty miles away on a creek that fed into the Great Miami River further down. The English called it New Coshocton.

"Why do you move?" asked Little Fox suddenly.

"I've told you before, Little Fox," answered Leith. "This isn't my store."

"Then why do we call it Leith's store?"

"I only manage it. The owners have each taken their share of the goods and gone their way."

Little Fox did not reply but stood looking at Leith with a frown, not satisfied with the explanation he had heard.

Noting this, Leith shrugged and tried again. "These belong to Mr. Robbins," he explained, pointing to the pelts. "As does the rest of the stuff in here. He is paying me to open a store for him at New Coshocton."

"This Robbins is a white man," said Little Fox, slowly drawing his tomahawk from his belt as he spoke. He raised it high and brought it down hard through the air. "One blow like this, and you have your own store."

Leith looked at the warrior and smiled. "Why do you so hate the white man, Little Fox?"

"White men killed my brother and my mother. They take our lands. I will fight them to the end, I will never stop."

"But I am a white man, Little Fox. Do you wish to kill me?"

"You are Delaware!" The words were sharp and bitter, resounding like an axe biting into a wood block.

"It is true, I was captured by the Delaware," said Leith quietly. "An old man, who had a white wife, adopted me and befriended me. I suppose he saved my life, but he and the others took all the goods from my employer's store."

"You were at the Moravian village," exclaimed Little Fox, surprised himself that he had suddenly remembered seeing Leith there.

"Yes, I was," replied Leith. "But how did you know that?"

"I saw you there but didn't know who you were. It was then that Red Storm lost his ear."

"I knew nothing about that. I was living at Moravian Town with my wife, Sally, and our children. We were forced to come to the upper Sandusky."

Little Fox said nothing, and Leith did not feel like recounting his life's story to this young Indian. He remembered his anger at having to pack up and move his family along with the Christian Indians and their missionary leaders. He had not felt endangered, for he was known to many of the Wyandots from his time as a trader with a store at the lower Sandusky towns.

Nevertheless, he had kept his distance from the missionaries. The hostile tribes were very upset with the missionaries for providing warnings to the Virginia settlers, and they were suffering from rough treatment. When he arrived at the upper Sandusky, where the Moravians were being settled, he proposed to open his own trading store. Although the British denied him this opportunity, five of them, including his former employers, Arundle and Robbins, agreed to pay him a wage to manage a store for them.

There he had stayed for about three years, except for one short interlude during the Crawford raid, when he had taken his inventory and removed it to the lower towns. It was those five men who had recently ended their business. He was thankful that Robbins was willing to continue his pay in return for establishing a post at New Coshocton. Leith continued to pile his goods near the door, aware that his Chippewa friend was still watching him.

"Where is your partner, Red Storm?" he asked after a while. "I haven't seen him here lately."

"He is with his wife who is near her time."

"Your wife is with child too, is she not?"

"Yes," said Little Fox, whose face turned dark as he stared at the floor.

"Is she not well?" asked Leith, who had noticed the young warrior's reaction.

"It has been very hard for her," he answered. "I must go."

With that pronouncement, Little Fox left the store, suddenly eager to get back to his lodge where Spotted Fawn was resting. The previous morning, she had awakened with a pool of blood in her bed, and Little Fox had gone to get one of the old women who sometimes helped with births. The woman, who was called Buffalo Woman, had put him out and spent several hours with his ailing wife. She had seemed better this morning, but now he felt bad that he had left her, and he wanted to know if she was well. He began running along the trail that led to his village.

For some reason he could not fathom, a sensation of doom had descended upon him, and he was sure that something was terribly wrong. He had several miles to go, and though the first part of the trip was along a well-formed trail through a grassland, when he reached Little Tymochtee Creek, the path along its bank was much harder. It took the better part of an hour for him to reach the village located between the Tymochtee and the Little Tymochtee. His heart dropped when he saw a crowd of women outside his lodge. He pushed through and was stopped at the door by Buffalo Woman, whose countenance was sad but determined.

"Stop," she cried. "It is your wife."

"What about her?" questioned the distraught Little Fox, although he already expected the answer.

"She is dead," was the reply.

"No, No! She can't be dead. Spotted Fawn," Little Fox shouted as he tried to push past the woman.

However, Buffalo Woman was quite stout, and she pushed him back. "It is no place for you now," she insisted.

"The child. The child. Is the child alive?" demanded Little Fox.

"The child was too early," she explained. "It was a boy, but he did not live."

The vision of his wife, whom he had come to regard as very lovely, appeared in his mind. He wanted to hold her and show her his love. The realization that this was never to happen again came crashing down on him, and he wanted to cry. Crying was not an option for an Indian brave, especially in front of these women. He turned and felt the sudden urge to get away. He was vaguely aware that someone was reaching to touch him, but he was running now and unwilling to stop.

Though he realized finally that it was his friend Red Storm, it made no difference. Indeed, Red Storm was the last person he wanted to have near him. Red Storm still had his wife. It was not right that this had happened to him. Little Fox did not stop running until he had splashed across the little creek and disappeared into a heavy stand of woods. He sat down then and cried.

April 28, 1785

The fish were definitely not biting, but John Leith did not mind. He leaned back against a small boulder on the river's bank and allowed the warmth of the late-April sun to envelop him. He propped his fishing pole carefully against another rock, closed his eyes, and drifted into a semisleep.

Much had happened in the previous months. He had moved with his family to the Delaware village called New Coshocton shortly after the tragic death of Spotted Fawn. He had felt great sympathy for his friend Little Fox, who had taken the loss of his wife very hard. Leith had tried hard to get Little Fox to make the move with him, but after the burial ceremony, the young Chippewa had disappeared. Red Storm thought he might have gone to visit their friend White Eagle, who was still living at the camp of Wingenund.

Leith had opened his store in the new location on the little creek named for the principal chief of the village, Buckongehelas, and as there was no other post nearby, he expected to do well. However, there was much unrest among the Indians over uncertainty about relations with the Americans and their new country referred to as the United States. In the last month of the year, a delegation of tribesmen was gathered to meet with the Americans at Fort Pitt. Representatives from four tribes—the Wyandots, Delawares, Chippewas, and Ottawas—were going, and Buckongehelas was one of the chiefs to be included. He had prevailed on Leith to go along.

By the end of the month, the delegation of Indians had gathered at Fort McIntosh, near the mouth of Beaver River, where the negotiations were held under the leadership of Arthur Lee, Richard Butler, and George Rogers Clark for the Americans. The chiefs included Half-King and Abraham Kuhn of the Wyandots, along with Pipe, Wingenund, and Buckongehelas of the Delawares. These men Leith knew very well. There was an Ottawa chief named Ottawerreri and a Chippewa called Waanoos. The others were unknown to Leith. He attended the sessions and helped with some of the translations, although he was ignored by the American representatives, who considered him to be an Englishman.

Leith understood why they would feel this way; although unknown to his English and Indian friends, John had harbored sympathies with the rebel cause. He did feel some empathy for his Indian friends, however, for the representatives of the United States had driven a hard bargain. The Indians were distraught that the old boundary formed by the Ohio River was no longer to be observed. Instead, new boundaries were drawn that removed the Indians from some two-thirds of their former territory in the Ohio region. Much of the area had been inhabited by the Shawnees, who were not even represented at the negotiations.

The chiefs had argued vehemently against these provisions, but in the end, seeing no other choice, they had signed, on January 21, 1785, the instrument known as the Treaty of Fort McIntosh.

Leith had tried to talk to General Butler to explain that there was likely to be trouble over this treaty, especially from the Shawnees, who would consider themselves to have been deeply wronged by the proceedings. "You are probably right," Butler had agreed. "But they have to realize that they are a conquered people and no longer have the British to fight for them. We will have to treat with the Shawnees and Miamis separately."

The major outcome of the conference for Leith, however, was a new partnership that he had formed with two men from Pittsburgh, one of whom was David Duncan. Duncan, who was well-known on the frontier, and the other partner, a man named Wilson, had come to Leith with a startling offer to form a trading association. As a result, rather than returning to New Coshocton, Leith had started westward with thirty-four horses loaded with trade goods valued at nearly 1,500 English pounds. He had gone to the old town called Tuscarawas, located on the south side of the river of the same name, several miles above the old Moravian towns.

After building a rudely constructed log structure to house his store, and getting well established, he had sent for his wife and family, who had arrived just a few days ago. There were only a few Delaware Indians living in the village, but it was well-placed on oft used trails, not far from the site of Fort Laurens. That fort, built in late 1778, had been occupied by troops constantly under harassment and attack from the Indians, and abandoned in the summer of 1779. Leith had walked by the ruins of the fort that very morning on his way down the river. Very little was left; most of the usable logs had been taken to build huts for the villagers.

John had left his wife, Sally, to mind the store. Business had been good, although just a few weeks ago, a competitor, Captain Hamilton, had set up a store of his own nearby. A former officer in the army, Hamilton seemed to be a good man, and Leith was not upset at this development. A feeling of contentment had been with him on this day, and it had led him to this lazy day of fishing. The spot he had chosen was at least two miles downstream from the town. The sound of a human voice broke into his reverie, and he came fully awake, reaching for his rifle, which leaned against a neighboring tree. The speaker was behind him, but very near.

"Hello there," said the voice again, and from behind Leith, a big hand grabbed the rifle barrel and pushed it back against the tree.

"No need to shoot me now," came the voice again. "I'm a white man and not lookin' for no trouble."

Leith jumped to his feet and turned to face this intruder. He was taller than the average man, with wide shoulders and long hair, and he carried a long rifle. The colorful tassels hanging from his ears made Leith think of the trader Le Clerk, but this man was much bigger than Le Clerk.

"Who are you?" stammered John, aware suddenly that he might be in great danger.

"I am Lew Wetzel from Virginia."

"My God," exclaimed Leith, without thinking. "You are Lewis Wetzel?"

"I reckon I am. What is that to you?"

"Well, I've heard lots about you," answered John, relaxing finally.

Wetzel was greatly surprised. "Where did you hear about me? I ain't nobody special."

"The French trader Le Clerk told me about you."

"Where did you see him? I only met him once myself."

"My name is John Leith," said John, extending his hand. "I am a trader with a store up at the village. I used to have a store up on the Sandusky, and Le Clerk came by there late last summer. That's when he told me about you."

"So what did he tell you about me?"

"That you've taken a bunch of Indian scalps and are a fearful opponent."

Wetzel was pleased to hear that his exploits were becoming known, but he thought it was not right to make a fuss over them. "I s'pose I might have once or twice," he said modestly. "Don't reckon it is much worth talkin' about."

"He said you brought four scalps in to Fort Henry the day he was there."

"Well John Frazier kilt one of them bastards. They ought not stole that girl."

"What brings you up here, Mr. Wetzel?"

"Just call me Lew." Wetzel shook his head. "I don't rightly know. I was huntin' on the Stillwater, and I just kept comin' north. I ain't never been this far up afore."

"You've been to Gnadenhutten."

"You mean the Moravian town? I never did get there."

"You got pretty close, I think. Close enough to get into a scrap with a young Delaware warrior."

Wetzel was astonished. "How could you know about that?" he asked.

"I know the warrior you fought. You cut off his ear, and he's sworn to kill you for it. His name is Red Storm."

"Well, he tried to kill me then, cut me a bit with his knife. But I still don't know how he would know it was me and my name."

"He's been lookin' for you ever since. Thinks he saw you once over in Virginia."

Wetzel found this hard to believe and could think of nothing else to say.

"He's got friends sworn to help him," continued Leith. "After what Le Clerk told them in my store that day, they are sure it is Lewis Wetzel they are after. Red Storm has a tomahawk with a W scratched in the head. He says it was yours."

"By God, if that don't beat all," exclaimed Lew. "I guess it's right though. I didn't know I'd sliced off his ear. I meant to bash in his head, but I missed. I had to skedaddle real fast after that."

"There was a Shawnee in my store that day who also knew the name Wetzel. The man he knew didn't fit Le Clerk's description of you though."

"Don't make no sense," said Lewis.

"Maybe he knew some relative of yours."

"Martin! My brother Martin was a captive of the Shawnee for more'n two years."

"Could be, I suppose," agreed Leith after a short while.

"This Red Storm," said Wetzel suddenly. "Is he at your store now?"

"No, he's still up on the Sandusky."

"Don't reckon he'll ever find me if he stays up there," grinned Lew. "Mebbe I'll go up to your store. Are there Injuns there?

"There might be a few, but they're peaceful."

"I didn't never know no peaceful Injun," said Wetzel.

"Well these are, and I don't want you causing them any trouble." Leith was becoming alarmed at what this avowed Indian killer might do if he came to the town.

Wetzel's temper began to flare at this turn in the conversation. "You sayin' I ain't welcome?"

"You're not welcome if you're bent on killin'."

Wetzel turned and walked away a few steps. He was calmer now.

"You a Tory, Mr. Leith?"

"I never took sides during the war." Leith thought it better not to mention that he had been employed by the British. "I'm an American now, just like you."

Wetzel leaned down to pick up his hunting bag, which he had dropped earlier at the base of a tree. "I've got a fox pelt in here. Will you take it in trade for some powder and a little food?"

John was not wild about trading for a fox skin, but it seemed like a good thing to do under the circumstances. "I guess that would work," he said finally. "Come along, I'll show you to my store."

August 16, 1785

It was late afternoon and the sky had become quite dark. Lew Wetzel had left the family homestead early that morning. "Goin' on a hunt," he had told his mother.

He was easing his way up a small run that emptied into Little Grave Creek, having been intrigued by a bear track he had discovered in the soft mud at the edge of the creek. He had certainly been here before, but the little creek had no name, at least none that he knew. A second track and then a third showed that the bear was moving in the same direction although it could have been the previous day. It would be a very successful hunt if he could find and kill this bear. The sound of thunder from not too far to the west caught the hunter's attention. A flash of lightning and another loud thunderclap followed.

"I'm gonna get mighty wet, it appears, before I find this damned bear." He thought for a moment about striking out over the ridges toward the Wetzel farm, or maybe to his Uncle Bonnett's place. As the raindrops began to fall, he rejected that idea and hurried on up the little stream. He remembered that there was an abandoned cabin a short distance away, which would provide good shelter. He had discovered it one day when hunting in this region, and though it was in some disrepair, it would serve nicely just now. The cabin was farther away than he had first thought; and by the time he found it, he was thoroughly soaked. The wind had arisen, and the rain was falling in sheets.

A lightning bolt had hit a tree close enough to make him jump, and he didn't like the feeling of fear that had come over him. There was very little that frightened him—snakes and lightning were the exceptions. There was no door covering the opening into the hut, but it was away from the direction of the wind, so the dirt floor was not muddy. It was dark inside, but his eyes soon adjusted, and he could see that the room was empty as he remembered it. There were a few puddles on the floor where leaks in the roof had allowed some dripping. Several loose boards lay near the north wall, and a crude ladder leaned against it. There was a loft built out over some two-thirds of the room below, but many of its floorboards were missing.

Feeling chilled, he thought of starting a fire, but there was no dry wood, except for the boards. He did have flint and steel with him, but he decided against it. He looked again at the loft. "I reckon it might be safer to sleep up there," he said aloud. "Hell, that old bear could wander in here."

He took the ladder and placed it against the outer railing of the loft, and after tossing the best of the loose boards up above, he climbed the ladder and arranged the boards over the holes in the floor of the loft. He removed his hunting shirt and shook the water from it, then put it on again. There was no alternative to just sleeping in the wet clothes. He found a dry spot in the corner and sat down, pulling a small pouch of parched corn from inside his shirt. It would have to do for his supper, although it wasn't enough to satisfy his hunger.

The rain continued to pound against the roof, and he resigned himself to an uncomfortable night. Having stretched out as best he could, he suddenly sat up again. His gaze caught the end of the ladder protruding above the edge of the loft. After getting onto his hands and knees, he crawled over and pulled the ladder up, laying it down so that it was out of sight from below.

"Just in case I have a visitor, I don't need to make it easy for him to get up here." He settled down and was soon asleep. The visitors were not far behind. The six warriors had come down Little Grave Creek and found the bear tracks just as Wetzel had a couple of hours earlier. It was nearly dark, and the rain was pelting them as they tried to decide what to do. Red Storm was the recognized leader, but it was a loosely held position, and most decisions were made collectively.

"This storm is getting stronger," said White Eagle, who had never really wanted to come on the trip but had consented finally, partly because he wanted to keep an eye on his friend Little Fox. "We will need shelter."

The other three members of the party pushed in closer. One of them was Fire Heart, the Shawnee, who was intrigued by the search for the white hunter called Wetzel. The others were Delaware friends of Red Storm named White Turkey and Frog Hunter.

"The woods here are not heavy," Fire Heart pointed out. "They will not protect us."

As if to punctuate what Fire Heart had said, a fierce gust of wind buffeted them, accompanied by a flash of lightning.

White Turkey pointed up the little stream in the direction that Wetzel had gone. "There is a cabin up that way."

"How do you know that?" asked White Eagle.

"I have been here before," explained the warrior.

"Are there white men there?" Red Storm thought he should assert himself.

"No, it is abandoned."

Nothing more was said, and the six braves moved quickly up the run. They fought against the wind and rain, hoping to see the cabin, but beginning to lose faith in what White Turkey had told them. Becoming discouraged at no sign of the supposed cabin, Red Storm grabbed White Turkey by the arm and pulled him to a stop.

"Where is this cabin?" he shouted. "I don't think there is any cabin."

"There is," was the reply. "Not much farther, I think."

"You think?"

"I know," declared White Turkey, water streaming from his face. He pulled away and plunged on, the others following but becoming convinced that this young warrior was confused about where they were. There was nothing to do, however, but continue on. White Turkey had pulled ahead of the others by several yards, anxious to prove himself right. Finally the dark form of the hut appeared in the blackness of the night a short distance ahead.

Relieved after beginning to lose faith himself, White Turkey gave a shout and pointed at the cabin. A loud shout came from the others, although it was swallowed up by the blustery winds and driving rain. The six fully soaked Indian braves pushed through the door and dropped to rest on the hard dirt floor. No one spoke for several minutes. White Eagle was the first to get up, and he tried to look around, but it was too dark to see anything. He pushed along the long wall where he found several scraps of wood from broken boards that Wetzel could not use. He turned to the others. "There is wood. We should make a fire."

Red Storm scrambled to his feet and produced some flint and steel. Fire Heart had produced a knife and, taking a scrap of the wood from White Eagle, began to whittle some small shavings to use in igniting the fire. Soon they had a small fire going just to the side of the door opening. They sat close to get warm and to eat their meal provided from a private store each carried in a buckskin pouch.

Little attention had been paid to the loft, although in the dim light provided by the fire, White Eagle had noted some water dripping from the loft floor. This had concerned him for a moment, but there were obviously many holes in the roof, for water dripped in several locations. He shrugged and went to take a seat with the others, not mentioning his observations to his companions.

In the loft, Wetzel had awakened immediately at the sound of the Indians coming through the door. Instantly he had come up on hands and knees to a point where he could peer through a crack in the boards. He drew his knife and laid it next to him, expecting to be discovered any minute. To his relief, the red men had hardly even looked at the loft. He had tensed when he saw that one of them had noticed the drops of water coming from puddles made by his own wet clothes.

The threat had passed, however, and Wetzel realized his wisdom in pulling the ladder up with him. His plan, if discovered, was to jump among them, slashing with his knife, hoping in the resulting confusion to make it to the door. Once free outside, he was confident that he could outrun them.

Getting to the door, of course, was going to be very difficult. He watched as they finished their meal, and after some quiet talk and friendly laughter, the braves began to get drowsy. The wind had lessened, and the rain became a slight, comforting drizzle. One by one, the six warriors drifted into a heavy sleep. Wetzel's spirits rose. The fire was nearly out, but in its soft glow, he could make out each of the sleeping forms, and there was a clear spot for him to lower the ladder. Although he could have jumped down without being injured, he figured the noise was sure to awaken the sleepers. The ladder was a better bet. It was difficult to move without the boards creaking, but he moved slowly and carefully until the ladder was lowered.

He replaced his knife in its sheath, and holding his rifle in one hand, he silently descended to the cabin floor. Once there, he gathered himself, rejecting a sudden notion to take his tomahawk and slay each of the sleepers in turn. Instead, he made his way around them and to the doorway, rushing into open air with a great feeling of relief. The rain had stopped, and he made his way across the tiny creek, now running with banks full, finding a good hiding place behind a fallen log lying between two big sugar trees. There he waited.

August 17, 1785

Dawn brought a dash of daylight on the little hut, and though the sun was still hiding below the ridge to the east, it was bright enough to awaken White Eagle. Sprawled near the door, White Eagle came awake, confused for a moment as to where he was. He glanced at his sleeping companions and struggled to his feet, seeing but not really noticing the ladder that had not been there before. Feeling the need to relieve himself, he turned and stepped into the open doorway.

Wetzel had been awake since reaching his hiding place across the stream but directly in line with the door. He had contemplated the wisdom of staying there facing so many adversaries, but he was annoyed at having been disturbed and felt that the intruders should be made to suffer. Intrigued by the story told to him by the trader John Leith, he could not help but wonder if this raiding party was looking for him.

He had thought once that one of them appeared to have a missing ear, but the light was poor, and he couldn't be sure. His gun was loaded and dry, ready to do his bidding. When he saw the figure in the doorway, he quickly lifted his rifle and fired. He saw his victim fall, and then he rose quickly and bounded away, heading in the upstream direction but partway up the incline, staying among the trees. The sound of the gunshot brought the five sleepers awake in the hut, and Little Fox rushed to the aid of White Eagle, who was lying on the ground just in front of the door. Red Storm grabbed Little Fox by the arm and pulled him away from the opening.

"Get back!" he shouted. "You will be hit too."

The five warriors spread out along the walls, staying clear of the door. Little Fox stayed close, able to see the body of his friend but unable to determine the extent of the injury. In vain he tried to detect any sign of breathing. A grunt from Fire Heart caught their attention. He was pointing at the ladder leaning against the edge of the loft. "Someone was up there," he said.

"And now he is out there," remarked Red Storm.

"There is only one then," concluded Fire Heart. "But he may still be there."

"I don't see anything," announced the brave called Frog Hunter. He had found a small crack between the logs on the front of the cabin, although his view was limited.

"If we all rush out, he cannot stop us," said Red Storm excitedly.

"Except one of us," observed White Turkey. "Which of us will it be?"

"Let me." Fire Heart had removed his hunting shirt and draped it over the end of his rifle. He moved up next to where Little Fox was standing and pushed the hanging shirt out into the open doorway. When nothing happened, he took his headband, which contained a single feather of a hawk, and dangled it into the opening. This too received no response. "I think he has gone," said Fire Heart after a few more minutes had passed.

Little Fox could wait no longer, and he moved outside, kneeling next to White Eagle and putting his ear against the chest of his fallen friend. The others watched in tortured expectation, wondering when the second fatal shot might ring out. Still there was no further response, and Little Fox jumped to his feet, screaming in agony, and then beginning a death chant. He had spent many hours mourning the death of Spotted Fawn and the unborn child; now his best true friend was dead. Little Fox stopped his chant and dashed across the little run, continuing in a straight line toward the fallen log where Wetzel had been only a few minutes before. There was no difficulty in seeing the signs in the mud that showed where the shooter had been hiding.

Jumping up on the log, Little Fox shouted to the others. "He was here. I will follow him and kill him."

"We are with you," yelled Red Storm.

The others gave a shout and rushed over to join Little Fox, who had already discovered a footprint, which showed the direction of Wetzel's flight and was moving quickly to follow.

"Wait," cried Red Storm. "We must take care of White Eagle."

It was common for the Indians to remove their dead from the battlefield when possible, but there was no way to do that here. Little Fox stopped and came back to the others. He was ashamed of himself, having forgotten about honoring his friend and taking care of his body.

"We should not delay the pursuit," noted Fire Heart.

"Yes," agreed Red Storm. "White Turkey, you, and Frog Hunter take care of the body, and then catch up with us."

"How can we bury him?" asked White Turkey. "We have nothing to dig with."

"Use your tomahawks or something from the hut. We will see you later."

Red Storm turned up the trail motioning the others to follow, leaving the two braves to carry out the unwelcome task. More than a mile ahead, Wetzel had abandoned any attempt at hiding his trail in the soft ground and instead had kept a steady and rapid pace. He had come to the source of the small unnamed run and ascended the ridge to his right. From here, he could descend to Big Wheeling Creek at a spot not too far below the Wetzel homestead. "That would lead the bastards right to our farm," he said aloud. That would clearly be unwise.

On the other hand, if he followed the ridge on to the north and west, he would be close to the settlements at Wheeling. Confident that he could maintain his lead on his pursuers, Wetzel made the easy decision and continued in the northerly direction, deliberately leaving an easy-to-follow trail.

Little Fox continued to lead the little party now consisting of himself, Red Storm, and Fire Heart. When they reached the spot where Wetzel had stopped earlier, Little Fox called a halt. He knew that his blood was running hot with desire for revenge. The sight of White Eagle sprawled in death at the cabin door was still bright in his mind's eye. He had been thinking of Bright Moon and the two children and how this news would be such a blow to them. He felt responsible for White Eagle having come along on this adventure. White Eagle had been a source of great comfort in his own time of mourning, and now he was gone. The only release for the pain he suffered was to strike back, and to strike back quickly. Still he knew that he must be under control.

"The tracks go that way," said Little Fox to Red Storm who had just come up to him. He pointed along the ridge to the north.

Red Storm, usually the one acting in fury, now took a more patient and reasoned stance. "That will lead to the fort at Wheeling where there will be many of the Long Knives."

"We will catch him first," insisted Little Fox, although he knew that was probably not possible.

"He is one man who knows where he is going. He will travel faster than the three of us."

"I agree," chimed in Fire Heart. "I think we have to give it up."

"We cannot," shouted Little Fox. "We must avenge the death of White Eagle."

"I agree, we must seek revenge," agreed Red Storm, who pointed down the hill to the east. "There are settler's cabins down there on Wheeling Creek."

"There are not enough of us for that," protested Little Fox. He was remembering attacks on the farms they had carried out several years ago, when they had many more warriors.

"We are fierce, and we are filled with rage," answered Red Storm. "We are enough."

They both looked at Fire Heart. "If we wait for our two friends, we will surely have enough," he noted after a few seconds.

"I hate to wait," said Little Fox immediately.

"Fire Heart is right. We must wait for them. They can find us easily here, but maybe not down there," replied Red Storm. "Besides, we will surely have enough if there are five of us."

Little Fox was not happy, but he knew he could not prevail.

Fire Heart could see the disappointment on his face. "It will be good to rest here while we wait for them to come," he said as he stood his gun against a tree and sat down. "I am hungry," he added.

In something less than an hour, White Turkey and Frog Hunter appeared along the path behind them.

"Ah," shouted White Turkey. "There you are."

"Surely we were not hard to follow," said Little Fox with considerable annoyance. "It took you long enough."

"You were not hard to follow," said White Turkey with some heat. "Your friend was not easy to bury."

"The white man has escaped us," explained Red Storm, trying to head off any skirmish between the two. "We plan to raid some settlers below. Do you need to rest and eat?"

"We rested and ate after the burying."

"Good," shouted Little Fox, whose patience was at an end. "Let us go."

He plunged down the hill to the east, and the others quickly followed. They came upon a shallow ditch with a slight flow of water and followed it down to where it spilled into Big Wheeling Creek.

The young Chippewa, still leading his companions, turned to the right as they came to Wheeling Creek and moved upstream along its bank. His anger having cooled a bit by now, Little Fox moved more slowly, not sure of what was ahead. The others filled in behind him, urging each other to be as quiet as possible. Finally he stopped and motioned to Fire Heart. "Have you been here before?" he inquired of the Shawnee.

"Not here," answered Fire Heart.

"What creek is this?"

"I think it is the one called Big Wheeling Creek," said Red Storm, who had crowded in close to Little Fox. "The one we followed from the fort with my uncle Pekillon."

"It must be," agreed Fire Heart.

"We never followed it down here. I've never been here before." Little Fox was thinking they had come the wrong way.

"We took one of the forks," said Red Storm, "and didn't come this way."

"But are there white men's cabins on this creek? That is all that matters."

"I have heard my uncle say that there are many cabins all along Wheeling Creek."

"Then we will keep going," said Little Fox, his confidence returning. "We must be quiet."

The little band began moving along the bank again, where it began a wide U-turn, and they followed it in a northerly direction until they could see where it began to turn to the east.

Suddenly Little Fox stopped and held up his hand. "Did you hear that?"

"Yes, it is a bell. White men put them on their horses sometimes," answered Fire Heart with some excitement.

The brave called Frog Hunter, who rarely spoke, had moved out to the right a little and then uttered in a loud whisper, "There!" He pointed to an open grassy area on the opposite bank, where a black mare stood grazing quietly. She shook her head at an annoying fly, and the bell sounded again. On her other side, a young colt stood, banging its head under her haunches, trying to nurse.

"White men's horses," shouted Red Storm, then quickly holding his own hand up to his mouth sheepishly, acknowledging the need to be quiet.

"Yes," said Little Fox. "This is a perfect chance. Surely someone will come to get them."

Without another word, the five Indians crossed the creek where Fire Heart caught hold of the mare, and producing a short cord, tied her to a tree near the creek bank. He took the bell and held it in his own hand. "This way we can make sure the bell rings," he said.

Each of the braves then found a hiding place so that the area was surrounded, except for the open field to the east. They settled down to wait, unaware that the field they were watching belonged to the family of Red Storm's sworn enemy.

Just outside the Wetzel house, fifteen-year-old John Wetzel was having an argument with his sister, Susannah.

"Please, Johnny," she said. "Please go after my mare. She has wandered away, and the colt is with her."

"Why didn't you have her tied up? You oughta knowed she'd run off."

"She was out by the shed, and I'd just give her some corn. I didn't think she'd go that quick."

"You forgot about her, didn't you?"

"Well what if I did? She run off, and I can't help it now."

"'Twas your fault. You go after her. Me and Fred have got other stuff to do."

Fred Earlywine was a neighbor boy and good friend to Johnny, although a couple of years younger.

Captain John Wetzel had just stepped from the cabin door, and he ended the argument.

"John," he said in a commanding tone. "Go look for your sister's horses."

"But Pa, me and Fred—"

"You and Fred will make fine horse catchers," said the elder Wetzel, cutting young John off in midsentence. "I ain't about to send your sister out there by herself."

"Johnny, if you find them, I'll give you the colt," offered Susannah.

"I reckon I'll hold you to that offer," replied Johnny, looking warily at his father as he spoke.

Captain John said nothing.

"What do I get?" asked Fred.

"You git to go along," said Johnny with a laugh.

"I'd go downstream if I was you," advised Captain John. "They'll probably stay close to the creek."

"She's got a bell on," added Susannah.

"And John," cautioned his father. "You'd better take a gun. It could be some red robbers have got those horses. Be careful."

The idea that Indians might be responsible had not occurred to Johnny. He didn't think it likely, and he figured the old man didn't either, or he wouldn't send him out. He didn't mind taking the gun though. He and Fred could surely find something to shoot at. In spite of their arguments, the boys were pleased to be on this assignment, particularly young John at the prospect of having his very own colt. They moved along the edge of Wheeling Creek, stopping occasionally to talk and play. They were tempted to shoot at an old turtle who had crawled out on a rock in the stream.

"Better not," said John sorrowfully. "Pa would hear it and think we were in trouble."

So they went on, staying close to the creek. They heard the bell at the same time and turned to each other, each shouting with delight.

"She's over there someplace," said John Wetzel, pointing off a bit to his right. "Over there past the bend in the creek."

"You're right," agreed Fred, "though I can't see her."

"She's there all right. Come on!"

The boys ran off into the open field and over a slight hill where they could see the mare standing next to a tree.

"There she is," shouted Fred.

"Yeah, but I don't see my colt." John was already thinking of the colt as his own. Neither boy had noticed that the mare was tied. They closed the distance quickly, and when he was within a few yards, young John finally saw the cord fastening the horse to the tree. He tried to shout a warning, but it was too late, for the five warriors, who had remained hidden until the last instant, suddenly appeared.

Frog Hunter had Earlywine in his grasp, and Fire Heart grabbed John by his left arm. John, however, managed to jerk loose and bounded away. Watching the action closely, Little Fox now raised his gun and fired, the ball tearing into the left wrist of the fleeing Wetzel. The shock of being hit and the rough ground caused him to stumble, and White Turkey caught hold of him, throwing him to the ground. The boys were pushed together, and their hands quickly tied behind them. John's wrist was causing him great pain and bleeding badly, but he tried hard not to show it. Young Fred, however, was whimpering and nearly in tears. John shook his head at him, trying to warn him against that kind of behavior.

The braves indicated to the boys that they were to come with them.

"No," cried Fred," I won't."

This was enough for Little Fox, who was still eager for the blood that would avenge the killing of White Eagle. He drew his tomahawk and drove it into young Earlywine's skull. After taking the scalp, he pushed the body over the bank and into the stream.

"Let us take the horses and go now," said Red Storm. "We'll bring that one with us. He might make a good warrior some day."

Fire Heart put together a rough bandage of mud and leaves to stop the bleeding in Johnny Wetzel's wrist; and with the horses in tow, they began the return trip, splashing across the creek and retracing their route from before. Frog Hunter was sent to the rear to watch for any pursuit.

At the Wetzel house, John, his wife, Mary, and daughter Susannah, were eating dinner and did not hear the shot, which would have been possible had they been outside and listening.

When the boys had not returned by midafternoon, Captain John became restless.

"Maybe I'd better check on what's happened to them two boys. Mary," he said after awhile. "They're prob'ly playin' around out there somewhere." He saddled one of his horses and rode out.

Captain John found the body of Fred Earlywine at the edge of the creek. He looked around with unspoken fear, hoping he would not find another body.

After a few minutes of searching, he was satisfied that they had not killed Johnny. He couldn't tell how many warriors there were, but he knew they had a long head start. He thought, *If only Lew were here, we could maybe track them*. But he had no idea of Lew's whereabouts. Jacob was at the Bonnett farm several miles down Wheeling Creek. Maybe if he went and got Jacob and his brother-in-law, Lewis Bonnett, the three of them could still catch up with the kidnappers. The trail would be easy to follow, he thought, but they would be a long way behind. He had pulled the body of young Fred up on the dry ground, and he realized that he needed to get it back to his parents. Finally he shook his head in despair. "There ain't much chance," he said aloud.

It was going to become another hard blow for Mary. Looking wistfully up the trail in the direction of the Indian retreat, he sighed and began the task of loading Fred Earlywine's body onto the horse. It would be a sad journey.

Little Fox and his raiding party kept up a brisk pace, retracing their earlier path. After ascending the ridge, they continued down its length, coming once again to the little hut where they had spent the night. White Turkey showed them where they had buried the body of White Eagle, and some time was spent at the grave.

"We have avenged you, Brother," whispered Little Fox. "Although we have not finished yet."

"Should we spend the night here again?" asked White Turkey after several minutes had passed.

"No," answered Fire Heart immediately. "We would be too easy to catch if we stay here."

"True," agreed Red Storm. "There could be those already tracking us. We must get far away."

There was still much light left in the day, and they moved out again.

Little Fox was feeling better, for he felt that their raid was more of a success than he could have expected. They had killed one of the hated whites and had two of their horses, which was maybe of even more value.

They came to Little Grave Creek, and with Red Storm once more in the lead, they walked for a ways in the shallows of the stream, making sure the horses were leaving no tracks either. They continued in this way for close to a mile. It was agreed that they should endeavor to cross the Ohio further away from the Wheeling settlements, so at a point where the creek made a wide bend, they turned to the south and climbed a high heavily wooded hill. At its summit, they found a good place to camp in a little open space, completely surrounded by several stately elms and a thicket of white pine.

There was to be no fire for fear of pursuit ran high, so each of them ate from his own private stock and settled down for the night. Frog Hunter was sent back down the trail in the direction from which they most expected a rescue party might come. Fire Heart had produced some sassafras leaves from his pouch, which he chewed and used to replace the mud and leaves dressing on Johnny Wetzel's arm.

There was general approval among the warriors for Johnny's behavior and his stoic acceptance of the pain he was suffering. Johnny had patiently waited for his captors to go to sleep, hoping for a chance to escape. He was not successful and drifted off to sleep in spite of his best efforts to stay awake.

Young Wetzel was awakened by the footsteps of Frog Hunter, returning in the early daylight from his post on the back trail. The others were stirring as well; and with urgency, they gathered their belongings and pushed on over the ridge.

Before long, they descended to the larger stream called Grave Creek and followed it toward its mouth on the Ohio River. Off to their right, they could see the abandoned cabins of the Tomlinson and Williams families, whose occupants were enjoying the safety at Fort Henry. Little Fox and Fire Heart continued with the horses while the others moved up to see what they might find among and in the empty buildings. They turned up a small group of hogs, which they chased down toward the landing.

Much to their delight, they discovered a large canoe belonging to the absent inhabitants. "This will ease our crossing of the great river," noted Red Storm as they examined the canoe. The pigs had stopped running, and one of the bigger shoats stood looking at the three Indian intruders. Red Storm raised his gun and shot the animal in the head. After uttering a loud squeal, the shoat fell dead, and the other hogs ran off into a scrub thicket a few feet away.

The three braves managed to drag the heavy carcass to the creek bank and got it into the canoe, which they eased out toward the mouth where Little Fox and Fire Heart stood waiting with the horses. They were quite pleased with themselves, although it had taken considerable effort and a good amount of time.

A mile upriver, having just crossed the mouth of Little Grave Creek, Isaac Williams, Hamilton Kerr, and a Dutchman named Jacob Hindeman were making their way on foot toward the Williams farm to tend to the livestock. A rifle shot and the squealing of a hog reached them and quickly caught their attention.

"Did you hear that?" cried Isaac Williams. "I bet it's some of them damned Kentuckians have landed there by the creek and are killin' my hogs. Goddamn them."

The three men began to run over the rough ground, and Kerr, being the youngest, soon outdistanced the other two. He reached the stubby growth into which the other hogs had fled, and coming out on the rise above the creek bank, he could see the canoe with three Indians standing in it. He caught sight of the hog lying in the bottom with five rifles laying against it. He could not make out the other figure lying at the feet of the Indian in the bow. He raised his rifle and fired, watching as the brave in the stern, White Turkey, fell into the stream.

By this time, Isaac Williams had come up and fired his own gun, striking Frog Hunter in the chest, toppling him over the side of the canoe. Red Storm, standing in the bow, had not recovered from the shock of this sudden attack and had not tried to pick up a weapon to fight back. As he saw a third white man appear, he turned to dive into the water. Kerr grabbed the rifle from

Hindeman and snapped off a shot that caught Red Storm in the fleshy part of his left side, just above the hip.

The current had begun to pull the little craft out into the big river, but it twisted to the side because Frog Hunter, in falling over the side had grasped the edge with one hand and was still holding on. Kerr had caught sight of Little Fox and Fire Heart, who were out in the Ohio a few yards, trying to swim the horse and colt across. Ignoring them for the moment, Kerr reloaded his rifle and, seeing the fourth figure in the canoe beginning to rise, drew a bead on him.

Able to see what was happening, Johnny Wetzel raised his good arm and shouted, "Wait, don't shoot. I'm a white man."

"By God, it's young John Wetzel," yelled Williams.

"I reckon it is," said Kerr. "Johnny, can you paddle to the shore?" Seeing that the Indian's hand was still grasping the edge of the canoe, Kerr shouted again. "Knock his hand loose and paddle to shore."

"I can't," called Wetzel. "My arm is broken." He was able to reach up with his right hand and dislodge the fingers of the dead warrior. This caused the bow to swing, although unseen by the whites on shore, the injured Red Storm was partly under the bow trying to keep on the far side from the direction of the shooting. The current was pushing the craft sideways when Red Storm lost his footing and his hold under the bow, the canoe swung around and against a rock protruding in the shallow water.

Wetzel was able to scramble out and make his way to shore while Red Storm remained out of sight. Kerr and Williams had turned their attention to Little Fox and Fire Heart who were swimming the horses across. Little Fox, seeing his friend Red Storm fall into the water, immediately slipped off the mare and handed the rope to Fire Heart, who was still sitting on the mare and hanging on to the rope tied to the colt. Two shots were fired from shore, kicking up splashes of water but missing their intended marks. Little Fox was swimming back toward the canoe, which was still wedged against the rock. He could not see Red Storm as he swam, but he knew that the guns were still in the bottom of the canoe and would be needed.

Kerr and Williams were watching Johnny Wetzel who was running toward them from the other side of Grave Creek. The Dutchman was watching the swimming Little Fox but made no move to shoot him. The Chippewa warrior, upon reaching the canoe just as it began to break loose, was relieved to find that Red Storm was alive. Holding his friend with one hand and the canoe with another, he allowed it to drift with the current, trying to keep both of them hidden from the danger on the shore.

Taking a quick peek at the figures on the bank of the creek, Little Fox took a chance and helped to boost Red Storm up into the canoe, then clambered into it himself. Grabbing one of the paddles, he began to row furiously, hoping to get out of effective range of the enemy rifles. Fire Heart had continued to swim the horses and was near the far bank of the Ohio.

Hindeman, observing the efforts of Little Fox, shouted to Kerr. "Hamilton, they've got the canoe and are gittin' away."

"Well, shoot at 'em then," hollered Kerr with some annoyance.

"My gun ain't loaded," came the reply.

"Damn," said Kerr, standing near the creek bank as Williams helped Johnny Wetzel across to their side. In the confusion, he had neglected to reload his own gun, and he could see that any chance of stopping the fleeing canoe was rapidly slipping away. "I guess we'll have to let 'em go. At least we killed some of 'em."

The canoe soon reached the other shore of the river where Little Fox helped Red Storm onto the dry land, and after retrieving the five rifles, pushed the craft, still holding the dead hog back into the stream. Exhausted, he fell to the ground next to his injured friend and waited as Fire Heart made his way toward them, walking now and leading the mare and her colt behind him.

11

FATHER

August 18, 1785

JOHN WETZEL HAD thought it best to bring Mary and Susannah, the family members still at home, to the safety of Fort Henry. Clearly there were Indians intent on terrorizing the settlers. He was still harboring thoughts of going after the ones who had carried off young Johnny, but he could not leave the two women by themselves.

It was about noon on the day after that tragedy when they arrived at Wheeling. John was always a bit dismayed when he saw the deteriorating condition of the old fort. They rode in through the east gate, which stood open. By the look of its dilapidated state, John figured it probably could not be closed. They rode by the main house where Catherine Zane, now a widow, was still living. They stopped at one of the little huts where the two women dismounted and carried in their belongings.

Captain John led the horses to the little corral and shut them in. He saw that Mary and Susannah were already walking over to pay their respects to Catherine, who had come out on the front step. He watched the two of them, knowing how they were struggling to keep from crying again as they spoke to Catherine. Mary had taken the bad news in stride, but Susannah was much more distraught, feeling personally responsible for Johnny having been placed in harm's way. No one else was in the fort, and John was disappointed, for he had hoped that Lewis might be there.

Now he walked quickly back out the gate and over to Ebenezer Zane's big blockhouse. He was pleased to find both Ebenezer and his wife, Elizabeth, at home.

"Why, hello, John." exclaimed Zane when he discovered who was knocking at his door. "What brings you here today?"

"Young John's been stole by the damned Injuns, Eb," answered John. "I came lookin' for Lew, or somebody that could help me track 'em."

"Come in, John, come in," insisted the colonel. "Damn, that's bad news. When did this happen?"

John removed his hat and stepped inside, continuing to tell his story while Zane led them over to a couple of chairs near the kitchen table. He indicated that John should sit, but John shook his head.

"There's no time for me to sit, Eb. They took Johnny sometime yesterday afternoon. He'd gone out with young Fred Earlywine to look for some horses. Fred was scalped and dead when I found him, but they took Johnny with them."

"Yesterday? God, they'll have a big head start on us."

"I know, but it was late when I found out about it. I came first thing this morning and brought the women in with me. Wasn't safe to leave 'em at home."

"I'm glad you did that, John. This is bad. I was hopin' we might not be havin' this kind of trouble this year."

"Have you seen Lew?"

"Well, yes, John. He came in late yesterday afternoon in bad shape. Exhausted and not feelin' good. This mornin' he came by here in a bad way. He was runnin a fever and all stuffed up in the head. Elizabeth rubbed him down with some spikenard and told him to lie down here in one of our beds."

"Is he still here?" John knew that having this kind of ailment was not that unusual for his son. He figured that his news might make Lew forget all about how bad he was feeling.

"No, you know Lew. He ain't about to accept an offer like that. I think that old wound in his chest was hurtin' him too. Anyway, he left. If he ain't over at the fort, then you might find him at Jones's tavern down by the river." Zane smiled now at John Wetzel. "There's more'n one way to cure what's ailin' you."

"I reckon that's where he is," said John. "His mother thinks he's takin' to likin' that medicine way too much." He walked quickly to the door, replacing his hat as he stepped out. Zane followed.

"John, I'll be glad to go with you to trail the bastards if you want. I think Jonathan is home too and would be glad to go along. Not sure we'd have much luck though, bein' a whole day behind."

Wetzel stopped and turned back to speak to Zane. "Thanks for the offer, Eb. From the looks of things around where I found young Fred, I'm pretty sure they was headed for Little Grave Creek and will probably cross there, or maybe on down at Tomlinson's. We'll see what Lew has to say."

With that, he hurried out and made his way down the hill, past the burial grounds below the fort, and then over toward the river.

A man named Palmer had built a small boathouse along the riverbank where the ground was flat and used for a landing. Israel Jones had built a small cabin nearby, which he had turned into a tavern. As soon as he entered the dark room, John saw his son sitting at a table near the back. Another man was with him, but he was unknown to Captain John.

"There you are," said John to Lewis, who looked startled.

The younger Wetzel scrambled to his feet and was a bit unsteady. The father wondered whether it was from the illness or the cure, a whiskey jug sitting on the table between the two men.

"Pa, what are you doing here?"

"It's young John," replied his father with considerable urgency in his voice.

"What about him?" questioned Lewis.

"Injuns got him yesterday afternoon."

"Good God," shouted Lew. "How did that happen? Where was he?"

"He went out west of the house looking for Susannah's mare and colt. Fred Earlywine was with him. I found Fred's body near the big bend in the creek."

Lewis, feeling a bit dizzy, sat down again. "Lord," he said after a short while. "How many of 'em was there?"

"I don't rightly know," answered Captain John. "There was four or five I think."

"Same bunch as had me treed, I reckon," observed Lew, feeling his senses sharpen a bit.

"What are you talkin' about, Lew?" asked his father.

Lew explained what had happened on the rainy night. "I thought they'd keep followin' me and not be going down to the farm. Hell, this is my fault."

"I don't see why that's true," said John. "Who can explain why an Injun does somethin'? Will you go with me and see if we can catch up with 'em?"

"Sure, Pa, we'll go after 'em right now."

Having come to his feet again, Lew shook his head. "Is Jacob with you?"

"No, he went off somewhere with his uncle Lewis. Eb Zane said he'd go, and maybe Jonathan too. They've got a big head start on us."

"No matter," said Lew, now feeling some confidence. "They're bound to cross the Ohio somewhere around Grave Creek, prob'ly yesterday afternoon. We'll pick up their trail on the other side."

"Want me to go?" asked Alexander Mitchell, who had been sitting with Wetzel.

Before John could answer there was some yelling from outside, and they all hurried out to see what was happening.

"Thank God," shouted Captain John at the sight of his youngest son, Johnny, holding his left arm, but standing up straight next to Hamilton Kerr. Kerr was grinning from ear to ear as he saw John Wetzel and Lewis emerge from the tavern.

"We brought your boy home, John. You need to keep a closer eye on him in the future."

The father ran to embrace his son but stopped short when he saw the bloody arm.

"It's all right, Pa. I ain't hurt too bad."

"We had to kill three of them red bastards to save him," noted Isaac Williams, who had pushed up from behind. Jacob Hindeman had also come up, but he said nothing.

"Where did you find him?" inquired Lew, who was examining the wounded wrist.

"Just below Tomlinson's," answered Kerr.

"They shot one of my hogs and had it in their canoe,"Williams pointed out. "We got there just in time."

John turned now to his young son. "Your ma's been cryin' her eyes out. She's up at the fort. Let me take you to her." Fishing some coins from his pocket, the grateful father tossed them to Lew. "Son, buy these heroes a drink. I'll be back and join you in a while."

After watching his father put his arm around Johnny and help him up the path toward the fort, Lewis turned with a smile to the three men and motioned them into the tavern. "Come on boys, the drinks are on me. You too, Alex," he said to his previous drinking companion. The five men pushed through the door, and Lewis made his way to the bar. Five whiskeys, Israel," he demanded of the bar owner. "My little brother is saved!"

August 22, 1785

The journey back to Wingenund's town had not been easy. Although the wound to Red Storm was not mortal, it was very painful, and the injured brave had lost a considerable amount of blood. Little Fox was certain that they would be followed and that haste was of the utmost importance.

For that reason, Red Storm was put on the mare and tied into position. The bouncing of the horse's back increased the pain for him, but they were able to move at a quickened pace. They had made their way along a small creek at first, hoping to hide the trail; but leaving it after a short time, they struck across the wooded hills. When they came to the creek now called Wills Creek, they followed it until they arrived at the old Delaware town of Coshocton. It had been mostly abandoned since the attack on it by Brodhead several years earlier, but the travelers found a few families living there, and Little Fox decided it would be safe to rest there for a day. Still worried about pursuit, he went back along the trail for more than a mile, then completed a circle around the town until he was satisfied there were no enemies anywhere on the town side of the Muskingum and its branch, the Tuscarawas.

Red Storm was grateful for the rest and was beginning to recover his strength. He was hoping that Little Fox might remain here for several days, but he knew that his friend felt driven to get to Wingenund's town where White Eagle's widow dwelt as yet unaware of her husband's fate. Fire Heart had actually made this same suggestion to Little Fox.

"We must go on tomorrow," was the reply with no further explanation.

The Shawnee had begun to argue but suppressed the thought when he saw the look on the face of the young Chippewa. Little Fox could think of nothing but the death of his friend, White Eagle, and the terrible task that fell to him to inform the widow, Bright Moon, and her two children. A plan had crossed his mind, and he refused, out of guilt, to let it settle. It returned often, each time bringing him a pleasurable feeling, but he always pushed it aside. He did so now and hurried off to ask one of the families for some food to take with them the next day.

When he had returned to the place where he and his companions were spending the night, he went off into a stand of trees along the creek and descended below an embankment that overlooked the stream. Kneeling there on the wet ground, he fished a small piece of fox skin from his pouch. This he had kept since he was twelve years old, it was his own personal manito or divinity.

At that time in his youth, his father had instructed him in the selection of such a special, personal spirit that would be his very own. He had been instructed to fast for several days, and then, in a special night of sleep, an animal or special omen of some kind would appear to him. His father had eagerly awaited his awakening on that day and asked him what had appeared to him in his dreams. In fact, Little Fox hadn't been aware of anything, but that would have not been a satisfactory answer.

Knowing of the reason for his name, he assured his father that a fox had appeared to him. Immediately, his father had insisted that he must kill a fox, and that the furry skin would be dried and prepared for him to keep with him always. His personal manito, represented by this fox skin, would then be his constant companion and would help him to succeed in all his undertakings. Of course, he had been instructed that he must worship and pray to the manito; and in this, Little Fox knew he had been quite delinquent. Perhaps this is why these bad things had been happening to him.

He brought the furry pelt to his face and bowed low, holding it tight. He tried to pray and promise his undying fidelity. After several moments, he raised his hunting shirt and traced with his fingers the small tattoo that had been carved into his right side, just above the hip. It was a crude drawing of a fox, placed there to be a constant reminder of the existence of this manito.

He stood and stared for a moment at the slow moving current of the river, noting how the pale moonlight reflected from it. He returned then to the camp, trying to tell himself that things would be better.

By midmorning on the fourth day after leaving Coshocton, Little Fox, Fire Heart, and Red Storm had reached Wingenund's town. All three were weary, but Red Storm was feeling better, and Fire Heart agreed to take him on to his family on the Upper Sandusky.

"Let us find two horses for you to use," said Little Fox. "This mare and her foal must be given to the wife of White Eagle."

"It will be done." Wingenund himself had come out to see who had just arrived in his village.

"I will take care of it," replied Fire Heart. "You do what you must do, Little Fox."

With heavy heart, Little Fox set out on his sad errand. He found White Eagle's lodge, and calling softly to Bright Moon, he waited patiently for her to appear at the door. When she did, he bowed his head, unable to speak the necessary words.

"It is you, friend of my husband," whispered the young woman, whose bright countenance had immediately darkened. "What has happened to him?"

Although Little Fox did not speak, his grim look told the story.

"He is dead?" It was a question, but the young widow knew the answer.

Little Fox could only nod his head. He knew that he had to say something, but he was fighting back tears that were not supposed to come to an Indian brave. He looked away for a moment, not able to bear the look on the face of Bright Moon.

"Was he killed by a white man?" Her voice was quiet but did not quiver.

"Yes," stammered Little Fox. It was all that he could muster. There was so much he wanted to say, but he wasn't sure it was right to do so.

"Did you avenge him?"

"Yes," answered Little Fox with a bit more firmness. "We killed a man and took two horses. I have brought them to you."

He felt it wasn't necessary to say that it was no more than a boy that they had killed.

"Was it the man who killed my husband?"

Little Fox hesitated, wanting to say yes, but he couldn't bring himself to tell such a lie to this young woman of whom he thought so much. "No, he got away into the fort before we could catch him."

Bright Moon lowered her head, staring at the ground.

"We could not bring your husband back with us, and we buried him near where he fell."

She was owed this bit of information, he thought, although Little Fox could not quite shake the feeling of guilt that he continued to feel at this failure.

A moment of awkward silence fell between them until Bright Moon spoke again. "Thank you, Little Fox. I must go now and mourn for my dead husband." She turned and started to reenter the lodge.

"Bright Moon." He wanted so much to speak of the other matter that was on his mind, but how to do it?

She looked back at him, her face softening, a small smile on her lips. She nodded to him and went through the door.

"You did not help me much, my manito," whispered Little Fox to himself before turning away sorrowfully. On the next day, a burial ceremony was held for White Eagle even with the absence of his body. A shallow grave was dug, and a few of his possessions placed in it. An elderly man called Old Swan, who played the role of a type of holy man, stood along the path to the grave and held a buckskin bag. The bag contained a sacred tobacco that came from the Canadian side of the lakes. Each person who came by would take a pinch of the tobacco and hold it while circling the grave, then pitch it in.

After Bright Moon and her children had passed, the old man followed and spoke some words over the grave site. As he spoke, he dropped in bits of the tobacco, and when he was finished, he dropped the remainder of the tobacco into the grave. At this point, four designated braves, one of whom was Little Fox, the ones who would have carried the body in a normal burial, filled in the opening with dirt. For the rest of this day and all of the next, Bright Moon gave in to her grief. After this, she was advised by Old Swan to choose a man to replace her departed husband.

She rested and ate in preparation for the third night. On that evening, her friends, both men and women, joined her for a night of cheer. A fire was built outside her lodge, and the people gathered around it. Stories were told by the women about the bravery of her man and theirs while the men added their stories and legends from the past as well as many jokes. The goal was to keep the young widow awake and interested.

At sunrise, Old Swan joined the group and took a place behind Bright Moon, who was seated. The crowd hushed as he began to speak.

"My daughter, your husband has gone and left you alone with your children, Swift Hawk and Many Winds. He was a very good man who was lost while on an important mission against our enemies. He did many fine things while he was here and was an excellent husband and father. However, he is gone and it is not good that you continue to grieve for him. He would not want it so. It is right now that you should select another man to be your husband and father to your children. Will you select a man to be your husband?"

When he concluded his address, Old Swan stepped back and held up his hand to signal to the others to await Bright Moon's decision. There was an expectant murmur from the listeners, then all was still. Little Fox stood near the back and looked down, unable to look at Bright Moon. Why hadn't he spoken up earlier? Now it was too late. Bright Moon rose slowly to her feet. She stared at the crowd and began to turn her head from side to side, clearly searching for someone. Suddenly she pointed, and Little Fox felt the eyes of the audience turning toward him. "I choose Little Fox to be my husband," declared Bright Moon in a strong, clear voice.

A loud cheer rose up all around, and the people began to shout the name, "Little Fox, Little Fox."

A feeling of exhilaration engulfed the Chippewa warrior, unlike anything he had ever felt before. A broad smile appeared on his face, and strong arms were pulling and pushing him to the center of the circle where Bright Moon stood, also smiling. The crowd began to melt away, and soon they were alone just in front of the door to the lodge.

"Were you surprised, my husband?" Bright Moon had taken both of his hands in hers. He was her husband, for the party just held was considered to be the marriage ceremony.

Of course, Little Fox could have refused, but he had no such idea. "Yes, I am surprised," he admitted. "I wanted to suggest it to you the other day, but I could not say it. Then I thought it was too late."

"I know what you wanted to say. It was not necessary. I always knew you would be my husband some day."

"I am so happy." It was all Little Fox could say.

August 24, 1785

The two scouts had pushed out in the canoe and around the southern end of Zane's Island aimed at the mouth of Wheeling Creek on the Ohio's Virginia shore. It was five days since they had made the decision to see if they could pick up the trail of the abductors of Johnny Wetzel.

Lewis Wetzel had made the decision immediately after the little celebration held in Jones's tavern. Alexander Mitchell was quick to say he would go along as soon as Lew had suggested it. The other men felt they had already done their part.

"The two of us will be enough," declared Lew. He and Mitchell had made their preparations, setting out that same afternoon. A rain squall had blown up while they were crossing the river. "This ain't gonna' help us find no trail," observed Lew as they fought their way across against the wind and rain. They had searched for miles up and down the shore across from Grave Creek where they knew the Indians had fled. There was no sign of a trail, so they had pushed inland for a considerable distance; but after three days, they had given up and begun their return to the settlements.

"By God, Alex, I'm lookin' forward to some of that good whiskey at Jones's place," said Lew, feeling the disappointment of this failed scouting mission.

"Me too," agreed Mitchell as they came ashore, just on the upriver side of the creek's mouth. After securing the craft, they made their way up to the tavern and went in. It was just past noon. Both men were surprised when they stepped inside, for the little room was full of patrons.

"Who are these fellas?" Mitchell asked of his companion.

"I ain't sure," replied Wetzel.

They pushed through to the bar, trying to get the attention of Israel Jones, who was pouring a drink. As he did so, Wetzel bumped into one of the men who took exception.

"Watch it, you damned fool," responded the man, who was short but stocky, with a bronzed face that featured a big scar under the bottom lip. "Who the hell are you, anyway? You look like a damned savage or a French trader, one or the other."

Mitchell stopped and backed up a step, fully expecting his friend to react violently to the insults. Instead, Wetzel, having reached the bar, turned toward the man, a wide grin spreading across his lips.

"No harm intended, friend. I reckon you don't like my tassels," said Wetzel as he reached up with his right hand and flipped the scarf hanging from his right ear. "The name is Lew Wetzel. And who are you and your friends here?"

"That name don't mean nothin' to me," replied the man.

"Don't reckon it should," said Wetzel, the warm grin now receding. "I guess I ain't too far from bein' a savage at that." His hand dropped to rest on the head of the tomahawk stuck under his belt.

Mitchell, fearing that Lew was about to erupt, stepped between the men. "Well, you ought to know who Lew Wetzel is, considerin' he's the best shot and best fightin' man anywhere 'round here."

"Well my name is Jack Wheeler," admitted the man, coming to the realization that he may have bit off more than he could chew. "I'm a private in Captain Tom Gibson's company of Pennsylvanians, regular army. These here fellas are in the same company, and I reckon we got a couple of sharpshooters that can outshoot your man."

A year earlier, Congress had resolved and recommended that a multistate militia be formed including 165 men from Connecticut, 165 from New York, 110 from New Jersey, and 260 from Pennsylvania. As the commander of the largest unit, Lieutenant Colonel Josiah Harmar of Pennsylvania was given overall command. Although the Congress was allowed almost no powers at all during this period after the Revolution had ended, the states had agreed that Congress was responsible for control of Indian affairs.

This tiny army, which Colonel Harmar referred to as the First American Regiment, was all that was left of the Continental Army, and Harmar was, in fact, the commander of the army of the United States. Although its members were really state militiamen, they came to be regarded as the regular army. Harmar at this time was located at Fort McIntosh, but he had determined that a new fort should be built somewhere along the Ohio below Wheeling. The fort was occupied, though still under construction, before the end of 1785 under troops commanded by John Doughty at the mouth of the Muskingum River, and named Fort Harmar.

"So what are regular army men doing here?" Mitchell wanted to know.

"We're on our way to the Muskingum to see about buildin' a fort."

"By God, you're just a bunch of carpenters. Who could you have who could outshoot Lew Wetzel, or even me for that matter?"

"You bastard!" screamed Wheeler, loud enough for the whole crowd to hear. "I'll show you who is a damned carpenter."

Wheeler lunged at Mitchell but was intercepted by the strong arm of Wetzel, who grasped the man's hunting shirt just under his chin and lifted him up a few inches, then set him down slowly.

"Rest easy, friend. We don't mean you no harm." Wetzel's voice was quiet but firm as he released his hold.

"What's goin' on here, Private?" The speaker was Captain Gibson, who had reacted quickly to the disturbance. Most of the other soldiers had pressed in behind him, eager to see what they thought was going to be a fight.

"These dumb farmers don't know no better'n to insult the American Army," explained Wheeler to his commander. "They claim they can outshoot any of us."

"We ain't farmers, and I never said we could outshoot any of you," protested Mitchell. "I will say, though, that my friend Lew here can outrun anybody in your company, and while he's runnin', he can load and shoot his gun oftener than any one of them can load and shoot standing still."

"That's a tall claim there, mister." Gibson was inclined to side with his man against what he considered to be two ruffians. "What have you got to back that up?"

"How 'bout a gallon of whiskey?" asked Mitchell. "Loser buys."

"How do we know you'll pay off when you lose?"

"By God, the bigger question is whether you will," replied Mitchell.

"I am on officer in the First Regiment of the United States, formerly of the Third Pennsylvania. Who are you to question that?"

"Are you related to Colonel John Gibson?" asked Wetzel.

"I don't reckon so," said Gibson quickly, "since I don't know who that is."

"He's a hero on this border," answered Wetzel.

"Well, he's got a good name anyway," exclaimed the captain. "Let's set up the rules of this contest."

Mitchell was surprised that this upstart captain wouldn't know the colonel with the same last name, particularly since John Gibson had once commanded at Fort Pitt. He shrugged it aside and worked out the arrangements for the contest. Wetzel, who was annoyed that his friend had gotten him into this, said little but ultimately agreed to go through with it.

Captain Gibson had sent for a man named James Clark, regarded to be the fastest runner, who had remained at the fort with some other members of the company. The best and fastest shooter was John Oliver, the captain and his men all agreed readily to that.

Big Wheeling Creek came from the east and turned to the north before making a big turn to the south. The field of combat was chosen to be a flat grassy piece of land lying between the back side of Wheeling Hill and the west bank of the southerly flowing creek.

Word had spread quickly through the settlement, and a sizable number of residents joined the men of Gibson's company as they made their way across the creek to the site of the contest. Both Ebenezer and Jonathan Zane had come along, but none of the Wetzel family was there, having returned home two days earlier. A course was laid out of some one hundred yards in length, a ways west of the creek bank and relatively free of obstacles. Wetzel and Clark went to the north end of the course and stood together, the former holding his rifle aloft in his right hand.

Gibson and Mitchell took a station at the finish line for the race, their job to determine the winner at which they must agree.

Oliver stood a few yards to the far side with an empty rifle. Wetzel would fire his gun, which signaled the beginning of the contest. The two men would begin running; and Oliver would begin loading his rifle, trying to finish that job and shoot before Wetzel while running at top speed, could do the same. The crowd gathered downstream from the finish line.

"I sure hope you got the money to buy that whiskey," said Gibson to Mitchell. "You surely know that your man has no chance."

Before Mitchell could retort, the smoke from Wetzel's rifle was seen, and the race was on. Wetzel had fallen behind at first, getting his gun under control, but soon gained the lead. The crowd could see that he was also already pouring powder into the end of the gun barrel. Oliver was doing the same and under much better conditions. Gibson smiled, for he was sure that even if the frontiersman Wetzel managed to outrun Clark, there was no way he would be able to get his gun loaded before Oliver.

Wetzel maintained a short lead on Clark, who had stumbled slightly when his foot caught on a high spot in the grass. He produced a ball, which he had held in his mouth (having noted that Gibson had failed to make a rule in that regard). He dropped it into the barrel, which he was careful to hold upright. Oliver, quite sure of himself, had taken the time to tamp the powder with the ramrod. Meanwhile, Wetzel, whose foot speed was extraordinary, had gained on Clark, clearly winning the footrace.

The time for the most difficult part in the muzzle-loading process had arrived. Wetzel preferred to stop for the act of priming the pan, but there was no way he could do that and maintain his lead on Clark. He gambled on a shortcut that sometimes, but not always, worked. Lowering the muzzle slightly, he turned the rifle on its side and tapped it hard, the idea being to shake some of the powder from the barrel into the priming pan. Even this was difficult at the speed he was running, and if the action failed, the contest was lost.

A few yards short of the finish line, he turned the rifle to his left, pulled back the hammer, pulled the stock against his shoulder, and squeezed the trigger. The discharge bruised his upper arm, for he hadn't been able to seat the stock tight enough against his shoulder, but he was exhilarated to hear the gun fire. He then flashed across the finish line as he heard the shot from Oliver's gun. He had won; there could be no question. But a question there was.

Jack Wheeler, still nursing the grudge he had acquired from what he felt were the insults by Alexander Mitchell, stepped forward from the men standing behind Captain Gibson.

"Captain," said Wheeler forcefully. "How do we know that scalawag even put a ball in that gun? He may have just fired off some black powder."

Wetzel, who had flashed past the point where Gibson was standing, had circled back in time to hear this question. Still breathing hard from his extraordinary effort, he pointed to the base of a tree some twenty yards distant. "If you look there," he said between breaths. "I reckon you'll find the ball I shot."

Gibson, Mitchell, Wheeler, and several others, including Ebenezer Zane, moved quickly to the tree. It was Zane who found the ball, burrowed into the bark a foot or so above the ground.

"By God, Lew was right," exclaimed Zane, pointing to the spot.

"Hell, that's probably Oliver's ball," argued Wheeler.

"It's not," said a voice that turned out to be that of Oliver himself. "My shot went much further to the right than that."

Mitchell erupted with a great cheer, and Gibson said quietly, "I guess I have to agree. Your man has won the bet. Quite remarkable, I must admit."

"We won the bet! Lew Wetzel won the bet." Mitchell's loud announcement brought a cheer from many of the onlookers, including a number of the soldiers, who could not help but appreciate such an unbelievable feat. Wetzel had remained at the finish line throughout the examination of the tree, joined there by Jonathan Zane, who had put his hand on Lew's shoulder.

"That whiskey's gonna taste mighty good, Lew," he observed.

"Reckon you're right," agreed Wetzel with a broad smile.

October 1, 1785

Little Fox did not suppose that he had ever been happier. His life with Bright Moon was better than he could have imagined. Summer was barely over, but already she was pregnant with his child. Wingenund's camp had broken up for the winter, and Little Fox had moved his new family to the village of Buckongehelas, the one also called New Coshocton, that was located near the Shawnee towns.

Bright Moon had thought they would go to Pipe's town, where Red Storm lived with his family, but Little Fox had no desire to return to the place where he had lived with Spotted Fawn. Buckongehelas's town was where his friend Leith had moved the previous year, although Little Fox knew that Leith was no longer there. Another attraction to this location was that it was within a few miles of Wapatomica, the home village of Fire Heart. Satisfied that it was a good move, Little Fox built a new lodge, and together with Bright Moon and her two children, settled in to prepare for the winter.

It was a time of considerable unrest among the tribes. The treaties at Fort Stanwix and at Fort McIntosh were highly unsatisfactory, as they had essentially removed the old Ohio River boundary between the whites and the Indians. Flushed with their victory over the British, the Americans had driven hard bargains, and though many of the tribes had agreed to the new conditions, they were not happy about it. The hotheads among the warriors were simply refusing to recognize the terms at all. In particular, the Shawnees had not been a part of the Fort McIntosh negotiations, and the Americans were pushing for a new session of talks, which would include that unhappy tribe.

Not long after Little Fox had arrived at his new home, important chiefs from a variety of tribes began gathering at New Coshocton, intent on holding a grand council. Some Chippewas had come in, including the chief Waanoos, who had signed the treaty at Fort McIntosh. It was good to talk with these brethren, although once again, Little Fox was disappointed that none of them knew anything of his father. On the day the council began, a short distance outside the village, Little Fox was greatly surprised to see his old friend Leith again.

The trader, along with his wife and two children, had arrived in the company of a delegation of Delaware and Wyandot warriors. The demeanor of the Wyandots indicated that they considered Leith to be something of a captive while the Delawares treated him more as if he were one of them. The Indians had a quantity of goods and furs with them. Little Fox was overjoyed at seeing Leith again and sought him out at the first opportunity.

"What are you doing here, my friend? Have you come to open another trading post?"

"Not exactly," replied the trader. "We were brought here from the Tuscarawas."

Leith went on to explain how Hamilton's store, operated by a man named Chambers, had been raided and destroyed by the Wyandots, who had tomahawked Chambers and thrown his body out on the doorstep. The Delawares had prevented a similar attack against Leith, leaving his store untouched. The goods from Hamilton's store had been divided between the Wyandots and Delawares. A Delaware called Loud Thunder had come to Leith and offered his protection.

"My stuff was not taken, and one of my friends there promised to take care of it for me." Leith did not bother to tell his Indian friend how he had determined to kill the Wyandot warrior who had slain Chambers. His wife and Loud Thunder, who had accompanied them on the journey, had talked him out of it.

"I am glad to see you," said Little Fox.

"I did not expect to see you here," said Leith. "They took us to the Shawnee towns first then brought us here. They said that a big council was in progress. Is that why you're here?"

Little Fox laughed at that. "I am not a chief," he pointed out. "I live here now. Come, I want you to meet my new wife."

As they walked to the lodge, Little Fox told the trader of White Eagle's death and what had transpired since.

"What of Red Storm? Have you given up your quest to find Wetzel?"

"I have not seen Red Storm in a while. He recovers from his wounds."

Little Fox was surprised at himself, for he realized that he had not been thinking about their great enemy lately, nor even about his hatred of white men in general. He had even felt some sympathy for the man Chambers, whom he did not know. What was happening to him?

"I met Wetzel myself awhile ago," declared Leith. "He came to my store."

This brought Little Fox to a stop. "You did? Then he does exist."

"Oh, yes. An impressive man."

"Did you find out where he lives?"

"Well, I didn't really ask. But it is somewhere near the Wheeling fort."

"You should have found where he lives."

"I told him about Red Storm and you coming after him. I doubt he would have told you where to come."

"You should not have warned him."

Leith felt it best to change the subject. "Tell me about this council. What is it about?"

"There is much anger about the treaties." Little Fox had attended some of the sessions. "Simon Girty has been here, and also the British soldier Caldwell."

"I know both of them," said Leith. "What are they up to, I wonder."

"They argue against attending the treaty talks at the mouth of the Miami."

Leith knew that the Americans hoped to have the tribes, especially the Shawnees, agree to stop their recent aggressive actions against the settlers. Apparently the tribes had been invited to meet for negotiations to be held at the point where the Great Miami River emptied into the Ohio. The British, who had refused to give up many of their posts in the northwest, continued to stir up the Indians against the Americans. This was not hard to do as the tribes could easily see their lands were shrinking and the American demands grew harsher.

John Leith and his family were being kept in a loose confinement, although the Delawares tried to make them as comfortable as possible. The Delaware chief, Captain Pipe, had come by to see Leith on the second day of the council and at its conclusion, and after the Leith family had been released from confinement, Pipe came by again, requesting that Leith accompany him to his own village.

Little Fox was there at the time, and Pipe invited him to come along as well. Though he was reluctant to leave Bright Moon behind even for a few days, Leith was insistent, and Little Fox agreed. They left the next morning, accompanied by another Delaware warrior named Que-shaw-sey, who liked to call himself George Washington.

After two hard days, they reached the Wyandot towns on the upper Sandusky. Simon Girty was there when they arrived, and he requested a conference with Captain Pipe. Little Fox was left with George Washington and several other warriors from Pipe's village.

"Why do you call yourself George Washington?" Little Fox wanted to know of Que-shaw-sey, after they had eaten a small meal together. Little Fox knew that George Washington was the name of the American commander during the recent war with the British, although he knew little else.

"Ah, I am named after the great chief of the Americans," answered the Delaware with a broad smile. "I met him once, you know. He is a very great man."

Little Fox was annoyed by Que-shaw-sey's jovial nature, which he thought was unbecoming of a Delaware warrior, but even worse was his praise for a white man, especially one who had led them in a war against the Delawares and other Indians.

"I would think you would be ashamed that you met him and did not try to kill him."

"Oh, one cannot kill George Washington. He is protected by the Great Spirit." Que-shaw-sey was taken aback by the bitterness in the voice of Little Fox, who turned and walked away.

"He is a very sad man," said George Washington to John Leith, who had been listening to the conversation.

"Yes, he has a great hatred for white men, and he is mourning some tragic deaths."

"But you are a white man, and you are his friend."

"Yes, and I think that troubles him."

The next morning Captain Pipe took them to his village on the Tymochtee. Little Fox was glad for the opportunity to see Red Storm, whom he had not seen since their return from the ill-fated raid in Virginia. He went immediately to Red Storm's lodge.

"Hello, friend," was the eager greeting by Little Fox. "Are you completely well?"

"It is you," exclaimed Red Storm. "I have wondered about you. I was told that you have a new wife."

"Yes, White Eagle's widow has become my wife. She is with child."

"That is good news," replied Red Storm, who smiled. "You may not want to go chasing W with me anymore."

"Ah," laughed Little Fox. "Leith says he has talked with this man."

That remark brought Red Storm all the way out of the lodge. "He did? What did he say about him?"

"He told him that you and I meant to kill him."

"Why did he do that? But I suppose it does not matter."

"Not since we are both becoming like old squaws."

"Speak for yourself. I am well and ready to go on another raid."

"How is your child? I do not know his name." The child had been born while Little Fox was still in mourning for Spotted Fawn.

"We call him East Wind. He grows very fast."

Leith was involved with helping to gather together again the goods that had been taken at the Tuscarawas to be returned to the owner. There seemed to be genuine sorrow at the events that had taken place there.

"Next we will go to the Wyandot towns and gather up what they have that was taken from the store at Tuscarawas," explained Captain Pipe to Leith. "We do not approve of what was done there. Que-shaw-sey will take some warriors and see that these things are returned."

"That is very kind," said Leith. "I was sad at the killing of Mr. Chambers."

"You can go with them if you wish," said Pipe, who, it seemed to Leith, was going out of his way to be friendly.

"We are for peace with the white settlers," mentioned Pipe as they journeyed to the Wyandot towns. "Many of our young warriors are angry, however, and it is hard to keep them down."

The Frenchman, Le Clerk, was at the Upper Sandusky towns, and he informed Leith that he was planning to go to Fort Pitt.

"I will go with you," said Leith. "I want to get some horses and go back to Tuscarawas to retrieve my goods. The Delawares promised that they would be kept for me."

"I am pleased to have your company. It was a surprise to find you here."

"It is a long story," sighed Leith. He nodded toward Little Fox, who stood near. "You remember my Chippewa friend?"

"Ah, yes," said Le Clerk. "The one who means to kill Lewis Wetzel."

"Yes," laughed Leith. "Little Fox, come here. We want you to go with us to Fort Pitt."

"Why should I do that?" Little Fox wanted to know.

"It might get you closer to Wetzel," Le Clerk offered. "Is that still your goal?"

Little Fox shrugged, and Leith answered for him. "He has a new wife, Le Clerk. And a very pretty one at that."

Little Fox parted from them and began his return to New Coshocton He had been tempted to go on the adventure suggested by Leith, but the thought of traveling with two white men was repulsive to him. Besides, Leith was correct; he did have a good reason to go home.

May 25, 1786

The remaining days of 1785 had passed quickly into the new year. Although there was supposed to be peace with the Indians because of the treaty negotiations held in the last couple of years, the settlers in the Wheeling region were still uneasy. The most recent negotiations held at Fort Finney, hurriedly constructed near the mouth of the Great Miami River, had led to a signing in January 1786, by some of the Shawnee chiefs.

The Indians were not happy with the terms, however, which had succeeded in shrinking their holdings in the Ohio country. The raids into the white settlements in both Virginia and Kentucky had continued. The fort under construction at the mouth of the Muskingum River was named Fort Harmar by Major Doughty, and a small number of troops of the First United States Regiment were stationed there. Much to the consternation of the whites, one of the missions of those troops was to prevent white settlement in the former Indian lands to the north and east of the Ohio.

Captain John Wetzel, in the fall of the previous year, had staked a claim on some land along Middle Island Creek, and he was anxious to visit and make some improvements on that land. He had waited patiently for the winter to end, and after the planting was finished at the homestead in May, he made arrangements to make the trip south.

"We need to clear some of the trees and brush away," John had explained to his wife. "Maybe build a small cabin, so the place will look occupied."

"Who you takin' to help with that job?" Mary wanted to know.

"Well, Tom Moore was around the other day, lookin' for some work."

Moore had lost his wife to a fever during the winter, and his two children were staying at a brother's place. John figured he would be doing Moore a big favor by hiring him for a few days.

"I can't see he'd be much help. He ain't as big as our Johnny, and he's a stone or two short of a full chimney, if you ask me."

"Tom's small, but he's wiry, and he knows how to cut down trees," John assured her. "Besides, he needs the work."

"What about Jacob and John? I guess Martin needs to stay here. Plenty for him to do."

"You're right about Martin. Jacob promised to help over at your brother's place and think I'd better leave Johnny here to keep you company."

"Phew," grunted Mary with a laugh. "Since when has anybody worried about me havin' company. Besides, Martin and his family provide me with plenty to worry about."

"I want John to be here with you," insisted the captain. "Moore tells me there's a young feller named Andrews up at Wheeling who's a good worker. I'll see if he'll go along."

"What about Lew?" wondered Mary. "You should take him."

“Ha,” laughed Captain John. “Lew’d be worthless at clearin’ ground. He’s no better at that than he is at farmin’.”

“I’m worried it won’t be safe down there where you’re goin’. The Indians are still stirred up, ain’t they?”

“I reckon they are,” admitted John. “You may have a point at that. He could keep us in meat too, I suppose. I’ll go to Wheeling tomorrow and see if I can find him and this Andrews feller.”

John had found his son Lew at the fort in Wheeling, although the idea of being part of a work party did not appeal to the young hunter.

“Hell, Pa,” he had said when informed of his father’s plans. “I ain’t no good at that kind of work.”

“I’m well aware of that, son,” replied John. “But your ma seems to think you might be of some use in case there might be some of them pesky red men around.”

Lew’s face brightened immediately. “Why, yes, I could serve as a guard for your work party.”

“And supplier of meat as well,” added his father.

“I’m glad Ma thinks well of me anyway, even if you don’t,” Lew said, grinning.

“Well, your ma tries to think of something good to say about most folks, even you.” John couldn’t hide his obvious pride in his son, in spite of his words.

The four men left from the mouth of Wheeling Creek early in the last morning of May. Although the plan was to stay for only a few days, the canoe was loaded with provisions and tools. It was more than sixty miles downriver to the mouth of Middle Island Creek, and they hoped to cover a large portion of it on the very first day.

The days had passed uneventfully with Lewis avoiding the hard work as much as possible. When they reached the claim, Lewis made a wide sweep around the site, satisfied that there were no Indians in the area. The hunting was good, and he had supplied the camp with enough venison to keep them happy.

The first job had been to build a rough lean-to shed, which had served them well when the showers came on the third day.

On the ninth day, Captain John announced that he was satisfied with what they had accomplished, and that they would begin the return trip on the next morning. This news was met with great joy by all, and they celebrated by breaking out the whiskey jug that had been brought along for just such an occasion. Although Lew was usually inclined to let people do as they wished as long as it did not affect him, he found himself annoyed with the antics of Tom Moore, who had become quite drunk. In spite of his small stature, he had become feisty in his drunken state.

"I may be small, but I can lick anybody twice my size," he boasted. "That includes you too, young Lew. I doubt you're as tough as everybody says you are."

Lewis stood up and after giving Moore a disgusted glare, he turned and walked away.

"Here, you ain't scared of me are ye," called Moore, who took a step as if to follow. John Wetzel caught him by the arm and pulled him to a sitting position.

"It won't do to get Lew riled up now, Tom," he said quietly. "You best sleep it off cause we're gonna get an early start in the morning."

Moore shook his arm loose and tried to get up again, but the struggle was too much. He slumped against the tree behind him and was soon asleep.

"Ma may be right," observed John as Lewis rejoined them after a few minutes.

"About what?" asked Lew.

"About Tom Moore," answered John. "She thinks he's a bit tetched." Realizing he maybe shouldn't have spoken in that way, he turned to Andrews.

"Sorry, Joe," he said. "I guess he's some kin of yours."

"Yeah, but not too close. His ma was a bit off herself, we all think. I'm just glad Lew didn't whack him."

"Yes, Lew, you showed good restraint there," said his father.

"It was mostly the whiskey talkin', I reckon," remarked Lew.

The next day was spent getting as far back toward home as the mouth of Fishing Creek, where they spent the night. Early the next morning, they resumed their homeward journey, but Lewis Wetzel was not feeling well. Shaking with chills and fever, he was unable to help with the rowing. He slumped against the side of the canoe, just in front of Moore, who was in the stern. Andrews was in the bow, and John Wetzel near the middle and just in front of Lewis. "What's wrong with Lew?" Moore wanted to know after they had managed to gain a few miles upstream. "He ain't lookin' good."

"He's got the ague," replied Captain John with some annoyance.

"We've just passed the mouth of Fish Creek," announced Andrews from up front. "There's Fish Creek Island on our left."

Lewis roused himself enough to speak to his father. "Pa, I'd be better off if you put me ashore."

"Ashore? I don't see how that'll work too good."

"I need to be able to lay down and cover myself for a bit. After some rest, I'll make my way up to Baker's Fort. You can wait for me there."

"Why don't you just wait until we get up Baker's? We'll put in there and let you rest."

"I can't wait, Pa, I've got to get out of this boat now or you'll all be sorry."

"All right, Lew." Captain John finally comprehended why Lew might have need of being on shore. "We'll put you off just up there, past the head of the island."

They slid past the island for some hundred yards and steered the canoe to the Virginia shore. Lewis scrambled out, carrying his rifle and a blanket he had fished out of the bag of gear, heading for a clump of trees just a few feet above the riverbank. John Wetzel watched his son for a few minutes and then directed the others to return the canoe into the river.

"Shouldn't we just wait here for him?" asked Joe Andrews.

"No, he wants us to go on. I think the motion of the canoe is makin' him even sicker," answered John. "We'll put in up at the fort and have somethin' to eat while we wait. He'll meet us up there afore too long."

"Let's hurry then," shouted Tom Moore. "Eatin' sounds good to me."

Moore had taken the spot in the bow, and Andrews was in the stern. All three men were paddling.

"Let's stay as close to the shore as we can," said John. "The current ain't so strong over here."

They had not gone far when a shout came from the shore some distance ahead. "Come ashore and help us," called a strange voice.

"That don't sound quite right to me," noted Captain John. 'Let's ease out from the shore a ways."

As they began to swing the canoe out more toward the main channel, Moore stood up, trying for a better look. "Hell," he cried, "them's Injuns!"

Before he had finished, three shots rang out from the riverbank in front of them and to their right. Moore was struck full in the chest, and he tumbled out of the canoe and into the water. Another of the shots struck John Wetzel in the right shoulder. The paddle dropped from his hands and into the water. He quickly reached to the front to pick up the oar that Moore had dropped when he was hit.

"We've got to keep movin'," John cried, trying to work the paddle with his left arm. His words went unheeded because Joe Andrews, seeing that his companions were both hit, had jumped into the stream on his left and was swimming for the opposite shore. Another shot had torn into John Wetzel's right side and into a kidney. He was still functioning, but his paddling on the left side had caused the bow of the canoe to turn to the right and toward the near shore.

Less than fifty yards away, three painted warriors had jumped into the shallow water and were making their way toward the crippled boat.

Having relieved himself and huddled under his blanket beneath the branches of a short willow tree, Lew Wetzel was trying to get warm enough to stop the shivering. The sound of gunshots brought him up immediately, and throwing the blanket aside, he grabbed his rifle and began running upstream.

He quickly came to a spot where he had a clear view up the river, and he could see the canoe turned and beginning to drift back downstream, although very close to the shore. There was no sign of anyone in the canoe, but he could see the three Indians who had nearly reached it. Two others were watching from the shore. Although he knew it was too far for any accuracy, Lew raised his gun to his shoulder and squeezed the trigger. The ball struck the water a few feet to the left of the front warrior. The three Indians stopped for a moment, then continued toward the canoe.

John Wetzel had slumped to the floor of the little craft, still breathing, but barely. He had taken a third ball in his chest that punctured a lung. He knew he was going to die. The sound of a rifle shot from downriver did register for a moment.

"Lew," moaned John Wetzel and then he died.

The Indians pulled the canoe to the shore and jerked John Wetzel's body out, throwing it down against a rock lying along the waterline. Five in all, the warriors began climbing into the canoe.

Lew Wetzel, having reloaded on the run, had kneeled and fired a second time. The ball had slammed into the top ridge along the side of the craft and through the hand of the brave who had been clinging to it.

Not knowing how many others might be with the one who was shooting at them, the warriors hurriedly put the canoe in the stream and began rowing rapidly for the other shore.

Wetzel could see the body of his father lying at the edge of the water. He was winded and out of strength, so much so that he gave up the idea of reloading again. He might have been able to kill one of the Indians had he done so, but now he was concerned about the condition of his father. He rested a moment and then pushed on. "At least I kept the bastards from scalping him, or worse," he said aloud.

He looked in the direction of the blockhouse that was Baker's Fort. It was close to a mile away from where he was, but he wondered why there had been no intervention from there. Surely they could hear what was happening. Maybe there's no one there, he thought. By the time he reached his father's body, the Indians were nearly to the far shore. He looked at them forlornly, then gave his attention to his father. He quickly saw that Captain John was dead. He dragged the body up out of the water and into a grassy spot next to some bushes.

He could not suppress the tears that came as he sat down next to his father's lifeless form. "I'm so sorry, Pa," Lew said aloud. "I did love you, I hope you knew that."

There needed to be a burial, but he didn't want to do that by himself. A flurry of thoughts went through his mind. Maybe he should go and bring back some family members. Maybe they should try to take the body home. Something else was nagging at him as well, and its intensity grew stronger. He stood again and looked across the river where he could see the abandoned canoe.

"Those damned murderers are getting away. That ain't right."

Suddenly filled with resolve, Wetzel picked up his rifle. He turned and looked down at his father's corpse.

"I'll be back for you, Pa. But I mean to make at least one of them bastards pay for this."

With that, all thoughts of illness and fatigue forgotten, he strode to the riverbank and plunged in. He swam purposefully, carrying his gun in his left arm, the muzzle and part of the barrel under the water and pressed against his left shoulder, with the lock and breech clear above the water so that the essential part of the gun was dry.

June 11, 1786

Red Storm had talked them into it, and he wasn't altogether happy about it. The winter had been somewhat pleasant in Buckongehelas's village, and his young son had been born just over one moon ago. His lovely wife, Bright Moon, had born the child with ease, or so it seemed to Little Fox. And after several days, they had settled on the name Eagle's Wing, which they felt showed their respect for White Eagle. When Red Storm arrived at the village, urging Little Fox to join him, Little Fox had refused at first.

"It has been a year since we have been on a raid. It is time, lest we become like old women, as you said before."

"I suppose you are wanting to hunt down this man, Wetzel." Little Fox had learned to say the name, tired of referring to him as W.

Red Storm had prevailed, however, and they had swung by Wapatomica, hoping that Fire Heart would join them. In that venture, they failed; but three young Shawnee friends of his had eagerly joined them. Red Storm had heard that the white men had built a new fort at the mouth of the Muskingum. He suggested that they see what it was like.

"It is on this side of the big river," he noted. "That is not good."

The last fort built by the whites in the Ohio country, the one called Fort Laurens, had not lasted long. The little band had observed the activities on the Muskingum but kept their distance. Later they had ascended the Ohio, and when they came to the creek the white men called Captina, they crossed the river. Just below where they crossed, they discovered the blockhouse of the Baker family. They spent two days in the vicinity but saw no one come or go.

"We should burn it down," said one of the young Shawnees, a man called Red Feather.

"Too dangerous," cautioned Little Fox. "But if there is no one there, it means the white families may be in their little cabins. They are easier to attack."

Staying out of sight, the five warriors moved down until they came to a sizable creek, the one called Fish Creek. They camped along the creek, inland more than a mile from its mouth; and two of the Shawnees went up the stream to see what they could find. They returned the next day, filled with excitement.

"There is a cabin not far," they reported, "with two women and three children there. No men!"

"You are sure about this?" asked Little Fox.

"Yes, we are sure."

"Let us burn it," exclaimed Red Feather.

"You are very anxious to burn things," remarked Little Fox, who was not too interested.

"Let us do it," urged Red Storm. "These young bucks need to be bloodied."

The decision made, the raiding party soon found the cabin, and following a favorite tactic, it was decided to attack the following morning. Having surrounded the little log structure, which was built some fifty feet from the creek bank, they watched silently as the women and children went about their evening tasks.

The night was warm, but all went inside at dusk and did not reappear. Red Storm and Red Feather had crept up near the cabin door during the night, and shortly after daylight, one of the women stepped out into the morning coolness. It was her last step, for Red Feather struck with his tomahawk while Red Storm burst through the door. The other warriors came round the building and followed him in. The four remaining inhabitants were too surprised to offer resistance, although the older woman had tried to reach for a gun hanging above the fireplace.

Red Storm brought her down with his axe, and the three children were quickly killed. A swift search of the contents of the cabin was made, but there was little to interest the raiders. They took the gun and some powder, along with some of the more colorful clothes, which could be easily stuffed in their hunting pouches. They then set fire to the building and stood outside with great satisfaction watching it burn.

"We had best not stay here long," announced Little Fox. "The smoke will bring men to investigate." He was not so proud of having killed only women and children.

"Yes," agreed Red Storm. "Let us go back to the big river. There are many white men traveling in boats along this shore. We might find one to attack."

"I think we should cross to the other side," said Little Fox. "There could well be an avenging party coming after us."

It was decided to follow the creek back for a short distance, and then angle over the ridges and arrive at the Ohio up near the empty blockhouse they had seen earlier. Having arrived a half mile below Baker's Fort, they saw the canoe with three white men coming toward them and close to the shore. One of the Shawnees, a man called Tall Shadow, could speak a little English.

"Look," whispered Little Fox, pointing to the canoe. "See if we can get them to come closer. We can kill them and get their canoe. Call to them, Tall Shadow."

Tall Shadow called out, saying he needed help, but the canoe had started to turn away. It was then that the warriors began shooting, and making their way out to retrieve the canoe.

The shot from downstream had surprised them, especially the second, which had hit Red Feather in the left hand.

"We need to get across the river quickly," shouted Little Fox. "We don't know how many are coming against us."

"There is only one in this canoe," pointed out Red Storm. "I saw three at first."

"I know I shot one of them, and he fell in the water," said Tall Shadow. "I don't know about the other."

None of the braves had seen Andrews swimming, for he had kept himself low in the water. The other action had kept them from discovering his escape. After discarding John Wetzel's body, the five warriors rowed the canoe quickly across the river. They pushed directly inland and, after going a short distance, made an interesting discovery.

"Horses!" exclaimed Little Fox. "White men's horses, five of them."

The others gathered around, examining the clear tracks. Red Feather was in some pain, and Red Storm helped him dress his wound.

"Let us follow them," suggested Tall Shadow.

"We can follow them to see where they go, but it is too many to attack," remarked Little Fox.

"Do you think the white men who were shooting at us will try to find us?" asked Red Feather.

"I doubt it," said Little Fox. "But let us get moving."

Both Little Fox and Red Storm would have been quite surprised if they had known that they were being followed, and by only one man—their sworn enemy, Lewis Wetzel. The swim had exhausted him, but Wetzel was still enraged and determined to avenge his father. He soon found where the Indians had stowed the canoe, and he followed their trail to where it crossed the tracks of the horses. Wetzel examined those tracks carefully. *Who could these white men be*, he wondered. He stooped to look carefully at one of the imprints of a horse's hoof and the shape of its shoe.

"Damn," he uttered suddenly. "I'd swear that track looks just like one that mare of Jacob's would make. S'pose he's with that bunch?"

Concerned now that this raiding party might be going after the white men, Wetzel pushed on in pursuit. It was not long, however, that the combination of fatigue and illness became too much for him. He stopped to catch his breath but realized that there was no way he could continue. Besides, his father's body was lying along the riverbank and must be attended. A small sapling stood next to the trail, and Wetzel broke a branch of it across the track, for he intended to return.

He had gone farther than he realized, for the return to the river took him much longer than he had expected. He found the canoe and pushed it into the river. Paddling as fast as he could, he aimed for Baker's Fort, hoping that he might find someone there after all. Upon reaching the Virginia shore, Wetzel pulled the canoe out of the water. He noticed the hole in the top edge along the right-hand side, and that there was blood around it. The thought struck him that maybe his second shot had made that hole, and perhaps he had hit one of Indians. There was no way to know that, of course, because the Indians had shot at the canoe, and the blood could be his own father's.

He made his way to the front of the fortified cabin owned by John Baker and his family. Pounding on the door, Wetzel was surprised when it was opened, and he was face-to-face with young Henry Baker.

"Why, hello, Lew," said Henry. "What in the world brings you here?"

"I'm glad to see you, Henry. I didn't think anybody was here. Didn't you hear the shooting earlier?"

"What shooting?"

"The damned redskins! They killed my pa."

"Your pa? Where'd this happen?"

"His body's lyin' along the bank, maybe a half mile from here. I've got to bury him."

"My God! I'm mighty sorry, Lew."

"I can't understand why you didn't hear any of the shootin'."

"Well, I just got here an hour ago. The whole family's up at Wheeling, and I came back for the night to tend the hogs."

Wetzel sat down on the doorstep, bending down, his head in his hands.

"Are you all right, Lew?"

"I ain't been feelin' too good, I guess," Lew muttered with a sigh.

"You know, I did find a couple of dead hogs. But they looked to be dead for a couple of days." Baker brought Lew a drink of water. "I suppose it could've been done by the same Injuns."

Refreshed a bit by the water, Lew stood again. "No tellin', but they did seem to be comin' from up this way. I've got to git Pa buried. Can you help?"

"Sure can," said Henry, who was about the same age as Lew. He came out and started for the small shed behind the house. "I'll get us some spades."

Wetzel watched as Baker went to retrieve the tools. His family had known the Bakers for a long time, first in the Shenandoah Valley, and later on Dunkard Creek. Captain John Baker, though born in Germany, had come to eastern Pennsylvania as a teenage boy, later married and, after several stops, had built this station near Graveyard Run. There were ten or eleven children, thought Lew, but Henry was one of the older ones.

"I've got a canoe," pointed out Lew when Henry had returned. "Let's take that."

It took them only a few minutes to go down the river and put in at the spot near where Lew had hidden his father's body.

"Do you want to bury him here?" asked Henry.

Lew had been thinking about that very question. He didn't think there was anyway he could take the body all the way back to the Wetzel farm, but he didn't like the idea of having his father's grave in this forlorn place. "I think it would be better if we took him up and buried him near your station. Maybe along Graveyard Run there someplace."

"That sounds good," agreed Henry. "Let's carry him down and put him in the canoe."

This was done, and they soon made their way back to the landing near the blockhouse.

"Sorry, you had to do most of the hard rowing, Henry," said Lew as they lifted John Wetzel's body from the canoe. "I don't seem to have any strength left."

"Just glad I can help, Lew."

They chose a spot along the south side of the little run, just east of a large beech tree. They quickly dug the grave, although it was probably a bit shallow, Lew thought. Considering how tired he was, it would have to do.

"Do you want me to read over him, Lew?" asked Henry.

Wetzel was embarrassed that he hadn't given any thought to such a thing. He realized that it would be very impolite to refuse such a kindness. "Why, yes, if you can do that. It would be good to be able to tell Ma that Pa'd had some good words spoken over him."

"Let me get the book," said Henry, who went back to the house to get his Bible. Although John Baker could barely speak any English, he had insisted that his children learn to both read and write the language of their new country. The Bible had been the principal textbook. When Baker had returned, the two young men stood beside the open pit. Lew had placed his father's tomahawk and hunting pouch next to his body.

Henry read in halting tones the stirring words from the first seven verses of John, Chapter 14. When he had finished, he turned to Wetzel. "Lew, I'll fill in the grave. There's some bread and cheese on the table, I just brought it down from Wheeling. You eat and rest a bit while I finish."

Wetzel did not argue but did as Baker suggested. It was late afternoon, and he knew that he needed to get home yet that evening and inform his mother. He needed the refreshment, and he was extremely grateful to Baker for all that he had done.

When Wetzel came back from the house, the grave had been closed.

"Do you plan to take the canoe, Lew?"

"No, I don't think I have the strength for that. I'll go on foot, and I'd better get started. It will be long past dark before I git there as it is."

"I reckon you're right," observed Henry. "I do have my horse here. I guess you could take him." Baker was a little hesitant as he made this offer.

"No thanks," answered Lew quickly. "I can't leave you here without your horse. Besides, I intend to go over the ridges, and I'm better off on foot."

After following the riverbank for close to ten miles, Wetzel came to Little Grave Creek. He turned upstream until he came to the same place where he had spotted the bear tracks more than a year earlier. It was dark by the time he passed the little hut where he had spent the rainy night. Following the path that Little Fox and his companions had taken on that same occasion, he came to Wheeling Creek. Rather than going immediately to his mother's home, he turned down the creek until he arrived at the little cabin owned by Henry Jolly. As he banged on the cabin door, Lew realized what fear that might cause inside. He didn't think they should have gone to bed already. Soon a hoarse voice came from inside.

"Who's out there?"

"It's Lew Wetzel, Henry. Can you let me in for a minute?"

"Hold on. I'm comin'."

The door opened slowly, and Henry Jolly's face appeared in the opening.

"What the hell, Lew. Do you know how late it is?"

"Yes, I do, Henry," he acknowledged as he pushed the door open further and stepped inside.

"Hello, Rachel," Lew nodded toward Henry's young wife, who stood near the fireplace. Seeing Rachel brought a flashback of the day, years ago now, when his brother George had delivered this same young girl, Rachel Grice, from the scene of the massacre of her family. "My pa's been killed, Henry."

"What? Your pa? How in the hell did that happen?"

"A band of raiders shot him in his canoe comin' upriver. I'll explain it all later. Right now I've got to tell Ma. Could you get word to my Uncle Lew. I'd like to get some men together and go after them red bastards. They went across down below Baker's Station."

"Sure, I'll go down to Bonnett's first thing in the morning. There's several men there. He's puttin' up a stable."

"Good. I'll meet you here later in the morning."

"We're awful sorry, Lew. Please tell your mother for us."

"Thank you," said Lew, and then he was gone.

Kentucky Forts and Towns

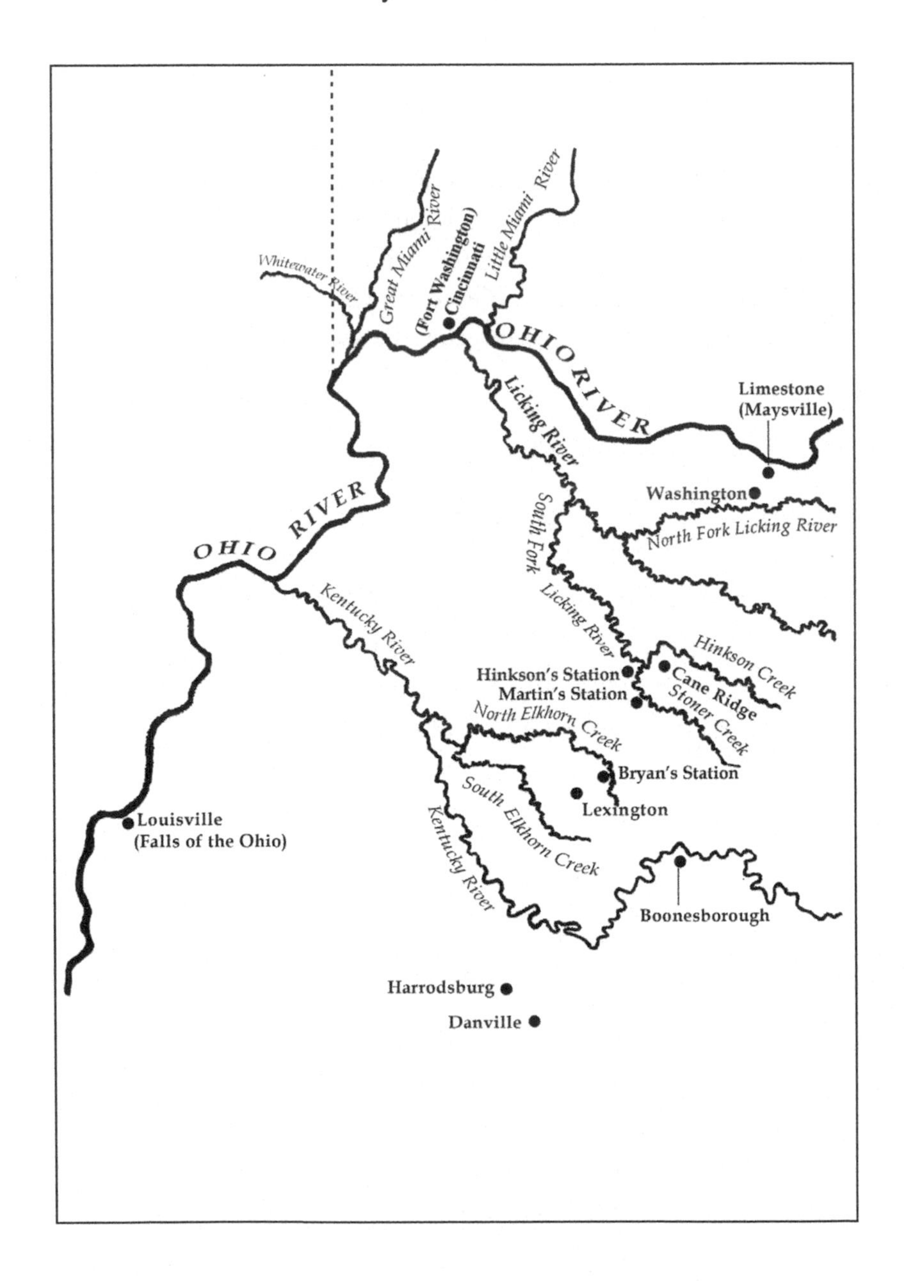

12

Kentucky

June 12, 1786

Awakened by the sound of a hammer, eight-year-old Lewis Bonnett Jr. sprang from his bed and looked out the small window in the loft where he had been sleeping. He could see his father going around the corner of the half-finished stone house, shouting something at the person with the hammer. Frustrated, Lewis grabbed his pants and shirt, dressing quickly and grumbling at himself.

"Damn," he said, a word he had learned to use recently after spending extra time around his father and the other men. He tried not to use the word in front of his mother, but his pa didn't seem to mind it too much. He was angry that he had slept so late, for he wanted to be outside where some of the neighbors were helping his father raise a new horse stable. He had assisted with the work the previous day and, in his mind anyway, had been a valuable contributor.

Still buttoning his shirt as he rushed to where the stairway descended to the ground floor, he noted that his two older sisters, Elizabeth and Barbara, were still deep in slumber. The daybed, where his five-year-old sister, Mary, slept, was empty. That didn't surprise him, but he did wonder a bit about why the older children, including himself, had been allowed to sleep. Scrambling down the stairs, which ended in the kitchen, Lewis settled into one of the chairs by the table and pulled on his shoes.

"Why, good morning, sleepyhead," said his mother cheerfully. She stood near the kitchen fireplace, holding the baby, John, now nearly one year old, under one arm. Mary, who was sitting on the ledge in front of the fireplace and eating a biscuit slathered in maple syrup, eyed her brother.

"Hi JuJu," she offered, her best effort at trying to say Junior, which the family often called him.

JuJu said nothing, continuing to fumble with getting his shoes on and secured.

"Cat got your tongue this morning?" asked his mother. "At least you can say something to your sister."

"Why didn't you wake me up?" said Lewis finally, ignoring his mother's suggestion. "I need to be outside helpin' Pa."

"Your pa said to let you sleep. Said you worked hard yesterday."

"Well, I'm goin'." His shoes in place, Lewis dashed toward the door.

"Wait," cried Elizabeth Bonnett. "You need to eat somethin'. Don't you want some nice biscuits?"

"I'll wait 'til dinner," shouted Lewis as he ran out the door.

The men were working on the other side of the stone house, whose walls had been built to a height of over six feet all the way around, but stood forlornly, awaiting completion. Lewis thought that the big frame house was plenty nice, but his father had been determined to build a fine stone house in the old German tradition. The building had been going on for at least two years, with the masonry work being directed by their neighbor and friend, Adam Grandstaff.

Not much had been done lately, thought Lewis, and now they were building the stable. He wondered if the stone house would ever be completed. As he rounded the corner of the building, he caught sight of his cousin Martin Wetzel perched on a ladder against a huge corner post, hacking a notch out of the top log. It was not going well, and Martin was accompanying his efforts with a few choice words. Lewis Bonnett Sr. stood nearby, watching the work with a slight grin on his face. Lewis could see that Adam

Grandstaff, along with his sons Lewis and Eli, were busy with something on the other side of the structure. He was surprised to see Moses Shepherd there as well.

"You ain't quite the carpenter your pa is, are you, Martin?" said the elder Bonnett with a laugh.

"I don't reckon I am, Uncle," replied Martin, with a bit more annoyance than he intended. "I'd be plenty glad fer you to take over if you want."

"Why, hello, JuJu," said Bonnett to his young son, ignoring Martin's offer. "'Bout time you stirred them lazy bones."

"Don't call me JuJu," protested young Lewis. "And I ain't lazy! You didn't wake me up."

"Damn!" shouted Martin. "This axe is dull. Maybe I should just get down and wait for Pa to get here since you think he's so much better anyway."

"Who knows where your pa is, and when he'll get back. I guess we're just stuck with you." Again, Bonnett laughed, hoping Martin knew he was just having fun with him.

"Lewis," he said, turning again to his son. "Run to the house and get that small axe hangin' next to the fireplace. We'd better help out our chief carpenter afore he quits."

Lewis started toward the house, glad to be doing something useful but was stopped short by a shout from Eli Grandstaff.

"Somebody's coming!" he yelled, pointing up the lane toward the main path that followed alongside Big Wheeling Creek. A rider was coming fast, shouting something they couldn't quite understand.

"That looks like Henry Jolly," said Adam Grandstaff. "He sure is in a big hurry."

"What's he sayin'?" wondered Bonnett.

"I think it's somethin about my pa," said Martin Wetzel, who had come down from his post.

The rider yelled again, and by now he was close enough for them to hear him clearly.

"It's Captain John," cried Henry Jolly as he pulled the horse to a halt. "The Injuns killed him down near Baker's."

"Oh my God," exclaimed Lewis Bonnett. "Was he by himself?"

"No, some others were with him. They were comin' back from workin' on his place on Middle Island Creek. Lew was along for sure, and he wants to go after the redskins."

"Where the hell is Lew now?" asked Martin. "How could he have let this happen to Pa?"

"Lew came to my place last night. He was on his way to tell your ma, Martin. He asked me to spread the word and wants us to meet him at my place this morning."

By now, the three Grandstaffs and Moses Shepherd had gathered around to hear what Jolly had to say.

"Let's get our horses," commanded Shepherd. "We'd better hurry."

"You're right," agreed Lewis Bonnett. "Junior, run and git your ma. I need to talk to her right now." He started back to get his horse when he thought of something else. "And Junior, go to the larder and put some of that salt pork in that deerskin that's hangin' there. Bring that and a bag of the parched corn mix."

The parched corn mix consisted of some parched corn pounded fine and mixed with sugar and sometimes chestnuts and beans. Martin Wetzel, after returning from captivity among the Shawnees, had explained to his family and neighbors how the Shawnees kept such a mixture on hand to be used for travel, along with some dried meat. The white hunters had learned the value of this preparation for their own use.

"No tellin' how long we might be gone," Bonnett explained to Adam Grandstaff, who had just come up, leading his own horse. In a very short time, the men were all mounted and waiting as Lewis Bonnett talked with his wife.

"Elizabeth, you need to go to Mary and see what she needs. Take Junior with you. Beth can look after the others 'til you get back."

Lewis, who had brought the foodstuffs as directed, protested immediately. "Pa, let me go with you."

"No, Junior, where I'm goin ain't no place for young 'uns. You go with your ma and help your Aunt Mary. She'll be grievin', and she may be all by herself. That's where you're needed, and I don't want no arguments."

With that he turned to mount his horse, and the men rode away. Elizabeth Bonnett watched for several moments until the riders were out of sight. She turned then to her son and hugged him tightly to her. "Life is sad sometimes, ain't it honey," she murmured, as she led him toward the house. "Let's hurry, I need to get some things together for your Aunt Mary."

The horsemen had ridden quickly, and by the time they reached the Jolly homestead, Lew Wetzel was there waiting.

"By God, Lew, you look awful," pointed out his brother Martin before embracing him.

"I reckon I've felt better," acknowledged Lew, pushing back and eyeing Martin, who was several inches shorter than Lew. "But them damned reds need killin', and I aim to do some of it."

"I hope we ain't too late," said Martin.

"I don't think so," said Lew. "I found their trail all right. They was followin' the path of some white men. That had me worried a bit. Could one of our brothers be in that bunch?"

"Yeah, Jake and Johnny was both in that huntin' party, I think. Mitchell was another one of 'em, and I don't know who else."

"Well, them Injun sons of bitches is on foot, so maybe we can catch 'em still."

"God, Lewis, I'm sorry about your pa." Lewis Bonnett had dismounted and came to where Lew and Martin stood talking. "How did it happen? How's your ma doin'?"

"We need to get goin', Uncle Lewis," said Lew. "I'll tell you about it on the way."

The eight men were soon mounted and on the way again up the big creek, headed through the hills to Baker's Station. It was shortly after noon when they arrived. Henry Baker, who had seen them coming up the Ohio shore, came out to meet them.

"Hello again, Lew," Baker greeted Wetzel, who was out in front. "How are you feelin'?"

"I ain't good, Henry, but I'm leadin' these men after them redskins that killed Pa."

"I figured as much. Why don't you all come in and get somethin' to drink. I'll get my horse and go with you."

The idea of some rest and refreshment went over well, and the men crowded into the house. The Wetzel brothers walked out to where their father was buried.

"We spoke some words over him, Martin," Lewis explained. "Do you think we should take him back home?

"Let's let him lie, Lew. Sounds like you did the best that could be done."

Overcome by a sudden coughing spell, Lewis dropped to his knees, his eyes watering and nose running.

"God, Lew, are you all right," asked Martin as he bent down, helping Lewis back to his feet.

"I ain't so good as you kin see," answered Lew. "I've got the damned chills too."

"You ain't in no shape to be chasin' Injuns. Why don't you stay here at Baker's and rest. We'll pick you up on the way back."

"No, no, I've got to go. I can't quit now after leadin' everybody this far. Forget it, Martin, and don't mention it to nobody."

"Don't mention what?" wondered Lewis Bonnett, who had just walked up to where the brothers were standing.

"Nothin'," said Lewis, trying to suppress another round of coughing.

"Lew ain't feelin' the best, Uncle Lewis," said Martin. "But I can't talk him out of goin' on."

"This is where Captain John is restin', I presume," observed Bonnett, kneeling to rearrange one of the stones Lew had put on the grave. "It's a nice spot, one John would have liked. He loved this river, you know."

"He did that," agreed Martin.

"I wonder though," interjected Lew hoarsely, "if we ought to take him back and bury him closer to home?" Lew couldn't shake the feeling that he had failed his father, even at the very last in giving him a proper burial.

"What did your ma say?" Bonnett wanted to know. "Did she want you to bring him home?"

"She never said," responded Lew. "She mostly just cried."

"Unless she says different, I think this is a fine spot."

"I agree," said Martin. "It is easy to find. We'll bring Ma down here sometime when she's over her grievin'."

They found a larger rock not far away and dragged it over to the head of the grave.

"We can chisel his name in sometime," suggested Martin, "but we ain't got the tools for it now."

This settled the matter, and the three men returned to the house to find the others eager to continue the mission. The day was warm, and it made the splashing and swimming of the horses across the river less onerous. Lew Wetzel quickly found the trail from the day before and pushed rapidly along until he came to the place where he had left the broken branch. He dismounted here and examined the ground. The others stopped and waited, remaining seated on their horses. Feeling a coughing spell coming on, Wetzel stepped off the trail amid a stand of pine trees, out of sight of his companions.

Moses Shepherd edged his mount up next to Martin. "Lew ain't well, is he?"

"He's sick all right but determined to track the Injuns."

"Maybe we should just turn back."

"I tried to tell him that, Moses, but he won't listen."

Lew reappeared. "Them sons of bitches are following the horse tracks left by that huntin' party. I guess we'd better git movin'." He pointed to the south along the open trail and, mounting his horse, moved out at a gentle trot. The others swung in behind. There was no talking, for there was no way to know whether they might be under watch themselves. They stopped twice more for Lew to check the signs, and after three miles or so, he stopped again, sliding to the ground and leaning for a moment against his horse's neck. He had seen something that surprised him. He walked off a short distance to the right of their line of travel and pointed to the ground.

"Look there," he said, following the words with a fit of coughing. "The bastards have turned aside."

Martin and Lewis Bonnett soon joined him and examined the ground for several feet around. "You're right, Lew," exclaimed Martin. "Looks like the hunters are headed for the Sunfish, but these buggers are following the ridge to the west."

"They've given up goin' after the hunters, you think?" wondered Lewis Bonnett.

"Looks that way to me," observed Martin.

"Could be they want to swing around and cut 'em off farther on," suggested Henry Baker, who had joined them at the front.

"Henry could be right," agreed Lew. "We'd best go after 'em anyway."

The men remounted and followed after the trail that the red men had left.

"They ain't bein too careful, are they?" noted Bonnett. "Their trail is pretty easy to follow."

"They ain't expectin' to be followed. Looks like they're headed for home," said Martin.

Lew continued in the lead, but he was leaning low, resting on the horse's neck.

"Look at Lew," said Baker to Martin Wetzel. "He's about to fall off that horse."

"You're right," answered Martin, who spurred his mount forward. Before he could come up even with his brother, Martin saw that he would be too late. He watched in horror as Lew lost his grip on the reins and slid to the ground with a thump.

"God, Lew, what's happened to you?" cried Martin, who jumped to the ground and ran to where Lew was sprawled in the grass. Martin helped him to a sitting position. "Are you hurt, Lew?"

"I'm sicker'n a dog, Martin, I can't go on anymore."

The other men had gathered around the Wetzel brothers stunned by this turn of events. Seeing Lewis Wetzel in such a vulnerable position was something they had never expected.

"He's mighty sick," explained Martin, turning and looking up at the circle of worried men standing behind him. "There's no way he can keep goin'."

"I think we should all go home," announced Henry Jolly, who had returned from a short scouting trip further up the trail. "There's no sign that the reds are still after that huntin' party. They're a day ahead of us, and I doubt we're goin' to catch 'em anyway."

"I agree," said Lewis Bonnett. "Let's git Lew back to your place, Henry, and let him rest there for the night. Martin and I can git him home the next day."

"I'm sorry," whispered Lew. "I wanted to get one of them for Pa."

"It's all right, Lew," said Martin. "There's plenty of time to git even."

They began the return trip with Lew riding together with Martin on Martin's horse. There were no further incidents, and the nine men reached Baker's Fort well before dark. The five-man hunting party returned to Wheeling the next day, their horses loaded with venison.

June 14, 1786

Little Fox felt a growing aggravation with the whining and complaining by Red Feather. In his view, an Indian brave should not show such behavior. He supposed the wounded hand was painful, but Red Feather should be quiet about it. Little Fox kept his distance as much as possible. The braves had followed the trail of the five white hunters for a few miles, but when it led over the ridge and down into the valley of Sunfish Creek, they had given it up and turned westward.

After a quiet and fireless camp on the first night, they pushed on until they came to Wills Creek putting in for the night along its banks, a few miles below the source. Little Fox and Red Storm were both concerned about pursuit, for they were sure the Long Knives would be out to revenge the killings for which they had been responsible.

"It has been a very successful raid, my friend," Red Storm had remarked. "We killed seven, I think."

"Yes, but we have only the scalps of the women and children," pointed out Little Fox. He had been thinking more and more that it was possible they were being followed. "I am worried that the ones who were shooting at us may have gathered others and come after us. We have been careless and left a trail that is easy to follow."

Red Storm had agreed and decided to go back along their path for a full day to see if anyone was behind them. Red Feather, who was anxious to get back to his home village, protested that this would cause too much delay.

"We will move on to Coshocton," said Little Fox to Red Storm, ignoring Red Feather. "We will wait for you there."

Red Storm had just this day rejoined them at Coshocton. He had gone all the way back to where they had left the trail of the white men.

"There were many tracks there," Red Storm reported. "Many white men on horses, but they did not follow our trail. We are safe."

This was good news. Even Red Feather seemed to have reduced his whimpering. They set out the next day for the Shawnee towns on the Mad River. In three days, they had reached Wapatomica, the town of Red Feather and Fire Heart. They spent two days there resting, but Little Fox was anxious to return to his family at New Coshocton, another nine or ten miles to the north. Red Storm was less interested in returning to his village on the Upper Sandusky and decided to accompany Little Fox to his town.

The reunion with Bright Moon was glorious, and Little Fox found himself to be very excited to see his son, Eagle's Wing, now barely six weeks old. On the second day, a runner arrived at their hut, sent by the old chief, Buckongehelas, and asking Little Fox to come to the chief 's lodge. "What is this?" asked Bright Moon. "Why does the chief ask for you?"

"I do not know, my wife," answered Little Fox, "but I had better go and see."

Much to his surprise and to his delight, although he would be loathe to admit that, he found his old friend John Leith waiting for him.

"Hello, Little Fox, it is very good to see a friend," said the trader. "I hear you have returned from a raid."

Little Fox felt a strong urge to embrace Leith but stopped himself in time. Instead, he spoke quietly. "I am surprised to see you here. I thought you were at Fort Pitt."

"I have been many places since we last met, Little Fox."

"We came through Coshocton just a few days ago," said Little Fox. "They told me you had lived there for a time."

"Yes, but we moved away from there a few moons ago. The Mingoes and Wyandots killed my man who was taking goods to Fort Pitt. They stole the goods. We went to live at Tapacon for a while, but the Delawares told us it was not safe, and that we should move to Fort Pitt." Leith went on to explain how the Mingoes had killed the four men working for the traders Dawson and McClain, who had been left in Coshocton. His Delaware friends were sure that some Mingoes and Cherokees were on the way to Tapacon to kill him and his family.

"I am glad that my friends the Delaware were kind to you," said Little Fox.

"Yes, and they hid my skins for me and took my horses and goods with them when they came back here. When I came again to Tapacon with some men, we found the skins and returned them to Fort Pitt where I sold them. But I came here to recover my goods and horses."

"I am very glad you were not killed, Leith," said Little Fox after hearing Leith's story. "But I do not blame the Mingoes and Wyandots. They are fighting for our lands."

Two days later, Little Fox was asked to come to the chief's lodge again, where he found Leith and the French trader Le Clerk. "Our French friend Le Clerk has come, Little Fox, and he brings news you will want to hear."

"What news is that?" asked the Chippewa.

"Le Clerk has just come from Wheeling. They are saying there that old John Wetzel was killed by Indians in the big river, near a place called Baker's Sation."

Little Fox reacted quickly to the name Wetzel. "Wetzel is dead?"

"Well, it's not your man, but Le Clerk thinks it is his father. I thought you would want to know."

"You think we killed the father of Wetzel?"

Le Clerk, who had been listening intently, now spoke up. "Did you kill a white man on the Ohio River?"

Little Fox stared at the French trader for a moment. Could he be in some trouble if he admitted this shooting? He couldn't see why, and the natural desire to tell again of this successful raid led him to answer.

"Red Storm and I and three Shawnees killed two white men, maybe three, in the river thirteen days ago."

"It was you then, most likely, who killed John Wetzel."

"Maybe the son was the other man, the one who fell in the water." Little Fox felt a leap of hope, thinking it quite possible that they had managed to kill their number one enemy after all.

Le Clerk smiled. "Not so. Lewis Wetzel is very much alive. The story is that he was on shore and fired shots at the attackers."

This was disheartening information for Little Fox, and his countenance darkened.

Leith took notice. "Is that right, Little Fox?" he asked. "Was someone shooting at you?"

Little Fox nodded, thinking about the opportunity they had missed. "Was he alone?" he asked after a short silence.

Le Clerk explained that he didn't know much more except that some men had gone with Lew Wetzel the next day to follow the Indian trail, which they found but gave up after a time.

Little Fox knew that these were the white men whose tracks Red Storm had found. He decided not to mention the injury to Red Feather. Why add to the acclaim for this dreaded man? He wondered if Red Storm was still in the village. Maybe the death of Wetzel's father would satisfy his frantic desire for revenge.

"Is Red Storm still here?" Little Fox asked of Leith.

"I think he left yesterday for the Sandusky towns."

"He would have been very happy to hear of the death of a Wetzel."

"I am sure he would," agreed Leith. "Tomorrow I am going with a hunting party to the Stillwater. Why don't you come along?"

"It is too soon for me to go away again," answered Little Fox quickly.

"Yes," said Leith with a chuckle. "Your wife is still new, eh?"

"New enough," said Little Fox, unable to suppress his own smile.

"Good-bye then, my friend," said Leith with some feeling. "I hope we meet again."

June 19, 1786

The four men were going through his father's shed, making notes of some kind, and Lewis Wetzel was annoyed. He did not see the necessity of this exercise, and he felt like ordering them off the place. One of them was his own uncle, Lewis Bonnett, and of the others, he knew James McConnell but was not really acquainted with the other two, Lewis Lindhoff and Martin Collons. They were appraisers, he knew, whose job it was to conduct an inventory of the goods and chattels of his father, customary when someone died. His brother Martin, who stood to inherit these items, was sitting on the steps to the house, watching the activity intently.

"I don't like it, Martin," said Lew finally. "I don't like them scavengers pawing through Pa's things."

"They ain't scavengers, Lew," said Martin. "One of them is our own uncle."

"Well, I still don't like it. 'Course the stuff will belong to you anyway."

"Does that bother you, Lew? Do you want something."

"Not really. It just bothers me, that's all." Lewis walked over to the side of the milkshed where several tools were piled together in a bushel basket. He knelt and sorted through the pile. Moving a long hoe whose handle stood against the wall, he lifted an old tomahawk.

"Well, look at this, Martin. I remember this old 'hawk. Pa used to carry it all the time."

Martin took the instrument in his own hands and examined it for a moment. "Yeah, I remember this one. It has Pa's letters carved in the handle."

"Well, maybe I'd like to take that with me after all," said Lew. "If you don't mind."

"Hell, no, I don't mind," retorted Martin. "I think they've already sorted through this stuff anyway. It's yours."

"Hey, Martin," came a shout from James McConnell. "Come over here a minute." McConnell stood next to Lewis Bonnett, taking note of several cows and calves standing inside the small fenced-in area next to the barn.

"I'll see ya around, Martin," said Lew, stuffing the old tomahawk in his belt as Martin began walking toward the others. He watched as his brother moved away, then went to where his horse was hitched near the house. He called to his mother through the open door. "Bye, Ma, I'm goin' over to see Jake Miller."

Mary Wetzel came out the door as Lewis swung up on the back of the horse. "Lew, ain't you goin' to stay for supper?"

"Can't, Ma," was the reply. "I'll see you soon." He had ridden for several yards before turning to wave. He could see the sad look on his mother's face, but he did not stop. He rode out and moved upstream along the narrow trail that followed the creek bank. "That's pretty bad behavior, Lew," he muttered to himself after a while. "You ought to be ashamed of yourself."

He couldn't seem to help himself; it had been difficult to be civil to anybody, even to his mother. The death of his father was proving hard to accept, and it didn't help to watch his mother grieving either. He couldn't explain why he was irritated with his brothers and sisters, and the latest news that his brother Martin and his family were going to move in again was more than he could take. Martin had been living in a small cabin on land that had been claimed in his name, but now it was thought best for him to bring his family into the larger house with their mother.

"Too damned crowded." Lew's thoughts escaped as he spoke aloud. He was thinking about Martin with his wife, Mary, and three young children, the youngest of whom, George, was barely a year old. His younger sister, Susannah, had married a man named Nathan Goodrich and moved out, but Jacob and Johnny still lived at the homeplace. Lew didn't mind the little ones that much; in fact, he loved playing with them. Still there would be way too much confusion to suit him, and he planned to ask his uncle about living with him for awhile.

Something was irritating him as he rode, and he realized it was the old tomahawk that he had stuck under his belt. It was rubbing against his hip bone, and he smiled as he pulled it out and shoved it into a pouch on his saddle. It pleased him to have this relic that had belonged to his father; and the sight of the letters JW carved into its handle made him think of the tomahawk he had lost years ago to the Indian up near the Stillwater. That was the brave whose ear he had sheared off, and who, according to the trader Leith, had vowed revenge. Where was old one-ear now, Lew wondered, thinking he'd be right glad to find him.

The Miller farm was on the Dutch Fork of Buffalo Creek across the Pennsylvania line and a couple of miles above the trail that led to Washington. It was dusk by the time Wetzel arrived at Miller's, which distressed him a bit, since he was really hoping to make it by suppertime. He hadn't had much to eat that day and had been looking forward to some of the good food that was often to be had here. He hoped that Jake was home, but he couldn't be sure. As he dismounted, he saw Jacob's younger brother, Frederick, emerging from the stable.

"Hello, young Fred," was Lew's cheerful greeting.

"Hello to you too, Lew," was the response, which brought a smile from Lew.

"It rhymes," laughed Wetzel. "Where's your lazy brother?"

"He's in the house. Come on in."

Once inside, they were met by Jacob Miller. Two younger sisters sat at a table trying to knit in the dim light from an oil lamp.

"I heard that remark," said Jake, breaking into laughter. "Who are you to be callin' anybody lazy. You ain't done a lick o' work in your whole worthless life."

"I may do a lick of work right soon, here, if you keep talkin'."

"I ain't too scared. All I gotta do is offer you somethin' to eat."

"That might work," agreed Wetzel.

The two men embraced.

"Too bad you missed supper."

"Sure is. I was countin' on it."

"Well, I reckon there might be somethin' left, even for a scoundrel like you."

Miller soon produced a piece of ham and some fresh bread, which he put on the table. The two girls nodded meekly to Lew and went off into a back room. Wetzel ate the food with relish, thinking it tasted better than anything he could remember.

Miller watched his friend eat with great amusement. "By God, Lew, I've seen hogs eat slower'n you. How long since you had anything to eat?"

"First today," said Lew as he swallowed a piece of the bread. "This is mighty good."

"You spendin' the night with us?" asked Miller.

"If you don't mind," answered Lew. "I'll sleep outside though. It's plenty warm."

"You're right about that. Maybe I'll join you."

Later the two friends lay side by side in the grass, staring at the dark sky above with its glittering stars.

"Right beautiful, ain't it, Lew?" observed Miller.

"Yes," noted Lew quietly. He was always amazed at himself, at how much sheer joy he felt just gazing at the starry sky. "Make's you wonder how they got there, the stars, I mean."

"I reckon God hung 'em there."

"I know, but I still wonder what's really out there, and how far it is out to them stars."

"God, Lew, I never figured you for such deep thoughts."

Wetzel chuckled. "Well, it probably ain't too healthy for me at that."

There was silence for awhile, only the crickets chirping. Then Wetzel brought up a new subject.

"I'm thinkin' of goin' to Kentucky, Jake. Why don't you go with me?"

"Kentucky! Why in hell do you want to go to Kentucky?"

"It's the land of opportunity, so I hear tell."

"Opportunity? What opportunity did you ever look for, Lew, 'cept maybe to kill some damned red bastard. You plannin' to become a farmer?"

Wetzel laughed. "You got me there, I reckon. No, I ain't plannin' to become no farmer. Simon Kenton is there. I want to meet him."

"I've heard the name, I guess," admitted Miller. "Supposed to be a pretty mean man, so I've heard."

"Best on the border accordin' to a feller I talked to over at Wheeling."

"Oh, so you want to see if he's as good as you, eh?"

Wetzel ignored that remark. "Martin thinks he might've met him during Dunmore's War. He went by the name of Butler then. 'Course, Boone's there too."

"Where in Kentucky would you go?" wondered Miller.

"Limestone is the place. Kenton's got a fort near there, so the feller says. This man is buildin' a flatboat and wants me to help him build it and then help him get a farm started once we're there. He says there are folks wantin' to start up a new town up above Limestone. Sounds excitin'."

"This feller is willin' to pay you to help him build a flatboat? Now there's a fool if ever I knowed one."

Wetzel tried to look angry but couldn't keep from breaking into a laugh. "You know me too well, you son of a bitch."

"I reckon I do." Miller changed to a serious tone. "Lew, I can't go with you. I'm runnin' this place, and I've got no time to go chasin' off on one of your wonderful adventures. Wish I could."

"Too bad," was all Lew could say. He had sat up during the conversation, and now he settled down again.

"Take Mitchell with you," Miller suggested. "You and him git along good, don't ya?"

"Naw, he's sparkin' some gal up on Short Creek. He ain't no good for nuthin' these days."

"Well, I might be sparkin' some pretty gal myself for all you know."

"I don't reckon so," laughed Wetzel. "You're no better with the girls than me, and I sure don't see 'em comin' after me too much."

"I reckon that's enough to shut us both up." Miller turned away and settled back. The quiet night took over again.

Neither of them were sleepy, however, and after a few moments, Miller decided to start the talk again, wanting to make sure that his friend wasn't angry with him.

"Surprisin' there ain't no skeeters out tonight."

Even before Miller had finished his sentence, Wetzel was slapping his arm.

"Spoke too soon, Miller. I just killed one of the bastards."

"Yeah, one just bit me too. Did you feel that wind change?" Miller noted the dark sky in the west. "See them clouds? It may get a bit wet here afore long."

In silent agreement, the two men picked up their blankets and went inside.

July 20, 1786

Thomas Nichols was feeling quite proud of himself. He stood near the center of the big flatboat looking past the pen at the back where the animals were kept, watching with satisfaction as Lewis Wetzel put in his time with the big steering oar at the stern. It had been pretty smart, Nichols thought, to have persuaded the big hunter to come along on this trip. Not only was it necessary to have someone strong enough to handle the large oars used in controlling the boat; but someone who could hunt for food and help defend the boat was invaluable. There was no one better than Lewis Wetzel for those duties.

Nichols was proud of the boat too, for he had built it himself. Well maybe not entirely, for he had purchased the flat bottom from a man who had changed his mind about pushing into new territory. He had built up the sides and ends at a height of about three feet. A pen at the rear was built to keep the animals he would need to start his new farm. There were two cows and a calf, three hogs, and two horses. They took up a lot of space and didn't help with the bad smell that lingered on the boat, but he was glad to have them along.

At the front of the boat, he and Wetzel had constructed a three-sided lean-to shed with a blanket covering the opening, which faced the back of the boat. It was not roomy but was enough for his wife and two daughters to have a warm dry spot for sleeping. He turned now to face the front, where a man was entertaining his daughters, aged six and four, with some kind of sleight of hand card tricks. The man's name was James Gridler, and Nichols knew nothing about him. Gridler had approached him in Wheeling, asking to be taken to Kentucky. "I'm a kind of entertainer," had been his answer when questioned about his occupation.

"That makes no sense to me," Nichols had replied. "I ain't heard that they were needin' entertainers in Kentucky."

But Gridler had persisted, pointing out that he could help man the big sweeps used in steering.

"Can you shoot?" had been Wetzel's question, and Gridler assured them that he was a crack shot.

"We can always use somebody who can shoot," Wetzel had pointed out, and Nichols had finally agreed.

"If you try messin' with my wife, I'll kill you. Just remember that," Nichols had warned the man.

His wife, Ann, was quite a looker he figured, and he was wary of men like Gridler, whom he suspected of evil intentions. So far, though, there had been no trouble of that kind. Nichols did suppose you couldn't blame a man for tryin' to better himself, which he guessed was what Gridler wanted. He was acting on the same instinct. After coming out to Wheeling Creek where his brother, Austin, had claims, Nichols had become disillusioned with the land that he was able to find. He became acquainted with Jacob Drennon, who constantly talked about the wonders of Kentucky. He had gone with Drennon to Limestone the previous fall and purchased some land from Simon Kenton near the new village being settled on the high ground above Limestone.

When he returned to Wheeling, he sold his acres to his brother and began planning for this current adventure. The big broadhorn, as flatboats were frequently called, was difficult to navigate in the fast river current, and it was definitely easier with at least three men as a crew. The name broadhorn came from the vast sweeps on the sides that were used to maneuver the boat in and out of the current. When raised out to the sides, the sweeps resembled giant horns. In addition to the sides and the big steering oar at the stern, there was also a short front sweep called a gouger. Ann Nichols was sometimes called upon to handle it.

It seemed to Nichols as if they should be nearing their destination by now. It was nine days since they left Wheeling, and he reckoned they were making thirty miles a day on the average. They stopped at night, always putting in on the Virginia side. Nichols had thought they might be able to travel in the darkness as well, but there were too many islands and obstructions that could cause disaster. Putting in to shore was also dangerous for it was difficult, and the ever-present possibility of Indian attack made stopping a precarious proposition.

On two occasions when they were stopped, Wetzel had managed to find time to hunt, adding a small buck to their foodstuffs each time. Wetzel was particularly sensitive to the Indian peril, noting that the threat could come from either side of the river, although it was most hazardous near the Ohio shore. A common practice of the red men was to put somebody, often a white captive, along the shore to cry for help, hoping to lure the boatsmen in close enough for ambush.

"We don't stop for nobody," Wetzel had explained to Nichols, who was already familiar with the dangers from his earlier trip down the river. Pushing past his daughters, still playing with Gridler, and the cooking station, Nichols ducked through the curtain and into the little sleeping cabin. Ann Nichols sat against the side, working her knitting needles. "Ain't you hot in here?" asked her husband.

"Yes, but it's better than that hot sun beatin' down on me."

"Well, suit yourself. I'm lookin' for Drennon's map."

"It's there under them books," noted Ann, pointing to a Bible resting on top of a worn copy of Paine's *Common Sense*.

Jacob Drennon had produced a rough map, drawn on several pages, of the Ohio River course as he knew it, noting some of the islands and creeks that spilled in from either side.

Nichols was glad to have it, imperfect though it was, and he fished it out from under the books. "Yeah, that's it," he said, giving his wife a loving smile. He patted her on the knee and went back outside.

"Hey, Gridler," he shouted. "Quit playin' and go back and take over for Wetzel. Tell him I want to talk."

Gridler, who held no liking for Nichols, made a face but did as he was asked.

When Wetzel appeared, Nichols held up the map, pointing to a rough drawing of an island with a creek coming in from the Indian side.

"I think that's what Drennon calls Brush Island," said Nichols. "We passed it a few miles back."

The passing of this island had caused some anxiety, for the channel on the Virginia side was too narrow, and the boat had passed quite close to the Ohio shore. However, nothing happened, and they came out again into the broad stream where it made a gentle curve.

"There's a dangerous spot just ahead though. It shows here on the map. Looks to me like there are two islands." Nichols pointed to the map, showing a small island on the left and another, much longer one, just to its right, looking downstream. The three river channels, thus formed, looked quite small.

"What's that word right there?" asked Wetzel, pointing at a word scribbled on the map with arrows pointing from it to each of the three channels.

"The word is *narrow*," answered Nichols.

"That's what I was afraid of."

"We don't know how accurate this map is," noted Nichols. "It may not be as bad as it looks."

"I know one thing," said Lew. "If I was an Injun wantin' to catch me a boat, that's right where I'd do it."

"I don't remember havin' any trouble here when I came through last year. Course we were in a canoe, not a flatboat."

"Well, we better git ready," warned Wetzel, holding his hand above his eyes and peering intently ahead. "I can see them islands up there right now."

"What should we do then?" asked Nichols, ready to defer to Wetzel's judgment in any event that might involve fighting.

"Git them girls inside the cabin, and then I think you oughtter take the stern, and let Gridler and me handle the side sweeps. Make sure you got your gun with you. We'll steer for the channel closest to the Virginia shore."

Nichols hurried his two daughters inside the cabin. "There may be trouble ahead, mother," he said to Ann.

When he came back out, Wetzel stood waiting. "Tom, have you got some extra guns?"

"Yes," was the answer. "There are three of 'em in the cabin."

"Does your wife know how to load a gun?"

"Sure she does."

"Have her load them guns and put 'em out here where Jim and I can get them."

Ann Nichols, frightened by the talk she was hearing had stepped outside. "What is goin' on, Tom?" she asked. "Are we bein' attacked?"

"We don't know, honey," answered Nichols. "There's a place ahead where Lew thinks there could be Injuns hidin'. We want to be ready. You load them three guns and put 'em out here. Then stay in there with the girls. Don't come out no matter what happens."

The islands were clearly visible now, and the three men tried hard to move into the channel on the far left. The boat rebelled against their efforts, however, and seemed headed straight into the small island.

"Lift your sweep, Gridler, damn you," shouted Nichols from the rear. "You're draggin' us into the island."

"We ain't goin' to make the far channel," yelled Wetzel. "Steer for the middle one, the current's strong there anyhow."

Gridler, trying to raise his oar, had slipped, and the big sweep dipped into the water. As it happened, this was a good thing for it caused the front to shift a bit to the right. Nichols was struggling to reverse his actions with the stern oar. Wetzel raised his sweep, and as he did so a shot rang out, then another. The first ball plowed into the side planking just to the left of where Wetzel was standing. The second whizzed by his head and splashed into the water on the other side of the boat.

"Damn," cried Gridler. "Where are those shots coming from?"

"Never mind that," hollered Nichols from the rear. "Pull on that oar and move us to the right. Can you see them devils, Lew?"

"They're on the far shore," answered Lew, who had dropped the oar, raising the sweep end in the air. He grabbed his rifle, which he aimed at some movement he saw along the Ohio shoreline. "Missed him," muttered Lew in disgust, shortly after the roar of his gun had quieted.

The boat was nearly at the entrance of the middle channel, with the left front dangerously close to grounding on the island shore. "Use your push pole, Jim. Shove us away."

Pulling in his oar, Gridler grabbed the pole lying at his feet and ran to the front where he began jabbing at the ground, trying desperately to push the boat into the channel. After a couple of false tries, the pole caught firmly, and the boat corner veered to the right. Suddenly they were clear and into the channel, caught up in the fast-moving current. There was no room for the side sweeps here, and the steering job was left in the hands of Nichols.

"Good job, Jim," said Wetzel. "That was close."

They were protected now from the Indians on shore by the trees and brush on the long island. However, Wetzel, noting the length of the tree line on their right, was concerned that the warriors might cross the narrow stream in front of them and get on the island. They were already passing by the small island on the left.

"The bastards may git on that island and hit us again on the far end," he shouted to his companions.

"Let's git as close to the Virginia shore as we can then," was the cry from Nichols.

Ann Nichols had poked her head out of the lean-to. "What's happening?" she wanted to know.

"We got some Injuns shootin' at us," answered Lew as he handed her his rifle. "Can you load this for me? We'll be all right once we get past this island."

She took the gun and ducked back into the shelter. Wetzel took up his oar again and tried to force the boat away from the island shore. In concert with Nichols, he managed to move them some distance to the left.

"Not too much, Tom," he warned. "We don't want to pile up on the shore. They'd be on us afore we could git off again."

"How many are there, do you think?" asked Gridler.

"Prob'ly four or five, I reckon," said Wetzel. "If 'n they was more, there'd have been more shots."

They were nearly past the tip of the island when the shots came again.

Most were aimed at Nichols, toiling with the steering oar. Nichols dropped to his knees, trying to get below the edge of the siding. Some of the shots were coming from the trees along the shore, but a canoe had appeared with two braves aboard. Wetzel took aim and hit the one in front while Gridler, who appeared beside him, was shooting at the other. Nichols managed to get off a shot as well, and there was silence for a moment.

"Damned red devils, they shot one of the hogs," shouted Nichols.

As if in answer, a second round of shots came from the trees, and all missed except one, which tore into the roof of the shelter. This resulted in a flying splinter which caught Gridler in the right arm as he was crossing to the other side of the boat. Wetzel picked up one of the extra guns and fired again, after which the canoe retreated, and the brief battle was over. Gridler had dropped to the floor, more startled than hurt, although the splinter was large enough to open a deep gouge in his arm, causing it to bleed profusely.

"I think we're safe now," pronounced Wetzel. "Jim, are you bad hurt?"

At the word *safe*, Mrs. Nichols reappeared and knelt beside Gridler, who was sitting up. The two girls came out, and she sent one of them back for a piece of cloth to use in binding the wound. Gridler said nothing but was enjoying the attention he was getting.

"We come outta that pretty good," observed Wetzel, retrieving his rifle, which had been reloaded. He went to the back to relieve Nichols.

"Thanks, Lew," he said gratefully, as Wetzel offered to take the oar. "I'm worn out. You saved us."

"Wasn't me no more than Gridler," Wetzel remarked.

"Your shootin' discouraged the bastards."

"Maybe, but Gridler saved us from goin' aground on that little island."

Wetzel knew that Nichols still thought he'd been wrong to bring Gridler along. "You ought to tell him."

Nichols could not bring himself to agree. Ahead the river made a curve to the left. "We ain't far from Limestone, Lew. I remember that big bend up ahead. There's another one a mile or two after that, and then we'll be real close."

He stopped to check on the dead hog, shooing away the other two, who were nibbling at the bloody and ragged hole left by the stray bullet.

"Hey, Lew, help me pull this pig outta here. Them others'll eat him up if we don't."

The two men hopped over the low fencing and pulled the pig to the edge. It was all they could do to hoist the carcass over and let it fall to the floor against the sidewall. Wetzel went back to his oar, correcting a drift toward the right bank. The remaining miles went by uneventfully.

"There it is," shouted Nichols. "The end of that tree line is the mouth of Limestone Creek. Let's head for that."

They managed to get the boat headed toward the left bank, with Gridler able to help in spite of his injury. The landing came just past the mouth of the creek; and as they pushed the front of the boat up onto the sandy beach, two men came out from a blockhouse built just a short distance above the landing. One of them was quite large, but he had a big smile on his face.

"Welcome pilgrims," was his greeting. Nichols helped his wife and daughters off the front and leaped down himself to shake the hand of the big man.

"Hello, Simon, it's Tom Nichols and family. We finally made it."

"I remember you, Nichols," replied the greeter, who took Ann Nichols by the arm and helped her to the ground. "Welcome to Limestone, Mrs. Nichols."

"This is Simon Kenton, Ann," explained Nichols to his wife. "He's the one who sold us our land."

"Yes, I've heard lots about you," said Ann.

"I'm James Gridler and glad to make your acquaintance." Gridler had jumped down and reached for Kenton's hand.

Kenton took note of the wrapping on his right arm.

"What happened to the arm?" asked Kenton.

"Injuns attacked us up the river a ways." Gridler was actually proud of his wound, although it was hurting some.

"They hit us at the islands up ten miles or so," added Nichols. "Lew managed to shoot one of 'em, I think. Anyway, they came up on the long island as we went past. Other than one hog and Gridler's arm, there was no damage."

"I didn't know they was around here that close," Kenton said. "That's a dangerous spot all right, but I don't recall nobody bein' hit there before."

Wetzel had stowed his oar and made his way to the front of the boat.

"Lew, Lew," cried Nichols. "Come here, come here. I want you to meet Simon Kenton."

To Kenton, he said, "This here is Lew Wetzel, Simon. Maybe you've heard of him."

"Reckon I have," was the reply. "I hear you've killed some Injuns."

"One or two, I suppose," was Lew's modest answer. "I've heard plenty about you." Wetzel had jumped to the ground and grasped Kenton's extended hand.

"This rascal's name is John Waller," said Kenton, pointing to the other man, short and stocky with a heavy beard. "He's got a cabin just down the way and could prob'ly put up you two men for a night or two if you like."

Turning again to Mrs. Nichols, he said, "You and your family can stay in the blockhouse there. There's a tavern attached where you can get some food."

He turned to Nichols. "Boone's here now runnin' that tavern."

"It's gittin' dark, and we're pretty beat," noted Nichols. "What should we do with the boat and my livestock?"

"Tie it up to that tree for the night. You can leave the animals on board, and we'll take care of things in the morning."

Nichols looked at Wetzel with an unspoken question on his lips.

Nodding, Wetzel said, "I'll sleep on the boat and watch out for things, Tom. You go with your family."

"Thanks, Lew," replied Nichols. "We'll bring some supper out to you."

Waller produced a rope that they used to secure the boat to the nearest tree. After Waller left, Wetzel looked up and down the shoreline and at the big hill, which rose up behind the little settlement.

"So this is Kentucky," he said aloud to himself. "Nothin' special 'bout it that I can see."

August 20, 1786

Preacher Wood was droning on, and Lewis Wetzel was standing uncomfortably at the back of old man Taylor's cabin. It wasn't a usual pastime for him to be at a religious service listening to a preacher. He did believe in God and figured that there was probably a heaven and hell, but he had never been much for church goin'. Although he'd never attended one, he felt somehow that if he did belong to some church it ought to be Lutheran. Of course, there were no Lutheran churches on the frontier; at least none he knew about. And Preacher Wood was no Lutheran, he was pretty sure of that.

Kenton had insisted that they come to this meeting at Taylor's cabin. It was a Sunday night, and it was common for the settlers to go to hear some preaching, but there was something else going on that had attracted many of the men in the settlements. Taylor was crippled with rheumatism, and for that reason, the preaching was often held at his house.

Wetzel had been spending many of his nights at Kenton's Station, a U-shaped collection of long log cabins shaped something like soldiers' barracks. The open end was picketed, but there was no gate to the interior. The cabin doors were made of planks three inches thick, which were barred at night with hand spikes; and on each corner, a second story had been constructed with edges jutting out to form a bastion. There were twenty separate living spaces, and Wetzel was using one of them.

The station was built on the west side of Lawrence Creek, not far from the spring that Kenton had named after Jacob Drennon. There were other cabins located nearby, and Taylor's was among them. It was nestled against the canebrake that stretched for miles to the south.

Wetzel watched Kenton who was sitting near a lovely young woman named Martha Dowden. She had caught Wetzel's eye as well, and he felt a bit of jealousy wash over him as he watched Kenton reach down and take Martha's hand. Simon Kenton had a reputation as a man who loved and was admired by the ladies. Martha was related to Kenton in some way by marriage through Kenton's brother, William. Simon had tried to explain it all one day, wanting to make sure that Lewis understood that there was nothing incestuous about his relationship with the girl. There were rumors about another girl involved with Kenton, but Lew doubted they were true.

It sounded to Wetzel as if the preacher was winding down, but he couldn't be sure. He'd thought that a time or two before, but then he wasn't really listening. William Wood had arrived at Limestone Landing on New Year's eve in 1784 along with the family and purchased land from Kenton in the cane lands across the ridge. He was heavily involved in the formation of a new town people were already calling Washington. The town was literally being carved out of the canebrake, with a path that would become the main street through the center. Wetzel helped Thomas Nichols clear out a space and build a rough lean-to that would serve as shelter while a sturdier cabin was built. There were more than a dozen such places established by now. Nichols had dismantled the flatboat and used the lumber to build the new house. Wetzel made several trips guiding a horse and hauling the lumber up the steep and winding trail from the Limestone Landing.

The night was warm and the moon was bright. Wetzel had noticed how it was showing through a large chink in the western wall of the cabin, and now had disappeared. He continued to stare at the spot for a moment, then saw the light appear again. This was curious.

The sermon ended, and Preacher Wood called for prayers. One of the men at the front began to pray as the others bowed their heads. All except Lewis Wetzel, who kept his eyes glued to the interesting chink in the wall. In a few minutes, he saw the light disappear. Then it flickered on and off again. Wetzel was several feet from the back door, and he began to inch his way toward it, moving faster as he saw the light appear once more. "Let me by," he whispered to a bearded man who had stepped up to block his way.

"Don't be rude," the man said. "They're prayin'."

Lew recognized the man as one of Kenton's Boys, one who he had been with on a hunt. "It'll get ruder if ya don't let me by, Jack," muttered Lew in a tone louder and more threatening than he intended. He managed to slip past and out the door before Jack could take further offense.

Once outside, Wetzel, hurried around the corner and found the spot where he thought the moonlight had been showing. It was difficult to see much, although he thought he could see where the grass and weeds had been mashed down a bit, as if someone had kneeled there. He stood up and listened, thinking he could hear a faint rustling amongst the cane off to his left. He could see nothing, however, and rejected a fleeting thought of pursuit. If an unfriendly someone was there, the pursuer might quickly become the pursued. He returned to the door of the cabin and went in.

The praying had ended, and Simon Kenton was standing at the front, addressing the crowd.

"Friends," Kenton was saying, "Henry Lee is here to talk to you about something, so pay close attention to what he's got to say. It's mighty important and has my complete support."

Simon Kenton was the most revered man in the area, the acknowledged leader and protector of the settlements. What he said was likely to be heeded. Henry Lee was also well-respected, and he took the floor with a flourish and a big smile.

"Brothers"—he began, and then with a nod and a grin—"and sisters too."

There were only a few ladies there, including Martha Dowden, whom Kenton had rejoined, but Lee knew the influence they could have. Wetzel found himself watching young Martha.

"You know we've been talkin about a new town," continued Lee, "and how we want to name it after our great general from the recent war, the Honorable George Washington. It is time we do something about it."

A loud cheer erupted from the audience. Lee acknowledged it by raising both hands high and shouting a loud, "Hurrah!"

"I'm very glad to hear, brothers and sisters," he went on, "that you agree with me. Now we've drawn up a petition to send to the Virginia legislature asking them to charter the town officially. We think it will be the first new town in America named after General Washington."

Another loud cheer went up, but Lewis wondered if they knew about Catfish Camp up in Pennsylvania that was now being called Washington. He guessed that it didn't matter.

"Reverend Wood there, and Arthur Fox have some papers for you to sign," Lee was saying, pointing to Wood who sat at a small table with papers and a quill pen in front of him. Next to him was Fox, a surveyor and a partner to Wood in the land purchase. "Line up there, and he'll write your name so you can sign or make your mark. Don't you leave now, you men, without signin' that paper. While you're at it, there's another one asking for a new county to be formed called Mason County. Sign 'em both."

A line was soon formed by eager signers, with Kenton and Lee circulating among the others, determined that no one would slip out before signing the petitions.

"Here, Lew," said Kenton when he found Wetzel standing at the back and making no effort to join the line. "We need you to sign too."

Wetzel had become good friends with Kenton and was a member of the unofficial militia that Kenton had recruited. Its purpose was to fight and chase the Indian raiders who continued to come into Kentucky to steal horses and kill or capture white settlers when they could. These men were called Kenton's Boys, and they were popular with people at Limestone, Kenton's Station, and the neighboring region. The Indian raids had been numerous in recent months, so much so that there was a shortage of horses. Some people estimated that as many as five hundred horses had been stolen since the first of the year. Kenton's Boys had managed to steal some of them back.

"Come here a minute, Simon," said Wetzel. "I noticed somethin' kind of funny." Lew went on to explain what he had seen earlier and his suspicions about what might have happened.

"We'll check it out in the mornin'," replied Kenton after listening with interest. "Right now I want to get these men's names on that petition, and that includes yours."

Wetzel joined the line, and when his time came, Reverend Wood asked him how to spell his name.

"I don't rightly know," admitted Lew. "Never did learn to write it."

"Well I've written it down here as best I could. Put your mark next to it."

Lewis took up the quill and made a large X right next to the name Lewis Whitsel.

"Thanks, Lew," said Wood. "Next man!"

Fire Heart stood with his friend Little Fox in a small clearing in the cane lands. He was watching for the return of their leader, Captain Black Snake, and the captive they had taken just a short time ago. He could see the bright moon clearly above, but he was nervous. They weren't far from the fort that Black Snake told them was called Kenton's Station by the whites. Butler lived there, according to Captain Snake, and Butler was a famous white man well-known to the Shawnees. He had been their prisoner once, but Simon Girty interceded on his behalf. The Indians never knew him by his real name. Anyway, if Butler was anywhere close, Fire Heart figured there was great danger.

It had been a long time since Fire Heart had been on a raid to the Kentucky lands. However, he loved the horse-stealing raids; his memory often retreating to the one several years ago when his friend Martin had betrayed him. Even now, that thought brought anger, and when this current raid was being organized, he determined to be a part of it. He sent a runner to Buckongehelas's village to invite his Chippewa friend Little Fox to join them.

It was a bit of a surprise when Little Fox had appeared. Captain Black Snake was a Shawnee war chief, but he was a strange man in Fire Heart's view. He had weird ideas and an unusual sense of humor. Their little raiding party had come upon a white man in the woods not far behind Kenton's Station who was obviously looking for some stray cattle.

"Come out of there, you damned fools. I can hear you," was the shout from John Kinsaulla, a Dutch farmer with a cabin not far away. "I know you're in there, I kin hear you."

What he heard was not his cows, but the Chippewa warrior, Little Fox, who stepped from behind a tree and grabbed the rifle from the startled settler's left hand. As he raised his tomahawk to strike a fatal blow, his arm was halted in midair by the strong grip of Captain Snake.

"Stop," commanded Black Snake. "I want to question him."

"What your name?" Black Snake asked in what little English he knew.

"John," answered Kinsaulla. "As if it makes any difference, you damned son of a bitch."

"Behave!" said Black Snake sternly in the Shawnee tongue. He didn't know exactly what the man had said, although he recognized the curse words. "Come," he said harshly in English.

Grasping Kinsaulla by the arm, the chief led them along the edge of the woods and into a small trail in the canebrake that came out close to the Taylor cabin. They could see a number of horses, indicating that there were many people in the cabin. Assuming that their little party, consisting of himself, Little Fox, Captain Snake, and three others, would now return the way they had come, Fire Heart was dismayed when Black Snake pulled the captive with him and approached the cabin. It was then that Fire Heart led the others into the cane.

Fearlessly, Captain Snake dragged John across the open field to the side of the cabin. He found a large crack in the wall and crouched in front of it, peering in to see the white people with heads bowed and someone talking. After a moment, he pulled Kinsaulla over and indicated that he was to look through the hole. Doing as he was told, John could see that the congregation was praying, probably wondering why he wasn't there too, he supposed. He scrambled back to his feet as the chief jerked on his arm. He wondered if he should sound an alarm, but he realized he would be dead before the sound stopped. He allowed himself to be led back into the cane and out of sight of the cabin.

"They praying?" asked Captain Snake in his limited English.

"Yes," answered John more politely this time. "They are praying to God."

"Uh," grunted Black Snake. "Great Spirit here. We not steal or kill."

When they joined the others, Captain Snake explained what had happened.

"The white people were praying. I think that the Great Spirit would not want us to harm them or steal their horses. We will go to another place."

Little Fox could not believe his ears. "What kind of war chief is this?" he asked Fire Heart. "Is he afraid to fight? Does he think there are too many?"

"Captain Snake is not afraid. He is very brave. He is also very strange."

"We could at least have made off with their horses," insisted Little Fox.

"If I know Black Snake, we will find other horses."

On this point, Fire Heart was right. They found the small settlement at Helm's Station only a few miles away, and after stealing a string of seven horses, they made their way across the Ohio and returned to the villages on the Mad River.

September 24, 1786

It was quite dark, and Lewis Wetzel, riding closely behind Simon Kenton, tried his best to keep the big man in sight. They were on the narrow trail through the cane going south from Kenton's Station, the trail that was already being referred to as the Lexington trace.

Henry Lee had a blockhouse a few miles south of the station, and this was their destination. A runner had come to Kenton's with the news that the two sons of Moses Phillips, who had been sent to the cornfield to gather corn, had not come home to supper. One was ten and the other six, and it was not their habit to be late for a meal. A short search had come up with nothing, and fearing a tragedy and for their own safety, Phillips sent for help.

Kenton and Wetzel were the responders. There had been several raids by the Indians in the last month. The first was the capture of John Kinsaulla back in August. Wetzel and Kenton had confirmed that someone had been outside Taylor's cabin that night of the petition signing, and Mrs. Kinsaulla had reported that John was missing the next morning. "I'd give up my little red heifer to get my old man back," had been her plea.

Kenton's Boys found the trail but had not tried to pursue across the river. Next, George Clark, a long-time friend of Kenton's, lost his fourteen-year-old son and one of his slaves to a raiding party. Three slaves were taken from Lee's station on another occasion. Now there may have been another strike at Lee's.

Ahead, Wetzel could see the dim twinkling of a lantern, indicating the clearing that was Henry Lee's place. The two hunters pulled in and slid from their mounts.

"Where's Henry?" Kenton asked of the Negro slave who came to take the horses.

"Not here," was the answer.

"He's gone up to Washington," explained Moses Phillips, who had come from the blockhouse.

Phillips had a small cabin of his own and a few acres that adjoined Lee's property. He and his wife had taken refuge in Lee's blockhouse.

"What's happened then," asked Kenton of Phillips, who was clearly in distress.

"The boys didn't come home," Phillips managed to say, fighting to hold back tears. "We went out to look but were afraid to go too far. If it's Injuns, we're afraid they're still in there."

"What do ya think, Lew?" Kenton was a bit disgusted with Phillips.

"I reckon they're long gone, prob'ly took the boys with 'em."

"That's what I think too," noted Kenton. "Shall we look tonight or wait until morning?"

"Mighty dark," observed Wetzel. "Nothin' we can do tonight anyway."

"Agreed. We'll start first thing in the morning." Turning now to Phillips and with a softened tone, Kenton said, "Come on Moses, you best get in and comfort your wife."

Daybreak found Kenton and Wetzel in the cornfield, and it wasn't long until Wetzel gave a shout. "I found 'em. They ain't captured."

"Alive?" Kenton asked, although he was afraid he already knew the answer. He made his way through the stalks to where Wetzel was standing, looking down.

The bodies of the two boys, scalped and mutilated, lay sprawled between the rows.

"Son of a bitch!" muttered Kenton and repeated. "Son of a bitch!"

"There's a bloody trail," said Wetzel, pointing down the row to the west. "Easy to follow."

"I'll send for some of the Boys to help us," was Kenton's reply.

"Take too long," said Wetzel. "They ain't but three or four of the bastards. You and me are plenty, and we can move much faster."

"Of course, you're right. But I need to tell Phillips. You find where their trail goes at the edge of the corn. I'll join you there."

Having finished his unwelcome task, Kenton found Wetzel in the woods, just west of the corn. He brought along their horses. "What have you found, Lew?"

"They're headed straight for the river."

"No surprise."

There was no more talk between the two as they led their horses through the entangled growth and down a winding trail from the ridge to a spot on the river's edge, several miles west of Limestone. The Indians were on foot and had returned to a place where they had evidently stashed a canoe to use for recrossing the river.

"I don't think there's much use in us going on," said Kenton.

Wetzel was thinking of his unsuccessful attempt to avenge his father's death a few months earlier. He couldn't bear to give up this chase so easily.

"Damn it all," exclaimed Wetzel. "I ain't givin' up that easy. Them bastards deserve killin'."

"Can't say I disagree," noted Kenton. "You think we can find their trail on the other side?"

"I aim to try!" was Wetzel's reply. With that, he mounted his horse and plunged into the stream. Kenton shook his head but followed suit. They came ashore on the Ohio side a mile or so downstream.

"They may have taken that canoe downstream a long way, Lew." Simon dismounted and was searching along the bank for any sign.

"I reckon they did," agreed Lew. "But let's mosey on down along the bank here, see if we find anythin'."

Kenton nodded his agreement and remounted. They took their time until they came to the mouth of Eagle Creek.

"I reco'nize this place," announced Kenton. "Just above, here's where the damned Shawnees grabbed me back in '78."

"Where'd they take you?" asked Wetzel.

"Well, first to the old Chillicothe town. But I was taken to several towns. Had to run the gauntlet every time."

"My brother Martin was there about that time, I think."

"Well, I never saw him. Never saw no white man 'cept Simon Girty later on. He saved my skin."

Wetzel said no more. He wasn't prepared to think kindly about anybody named Girty. He rode out into the shallow waters of the creek and began moving upstream. Kenton understood that the original chase was over, but Wetzel was thinking they might find some other party of red men farther up. Seemed all right to him, and he fell in behind. They moved a short distance and then through a gap in the hills that flanked the stream. A discernible trail was evident, one obviously used regularly by the Indians.

They traveled westerly for a couple of miles before the trail swung to the north. When it turned again to the northwest, Kenton spoke up. "By God, I remember this trail. This is the way they took me up to Chillicothe. Hell, we may still be following them child killers. They're on the way home."

"Could be," said Wetzel. "Though there's lots of tracks along here."

The two men spent most of the time leading the horses and searching the trail closely for fresh tracks. Occasionally, Wetzel would drop the reins and walk off into the woods for a few feet. They came to a small run, just a tiny rivulet winding its way down a low hill, and it was there that Wetzel found something that interested him.

"Come here, Simon. Tell me what you think of this."

After examining the ground in the area at which Wetzel was pointing, Kenton stood, staring off to the southwest in the direction the little run was flowing. "Moccasin tracks in the soft mud," noted Kenton. "A single warrior headed off by himself."

"And in a direction different from the rest."

"Reckon we ought to follow. It's gittin' late though," observed Kenton, pointing to the west where the sun was disappearing below the tree line.

"It is, but them tracks are fresh. Mebbe we can find the bastard's night camp." Wetzel was suddenly energized. They eased their way along the edge of the run, noting a high ridge rising to their left. Wetzel stopped again and held up his right hand. "Do you smell that?"

"I smell smoke for sure," answered Kenton, smiling. "Mebbe we kin drop in fer supper."

The run cut through a low hill in front of them, and Wetzel left his horse standing while he dropped to all fours and crawled carefully up the hill to where he could see beyond it. The grass was tall, and he extended himself in a prone position, holding the grass aside to get a better view. Kenton sprawled out beside him. They could see the campsite and several figures tending the small fire. It was nestled into the Y-shaped region bounded by two tiny steams that collided to form a larger one flowing to the south. There were scattered bushes and a few trees bordering the streams, but the wide end of the Y was open, covered only by the dense grass. The last streams of daylight framed the little camp, a picturesque scene.

"They look mighty relaxed," observed Kenton. "They might invite us in."

"We'll wait here 'til they're sleepin', then we'll hit 'em," said Lew in a matter-of-fact tone. He was in no mood just now for his usual lighthearted banter.

"There's too many of 'em for that, Lew. There's at least ten of 'em down there."

"We can kill three or four afore they know what hit 'em."

"Yeah, and that leaves six or seven more. We might be able to run off their horses, they got 'em stashed up on that far creek. Maybe even steal a couple and get away. Not wise to attack the camp directly though."

The two men waited patiently for the darkness to descend and the Indians to settle in for the night. It took over two hours; but patience was an important virtue for any hunter, and these two men were among the best. Wetzel had even slept for a few minutes. Now he again took a long look at the camp, which was completely quiet. The fire had dimmed to a soft glow.

"I think it's time," he whispered to Kenton. "They're all asleep."

"Any guards still awake?"

"Just one that I can see," replied Wetzel. "He's sitting by that big maple just outside the circle and closest to us."

"So how do you want to do this?" Kenton was normally in charge in a situation like this, but he found himself treating the younger man as an equal.

"One of us needs to work around to the far creek and get in among their horses. The other's got to kill that guard."

"You think you can get in there without him hearin' you?" asked Kenton. "If you don't we're dead men."

"I can, and we ain't about to be dead."

"Give me some time to get around there." Kenton started to move away, and then, as an afterthought. "Only the guard, Lew, not any of the others."

"Well, not unless it's needed." He pointed to where their two horses were tied to some small saplings just down the slope. "We meet back here."

Kenton waved and moved off. He took a wide circuit well away from the Indian camp until he reached the little run that formed the far arm of the Y. He worked his way slowly down to the place where the Indian ponies were hobbled. He watched to see if he could tell when Wetzel made his move. After a short wait, Kenton decided to remove the hobbles; and when he was among the horses, he realized that there were only five of them, and they had been stolen, no doubt, from somewhere in Kentucky.

He decided to take two of them with him and scatter the others. It would be best to wait until Wetzel had silenced the guard, but he might as well be mounted. He didn't have a clear view of the spot where Wetzel would attack, but he was sure that he would be aware when it happened. As he boosted himself up on the horse's back, a shot rang out, and he heard the whizzing of the ball beside his head. *My God, there's another guard we didn't see*, he thought as he dug his heels into the horse's flank, spurring him forward while hanging on to the rope tied to the second horse.

The others scattered at the sound of the shot. *I hope Lew can get out of there.* He rode hard toward the low ridge that ran for some distance back around to where he and Lew had left their mounts. A second shot rang out, the ball falling errantly behind where Kenton was riding.

Wetzel realized that he was in a tight spot. He had made his way to within ten feet of where the Indian sentry waited by the tree and was ready to pounce. He laid his rifle in the grass and reached for his tomahawk. It was then that the first shot was taken, and the Indian picked up his gun and began running in the direction of the shot. To follow him would likely result in disaster, thought Lew, and his next idea was to get his rifle and shoot the brave. That would reveal his own position, however, and at this point there was no reason that the Indians would know that.

He turned, picked up his rifle, and ran back in the direction he had come, running as low as he could. He figured it was at least two hundred yards before he could reach some measure of safety. As he ran, he could hear more shots as the sleeping Indians responded to the commotion. Fortunately, they were shooting toward the area where their stolen horses had been tied. He would be nearly invisible running in the dark through the tall grass, and he made it to the little ridge without being seen. Once on the other side, he took a prone position where he could see back to the Indian camp.

The Indians boiled out of the camp and fired their guns. Now they were reloading while the original sentries reached the horse stand, only to find the horses scattered. Even in the darkness, they saw the fleeing Kenton but were not sure whether to follow. Within the camp, the fire had nearly gone out, but Wetzel could see its dim glow and saw the warrior approach it, kicking dirt on the fire to extinguish it.

Raising his rifle, Wetzel figured he could hit that brief target, but then thought better of it. So far, the Indians had no knowledge of his presence. He would wait here as long as he could, hoping Kenton survived and would return to where he and Lew had secured their own horses. It was only a few minutes until Wetzel heard the sound of riders off to his right. He retreated behind a small bush and raised his gun in the direction of the sound.

"Don't shoot me, Lew," was the muffled shout from Simon Kenton. "I'm here with two horses."

Wetzel emerged from his hiding place and took hold of the rope tied to the second horse. Kenton dismounted.

"My God, Lew, I'm glad to see you. I thought the devils had prob'ly kilt you."

"It ain't happened yet, but I reckon we best git outta here real quick."

"Let's git our horses," said Kenton, "and we'll take these two back with us. There was only five of 'em to start with, stolen from somewhere in Kentucky, no doubt."

They rode back along the rough trail next to the tiny stream until coming to the main trail traveled the day before. It was more open, and they were able to move at a brisk rate, leading the stolen horses behind them. After a hard half hour, Kenton called a halt. "It's hard going in the dark. Let's rest here until daybreak. I doubt the bastards will come after us anyway."

"I think you're right about that, Simon," agreed Wetzel. "They couldn't know how many of us there was, and it is too dark for tracking."

At dawn, Kenton and Wetzel resumed their trek toward the Ohio River. The trip was uneventful; and by noon, they arrived along the river across from Limestone.

"I was surprised to find Daniel Boone runnin' a tavern in Limestone," Wetzel was saying.

"Boone has had some hard times. The damned land robbers took his place at New Station, and when he came to Limestone, there was a need for somebody to run the tavern."

"I heard some fellers say some bad things about Boone."

"Well, some Kentuckians don't like him much. They think he was a traitor when he surrendered the salt boilers at Blue Licks back in '78." When Wetzel said nothing, Kenton continued. "Fact is, Dan'l saved a lot of lives, even though the men were taken prisoner along with Dan'l hisself. He gets no credit for what he did."

"The river's a bit high," observed Lew. "Hope these nags'll be willin' to swim it."

"Do you see that?" asked Kenton, pointing across and to the west of the village of Limestone. "There's men camped there with lots of horses. Somethin' must be happenin'."

"Only one way to find out," said Lew, who spurred his horse into the river, with Kenton following close behind.

Forts and Indian Towns in Ohio

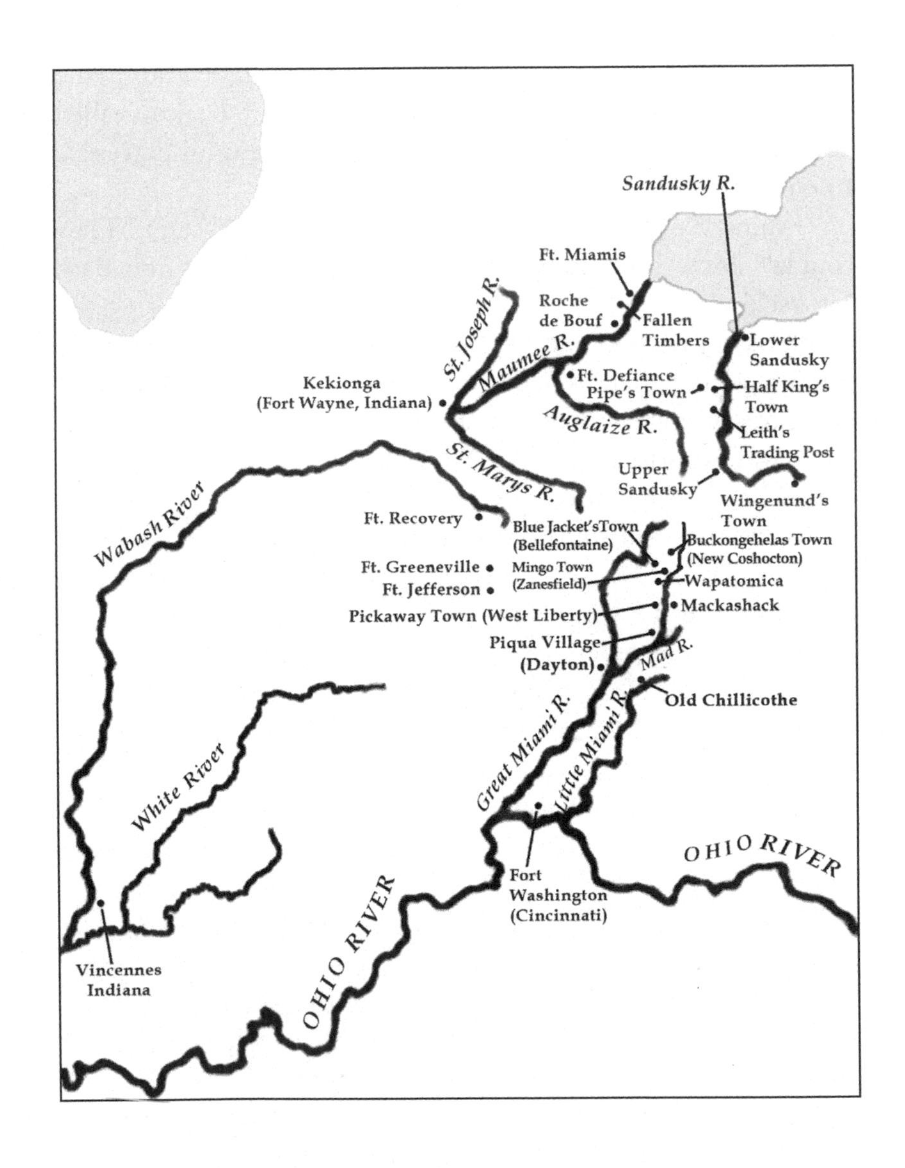

13

LOGAN

September 28, 1786

THE WESTERLY BREEZE provided its own announcement of the presence of the militia camp outside Limestone. More than seven hundred men with their own mounts had been there for a few days, and others were arriving daily. A herd of fifty cattle had been brought along to provide fresh meat for the troops. The smell arising from so many men, horses, and cattle, along with poorly designed latrines, had created plenty of grousing from the regular inhabitants of the small river town.

It was understood that General Benjamin Logan was assembling these Kentucky men here under orders from George Rogers Clark, and so the annoyance had to be endured. Indeed, the women in the nearby settlements were working hard to provide parched corn and johnnycake to be added to the stores of provisions.

Lew Wetzel, who was usually unaffected by the natural sights and smells associated with men and animals, found himself irritated by the presence of these soldiers and had deliberately stayed away from the camps. The odorous breeze seemed especially disagreeable this evening, and he ducked inside the tavern to avoid it.

"Hi, Lew, come and join us," was the command that greeted him as he stepped inside; and though it was hard to see in the dim light of the room, he easily recognized that it was Simon

Kenton who called to him. As he moved closer, he could see that Kenton was sitting at a table with two other men. One of them was Daniel Boone, to whom Wetzel gave a nod. The other man Wetzel had not met, but he knew who it was.

"Evenin' Simon, Daniel."

Wetzel bowed his head slightly toward the dignified dark-haired man sitting between the two frontiersmen. "Good evening to you, Sir, Colonel Logan," he added.

"Ben, this is Lew Wetzel," broke in Kenton. "And it's General Logan now, Lew." Turning back to Logan, Kenton explained, "Lew ain't too informed on army things, Ben. You'll have to forgive him."

Logan stood and extended his hand to Wetzel. He was tall and broad shouldered, and his eyes, which were keen and penetrating, held Lew's attention. Logan had marched with Bouquet against the Indians in 1764 and had been an officer in Dunmore's War. He was one of the prominent men of Kentucky and had served during the Revolutionary War and since as an active and successful commander under Clark.

"I am pleased to meet you, Lew. Simon has been telling me all about you," Logan said with a wide smile. As he sat back down, Logan indicated to Wetzel that he should sit with them. Boone shifted his chair over to make room for the one that Wetzel pulled up to the table.

Although always pleased by compliments, Wetzel was also uneasy about them. He felt it necessary to respond. "I ain't too sure what Simon might be sayin' about me."

"Oh, it was all good, that's for sure," replied Logan immediately. "He claims he's never seen a better tracker, and that's just what I'm lookin' for." Logan turned back to Boone. "Daniel, you know I was with Clark earlier at the falls of the Ohio where he is planning an attack up the Wabash. He is determined to punish the Shawnees. We had information that they had many warriors on the way to fight with the Wabash Indians."

"Yeah, we knew about Clark headin' toward Vincennes. How many men does he have?"

"He had planned on about 2,500, but there was a great reluctance to join up. There have been some desertions, but I think he still has about 1,200."

"What's happenin' with Clark?" asked Kenton. "We heard he'd been drinkin' pretty bad."

"Vicious rumors," exclaimed Logan with feeling. Although Logan and the people of Lincoln County had sometimes had their disagreements with Clark, he could not countenance outright lies. "There just wasn't much enthusiasm to fight against the Miamis and that bunch as there would be against the Shawnees."

"There were lots of deserters?" Boone wanted to know.

"Some, but most just refused to go in the first place. But George and I had already decided that a strike at the Shawnee towns would be a good idea. That's why he sent me back. There's been too damned many raids on our settlements here, and most of them come from them towns on the Mad River."

When nothing was said by the other men, Logan continued. "We decided against any punishment for the men who left us. I've recruited some of them to go with us. Plus other men were much more interested in going to the Shawnee towns and volunteered to go this time."

"I ain't too happy to have a bunch of quitters," noted Kenton.

"They're anxious to go on this one, Simon, and there ain't that many. I don't expect any trouble."

"What is your plan, Ben?" asked Boone, tired of the conversation about the Clark expedition.

"We've got close to nine hundred men by now, I think," began Logan. "All but eighty or so have horses. I think we can begin crossing the river by tomorrow."

"Where are we going exactly? I heard you say something about the Mad River."

"That's where the towns are. Simon, you, and Lew were out that way just a couple of days ago, weren't you?"

"Not up that far," answered Simon. "But I know the towns. I ran the gauntlet in most of them."

"What about you, Lew," Logan wondered. "Have you been to any of those towns?"

"Never have," replied Lew, who offered no more information.

"Well it doesn't matter. I have a rough map, and we'll send out scouts, one of whom will be you, Lew."

Wetzel looked quite uncomfortable, wanting to say something but unsure of what it should be. "I didn't know I was goin'," he said finally.

Logan, who had turned to say something to Boone, was clearly surprised at what he had just heard. "What? I thought Simon said you were planning to go with us."

Kenton spoke up immediately, "I guess I just made the assumption, Lew. Why wouldn't you go? The rest of my boys are goin'."

Wetzel looked down at the floor, and a tiny grin appeared on his face. "The truth is the last time I went along on one of these army raids, I swore I'd never do it again."

"That ain't no good reason," exclaimed Kenton. "Why did you swear that?"

"I ain't much good as an army man," replied Wetzel. "I'm much better by myself or with one or two others."

"That's how it would be this time, Lew," said Logan. "You'll be a scout, out by yourself or with one of Simon's men."

Wetzel continued to stare at the floor and said nothing.

Becoming impatient, Logan said in an angrier tone, "Well, the pay is fifteen dollars. You can take it or leave it."

Wetzel looked up at Kenton, who spread his arms and eyed Lew with a look of bewilderment. The thought that Kenton would be disappointed in him, as well as the monetary offer, which he had not previously considered, brought Wetzel to a decision. "I reckon I'll go along then," he said.

"Good!" was Logan's response. "Daniel, I expect you and Simon to lead sections of the troops. Come with me, and we'll go out to the camp. We need to be ready to move out tomorrow." The three men stood up, but Wetzel remained seated at the table. "Wetzel, you report to Simon in the morning. You're responsible to him. He'll tell you what we want you to do."

Logan went out the door with Kenton behind him while Boone walked over and said something quietly to the man behind the bar. Wetzel had met him earlier. His name was Ben, and he was related to Boone in some way, perhaps a cousin. Boone turned and went out the door, nodding to Wetzel, who watched him go. He continued to sit, running his hand through his heavy locks, then called to the tavern keeper. "I'll have a whiskey, Ben," he said quietly.

October 5, 1786

It was shortly after dark at the small Maykujay Shawnee village called Machachack, which straddled the stream with the same name a mile east of its junction with the Mad River. The village consisted of two distinct settlements, one on each side of a branch of the creek that flowed from the north before a right turn took it toward the Mad.

The west side part of the town consisted of more than twenty wigwams while the one to the east, sometimes referred to as Moluntha's Town, was a bit smaller. It was here that the old chief, Moluntha, had his residence. Moluntha was the chief of the Maykujay sept of the Shawnees and even regarded as a titular chief of the entire Shawnee tribe. He lived here with his three wives, one of whom was Nonhelema, the famed Grenadier Squaw, the sister of Cornstalk.

The day had been warm, but late in the afternoon, a shift in wind direction brought a change, and a sudden chill had settled over the village. Moluntha sat by a small fire that had been built just outside his lodge. He watched with pleasure as his youngest wife, Bright Star, played with his young son near the door. He was proud that he could produce such a lively youngster at his age, and especially with such a beautiful young woman.

He shifted his gaze to Nonhelema, who stood at the other side of the entrance. She had become his wife in more recent years, and he found her fascinating. She was very tall, much taller than he, and she had a commanding presence that had come from many years of prominence and association with leaders among both the Indians and the whites. Moluntha smiled at her, and she nodded to him. She had spent much time among the whites he knew and often took their side in the conversations among the chiefs.

Many of his colleagues were offended that she was sometimes allowed to speak in their councils. She had become a Christian convert many years earlier and given the name Catherine after her baptism. Moluntha knew something about this but did not really understand it nor did he make an issue of it. He himself had become friendly toward the white men in recent times, although he was troubled about it. Moluntha had gone to Fort Finney and participated in the treaty negotiations there in January of the present year. This he had done in spite of the pleadings of Simon Girty and other Tories. He was accompanied by two of his fellow chiefs, Aweekony and Musquaconacah, all three of whom had signed the document. Moluntha was determined to keep the peace and had continued his efforts at cooperation with the Americans, even sending warnings to them about hostile raiding parties.

Later, however, under the influence of the British agent Matthew Elliott, who lived in the Mackachack village, he had sent a message to Detroit assuring the British of his allegiance to them and asking for assistance. He smiled to himself now as he thought on these things. It was not good, he believed, to break all his ties, and he had sent another friendly message to the Americans at Fort Finney, explaining how difficult it was to keep the young warriors in check, asking the Americans to have patience with him and the people of his village.

His fellow chief Shade, who lived in the section of Machachack on the west side of the creek, was a bit more militant and sometimes encouraged the young braves in their raids on the white settlements. The old chief continued to watch his young wife, the warmth of the fire making him sleepy. He nodded off for a few moments and awakened to find Bright Star sitting next to him, the child on her lap. It would be good to spend the night with her, thought Moluntha, and he reached out to touch her on the knee.

Suddenly there was a loud commotion in the village across the river, shouts from several of the men rising clearly above the din. Moluntha could not understand the words, but the excitement was plain. His lodge was situated on a high point of land a short distance from the bank of the creek, and the chief stood quickly, trying to make out in the dim light what was happening. It was too far for him to see what it was. Several minutes had passed when a young Indian boy came from behind the lodge and stood next to Nonhelema.

"Ah, High Horn," exclaimed Moluntha. "Come here and help an old man."

The boy, who was a little more than twelve years old, quickly moved toward the chief. His father and mother had been dead for two years, and he had been adopted by Moluntha and the Grenadier Squaw. He was close to them both and very eager to please them. His name, in the Indian tongue, was Spemica Lawba.

"Go," shouted Moluntha, pointing in the direction of the noise. "See what is happening in the camp and bring me the news."

High Horn, overjoyed to be given such an assignment, bounded down the trail past the springs at the bottom, and out toward the creek. It was dark, but he knew the ground very well. Before he reached the stream, he stopped for he could hear the sounds of approaching horses splashing through the water. In the darkness, he could not tell who was coming, and he felt a quick stab of fear. He was relieved when they came close, and he could see that one of the riders was Shade. The other was a white man.

"Where is the chief?" asked Shade, speaking quickly and with impatience.

"At his lodge on the hill," answered High Horn.

The two horses plunged ahead, with the boy following as fast as he could. He arrived just after the two men had dismounted in front of Moluntha's lodge, and he was able to hear the beginning of the conversation.

"Hello, Shade, my brother," Moluntha was saying. "And who is this?"

"I am glad to see you, my chief. This man brings troubling news."

"Come, sit down, and tell me this news."

Shade was impatient with Moluntha's calm manner, but his respect for the old chief restrained him. He waited until the three men were seated by the fire before speaking again.

"This man is Jean Celon, a French trader. He has been in Kentucky."

"We welcome you," said Moluntha with a nod and a smile. "You have news for us?"

Shade spoke for the Frenchman. "He says many soldiers are coming to attack us under the man named Logan."

"That cannot be," Moluntha said quietly. "We are at peace with the Long Knives. I am their friend."

"It is true, I am afraid," proclaimed Celon, who was quite competent in the Shawnee language. "I was with them until yesterday morning."

"Were you their prisoner? Did you escape from them?"

"No, no," answered Celon. "They brought me along to be an interpreter."

"There," said Moluntha, turning to Shade. "They are wanting to negotiate with us. Otherwise, they would not have brought this Frenchman."

He shifted attention again to Celon. "Why did you leave them and come to us? Did they send you."

The Frenchman, in his eagerness to make his point, stood up, forgetting that the chief would consider this an insult. "I left them in order to warn you. I do not want your people to be killed."

Moluntha stood up now as did Shade. "You are betraying your friends to warn us?" asked the chief. "The Shawnee do not admire such behavior."

"That is true, my chief," interjected Shade. "Some of my warriors wanted to kill this man, but I prevented it. He wants to help us, and he brings us valuable information at great danger to himself."

Celon had not expected resistance to his message and was uneasy about his own safety. He was thankful to Shade who continued to defend him. "My chief," began Shade again in a pleading tone. "You are the Shawnee king, but these soldiers who are coming may not know you at all nor care who you are. They are determined to destroy all the Shawnee towns, and they will kill us all, even our women and children. Our warriors are mostly gone to fight Clark. We must flee now. Our friend here says they will be here by tomorrow afternoon, if not before."

"My brother, Shade," said Moluntha calmly. "You may do as you please, but I will not flee. I do not believe this man."

"Would you believe Le Clerk?" asked Shade.

"Where is he?"

"In Buckongehelas's Town, I think."

"Send for him then," said Moluntha. "We will see what he thinks about this."

Turning to the boy, Moluntha directed him to get the flag with the stripes and stars. "We will put up this flag on my lodge. The Long Knives will not attack this flag."

Wetzel could hear riders approaching, and he left the trail, leading his horse back some distance before returning to see who might be coming. It didn't seem likely that it was Indians, but he had to be very cautious. He had been on a long ride since leaving Logan's army somewhere below Old Chillicothe, under orders to scout the Indian towns on the Mad River. He had struck that river just a mile below a small village on its eastern bank, which Wetzel supposed was the one Kenton had called Wapakoneta.

Simon had shown Wetzel a rough map he had drawn from his own recollections. Kenton had been a captive of the Shawnee and had run the gauntlet in several of the towns. Lew could not read the names, of course, but he had tried hard to commit to memory the locations and names as Simon had recalled them. Thinking that the horse might make it difficult for him to do his scouting and remain undiscovered, Wetzel tied his mount to a small birch in a heavy stand of trees and bushes alongside the stream. Satisfied that the horse could reach the water to drink and that there was sufficient grass for him to eat, the scout had skirted the edge of the village and moved north where Kenton had assured him there were a number of Shawnee towns.

He found the one Kenton had called Pickaway town, the two villages on Mackachack Creek, and up past Pigeon Town to the big village that he knew had to be Wapatomica. In each place, he noted that there were few warriors. When the darkness fell, Wetzel had decided to take advantage of it, and he pushed on north along the riverbank. Sometime after midnight, he came upon still another village, which was scattered out and seemed larger than it really was. He decided to wait until daylight to check it out further, crossing the stream to lower the chances of accidental discovery.

He had slept awhile but was awake and alert by the time daylight arrived. He worked his way around to the north, crossing the river again, and finding a place where he could observe the awakening of the residents. There were two distinct parts to the town formed, he guessed, by different tribes. Kenton thought there was a place called Mingo Town in this region, but Wetzel thought it might also be the town where Isaac Zane lived with his Indian princess. He meant to find out. More than two hours had passed before Wetzel saw a white man walking out from the village straight toward his own hiding place. Was this Zane? He looked like the Zanes, but how could he be sure? It was well-known that there were often white men living in the Indian towns. Should he make contact and warn the man of the oncoming Kentucky militia. He rejected that idea immediately, for that would be considered treasonous.

Zane, if that's who he was, had turned aside, and Wetzel stayed put, trying to observe whether there were many warriors present. Satisfied after another hour's observation that this town was short on defenders, just like the others, Wetzel had made his way to the west, staying well away from any obvious trails. He had completed a circuit that took him past another village, the one called Blue Jacket's Town, then to the south and past McKee's Town, named for the British agent who lived there with his Shawnee family.

Having completed this long scout by evening on the fifth, he had retrieved his horse and started back down the trail to report to Logan. Now that he could hear riders approaching, he thought it would be a shame to be caught here after he had gone by so many towns undetected. His anxiety eased when he realized the riders, now very close and having slowed their mounts to a slow walk, were speaking English.

"Haloo, men," shouted Wetzel as they passed on the trail just opposite where he was hiding. "Don't shoot, it's just me, Lew Wetzel."

Startled by the shout, Simon Kenton had quickly slid off his horse on the far side and raised his rifle, resting it on the horse's back. His partner, George Nokes, one of Kenton's Boys from Limestone, had turned aside on the opposite side of the trail and remained mounted. Wetzel stepped into the open where Kenton could see him.

"By God, Lew, I coulda shot you," shouted Kenton, trying to calm himself.

"I reckon I coulda shot you first. Didn't ya hear me yellin?"

"I heard a shout, but I thought it might be an Injun."

"You got off that horse mighty quick. I'll give you that. Who's with you?"

"George Nokes," answered Kenton, nodding toward George as he rode out of the trees on the other side. "Hugh Ross was with us too, but I sent him back to Logan."

"Hello, Lew," said Nokes, who had dismounted and joined the other two men. "I thought I heard you say Wetzel, but I wasn't takin' no chances."

"What are you fellers doin' this far up? I figured tomorrow afternoon before the army got here."

"That damned Frenchman slipped away last night on his way to warn the red men," explained Kenton. "We came after him but are too late. He must be at one of the towns by now. You didn't see nothin', I guess."

"I came from the other side of the river. If your man was on this trail, he's prob'ly in the town just up the way, not even two miles from here. The town you called Machachack, Simon."

"He left a clear trail, but we've lost track of it now that it's dark."

"Well, there's a town below us over on the river," noted Lew. "But I doubt he went that way."

"We're too late. Not much we can do now but wait for the rest of the men to come up."

"I don't think it's too important," said Wetzel. "Most of the warriors are gone anyway, just a few around. The rest are women and kids."

"Let's go up to Mackachack then and see what's happenin'," suggested Kenton. "We'll wait there for the army."

The three scouts arrived in a grove of trees below and on the opposite side of the creek from Shade's section of the village. They noted that there was no feverish activity indicating a desire to flee by the Indians as a result of the Frenchman's warning. They settled in for a long wait, scattering apart to prevent them all being discovered at once. Nokes agreed to take the first watch. At daylight, Lew Wetzel was awake, serving his term on watch.

The fear was that a party of braves might fan out to discover if the American army was coming. Strangely the village came to life in a normal manner, with none of the activities aimed at facing an attack. Wetzel eased out of his hiding spot and began to circle around to get closer to the eastern part of the town, which lay a half mile to the north and east. Kenton and Nokes had agreed to wait where they were. Within a half hour, Wetzel had worked his way into a stand of hazel bushes some two hundred yards east of the small prominence upon which Moluntha's lodge stood.

Wetzel could see the American flag flying high above the lodge. This was a surprise to him. What did it mean? Was this a village of friendly Indians? That was foreign to Lew's way of thinking. To him, all Indians were enemies, flag or no flag. Still it made him uneasy as he thought about what was to come when the army arrived. He watched for another hour, then returned to where his partners were waiting.

"Nothin's goin' on in either side of this creek," said Wetzel. "Are you sure that Frenchman came here."

"Don't know where else he'd have gone," answered Kenton.

"Pickaway town is about two miles west," noted Wetzel. "Over on the Mad."

"But that ain't the way he was headed," insisted Kenton. "And besides, you came in from that way."

"Maybe they didn't believe him," said Lew. "Funny thing though, the stars and stripes are flyin' over in the other town on a high pole."

"I'll be damned," exclaimed Kenton. "That might be the old chief, Moluntha. They say he's friendly."

Nokes, feeling a bit nervous, joined the conversation. "I think we ought to go back a ways and get the horses. If one of them young bucks gits frisky and comes out here lookin' around, we might be in trouble."

"You're right George," agreed Kenton. "There ain't many braves but more than we might be able to handle if they discover us."

October 6, 1786

The army arrived at Mackachack by noon. The three scouts intercepted them no more than a half mile from the town. Logan had pushed the troops forward without a rest, hoping to reach the Indian towns well ahead of schedule. He halted them when he saw Kenton and Wetzel standing in the trail in front of him.

"What is happening?" he asked as he dismounted.

"You're here quicker than we thought," said Kenton.

"Not quick enough, I'm afraid," answered Logan. "Did that damned traitor get here and warn them?"

"He came this way all right, but we never saw him."

"The Injuns ain't runnin'," interjected Wetzel. "There's mostly just women and children in the towns though. Only a few warriors are here."

"Did you scout all the towns?" the general wanted to know.

"I saw seven or eight towns. They're all the same. You won't have much opposition that I can see."

Logan called for his commanders to gather around.

"What's just ahead of us?" he asked Wetzel.

"About a half mile ahead is the town Simon calls Mackachack. It's split into two pieces, one on each side of a little creek, mebbe a half mile apart. One of the lodges on the east side is flyin' the stars and stripes."

"The flag? Flyin' our flag?"

"Might be the old chief, Moluntha, General," offered Kenton. "He lives in one of these towns."

"I think he was at Fort Finney and signed that treaty," said General Logan. "Well here's what I want you to do. Colonel Peterson, I want you to hit the first village, the one on the west side of the creek."

"Yes, sir," exclaimed Peterson. "We'll wipe 'em out," he promised, turning to go.

"Hold on now," cautioned Logan. "Don't go off hell-bent till you hear all I've got to say. Colonel Kennedy, you are to take your men and swing far around to the right of the upper village to stop any escape in that direction. I will lead the rest of the men against the eastern town. Simon, you, and Daniel will be with me. Now listen to this, I don't want us slaughtering women and children, and if you take prisoners, they're not to be harmed. Is that clear?"

There was a bit of scuffling and a grunt from Colonel McGary.

Colonel Kennedy, who was standing next to him, spoke up, "I ain't sparin' nobody if one of my men is in danger, General."

"That might be different," acknowledged Logan. "But I expect to be obeyed." He glared at Kennedy for a moment, then turned to Wetzel who was standing with Kenton a few feet away from the rest.

"Awful lot of colonels in this army I'm noticin'," Lew had just mentioned to Kenton.

"You're right," laughed Simon, "and I reckon I'm one too."

"Wal, you're a good one, and I ain't so sure about the others. Oh, oh! The general's lookin' at me."

"This man will show us the way," announced Logan, pointing to Wetzel.

Nodding assent, Wetzel mounted his horse and began riding to the north. Logan and the army following after. When he came to the creek, he stopped and motioned to Logan.

"This creek bends around, and the western village lies across the creek, no more than a quarter mile from here. To hit the other part of the town, you need to skirt that clump of trees ahead and ride through an open field. The town's mebbe a half mile up."

Logan motioned for Peterson to move to the left and cross the creek, then pointed for the rest to go in the direction Wetzel had indicated. "Now let me say again, I want prisoners, and I want 'em unharmed. We want to trade for George Clark's son Robert if we can. Now let's go," shouted Logan. "Full charge."

With that the men spurred their horses to a fast gallop, and it wasn't long until the lines were spread widely, and there was little semblance of any organization. It wouldn't matter, though, because at the sight and sound of the charging men, the few Indians still in the villages were in rapid flight. A handful of warriors held their ground and began shooting at the oncoming soldiers, but it had little effect.

Wetzel turned aside to the right and headed for the trees and bushes to the east of the upper town. He had been there earlier that morning, and he thought he might be able to pick off any warriors who might want to be escaping in that direction.

Kennedy's men had been given that same task by General Logan, but Wetzel figured that there would still be opportunity for him. His guess was correct, for Kennedy's men, who had been first to begin the charge, soon decided to attack straight into the village, and they veered to the left, mixing in with the troops led by Kenton and Boone. It was clear to Wetzel that the officers had lost control. The charging Kentuckians had soon enveloped the village.

Lieutenant William Lytle was a sixteen-year-old who, though too young to be drafted, had volunteered to come along and had resolved to stay close to the commander, General Logan. He was mounted on a very fleet horse, and almost before he realized what was happening, he was through the village with fifty men following him. Ahead, he saw several Indians running along the edge of a thicket of hazel and plum bushes. He motioned for the men behind him to come on and then angled across the plain trying to get ahead of his quarry. When he closed to within fifty yards, he dismounted and raised his gun.

The Indians had also stopped, and their leader held up his hand in surrender. As he came closer, Lytle saw that the Indian leader was just a boy, not as big and definitely younger than Lytle himself. With him were two children not more than ten years old. The three of them waited as Lytle walked up to them. Hearing his men coming up behind, he turned and shouted at them to stop, "These have surrendered, and they are only children. We will take them back with the others."

As he gathered the youngsters to him, Lytle heard a commotion close by and saw that Colonel Kennedy was riding after four women who were trying to reach the creek. Kennedy was holding his sword high above his head, and as he came near the women, he brought it crashing down on the head of the one closest to him. The woman threw up her hands, and the sword sliced off three of her fingers before she fell. The horsemen charged by, then turned back intending to finish the job.

Watching what to him was a horrible sight, Lytle cried out, "Colonel, stop."

Two of Kennedy's men had dismounted and were leaning over the woman who was crying in agony. "Stop, Colonel," one of them shouted. "She's a white woman. She's white!"

"Hell, I couldn't tell that," said Kennedy, who had stopped his charge and dismounted. "She's prob'ly Injun now anyway."

His men had rounded up the other three and brought them to the spot where the wounded woman was lying. One was an adult, also white; and the others were young, apparently daughters of the two women. Lytle came up to them with his three prisoners in tow.

"We should take them back with the others," he said, noting Kennedy's angry look.

"Who put you in charge, you young sprout?" sneered Kennedy.

"I'm not in charge," replied Lytle. "But I heard what the general said."

One of the men had helped the woman to her feet, the hand bleeding profusely. The others crowded close to her.

"Who are you, women?" asked Kennedy, his tone softer now. "When was you captured?"

The women looked down and did not answer, shaking their heads.

"They've been Injuns for too long," said Kennedy, his sneering tone returning. "Forgot how to talk." Looking again at Lytle, he waved his hands. "Well, take 'em in then, sonny. Me and my men are goin' to burn these towns."

Lytle was glad to have this opportunity, and he asked one of the men who had come with him to find something to bind up the woman's hand to stop the bleeding. Gathering up the horses, they led the prisoners back to the center of the town near Moluntha's lodge, where a number of other prisoners, all of them women and children, were being held. A large crowd of men stood around the area.

Lytle stepped aside looking for a place to secure his horse, and the young boy, High Horn, stayed by his side. A man named Curner, coming up from the spring, suddenly began running directly toward them, apparently intent on attacking. Lytle felt the boy tense at his side, and much to his surprise, produce a bow and arrow that he had kept hidden in his clothes. Thinking what a fool he had been not to have searched the boy for weapons, Lytle managed to catch the Indian boy's arm as he let fly the arrow. It passed through Curner's shirt and grazed his side. Curner stopped and examined his side, realizing that the wound was slight.

"You damned red pup!" shouted Curner, his face twisting into a look of pure hatred. "I'll fix you." He pulled a long knife from his belt and began advancing toward High Horn. Lytle had grabbed the boy and took away the bow and remaining arrows, tossing them into the grass several feet away.

"Let him go, Lytle," shouted Curner. "I'll fix his red ass right quick."

"No you won't," said Lytle sharply. "This boy is a prisoner and won't be harmed."

"He tried to kill me," snarled Curner. "I've got a right to defend myself, and that's what I aim to do. Now get away."

"He thought you were coming to attack him, so he was defending himself. He's my prisoner, he's disarmed, and you won't touch him."

"The boy's right," said Daniel Boone, who had observed the action from further up the hill. "Now back off." Boone took Lytle and High Horn on each arm and led them up and inside the circle of onlookers.

Simon Kenton had led his men straight up the incline toward Moluntha's lodge, keeping his eye on the American flag waving in the slight breeze, high above the lodge. He found the old chief standing outside his door, sadly watching the action all around him and holding some papers in his hands. Kenton signaled to the men behind him to withhold any shooting, then dismounted and approached the Shawnee king.

Moluntha watched Kenton as he came near, nodding his head, his thin lips breaking into a weak smile. "Hello, Bawdler," he offered in broken English.

Kenton was taken back, wondering how the chief would know to call him by that name. He knew this must be Moluntha, but how could the old man know him. They had never met as far as he could remember.

"You are Moluntha, I reckon," said Kenton, nodding his head as a gesture of friendship.

"Friend to Americans," attempted Moluntha in his limited way, holding the papers high above his head.

Kenton knew a few Shawnee words but realized he could not carry on a meaningful conversation. There was no good interpreter among his men either. Seeming to understand the dilemma, Moluntha turned toward the door of his lodge and said something in Shawnee. Shortly after, a white man emerged from the dwelling. The Grenadier Squaw and Moluntha's two other wives came out behind him along with the baby and two other children. The man offered his hand to Kenton.

"My name is Pierre Le Clerk. You are Simon Kenton?"

"I am."

"I've heard lots about you."

"Well, I ain't so sure I'm glad to meet no Frenchman. A Frenchman was with us and deserted to warn the villages here."

"Yes, Jean Celon. I was called here to talk with him."

"If the men find him, they'll make short work of him."

"Well, he's gone by now. The Indians sent him to Detroit. They didn't really believe him and didn't treat him that well anyway."

Moluntha grasped LeClerk by the arm and shook the papers in front of him.

"The chief wants to remind you that he is a friend of the Americans and signed the treaty at Fort Finney," Le Clerk explained. "He has his copy of the papers here. He wonders why you are attacking him."

"There's been too many raids in Kentucky," said Kenton emphatically. "We know the raiders come from these towns."

Moluntha stood watching the two men talking. Then he stepped forward, first pointing a finger at Kenton, then toward the creek, sweeping his arm past the wide fields where militiamen could still be seen chasing a few fleeing women.

"You kill," Moluntha rasped, tears forming in his dark eyes with the wrinkled lids. "You kill."

Kenton felt a moment of regret, then said, "You and the other prisoners will not be harmed. The general has promised this."

The chief looked down not raising his eyes, and he did not answer. A horseman approached, and the circle of men opened to allow him to pass through. It was General Logan. He stopped his mount just short of where Kenton, Le Clerk, and Moluntha were standing, but he did not get down.

"What do we have here, Simon?" he asked.

"General Logan, this is Moluntha, the Shawnee king, and those are his wives." Simon pointed to the women who had crowded in behind the old chief.

"By God," exclaimed Logan. "Is that the Grenadier Squaw? I didn't know she was living here."

Nonhelema, who understood English, nodded but did not speak.

Le Clerk stepped forward to introduce himself. "I am Pierre Le Clerk, General. Pleased to meet you."

"And what is your role here, Le Clerk? French traders ain't exactly popular with this army just now."

"I understand that. I happened to be in the area, and Moluntha asked for my advice. He could not believe that his village would be attacked."

"Well, it's unfortunate for I know he has been friendly, but we did not know he would be here."

"He thought you were coming to negotiate."

"Hell, we're in no mood to negotiate. Tell the old boy that he is our prisoner and that he and his family will be well treated. But they must come with us to Kentucky. We intend to make an exchange later."

Moluntha, who realized that he was facing the American commander, came close to where Logan sat on his horse. He gave a low bow and turned to point at the stars and stripes still waving in the breeze, high above his lodge. "American friend," he said loudly to Logan, but he did not smile.

"I know," acknowledged Logan, giving a slight nod toward the chief. He spoke again to Le Clerk. "Is there a prisoner here named Robert Clark?"

Moluntha stiffened at that name. Even his wives took notice.

Le Clerk shook his head, indicating that the answer was yes.

"He was here, but I believe they moved him to one of the other towns. They regard him with value, believing him to be the son of George Rogers Clark. Is that true?"

"No," answered Logan. "He is not related to George Rogers. But his father's name is George, who is with this army, a good friend of mine and of Colonel Kenton's. We will exchange any two of our prisoners for him. We are posting notices of that intent."

"Is that the purpose of this raid, to get back a special prisoner?"

"Don't be impertinent. I am under orders of the authorities of Virginia. You should keep in mind that you also are my prisoner."

Logan was finished with this interview, and he spoke now to Kenton.

"Simon, come with me, we must organize the burning of these towns and the destruction of the crops. Plus, we must move against the other towns. Where is Boone?"

"He was here before, but I guess he rode off."

"Well, we'll find him. Colonel Whitley!"

"Yes, General," responded Whitley, who had ridden in with Logan and had waited patiently in the background.

"I want you to organize a guard for these prisoners. All the prisoners will be gathered here. They are not to be harmed. Is that understood?" He glared at the other men standing by, making sure they had heard him. His eye fell on Lt. Lytle, who stood not far away, with his arm around the Indian boy, High Horn. "Lieutenant Lytle, you will help Colonel Whitley with setting up this prisoner camp."

Lytle gave a salute but did not let go of the boy. Logan took notice.

"Who is this boy with you, Lytle?"

"He is my captive, sir. He was bravely leading some young children to safety when I caught them."

"He appears to be a strong lad," said Logan with a smile. "I would like to talk with him later." With that, Logan wheeled his horse and rode away; Kenton following.

Watching the panorama unfolding before him from his position above and to the east of Moluntha's town, Lewis Wetzel was disappointed that none of the fleeing Indians had come his way. The afternoon sun had suddenly broken through the light clouds, bringing some warmth. Strangely Wetzel was struck by the beauty of its rays against the tree leaves, bringing out the multicolors of red and brown and yellow. The thought prompted a laugh from Wetzel, who was surprised at himself. For him to make such an observation in the midst of all the running, shooting, and screaming going on below was definitely unusual.

Far up to his right, Wetzel's eye caught sight of some movement near a clump of trees. Although the figure was more than two hundred yards away, Wetzel could see that it was a young warrior carrying a dead buck on his shoulders. The Indian stopped, perhaps seeing for the first time the flames rising up from the town across the creek. Closer to him and near the creek, Wetzel could see a small group of riders led by a man he recognized as Captain Irwin. Just in front of these horsemen, a man rose up from the tall grass and fired his rifle at the target who was standing in front of the trees, shading his eyes as he looked at the burning village.

The Indian dropped the buck, grabbed his leg, and dove into the grass completely out of sight. Captain Irwin rode up to the man who had taken the shot, apparently asking him where the Indian had gone. Wetzel recognized the man as Hugh Ross, and after Ross pointed to the appropriate spot, the captain led his men in a charge in that direction, shooting as they rode.

Wetzel could see that they had missed and he stood, crying, "Watch out!"

Of course, Wetzel was too far away to be heard, and he watched with dismay as Irwin wheeled his men for a return charge. The warrior rose quickly and leveled his gun, the shot striking Irwin in the chest, knocking him to the ground and killing him instantly. Wetzel brought his own rifle up and tried to aim, but he could not see the Indian, who had scooted away in the tall grass.

Other men now came running to the scene and managed to find the warrior before he could reload, ending his life with a tomahawk blow. Wetzel could not help but admire the gallantry of this young brave's fight. Wetzel had watched also the gathering of the women prisoners near Moluntha's lodge, and he had seen Logan ride away with Kenton. He retrieved his own horse and decided to make his way down to that location. "I sure ain't been worth much today," he muttered aloud to himself.

Lieutenant Lytle had moved inside the circle of guards to a position close to where the old chief Moluntha was seated. The boy, High Horn, had stayed by Lytle's side. A stirring of the crowd to the south attracted their attention, and they could see a rider coming whom Lytle easily recognized was Colonel Hugh McGary. Instinctively Lytle was alarmed, for he knew McGary's temperament, and he could see the look on the colonel's face when one of the guards stopped him.

"Get out of my way, goddamn you," shouted McGary.

"Colonel McGary," said Colonel Whitley quietly. "You are not to molest these prisoners. That is a direct order from General Logan."

"I'll see to that," answered McGary. "Now let me through."

Whitley started to argue but shrugged and nodded to the guard. The crowd opened, and McGary rode through, slamming to a stop near where Moluntha sat, cutting some tobacco with his knife. He stood and walked close to where Lytle and High Horn were standing, waiting while McGary dismounted and strode briskly toward them. Moluntha extended his hand; a weak smile forming on his face. McGary was having none of that, ignoring the friendly gesture. "Were you at the Blue Licks?" McGary asked the chief in an accusing tone.

As he did so, he noted the small axe tucked into the belt of the Grenadier Squaw, who stood nearby. Moluntha, who did not know what McGary had said, mumbled something that might have sounded like a yes, especially to the embittered McGary, who had often been blamed for the terrible defeat at the Blue Licks battle in Kentucky a little more than four years earlier.

Suddenly McGary grabbed the axe from the Grenadier Squaw and raised it high. Lytle saw what was about to happen and threw up his arm to try to ward off the blow. Although the handle of the axe struck his wrist, it was not enough to prevent McGary from bringing it down upon the chief's head, where it sunk all the way to his eyes. Moluntha fell dead as the Grenadier Squaw gave a shriek. After quickly taking the scalp, McGary pushed Lytle aside and went immediately to his horse. The crowd was stunned into silence. Colonel Whitley appeared and grasped the bridle of McGary's horse.

"Colonel McGary, what have you done?" shouted Whitley. "You've killed our prisoner."

"Yes," cried McGary, still holding the bloody axe. "And I'll chop up anybody who tries to tell me it was wrong."

He jerked the reins, pulling loose from Whitley, and rode away through the scattering crowd.

As he was riding down near the center of the town, Wetzel had not been able to see everything that was happening, but he knew something had exercised the men who were encircling the area around Moluntha's lodge. He dismounted and led his horse for the last thirty yards where he met Andrew Thompson, a man he knew from Limestone, who was walking away from the scene.

"What's goin' on Andy?"

"Hell, they killed the old chief."

"By God, who had the guts to do that?"

"It was Hugh McGary. I seen the whole thing!" Thompson was glad to have the chance to tell what he had seen.

"Did the old bugger attack him or somethin'?" Wetzel wanted to know.

"Naw, he was just cuttin' some tobacky when McGary went after him. McGary accused the bastard of bein' at the Blue Licks."

Wetzel nodded, for he knew about McGary and the Blue Licks. "So does Logan know about this?"

"Not yet, but he's goin' to be mighty mad when he finds out. Colonel Whitley thinks McGary should be court-martialed."

"Well, I ain't sure a man should be punished for killin' an Injun."

"I agree about that, 'cept that old chief was no threat to nobody. He claimed to be a friend. Besides, the general had ordered that he be unharmed."

"Yeah, I guess he did." Wetzel looked up and pointed. "We're about to find out what Logan thinks, I reckon. Here he comes with Kenton and Boone right behind."

The two men moved back to where they could hear what was being said. Colonel Whitley was quite upset and explaining to Logan what had taken place.

"By God, he should be thrown in jail and charged with murder," Whitley was shouting.

Moluntha's body still lay where it had fallen, and Kenton, who was also visibly angry, bent down to examine it.

"I see the damned fool took the scalp too," noted Kenton, looking up at Logan who was still astride his horse. "If I'd been here, I'd have struck him down on the spot. Where is he anyway?"

"I'll send some men to find him and bring him here," said Whitley. "We can try him right here."

"Let's slow down, men," cautioned the general. "It's a terrible thing and was contrary to my orders. But we're in a middle of an action, and we can't get bogged down in a trial just now."

"Hell, it won't take long, General," cried Whitley. "He's guilty as sin!"

William Whitley was a very good friend of Logan's and brother-in-law of George Clark, another of Logan's friends. However, Logan was becoming annoyed with Whitley's insistence on punishing McGary. McGary had a large contingent of men following him who might take exception to any such action. Beyond that, Logan knew that this very expedition, although sanctioned by George Rogers Clark and Kentucky authorities, was probably not legal in the eyes of the United States government and was violating treaty agreements. It wasn't a good time to have trouble within the ranks.

"Colonel Whitley, we will consider bringing charges once we are back in Kentucky. Right now it would be difficult to have a fair trial, and we have other things to do. I'll hear no more of court-martials."

Logan set his gaze on several groups of the men standing there, making it clear that he expected no more arguments. Kenton was still angry but not inclined to push the point. Boone said nothing. A moment passed before Logan spoke again. "All right, let's get busy burning these towns and destroying the crops. Gather up anything that might be useful. Some of the men have already gone over to burn the Pickaway town. Tomorrow we will burn some of the other towns. Now let's get moving."

Satisfied that he had adequately defused a simmering firestorm, Logan rode away.

It had been an uneasy night in the camp. Some of the men had advanced as far as Wapatomica and finding the town abandoned had begun its destruction when night fell. Deciding to return to the main camp, they had become lost, and imagining that they were being attacked by Indian warriors who were roaming the woods in the darkness, the men had created quite a stir when they finally found their way back.

The morning had brought a feeling of calm, and the commanders organized renewed attacks against the remaining villages. Lewis Wetzel was guiding one such band of men under Colonel Peterson toward the village called Mingo Town. He had volunteered for this assignment since it was in his mind that he might need to provide some measure of warning or protection for Isaac Zane. He was sure now that it had been Zane whom he had seen two days earlier while scouting the towns.

Wetzel had had a short conversation with the trader Le Clerk after noting that the Frenchman was one of the captives. Le Clerk had confirmed that Zane was living at Mingo Town. The town was inhabited by the Wyandots who were not hostile at this time, but the eastern side of the town was made up of Mingoes and Cherokees. Le Clerk was quick to point out that it was from there that much of the mischief was carried out against the whites. Le Clerk had not been sure as to whether the town had been abandoned. He thought that if there were many Cherokees around, they might put up a fight. That would be welcomed by Wetzel, but his close friendship with the Zanes made him apprehensive about safety for Isaac.

The trail led past the village of Wapatomica, once a strong and powerful stronghold for the Shawnees. Now it was abandoned and mostly on fire as they rode past. More than one hundred troops rode behind Colonel Peterson. Far more than needed, thought Wetzel. He supposed that some of them were to swing over and finish the destruction of Blue Jacket's Town, which lay several miles to the west. Wetzel had kept the men following him to the east side of the Mad River, for he knew that the Cherokee side of Mingo Town straddled the river. It wasn't long before they had traversed the two miles that separated the town from Wapatomica. He stopped when he could see some of the small huts lying to the east of the stream.

"What is it?" asked Colonel Peterson, who had ridden up beside Wetzel.

"There's your town, Colonel," said Wetzel quietly, pointing at the huts. There was no sign of human occupancy. "That's the Cherokee side, although I reckon there's some on the other side too. The Wyandots are farther to the west."

"Looks like the place is deserted," observed Peterson.

"Reckon it might be. There was some women and children there two days ago, a few warriors too."

"Well, we'll charge it and see what happens." Peterson turned and waved his arm at the men, who were anxious to make the attack.

Wetzel started to suggest that the colonel send some of the men across the river to attack from the southwest as well, but thought better of it. Peterson spurred his horse forward with a yell, and the men charged after him. Wetzel let them pass, then rode toward the trees along the river, splashing across the narrow stream and riding hard toward the west end of the town. He saw that some of Peterson's men had swerved aside to follow him. If Zane was still in the village, it might be hard to protect him, but Wetzel was determined to try.

The village appeared to be completely deserted, but Wetzel approached with some care through a patch of pumpkins and gourds. Fields of corn bordered the town to his west and around to the north side. Abandoned items were strewn among the alleyways between the lodges. There was a fairly large blockhouse near the center of the town, which surprised Wetzel, who had not noticed it in his earlier scout. It must have been built by the British, he thought. He could hear shouting and scattered shooting as Peterson's men entered the village from the east.

The men behind him had spied the big blockhouse, and they immediately moved, with excited shouts, to set it on fire. Wetzel continued on toward the lodge that he believed belonged to Zane. He slid down from his horse, and with his rifle cradled in his arms, began walking slowly toward the door of the crudely constructed log hut. Having become convinced that there were no humans anywhere in the village, he was startled when a figure stepped out from the far side of the house. The man, who was white and unarmed, stood between Wetzel and the door.

"Who are you?" asked the man in good English.

"You must be Isaac Zane," said Wetzel rather than answering the man's question.

"I am, but who are you?"

"Lewis Wetzel."

"Ah, yes. My brother has spoken of you. What are you doin' with a bunch of Kentuckians?"

"I've been livin' around Limestone. Not many folks in your town I see."

"They've fled. We received word yesterday that an army from Kentucky was coming under Logan."

"Why didn't you go too?"

"I was hopin' to save my home. My family is still here with me."

Wetzel could see that some of the men had seen him talking with Zane and were approaching, quite determined to take him as a prisoner.

"I don't know if you'll be safe. These men are out for blood."

As the men came near, Wetzel turned to face them.

"Hold up, men," he shouted. "This man is a friend."

"He ain't no friend of mine," barked Silas Dexter, who lived in the Limestone area. "He's a friend of the damned redskins. Now get outta my way, Wetzel."

Wetzel's temper flared. "Damned if I will!' He took a step toward Dexter, pulling the tomahawk from his belt.

"I wouldn't do that, Silas," said Nicholas Washburn, who had come up beside Dexter and grabbed his arm just as he tried to raise his gun and aim it at Wetzel. "You don't want to tangle with Lew."

Washburn was one of Kenton's Boys, and he knew Wetzel quite well. Dexter pulled away from Washburn but thought better of continuing his threat. He gave Wetzel a dark look, then spoke to Washburn. "He ain't no commander here. We don't have to listen to him."

At this point Zane spoke up. "I am Isaac Zane. My brothers Ebenezer and Jonathan live at Wheeling. Though I live with the Wyandots, I have never lifted my hand against a white man. I did not flee because I did not think I had anything to fear from my own kind."

"I still think we should take him back as a prisoner," insisted Dexter.

"Before you take him, you'll have to take me," said Wetzel, still holding his tomahawk in his right hand.

"Let's cool off, both of you," said Washburn. "It's up to Colonel Peterson, I reckon."

Wetzel stood his ground, and the others moved away.

"Thank you, Lew," said Zane gratefully. "I guess you saved my life and my family's."

"It ain't over yet, mebbe," cautioned Wetzel. "You'd better keep your family inside."

Dexter and Washburn went to find the colonel. Peterson, who had heard of Isaac Zane and knew that he had served as an interpreter at the Fort Finney treaty negotiations, decided to leave Zane and his family in their home, which was to be left unharmed. He ordered that the remainder of the village be burned and the crops destroyed. By sunset, the troops had returned to the main camp from burning the surrounding towns.

Wetzel had gone by the place where the prisoners were being held. The prisoners were mostly Indian women and children, plus the four white women. Of course the Frenchman Le Clerk was also being held. The count of Indian casualties was not known, but there were ten scalps thrown in a pile, and that didn't count that of Moluntha. Wetzel guessed this expedition would be considered a big success when they got back to Kentucky.

Logan's men had found plenty of evidence that Robert Clark had been held there, including bits of paper with his name and the names of his family members stuck in cracks in one of the huts. Logan directed that advertisements be posted along the trail as they returned to Kentucky, indicating that two prisoners would be released in exchange for young Clark. Wetzel knew that this would be a useless exercise. He had learned from Zane that the Indians thought the present attack was just to rescue young Clark. Infuriated, they had made sure he was on his way to Detroit before the soldiers could find him. He supposed he should inform Logan about that, but then it might lead to trouble for Isaac Zane, or worse, for himself. He decided to remain quiet.

The army began its retreat to Kentucky that very night, marching south until midnight. There was some worry that the Indians might regroup and mount a counterattack. This fear heightened the next day at midmorning when some stragglers came in with a rumor that a large band of warriors had returned from the Wabash and was planning to strike at the rear of the marching troops that very afternoon. Logan had some signs made up and placed in the path stating that all the prisoners would be killed if he were attacked. Wetzel and two others were sent back up the trail to watch for any threats. The rumors turned out to be false.

October 21, 1786

The Shawnees had been greatly disappointed. More than two hundred warriors had left the towns near the Mad River and gone to join the Indian confederation that had gathered in the Wabash country to oppose the intruder, George Rogers Clark and the army he was reported to be leading against them. The main camps were near the mouth of Pine Creek as it flowed into the Wabash. There were braves from a variety of tribes, including the Miamis, Weas, Pottawatomies, Ottawas, Delawares, Kickapoos, and the later-arriving Shawnees.

Little Turtle, the great Miami chief, was the acknowledged leader. To the chagrin of the Shawnees, who expected to move quickly against the invaders, Little Turtle was holding back. The Shawnee war chiefs, Black Snake and Blue Jacket, were not along, for they were engaged in their own raids against the Kentucky settlements. However, Black Hoof was there and pressing for action. Little Fox and Fire Heart had been quick to join the Shawnee war party, along with their friend Red Storm, who had moved his family to New Coshocton in the last month, desiring to be closer to the action, as he put it.

It was well-known that Clark's army had stopped at Post St. Vincent for a number of days and then had advanced up the Wabash to a point not more than thirty miles away. Then the Indian scouts had brought word that the white men had started back down the river again.

"We should attack them now," Red Storm had shouted on hearing this news.

Black Hoof had gone to the council with this very same demand. "If we move quickly, we can catch them as they are moving," Black Hoof had said at the meeting of the chiefs presided over by Little Turtle.

"We have defeated them without fighting," explained the great Miami chief. "Why should we risk a life? We do not know what they intend. It is Clark we face, and he is not known to retreat so easily."

Black Hoof wanted to say much more, but the respect for Little Turtle was so great that one must proceed carefully. Others spoke, but no one could budge the Turtle from his position. "We will remain here and watch."

Further intelligence reports indicated that some of Clark's troops had left him, but those reports were generally not believed. After a few more days, a letter was received from Clark, and also from Colonel LeGras, the leading French citizen in Vincennes or Post Vincent as it was usually called. Clark's letter was stern but offered peace, calling for a peace conference to be held at Clarksville on November 20. The letter from LeGras explained that he had persuaded Clark to stop the army's advance and return to Post Vincent, promising that his Indian brothers would remain quiet.

The Indians had observed the retreat and were also aware that some of the army had left the post and were returning to Clarksville. The Shawnees, who were strongly in favor of attacking Post Vincent, were now met with a conflict of interest. Runners had arrived from the Mad River country informing of the destruction of the Shawnee towns by the Kentuckians under Logan. While the chiefs of the congregated tribes continued to debate, the Shawnees began to slip away, anxious to get back to their families and see what had happened to their homes.

"If you want to go against the Long Knives now, we will be with you," pleaded Black Hoof at the council discussions. "But if you continue to wait, there will be no more Shawnees left. We must get back to our towns, which are under attack as we speak."

Fire Heart, Red Storm, and Little Fox did not wait but set out for the Mad River as soon as they heard the news. The messengers had been unclear as to just which towns were attacked and could provide no information on what had become of the inhabitants. It was a long way back; and the three friends, who had been joined by a handful of other warriors, decided to take a straight line across country rather than follow the Wabash, which made a long curve to the north before coming back down to a point nearly due west of Blue Jacket's Town.

The trails were less traveled, but they were able to take a route, which followed the south fork of the Wildcat River. They had little food with them; and on the third day, after crossing the Mississinewa Creek, they stopped to hunt. One of them managed to kill a small doe, and they built a fire to roast it.

On the fourth day, they had encountered the Wabash again, where it curled back to the south. In two more days, near evening, they came to Blue Jacket's Town. The devastation stunned them. Most of the permanent huts were burned to the ground, and the cornfield was barren except for a pile of charred stalks in the center. There was no sign of life.

"This is very bad," remarked Fire Heart. "I am afraid it will be the same at my village." He stared off in the direction of Wapatomica.

"Where are the women and children?" wondered Little Fox, who was suddenly fearful about the well-being of his own family.

The messenger who had reached them on the Wabash had indicated that most of the inhabitants of the attacked villages had escaped. The sight of the ruined town reawakened his anxiety.

"Do you think they attacked the Delaware town too?" Red Storm had picked up on what was bothering Little Fox.

"They wouldn't know one from another," said Little Fox. "I think we should go to Buckongehelas's Town right now."

Noticing the look on Fire Heart's face, Little Fox spoke again to Fire Heart. "It is closer than Wapatomica, and it is very late. We will go with you there tomorrow."

The three friends made their way through the burned-out town and took the trail north to New Coshocton, Buckongehelas's Town. Although they were tired, they walked swiftly and had negotiated the three miles in less than thirty minutes. Night was falling, but they were overjoyed to find the town intact and inhabited.

Red Storm and Little Fox grasped each other's hands. "Maybe they are here," cried Little Fox. "They must be here."

"Yes," agreed Red Storm. "Let us go to our homes now."

"Come with me, Fire Heart." invited Little Fox. "You can stay at my lodge tonight."

Not waiting for an answer, Little Fox took the Shawnee by the arm and pulled him along, half running now to his own hut. As they neared it, Fire Heart stopped, pointing toward Bright Moon who was standing just beside the door.

"You must greet your woman without me. I will join you shortly."

Little Fox, not arguing, ran to Bright Moon, lifting her high in his embrace. "Bright Moon, Bright Moon, you are safe."

"Yes, husband, I am safe," she laughed. "Now put me down."

"The Long Knives did not attack you here?" asked Little Fox. "We have come from Blue Jacket's Town, which is destroyed."

"Yes, many towns were burned," explained Bright Moon. "But they did not come here. We had all run away, but in two days we were able to return."

"I thank the Great Spirit that you are safe. And Eagle's Wing, he is all right too?"

"Yes. We were never in danger. Many of the women from the other towns have come here."

"Do you know what happened?" asked Little Fox.

"I will tell you what I know, but first we should invite your friend who waits over there." She nodded toward Fire Heart, who stood watching them.

"He is worried about his family," noted Little Fox, who waved at Fire Heart, indicating that he should join them. "They were at Wapatomica."

"Some of those people have come here. Maybe his wife is one of them."

After Little Fox had introduced Fire Heart to Bright Moon, he asked her to tell them what she knew about the American attack. She did not know much other than that there had been some warriors killed and women taken captive, mostly from the Mackachack towns. She told them of the killing of Moluntha. They were saddened to hear this. Fire Heart was excited to learn that some of the refugees were in this very town. Bright Moon prepared a meal at which they ate heartily. Fire Heart would wait until morning to search for his wife and children.

The two men talked for some time, agreeing that they would plan a raid against the Long Knives in revenge for what they regarded as a cowardly attack, especially the killing of Moluntha. They were confident that Red Storm would join them.

"Moluntha regarded himself as a friend of the whites. Why did they kill him?" Fire Heart could not believe this should happen.

"White men are evil," snapped Little Fox. "Nothing they do makes sense."

"They are good at betrayal," agreed Fire Heart, recalling the day Martin Wetzel had left him.

"Do you think the man Wetzel was with the Long Knives?" wondered Little Fox.

"Your woman said the men were from Kentucky. Is Wetzel in Kentucky?"

"I don't know, but we will tell Red Storm that he was here. That will make sure he will want to go with us." *We will definitely make Wetzel the target of our revenge*, thought Little Fox. *We are sure to kill him.* The thought pleased him.

November 13, 1786

It was late in the afternoon, and Colonel Josiah Harmar sat at his desk in the commandant's office in the fort that was named for him. The desk faced the small window through which the colonel could see the murky waters of the Ohio River.

The fort had been built in the corner of land between the Ohio and the Muskingum, which flowed into the Ohio just to the east of the fort. There was still some construction going on; and only a few days earlier, the men had finished putting shingles and chimneys on the barracks. Harmar was pleased that his name had been attached, an honor provided by Major Doughty, who had supervised the building, which had begun the previous year.

His time at the fort had not been easy. Supply was a problem, and keeping enough provisions to feed the troops was a constant worry. Fortunately, a trader had brought in some provisions a week ago, and then a few days later, some hunters he had hired had brought in thirty deer and a large quantity of turkeys. Relieved of these worries now, he began to think of Captain Hamtramck, who was in command of a company of troops up on Indian Wheeling Creek guarding a surveying party.

There were indications that the Indians were becoming upset with these surveyors, although there had been a period of relative peace in the area. Harmar suspected that the increase in Indian activity might be related to recent actions by the Kentuckians. Although he had heard of an expedition by Logan, he had no facts.

A knock at the door interrupted his thoughts. "Who is it?" he asked with a hint of annoyance.

"Sergeant Shambough, sir."

"Well, come in then, Sergeant."

"Sir," said Shambough, a tall skinny man with reddish hair. "Three men have come in from Limestone, or so they said."

"And why do you bother me with that?"

"They claim they were with Logan, sir."

"With Logan? Are you sure?"

"One of 'em's just outside, sir. He's kind of a rough lookin' character."

Shambough watched the colonel for some reaction, but Harmar just stared at him expectantly. "He says he figures you might want to hear what he's got to say."

"Bring him in then, Sergeant."

This was a pleasant surprise, for Harmar was anxious to know something about Logan's raid. In spite of the sergeant's warning, the colonel was taken aback by the appearance of the man who walked through the door. A gust of cold air came in with him.

"By God, man," exclaimed the colonel. "You look spent. Sergeant, shut that damned door. That wind is cold as hell."

The courier took off his heavy outercoat and laid it on a chair against the wall. "We've had a long ride," he said quietly. "We're hopin' you can put us up for a night or two."

Harmar looked his visitor up and down, noting the soiled and torn buckskin jacket and the leggings caked with dried mud. The tassels dangling from his ears made the colonel think he might be a French trader. The glaring dark eyes revealed that this was not a man to be crossed.

"Who are you, and what brings you here?"

"My name's Lew Wetzel."

"You came from Limestone?" Colonel Harmar thought he had heard the name Wetzel before, maybe from one of the hunters he hired from time to time.

"That we did," said Wetzel, "and we've been five days doin' it. The trails 'tween here and there ain't too friendly."

"Well, it's better to travel by water. The sergeant here says you were with Logan. Is that right?"

"I was. All three of us. When Kenton heard I was goin' back to Wheeling, he said I ought to stop here and report what happened."

"Who is this Kenton?"

"Hell, don't you know Simon Kenton?" Wetzel found this hard to believe.

"I guess I've heard the name," admitted Harmar. "Is he a militia officer?"

"I reckon he is, a major or colonel, I think. One of the most important men in Kentucky, most would say."

"Well, I'm glad he sent you along to us. So tell me about this affair with Logan."

"General Logan gathered up a bunch of Kentuckians and led us to the Mad River towns."

"General Logan you say? He's only a colonel as far as I know." Colonel Harmar was quite sensitive about rank, figuring he ought to be a general himself.

"Kenton calls him a general. Not the kind of thing I'd know about."

"It doesn't matter. Tell me how many men did he have?"

"There was around nine hundred I would say. Don't rightly know the exact number. There was enough of us, and that's for sure."

"What can you tell me? Anything at all will be of interest."

"There weren't much of a battle. Most of the warriors were gone, off to fight Clark, I reckon. We hit Mackachack first. Burned both parts of the town, then the next day burned Pickaway, Wapatomica, McKee's Town, Blue Jacket's, and the Mingo Town. There were some others, but not many. We burned 'em and destroyed all the crops."

"What about losses, yours and theirs?" Harmar knew that secretary of war, Henry Knox, would be interested in such figures. He also knew the inclination of frontiersmen to exaggerate these numbers, but this man Wetzel didn't appear to be one who would do that.

"I think three of our men was killed and three wounded. I don't know how many of the Injuns was killed, but we took eleven scalps, all warriors." Wetzel paused for a moment, then added, "The General said we wasn't to harm no women or children."

"Well I'm glad to hear that," remarked the colonel. "Logan showed some good sense."

"There was a bunch of prisoners, about twenty-five women, I think, and two children," continued Wetzel. "Also there was four white women who'd been taken sometime before and one Frenchman."

"Where are these prisoners now?" asked Harmar.

"I believe they took 'em to Danville. I didn't go that far, but I think the general was hopin' to set up an exchange."

"When did the army leave from Limestone?"

"I ain't too good on dates, but I thought I heard Kenton say sixth of October. We was about fifteen days on the whole trip."

"Anything else of importance?"

"Well, one of the Injuns killed was the old Shawnee king, Moluntha."

"Moluntha you say?" Harmar was shocked. "He has been friendly to us. Was he fighting?"

"Well no, he didn't fight, and he didn't fly. He was a prisoner when he was killed."

"My God, my God. Did Logan order this killing?"

"No, the general was unhappy about it. The old chief was flying our flag and holdin' up some papers when he was captured. Simon says it was the Miami Treaty he was holdin'." Wetzel was not sure what more he should say. He knew the name of the killer but thought it best not to mention it. Harmar didn't ever ask that question.

"The chief was flyin' the thirteen stripes?"

"He was, I saw it myself."

"He assumed he was safe. What a tragedy."

The colonel watched Wetzel closely but saw no indication of what the hunter thought about this killing. He decided not to examine him further.

Wetzel remained silent.

"What do you know about General Clark?"

Harmar knew something of a campaign by Clark from the falls of the Ohio to the Wabash country.

"Not much. The word in Limestone was that he had got to Post St. Vincent, that there was a body of warriors waitin' for him. Four hundred of his men left him and went back to Kentucky. Don't know anymore than that."

"That sounds bad. I fear his push will be unsuccessful."

The news was discouraging, especially the story about the murder of Moluntha, for this was how Harmar regarded it. He called for Sergeant Shambough. "Sergeant, see that this man and his two friends have a place to sleep and something to eat."

Turning to Wetzel again, Harmar asked, "Where are you headed, Mr. Wetzel? Are you returning to Limestone?"

"No, sir," answered Lew quickly. "I'm headed to Wheeling. I think I said that before."

Harmar ignored this little put-down. "Well, I am sending a boat up the river the day after tomorrow under the command of Major Denny. You're welcome to go along. Much better than by horseback, I'm sure."

"But we have horses," noted Wetzel. "Is there room on the boat for them?"

"Afraid not," said the colonel. "But we can use some more horses here. We'll buy them from you."

"I'll think about it."

"All right, but go with the sergeant now. He'll take care of you and your friends for the night."

Wetzel left the room, and Harmar stood watching for several minutes.

"Damn," he said finally. "I'm afraid we're in for some big Indian trouble now. They won't take kindly to what has happened to old Moluntha."

14

REWARDS

April 25, 1787

IT HAD BEEN a very hard winter, and Little Fox was finally enjoying the spring weather. He watched as his friends Red Storm and Fire Heart emerged from the woods to join him at a grassy spot along the northern bank of Fishing Creek. They were part of a war party of some twenty-five braves who had established a camp along the Muskingum a ways below the old Delaware village of Coshocton.

This party was bent on finding and killing as many of the Long Knives as they could. Little Fox, Red Storm, and Fire Heart had undertaken a long tour of their own that had taken them deep into Virginia. They were returning now to the point where they had crossed the Ohio, intent on visiting a settler's cabin they had observed earlier. The attacks back in the previous fall by Logan's army had created a furious mind-set for revenge among many of the Indian tribes, not just the Shawnees, who had born the brunt of it.

The story of the killing of the old chief Moluntha had spread like wildfire through the Indian towns. Although Little Fox's village at New Coshocton had been spared the burning and destruction, it was soon overrun with refugees; and as winter set in, the food supplies had dwindled to nothing. Fortunately, Fire Heart had located his family, which had fled to safety at New Coshocton. Within a few weeks, Red Storm had suggested they all return to his home village on the upper Sandusky. In

December, word had come of an Indian council to be held at the Wyandot villages near Detroit.

Little Fox had been determined to go, and he talked his two friends into going along. They took their families with them, unwilling to face again the type of homecoming of the previous summer. The time spent in the villages along the Detroit River had been very interesting. Many of the leading chiefs from a variety of tribes were there, along with the Indian agents McKee and Elliott, as well as Simon Girty, who came from his new home in Canada just across the river.

The council itself was held in the Wyandot village on the Canadian side. Little Fox had made the acquaintance of a French trader named Baptiste Ariome, who reminded him of his friend LeClerk. The Frenchman had with him a young American named James Moore, who had been captured by the Shawnees and eventually purchased by Ariome. As they talked one day, the trader mentioned that young Moore was looking for his sister, who he heard had been captured during the summer and brought to the Mad River towns.

"Yes, I know of this girl," Little Fox had replied. "She came here in the same group as I did."

This information excited Ariome, and he immediately asked, "Where is she now? James and I wish to find her. Tell me all you know of her."

Although Little Fox was not inclined to do anything to please one of the Long Knives, he did proceed to explain to Ariome what he knew of the girl, who, he was quick to point out, was surely less than ten years old. Some of what he knew had come from Fire Heart, for the girl, along with her mother and a sister, had been brought to Wapatomica. A Shawnee war party had gone deep into Virginia to attack the home of this family. The father had been killed along with another son and infant daughter along the way. The young girl, Mary, had been taken in for awhile by Moluntha himself, but her mother and sister did not fare so well.

While in the Shawnee town of Wapatomica, some Cherokees had taken advantage of the fact that many of the Shawnees were engaged in a drunken orgy and burned the mother and sister at the stake. After this, Mary had stayed with another Shawnee and was brought along to Detroit. Looking for money to buy liquor, the Shawnee sold the girl to an American named Stockwell. It was thought that the man Stockwell, who had remained loyal to the British, may be living in Frenchtown.

Little Fox had felt himself defiled at having to divulge so much information to a white man, especially at having to report such foul behavior by his friends, the Shawnees. He deplored the drinking habits, which led to such actions, although he blamed the whites for having introduced the filthy rum, as he thought of it, in the first place. But the French trader had been very good to him and his family, making sure they had plenty to eat. Ariome was overjoyed and hurried to pass the information to Moore. Little Fox had also decided to take the opportunity to go north to visit his home village.

There were a number of Chippewas living in the area of Brownstown, on the Detroit side of the river, and he had tried to find someone who might know his father. Failing this, he decided to go and see for himself. Bright Moon had declined to go along for the child was ill, and she did not relish any more traveling. The trip had been uneventful, although it brought back the memories from his journey more than five years earlier when he had left his father's lodge to undertake his own battle against the white men. He recalled his father's words that they would never see each other again. "I will show him now that he was wrong," Little Fox recalled saying to himself. "He will be surprised!"

Unfortunately, when he reached the Saginaw River, the young brave found that the home village was no longer where he had remembered it. The disappointment was keen, but then he supposed he should not have been surprised. He continued down the river until he found a Chippewa village not far from where the river emptied into Saginaw Bay. He soon learned that some of the people were from his old town, and one of the first that he encountered was Wild Buffalo, the father of his friend Red Bird.

Overjoyed, Little Fox had embraced the elderly man. "Wild Buffalo, I am so glad to find you. Do you remember who I am?"

Stepping back and pushing a short distance away, the old man looked up and down at the figure in front of him, finally nodding in recognition. "Yes, you are Little Fox. You have been away many winters."

"It is true. It was Red Bird who showed me where to go. Is he here now?"

"My son, Red Bird, was killed over four summers ago in a battle against the white devil, Clark."

"I am sorry to hear that. Another reason for killing the Long Knives."

Little Fox had turned away from the sadness in the old man's face, and then back again. "My father, Black Wolf. Do you know where he is?"

Little Fox was not surprised by Wild Buffalo's news. "Black Wolf died two winters ago with a very bad fever."

The realization that he was all that was left of his childhood family had filled him with an overwhelming sadness. "There is nothing left for me here now, I see," he had said to the old man.

He left the next day to return to his wife waiting for him at Brownstown.

Red Storm shouted at Little Fox, beckoning him to follow into the woods to join Fire Heart and the others. Fire Heart, who was the oldest, had assumed leadership for the little party, which included Little Fox, Red Storm, and two Cherokee braves named Bloody Knife and Dark Warrior. Little Fox was glad to have the Cherokees along, for their hatred of the whites matched his own. In recent times, many of the Delawares and Wyandots had favored peace with the white men, a stance that was strongly disapproved by both Little Fox and Red Storm.

The two Cherokees had not been along at the beginning. They had joined when Little Fox discovered them, along with one other, coming down the Cheat River, not far above its junction with Big Sandy Creek. When Little Fox explained that they were planning an attack on a settler's cabin back near the Ohio, Bloody Knife and Dark Warrior were quick to agree to come along. The third Cherokee was a chief named Grey Bear. He had little to say and was not interested in coming along with the rest of them. Bloody Knife explained that the chief regarded himself as a man with powerful medicine and was bitter that his people had rejected him. He intended to go on alone, looking for a place where he could meditate without interruption.

"Let us leave him," Bloody Knife had said. "He is nothing but trouble anyway."

They had left the Cheat at that point and reaching the valley of White Day Creek, crossed the Monongahela near the mouth of what the white men called Indian Creek. Proceeding up that creek to its source, they crossed the ridges to the west and came to the North Fork of Fishing Creek, following it down to their current location.

The terrain reminded Little Fox of their adventures in the previous summer, although he knew it was not the same creek. There was no clear path through these woods, but it was thought that traveling too close to the stream might lead to discovery. In many places, there was no choice, for the high-wooded hills enclosed the stream on both sides.

It was late afternoon when the smell of wood smoke announced the presence of the target they had noted on the way in. They angled back toward the creek until they came to a cleared area. At its far edge stood a lone cabin, a puff of smoke curling above the chimney and dispersing in the light southerly breeze. A man was in a small-plowed field bending low, planting his corn. A woman stood at a tub near the front stoop, washing clothes. Nearby, a young boy played in the dirt.

Fire Heart and Little Fox exchanged glances, nodding in agreement. Without speaking, they both saw that now was the time to attack, as the cabin's inhabitants were out in the open. No need to wait for morning, which was a common tactic. With a motion of his hand, Fire Heart indicated to the two Cherokees that they should circle around the clearing and get into position to prevent anyone escaping into the cabin. Little Fox and Red Storm went in the other direction, finding a place behind some bushes near the open field and not far from where the man was working. It was plain that Fire Heart would begin the attack by shooting the white man.

In only a few moments, everyone was in place, and Fire Heart raised his weapon and fired. His bullet tore into the ground just in front of where the man was kneeling. Startled, the planter raised up just in time to be hit by a shot from the rifle of Little Fox. Red Storm was already running to the spot, intent on finishing the job with his tomahawk. As soon as the first shot rang out, Bloody Knife sprang from his hiding place and killed the woman with one quick blow from his tomahawk. Her body fell against the tub, knocking it over with water and clothes spilling everywhere. Dark Warrior came from behind the cabin to grab the little boy, holding the boy's arms tight and raising the body high above his own head, as if to dash it against the nearby tree stump. The boy began to kick and scream, which brought a laugh from his captor, who suddenly lowered him and slung him under his arm as if he were holding a bag of grain. He cuffed the boy hard in the face, trying to shut him up. He laughed out loud as he watched Bloody Knife finish lifting the scalp of the woman. "If this boy ever stops screaming, I will take him with us. He will make me a fine slave."

"Well, he'd better stop that noise, or I will shut him up forever," responded Bloody Knife.

They were joined now by the other three who had run across the plowed field, Red Storm carrying his bloody trophy.

Fire Heart pointed to the cabin. "Is there anyone inside?"

"I will see," said Bloody Knife, who quickly turned back and entered the cabin.

They heard a cry and then a loud thump. The warrior appeared again at the door and threw to the ground the body of a small baby. The head was caved in and gushing blood.

"Not anymore," said Bloody Knife with a laugh.

In spite of himself, Little Fox was sickened by this sight. He thought it was probably necessary, but he had never grown used to the killing of babies and children. Standing now beside his captor, the little boy's eyes were wide with horror and fright, but he seemed to know that it was better for him if he kept quiet. The little cabin rested on a small knoll that sloped down toward the creek some fifty yards below. The Indians found a cow and horse grazing among a small stand of birch trees close by the bank of the stream.

"Kill the cow," ordered Fire Heart. "We will have fresh meat for our supper. Tonight we will sleep in this lodge and take the horse back with us tomorrow."

This met with great approval by the others, for the wind had changed and a light rain had begun to fall.

April 26, 1787

The afternoon was fading as the two hunters made their way along the left bank of the Cheat River. The tangled bushes and stands of twisted cottonwoods had made the going difficult for the horses, so the men were leading them along this part of the trail. The larger of the two brothers who was leading had stopped, lifting his face and sniffing at something in the light breeze. When Jacob began to ask a question, he was quickly silenced by his brother's upraised hand. Standing motionless for a moment, Lewis Wetzel finally turned to his companion, whispering softly. "I smell wood smoke, Jake. Comin' from upriver."

"I can't smell nothin' but this damned horse," answered Jacob, keeping his voice down.

"Well, it's wood smoke all right. Somebody's got a fire goin', and we ain't close to no settler's cabin that I know about."

"Hell, Lew, what do you know about the country round here? This ain't your usual stompin' grounds."

"We've visited Sis down here before, and I don't remember any white men livin' along this part of the river."

Jacob shrugged, knowing it was no use arguing with Lew. "So what do you think then. It could just be some hunters out who made a night camp."

"I reckon it could, but there's other possibilities too. You stay here with the horses. I'm goin' to find out who it is. We're not far from where the Big Sandy comes in. That would be a natural spot for a night camp."

"Why don't we both go?" suggested Jacob.

"'Cause one man'll make less noise. Stay here and off the trail. I'll be back afore you know it."

Lew handed the reins of his horse to Jacob and disappeared into the woods. It always amazed Jacob even as well as he knew his brother how Lewis could slip away so quickly and quietly. The brothers had left home two days earlier, having decided to visit their sister, Christiana, and as a bonus, avoid helping Martin at a busy time on the farm.

Christiana had married Jacob Wolfe several years earlier, and the two had eventually settled on a place near where Muddy Creek entered the Cheat River. It was a long way from the homeplace on Wheeling Creek but not far off the well-traveled trail that led to the settlements on the south fork of the Potomac, where the family had lived prior to coming to Wheeling Creek.

Lewis and Jacob had spent the previous night with their relatives near the mouth of Dunkard Creek and, earlier in this day, had crossed the Monongahela and followed the Cheat River down to the current location. Jacob was annoyed at having been left to hold the horses, but he was looking forward to seeing his sister and her family, which now included little Jacob, aged three, and the baby, Sallie, who was about one. He was especially fond of Jacob, who he liked to think had been named after him, even though he knew it was more likely that the boy was named for his father.

Having drifted into a deep sleep, Jacob awoke with a start, first noting with relief that the two horses had not strayed but were standing patiently in the small glade just a few feet away. His brother stood just three feet away holding a leafy branch, which Jacob realized had been brushed across his face in order to awaken him.

"By God, Jake," said Lew in a loud whisper, "I'm glad them horses didn't know you was sleepin'. They might of been a mile away by now."

"I wasn't asleep very long," protested Jacob.

"Long enough," said Lew.

"What did you find out?" asked Jacob, anxious to change the subject.

"It's an Injun camp," said Lew, "but I only saw one there. I couldn't find no sign of any others, but I suppose there could be, and he's waitin on 'em to come in."

"So what are we goin' to do about it?"

"We're gonna go up there and watch to see if any others come in. When the right time comes, I reckon we'll reduce the Injun population a bit."

"Where is the camp?"

"It's right in the neck between the Cheat and the Big Sandy. No more'n a mile up river."

"So we'll have to cross the Cheat to get at the camp?"

"By God, Jake, I never knew you was that smart." Lew couldn't suppress a laugh. "We'll cross here and lead the horses up to within a half mile or so. We'll leave them there and go the rest of the way on foot."

"Hell, Lew, why don't we just go around and head on down to Wolfe's. That's what we came for anyway."

"We can't leave this bastard just sittin' there, Jake. We don't know what he's up to. Mebbe he's heading up river too and figurin' on some mischief at one of the cabins. He might even be after Christiana's place."

"Not if we're there, he won't," said Jacob. He knew that his arguments were hopeless.

"Sis doesn't even know we're comin', so it don't matter if we get there later tomorrow. It's too far to go tonight anyway."

"Well, your blood is up, so I know I ain't goin' to convince you," admitted Jacob. He walked over to get the horses. "Where should we cross this river?"

"There's some shallow rapids just up the way. We'll cross there."

After crossing the Cheat, they left the horses in a wooded glen on the banks of a little run some distance from the river. They made their way through the woods in the dark until they could see into the camp, dimly lit by the small fire. A lonely figure sat by the fire with his back to the juncture of the two streams, the Big Sandy emptying into the bigger Cheat River from a northeasterly direction.

"He ain't movin'," observed Jacob. "You reckon he's asleep sittin' up?"

"Could be," allowed Lew. "You're pretty good at doin' that yourself."

"Hell, can't you let that be?" Jacob's voice had risen to a level above what Lew thought was acceptable.

"Shsss. You'll have him awake for sure."

"Let's just take him right now and be done with it," argued Jacob, picking up his rifle, which had been stashed against a tree.

"Not now," said Lew, putting his hand on his brother's arm, and pushing the gun away. "I want to see if there are others comin' in. Don't want to scare 'em off."

"Well, I hope they don't come in behind and scare us off."

"They ain't likely to come in on us from up here." Lew had placed them partway up on the side of a hill, which sloped away from the camp. "Here, chew on this awhile, then get some sleep. I'll take the first watch."

Jacob took the piece of dried venison that Lewis handed him and sat back against a wide tree trunk. There was a bit of a chill in the air, and Jacob was wishing they had just gone on and spent the night in Christiana's warm snug cabin. He was glad for the blanket he had brought along; and after finishing the venison, he pulled the blanket over himself and soon fell asleep.

Dawn came with Jacob watching carefully for any sign of life from below them. Lewis was sleeping soundly next to him, having traded places sometime in the night. Proud of himself that he hadn't fallen asleep this time, Jacob was glad to wake his brother with a rough shake. Lewis came awake without any sound and quickly rose to his feet.

"Has our boy accumulated any friends during the night, Jake?"

"Nary a one," answered Jacob. "But he's awake all right. Looks to me like he's prayin' or something."

"I reckon he is, and it's good cause he's about to meet his maker."

"Seems a shame somehow, Lew. He ain't hurtin' nobody, and God did create him, I guess."

"Hell, Jake, he's an Injun. God made skeeters too, and you don't mind killin' them."

"Well, it ain't the same as killin' a skeeter."

"Reckon you're right about that. I think we better take him with a 'hawk since a gunshot might attract unfriendly guests."

After a short discussion between the two, Jacob made his way around to the opposite side so that he could approach the unsuspecting Indian from out of the rising sun. Lewis eased down to a spot behind a big maple and only a few feet from where the intended victim, Grey Bear, was now trying to resurrect the fire from a few live coals remaining from the night before. The plan was for Jacob to provide a distraction while Lewis rushed in to deal the killing blow. It worked to perfection, for the chief jumped to his feet and turned, squinting into the sun to see what was making the noise. Lewis bounded from behind the tree with a loud yell as he swung his tomahawk in a high arc, crashing it down on the right side of Grey Bear's face and neck. The stricken man slumped to the ground, dead by the time he had fully landed.

"You've kilt him for sure," shouted Jacob as Lewis stepped back to avoid the blood spurting from the severed artery.

"I reckon I did, Jake. You take his scalp while I go back for our horses."

"Whoa," exclaimed Jacob. "I ain't never took no scalp before."

"Well, it's time you did then," said his brother, already disappearing among the trees.

"Damn it all. It's his kill. Why should I be the one to do the scalping?"

Annoyed with his brother and muttering to himself, Jacob took out his hunting knife and set about the task of removing the topknot. It wasn't easy, but he managed to do it, noting the long tuft of hair interwoven with silk and silver beads. He shook it out as best he could and used Grey Bear's hunting shirt to wipe off the blood from the skin side. He found a string in the dead man's pouch, poked a hole in the scalp, and looped the string through the hole so that the scalp could be easily carried. He began to feel some pride in his work and was standing there admiring it when Lewis returned with the horses.

"I see you got the job done, Jake," noted Lewis as he rummaged through the chief's belongings, looking for anything of value. He settled on a blanket and an old musket along with some powder and balls.

"Why do we take scalps anyway, Lew?" asked Jacob as he watched his brother. "It's kind of a messy business."

"We do it because they do it to us. And it's an insult, I suppose. It's hard to be a hero in the happy huntin' ground if you ain't got no scalp." Lewis grinned at Jacob. "Besides, it's a way to prove what you did."

"Well, I didn't do the killin'. You did."

"Your part was just as important. Anyway, let's get movin'. I'm ready for some of Sis's good eats."

Lewis tied the blanket up behind the saddle and stuffed the ammunition into his pouch. He handed the gun to Jacob. "Here, stick this in your sling if you can. It ain't much of a weapon, but maybe Wolfe can make use of it."

Lewis had never thought too highly of Jacob Wolfe, Christiana's husband.

They splashed across the Big Sandy Creek, which was shallow and narrow and began to move along the right bank of the Cheat.

"How far do you reckon it is up to Christiana's place from here, Lew?"

"I'd say six or seven miles."

"Shouldn't take us too long then." Jacob was feeling pretty hungry.

"Well, I want us to look around some on the way. I'm goin' to cross back to the other side. I ain't convinced that bugger was all by himself."

It wasn't long after Lewis had crossed to the western side of the river that he pulled his horse to a stop and dismounted. Something had caught his eye, and he stopped to examine what he now saw was a clear imprint of a footprint in the soft mud a few feet in from the river's edge. He looked across to see if he could spot his brother who was riding slowly down the other shore. Jacob was not visible, and Lew decided not to shout. Instead, he pushed into the woods near where he had seen the print. He quickly found evidence of what he guessed was the passage of at least three or four humans.

"Red devils for sure," he said aloud softly.

He followed a trail along a small run that cut through the low hills that rose above the valley along the river. He found more sign, enough to convince him that this party was moving to the west and no longer posed a danger to him or to his sister and her family. He returned to where his horse had been left standing, but did not mount. He led the horse along the bank, watching to make sure there was no more Indian sign. After walking for more than a mile, Lew saw his brother reappear in a grassy opening on the opposite side of the river.

"There you are," shouted Jacob. "I was wonderin' what happened to you."

"Be still," cautioned Lew. "There are more of the devils around here. I saw signs of a party headed out to the west. Keep a sharp eye out on your side too."

April 27, 1787

The two brothers continued their journey on parallel paths along the river, both walking now and searching for any new sign. After an hour, they were close to their destination. Lewis recrossed the river, which was deeper here, and he was forced to urge his mount to swim through the current. He joined Jacob on the east side of the Cheat, just short of where a murky stream emptied into the river. The stream was lined on both sides with an assortment of trees and bushes; and beyond it, an open meadow with a covering of grass brought to a healthy green by the spring rains.

"This is Muddy Creek," said Lew.

"Don't know why they call it Muddy," Jacob noted with a laugh. "It's mighty clear up the way a bit where it tumbles down over the rocks."

The stream was wide at the mouth, so the two men led the horses upstream a ways before crossing at a shallow spot. More than a quarter mile upstream they could see the cabin on a low hill above the creek. Smoke was coming from the chimney at the far end.

"Looks like they're awake and maybe fixin' breakfast," said Jacob, who mounted his horse and urged him into a fast trot.

"Better be careful, little brother. Wolfe might take you for an Injun and spoil your breakfast real quick."

They made it to the cabin without incident, and their shouts of hello were met by the emergence of a young woman who stood on the front stoop with a big smile.

"Well, I'll be," said Christiana. "If you two ain't a sight fer sore eyes. Get down here and give your sister a big kiss."

"You may want to wait on that," said Lew. "We don't smell too good, I'm thinkin'."

Christiana laughed. "On second thought, I believe you're right, Lewis. So come on in then, little Jake will be glad to see you."

"You got any thing we can feed these horses?" asked Lew.

"Sure, take 'em round back to the little shed. There's some hay there they can eat."

"That's your job, Jake," said Lew, smiling at the sour look his little brother gave him. "But hurry up cause I'm mighty hungry, and I'll bet Sis has some fresh biscuits or something for her two favorite brothers."

"As a matter of fact, I do, and you can slather 'em with some fresh maple syrup. There's a little salt pork to go along with too. You're lucky you came today. I guess I must have known you was comin' somehow, so I suppose you are my two favorite brothers today. The others ain't here to defend themselves."

Little three-year-old Jacob came running from the far end of the cabin and jumped into Lew's arms.

"Uncle Lew, Uncle Lew. What you got for me?"

"Well, now," said Lew, giving the boy a hug and setting him down on his feet. "What makes you think I got something for you?"

"Cause you always do," exclaimed the boy.

"Let me see," said Lew, reaching into his pouch and pulling out a small wooden whistle he had fashioned for just this purpose.

Little Jacob took it and immediately began to blow on it.

"Thanks a lot for that," laughed Christiana. "Just what we need around here, more noise."

"I try to be helpful, Sis. Now who do we have here?" said Lew as he walked over to where a baby girl stood unsteadily against the side of the cradle in which she was standing. "This must be my little Sallie." Reaching again into his pouch, Lew pulled out a small piece of red ribbon. He had found it among Grey Bear's belongings and knew it might be just the thing for his young niece. He put it in her little hand, and it went immediately to her mouth. Lew retrieved it and placed it on top of her head.

Christiana was touched at this sight. She knew her brother's reputation, and yet his thoughtfulness and gentleness with children was remarkable. She walked over and took the ribbon. "Very nice, Lewis. I'll fix it so it stays in her hair."

The soft moment was broken by the noisy entrance of Jacob coming in from feeding the horses. "Hey, Sis," he shouted. "I've got a present for you."

He kept his right hand behind his back.

"A present for me? Why, Jake, how nice. What is it?"

Grinning widely, Jacob tossed Grey Bear's scalp to the floor at her feet.

"Oh my God," cried Christiana, jumping back. "What is that?"

"Why it's an Injun scalp, freshly taken. Took it myself."

"Jake, you idiot," said Lew, aghast at what his brother had done. "You oughta have more sense than that." After a moment he added, "That's more like somethin' Sis would expect me to do."

Chagrined at the reaction, Jacob stooped down and picked up the scalp.

He held it up and pointed to the shiny beads. "Hell, I was just havin' some fun. I thought you'd like these decorations on it."

Having recovered from the shock, Christiana tried to ease the tension.

"It's all right, Jake. It just surprised me, that's all. Sit down, both of you now, and I'll get you some biscuits."

Jacob stepped back through the door and hung the scalp on a small peg protruding from the side of the cabin. He came back in and greeted both children before sitting.

"Where'd you git that whistle?" he asked little Jake, who was still playing with his new toy.

"From Uncle Lew," the boy answered. "Ain't it swell?"

"I guess it is for sure," said Jacob, suddenly ashamed that he hadn't thought to bring presents for the children. He walked over and planted a kiss on the top of Sallie's head, then sat at the table without further talk.

"Where is that no good husband of yours, Sis?" asked Lew, his mouth still half full of biscuit and syrup.

Christiana laughed. "My good husband is up north on the ridge helping the Watsons build a new cabin."

"Well, he needs to be here," said Lew emphatically. "The Injuns are out and about. We took that scalp just a few miles down the Cheat, and I found tracks of three or four others. It ain't safe for you here by yourself."

"Well, we're lookin' at findin' some land up there, closer to other settlers. He should be home tonight or tomorrow at the latest."

"Jacob, I intend to go back and follow that trail I found. I want you to stay here with Christiana and the kids until Wolfe gets home."

"I need to go with you, Lew," argued Jacob.

"No, you're needed here. I reckon Sis can find you a nice soft place to sleep. It won't be all bad."

"Ain't you goin' to spend the day and night here, Lewis?" asked Christiana. "You just got here."

"I'd like to, Christy, but them reds is up to no good. Maybe I can catch up to 'em before it happens."

"No use arguin' with him, Sis," laughed Jacob. "He's more stubborn than any mule you ever saw."

"I reckon he's right," admitted Lew. "This is the best food I've had in a long time. How about givin' me a chunk of that salt pork. I'll take it with me."

When they had finished eating, Lew prepared to go on the trail again. Christiana fixed him a small bag with salt pork and a couple of the biscuits. "Be careful, Lewis," she cautioned. "I don't want some devil gettin' that beautiful hair of yours."

"I'm always careful, Sis. Jacob, I'm gonna leave my horse with you. I think it will be easier following that trail on foot. You can bring both horses back home when you come." Smiling, he reached into his carrying pouch and pulled out the tassels, fishing them through the holes in his earlobes and securing them.

"Lewis, what is that?" Christiana was surprised to see Lewis wearing tassels in his ears. "You look like an Injun yourself, or maybe a French trader."

"Well, if I can't kill 'em, mebbe I'll skeer 'em to death."

With his rifle slung under his arm, Lew waved his good-byes and moved off quickly down the creek.

April 29, 1787

Red Storm was exhilarated. Along with his five new companions, he stood at the edge of the woods alongside a small run that tumbled down between two high ridges before ending at the north fork of Fishing Creek. In the valley between was an open clearing in the center of which stood a lonely cabin. They had been watching the cabin for more than an hour when Red Storm turned to the group's leader, a tall Shawnee named Bald Rock.

"There does not seem to be a man at this place," said Red Storm.

"No, we have seen only the two girls. The man and woman might both still be inside." Bald Rock continued to stare at the cabin's front door.

"It would seem strange if that were so," said Red Storm. "The sun is high, and the white man is usually working in his field on such a day."

"We have seen no grown woman either," noted Bald Rock.

"Let us take the girls as captives and move on," argued Red Storm. He watched as the two young white girls chased each other around a wide tree stump, one that had been too large to root out. The girls looked to be much the same age, and he thought they might be twins. The stump was only about ten yards in front of the cabin door and more than fifty yards from where the Indians were hiding.

"They would be able to get inside the cabin before we can get to them," said Bald Rock, "which makes their capture more difficult."

"One of us can circle around and come in from the back side. They will not see us until it is too late."

"There must be a man or woman inside the cabin."

"There might be a woman, but no man, I think," insisted Red Storm. "We will have the girls before it is even known we are here. If there is someone in the hut, we can easily take care of them. I will go around and come in from behind."

Not waiting for an answer, Red Storm moved up alongside the little stream until he had gone past where the clearing ended. It was easy to move through the trees to a spot directly behind the cabin, although the distance to the cabin was more than twice what it was from where Bald Rock and the others waited. Red Storm noted that there was a small window in the back side of the cabin and a low shed only a few steps behind it. Although the grass was tall, he would be visible from that window for part of the way. He crept out into the clear, bending as low as possible, advancing at a slow walk. He supposed he should be crawling to avoid detection, but the ground was wet in places, and he decided that speed was more important than stealth.

The excitement built in Red Storm as he moved through the grass. He had grown to love these moments just before an attack, and he was glad now that he had decided to come along with Bald Rock and his warriors. He had tried to talk Fire Heart and Little Fox into continuing their raid even after the killings four days earlier. But that party had decided it was time to return to the base camp, especially since they had a captive.

On the way back from Virginia, they had encountered Bald Rock's party on the way in. Red Storm saw the chance to participate in more attacks, and he had asked to come along.

Bald Rock was happy to have another hand, especially after he learned that Red Storm had some knowledge of the land they were entering.

Almost before he knew it, Red Storm had reached the back of the small shed. He moved around to the far end of the cabin and up to where he could see the girls, still innocently playing near the stump. Stepping out into the open, he gave a shout and waved to Bald Rock. The two girls looked at him in shock, then began screaming and running directly toward Fishing Creek.

Red Storm quickly overtook them, but they split as he came near and began to run in opposite directions. He easily caught the one running to his left, confident that Bald Rock and friends would catch the other. It was all over in less than a minute. There had been no interference from inside the cabin. The girls had stopped their screaming and were now quietly sobbing.

"These girls will be fine helpers in our village," said Bald Rock, handing both over to two of the other braves.

"I would rather have two scalps," said Red Storm. "We'd better see what's inside."

As he turned toward the door, a shot rang out and the ball whizzed by Red Storm's shoulder and into the cabin just to the right of the door jam, about halfway up. The sound of the shot was followed by a loud yell from a good distance upstream. The six Indians made a rush for the woods from which they had come, dragging the two girls with them. It wasn't long before there was a second gunshot. Upon reaching the woods, the six braves stopped for a moment.

"Let us go quickly," shouted Bald Rock. "We don't know how many there are. Let us take our captives and go home."

Red Storm wanted to argue but gave up on it. He raised his gun and pointed it in the direction from which he had heard the yelling, firing without seeing a real target. He then turned and ran after the others.

Lew Wetzel had been following cold tracks for two days. After leaving his sister's place, he had rediscovered the place on the west bank of the Cheat River where he had found the Indian sign the previous day and managed to follow the trail to a point near where he assumed the party had crossed the Monongahela, close to the mouth of Whiteday Creek. He had spent the night there after rejecting his first thought of going to Prickett's Fort, which was not far away. He continued the next day, finding the trail again along Indian Creek. He had wondered about the route, for it seemed to him not the best or quickest way to get to the Ohio. "This bunch has got some other ideas, I'm thinkin'."

It had caused him great difficulty, but he had found where the Indians had struck out across the ridges, angling a bit to the south, and he followed until he came to a creek that was a bit more substantial than the multitude of streams and tiny runs that had been encountered most recently. "I wonder if this is Fishing Creek?" he asked himself. Indeed it was the north fork of that creek, although Wetzel had not ever been on this part of it, as far as he knew.

He traveled along the north bank for another mile or two before stopping for the night. Fatigue had set in, and he had given up any hope of finding this raiding party before they had crossed the Ohio. He slept later than usual on the next morning and then resumed his trek. It wasn't long until he stopped, having stepped across a tiny stream flowing down from the right. He stared intently at the ground among the weeds and vines along the bank of fishing Creek.

"What is this?" he said aloud. "These are new tracks."

The new tracks had suddenly appeared, and they were fresh. It was clear to the tracker that another party had crossed here from the other side of the creek and had begun to move downstream. A heavily wooded ridge began here, sloping up to the right and widening. The tracks turned toward the creek and disappeared. Puzzled, Wetzel stood still for a moment, wondering what to do. "They've crossed the creek again. Strange behavior!"

It was then that he heard the screaming. He pushed through the brush along the bank to an opening through which he could see the clearing and the log cabin. He could see the figures well enough to know it was likely the party whose tracks he had just found; and though he could not see who was screaming, he could tell that someone was being held behind two of the warriors. He raised his rifle and fired toward the cabin door. The distance was too great for a shot well-aimed. He quickly reloaded, doing so as he moved to his right a few yards.

"Maybe they'll think there's more than one of us," he grunted as he snapped off a second shot. He moved further along the base of the ridge when the answering shot came. He stood for a moment watching the Indians retreating into the far woods. His inclination was to rush to the house to see whether there were any survivors. But he was cautious, realizing that if the enemy warriors chose to stand and fight, he would be at a serious disadvantage. "At least I've kept 'em from burning the place," he said with some satisfaction.

He edged further up along the tree line until the cabin and shed were between where he stood and where the Indians had disappeared among the trees. He figured the devils had taken at least one captive, and he resolved to follow, hoping for a chance at a rescue. However, he had to be patient and wait for his chance. After watching for another fifteen minutes, he eased out in the clearing, making his way toward the cabin.

"Mister, mister," came a voice from out of the woods behind him and to his right. "Wait for me. Don't leave me."

Wetzel stopped and turned in the direction of the sound. He was astonished to see a woman step into the clear, pulling on a rope attached to a scraggly red cow. "What the hell," exclaimed Lew. "Who are you?"

As bad as the cow looked, the woman seemed worse. Her eyes were red, her hair was tangled, and the dress she wore was dirty and torn, hanging loosely from her body. She had no shoes, and her feet were bleeding. She did not answer his question but stared toward the buildings. Her face took on a vacant look. The cow, disinterested in the proceedings, tried eating the tall grass.

Wetzel moved toward her, and she tugged at the rope. "Must get the cow in the shed," she said.

In spite of her appearance, Wetzel could see that she had at one time been quite pretty. He felt an attraction to her that was unexpected. "Ma'am," he began gingerly. "Did they take your children?"

He had been able to see that the warriors had two children with them as they went into the woods. He could also see that the woman was not in full possession of her senses.

"Had to get the cow," the woman said finally. "She ran off. Had to get her."

Lew put his arm around her shoulder and took the rope from her. "We've got the cow all right, ma'am. Is there anyone in the house?"

She slumped against him but said nothing. She was crying. They made their way to the little shed with no more words. Wetzel opened the door and led the cow inside. A pile of hay stood behind a wooden barrier near a low trough, and Lew pulled some of the hay into the trough so the cow could easily reach it. The woman had followed him in, and she stood watching.

"Had to get the cow," she said again.

Feeling very uneasy, Wetzel tried to get some information from the woman. He did not know how to deal with someone in this condition. He wanted to get on with trailing the marauders and trying to recover the captives. This is what he knew how to do, and he thought it would still be easy to catch up with them when they camped for the night. Whenever he suggested that he should move on, the woman clung to him and begged him not to go. However, she would not answer his questions at all.

He took her arm, after a time in the shed, and led her around to the front door of the cabin. Lewis was still wondering where the man of the house was and half expected to find him dead inside the house. Once inside, though, he could see that the raiders had never got in. Everything was in its place, and there was no man there. The fireplace was directly opposite the door, and he was surprised at the furnishings. On the right side, there was a large four-poster, quite unlike the usual built-in bunks that were common in many of the settler's homes. A chest with four drawers stood next to the bed, and a smaller bed was in the opposite corner. To the left of the fireplace stood a table and four three-legged stools while at the far end, snug against the wall, there was a daybed covered with a black and red quilt. Two small rag dolls lay on the floor in front, with clothes and coats hung on pegs around the walls.

This woman spent some money for all these things, thought Wetzel, *I wonder where her man is?* He had asked this question of the woman several times but as yet had received no answer. A wooden bucket stood on the low ledge just to the side of the fireplace with a wooden dipper lying next to it. The woman looked at Wetzel and then went to the bucket, filling the dipper and handing it to him, indicating with a nod that he should drink. Realizing that his mouth was very dry, Wetzel took the dipper from her and drank, wondering as he did so where she got the water. There must be a spring close by, he assumed. The water tasted good.

"Thank you, ma'am. You should have a drink too." He filled the dipper himself and handed it to her.

She drank it greedily. She knelt in front of the fireplace and lifted an inverted kettle from off a small pile of ashes. A tiny puff of smoke greeted her. Wetzel was impressed. She had kept the fire alive by covering it with the kettle, an object he had heard called a curfew. She looked up at him, her facial expression pleading with him to help. He understood at once and went outside and to the back of the cabin where there was a very small pile of wood. He picked up as much as he could carry and took it inside, where he piled it next to the open hearth.

"Your wood is almost gone," he said to the woman, who was stirring the coals to free up some live embers and placing fresh pieces of wood on top. "I'll chop some more for you."

Although he was very anxious to get on the trail, he realized that he must do this chore before going. He found an axe near the now-depleted woodpile and a chopping block at the side of the shed. Several short logs were lying next to it, which saved him from going into the woods to find more. He spent more than two hours chopping the logs into pieces suitable for burning in the fireplace. The afternoon was more than half spent, and he was sweating profusely when he returned to the house. "There's enough chopped to keep you goin' for a week or two now," Wetzel informed the woman as he came through the door.

She stood at the table crying and mixing something in a small pan. The fire was blazing.

"Can you just tell me your name?" he asked for what he supposed must have been about the tenth time. She stared at the pan and said nothing.

"Well, I guess I'll be goin' then," he announced. "I aim to catch them varmints and get your little ones back for you."

"No, no," she cried, dropping the spoon in her hand and rushing to him, grabbing him by the arm. "No, stay with me."

Wetzel could think of nothing to say at first. It dawned on him that leaving her here by herself was not a good thing. He could take her along, he supposed, but that was not something that appealed to him either. The worst option was to stay here with her.

"Esther," she whispered, looking away.

"Esther. Is that your name?"

"Esther," she said again very quietly.

"I'll stay a little longer," he said. "But if I wait too long, I won't catch them Injuns."

She looked at him now, an entreaty in her eyes that he could not withstand. His resolve melted, and he felt a stirring inside, something more than just pity and compassion. It was clear that she intended for him to spend the night with her.

"All right, I'll stay."

Relief showed on her face, and she reached up and tenderly touched his cheek. He felt a sudden self-consciousness about the pockmarks, the remnants of his childhood smallpox. Embarrassed, he went back outside for a few moments, then returned with another armload of wood. Nothing more was said between them.

She prepared a meal consisting of the corn pone, which she had baked in a small oven formed from an iron pot. She covered the corn pone with maple syrup and produced some salt pork along with a jug of sweet cider. Wetzel could not remember a meal he had enjoyed more. It was well past dark now, and Wetzel sat at the table watching as Esther went about the after supper cleanup. In spite of what he thought was her madness, she went about the mundane tasks in a natural manner. Suddenly she turned to him.

"He had only one ear." The statement was made in a matter-of-fact manner, but it was shocking to Wetzel's ears.

"Who had one ear?" he asked after a short interval.

She raised her left hand and covered her left ear. She removed the hand slowly. "Gone," she whispered.

Wetzel stood up, staring at Esther, and shaking his head. "One of the Indians?"

She nodded almost imperceptibly.

Wetzel wondered how she could have been close enough to see that an ear was missing. Could it be his sworn enemy, the one whom Le Clerk had said was determined to kill him? Entirely possible, he realized, but he could also see that he would learn nothing more that was useful from Esther, for she was softly crying again. It would be interesting, though, if he were able to catch up with the marauders. That possibility was becoming much less likely, he knew.

Esther had stepped outside then, and he started to follow when it occurred to him what might be her purpose. When she returned, he went out himself. It had cooled off, and a light breeze was blowing. "I should just take off right now," he said aloud. He had promised her, however, and he went back inside.

"It is time for us to sleep now," Lew said to Esther. "I'll sleep over there on the old daybed." It was at the far end of the cabin, on the opposite end from the big bed. He thought this would be the best and safest place for him.

Esther came to him and pulled him toward the feather bed. "Sleep there," she said, pointing to it.

"No, no," protested Lew. "That's your bed."

"Your bed too," she insisted, holding both his hands and giving a coquettish smile.

"Oh no, that wouldn't be right," argued Lew, but in spite of himself, he could not completely put the idea out of his mind. "Your husband wouldn't like that now, would he?" He laughed, pulling away from her, hoping this would end the matter.

"No husband," she said with emphasis. She looked at the floor and shook her head sadly.

"What happened to him?" asked Lew immediately.

Esther had turned away, and Wetzel knew she would tell him no more. He walked to the daybed, removed his hunting jacket and his shoes, flopping onto the bed. He pulled the old quilt up and turned his face to the wall. He heard her walk to her own bed and could hear the rustling of clothes. He resisted the strong urge to turn and look, until he heard the squeak from the bed, which let him know she was finally lying down.

Sleep had not come easy; but eventually, Wetzel had dozed. When the hand shook him awake, he jumped to a sitting position startled and confused, reaching instinctively for his rifle, which stood propped against the wall just to the left of the bed. He set it down again when he remembered where he was. Esther stood in front of him. In the dim light from the softly glowing coals of the fireplace, he could see her clearly enough. She was naked.

"Sleep with me," she said in a husky and seductive voice. He stood and followed her back to her bed.

April 30, 1787

Wetzel was on the Indians' trail, but he was paying little attention to it. He was pretty sure they would continue down Fishing Creek to the Ohio. No doubt they had crossed it by now. He would decide whether to continue his pursuit once he got there. His mind was more focused on the guilty feelings, which were overwhelming him. His behavior had been inexcusable, he felt. He had taken advantage of a mad woman. Yes, she had come to him in the night and insisted, but he couldn't suppress the sense of shame. Even as he berated himself, he also remembered the pleasure he had enjoyed, so much better than his adventures in Pittsburgh. Perhaps it had been pleasurable to her, so he hoped, for it eased the harshness of his self-reproach.

"What would Ma think of me now?" He had stopped near the creek bank, quite without realizing it.

Perhaps even more reprehensible was his decision to leave without saying a word. How could he justify leaving her alone in such a state?

"Well, she can take care of herself. She can do the usual things. She can fix her own food and take care of the cow." He spoke these words aloud as he often did when he was alone and trying to think. Still how could she work the soil and plant crops? It was a bad situation, she couldn't stay there very long. But Wetzel knew he couldn't stay there any longer either. He wondered if there were any neighbors who could look in on her. He was moving again now, and it wasn't long before he heard someone singing. It couldn't be an Indian. He hurried toward the sound.

Wetzel reckoned that he had come at least four miles from Esther's place. A high wooded hill rose above him to his right, leaving a narrow band of level ground alongside the creek. The banks on both sides supported some low bushes, now green with their new leaves. There was an open spot on the opposite bank, and a man sat there, holding a fishing pole and smoking a pipe. He hadn't noticed Wetzel's approach.

"Hello there, mister. How's the fishin'?"

The man dropped the pole and jumped to his feet. "What the hell," he exclaimed at the same time reaching for his rifle propped against a nearby rock.

"No need to reach for your weapon," cautioned Lew. "If I was unfriendly, you'd be dead by now."

The man gathered himself and then relaxed. "I reckon that's so," he replied. "Will you favor me with your name?"

"The name's Lew Wetzel."

"By God, I've heard of you," was the reply.

"Well, you've got the advantage then," noted Lew, "since I don't know your name yet."

"Sam Johnson. Glad to meet ya. Why don't you come on over here. I've got a jug, be glad to share."

"Don't mind if I do," answered Wetzel, splashing across the creek, which was shallow just above the deeper hole where Johnson had cast his line. "Sorry about disturbin' your fishin'."

"Well, the damned fish ain't discovered I'm here yet. What brings you to these parts?" asked Johnson, handing the jug to Wetzel, who sat in the grass.

"I'm trailing some red varlets," said Lew. "They captured a couple of kids from a place back up the way a few miles."

"By God, I ain't seen no sign of 'em," said Sam.

"They would've come through here yesterday. Where do you live?"

"A few miles south down on Middle Fork."

"Do you know the lady who lives back up Fishin' Creek, here just past the falls? It's her kids was taken."

"That'd be Esther Cale, I reckon."

"She said her name was Esther, but that's about all I could get out of her." Wetzel couldn't help thinking about something he did get from her. He pushed it out of his mind. "She seemed a bit off."

"Yep, Esther's tetched all right. Don't know if that happened afore or after her man left her."

"So her husband ran off? I couldn't get her to tell me about him."

"He left back in the winter to get supplies is what I heard. Never came back. They had two girls aged about eight and ten, I think." Johnson had picked up his pole again.

"That's bad. Left her out here all by herself with them girls. What kind of man is he, anyway?"

"Dan seemed like a good man to me," offered Johnson, pulling his line out to examine the hook. "She was a handful though. Her folks back east had money, so Dan said. She liked nice things, that's for sure."

"I could see that," said Wetzel.

"She showed up at our cabin a month or two back. Wanted to know if we'd seen Dan. My wife tried to get her to stay with us, but she insisted on goin' back. Said she'd have to do the planting."

"I saw no sign of any planting. All she's got there is a cow. She seems to have plenty of food there now, and she seems able to do what's necessary. Still I don't see how she can last very long."

Lew was wondering now how he could have gone off and left her.

"Where are you headed?" wondered Johnson.

"I'm trailin' them reds, although I doubt I'll catch 'em now."

"Want me to go with you?"

"I'd rather you'd do somethin' about Esther. I felt bad goin' off like I did."

Johnson was not excited about trailing Indians. Seeing to Esther seemed the lesser of two unwanted tasks. "I'll look in on her," he said after a minute. "I'll try to get her to come home with me."

"That's good," agreed Wetzel. "I'll be on my way then."

The two men parted going in opposite directions. Wetzel crossed the creek but continued along it's bank, trying to avoid climbing over the ridges. Once, he cut across to avoid a large bend in the stream, but the difficulty in traversing the rough terrain convinced him to stay with the creek. As it began another bend to the south, the ground flattened out a bit in front of him, and he could see there was a clearing. He noticed several tracks left, no doubt, by the warriors he was following.

"They ain't takin much care to hide their tracks," Wetzel muttered aloud. "God, what's that?"

The light breeze blowing from the west had brought an incredible stench to his nostrils. He pushed through some bushes at the edge of the clearing and could see the remains of a burnt out cabin. The smell of ash was there too, along with the odor of decaying flesh.

This wasn't done yesterday, he thought. *I bet it was that first bunch I was tracking.*

When he reached the ruins, he disturbed two large vultures who were feeding on the dead bodies. He could still tell that one was a woman and the other must have been a baby, although not much was left. He noted that the vultures had landed out in the plowed field some fifty yards from where he stood. He found what was left of the man's body there, a sack of seed corn partially spilled and lying nearby. He moved a few feet past and into the breeze, breathing deeply in the fresher air.

"I guess I better bury 'em," he said aloud. He went back to the shed, which the Indians had not bothered to burn, where he found a spade. He dug shallow graves and buried each body close to where it lay. He found some footprints that had to be those of a small boy.

"Looks like they carried off somebody too. The damned bastards have sure been busy."

Anxious to leave this horrible scene behind him, Wetzel took off at a run, reaching the edge of the creek and following it to its mouth on the Ohio. Here he turned north, deciding that it might be best for him to report his findings to Colonel Zane at Wheeling.

August 4, 1787

It was midmorning and already hot. The heat waves rising from the swampy ground were almost visible. Standing back among the bushes along the west bank of the Ohio River, Little Fox watched the canoe making its way across the river from the settlements on the Virginia side. A lone white man occupied the canoe, paddling hard now to avoid the pull of the current, threatening to sweep him far afield from his targeted landing spot on the opposite shore.

A smile curled on the lips of Little Fox, and he waved to his friend Red Storm, who waited nearby. With a nod, Red Storm left his post and moved upstream. Their clear intent was to bracket the area where they expected the canoe to land. Little Fox was feeling especially good.

The spring and summer had been filled with successful raids against the hated Long Knives. There had even been time for a quick visit back to the home village to see his wife and family. The towns on the Mad River had not been established again, and even though New Coshocton had been unharmed by Logan's soldiers, the chief, Buckongehelas, had decided to move his town. Far to the west and a ways north, the new Delaware village was located on the Auglaize River, a few miles to the south of its junction with the Maumee.

Little Fox had been dismayed to learn that this move had happened in his absence, but Bright Moon had managed, with help from some of her relatives, to make the change and get settled into a new home. When he finally arrived, Little Fox was pleased at how well the new lodge had been built, although he felt guilty that he had not been there to do it himself. The reunion with Bright Moon was joyous as it always was. He was so happy and proud that she was his wife. He loved her children by White Eagle, the oldest, Swift Hawk, now more than six years old. The little girl, Many Winds, was almost four. His own son, Eagle's Wing, was just past one and still shy around his father, who had not spent much time with him.

The time went quickly, and Little Fox found himself eager to return to the warriors' camp along the Muskingum. When Red Storm came by suggesting that they go, Little Fox bade his family farewell, and the two braves made their way back to what they considered their killing ground.

Shortly after they had reached the camp, a party of Chippewas had come in, fresh from a raid in the area near Wheeling Creek. They had stolen some horses, but a band of whites had surprised them at their night camp. They had fled, leaving their possessions and one of their number who had been killed behind. This had disgusted Little Fox, ashamed of such behavior by his fellow tribesmen, and motivated him to undertake the current mission.

As he waited for the white man's canoe to come ashore, Little Fox thought about what he knew of recent treaty agreements with the hated enemy. He knew the land where he stood just now was supposedly ceded to the Americans. Even now, there were surveyors in the area sent by the American government to lay out plots for Americans to occupy. He didn't really understand what that was all about, but like many of his more militant friends, he regarded the Ohio River as the border, and any white settlement as an illegal invasion. Some of the chiefs had warned the American officials that the surveyors would be killed if they continued to do their work, and the Americans had responded by sending troops to protect them.

A fort had been built only a few miles above where Little Fox now stood, but it had been abandoned. He and Red Storm had investigated that just the day before. Although there were many white settlers just across the river, Little Fox felt no danger at all. Excitement rose in him as he anticipated the action that was soon to occur. He thought of White Eagle, and for some reason remembered the day many years ago when the two of them had found White Eagle's slain uncle at Coshocton. They had vowed to avenge that death. "I will do that now, White Eagle," said Little Fox softly.

The canoe put in at the mouth of a tiny run, and the man pulled the craft out of the water. He did not bother to hide it, for he hadn't planned to stay long. He had a small oak basket in his hand, and he walked deliberately up the run until he came to a clump of bushes laden with ripe blackberries. He paid no attention to his surroundings, intent only on gathering the berries.

Little Fox had kept out of sight but followed the white man's movements, curious as to his intent. Once the man began picking the fruit, Little Fox found a spot from which he had a clear shot and brought the rifle to his shoulder. A quiet attack with a tomahawk would have been easier and safer, but Little Fox wanted the people across the river to hear and be afraid. He knew that Red Storm would support his attack however it was made. He took aim and squeezed the trigger.

The shot hit the man but in the leg rather than in the side, where Little Fox intended. Throwing the bucket of berries into the air, the victim screamed, looking back to where he could see his assailant was approaching.

"Don't kill me, don't kill me," he begged, screaming as loud as he could. A second shot rang out, and the man crumpled, struck in the back just under his right shoulder. He was still screaming when Little Fox ended it all with a tomahawk blow to the head. He was taking the scalp when Red Storm arrived.

"This is good," exclaimed Red Storm. "Only I wish it was W who we killed."

"Maybe W will come after us now," said Little Fox with a grin. "If he is over there, he will come."

"If we knew where he lived, we could find him and kill him," answered Red Storm, who had expressed this thought more often than Little Fox could count.

"They will have heard the shots over there," noted Little Fox, pointing across the river. "We should probably get away from here."

"Let us wait until we see how many come," suggested Red Storm.

The confidence he had felt earlier had dissipated somewhat for Little Fox. "They will come with many. We should go now." He moved at a quick pace up the run not waiting to see if his friend was coming.

Shaking his head, Red Storm followed along. When they had reached the top of a hill a short distance from the river, Red Storm was able to see that a group of the Long Knives was already at the shore, preparing to cross. He turned and followed after Little Fox with more determination.

John Mathews was walking along a ridge not far from the edge of the Ohio and in sight of a small settlement when he heard the shots from across the big river. He made his way down toward the buildings as fast as he could, wondering what he might find. By the time he arrived, some men had already crossed the river to investigate.

Within an hour, two of them returned with the body of a young man named Wheaton, whose father lived on Short Creek, several miles downriver. Others had undertaken a pursuit of the Indians who had killed young Wheaton. Esquire McMahan arrived not long after Mathews and took charge of the situation. Someone said they thought there had been some Indians fishing near the mouth of Cross Creek, a short distance farther to the north.

Mathews was staying at McMahan's and was part of the surveying party that had been charged with surveying the so-called Seven Ranges. That task had been going on since the previous summer but had been interrupted several times by rumors of hostile Indian attacks. Soldiers under the command of Captain Hamtramck had built Fort Steuben the previous winter; and in the past February, Mathews had been asked to take charge of the commissary department at the fort.

Fort Steuben was located three miles above the mouth of Indian Cross Creek on the west side of the Ohio. In May, however, the army had decided to abandon the fort, and Mathews was ordered to move the stores to Wheeling. After carrying out a number of errands in June and July, he had returned to McMahan's at the end of July. He had been ordered to go to Fort Harmar and was planning to depart for there in two days. It wasn't long before the pursuing party returned, having given up the chase.

"By God, I've had enough of this nonsense," Mr. McMahan announced to the crowd that had gathered near the riverbank. "I'll put up one hundred dollars to go to someone who will catch and scalp one of those red bastards."

This announcement created quite a stir, and runners were sent to Wheeling and other nearby settlements, asking for men who would go on such an expedition. The volunteers were asked to gather at Esquire McMahan's that same day if possible. This news reached Lew Wetzel at Zane's store where he was spending the afternoon. Although he was not usually interested in going out with large parties, the reward money caught his attention.

"Will you go with them, Lew?" asked Colonel Zane.

"I reckon we need to do somethin'," he answered. "The red bastards have made this into a damned bloody year."

It had been just over three months since Wetzel had gone with his brother to visit the Wolfe's, and he had followed the

Indian trail, finding the results of the attacks on settlers along Fishing Creek. He had brought the report to Colonel Zane of at least three deaths and three taken prisoner. It was then that he learned from Zane about the killing of Adam Grandstaff, the husband of his first cousin, Maria Wetzel Grandstaff.

Adam was returning to Shepherd's Fort after spending the day at his farm along Wheeling Creek, a couple of miles below the Bonnett farm, when the Indians intercepted him. This loss had greatly saddened Wetzel, and he had recently spent time with the survivors who had returned to the farm. The oldest son, Lewis, had taken over and at the time was living at the homeplace with his mother, a sister, and three other brothers. Wetzel had thought it wise to stay close to his family in these days with so much Indian threat, but the recent reports of action close to Wheeling had brought him into the town. He had been planning a scouting mission anyway, so the invitation by Esquire McMahan came at just the right time.

"I better get movin' if I aim to join that party," he said to Zane.

It was already past midafternoon, and it would be nearly dark by the time he made the sixteen miles up past Beech Bottom.

"Take this with you, Lew," said Zane, who handed him a pouch filled with gunpowder. "It'll be my contribution to this affair."

It was dark when Wetzel reached McMahan's, which was about a mile from the mouth of Buffalo Creek. He found a group of men camped near the river. The night was still warm, but the men were gathered around a small campfire. He recognized a friend, Absalom Wells, who had a flour mill up on Buffalo Creek.

"By God," exclaimed Wells, jumping to his feet at the sight of Wetzel who had dismounted and was leading his horse toward the fire. "It's Lew Wetzel. We can make good use of you!"

"Hello to you too, friend Absalom. Who's in charge of this bunch?"

"Well, Esquire McMahan, but he ain't here now. He's gone up to the house for the night, but he'll be back first thing in the mornin'."

Some of the other men had gathered around them. Lew nodded to John Bukey, a man he knew quite well.

"Is there still time for me to sign up?" Lew felt strange asking such a question. Indeed, he didn't much like the idea. Still there was this reward.

"Don't worry, Lew, the major ain't about to turn you down."

"Is there a place for my horse, maybe somethin' for him to eat?"

Wells pointed to a barn and fenced-in lot that was barely visible in the dim light. "You can put him in there with the rest. The Major had some feed put in for 'em."

When he returned from putting his horse away, Wetzel was met by a man and a boy of about twelve years of age.

"Mr. Wetzel, my name is James McDonald, and this is my boy, John. He wanted to meet you."

"Nobody calls me mister," said Wetzel with a laugh. "They call me Lew, and that will do for you too. I'm pleased to meet you. But why does young John there want to meet me?"

"Why, you're famous in these parts, mister, uh, that is, Lew."

"I reckon you mean that kindly, James, and I thank you. But I ain't all that famous."

"I think you are, specially when it comes to huntin' Injuns."

"Hell, there's lotsa good Injun fighters around here. John Bukey there, he's as good as any."

"That's not what we heard," interjected John McDonald, who backed away a step or two, expecting a reprimand from his father.

"Well, shake my hand then, young John, for I'm mighty happy to meet you." Wetzel grasped the boy's hand and gave it a squeeze. He looked hard now at the father.

"You ain't figurin' on takin' him along are you?" he asked.

"Oh no, Major McMahan would never go for that. He just wanted to come with me tonight. We live close by, and I'll take him home first thing in the morning."

"Will you have time for that?"

"Oh yes. Some others are still comin' in. I think the major hopes to get away by noon."

"That's what I was afraid of," muttered Wetzel to himself. "Good night then," he said loudly to the McDonalds, walking away and spreading his blanket on a flat spot a few feet away from the others.

August 5, 1787

It was just past noon when the McMahan expedition crossed the Ohio and began its trek toward the Muskingum, where it was thought the marauding Indians were gathered. Major McMahan had been very happy to see Lewis Wetzel and quickly signed him up as one eligible for the reward.

It had been decided that if the effort was successful, each man would receive four dollars for going along, and the one who took the first scalp would receive twenty dollars. There were twenty men in all, McMahan having rejected a couple of latecomers whom he didn't know very well. Wetzel had no doubt that he would snag the main prize and was feeling good about having a little bit of spending money. Of course, he was quite willing to hunt Indians, money or no money.

It took them two days to reach the vicinity of the Muskingum, having angled to the southwest to a point a few miles below the old town of Coshocton. There they halted while a three-man scouting party was sent ahead to see what they might be facing. Wetzel was not among them, an arrangement that had surprised him, and about which he was not altogether pleased. He grumbled about it to John Bukey and Absalom Wells.

"The major was afraid you'd git into a scrape and spoil the whole thing, Lew," explained Bukey. "I tried to tell him you was the best spy we had, and he agreed. Still he thought it best to send the others."

"I thought we came here to git into a scrape," answered Wetzel petulantly. "Hell, I know when to pick my fights."

"I agree with you, Lew," said Wells, always ready to cheer up his friend. "You're the best, but I suppose them other men will get the job done."

The other men returned with a depressing report. A man named Jeremiah Devore served as the spokesman.

"It's a mighty big village, Major," Devore reported to McMahan. "There might be more'n a hundred of the beggars. No way we can handle 'em."

"Are you sure there are that many?" asked McMahan, looking as he did so toward the other two scouts who quickly nodded in agreement. "Did you get close to the camp?"

"We got close enough," answered Devore. "We watched from just across the river last night."

"They're on the west side of the Muskingum?" McMahan wanted to know.

"Most are. We damned near stumbled into a bunch that was on this side though."

The news from the scouts brought some heated discussion, but Wetzel could see where it was headed. He withdrew and took a seat on a partially rotting log lying on the edge of the clearing. As the men talked, he took a rag from his pouch and began wiping down the barrel of his rifle. It wasn't long until an agreement was reached that the prudent course was to turn back and return to their homes across the Ohio.

"I agree with this decision," McMahan announced. "But I don't aim to pay out any money since we haven't accomplished anything."

"To hell with the money," one of the men shouted. "I'd rather go home with my hair."

This sentiment summarized the discussions, and the men quickly mounted their horses and prepared to ride away. Wetzel, however, remained seated on the log.

"You ain't had much to say, Lew," noted Absalom Wells. "What are you thinkin'?"

"What I'm thinkin' ain't goin' to sound too nice to you men, I reckon," remarked Lew after a pause. "I came out here to kill Injuns, and we ain't done that yet."

"We've decided against that, Lew," said Major McMahan. "We're going home, and I believe you should come with us."

"Well, you men should go right along then." Wetzel stood now, staring hard at them all. "I'm goin' huntin'!"

"Are you sure, Lewis?" McMahan felt obligated and responsible, but he was also aware of Wetzel's reputation for stubbornness.

Wetzel walked over to where he had left his horse, removing his rolled-up blanket and another pouch. He led the horse back to where McMahan was still waiting and handed him the reins. "Would you take my horse back to your place, Major? I'll pick him up when I come in."

"My God, you intend to stay out here on foot?"

"I'll be harder to find that way in case some young buck has an idea to track me."

John Bukey watched the interchange between Wetzel and McMahan with a tinge of guilt. He was a tough, experienced frontiersman, an able Indian fighter or so he thought of himself. He knew he should offer to stay with Lew, but he couldn't bring himself to make the move.

Wetzel's gaze settled on him, and he could feel those flashing black eyes accusing him. But then, Wetzel grinned and nodded to him. Bukey nodded back and turned his horse away. There was no more talk. The major waved his hand, and the men rode off satisfied with their decision, and thinking Wetzel was mad. For his part, Wetzel tied the blanket roll on his back, slung a pouch over each shoulder, and with rifle in hand, headed into the woods.

The general direction was upstream, but Wetzel stayed well away from the Muskingum itself. In spite of his self-confidence, he thought it best to move away from the big village and hope to run across a small party out on its own. He took his time, searching every small trail for sign that someone had traveled through recently. He decided to cross to the other side of the river near the old settlement of Lichtenau, a few miles below Coshocton.

He knew that there might be some Indians still living in the old Delaware town, so he moved a good distance to the west before turning north with the intention of striking White Womans Creek. It was dark by the time he reached the creek, and a change in wind direction, together with the dampness of his clothes from crossing the river, brought a chill that Wetzel would not have expected on a summer evening. He moved downstream a short distance until he came to a place where the bank was high above a broad rocky beach next to the stream. "By God, I'm cold," he said aloud. "I need a fire."

Building a fire carried a big risk at attracting unwanted visitors. Understanding that better than most, Wetzel set about digging a small hole in the sandy ground. It was a couple of feet in diameter and only a few feet in from the high bank. He gathered some bark and leaves, along with a number of twigs. Lining the hole with the bark, he piled the twigs and leaves in the center, covering it with the bark and some loose dirt. He left two air holes and, producing flint and steel, managed to get the dry leaves ignited. He sat down with his legs encircling the hole and pulled the blanket up over his head so that all was covered like a tent. The heat was kept in, and he was soon warm.

"It's like a stove room," he remarked to himself. "Feels mighty good."

He took some dried venison from his pouch along with some parched corn mix and enjoyed his supper. The fire smoldered comfortably, and it was almost impossible to detect unless one was in the riverbed itself. Wetzel was soon asleep, not waking until the sun was high enough to be seen over the trees that hovered above the riverbank. The fire had gone out, but it had served its purpose quite well. After munching on some of the dried venison, Wetzel gathered his things and began moving downstream where he knew the creek would join the Tuscarawas branch of the Muskingum.

When he came to a narrow place where there was a slight rapids, Wetzel crossed to the north side of the stream. He did not want to approach the forks from the south side, for he had decided to make his way upstream on the Tuscarawas branch. He swung far to the north, staying well away from Coshocton; and when he was a good distance past the forks, he angled back toward the Tuscarawas. He kept away from any open areas as much as he could, preferring to stay in the woods, even though it made the going difficult at times. Late in the afternoon, he smelled wood smoke wafting gently in the breeze.

"Ah," he exclaimed quietly, "mebbe one of my red friends has built himself a fire."

He began a stealthy advance toward the source of the smoke. When close enough to see the campsite, he stopped and watched for several minutes. There was no movement, and he worked in closer until he could see clearly. There were two blankets and a copper kettle sitting next to the fire, which was nearly out. The camp was in an open area on the bank of the creek with a line of trees and bushes all around it.

"Two of the bastards, I reckon," muttered Wetzel.

Looking around carefully, he spied a heavy undergrowth, which would afford him safe cover. He made his way into it and settled down to wait. About sunset, a warrior came in from upstream and began to build up the fire. He filled the kettle with water from the river, put in some ground corn mixture and cut up some dried venison, which he dropped into the pot. He placed the kettle on the fire and sat back to wait. It wasn't long until his partner arrived, carrying a fish he had obviously just caught. The two warriors talked a bit, and then the second one took his knife and skinned the fish. He cut it into several pieces and tossed them into the kettle, turning to his friend and laughing.

Hell, I'd never eat that mess, thought Wetzel. He picked up his rifle and thought about firing a shot. He could kill one with the shot and then attack the other with a rush. On the other hand, the Indians had their guns within easy reach, and it might be possible that the one left alive would be able to shoot Wetzel before he could get there.

"Ain't no need to take a chance," he reasoned. "I'll wait 'til they're asleep." He put his rifle down and settled in for a long wait.

Wetzel sat quietly while the two braves enjoyed their meal and then spent time telling stories amid a great deal of loud laughter. *They wouldn't be so happy if they knew what was about to happen*, he thought. Another surprise was in store for him, however, for the fisherman put his blanket around himself, picked up a chunk of the fire, waved to the other warrior, and left the camp, moving downstream.

"Damn," whispered Wetzel. "He's off to some deer lick, I suppose. He'll prob'ly come back afore dawn, so I'll have to wait." He settled back to watch and fell asleep. The chatter of a songbird awakened him, and he sat up with a start. The Indian camp lay undisturbed, but only one sleeping form was visible in the dim light of the fire. "He never came back," noted Wetzel. "But I can't wait no longer."

Drawing his hunting knife, the determined hunter left his sanctuary and moved silently toward the sleeping figure. He stopped and looked carefully around, making sure that the fisherman hadn't returned and was on watch somewhere on the perimeter. He saw and heard nothing, so he made his attack on the run, stooping to drive the knife into the sleeping warrior's heart. He stifled his usual scream, still not satisfied that the other Indian was not anywhere near. The victim died with no more than a quiver and a gurgle, and his slayer quickly took his scalp.

Wetzel shook the scalp violently to remove as much blood as possible before fastening it to the pouch hanging from his right shoulder. He went back to retrieve his rifle and other belongings before striding off upstream. Toward evening of the next day, Wetzel reached the vicinity of Mingo Bottom where he discovered a canoe left conveniently in a place where he could easily find it. He pushed it into the Ohio and paddled across. He made his way down to the McMahan farm. It was past dark when he knocked on the door. The major answered it for himself.

"Well, I'll be damned if it isn't Lew Wetzel."

"I reckon it is, Major, and I've brought you a scalp." He handed the scalp to McMahan, who was astonished.

"I guess I should never have doubted, but some of us wondered if you'd make it back this time."

"Well, I did, and I figure I've earned that reward you offered."

McMahan was taken aback by that request. He had already assumed he would not be required to pay anything. He started to protest; but even in the dim light, he could see the determination on Wetzel's face.

"I guess it is only fair. Step inside, Lew, and I'll get it for you."

McMahan returned with the money in paper bills. His wife came with him but took a step back when she saw the wild-looking man standing just inside the door.

"My dear," said McMahan. "This is Lewis Wetzel."

"How do you do, ma'am?" said Wetzel.

Mrs. McMahn nodded but did not speak. Her husband handed the cash to Wetzel and shook his hand.

"Congratulations, Lew, it is well deserved."

"Thank you, sir," replied Wetzel, a broad smile on his lips. Nodding to them both, he turned and walked out into the night. "God," he exclaimed. "I ain't never had this much money in my whole life."

15

ADVENTURES

September 25, 1787

THE WELL-DRESSED STRANGER who stepped into Zane's store quickly caught the attention of everyone. He was not a large man, rather slightly built and barely as tall as Elizabeth Zane, who stood immediately at his entrance and looked to see if her husband, the colonel, had noticed.

The man carried himself as one who commanded respect and deference. His woolen frock coat looked expensive, as did his knee-length trousers, tucked tightly around stockings that were silken in appearance. He wore a wide-brimmed felt hat, which he had not removed upon coming inside. He stood just inside the door and noted the store's inhabitants. He stared for a moment at the French trader seated at the back near a pile of furs, then nodded at two women standing by a table containing some cooking implements. They stopped talking and watched the man but did not respond to his nod. When his gaze turned to Elizabeth, a smile appeared on his lips.

"Sir, may we help you?" asked Elizabeth after an awkward pause. Colonel Zane moved out from behind the counter and stood next to his wife.

"Why, yes, I expect you can. I was told to look up Colonel Zane that I could get provisions at his store. Am I in the right place?"

"I'm Zane," asserted the colonel. "And who might you be?"

"Oh, forgive me. My name is John Madison. I'm from Orange County, Virginia." Madison pointed to the door. "That's my man, Zeke, just outside."

Having heard his name, Zeke, a young black man, stepped into the doorway, smiling and waving, then moved back outside and out of sight.

"Madison is a famous Virginia name," noted Ebenezer Zane. "Are you any relation to James?"

"Why, yes, James is my first cousin. What do you know of him?"

"I've followed some of the stories coming from the constitutional convention. I know that your cousin is one of the principal voices. But then I served with him in '84 and '85 in the House of Delegates. Him, and Randolph, and Governor Henry too."

"Just before we left home, I heard that the convention work was done. A document will be submitted to the states for ratification."

Elizabeth Zane, who had been listening carefully, couldn't keep quiet any longer. "My Eb's bein' considered as a delegate to Virginia's convention," she announced with pride.

Madison nodded and smiled. "Well, I know James'll be hoping for a yes vote. I ain't so sure about it myself. From what I've heard, they may be givin' too much power to a national government."

"Our current national government hasn't worked too well, I'm thinkin'," said Zane. "I think we need something new."

"Well, I ain't a politician, so I'm not wastin' any time worrying about it." Madison walked over to a barrel and lifted the top. "I didn't bring enough flour with me, I can see that now."

"We don't have much here," explained Zane. "You should have stopped up on Buffalo Creek. Absalom Wells has a big mill there."

"I think this barrel would do me fine," remarked Madison. "I've got a good-sized canoe, but there is a limit to what I can take."

"Where are you headed, if I might ask?" wondered the colonel. "Kentucky?"

"I'm checkin' out some land down below the Kanawha somewhere. I learned about it through James from George Washington himself."

"Well, Washington went down this river and chose land all right."

"I think the land I want to see is up the Big Sandy River."

"Well, that's a long ways. Probably is Kentucky ground as far as I know. You got someone to help guide you, or do you know how to find it yourself?"

"Hell, no, I need a guide all right. So far, my party just consists of Zeke and me." When Zane did not respond, Madison continued. "I was told at Fort Pitt that there was an excellent man here that I might be able to hire as a guide. His name is Lew Wetzel. Do you know him?"

The French trader LeClerk sat up straight at the mention of Wetzel. He listened to the conversation with great interest, although Madison and Zane had forgotten that he was there.

"Why, yes, everybody around here knows Lew," laughed Zane. "I guess they know him at Pitt too."

"Hell, I don't care who knows him. I want to know if he's a good man to hire, and if so, where do I find him."

"Well, Lewis Wetzel is about the best man in the whole damned country if you need an Indian killed or you need to track somebody. I don't know if he'd want to take on the job of guidin' some greenhorn who's lookin' for land."

"I don't consider myself a greenhorn," said Madison somewhat testily. "I've done plenty of trackin', and I been a soldier in the damned war too."

"It don't matter none what I think," remarked Zane again with a chuckle. "It'll be what Lew thinks."

"I don't expect he'll argue with me too much. I intend to pay well." Madison said this last with emphasis. "Now would you tell me where I can find this high and mighty tracker?"

"Oh, Lew ain't high and mighty. And he won't be impressed by money. He's out on a hunt right now, and he'll be back here sometime. Could be several days though."

"That's not what I wanted to hear. I guess I can wait a few days."

"You're welcome to stay with Beth and me if you like. Your man can sleep here in the store. Otherwise, there's Gooding's place over on the river or Jones's tavern, though he may not be takin' in boarders. Jones is partial to drinkers."

"That's very kind of you, Colonel Zane, and if you're sure its all right with the missus, I'll take you up on that offer. I could use some interesting conversation. Young Zeke's not much at making reasonable talk."

September 27, 1787

It was two days before Lew Wetzel came in. He entered Zane's store a little before noon. Hamilton Kerr was there talking with Colonel Zane, and Pierre Le Clerk was in the back where he had spent many hours in recent days. Zane had quizzed him some, curious as to Le Clerk's constant presence. The trader had been evasive, but Zane surmised he was waiting for someone, just not sure who it could be. Perhaps it was Wetzel, but the colonel couldn't imagine what business Le Clerk might have with him. He knew that the French trader spent a considerable amount of time among the Indians, but he had always seemed to be neutral in regard to the conflict between whites and Indians.

When Zane asked Le Clerk where he had been, the trader had mentioned Kentucky, but not much else. In fact, Le Clerk had been in Kentucky for several months, having been taken with the Indian captives at Mackachack following Logan's attack on the Shawnees there the previous October. They had been kept at Danville for ten months until an exchange was arranged at the treaty of Limestone, effected on the twentieth of August of the current year. The gathering that led to this agreement was held directly across the Ohio from Limestone.

General Logan was there along with Simon Kenton and Daniel Boone while the Indians were led by the chiefs Black Snake, Wolf, and Captain Johnny who gave a long speech. John Kinsaulla, who had been taken near Washington a year earlier, was one of the white prisoners returned by the Indians. Le Clerk was released along with the Grenadier Squaw and the other Indians taken from the Mad River towns. Le Clerk had fumed during his captivity, arguing that he was not an enemy of the Americans but had simply been plying his trade among the Shawnees at the time of Logan's attack. He received a sympathetic ear from several of his jailers, but nothing ever came of it.

As time went on, his anger and desire for revenge rose to a level that demanded relief. He came to Wheeling looking for a way to answer this desire, and the appearance of John Madison looking for Lewis Wetzel had given him an idea.

"Well, Lew, did you have any luck?" asked Hamilton Kerr with a wide smile. There was never any doubt about what Wetzel had been doing.

"Not much, Hamilton," grinned Lew. "I treed three of the bastards, but one got away."

"My, my," put in Ebenezer Zane. "Most hunters would be happy with two out of three."

Wetzel just smiled but gave no answer.

"Say, Lew," continued Zane, "there's a man here lookin' for you."

"My God," exclaimed Lew. "He ain't no sheriff, is he?"

"No," laughed Zane. "He's not a sheriff. What have you done to be worried about some lawman?"

"Who knows?" said Lew. "Some folks say it's a crime to kill an Injun."

"His name is John Madison." Zane stopped for a moment as a young boy came from behind the counter where he had been playing. "Noah, run up to the house and tell Mr. Madison that Lewis Wetzel is here."

The boy, glad to have an important part in the proceedings of his father and the other adults, ran quickly out the door on his errand.

"Why does this Madison want to talk to me, do you know?" asked Wetzel.

"He wants you to guide him somewhere down the river to look at some land." Zane did not say anything about Madison's connections with famous Americans, knowing it would have little effect on Lew Wetzel.

"Hell, that don't sound like my kind of work," observed Lew.

Le Clerk had moved closer to where the conversations were going on, wanting to make sure he could hear what was discussed between Wetzel and Madison. He pretended interest in some traps that were displayed on the table. It wasn't long before John Madison made his entrance, with little Noah Zane slipping in behind him. Madison stopped when he saw Wetzel, who was sitting on a flour barrel, smoking a pipe. John noted the rugged appearance and, in particular, the dark eyes, which were staring at him intensely.

"So you're the famous Lew Wetzel," he exclaimed, even before Colonel Zane could make the introduction.

"I don't know nothin' about bein' famous, but you got my name right."

"Well, you're famous at Fort Pitt, that's for sure."

Wetzel wondered what they did know about him at Pittsburgh. "The colonel says you wanted to talk to me. Well, here I am."

"I've been told you are a great hunter and tracker. I want to hire you to help me find some land."

"Where is this land?" wondered Wetzel.

"It's on the Virginia side, down below the Kanawha."

"There's a lot of land below the Kanawha. Don't sound too good to me."

"I believe the river that was mentioned by my cousin was the Big Sandy."

"There is such a river, I think," said Wetzel. "It's more'n two hundred miles down from here, I reckon. 'Course there's lots of little streams comin' into the Ohio around there."

"So you do know that country." Madison was already sure that he had the man he wanted.

"I know it some, but that ain't the big problem."

"What is the big problem, then?"

"Injuns! There's been a helluva lot of killin' goin' on this summer. They love to raid in that part of the country."

"That's just another reason that I'm lookin' for you. Colonel Zane there says you're the best Indian hunter in the whole country."

"I'm not bad at huntin' them, I reckon, but I don't much like it when they're huntin' me."

"I'll pay you a hundred dollars, plus any expenses."

"And how long do you expect to be gone on this trip?"

"I figured you might know better'n me about that. I would guess a couple of months, maybe more." Madison had brought little more than a month's worth of provisions and had already realized he might need to take more. His canoe was pretty big, he thought.

"If you stay too long, you'll be stuck all winter." Wetzel's tone was clear evidence of his doubts about going along on this journey. "How many men you got?"

"Well, so far there's just me and my man, Zeke. I'm hopin' to hire another besides you."

"So far you shouldn't be countin' me. Can this Zeke shoot?"

"I don't rightly know if Zeke can shoot. We're not in the habit of arming our servants."

"You'd better have men who can shoot. That's the most important thing." Wetzel picked up his rifle that had been leaning against the counter. He nodded toward Zane. "See you later, Colonel. I'm off to see my ma right now." He took a few steps toward the door when he stopped and acknowledged Madison. "Pleased to meet you, Mr. Madison. I ain't much in the mood to go off down the river just now. You might try Alexander Mitchell if he's around. He's a good man."

As Wetzel began to move again, Madison reached out and grabbed him by the arm. He shrank back when Wetzel turned, jerking his arm loose, his eyes blazing.

"Don't ever do that!" shouted Lew. "I don't take to bein' grabbed."

Madison moved back two steps and then held his ground. "I meant no harm, Lewis. I just can't let you go so easily. I really need you on this venture. I'll give you five thousand acres of the land if you go with me."

The idea of owning land was a new one for Wetzel. His father and brother Martin were landowners, but Lewis had never once thought about it for himself. Maybe he was being hasty in turning down this offer. "All right, I'll meet you here tomorrow with my answer. It'll help if you get another man to go along who can shoot."

Madison watched Wetzel as he strode out the door. Turning to Colonel Zane, he smiled. "He'll do it."

September 30, 1787

Wetzel had returned as promised the morning following his meeting with John Madison. Le Clerk, who had been watching, followed him into Zane's store where Madison waited.

"Hello, Lew," greeted Madison eagerly. "Do you have the answer for me that I'm wantin'?"

"I reckon so," answered Wetzel with an attitude of resignation. "Prob'ly one of the dumbest things I've agreed to."

"I don't see why you'd think that. Cash money and five thousand acres don't sound dumb to me."

"Money and land don't do you no good when you've lost your hair," replied Lew with a laugh.

"How soon can we leave?" asked Madison with excitement.

"Right away. But you need to hire another man at least."

"I'm workin' on that. Fellow named Josh Martin is willing, I think, but I wanted your advice."

Le Clerk had not waited for Wetzel's answer. He left immediately, gathering his horse and belongings, determined to get this information to his friends Red Storm and Little Fox. He assumed they were at Buckongehelas's new village on the Auglaize. However, he knew there was a chance they might still be in the big camp along the Muskingum, and he thought it worth looking there first.

He was overjoyed to find them both there, along with Fire Heart. They were quite pleased with his news. Le Clerk knew where the Big Sandy River was, and he thought that if they were quick, Red Storm and Little Fox could lead a war party to the area and ambush Madison's group.

Today the three friends had left with five other braves, hoping to find Wetzel at last. Le Clerk, who had declined their invitation to go along, had nothing against Wetzel in particular, but the hunter had been with Logan, and that was enough reason for him to deserve this fate. Besides, the killing of Lewis Wetzel would be a blow to the entire frontier community. The trader smiled at that thought.

The intended victim was at the moment paddling a canoe down the Ohio, his mind on other matters. The Madison party had left Wheeling just that morning and was nearing Grave Creek on the Virginia side. Baker's Station was not much farther ahead. Josh Martin, a man whom Wetzel knew slightly, had agreed to come along. He had served for a time with Sam Brady, and that was enough for Lew to agree that he would be a good man to hire. Madison had also brought along his dog, Wolf, over Wetzel's strong objections.

Wetzel's mother, as always, had been glad to see him, but Lew, who for some reason unknown to him, was impatient as usual in his old home. Jacob, who was living there now along with young John, was not there, and Martin was gone as well. Mary Wetzel thought the men had gone off to hunt but was unsure maybe Indians were involved somehow. John said that they were going to help John Baker, who had reported Indian activity across the river from his place. Anxious to find more about this, Lew soon left for Bonnett's, where he was staying.

His uncle had confirmed what Johnny Wetzel had said, and Lew had decided to go back to Wheeling the next morning and agree to go with John Madison. He figured that they could stop at Baker's and help with whatever was going on there. Frustrated at the delay in leaving Wheeling, Lew was pleased that they were nearing what was his intended destination all along. He had said nothing of this to Madison, but he reckoned events would take care of that when the time came.

"We're goin' to put in at Baker's Station," announced Wetzel, all the while keeping his eyes on the far Ohio shore. He thought he had detected some movement there.

"Hell, we don't need to stop yet, do we?" shouted Madison. "Seems like we just got started."

Before Wetzel could answer, a shot rang out. The ball splashed the water just off the bow of the canoe, while the men were turning toward the shore. A second shot sailed over their heads landing in the tall weeds at the shoreline. In answer, two shots came from the second floor of the blockhouse that was Baker's Station. The four men hauled the heavy canoe out of the water and up among a thicket of reeds and scrub trees so that it was partially hidden.

"Damn, I don't want them redskins to get my supplies," cried Madison.

"You'd better be more concerned about your hair," replied Wetzel. "Let's git inside that blockhouse."

The men ran through the weeds and trees fifty yards to the back entrance to Baker's house. There were more shots from across the river, but they fell far short. Henry Baker met the four fugitives at the door as they came in. The dog squeezed past him and entered the house as well.

"By God, it's Lew Wetzel. You're a sight fer sore eyes."

"What's goin' on here, Henry?" asked Wetzel.

"There's a passel of braves across the river. They've been pesterin' us for days. We sent for help, and there are seven of us here now."

"My brothers here?"

"Yep, Martin and Jacob both. They're upstairs with my pa."

Lew and Josh Martin went to the stairs and began climbing. Madison had slumped into a chair near the door, still muttering about the canoe while Zeke stood next to him, holding their guns. The dog was lying at Madison's feet.

The second floor of the Baker's Station blockhouse was one big room, and on the wall facing the river, there were three windows. Each window was small—three feet above the floor, with an opening only two feet wide and maybe six inches in height. Essentially they were shooting ports. John Baker was at the center window with Martin Wetzel at his side while Jacob Wetzel crouched at the one to the north. A man named Leonard Raigor was at the window to the south.

Martin turned and smiled when he saw his brother at the top of the stairs. "Hell, it's Lew. Where did you come from, brother?"

"With a party comin' down the river. Johnny said you was at Baker's, and there was Injun trouble."

"The rascals took to shootin' at us a couple of days ago, and we ain't been able to do much about it so far."

"Well, I plan to just about now," announced John Baker, who was taking aim with his long rifle. "One o' them bastards is wavin' at me, and I've got a bead on him." He pulled the trigger, shouting, "Take that, you son of a bitch," in a heavy German accent.

"You got him! You got him!" shouted Jacob Wetzel, watching from his window.

"The others are runnin'," yelled Raigor. "What a sight. Look at 'em go."

Lew rushed to the window to see for himself. "I ain't so sure about that," he said quietly.

"Hell, they're on the run, and I'm goin' to claim my scalp." With a great smile of satisfaction, John Baker stood and began walking toward the stairs. "Come on Lew and Martin. Let's cross the river and see what else we can find."

Baker was down the stairs in a flash, where he was met by his son, Henry. "Pa, what are you up to?" he wanted to know.

"Git me a canoe, Henry. Me and the Wetzels is goin' over the river. I aim to claim that scalp."

Martin Wetzel had grabbed his brother's arm as he watched Baker descend the stairs. "Lew, I don't think it's such a good idea to go over there just now. Them Injuns have likely stopped back in the woods."

"Prob'ly so," agreed Lew. "But there ain't no stoppin' the man. I may as well go along. Maybe I can keep him outta trouble." He started down the stairs, and Jacob had pushed past Martin to follow him closely.

When they were outside, John Baker was helping Henry carry a canoe down to the water's edge. He saw the three Wetzel brothers as they came out. "Ain't you Wetzel boys comin' along? I thought you had sand."

"We've got enough sand, John," answered Martin, "but we ain't dumb neither."

"We're comin'," said Lew with a clipped tone. "But keep an eye out. I doubt them bastards has run too far."

The trip across the river did not take long with Lew and Jacob doing the rowing. They aimed for the spot where the body of the dead Indian was lying, just above the water's edge on the grassy bank. As soon as they reached the shore, John Baker, hunting knife in hand, leaped out of the canoe and scrambled up near the body.

Three shots rang out, and Baker was hit. He stumbled and fell to the ground. The Wetzel brothers pulled the canoe out of the water and dove into a stand of reeds and heavy bushes off to their right. Several shots whizzed by them, but they were not hit. Five braves appeared and ran to where Baker lay moaning in the grass.

Two of them tried to pick him up but quickly gave up on that when a shot came from the bushes where the Wetzels had taken refuge. The warrior holding Baker under his arms dropped him when the ball struck his shoulder. He gave a cry of pain, then ran off with the others to safety among the trees.

"Now what?" asked Martin Wetzel. "We're in a bad way."

"I think John is still alive," said Lew, who was completing the job of reloading his rifle. "We need to git him in that canoe and git outta here."

"How're we gonna do that? If we get out of these bushes, they'll shoot hell outta us."

"I don't know how many of them there is, but it's a couple less than it was. You boys stay here and be ready to shoot. I'm gonna see what we're up against."

With that, Lew crawled out of their sanctuary and into the woods behind, moving away from the river. He moved carefully from tree to tree, in the direction toward where the Indians had retreated. He was able to see one of the braves crouched behind a large maple. He knew there were others just past there but could not see anything. He took careful aim and fired.

The Indian screamed and rushed away, wounded in the left side. Several other shadowy figures could be seen retreating further into the woods. A shot rang out from where the other two Wetzels were hiding. Lew was glad that one of them had held back so that there was a shot left. He quickly reloaded his own weapon and pushed on in pursuit of the Indians. He wanted to force them further back, and he hoped that Martin and Jacob would understand that they needed to take advantage of this time to get Baker into the canoe.

There were seven braves left in the forest, and two of them were injured. One had taken position in a small gully, watching for an opportunity to fight off the pursuit. Wetzel saw the top of the Indian's head as he raised it slightly, searching for his foe. Lew moved a few feet farther to his right where he could get a clear shot. He could barely see his target, but he figured the effect would be good whether his shot hit its mark or not. He fired, and the brave, surprised at the direction of the shot, jumped up and ran away. Satisfied, Wetzel began running back toward the river, loading his gun as he ran.

Lewis was overjoyed when he burst out of the woods at the riverbank to find that Martin and Jacob had managed to get John Baker in the canoe and were ready to push off when Lew appeared. This was accomplished quickly, and they were soon well out into the river, paddling hard. The Indians had not reappeared, and it was not long before the canoe reached the opposite shore, just below the blockhouse. John Baker was bleeding badly and in horrible pain.

"He ain't gonna last," pronounced Martin as they lifted the stricken man out of the canoe. Henry Baker was already there, trying to soothe his father who was moaning desperately. By the time they reached the house, the old man was dead.

Henry Baker sat down on the stoop and cried. The others stood there helplessly. Finally Henry managed to stop the tears.

"Thank you, boys," he said. "Thank you for bringing him home. We'll bury him next to mother."

John Madison had come out, watching quietly. "My God, I never expected nothing like this," he said after a few moments. He was thinking about his good fortune at having hired Lew Wetzel. On the other hand, he was anxious to get on down the river, and he wondered if this event was going to prevent that. "The day's well on by now," he said, directing his words to Lew Wetzel. "I reckon we should stay on here 'til morning."

"I reckon I'll stay until old John is buried," said Lew with quiet determination.

Madison started to flare up, then thought better of it. "How long will that be, I wonder."

"A couple of days, I suspect," answered Lew. "It'll be up to Henry there."

"I want a real funeral," said Henry. "Day after tomorrow."

Madison couldn't stop himself. "Damn, I can't wait that long. I don't even know the man."

"You can go on if you want, I reckon," said Lew. There was steel in his voice.

"You're my hired hand, Mr. Wetzel," said Madison, feeling wronged. "I'm payin' you, and you'll do as I say."

"I ain't seen no money yet, that I know of," replied Lew. "And I don't do what anybody says if I don't want to. Now that's the end of it!"

"Hell," exclaimed Madison, but he said no more.

October 5, 1787

Little Fox had been watching the river for several hours. Red Storm waited with him for most of the time, but Fire Heart and the others had gone back into the woods to look for some fresh meat to eat. The little war party had been in the area for a day, hoping that Wetzel and Madison had not yet come that far. They had located the river called the Big Sandy by the whites but had moved back up river opposite the mouth of another stream they had noticed on the way down.

They had pushed hard to get to where they thought the white men might be going, coming down the Muskingum by canoe, then overland to the present location. It would have been easier to continue down the Ohio by canoe, but they feared discovery by others on the river. The traffic was often heavy, although it had let up some as autumn had arrived. The Indians had hoped to find canoes hidden along the Ohio side when they reached their destination, for this was a common practice among their brethren. But there were none to be had.

"We will build a raft when the time comes," Fire Heart proclaimed.

"Ah," uttered Little Fox suddenly, his patience finally rewarded.

From the spot where he knelt, he could see upriver for a good distance. The big river made a westerly turn some two miles up from there and then flowed in a fairly straight line past Little Fox's position and on to the west before bending back to the north at the point where the Big Sandy flowed in. Little Fox could see the canoe clearly, and as he watched, he was able to count four men—the number that Le Clerk had told them to expect.

"This has to be them," he exclaimed aloud to Red Storm, who had come up when he heard Little Fox first sound the alarm. "Is the big one in the back your man Wetzel?"

Red Storm had never admitted that he had not really had a good look at his adversary that evening so long ago in the woods above Gnadenhutten. Still he always felt he would recognize the man if he ever saw him again. Now, however, he was unsure.

"They are too far away," was his reply. "I think so, but let them get closer."

The two warriors stood, watching intently as the canoe and its inhabitants drifted down toward the mouth of the stream, the one called the Guyandotte, although the name was unknown to the Indians. They had a good view, for they themselves were hidden by the tall reeds, which grew up from the streambed and above the riverbank.

"I think we should shoot the big man right now," said Red Storm. "I don't want him to get away from us."

"That would be unwise," cautioned Little Fox. "We could easily miss, and they would be warned. Besides, there are only two of us here now. It is best that we wait for them to camp for the night and then attack in the morning while they sleep."

Red Storm could not refute this logic, but he was disappointed. They continued their observance.

The Madison party was quite unaware that it was under observation, for the men were arguing about whether the tributary they saw ahead might be the Big Sandy. Wetzel, who was the supposed guide, was embarrassed that he could not be sure.

"I don't think that is the Big Sandy," he announced, quieting the others for a few moments. "It don't seem big enough to me. I remember Drennon mentioning another river before the Big Sandy." Wetzel was trying to visualize the rough map Jacob Drennon had provided for the trip down to Limestone the previous summer. It was of little help because he had been unable to read the names.

"I think there's a stream called the Guyandotte around here somewhere," offered Josh Martin. "I've heard Brady mention it."

"That could be right," agreed Lew.

"Well, it looks like what they said the Big Sandy would be like," said Madison. "I like the lay of the land around here anyway. Let's pull in and check it out. Maybe I'll choose some land right here. If nothing else, it will make a good spot to spend the night."

Wetzel could think of no reason to argue, and he began to steer the canoe in toward the shore. "We'll come in below the mouth. It looks like a better place to land," he said.

Nothing more was said as they brought the vessel ashore and pushed it up onto the low bank.

"We need to get this thing outta sight," declared Lew. He noticed a thick stand of cottonwoods, a short distance further down the Ohio shore. "There," he pointed. "Let's float it down and pull it up among them cottonwoods."

Once the canoe was stowed away, Madison began to gather some provisions to be used for the night's camp. They had a couple of small tents with them, and as he pulled one of them out, Wetzel stopped him. "The night is clear and warm," he noted. "We don't need them tents."

"But I might want to stay here a few days," protested Madison.

"Then we can put up the tents tomorrow. Let's keep it light and simple tonight. I want a chance to look around a bit afore we git too comfortable."

They walked a good distance along the left bank of the Guyandotte when they discovered an abandoned camp.

"By God, what's this?" exclaimed Madison. "Is it an Indian camp?"

The others held back while Wetzel searched through the remains. "No, it was white men. They sure must have left in a hurry."

Some blankets and cooking utensils had been left behind. Madison picked up the blankets. "We can use these."

"You men stay here while I see if I can figure out what spooked these men."

Wetzel was gone for close to an hour before returning.

"I don't see no fresh Injun sign," he reported. "Nor any idea of where the men went who were camped here. Too much time and too much rain."

As it was nearing evening, the decision was made to spend the night at the current location. No fire was built, and they ate a cold supper. Wetzel was satisfied with the surroundings. It was a pretty little forest glade surrounded closely on three sides by heavy woods, with the stream on the remaining side. Although it was somewhat open there, a scattering of weeds and small bushes helped to hide the camp. An enemy could use the woods as cover, but he would have to get close to have a clear shot.

"I think we'll stay in this area for a few days," announced Madison as they began to settle in for the night.

"I'm pretty sure this ain't the Big Sandy," said Lew.

"No matter," responded Madison. "Land is land, and I like the looks of it around here."

Wetzel and Martin agreed to split the night as sentries, with Martin taking the first watch. It was not long after darkness had fallen when all but Martin were fast asleep, completely unaware of what was happening on the other side of the Ohio.

October 6, 1787

Little Fox and Red Storm had watched the Madison party beach and hide their canoe, then moved up the little stream and out of sight among the trees. Their comrades had returned with a freshly killed buck and also some small sapling logs to be used for a raft. After finishing its construction, they had gone deep into the woods where a small fire was kindled, and the venison cooked for their supper.

A watch had been kept until after dark, making sure the white men had not returned to the river where they might detect the activities of the warriors. It was well into the night when the raft was launched, and they crossed to the Virginia side. Four of them had ridden on the raft while the others held onto the sides and helped guide it across. The landing was made nearly a mile downstream, but it did not take long for them to move back up to the mouth of the Guyandotte.

A quiet council was held in the early hours before dawn after a scout by Red Storm had found where the whites had made their camp. Silently, the attackers slipped through the woods into positions that surrounded their enemy. Tall Shadow and Red Feather, who had been on the raid that resulted in the death of John Wetzel, were along this time as well.

Little Fox sent them across the Guyandotte to prevent any escape in that direction. Once in place, the eight warriors settled down to wait for first light when the attack would begin. It was Wetzel's watch, but he had dozed, his back resting against a big cottonwood at the upstream side of the camp. He came awake suddenly, not sure what had caused it, but relieved and feeling ashamed that he had been asleep.

Something is wrong, Wetzel thought to himself. It was still very dark, but the first beginnings of dawn could be seen through the foliage to his far right. The dog, Wolf, lying near Madison's head, had roused himself and emitted a low growl.

"Even the dog is worried," muttered Lew quietly. "I'd better have a look around." He slid down and rolled over, crawling back among the trees, reaching out as he went by to snatch his rifle that was leaning against the tree. He continued to creep along, angling off the corner of the glade, reasoning that an attacker would be more likely to locate off the middle of one of the sides.

Wetzel was correct in this assumption, for the Indians had arranged themselves with two warriors on each side of the camp. Little Fox and Red Storm had stayed together on the Ohio side of the clearing, and they were wide awake, anticipating an attack they had been thinking about for a half-dozen years. They were aware of the presence of the dog, and for that reason, the braves had been forced to stay farther back than they might have wished. The two close friends moved nearer, trying to see what was happening in the camp itself.

"I think they are still sleeping," whispered Red Storm.

"One is awake and on watch, I think," said Little Fox. "But I cannot see for sure. Let us move closer."

It had been agreed that Red Storm would have the first shot at the big man, but that meant they had to wait for enough light. Little Fox was beginning to think that it might be better if they simply stormed the camp while it was still dark. It was at this moment that he thought he detected some movement among the slumbering white men. He turned toward Red Storm, who was advancing just a few feet away, and waved his hand. "We should attack now," he said in a very low voice.

"Yes," agreed Red Storm. "I will give the signal."

The signal was to be three hoots of an owl, and it didn't really matter how well it was done. Upon hearing this, the braves were to charge the camp, shooting first, then following up with knives and tomahawks. Tall Shadow and Red Feather were to remain across the stream, ready to stop anyone trying to escape in that direction.

Wetzel heard the owl hoots and knew immediately what was happening. He stood and lifted his gun as a figure rose up from behind a tree no more than fifteen feet to his right. He knew that an attack was on and that he would be unable to prevent it. "Injuns!" he shouted at the top of his voice. He tried to take aim at the warrior he had detected close by, but he had no clear shot. From the sounds around him, he knew there were at least five or six braves, and there was little chance for the sleeping men to survive.

His own position was also precarious, for his shout had revealed his location. The smart thing for him to do was to turn back into the woods and get as far away as possible. He knew from his scouting the night before that the Guyandotte made a turn back to the east, and if he could get past that, he could make his way back to the Ohio. However, he felt some sense of duty to try to help the others even though it seemed impossible. He moved back toward the big cottonwood he had been leaning against just a few minutes earlier. There was complete chaos in the camp. The sleeping men had come awake at Wetzel's shout, but a shot from Little Fox's rifle struck Zeke before he could rise.

Fire Heart had taken aim at one of the sleeping bundles that he could barely make out in the dark, but his shot only hit the leg of Josh Martin who was struggling to his feet. Madison had jumped out of his blanket and headed toward the stream when he was attacked by a charging warrior swinging his tomahawk. The dog dashed away into the woods. Wetzel had dropped his rifle and drawn his knife, thinking it impossible to shoot accurately among such confusion. He had taken a step toward the Indian who was engaged with Madison when a big brave came at him from his left. He turned and drove the knife hard into the belly of his attacker, who uttered a grunt of surprise and dropped the tomahawk he was trying to slam into Wetzel's skull.

Wetzel jerked the knife free and retreated back into the trees, picking up his gun as he did so. It was clear now that he could not save any of his companions, and he executed his earlier plan. It was all over in the camp. Although Martin had been hit only in the leg, he was unable to fight off the two warriors and their swinging tomahawks. Zeke died from the gunshot, and Madison had succumbed to the tomahawk attack. All three were scalped.

"Wetzel is not here," exclaimed Red Storm with great disappointment. "Where is he?"

"He was here," stated Fire Heart. "Black Wing has taken his knife." He led the others to where Black Wing was lying, blood seeping from the jagged wound in his belly. Little Fox knelt beside the wounded warrior. "Where was he, the man who knifed you?" he asked.

Black Wing struggled to speak, shaking his head from side to side. "I think he came from back there," he muttered finally, rising slightly and pointing at the cottonwood.

"He must have gone back that way," noted Red Storm, pointing into the woods past the tree. "Let's follow. We can catch him back there."

It was agreed to leave one man with the injured Black Wing, and the other four would begin pursuit in a wide arc in the direction in which they thought Wetzel had gone. Tall Shadow and Red Feather were to remain on the other side of the stream.

"Move upstream, for he is sure to try to cross someplace and not too far up," Little Fox had instructed them.

Wetzel had made good progress before the Indian pursuit had even begun. He passed the point where the little river made its curve to the east, and he turned with it. The path was surprisingly open along here, and although there were scattered trees, it was easy for him to slip through them. The sun was making an appearance, and the increased light helped considerably, although it would aid his followers as well. He ran for another fifty yards when he decided, partly because of some obstructions ahead, that it was time to cross the creek. He did not think it would be deep, but he figured he could swim it if necessary. As he began to crawl out on the other side, he heard movement in some bushes back to his left.

"Damn, what's that," he said aloud. "There must have been more of the bastards on the other side of the river."

This was unexpected, and he wondered how many more there could be. He stayed at the edge of the water and raised his head slightly above the level of the bank. There was enough light that he could clearly see Red Feather as he emerged from the bushes. He too had thought he had heard something, but he could see nothing. Wetzel quickly raised his rifle and fired a shot that caught Red Feather squarely in the chest.

Knowing that he had given away his position, Wetzel quickly scrambled up out of the river and began to run at an angle, which he thought would lead him toward the Ohio. He knew there was a path along that big river, and if he could reach it, he was confident that his foot speed would enable him to escape. Tall Shadow, who was some 150 yards away, ran toward the sound of the shot, hoping it was his partner who had fired it. Little Fox and his party, unaware of the turn in the river, were confused at the direction from which the shot had come.

"He must have crossed the river," said Red Storm. "Perhaps Red Feather has killed him."

"I doubt it," said Little Fox. "Let us get there quickly."

They decided to split up, with Little Fox and Red Storm crossing the stream immediately, and Fire Heart and the other brave following the trail that they thought Wetzel had taken. The bend in the river had puzzled them further, but they continued along both sides. In a few minutes, they reached the spot where Tall Shadow was standing above the fallen Red Feather.

"What happened?" shouted Red Storm.

"I don't know." explained Tall Shadow. "I found Red Feather here. He is dead."

"Did you see the white man?" Red Storm had grabbed Tall Shadow by the arm. "You should have seen him."

"He was down here," called Fire Heart, who had discovered the place where Wetzel had crossed the stream.

After a short conference, it was determined Little Fox, Red Storm, and Fire Heart would continue the pursuit while the others would take care of the dead and wounded. The three good friends hastened to find the trail Wetzel had left. Feeling that speed was more important than stealth, the white hunter had left some signs that were easily followed.

"His trail is easy to find," said Little Fox confidently. "Let us hurry, and we will catch him before very long." This was said partly to encourage Red Storm, whose scowl made it clear that he was distressed at another failure to kill his sworn enemy.

By noon, the confidence of the three was lagging. Although they were certain that Wetzel was somewhere ahead of them, there was no evidence that they were gaining on him.

For his part, Wetzel was pushing hard. He reckoned he was making close to four miles an hour, even counting the short rests he was taking. He felt that his pursuers could not do much better, and by evening he would be at Point Pleasant and the old Fort Randolph. Even though that fort was no longer occupied, there were settlers in the area, and his safety would be secured.

It was midafternoon when Little Fox called a halt. "It is of no use to continue this chase," he said sadly. "He is surely close to the white settlements on the Kanawha River."

"I agree," said Fire Heart.

"I am sorry, old friend," he said to Red Storm. Although he wanted to keep on, Red Storm was near exhaustion, and he knew that they had failed once more. "I don't see how he got away. I thought we had them for sure."

"I think he had left the camp before we attacked. He is very slippery." Little Fox patted Red Storm on the shoulder. "There will be another time, I promise. But now, I think we should go home to our wives."

September 20, 1788

There was a definite chill in the air that morning as Lewis Wetzel waited impatiently for Judge Symmes to appear. Wetzel had spent the night in a small lean-to shed that was one of three that had been hastily constructed by him and eight Kentuckians since they had arrived at the mouth of the Great Miami River just a few days ago.

Symmes spent his nights in the cabin on the flatboat that had brought them here. John Cleves Symmes was a former congressman who had been appointed one of three judges for the territory north and west of the Ohio River. His fellow judges were S. H. Parsons and James M. Varnum, who were residing in the new settlements across the Muskingum from Fort Harmar. Symmes had arrived at Fort Harmar in late August, and having obtained a contract from Congress for over one million acres of land between the Little and Great Miami Rivers, was anxious to visit the land. He needed guides and surveyors, and as Wetzel had been present at the time of his visit, Symmes had persuaded the hunter to go with him and his friend, Benjamin Stites, who had come with him from the east.

"We will be joined in Limestone by some men I know from Kentucky," Symmes had assured him, and Wetzel had agreed to go along. The two men had become well acquainted during the trip, and Wetzel, although it was quite unlike him, had told the judge a considerable amount of his life's story. As promised, they had stopped at Limestone, where the eight men, including John Filson, had joined them.

Stites had stayed in Limestone, planning to lead several families to the area a bit later. Much to the chagrin of the Kentuckians, Symmes had been talking with a small band of Wyandot Indians who were camped a few miles up the Great Miami River. Filson had recommended attacking the camp after it had been discovered on one of the early scouting expeditions. Symmes had refused, finding the Indians, led by an old chief named Black Fish, to be rather friendly. Filson was threatening to leave unless Symmes changed his mind. Symmes had returned from the Indian town the previous day in a happy mood and had mentioned to Wetzel that he had something special planned for him the next morning.

As he waited to find out what this was, Wetzel began to regret that he had come along on this adventure. It was a little short of a year since his unfortunate episode with John Madison. He still felt some embarrassment at what he considered his failure to do the job he had been hired to do. Of course, he was unable to figure out what he could have done to prevent the attack by what he now thought was at least eight Indians. His own life had been in danger for a time, but he had managed to get to Point Pleasant safely.

He found a boat going upriver that very day and made it back home in three days. He had taken his brother Jacob and Alexander Mitchell with him and returned to the scene on the Guyandotte in order to bury the dead. The three men were astounded to find Madison's dog, Wolf, lying next to Madison's body.

"He's near dead," Jacob remarked.

"Fightin' off the wolves, I reckon," said Lew. "Quite a dog. Deserves to be rescued." He picked up the dog and carried him over to their canoe, gently placing him on the floor. The dog did not move.

They had buried the three bodies with no further comment. The return home had Wetzel in a sour mood, and his two companions left him to his own thoughts.

In the spring of the year, Wetzel had signed on as a scout for Ohio County, Virginia. His friend Vachel Dickerson and brother Jacob had served in that capacity, as well as Sam Brady. It gave Wetzel a chance to do what he liked and receive a little pay for it. He had promised to resume those duties again early in the new year.

"What am I doing way down here?" he said aloud. "I'll have to get back to Wheeling pretty soon."

His thoughts were interrupted by the appearance of Judge Symmes, striding briskly up the path from where his boat was moored.

"Ah, good morning, Wetzel," he said cheerily. "Glad to see you here already."

"Good mornin' to you, Judge," answered Wetzel. "Where are we goin'?"

"We're goin' upriver to the Wyandot village. The chief wants to meet you."

"What?" exclaimed Wetzel in sheer disbelief. "I ain't never been invited to meet no Injun in my whole life."

"Well, this chief claims he led a party that captured two boys near Wheeling several years ago and that they escaped. I told him that one of those boys was with me right now. He didn't believe me at first, but then he asked to meet you and see for himself."

"I doubt it's the same Injun. Besides, ever since then, I've been plannin' to kill any of them sons of bitches if I ever run across one of 'em."

"Now, Lew, I have to ask you to scrap any such plans. These Indians have been nothing but friendly."

"What if that chief has been plannin' on gittin' even with me after all them years? I think I'll pass on this invitation."

"Lew, it's a small village, hardly any warriors there. I think it's mostly just the old chief's family. Aren't you just a little curious?"

The argument continued for another five minutes before Wetzel finally agreed to go. Two other men were chosen to go along, although Symmes was adamant that there was no danger.

It took a little more than an hour before the four men reached the Indian town. It was located on the site of the fort called Fort Finney that had been built as a temporary fortification used during the Great Miami Treaty negotiations held in January of 1786. The Americans had promised to dismantle it after the negotiations were over, but the job had been done for them during a flood several weeks later. The Wyandots had used some of the debris to build temporary huts for their current use.

The old chief, Black Fish, came out to meet them. "Hello, my friend, Symmes," he said in broken English.

"Hello, Black Fish." Taking Wetzel by the arm, the judge led him close to where the chief was standing. "This is Lewis Wetzel. I believe you have met before."

Wetzel was astonished. In spite of the passage of time, he could not mistake the small Indian leader that he and Jacob had called Little King. Strangely, he felt no animosity toward the man. For his part, Black Fish was not convinced. He did note the pockmarks on Wetzel's face, but otherwise, there was no way he could be sure that this was the boy he had captured. He held out his hands, palms up, to show his lack of belief.

Although it was quite surprising to him, Wetzel found himself wanting to prove to this old chief that he was indeed one of the boys they had taken. He ripped open his shirt far enough to reveal the old scar on his breast.

Immediately a smile appeared on the face of Black Fish, and he began to laugh and slap his hands on his thigh. "Yes, yes," he shouted, turning quickly and calling to an old woman standing near the door to his hut.

"By God, I think he believes it now," exclaimed Judge Symmes. "If this don't beat all. I don't imagine you thought you'd ever see that old man again, eh, Lew?"

"I had a lot of dreams about seein' him in my gunsight," allowed Wetzel.

The chief returned with his wife right behind him. She was smiling and nodding her head, saying something in her native tongue. Her husband made several gestures with his hands and managed a few words in his tortured English. "Stay with us."

"They're happy to see you, Lew," explained Symmes. "They want you to stay here with them for a while, I think."

"I don't think so," replied Wetzel.

"But, Lew, if you refuse to stay, they'll be insulted."

"I've insulted quite a few red devils in my day," laughed Lew.

The chief made it clear he wanted Symmes and Wetzel to join him in his hut, which they agreed to do. He pulled out a long pipe and stuffed it with tobacco he retrieved from an old pouch. The three men sat and smoked, passing the pipe around several times. The woman brought them bowls of a kind of corn soup, and they ate without any talk. When that was finished, they went back outside. Black Fish seemed to be waiting for an answer to his invitation. Judge Symmes felt it was in his interest to have good relations with the Indians, considering his large land holdings in the area.

He pleaded with Wetzel to respond to what he felt was the kindness of Black Fish. The white men withdrew to discuss the matter. The two Kentuckians wanted to return to their camp, and Symmes knew that he must return also. Even though he recognized that it was probably foolish to think that Wetzel would agree to stay with the Indians by himself, he continued to press the issue. "Lew, I'm asking you to stay with them. Just for one night. Please do it for my sake."

Wetzel was convinced it would be a bad idea. He couldn't help but wonder if the Wyandots weren't just hoping to finish the job they had started so many years ago. On the other hand, he couldn't admit that he had some fear for his own safety. That would not be expected of Lewis Wetzel. But his hatred for Indians was well-known also. Lewis Wetzel spending a night in a friendly Indian village? Who would believe that? In the end, Wetzel agreed to stay, and he watched with some dismay as his companions left him behind late in the afternoon.

September 21, 1788

The evening had passed without incident. The chief made it clear that Wetzel was to sleep in his hut. They had enjoyed a late meal of fish and a corn cake covered with maple syrup. The little village, which consisted of only four small huts, became very quiet as darkness fell. Wetzel was uncomfortable as he stretched out on a blanket on one side of the little structure while the chief and his wife bedded down on the opposite side.

Sleep hadn't come easily, and now Wetzel had come wide awake, certain that he had heard an unusual noise of some kind. He raised his head to look at the other two occupants, but they were sleeping quietly. There were two other warriors in camp, and Wetzel figured it was quite possible that one of them might be planning to become a hero. He had no way of knowing if these Indians knew anything about him. He found his knife and placed it within easy reach. His rifle was lying next to him on the other side, but he didn't think it was likely to be of any use if an attack were to come. He thought morning was not far away, and he had best stay awake.

Wetzel had settled down, but in just a few minutes, he heard something again. This time, he identified it as a footstep, just outside the wall beside him. He grabbed the knife and pulled it under the blanket. He would feign sleep, he decided, and surprise the attacker, for he was sure now that one was coming. Suddenly there was a loud disturbance outside, loud enough that it awakened Black Fish. There was angry talk, although Wetzel had no idea what it was about.

Black Fish had jumped up and was outside quickly while his wife had stepped behind him and stood in the doorway. She turned and held up her hand to Wetzel, who was up with his knife held in readiness. Her facial expression indicated that there was nothing to worry about. There was more shouting, some of which Wetzel could tell was coming from the chief. Black Fish reappeared and indicated to Wetzel that he should lie down again.

Lew could guess what had happened. One of the warriors may well have intended harm to him, just as he suspected. Another had intervened, and the chief had restored order. Wetzel settled down, as did Black Fish and his wife, but Lew did not sleep. He was very glad when dawn arrived and the little village came to life again. When he came out of the hut, he saw that a tall warrior was standing near the door. Lew nodded to him, and the man responded with a smile.

"Looks like I had my own guard," said Wetzel quietly to himself. Nothing more was made of the incident in the night, and the villagers all made effort to show Wetzel some kindness. After breakfast, a piece of buckskin was fastened to the limb of a tree near the river, and Black Fish signaled that there was to be a shooting match. This appealed to Wetzel, and he retrieved his gun and joined the two warriors and Black Fish at a spot some fifty yards away from the target.

One of the warriors was quite sullen, and Lew realized he was the one who had caused the trouble during the night. He was the first to shoot, and Wetzel, seeing that the gun was an old British musket, knew that he was unlikely to hit the target. After the shot, which missed everything, the warrior pointed at Wetzel, indicating he was to shoot next. Taking careful aim, Lew put a ball through the center of the mark. A cheer went up from the onlookers who now encouraged the tall brave, the one who had been guarding the chief's hut.

Lew could see that he had a rifle and handled it with some expertise. His shot hit the mark, but on the edge. Still he was pleased with himself, and the villagers cheered him wildly. A new mark was put up and the contest continued.

After awhile, Wetzel indicated that he wanted to show them something new. After proving to them that his gun was not loaded, he moved back a good distance from the place where they were standing and began running toward them, loading his gun as he ran. When he pulled up and fired a quick shot that again hit the mark, the crowd erupted. Even the scowling brave who had intended to harm the white visitor was impressed and slapped Wetzel on the back.

Wetzel was pleased that he had been able to perform so well, and he was surprised at himself that he could feel at ease among sworn enemies. Various games continued, and as the afternoon waned, Lew indicated that he must now return to his camp on the Ohio. Black Fish understood, but he asked Wetzel to wait while he went to get his wife.

It wasn't long before the old woman appeared, carrying in her arms a fine suit of buckskin. It included a hunting shirt, leggings, and a breechclout ornamented with several silver brooches. There was also a pair of moccasins, finely worked with colored porcupine quills. She presented these items to Wetzel with a wide smile. She pointed at her husband and laughed. Black Fish tried to explain as best he could. "She give for you, smart to escape from me."

Wetzel laughed and thanked her. Who would ever believe this, he thought. With a wave to all who stood watching, he turned and began his walk back to his home camp. "By God," he said. 'I'm goin' to keep this suit. It's nicer'n anything I ever had."

16

GEORGE WASHINGTON

June 20, 1789

THE WINTER HAD been long and hard, although Little Fox had found it enjoyable to spend so much time with his lovely wife, Bright Moon, and the three children they were raising. While he loved Swift Hawk and Many Winds—Bright Moon's son and daughter by White Eagle—Little Fox clearly favored his own son, Eagle's Wing, now nearly three years old. He had brought the boy a brightly colored fringed belt taken from the white men's camp. It had belonged to Madison's slave, Zeke, and Eagle's Wing had listened with great interest at his father's description of the black man.

Red Storm had brought his family to Buckongehelas's little village on the Auglaize as well, but Little Fox found it difficult to be around his friend, mostly despondent at their most recent failure to kill their great enemy.

"We will go there this spring to where he lives, Red Storm," Little Fox had finally promised one day. "We will bring back his scalp to hang by our fire."

Of course they did not know exactly where Wetzel lived, but they knew it was somewhere near the place the white men called Wheeling. They were in the area now, having crossed the Ohio and landed near the mouth of Short Creek. Red Storm was the leader of this raid, having stuck his tomahawk in the council house door at the Auglaize town. This act, announcing the intention to organize a raid, was really a custom of the Shawnees, but Red Storm had used it to his advantage.

There were a number of Shawnees living at the Delaware village of Buckongehelas, and Red Storm's act brought a quick response. Black Wing, the Shawnee who had been injured by Lew Wetzel's hunting knife, was especially eager to avenge himself. Tall Shadow was another who had been with Little Fox and Red Storm on a number of missions. Bald Rock was visiting in the town and was glad to have an opportunity to repeat the successful assault on Fishing Creek two years earlier. The other three were young Delawares who were friends of Red Storm. Their names were Black Buffalo, Red Beaver, and Young Deer.

Little Fox regretted that Fire Heart was not with them, but their Shawnee friend had gone with his family to one of the new Shawnee towns on the upper Maumee. The majority of the Delaware warriors was no longer on the warpath against the whites. Captain Pipe, one of the principal Delaware war chiefs, was considered friendly to the Americans and was a frequent visitor to Fort Harmar, where General Harmar considered him to be a peace emissary. He had participated in the negotiations, which led to the treaty of Fort Harmar that had been concluded in the January just past.

Both Red Storm and Little Fox were disgusted with their Delaware brethren and were pleased that several of the tribe were along on this expedition. The French trader, Le Clerk while visiting their village during the winter, had explained to Red Storm that his enemy, Wetzel, was acting as one of the Virginia rangers. It would be his duty to respond to any Indian raids in the Wheeling area. The plan, then, was to carry out an attack in the region and hope that Wetzel would appear in order to catch and punish the raiders. Little Fox put little faith in this plan, but Red Storm was excited about it, and Little Fox was very glad to see his friend's spirits restored.

There were a number of white settlements on Short Creek, including Fort Van Meter. Because of their small number, only eight braves, Red Storm's party knew that it should find an isolated homestead. They had moved along the creek very carefully, avoiding any detection and turned south at a point where a north fork took a turn toward the location of the fort and the town of West Liberty. They had set up a cold camp for the night in a clump of heavy woods near the creek and at the foot of a fairly big hill. Young Deer and Bald Rock had undertaken a scouting trip and returned to report on the existence of a cabin in a clearing on the flat section at the top of the hill.

"That is good," announced Red Storm. "We will attack them just after the sun sets this night."

The cabin in question was owned by a man named Robert Purdy who, with his wife and family of four children, had come to Ohio County only the previous year. He had chosen this land on high ground with great satisfaction, confident that the rich soil would help provide him with excellent crops. He was told that there had been few Indian attacks in the area in the last year, and it was close to the settlements in Wheeling and the town of West Liberty, which had been laid out and organized some eighteen months earlier and was the location of the county courthouse.

Purdy and his oldest son, Jonathan, had finished hoeing a field of corn, and as darkness neared, they hurried inside, captivated with the wonderful smells of pork chops frying in the big pan hanging over the fire.

"By God, it was a good day, and we finished the hoeing," Purdy said to his wife Ellen, who was already scooping up the chops and placing them in a big dish.

A little girl, Annie, just six years old, ran over and jumped into Purdy's arms. "Daddy, daddy," she cried, "the old cat had her kittens today. Ain't that wonderful."

"Well, I guess it is," agreed Purdy. "Did you know about that, Johnny?"

The boy allowed that he did, and eight-year-old Sally chimed in that the mother and kits were out in the little milkshed.

"How will we feed all of them?" she wanted to know.

"Well, her ma will take care of that for awhile," noted Ellen. "Now get up to the table and eat while everything is still hot."

"Where is the baby?" asked Robert.

The little boy, named Edward, was nearly two, but his father still referred to him as a baby.

"He's back on our bed asleep," answered Ellen. "I fed him earlier."

Purdy, a religious man, led in a prayer, and the conversations ended as the eating began. Suddenly the cabin door burst open, and five Indian braves rushed in. Red Storm attacked Purdy, who had immediately sprung to his feet but too late to defend himself. Repeated blows by Red Storm's tomahawk left him bleeding and lifeless on the floor.

Bald Rock had disposed of young Jonathan with one blow while Little Fox grabbed both of the young girls and pulled them back toward the door. Tall Shadow struck Mrs. Purdy with his tomahawk, and she fell to the floor. He took his knife and quickly scalped her, although he was a bit disappointed when he saw that he had only removed a very small piece.

In the meantime, Black Wing had found little Edward and was holding him by the feet, dangling him upside down. He gave a loud shout and swung the child hard against the wall, cracking his skull and killing him instantly. He threw the corpse on the floor and started toward Little Fox, holding out his hand, asking for one of the girls.

"No," said Little Fox. "We will take the girls with us. We want the whites to try to get them back. That is our plan."

"Yes," said Red Storm. "Let us go now and see if we are followed. I am hoping Wetzel will come."

"I do not care about this Wetzel," shouted Bald Rock. "But I do want these scalps."

The scalps were taken, along with a gun, some blankets, and other plunder; and the five warriors went out where they were met by the three Delaware boys.

"Shall we burn the cabin?" asked Tall Shadow.

"No, no," replied Red Storm. "We want them to see what we have done."

The eight warriors divided into two groups, one party of five led by Bald Rock, including Tall Shadow and the three young Delawares. The other group consisted of Red Storm, Little Fox, and Black Wing.

Little Fox spoke quietly to Bald Rock. "Take the two girl prisoners and return to the mouth of the creek on the big river. Leave a trail that can be followed, but not too obvious. Make sure that there are tracks by the little girls. We want any followers to know they have been taken."

Bald Rock nodded that he understood.

"We will go by another route," continued Little Fox. "If you are followed, we will be there to ambush them. We needn't hurry since it will be another day before any pursuit can begin."

The two groups moved off in the darkness. "Surely Wetzel will come," whispered Red Storm.

June 21, 1789

Wetzel was coming! Ellen Purdy had been knocked senseless with one blow of the tomahawk, but it had been a glancing stroke. Although she was gashed and bleeding, there had been no penetration of the skull, and she came back to consciousness about the time the Indians had left the cabin. She continued to lie still, thankful that the raiders had not disturbed the fire and tried to put the cabin aflame. Her head was throbbing, and there was a sharp pain coming from the top where the patch of scalp had been removed. She wanted to jump up and run but was afraid the Indians might reappear. She forced herself to remain still, feigning death for anyone who might be watching her.

After what seemed to be at least an hour, Ellen had roused herself and made her way to the open door of the cabin. It was quite dark, and she listened for several minutes without hearing any sound of human activity. She shuddered at the sight of her mutilated family, but in her fear and pain, she concentrated on only one thing, she needed to get someone to help.

She moved carefully through the door and ran through the darkness to the woods closest to the clearing on which the cabin stood. Upon reaching the edge of the forest, she dropped to the ground, deciding to wait there for daylight. As soon as the morning sun made its appearance, Ellen Purdy set out for Wheeling, at least a half-dozen miles away.

In spite of the terrible distress, her mind was focused on one thing, and her determination carried her to Ebenezer Zane's house in less than three hours. She pounded on the door, and Zane found her slumped against the threshold. He brought her inside, where his wife Elizabeth tended her.

"Noah," shouted Zane. "Where are you?"

"I'm right here, Pa," replied Noah, coming down the stairs from the second story.

"I need you to find Lew Wetzel," answered his father. "I think he spent the night down at the fort."

By the fort, Zane meant the new Fort Randolph, which had been constructed near the mouth of Wheeling Creek more than two years earlier. The old Fort Henry was no longer in use, many of its logs used in the building of the new one. People were more apt to just talk about Wheeling Fort than to use the actual name, which was given to honor the governor, Edmund Jennings Randolph.

Ten-year-old Noah, as always, was proud to run an important errand and immediately headed for the door.

"Tell him to get some men and come here real quick," Zane hollered after his retreating son.

Wetzel was talking with Veach Dickerson when Noah came rushing into the fort.

"Lew, Lew," Noah shouted breathlessly, not thinking it would sound right to address the man as Mr. Wetzel. "My pa says to come quick and bring some men."

"Whoa there, young Noah," laughed Wetzel. "What're you goin' on about?"

"There's a lady at our house, and she's hurt. Pa says for you to come."

"Come on, Veach, let's see what this is all about," said Lew, grabbing Dickerson by the arm.

Noah ran back up the path toward his father's house, looking back frequently to see if the men were coming. Ebenezer had come out to meet them. "Thanks, Noah, I see you were successful."

"What's up, Colonel?" asked Wetzel.

"I've got Ellen Purdy in the house. She's bad hurt, but she managed to tell me about an attack on her family by some Indians, at least four or five, she thinks. They killed her husband, Robert, and her two boys. She thinks they might have taken the girls with 'em."

"You want us to chase 'em?" asked Dickerson.

"I want you men to go up and see what's what. If you think you might rescue the little girls, then that would be good."

"Purdy. Is that the new family that settled up north?" Wetzel wasn't sure he'd ever met the man.

"That's right, Lew," said Zane. "Their place is up on the ridge 'bout halfway between here and West Liberty."

"We'll go, but there ain't nobody else around here just now. Can you get word to Brady? He's got some men with him, and they should be up around Van Meter's somewhere." Lew had only recently finished a term as a scout for the county, and he knew Sam Brady was still serving in that capacity himself.

"I'll find somebody to ride up there as soon as I can."

"Tell him to meet us at the mouth of Short Creek," said Wetzel. "I'm guessin' that's where the bastards will go to cross the river."

The two men reached the Purdy farm by noon. "God, what a mess," exclaimed Dickerson. "I reckon we need to bury these bodies before the coyotes get 'em."

"We should, but I want to get on the trail of them redskins as soon as we can." Wetzel looked longingly in the direction that the marauders had clearly taken. "But you're right, let's git it done."

They found a couple of spades in the little shed and quickly dug three shallow graves. When the bodies were covered, they replaced the spades and began following the trail.

"Someone will need to come up here and do a better job of buryin' than we did," said Dickerson.

"I agree, Veach, but we ain't got no more time if we hope to catch them sons of bitches."

They soon found the south fork of Short Creek and followed it down to where the north branch came in. Dickerson suggested they rest for a time before going on.

"You know, Veach, somethin' ain't right here."

"What are you talkin' about, Lew?"

"I ain't never seen them red bastards bein' so careless as this bunch. A blind man could follow this trail. You'd think they was wantin' us to follow 'em."

"Prob'ly they figure they got plenty of time. Hell, they should be across the Ohio by now."

"Could be, but it's mighty strange."

After continuing in silence for more than a mile, they came to a place where the creek, for no apparent good reason, took a sharp turn to the right before making a wide loop and returning to the original northwesterly course. The land inside the loop was mostly flat and covered with heavy grass and short bushes. The Indian trail cut directly through.

Wetzel knew the land well, but he stopped and searched the ground carefully. "They've definitely got two young 'uns with 'em. Here are their tracks." Wetzel stood, pointing to the clear footprints.

"That'd be the two daughters, I guess," observed Dickerson. "Six and eight, I think, is what the colonel said they was."

"Why do they want us to know they've got those little girls with 'em?" wondered Wetzel. "They would know that would make us want to follow 'em even more."

"Well, they ain't afraid of bein' followed, that's for sure."

"They'll have to cross the creek sometime," noted Lew. "There's a big hill on this side afore you git to the mouth. I wonder." He didn't complete the thought, and Dickerson decided against asking.

The sky had darkened, and a clap of thunder greeted them just ahead. The growth along both sides of the creek was thicker here, and several tall cottonwoods stood alongside the trail.

"By God, Lew, there's a storm comin'." Dickerson stopped and was looking around, hoping to find a good place to wait out the rain, which had begun to pelt them with some force.

"We may be in for more than just gittin' soaked," warned Wetzel. "Keep your powder dry, Veach, if you can."

"What are you talkin' about, Lew?" shouted Dickerson, as Wetzel began to run through the spindly growth along the left bank of the creek.

The hard shower stopped as suddenly as it had begun, but the ground had become muddy and slippery. The answer to Dickerson's question came as three shots rang out almost simultaneously. One tore through Dickerson's hat, and he dropped to the ground behind the nearest tree. Wetzel, who had swerved instinctively to his right, realized how lucky he was that the bullets had missed. He fell to the ground and raised his rifle just as Black Wing burst out of his hiding place and began running toward what he thought was a fallen foe.

Although Wetzel had no idea that this was the same Indian he had knifed back on the Guyandotte, he quickly aimed and fired a shot that felled the charging warrior immediately. A loud scream to his right brought Wetzel to his feet as he saw the threat coming from across the stream. As he attempted to move, he felt his foot slip at the edge of the creek bank, and he stumbled into the water and onto a pile of driftwood and dead tree branches.

Red Storm was wading rapidly through the water toward Wetzel with his tomahawk held high. Wetzel struggled to get up, but his right foot was jammed into a crevice between two logs and a piece of entangled vine. As he rose, he felt a sharp pain in his ankle, and he sank down again as the enraged warrior came near. He could see that one of the Indian's ears was missing.

"Kill Wetzel," shouted Red Storm, stopping to savor this moment that he had been anticipating for years.

Wetzel continued trying to jerk his foot free, but could not manage it.

"You're the one Leith told me about," said Lew, tensing to try to ward off the blow that he realized he could not avoid.

A look of surprise flickered across the face of Red Storm before he again made ready to strike. "Kill now," roared Red Storm, but his intention was thwarted when a bullet from Dickerson's gun struck his wrist, and the tomahawk tumbled from his hand and into the water. From the corner of his eye, Wetzel could see Little Fox racing toward them from just across the stream. He gave one last hard pull from his right leg, and suddenly he was free.

Red Storm was bent over in pain, and Wetzel thought to try to get his knife out and attack, but another brave had appeared and was taking aim with his gun. Wetzel dove onto the bank, and grabbing his rifle that had dropped when he fell, he rolled into some underbrush as the errant shot flew over him. Little Fox had reached Red Storm and was pulling him back to the other side of the creek. Tall Shadow, whose gun was now empty, retreated into a small stand of shrub oaks and began to reload. Veach Dickerson was doing the same.

Wetzel took advantage of the brief lull in activity to move back toward his partner's position, loading his gun as he ran, or more accurately, limped along.

Little Fox was helping Red Storm back along the right bank of the creek, determined to get him into the one canoe left a short distance downstream from where they were. Bald Rock and the three others had taken the two little girls across the Ohio early that morning. Little Fox was glad he had insisted the other canoe be brought up close to where they had set up the ambush. Red Storm was protesting, wanting to fight on, but his arm was bleeding badly, and he felt faint.

"We should get Black Wing and take him with us," said Tall Shadow.

"We should," agreed Little Fox, "but there is not time. They will be coming, and they can outshoot us."

Reluctantly, Tall Shadow turned back and helped Little Fox as he struggled to drag Red Storm toward the hidden canoe. "You may need to shoot to hold them back," said Little Fox to Tall Shadow. "The water's barely deep enough here to float the canoe. You will need to follow on the bank until we get to the big river."

Wetzel finally came to where Dickerson was kneeling behind a fallen tree trunk. "They're movin' back, Lew, and there's just three of 'em, I think. One of them is hurt too. We can rush 'em if you want."

"I'm afraid I ain't up to rushin' anybody," answered Wetzel, rubbing his sore ankle, which was sprained. "My ankle is hurtin' too bad."

"Are ya sure, Lew? I think we could take 'em."

"The girls ain't with this bunch," argued Wetzel. "I reckon they've already been taken across the river. We can follow later, but we might need more men. Brady ought to be showin' up afore long."

Wetzel reached out and squeezed Dickerson's shoulder, a gentle gesture meant to convey his gratitude.

"That was quite a shot, Veach," he said with a laugh. "You got him right in the wrist."

"Well, I was aiming fer his head."

"Maybe you should have aimed at his wrist."

"Well, maybe I should've let the bastard whack you in the head, you son of a bitch," cackled Dickerson.

"Well, this son of a bitch is mighty glad you didn't."

"Damn!" exclaimed Dickerson. "This sure didn't turn out the way I expected."

June 25, 1789

Veach Dickerson and Lewis Wetzel were stationed in a stand of oak saplings on a small ridge in the notch of a fork, which gave rise to two well-traveled Indian trails. The scattering of birch lodges that made up the old Indian village of Tuscarawas lay below them, and the Tuscarawas River was just beyond. They were partially blinded by the morning sun, rising to the east but determined that no one would get past them on either of the trails.

"What the hell, Lew? You think one of them bastards we been followin' will show up in front of us?"

"Prob'ly not, Veach, but some Injun's got to pay for what happened to the Purdys."

It had been three days since the two men had crossed the Ohio, following the rapidly diminishing signs of a trail left by Little Fox, Red Storm, and their friends. Sam Brady had shown up in the late afternoon after Wetzel and Dickerson's brief battle with the Indian raiders near the mouth of Short Creek. Brady was accompanied by four other rangers, all on horseback.

"Looks like we're a little late, Lew," he remarked as they rode up to where the two hunters were sitting. In spite of the difficulty in walking, Wetzel, with help from Dickerson, had made it up past the point where Little Fox and Red Storm had put the canoe into the creek.

"'Fraid so, Sam," agreed Lew. "You missed the party."

"I see you got one of 'em," noted Brady. "We saw the body on the other bank upstream."

"Got his scalp too," said Dickerson with a laugh. "Want to buy it?"

Brady just shook his head. "What all happened anyway?"

"A small war party came down the south branch of Short Creek and attacked the Purdy family, living on the ridge up there," explained Wetzel.

"I don't think I know that family," said Brady.

"They was new. I didn't know 'em either, but Colonel Zane filled me in. Anyway, the devils killed the old man and two sons, one just a baby. They scalped the mother, but she wasn't dead. Somehow, she made it to Zane's the next morning. They had two young daughters, and the Injuns carried them off. Veach and me was hopin' to get 'em back."

"They had too much lead on you though. Was that it?"

"Well, they split into two bunches. We was followin' the ones that had the girls, but the other bunch jumped us."

Brady shook his head. "It ain't like you to get caught with your pants down like that, Lew."

"Well, I was gittin' suspicious but didn't figger it out in time."

"That damned hard rain squall didn't help none either," offered Dickerson.

"It seems one of the bastards has been out to git me for a long time," said Lew. "I don't know how he had any idea I was around here."

"I suppose, Lew, you have made some enemies among the reds," laughed Brady.

"A trader named Leith told me about this son of a bitch a couple of years ago. Seems to think I'm the one who cut his ear off back in '81 up by Gnaddenhutten."

"That would rankle a fella a mite," said Brady, again with a chuckle.

"Well, me and Veach would like to keep after 'em, but we need horses. It's goin' to be awhile before I can walk very good."

"What's wrong with your leg?" asked Brady.

"I fell into the creek and got my foot caught up in a damned pile of driftwood. Twisted it bad tryin' to get away before that damned one-eared bastard conked me with his axe."

After some more talk, the Cox brothers, who had come along with Brady, offered to lend Wetzel and Dickerson their mounts.

"I don't want you goin' too far though," Brady warned. "We ain't suppose to be over there now chasin' Injuns since the latest treaty was signed."

"I reckon they ain't supposed to be over here killin' people neither," growled Wetzel.

"Well, no more'n ten miles or so, Lew, that's what I'm tellin' you."

Armed with some extra food and powder provided by Brady, Lew and Veach left the next morning. The cold trail was hard to follow, but it became clear that the Indians had taken a turn to the north and struck the old warrior path that went between Pittsburgh and the site of the abandoned Fort Laurens. On the previous evening, the two white hunters had come upon the place where the path crossed the Tuscarawas, and where the old town lay just beyond.

They had watched to see if there was any sign of the war party they had been trailing somehow staying in the village. There weren't more than twenty people in the town, including women and children. Disappointed, Wetzel and Dickerson had ridden a ways downstream, and finding an easy place to cross, they made their way to their current location. The horses were hobbled and left to stand a good distance back among the trees behind them.

More than two hours passed without a word between the two men. Wetzel had been enraged at what had happened to the Purdys and was determined to exact some vengeance. His attitudes toward the reds had been skewed somewhat, however, after his encounter with the Wyandots on the Great Miami. He realized that any victim who might come within his power right now would likely be completely innocent. But then, was any Indian really innocent? He never thought so before, so it was surprising that these thoughts were with him now. He knew this was not something that would be bothering his friend, Veach Dickerson. Their patient vigil was soon to be rewarded.

"Hey, look, Lew," whispered Dickerson, pointing to where the trail came out of the town.

"I see him," answered Wetzel quietly. "He's comin' on the south trail."

An Indian brave had ridden out from the town on a short pony. He was clad in buckskins, and his black hair was adorned with a single eagle's feather. Although it was unknown to Wetzel and Dickerson, the warrior was known as George Washington, and he was well-known down at Fort Harmar and was a favorite of General Harmar. He rode slowly but with confidence, completely unaware of any danger.

"He looks familiar to me," said Wetzel, "but I don't know why."

"He's a Delaware, I think," said Dickerson.

"Well, whoever he is, he was in that town when those killin' bastards went through with their prisoners. That's good enough reason for me." Wetzel lifted his rifle and took aim as George Washington, whose real name was Que-shaw-sey, rode by on the trail in front of them.

Dickerson was also ready, and they both fired their guns within a second of each other.

"By God, you hit him, Lew. I saw him start to fall."

The horse and rider had disappeared behind a clump of cedars, but they burst suddenly out and back along the trail at full gallop toward the town. Both Wetzel and Dickerson were frantically reloading, but by the time that task was finished, the wounded Indian, leaning flat against the horse's back, was nearly out of range.

"Well, he ain't dead yet," observed Wetzel, "and we ain't gonna git another chance."

"Mebbe we'd better skeddadle," suggested Dickerson. "Some of his friends may come out lookin' for us."

"I don't think there's any warriors much in that town. But I guess we may as well go home. At least we left one of the buggers with somethin' to think about." Wetzel shrugged and started back to get the horses.

June 28, 1789

The day was hot and muggy, and General Harmar had removed his powdered wig to let his bald head cool a bit from the very slight breeze coming in through the south window of his headquarters at Fort Harmar. He stood for a moment, feeling some relief from several hours hunched over papers at his desk.

He was a tall man, something that he felt some satisfaction about, and well proportioned, except for a bulging stomach that threatened to give him a portly look. He pulled his chest up and out, but he knew he was losing that battle. Just then his aide, Major Denny, came through the door.

"What is it, Major?" growled Harmar, annoyed that Denny had caught him without his wig.

"There's a Delaware runner here, General," explained the major. "He's sayin' that George Washington's been shot."

"The president?" began Harmar, before noticing that Denny was shaking his head vigorously. "Oh no, you mean the Indian?"

"That's right, sir. Your friend, the Delaware."

Denny had never really approved of his commander's feelings toward that particular Indian.

"So what happened? Is he dead?"

"I don't think so, sir. The runner's name is Cold Wind. He wants to tell you himself."

"Can he speak English?"

"Actually, he can, sir. Pretty well, in fact."

"Send him in then."

Harmar reached for his wig and quickly placed it on his head as Denny went out. He sat down and began shuffling through some papers as the major returned with Cold Wind.

"General, this is Cold Wind, the runner I told you about." Denny nodded at the Indian and took a step back. Both men waited for the general to respond. After a short time during which Harmar appeared to be deeply involved with what he was reading, the general raised his head and seemed to acknowledge his visitor for the first time.

"What do you have to tell me?" he asked.

"Que-shaw-sey has been shot," Cold Wind reported simply. "He wanted you to know."

"Where did this happen?" asked the general.

"Up on the Tuscarawas branch of the Muskingum," interceded Denny. "There's an old Indian town there where George Washington was staying."

"Is he dead?" The general realized that nobody had said anything about the nature of the injury.

"Badly hurt," said Cold Wind quickly.

"Do we know who did it?"

"Some of the townsfolk think it might have been somebody from Brant's people, but others insist it is militia from Wheeling," answered Denny.

"What do you think my friend?" The question was directed to Cold Wind.

"White men do it," he said coldly.

"That's probably right," said General Harmar. "What reason would Brant have for such an act?"

"Well, Brant doesn't like anyone who is friendly with us," responded Denny.

"White men do it," repeated Cold Wind.

"I think the Indian is right," said Harmar. "See what you can find out, Major. Send somebody up to Wheeling."

"But ain't this a civilian matter, General?" Denny didn't think it was right to send off any soldiers on such a duty.

"We'll notify Judge Parsons, but we'll have to help find the guilty party and deliver him to the judge."

"Yes, sir," agreed Denny, resisting the urge to argue further. "I'll send four men."

"That many?" The general thought Denny was trying to be difficult.

"Sir, four may not be enough. Them tough old frontiersmen ain't likely to give anybody up easy."

"Well, their first job is to find out who did this, then we'll worry about arresting him." Dismissing Denny, he turned his attention to Cold Wind. "We will send some food back with you. Please tell my friend Que-shaw-sey that he is welcome to come here and be treated by my doctor. Do you understand?"

Cold Wind indicated that he understood, and Harmar escorted him outside.

"Orderly!" he shouted. "Get this man some provisions and a fresh horse and send him on his way."

The general returned to his office, muttering to himself. "Those damned militia. They're going to get us into a fine mess, shooting innocent Indians. This one was a real friend to us. It's a damned shame."

July 9, 1789

General Harmar had just finished his latest letter to General Knox, the secretary of war, located in New York City. He sat back satisfied, resting a moment before calling an orderly to make arrangements for its delivery. He was thinking about the part involving the shooting of the Delaware George Washington. Harmar had explained to Knox that this was a

> trusty confidential Indian, and was wounded by some vagabond whites from the neighborhood of Wheeling. He is well-known to Governor St. Clair, and I believe there is not a better Indian to be found. The villain who wounded him I am informed is one Lewis Whitzell. I am in hopes to be able to apprehend him and deliver him to Judge Parsons to be dealt with; but would much rather have it in my power to order such vagabonds hanged up immediately without trial.

Of course, the general knew that he had no such power, that it was a civilian affair. He had sent some soldiers to Wheeling to investigate the shooting, after informing Judge Parsons of his intent. Someone in Wheeling had eventually suggested that Lewis Wetzel was the likely shooter. The four men had gone to the Wetzel farm and to the Bonnett farm but were unable to find their quarry. At least they had returned with a name, and Wetzel had been duly charged by Judge Parsons.

The general knew the man Wetzel, of course, having first met him when Wetzel showed up with a report on Logan's expedition. He had also served on more than one occasion as a hunter for the fort. As with most officers in the army, and also the British officers from times gone by, Harmar held a low opinion of militiamen, and especially the frontiersmen. He wasn't surprised that it was such a man who had shot a friendly Indian, but it irritated him greatly, and he very much wanted to see justice done in the matter.

He stood up and walked to the door when he was met by Major Denny, who burst in, nearly out of breath. "General, there's a big commotion out on the river. They tell me that Lewis Wetzel is on that big flatboat just outside the mouth of the Muskingum."

"What?" shouted Harmar. "The man that we've been looking for is right out there?"

"That's what they're sayin', General."

"Well, tell Kingsbury to get some men and go arrest the man."

"He's on the water, General," Denny pointed out.

"We've got boats, haven't we? Tell Kingsbury to get with it quick. I want that man in custody."

Lewis Wetzel was indeed on the water. When word had come to him that he was being sought for the shooting of an Indian, he had not believed it, but eventually he accepted the fact, and a growing anger began to consume him. Normally he would have laughed at what was an absurdity to him, but the more he thought about it, the more furious he became.

"By God, Veach," he complained to his friend and companion in the supposed crime, "we were chasin' them bastards that murdered the Purdy family. Why would them sons of bitches think I was some kind of criminal?"

"I agree it don't make no sense," sympathized Dickerson. "But they was up here lookin' for you."

"Well, I wish they'd found me. I'd a put 'em out of their misery, I reckon."

"I was told they had some writ from a judge down in Marietta. But the troops came from General Harmar."

"Hell, Harmar knows me. Why would he send soldiers after me?"

After a couple of days, Wetzel had decided to go to Kentucky, and he found a flatboat headed downriver owned by a man named Downs. Thinking it might be wise to have this famous frontiersman along, Downs agreed to take Wetzel with them. He had mostly kept to himself, but Downs could sense that Wetzel was seething about something.

For his part, Lewis had spent much of his time arguing with himself. What he planned to do was obviously foolish, but he could not seem to keep himself from doing it. The flatboat approached the mouth of the Muskingum shortly after noon on their third day out. Downs had originally planned a stop at the new town of Marietta, located across the Muskingum from Fort Harmar. But one of his men had let him know that they had a man on board who was wanted by the authorities in Marietta.

Downs didn't have to ask who that was, and he was sorry now that he had agreed to let Wetzel come along. Still he had no desire to give up one of his men to anybody, and he determined to push past the town and fort as fast as possible. The boat had swung toward the Ohio shore, where the elements of civilization were present, several acres having been cleared of the towering sycamores and other trees. The first settlers had arrived in April of 1788, and by July 2, the official name Marietta had been established, done so in honor of

Marie Antoinette. By now, a garrison with blockhouses at the corners had been established a short distance north along the east bank of the Muskingum. This garrison had been named Campus Martius.

Some semblance of policing and government had been set up under the broad guidelines of the Northwest Ordinance, but the principal enforcers of order were the three newly appointed federal judges, Parsons, Varnum, and Symmes.

A few people had gathered at the corner of land bordered by the north shore of the Ohio and the east bank of the Muskingum to watch the flatboat come toward them, assuming it was intending to make a landing. It was at this moment, as the boat came close to this point—later called Picketed Point—that Lew Wetzel made his appearance, "cutting a high swell" as his friend Henry Jolly would later describe it.

Holding his rifle high above his head, Wetzel gave out his patented scream, the one that sometimes accompanied his attacks against the Indians. "Come and get me, you bastards," he yelled. "It's Lew Wetzel right here in front of you."

Caught in the current flowing from the Muskingum, the boat swung out into the main Ohio channel, soon passing the point off Fort Harmar. Wetzel repeated his challenge, and it was not long before a boat, filled with a squad of soldiers led by Lieutenant Jacob Kingsbury, had put out from the shore and was giving chase. Aided by four men rowing, the boatload of soldiers was quickly closing the gap with the flatboat. Wetzel had moved to the back and raised his rifle as if to shoot at the pursuers.

"My God, man," said one of the flatboat's crew. "You can't shoot them soldiers. They'd kill us all afore it was over."

"The hell they would," snarled Wetzel. "They're just after me, I reckon, and I don't aim for them to catch me."

"You should have kept your mouth shut then," said Downs, who had come up behind them. "Put that damned gun down."

Wetzel turned and raised the gun, preparing to strike Downs with it. His black eyes were flashing, and his teeth were grinding together as he prepared to do battle. Downs shrank back, realizing that he was in real danger, and the soldiers would not arrive in time to save him. The other man moved back beside him. Suddenly, and surprisingly, Wetzel lowered the weapon, and shook his head.

"It ain't your fault, I guess. It's mine." He sank against a bag of flour that was stacked near where he stood.

Relieved, Downs moved past him and stared at the boat of soldiers bearing down on them. He turned back to Wetzel. "There's nothing I can do now, Wetzel," he said quietly. "We can't outrun 'em, and I ain't about to fight 'em either."

Wetzel gave a brief thought to rushing to the other side of the boat and trying to swim to the opposite shore. He knew this was hopeless with the soldiers so near, and he resigned himself to what was coming. His anger and foolishness had put him in this fix, and he didn't want to fight it any longer. He had never killed a white man that he could remember, although he'd given some serious injury to the thief in the Pittsburgh brothel.

Lieutenant Kingsbury signaled to the flatboat captain that he wanted the boat to put in on the Ohio shore. By this time, the two boats had gone past Fort Harmar for more than half a mile, but there was a clear landing spot just ahead on the shoreline. Downs, somewhat put out at the order, but feeling that he had no choice, executed the maneuver that soon brought them ashore.

The soldiers were out of their boat quickly and splashed through the shallow water to where Wetzel stood at the very back of the flatboat. He said nothing and made no move toward the soldiers, but when two of them jumped aboard and started to grab him, Lew suddenly pushed them away, pointing at the one who had grabbed at his right arm. "Keep your hands off me," he shouted. "I ain't no criminal."

"We've got orders to arrest you," replied the man, a sergeant named Sprague. "Come on, easy now." Sprague was joined by two other men, and the three of them crowded around Wetzel, who had begun waving his arms in protest, still holding his rifle in his left hand. When one of the men reached for it, Wetzel cuffed him hard against the side of his face, sending the man sprawling. Lieutenant Kingsbury, who had come aboard, drew his sword and pointed it at Wetzel.

"Stop it, man," he bellowed. "Or I'll run ya through."

"Easy, men," said Captain Downs, who had stepped up between the soldiers and Wetzel. "The man will come peacefully if you let him. He told me so himself."

"He ain't much actin' like it," offered Sergeant Sprague, looking at his fellow soldier who was getting up from the deck where Wetzel's blow had put him.

"I'll come," barked Wetzel, "but keep your hands off me." Lew had flared up at the sight of the lieutenant's sword, figuring he could still make it pretty hard for the men to take him. It took every bit of his willpower to get himself under control, and he knew that further resistance would only make things worse.

"All right," said Kingsbury, replacing his sword in its sheath. "But we have to tie your hands. That's standard procedure."

"This man is a civilian," noted Downs. "By what authority is he arrested by the army?"

Kingsbury had anticipated this question. "We are acting under the order of Judge Parsons, a federal judge of the Northwest Territory."

"And what is the charge?" asked Downs, not sure why he was coming to the defense of a man he barely knew.

"What business is that of yours, friend?" asked Kingsbury.

"I'm captain of this here boat, and you're arresting one of my crew."

"He's charged with shootin' a peaceful Indian, in violation of the new treaty signed at Fort Harmar just a few months ago."

Downs turned to Wetzel and gave a shrug. "There's nothing I can do. I think you need to go along with this. I doubt too much will come of it."

Wetzel allowed his hands to be tied behind his back, and the soldiers led him back along the riverbank to the fort. One of them carried his rifle and his pouch, which Downs had given them. They put Wetzel in the guardhouse, a log structure with no windows, built against the south stockade wall and equipped with a heavy door. A short time later, four men returned and replaced his rawhide bonds with iron cuffs, one on each wrist and joined with an iron chain. His hands were now in front of him, but the cuffs were painful. The men left him slumped against the wall, the picture of dejection.

An hour passed in which an observer would have detected not a single movement by the prisoner. Then he jumped to his feet and began to pace. The room was absolutely empty. There was no furniture, no water, not even a pail for him to relieve himself. This was a new experience for a hunter and woodsman accustomed to the freedom to do what he pleased.

"By God," he muttered. "What have I got myself into?"

He walked along the walls, forlornly hoping for some way to escape, but he quickly saw that there was no way to get out without some kind of help.

He had friends across the river. Hamilton Kerr had a place on the island in the river just across from Marietta, and Isaac Williams had lived for the past two years on a farm a few miles downriver on the Virginia side. Of course, neither of them would even know that Wetzel was in the area, and he didn't know if he could get word to them. He assumed there must be a guard outside the door, so he went there and pounded on it.

"Hey, guard."

There was no answer, and he pounded again.

"Hey, can I ask you somethin'?"

An answer finally came, and it was hardly friendly. "Whatta you want?"

"Can a man get some water to drink? I'm powerful thirsty."

"It ain't time for you to eat yet, so shut the hell up."

"Look, I ain't mad at you. I know you're just doin' your job. Askin' for a little water ain't much."

There was no more reply from the guard, but Wetzel continued to talk, explaining his predicament and how sorry he was. The guard, a private named John Stockley, began to sympathize with the prisoner. He didn't think it ought to be a crime to shoot an Indian. Stockley was no great lover of authorities himself, having been severely punished two years earlier for desertion. He had never really gotten over the humiliation the officers had caused him.

After another hour of intermittent conversation, Stockley agreed to procure not only some water, but Wetzel's pipe and tobacco from the storeroom where his belongings had been stashed. Just after dark, two men came with Wetzel's supper: a bowl of corn soup and a piece of hard bread. One of them was there to relieve Stockley, but all three stayed and had a pleasant conversation while the prisoner ate. It did not escape Wetzel's notice that the door was not latched from the outside.

He thought of making a break right then, but he would still be inside the fort. Better to wait for another opportunity, and a plan was already forming in his mind. It would depend on the goodwill of his guards. The men were still there when Sergeant Sprague came by to check. He quickly got the men outside and set the heavy latch to lock the door. He set two of the men to guard the door, and sent Stockley to take the dirty bowl back to the kitchen. The new guards' names were David Gregg and John Burton.

Wetzel waited patiently inside, letting more than two hours go by. Then he called to the guard whose name he had learned earlier during their friendly conversation.

"David," he called. "I need to go, you know?"

"What?" asked Gregg. "What do you want?"

"I have to go, David, and I don't want to do it in here."

"Well, you'll have to. I can't let you out."

"Come on, David," pleaded Wetzel. "You don't want me to do it in here. It ain't civilized."

"I told you, it ain't allowed," insisted Gregg. "They'd skin me alive if I was to let you outta there."

"Who would know? Get your friend Burton to help. I've got these damned irons on, I can't do nothin'."

He heard the two men whispering outside the door. Soon he heard the latch lifting, and the door swung open.

"Come on then," said Gregg. "But be damned quiet."

"Thanks, David," said Wetzel gratefully.

"Shut up and get out there quick. But don't go too far."

"Go ahead of me David, and show me where you want me to go. Burton can cover me from behind."

"Keep close," whispered Gregg as he opened the main gate and led the way out with Wetzel just behind him, and Burton holding his gun and crowding up closely in the rear.

"Damn, it's dark," said Burton. "Don't go too far."

Gregg and Wetzel moved out to the right, and Burton held back, deciding he didn't need to be so close to this action. Sensing that the distance between himself and the rear guard was widening, Wetzel made his move. He raised his arms and crashed the heavy iron cuff on his left wrist down hard on the back of Gregg's head. The man went down in a heap, and Wetzel leaped past him and was soon in a dead run across the grassy meadow, heading for the deep woods less than fifty yards away. Burton was momentarily stunned by the action and at first not sure who was down.

Even in the darkness, however, he saw the running figure and knew it must be Wetzel. He shouted at him to stop and raised his gun to fire a shot. He pulled the trigger, but nothing happened, and he realized the gun was not loaded. He rushed to see what had happened to Gregg. Having reached the safety of the woods, Wetzel pushed on. The moon had suddenly appeared, but the density of the foliage above prevented any of its light from being useful to the fugitive. His uncanny ability to navigate in these circumstances served him well, and Wetzel continued to move inward, although he intended to stay as close to the river as possible.

After what he judged to be well over a mile, he came to a large tree that had fallen across a huge dead log. The limbs were still intact with large green leaves, and he was able to burrow under to a place where it would be impossible to see him from above, even in daylight. Thankful for this place of refuge, he settled in, listening carefully for any signs of pursuit.

Burton found his colleague stunned and confused, but with no serious injury save a large knot on his head. The two stumbled back into the fort, not sure whether to raise an alarm, which would likely lead to their own punishment.

"I should never have trusted that son of a bitch," exclaimed Gregg. "Now what do we do?"

"We'd better tell Sergeant Sprague. We'll tell him Wetzel claimed he was sick, and when you checked, he hit you from behind and ran out." Burton was trying hard to think of some excuse for himself as well.

"Well, I got the knot on my head to show it," agreed Gregg. They found the sergeant fast asleep, and he wasn't happy when he heard the news.

"You stupid fools. I should have known you'd let somethin' like this happen." Sprague seemed to believe the part about Wetzel claiming to be sick, but he was curious about Burton's part in it.

"Where were you, Burton? I figured it would take two of you to keep an eye on that bastard."

"I had to take a piss, Sergeant. I wasn't gone that long."

"Long enough, I guess," snapped Sprague. "We'd better alert Lieutenant Kingsbury."

Lieutenant Kingsbury was awake, since he was the officer on night duty. He immediately rousted a detail to begin the search.

He sent one man over to the Indian camp that was present just to the north of the fort. The Indians were invited to help find this man who, it was pointed out, was their "great enemy."

Burton was able to point them in the right direction, and within the hour, there were at least fifteen men headed into the adjoining woods. Wetzel could hear them coming, and he sprawled out as close to the ground as he could, thankful for the small depression and the heavy branches above him. He could only hope that they would somehow miss him. They would not be able to find any tracks in the darkness, but there sounded like so many of them, he was afraid they would stumble upon him by accident. He heard footsteps very close, and then could hear someone climb up on the fallen tree trunk just a few feet from where he lay. He heard a grunt and some words in what he thought was the Delaware language.

"By God, they've got the reds after me too," he muttered silently. He didn't expect the soldiers to conduct a very thorough search, but the Indians were a different matter. He shrunk down even more, expecting now to be discovered at any time. Imagining he could hear his own heart beating, he thought the brave standing near him might hear it as well. After what seemed an eternity even to the patient Wetzel, the Indian moved on, and Wetzel allowed himself to breathe again. For the first time, he was conscious of how badly his feet were hurting. The soldiers had removed his shoes when he was thrown in the guardhouse, and he had made his flight while barefoot.

Twice more, he heard the searchers pass close by, but eventually all was quiet. He waited another hour before emerging from his leafy haven. He knew that he must get across the big river somehow. No doubt, the search would resume in the morning, and any decent tracker would soon find where he had been hiding.

"Isaac Williams has a place down here somewhere," Wetzel said aloud. "He'll help me for sure."

By dawn, he had circled back and was now along the right bank of the Ohio. The sun had burst out, and he could see clearly across to the opposite shore, where he was hoping to see some sign of the Williams farm. *I guess I came too far*, he thought. He began to move back upriver, realizing as he did so that he was also moving closer to those who were in pursuit. He thought about plunging in and swimming across, but the heavy cuffs on his wrists and their connecting chain made that seem to be an impossible task.

There was no flatboat traffic on the river, which was surprising, but it was very early, and those that had stopped in the night would not be out yet. Fort Harmar and Marietta were common stopping points not likely to be passed by in the night. Wetzel eased upstream a bit further and then stopped, not willing to go any closer to the fort. He stayed behind an overhanging tree limb and waited to see what might develop. He could try to hail a passing flatboat, although he knew the boats would be hesitant to respond, since that was a common ruse used by both Indians and river pirates.

His heart jumped when he saw something moving downstream close to the far bank. After a few moments, he could make out that it was a canoe, and he was overjoyed when he thought he recognized the single occupant.

"Hell, that's Isaac Williams as sure as anything, and he's out fishin'. By God, I may be saved."

By the time the little craft was almost directly opposite, Wetzel was sure it was Williams, and he began to shout.

"Halloo!" he cried as loud as he could. "Halloo, Isaac. It's Lew Wetzel, and I need your help."

Lew had removed his buckskin jacket and was waving it back and forth as he shouted. There was no immediate response, although Williams stopped paddling and seemed to move even closer to the nearby shore. Wetzel stepped out from where he was standing and down to the edge of the water. During most of his flight, he had ignored the pain coming from his feet which, he could see as he stood in the sand, were badly torn and bloody. Again, he waved his jacket and yelled across the water.

Williams at first suspected some kind of trick. He had no reason to think that Lew Wetzel would be yelling at him from across the Ohio. As he continued to watch and listen, he came to the conclusion that it was Wetzel, and he was clearly in distress. He pushed out into the flow and began to paddle furiously. Although the current carried him a bit downstream from where Wetzel was standing, he managed to cross fairly quickly, and Lew was making his way toward his intended landing spot. He could see the irons and chains, which Wetzel was holding closely in front of him as he walked.

"Good Lord, Lew, what has happened to you?" he asked as he brought the canoe up against the riverbank.

"The damned soldiers arrested me, but I got away." Lew climbed into the canoe and pointed across the river. "Let's git over there quick before them fools show up tryin' to catch me again."

Williams pushed the canoe into the water, and it was not long before they were well out into the current.

"Your feet are all chewed up, Lew. Tell me what the hell happened."

"I had to make a run for it last night, and they took my shoes."

"But why did they arrest you? What did you do?"

"I shot a damned Injun, that's all."

"What? They don't arrest a feller for shootin' no red man."

"That's what I thought, but them soldiers had a different idea."

"I don't know much about the law, but I didn't think the army could just arrest a man for shootin' somebody, let alone an Injun." Williams figured he wasn't getting the whole story.

"They claimed they was actin' for some federal judge. It's against some treaty to shoot an Injun, they claimed." Wetzel explained everything that had happened as they made their way across.

It was decided to put Wetzel ashore at the first opportunity, and Williams would return the canoe to his homeplace and then come back for Wetzel.

"I'll bring some tools back with me, and we'll get them chains off," said Isaac. "You get back out of sight and rest for a while. You should be plenty safe over here."

Back at the fort, General Harmar was in a rage. All the principals, including Lieutenant Kingsbury, Sergeant Sprague, and Privates Gregg and Burton, had been called in to endure the furious words of the commanding general. He singled out Sergeant Sprague for most of his invective.

"You should all be court-martialed," he had shouted at the conclusion, "for letting a dumb militiaman outsmart you."

Notice was sent to Judge Parsons, and General Harmar suggested that a reward be offered for Wetzel's capture. Parsons did not agree but made it clear that Wetzel was a fugitive and still subject to arrest.

"By God," complained Sergeant Sprague to his friend Sergeant Lawler. "I hate that damned Wetzel. He's got me into trouble with the general who's threatenin' to take away my stripes."

"I don't blame you," said Lawler.

"I'll shoot the bastard if I ever see him again," promised Sprague.

"Well, you just might get that chance sometime, Jim," answered his friend. "And I just might help you."

August 24, 1789

Lewis Wetzel was sitting quietly in Boone's old tavern, thinking about how fortunate he was to be here, out of the clutches of General Harmar and his soldiers. Boone no longer operated the tavern, nor his cousin either, but the place was still referred to as Boone's. Lew had been in Limestone now for a month since leaving the Marietta area and was staying with his friend John Young. Isaac Williams had kept him several days at his farm while he rested and recovered from his ordeal. Isaac had found some old boots for Wetzel to wear and gave him a rifle and hunting knife.

"I think you need to be movin' on, Lew," Williams had said one morning. "Them soldiers could come callin' any day, and I don't need any trouble."

"You're right, Isaac. I'm much obliged to you for all you've done for me. You saved my life, sure enough."

"Glad I could do it, Lew, but I reckon I've done about all I can."

"I'll leave right away," said Lew. "I think I'll head down toward Limestone. I doubt they'll try to follow me that far."

"Sorry, I can't supply you with no horse, Lew, but the wife has put together some fixin's that ought to keep you going for several days." Williams produced a buckskin satchel filled with a variety of foodstuffs.

He thought about Isaac just now, marveling again at his good fortune in having such a loyal friend who was available at just the right time. He had made it to Limestone several days later and with no trouble. For a while, he had stayed away whenever a boat had put in at the landing, aware that he was still a fugitive.

In the last week or so, he had begun to believe that there was no more danger. He had even worked a few times at helping to unload flatboats. He had also made some money winning the prize at a pair of shooting matches in which a purse had been established. It was nearly midnight, and Lew knew he had consumed more whiskey than he should, and he was feeling unsteady. He never liked that feeling, and his friend Young was in even worse shape. He started to stand up but sat back down, laughing.

"By God, Young, you're drunk," he managed to say, though the words were a bit slurred. "And so am I."

Young had put his head down on the table, holding it with both hands. Before he could say anything, there was a commotion along the riverbank loud enough that it could be heard even in the tavern. The man behind the bar went to the door and stepped outside to see what was happening.

"Some soldiers just landed and have scattered out on the street," he announced as he came back in. "I reckon some will soon be in here. That'll liven up the place."

Even in his drunken state, Wetzel had heard the word *soldiers*, and it got his attention.

"Surely they ain't after me," he said aloud.

John Young did not move at first, then slowly raised his head. Soldiers and Wetzel did not mix, he was aware of at least that much.

"We'd better go home," he managed to say.

It was too late as four of the soldiers came into the room. They went straight to the bar and demanded whiskey. Wetzel and Young got to their feet and ambled out the door, hoping they had been unobserved. One of the soldiers took notice.

"Who are those two old drunks who just left?" he asked the bartender whose name was John Porter.

"Why would you want to know that?" wondered Porter.

"Never mind why, just tell me," insisted Sergeant Lawler. "I think I may know one of them."

"It ain't my business to be givin' out the names of my customers." Porter was becoming annoyed with this nosy soldier.

"Listen to me, you son of a bitch. You're talkin' to a sergeant in the United States Army. We ain't used to bein' sassed by no bartender." Lawler pointed his finger at Porter. "I've got enough men out there to turn this place into a pigsty. You'd better think again about answering my question."

"I don't think the army's got no power over innocent citizens," argued Porter.

"Oh, we've got power, all right. You want to try me?"

When Porter said nothing, Lawler hollered at one of his friends. "Delany, come over here."

Delaney, already working on his second shot of whiskey, set down the glass and came over next to Lawler. "What do you need, Sergeant?"

"I need you to convince this dumb bartender that I ain't a man to be reckoned with. He's refusin' to answer a simple question."

"I reckon I'd tell him what he wants," he said to Porter with a sneer. "He's about the baddest sergeant in this whole army. He gives the word, and we'll tear this place apart."

Porter was angry, and before he knew it, he had said more than he intended. "Wetzel's a pretty bad man himself," he barked. "I wouldn't mess with him if I was you."

"Wetzel, eh? That's his name? Well, I'll be damned. We've got business with him, Delany."

"We do?" responded Delany.

"Yeah, but it'll keep. Let's get back to some serious drinking."

The night passed although the soldiers had been active during the night, plundering gardens and sheds of several of the inhabitants. Several men had entered the bakery of William Caldwell and bullied him into giving them all of the bread he had baked, offering no compensation. Toward morning, Captain McCurdy, who was in command of the seventy men, had managed to get them under some kind of control. It was then that he was approached by Sergeant Lawler.

"Captain McCurdy," he said. "I happen to know there is a man here that General Harmar has been trying to arrest."

"What are you talking about, Sergeant?" asked McCurdy.

"Lewis Wetzel. Do you remember him? Escaped from the guardhouse at the fort about a month ago."

"Well, yes, I do remember that. What about it?"

"I know where he is. If we take him in, the general will be real pleased with you, I imagine."

"He's here in Limestone?" McCurdy was beginning to be interested.

"Just down the street. He's stayin' at the house of a man named John Young."

"Seems you've been busy findin' out all this information." The captain was wondering why Lawler was so interested in the man Wetzel. "All right, take a squad and arrest him. We'll take him down and deliver him to Major Doughty, who has a garrison down on the Miami."

It was shortly after dawn when Lawler, Delany, and five other men found their way to John Young's log house, just a short way down the street from Boone's tavern. Delany pounded on the door, but Lawler did not wait for someone to answer. Finding the door unlatched, he pushed through, and the others followed closely behind. Young scrambled out of his bunk and met Lawler in the middle of the room.

"What the hell are you men doin' in here?" he managed to shout before Lawler pushed him aside.

"We're here to arrest the criminal, Lewis Wetzel."

"You've got no right—" Young started to say when Delany grabbed him.

"Shut up and stay out of the way, or we'll arrest you too."

Wetzel was lying in a bed against the far wall. Awakened by the shouting, but still groggy from a hangover, he struggled to his feet and reached for his knife hanging from a belt at the foot of the bed. He wasn't quick enough, and three men descended on him. He grabbed an arm and gave it a twist. The man screamed in pain and dropped out, quickly replaced by two others. Not without difficulty, the men managed to pin Wetzel's arms behind him, and he was helpless. When they had him securely tied, they dragged him out of the house and down toward the landing where the rest of the troops were boarding the three boats that had brought them downriver.

"Well, well, Mr. Wetzel. What do you think now?" chided Sergeant Lawler. "Sergeant Sprague sends his regards. You remember him, I suppose."

When they reached the landing, they were met by Captain McCurdy. "I see that you have accomplished your mission, Sergeant," he said, addressing Lawler. "Get him on board and let's be on our way."

When Wetzel tried one last time to resist, Delany grabbed him by his long hair and dragged him onto the boat. McCurdy thought this was unnecessary, but he said nothing. *In the end,* he thought, *maybe this will lead to something good for me, especially if it makes Harmar happy.*

August 25, 1789

Major John Doughty stood on the path smoking his pipe and observing the landing of a boatload of soldiers along the shore near the mouth of the Little Miami River. He had been sent by General Harmar to locate a place to build a new fort somewhere along the northern Ohio shore and between the Little and Great Miami Rivers. He had selected a site just opposite the mouth of Licking Creek on the opposite shore. Just four days earlier, he had sent a letter to Harmar informing him of his choice. He wondered if the boats brought soldiers here to help in the new construction, although he knew that Harmar had sent them before his letter could have arrived.

His aide, Ensign Hartshorne, had come to his headquarters earlier to inform him of boats arriving from upriver. Doughty had found an abandoned cabin at the edge of a little settlement more than a half-mile from the mouth of the Little Miami. The settlement had been established by Benjamin Stites nearly ten months earlier, and Doughty was pleased to find a place to set up his headquarters as well as a good place to live until permanent quarters could be constructed. He had a small contingent of men with him, and most had been able to find sleeping accommodations among the settlers. He sent Hartshorne back to find out more about the arriving boats, while he followed along a few minutes later. Now he saw his aide coming back up the path.

"Major, there's three boats coming in, seventy men in all."

"Who's in command of those men, Ensign?"

"Captain McCurdy is the officer in charge, sir. He arrived on the first boat, and he has a prisoner with him."

"A prisoner? Why would these men have a prisoner?" Doughty was not pleased about that. What was he supposed to do with a prisoner?

"I don't know, sir, but he intends to deliver him to you, he said."

Although it was dark, Doughty figured he had better find out what this was all about. He knocked the ashes from his pipe and stuffed it in his pocket, following Hartshorne down toward the landing. He met McCurdy, who was coming up the path, led by a soldier with a lighted torch and followed by a squad of four men pulling a big man with his hands tied behind him.

"Hello, Captain McCurdy," was Doughty's greeting. "I'm told you have a prisoner. Who is it, and why do you have him?"

The men holding Wetzel had stopped several feet short of the officers and were still in the dark.

"Hello to you, Major," said McCurdy. "The man is Lewis Wetzel. He is accused of killing an Indian and escaped more than a month ago from the guardhouse at Fort Harmar. We took him into custody at Limestone."

"I've heard of Lewis Wetzel. Is he a prisoner of the army?"

"Well, not really. He was charged by Judge Parsons at Marietta. He was being held at the fort since there ain't no jail in Marietta."

"I didn't kill no Injun!" shouted Wetzel, who could hear what was being said about him.

"Hell, Captain," said Doughty, clearly annoyed and ignoring Wetzel's outburst. "We've got no jail here either."

"I thought General Harmar would be pleased that we had captured him," explained McCurdy.

"Well, you're probably right about that. Have your men bring him up to my cabin so I can talk to him. In the meantime, you need to make arrangements for your men to make camp."

"Most of them will just stay on the boats, Major. We'll be off again in the morning."

"Off again?" asked Doughty. "Aren't you here to help with the construction of the new fort."

"Don't know nothin' about that, Major? We're supposed to go on to Post Vincent."

"Well, see to your men then and have the prisoner brought to my cabin. Ensign Hartshorne will show you the way." Doughty began to walk away, then stopped and turned back. "You come along too, Captain. I need to know the whole story about this man Wetzel."

Doughty returned to his hut and waited. It wasn't long until McCurdy returned with Sergeant Lawler and four other men along with Wetzel. The prisoner had ceased his resistance, sensing that perhaps this Major Doughty might listen to him. They crowded inside the cabin and faced the major, who sat at a small table.

"So tell me what you know, Captain McCurdy." Doughty eyed Wetzel closely as McCurdy began to talk.

"General Harmar explained to me that Wetzel had shot an Indian called George Washington, was charged by Judge Parsons, and put in the guardhouse at Fort Harmar. He escaped from there, and his whereabouts were unknown."

"I've heard of that Indian. He was friendly with General Harmar, I think," said Doughty.

"That's right," agreed McCurdy. "I'm not sure if he died, but I don't think he did. The general told me to keep an eye out for Wetzel because he might have gone to Kentucky. The sergeant here spied him in a tavern, and when he reported that, I ordered him to be arrested. They found him in a house near the river, and we brought him here to you."

"Did you have a warrant, Captain?" Doughty could already see that there could be some trouble coming over this.

"Well, uh, no, we didn't have a warrant. But General Harmar says there was one."

"Are there witnesses against him do you know?"

"From what Harmar said, I don't think so. If there was, he's gone from Marietta."

Doughty had not taken his eyes off Wetzel all during this conversation.

"Is there something you want to say for yourself?" Doughty asked, directing the question to Wetzel.

"Well, I did shoot an Indian all right, but he wasn't dead. He was ridin' off on his horse last I saw."

"So you admit that you're guilty?"

"I never knew it was no crime to shoot an Injun. I've been fightin' 'em all my life." Wetzel searched the major's face in the dim light for some sign of agreement. "'Course, I didn't know he was the general's pet."

Doughty couldn't prevent a smile.

Sergeant Lawler spoke up. "This man is dangerous, and he's caused all kinds of trouble, sir. He needs to be locked up."

"Sergeant!" cried McCurdy in a reprimanding tone. "The major didn't ask for your opinion."

"This man broke into the house of a private citizen to take me prisoner," shouted Wetzel. "I think he ought to be locked up."

"Be quiet, both of you," commanded McCurdy.

"I've no place to house a prisoner here," said Major Doughty after a short pause. "This is a matter for Judge Symmes. Captain, tomorrow I want you to take the prisoner to Judge Symmes over at North Bend. We will deliver him into civilian custody."

"How do I find him?" McCurdy was not happy with Doughty's orders.

"I'll send one of my men, Sergeant Cain, with you. Now secure the prisoner for the night, Captain. Godspeed in your journey to Post Vincent."

As McCurdy and the others turned to go, the major addressed him again. "And Captain. See that the prisoner gets something to eat. He doesn't look too good to me. He does not need to be treated badly."

August 26, 1789

The large flatboat eased in toward the shore, having just passed the mouth of a river that one of the men had assured Henry Lee was the Little Miami. Lee stood at the bow and eyed the shoreline in the morning sun. He and his twenty men were on an urgent errand, and he was searching for the military garrison that he thought was established somewhere in this region.

Lee spied the American flag flying in front of a small cabin at the edge of what appeared to be a small village. "That must be Benjamin Stite's settlement," he said, turning to John Young, who was standing next to him.

"I wouldn't know, Henry," answered Young.

"Well, it has to be, and maybe that cabin with the flag is the headquarters for Major Doughty."

Doughty had called on Henry Lee in Limestone two weeks earlier on his way downriver. Henry Lee was the county lieutenant for the new Mason County in Kentucky and was the person John Young and William Caldwell had come to the previous morning to report what had happened to Lewis Wetzel.

Lee had expressed the appropriate outrage at such a violation of the rights of a private citizen and immediately set about organizing an expedition to go and find out what had happened to Lewis Wetzel. He assumed that Captain McCurdy would take the prisoner to the garrison in the Miami country. Lee and his men had set out in the afternoon of the previous day and had reached their destination in midmorning. The boat made its landing, and Lee with five others walked up the path toward Doughty's cabin. Ensign Hartshorne met them there.

"Where is Major Doughty?" asked Lee. "I am Henry Lee, lieutenant of Mason County in Kentucky."

"The major isn't here, sir," explained Hartshorne. "He took some of the men downriver to the new headquarter's site."

"What about Captain McCurdy and his men? Where are they? Did they stop here?"

"They came in last night, but they've gone on."

"Did they have a prisoner with them?"

"Yes." Hartshorne was becoming a bit uneasy, sensing that Lew Wetzel might be the reason for this visit by the men from Kentucky.

"Where is he now?"

"I can't answer that," said Hartshorne quickly. "You need to talk to Major Doughty about that."

"Tell me then where I can find the major."

"He is at the site just across the river opposite the mouth of the Licking River. The men are putting up some temporary quarters there."

Many of the men from Limestone had left the boat and were looking up friends who lived in the new settlement. Sensing that it would take too long to gather them together again, Lee inquired of Hartshorne about borrowing a canoe to go downriver. Young and Caldwell, who had stuck close to him, volunteered to go along.

An available canoe was found, and the three men were soon on the way to find Major Doughty. It wasn't far, although the Ohio took a big bend to the north and then back down. They could see the men working to clear some trees, and already the outlines of a small log building that would serve as temporary quarters were in place. Landing quickly, Lee and his companions soon found the major.

"Major Doughty," said Lee, extending his hand, which Doughty grasped. "It is good to see you."

"And you too, Lieutenant Lee. What brings you here?"

"We were following Captain McCurdy, who illegally took a man from our county and made him a prisoner." Lee felt there was no need to hold back. His tone indicated his displeasure.

"Well, I wouldn't say it was illegal," replied Doughty. "It was a man wanted for a crime after all."

"I don't think it is legal for the army to go into a private home, take a citizen captive, and then deliver him to a military garrison. Besides, those soldiers committed all kinds of outrages against the citizens of Limestone." Lee was red-faced and had unconsciously stepped very close to Doughty.

"Well, if those things are true, then you certainly have reason to protest." The major moved back a step, and Lee, realizing what he had done, did not follow. "But Captain McCurdy is gone on to Post Vincent, and I have no authority over him."

"With what offense was Lewis Wetzel charged, and under what pretense was he seized by federal troops while in the state of Virginia?" Lee was upset, but he was also well aware of his political position, and he wanted Doughty to appreciate that.

"It is my understanding that Wetzel had been accused of the murder of an Indian, although it may be that the Indian recovered. Anyway, he was first arrested under a warrant issued by Judge Parsons in Marietta. When I questioned McCurdy further, he thought maybe that the only witness had left the country as well. Still McCurdy says that General Harmar wanted the man caught since he had escaped from custody at the fort."

"Did McCurdy have a warrant?" Lee wanted to know.

"I didn't see one," replied Doughty. "Frankly, Mr. Lee, I doubt that any charge will be supported in the end. In any case, I directed McCurdy to deliver the prisoner to Judge Symmes, who is the civilian authority in the area."

"I know the judge," said Lee. "Where can I find him?"

"The judge has a place down at the north bend, about fifteen miles downriver from here. He uses his house as a courthouse, and he has a jail there as well. I would assume he has Lewis Wetzel there."

"By God, I don't mean to leave Wetzel there in jail. I've got twenty men with me, Major, all Kentuckians and mad as hell about the army taking one of our citizens." Lee had begun pacing and had turned back, pointing his finger at Doughty.

Although he was angered by Lee's outburst, Doughty decided to remain a peacemaker. "Mr. Lee, I understand your ardor, but I advise against taking all those men with you down to see the judge. I think you'll find him sympathetic to your cause."

"Well, I left them back at the Little Miami, and I reckon they can stay there for now." Young and Caldwell had come up and were standing just behind Lee.

"Do we know where they've got Lew, Henry?" asked Young, casting a dark look at Major Doughty.

"He's downriver a ways, John," replied Lee. "We're goin' down to get him right now."

"I'll send one of my sergeants with you, Mr. Lee," said Doughty, eager to get the three men on their way. "Sergeant Cooper," he called to a burly man, carrying a log toward the structure under construction. "I want you to take these men down to see Judge Symmes."

Sergeant Cooper dropped the log immediately, glad to have a less strenuous assignment. "Yes, sir," he answered, walking directly down toward the shore, and motioning for Lee and the other two to follow.

Before leaving, Lee approached Major Doughty again. "I want to make a formal protest against the actions of Captain McCurdy and his soldiers."

"As I told you before, I am not the person to receive such a formal charge. You will need to write to General Harmar."

"Well, then, by God, that's just what I'll do!" Henry Lee stomped off, following after Sergeant Cooper.

It took over two hours to reach the judge's house at North Bend, so-called because the river made a wide loop to the north at that spot. Cooper led them up the path and knocked on the large front door.

"Quite a place," said Young to his friend Caldwell. "You reckon they've got Lew locked up in there?"

"Prob'ly not," surmised Caldwell. "I bet he's in that cabin out back. I'd guess that's the jail."

The door was opened by a black servant, and Henry Lee pushed past the sergeant to address the servant. "We're here to see Judge Symmes. Tell him Henry Lee of Mason County, Kentucky, is here."

The man said nothing, simply nodded, and turned back inside. Lee waited impatiently, and after a few minutes, the slave returned and invited the men to come in. He led them through a long hallway, and then to a large room that held a desk and a pair of chairs sitting at either corner of the desk. On the wall behind the desk were two shelves partially filled with books. Judge Symmes was seated in front of the shelves, watching the men file in behind his servant, whose name was John.

"Thank you, John," said the judge, who rose and offered his hand to Lee. "Hello, Henry. What brings you here?" He nodded at the others.

"Greetings, Judge Symmes. I'm here to inquire about a prisoner I believe you have in custody."

"Have a seat, Henry," said Symmes, who sat down again. "I'm afraid the rest of you will have to stand," he said to the others with a slight smile.

"This is John Young and William Caldwell, who came here with me along with eighteen other men from Limestone. The sergeant there was sent along with us by Major Doughty."

"Yes, I've met Sergeant Cooper before." Symmes smiled again, then turned his attention to Lee. "Now Henry, you must be asking about Lewis Wetzel."

"That's right," answered Lee, becoming highly animated. "Them damned soldiers took him illegally right out of a private house."

"I don't see that it was illegal. He escaped from custody at Fort Harmar. Isn't that right?"

"I don't know nothin' about that," said Lee. "I don't see that the army has any jurisdiction here."

"Captain McCurdy delivered him to me on behalf of the civil authorities. He was charged by Judge Parsons in Marietta."

"Did McCurdy have a warrant? You can't arrest nobody without a warrant."

"Now, Henry, you need to calm down. There was a warrant, according to Captain McCurdy. Now I know Lew Wetzel, and I know what he is capable of doing."

"Where is Lew, what have you done with him?" Lee had risen from the chair as he spoke.

"Lew is out back in the jail, Henry," said the judge. "Do you want to see him?"

"Of course, I want to see him," exclaimed Lee. "I came here with twenty men to take him home."

"Henry, you must not forget that I am the law here. Let us go out to the jail so that you can see the prisoner is all right." Symmes rose and lifted a large key off a hook behind his desk. He handed the key to Sergeant Cooper and indicated that they should all go out back to the jail.

The jail consisted of a log cabin with no windows and one heavy door with a latch and a big lock. Cooper unlocked the door, and they went inside. In the far corner was another room with a door secured on the outside by a heavy-wooden bar. Sergeant Cooper moved to raise the latch, but the judge stopped him.

"Lew," he called. "Step back from the door. You've got some visitors."

"I ain't at the door, Judge," came the answer in a voice that was strong. "You can open the door, I ain't goin' anywhere."

Symmes nodded at Cooper, who opened the door. He stepped inside, followed by Judge Symmes and Henry Lee. Young and Caldwell stayed outside.

Lee was taken aback. "God, you've got him in chains!"

Wetzel had been sitting on a bench against the back wall, which apparently also served as a bed. He had irons and chains on his legs and arms, which made it difficult for him to rise, although he managed it.

"I know, I hated to do it, but it is what is required," said Symmes. "Otherwise we can't secure a prisoner here."

"Goddamn it! Lew Wetzel ain't no criminal, and you should know that."

"That's right. Lew ain't no criminal," shouted John Young from outside the door.

"Is that you, John?" asked Wetzel, who took a step forward and tried to peer outside.

"Yes, John Young and William Caldwell are here with me," explained Lee. "We've come to git you outta here."

"Not so fast, Henry," protested the judge. "You seem to forget that I am in charge here, and Lew is in my custody. Everything has been done legally, including the proper writ of habeas corpus."

"Well, what do you plan to do with him? Major Doughty and I had a conversation about this, and he doesn't think these charges against Lew can be supported." Lee turned to Wetzel. "Are you all right, Lew?"

"Lew Wetzel was arrested, to begin with, on a warrant from Judge Parsons," explained Symmes, answering Lee's original question. "I will write him and request him to forward the charges."

"Was a warrant brought along with the prisoner, Judge?" asked Lee, who already knew what the answer would be.

"No, but I assume Judge Parsons will send it to me along with the charges."

"And how long will that take, do you suppose?"

"I would guess it will be sometime next fall."

"Humpf," snorted Lee. "I don't believe the people of Kentucky are about to submit to a fellow citizen being detained in irons when no charge is made against him and none likely to be supported. I've got twenty men here with me now, and there's plenty more back home ready to come if needed."

"Well," said Judge Symmes, "the crime is surely bailable."

"We'll stand for his bail," said John Young immediately.

It was here that Lewis Wetzel entered the argument. "What about the money and gold them damned soldiers robbed me of?"

"What is he talking about?" inquired Lee, his voice rising again with impatience.

"Captain McCurdy did inform me that he had twenty-two dollars and a half that belonged to the prisoner," explained the judge. "And when called upon, he would be answerable for that."

"Did you get the money from him?" Lee wanted to know.

"No, he did not have it with him, and since Lew was in custody, I didn't feel it necessary to recover it just then."

"And what about my twenty-eight and a half guineas of gold that they took?" Wetzel had moved a step closer to the door.

"McCurdy said nothing about any gold," answered Judge Symmes. "That's the first I've heard of that."

"The prisoner told me about it," interjected Sergeant Cain, who had just joined them. He had stayed at North Bend after accompanying Captain McCurdy in delivering Wetzel to Judge Symmes.

"Well, this is new information, and I need to investigate further." Symmes motioned for the men to come out and for Sergeant Cooper to lock the door.

They walked back toward the front door of the house, when the judge turned again to speak to Henry Lee. "Henry, there is nothing more for you to do here. I must look into this some more, and I cannot do it under pressure from you."

"Judge," said Lee with some heat. "You don't realize how angry the people in Kentucky are about this affair."

"I think I do, Henry, but it has to be done in an orderly fashion. You need to leave now and go back to your men. I will make a decision about bail very soon. I have no hard feelings toward Lewis Wetzel. Indeed he helped out here just a few months back, and I will look out for his welfare."

"He doesn't look too well to me, Judge."

"He was brought to me only yesterday. I will treat him fairly, Henry, you have my word on that."

Lee was prepared to put up further protest but decided it might be better to give Symmes some room to resolve the problem. "All right," he said finally.

"Good," responded Symmes, who began to smile. "And take these two gentlemen with you. I'm taking no chances on them helping Mr. Wetzel break out of jail again."

Two days later, Wetzel was released, and he returned to Limestone with his friends.

17

Beaver Blockhouse

October 18, 1790

The Indians had watched with dismay as the American army marched northward toward their towns near the portage connecting the Maumee, St. Joseph and the Wabash. Villages had been abandoned all along the route, and the inhabitants had retreated back toward Kekionga, the name often used for the capital of the Miami nation.

At least seven towns were in the vicinity, and in addition to the Miami, there were many Shawnees who had established a new Chillicothe, their capital, in the region. There was a scattering of people from other tribes, including some Delawares who had relocated, including Little Fox and Red Storm and their families. Even Kekionga had been deserted by this time; the women and children hurried off into the forests far to the northwest.

The warriors—under the command of Little Turtle, aided by the Shawnee war chief, Blue Jacket—kept watch, hoping for a chance to strike a blow. The Indians had been warned of this expedition led by General Josiah Harmar. Arthur St. Clair, governor of the Northwest Territories had written a letter to Major Patrick Murray, the British commander in Detroit, telling him of the American intent. President Washington and Henry Knox, secretary of war, wanted to assure the British that this raid was not aimed at them or any of their posts.

The Indian interpretation, when Murray had informed them of the American plans, was that the force must be so great that no surprise was necessary. Rumors had it that the army was more than eight thousand strong. Their response was to get out of the way.

Harmar had left Fort Washington on September 30 with a force of 320 regulars and 1,133 militiamen, of which nearly one third were mounted. The march north went unmolested, past the old Chillicothe town on the Little Miami, up to the Mad River, then across to the headwaters of the Auglaize, and down to its mouth on the Maumee. Harmar and his officers were perplexed about the absence of any Indians.

There were scattered scouts around the periphery of the army, and on one occasion, the soldiers captured one warrior who had been careless. When questioned, the brave told them that the Indians were gathered around the new French store, now being called Miamitown, next to Kekionga at the source of the Maumee River. His revelation that Simon Girty was with the Indians and had gone across Lake Erie to obtain allies was particularly disturbing to General Harmar.

The soldiers continued their march up the Maumee, going past the new Chillicothe town, which was abandoned like all the others. After setting up their main camp, they began to burn the deserted towns near Kekionga, destroying five in all, as well as the crops. Harmar later reported the destruction of over twenty thousand bushels of corn. They had also looted and burned the trading post at Miamitown, which had been operated by the British traders, Henry Hay and John Kinzie. The traders had given much of their arms and ammunition to the Indians and took most of the rest of their goods off to Detroit.

General Harmar had worried a bit when he learned of the destruction of the trading post, since St. Clair had promised the British that none of their possessions would be bothered. The Miami chief, Little Turtle, was pelted with demands from Indian leaders to strike back, the sight of their villages in flames more than they could endure. But the crafty chief held back. "They are too many," he insisted, and Blue Jacket, who wanted to maintain some kind of unity among the warriors, backed him.

There were not many more than 150 warriors present, including more than 50 each of the Miami and Shawnee, as well as a band of Ottawas that included some of Little Fox's brothers from the Chippewa tribe. Red Storm, whose right hand was nearly useless as a result of the ball he had taken through his wrist on Short Creek in Virginia the year before, was extremely agitated and demanding action against the whites. He could not effectively grip anything with his right hand, but had, with great determination, learned to shoot a gun with his left hand.

Little Fox put scant trust in his accuracy, but he had teased his friend by observing that he had not been too accurate with his right hand either. Red Storm's militancy was undiminished, however, and he had been railing against both Little Turtle and Blue Jacket with a ferocity that was becoming an annoyance to Little Fox. "They are both cowards," insisted Red Storm as they sat watching the two chiefs talking near the bank of the Eel River, just a few miles northwest of Kekionga. "Why do they not lead us against the soldiers? Why do they let them destroy our crops. We will starve this winter for sure."

"They are not cowards, and you had better be careful who hears you say that," cautioned Fire Heart, their old Shawnee companion who had been living in the Shawnee capital on the Maumee.

"Fire Heart is right," agreed Little Fox. "We are badly outnumbered, and the chiefs are waiting for an opportunity. It will come, my friend, but you must be patient."

"You are always advising me to be patient. Well, I don't want to be patient. I want to strike a blow at those dogs." Red Storm sprang to his feet and glared at his friends. "We can steal their horses. You saw how loose they were keeping them at their camp."

"Maybe he has a good idea there," said Little Fox, looking for some indication of agreement from Fire Heart. "It will shut him up, perhaps, if we agree to go with him."

"That is doubtful," laughed Fire Heart.

"Ah, you two are like old women," snorted Red Storm, who walked away. "I'm going, with or without you."

Late in the evening, the three friends had crossed the St. Joseph River and worked their way up close to the northern outskirts of the white soldiers' camp, spread out across the Maumee from where they stood. What seemed like the lights from at least one hundred campfires were sprinkled through the darkness for a distance of at least a half mile.

"They are many," noted Fire Heart. "Just as Little Turtle has said."

"Yes," agreed Little Fox, whose ardor for action was cooling a bit. In the front section of the camp were the fires of the 320 regular troops, and in the light of one of the fires, the three braves could see the three cannon that had been brought along, parked in a row.

"They have big guns," said Fire Heart, pointing to the artillery.

Little Fox stared intently, having seen cannon before, and although he had never seen them in action, he had heard their effect described often enough. "There are horses and cattle back in the center," he said, pointing in that direction. "We will have no chance to steal them."

"No, but near the back are other horses kept by the soldiers who ride them," explained Red Storm. "I think we can steal some of those, for the soldiers there are not careful."

Red Storm was speaking of horses ridden by some of the Kentucky militia, who were bivouacked at the far end of the line. Without another word, he began to move downstream, and the other two followed. After about fifteen minutes, they had reached a point where the last of the campfires flickered at them from across the river. A few men were still visible in the low light, but most had settled in for the night. Motioning for Little Fox and Fire Heart to follow, Red Storm moved down through the weeds lining the north bank of the Maumee and stepped into the stream.

"It is not deep here," he asserted and quickly crossed with his companions following along quietly. They had moved well past where the last of the campfires was visible, and it was quite dark. They listened for a short time, finally satisfied that there was no sentry anywhere close. Keeping close together, they made their way through a small stand of cottonwoods and then some low bushes, stopping often to listen for sounds of a sentry, and also for sounds that would indicate where the horses were being kept.

"There," whispered Red Storm, reacting to a soft whinny, and pointing off to their left.

They moved in that direction, keeping in among the trees and bushes that angled off toward the southeast. Shortly they came up to where a small herd of horses stood huddled together. The militiamen had foolishly left the horses hobbled on the outside of their camp. The sentry on duty in that area had left his post in order to get a cup of tea from the pot dangling over the remains of the fire.

It was warm there, and as the night air had cooled considerably, the sentry lingered longer than he had intended. Fire Heart was designated to attack the sentry with his knife in case he returned too soon while the job of Red Storm and Little Fox was to liberate three of the horses. The two braves approached stealthily and found it easy to cut the hobbles and lead away the three mounts closest to them.

"Come quickly, Fire Heart," hissed Little Fox. "We have three of them."

Overjoyed that it had not been necessary to alert anyone in the camp, Fire Heart quickly joined his companions as they led the horses back through the trees and across the river, trying to avoid making enough noise to arouse any of the soldiers. Once across, they mounted and rode back upstream, wanting to shout with joy over their successful mission but aware that there could be soldiers on the north side of the river.

They kept silent until they had crossed the St. Joseph again, but then began to shout and sing of their triumph. They were received with great enthusiasm when they rode into the Indian camp along the Eel River. Many braves were still awake and sitting around a bright fire. Even the Shawnee war chief, Blue Jacket, was there to greet them.

"Well done," exclaimed Blue Jacket when he heard their story. "Many of their horses have been stolen now. Maybe it will lead to some action that is to our advantage."

October 19, 1790

Colonel John Hardin appeared at General Harmar's tent before 9:00 a.m.

"What brings you here so early, John?" asked the general.

"We lost a bunch more horses last night. There's got to be Indians close by."

"You're probably right, John, but we haven't seen them. Where do you think they are?"

"Some of my scouts figure they're out to the west and north, waiting to pounce on us if we get strung out."

The general sighed and got up, walking to the door of his tent. He turned back to face Hardin. "So what do you suggest be done about it, Colonel?"

"Let me take some men out and look for the bastards, General. We came here to teach them a lesson, didn't we? Maybe we can get some of our horses back as well."

"Perhaps we have done enough already, burning their towns, and destroying their crops."

"The men are already grumbling about what a wasted trip this has been so far. What will they say if we go home now?"

Hardin could see that he was treading dangerously close to angering the general, but he did not back down. The discussion continued, with Harmar expressing his reluctance to divide his force in any way. Eventually the general agreed to send out a small force of militia under Hardin's command.

"You should take some of the regulars with you," advised Harmar. "Let Captain Armstrong choose thirty men to go along. Also, take the cavalry unit under Major Fontaine. Those Kentuckians should be a big help."

"Thank you, General. I will get started immediately." Hardin's glance fell on the open brandy bottle sitting on the table next to the bed. Harmar noticed and frowned.

"That was from last night, Colonel," he stated bitterly. "I have not been drinking this morning. In spite of what is rumored about me, I am not a drunkard!"

"Sir..." stammered Hardin, embarrassed and unsure of what to say. "I never—"

"Never mind," exclaimed Harmar, cutting him off. "Just go and do your duty."

Within two hours, Hardin led some 180 troops out of the camp and west toward the St. Mary's River. Thirty of the troops were regulars under Captain John Armstrong, forty mounted Kentucky riflemen under Major James Fontaine, and the rest were militia from the Kentucky regiments. Many of these men were new to the frontier and complete novices when it came to fighting Indians. They moved steadily and crossed the St. Mary's before turning to the northwest, following a trail that Hardin had been assured was traveled recently by a band of Indians.

This movement by a small detachment of soldiers was viewed with interest by Indian scouts who kept a close observance on the army camp. Word was sent immediately to the headquarters of Little Turtle across the Eel River.

"This gives us an opportunity," the Miami chief said to Blue Jacket.

"Yes, it does," exclaimed Blue Jacket with excitement. "We can lead them into an ambush right here."

"Have a small band set up in front of their advance and tell them to be seen and then run away."

"Yes, right toward us," said Blue Jacket. "But we are still too few. Our warriors are scattered all about."

"Send runners and have them brought here at once," ordered Little Turtle. "We could never have attacked that huge army, but they have given us a target that is more our size."

A small band of warriors was chosen by Blue Jacket to serve as the decoys, led by a Miami brave called Running Bear. Little Fox, Red Storm, and Fire Heart had all volunteered for this duty, and they set out on horseback. After going for a mile in the direction of Kekionga, they were met by another runner coming from the south.

"Some soldiers on horses have separated and are coming toward us here," reported the scout.

"Let us dismount," commanded Running Bear, "and let them see us. Then we will run straight back to where our brothers are waiting."

"Shouldn't we stay on the horses?" asked Red Storm.

"No," answered Running Bear. "We want them to think we are few and easy to catch."

"Well, that will be true," grumbled Red Storm, but he obeyed as did the others.

They positioned themselves along the trail at the top of a low rise, which gave them a good view of where they expected the soldiers to appear. Colonel Hardin stopped his advance and sent Major Fontaine and his cavalry forward to see what was ahead of them. They had not gone far when they saw the Indians under Running Bear more than a quarter of a mile ahead.

Fontaine was unsure of what to do when he saw the warriors begin running. Being a cautious man, he decided to return to Hardin and tell him what they had seen. Hardin was greatly excited at what Fontaine told him, and he ordered his men to advance immediately. This quick movement was not understood by the entire force, and nearly half of the militia under Captain Faulkner was left behind.

When Hardin realized what was happening, he sent Fontaine and his cavalry back to retrieve the rest of the men. The detachment was strung out, and this predicament did not escape the notice of Little Turtle. The leading part of the army had nearly reached the Eel when the Miami chief sent his warriors storming out of the bushes and across the shallow stream, striking the surprised soldiers with great force. Although the regulars stood their ground and fought back, the militia who were near the front dropped their weapons and began running back to what they were hoping was safety.

The Indians, after firing their muskets, attacked with tomahawks, and the regular troops were slaughtered. The Indians had moved out on both sides and had the troops surrounded. They killed many of the retreating militia; and even the men under Faulkner and Fontaine, who had been advancing slowly, stopped as the frightened men streamed through them. Soon they were retreating as well, and Hardin, unable to gain any control, gave up and called for a general retreat back to the main camp. The regulars had put up a good fight, but twenty-two of the thirty had been killed. No doubt, their actions had made it possible for most of the militia to make their escape, although forty-eight of them had lost their lives as well.

Captain Armstrong had managed to secret himself in a nearby swamp and during the night made his way back to the main army. Although the Indians followed the retreating troops, they stayed out of sight as the men neared the army camp. Harmar was dismayed at the results, and when Armstrong reported to him the next morning, detailing how the militia had deserted at the beginning of the fighting, he became enraged. "If the damned militia behave like this again, I will turn the artillery on them!"

October 22, 1790

Simon Girty stood talking with Little Turtle and Blue Jacket in one of the partially burned lodges still standing in Kekionga. The Indians had moved back into the town the previous day after an expected attack from Harmar's army had failed to materialize. Although it was quite early in the morning, word had come that the soldiers were moving again.

"It is another small detachment," Little Turtle was saying. "I do not understand what the white general is thinking."

"Perhaps he isn't thinking," laughed Girty. "He's pretty much showed already that he ain't no George Washington."

"Maybe they are coming to bury their dead," offered Blue Jacket. "We thought they would have done that two days ago."

The Indians had expected Harmar to come back with his entire army after the defeat of Hardin, but instead, the white soldiers had began a march yesterday morning back down the Maumee, apparently determined to return home without anymore fighting. Harmar had been badly shaken by the rout of Hardin's troops and the performance of the militia. He decided to go home, thinking he could declare victory because of the towns and crops they had destroyed.

"We have struck them a hard blow," Harmar explained to Majors Wyllys and Doughty who commanded the regular soldiers. "It will take them time to recover and should help relieve the settlers from the constant raiding."

"I'm not so sure the savages will see it that way," argued Major Doughty. "The last thing they will remember is that they won a stunning victory against white soldiers."

"I don't call that a victory," growled the general. "I call it a big failure by the damned militia."

"That may be," said Doughty, unwilling to give in easily. "But it's not how the reds will see it."

"I must think about our general welfare," continued Harmar. "Our supplies are dwindling, and I am worried that some of the militia will desert and take our provisions with them. An orderly retreat is a better option."

On October 21, the army had begun its retreat, and the grumbling among the men grew louder as the day went on. Numerous officers approached Harmar and complained until the general finally ordered a halt after a march of no more than eight miles. Soon after they made camp, Colonel Hardin came to the general with the news that fewer than two hundred Indians had moved back into Kekionga.

"Let us go back and attack them," pleaded Hardin, who was smarting under the criticism of the militia and his own failure. "We should take a large force this time. I know the men will do much better. They want to fight, General."

Harmar was well aware of what was being said about him in the ranks, and the old charge of drunkenness was being brought up again. He had more than two hundred regulars left, but he was reluctant to send them all out at once. He needed dependable men to make sure chaos did not develop within the camp itself.

Major Wyllys had joined Hardin in the argument, and Harmar placed a great deal of trust in Wyllys, an experienced Revolutionary War veteran.

"All right," General Harmar said finally. "I think you are right. We need to strike another blow."

After further discussion, it was decided to send sixty regulars, forty mounted cavalry under Captain Fontaine, and another three hundred of the best riflemen from among the militia. Hardin would command the militia, but Wyllys would have overall command. The detachment moved out shortly after midnight on the twenty-second. Now, as Girty and the two chiefs continued to talk, a second runner arrived with interesting news.

"The soldiers stopped and have divided in three ways," reported Little Turtle, who had interrogated the messenger. "This will give us a good chance."

"How have they separated?" asked Girty, who had returned several days ago, having mostly failed in bringing warriors from other tribes to help. He had informed Little Turtle that he had received word that a large contingent of Sac and Fox warriors were coming in from the Illinois country, but as yet there was no sign of them.

"One bunch goes to cross the St. Mary's. A second, which includes horse soldiers, is coming straight toward us while the third is going around to this side," explained Little Turtle, pointing to the east of where they stood.

"They will try to drive us back and then hit us from three sides," said Blue Jacket.

"We will put decoys in front of each group," said the Miami chief. "Now let us prepare."

Indian scouts had followed the troops from the time they left the main army camp until they stopped two miles short of Kekionga. Major Wyllys ordered his commanders to come to a conference, just as the first streams of light had begun to appear in the east. After a short discussion, the major's plan was put into operation.

Major Hall, with half of the Kentucky militia, began a move to the west where he was to cross the St. Mary's, go north for a ways, and then turn eastward to cross the St. Joseph and enter the town from the west. Major Wyllys would lead the sixty regulars, and Captain Fontaine's cavalry straight north across the Maumee and into the town from the south. Major McMillan, with the remainder of the Kentucky riflemen, would swing to the east before pushing north across the Maumee and then into the village from the east. The idea was to trap the Indians in the town with this giant pincers movement. The success of the plan depended on good coordination and surprise, both difficult to attain, especially since every move was under observation.

Major Hall was the first to move, for he had the greatest distance to travel, and the hope was that he would move in across the St. Joseph and into the rising sun just as the other two claws were ready to clamp down on the intended prey. As they were crossing the St. Mary's, some of Hall's men spotted an Indian scout moving in the tall weeds along the west bank. A flurry of shots rang out, but the brave managed to escape.

Hardin, who was riding along with Hall's unit, was furious, shouting at the men to stop shooting. Wyllys, waiting to begin his movement in the center, heard the shots and realized that all hope of surprise was gone, and he moved his men forward rapidly, with Fontaine's mounted men taking the lead. Red Storm and Little Fox waited among the bushes on the north shore of the Maumee and watched as the mounted soldiers approached the steep bank opposite them and plunged down into the shallow stream.

As the men reached the middle of the river, the more than thirty warriors waiting with them among the bushes began to fire. Several riders went down, but the leader, yelling for his men to charge, came directly at them shooting with a pistol in each hand. He turned to see that only one man, George Adams, had followed him, and then he went down in a hail of bullets. Adams was also hit by several shots but managed to stay on his horse and turn back, reaching the southern shore before dismounting.

"A very brave man," observed Little Fox as he watched Adams riding away.

"Yes," agreed Red Storm, grinning because he knew one of his bullets had hit the man. "I thought he would surely fall when I shot him."

McMillan, crossing further to the east, heard the firing and quickly directed his men in that direction. They reached the battle site just as Fontaine's men, now without their leader, had reformed and were crossing the river.

Little Fox and his fellow warriors sensed that it was time to run away as they had been ordered to do, and they ran back through the town, a ruined cornfield, and into a swampy area that went all the way back to the St. Joseph River. The cavalry and McMillan's men, thinking they had the dreaded savages on the run, pursued with vigor, charging through the town, the cornfield, and into the swamp.

Major Wyllys, with the sixty regulars, crossed the Maumee and made their way through the abandoned town. When they came into the cornfield, Little Turtle sprang his trap. From the edge of the field, the combined forces of Miami, Shawnee, and Ottawa—more than one hundred strong—fired their weapons into the helpless regulars and then attacked with their knives and tomahawks. Wyllys was among the first to fall, shot in the chest and finished by a tomahawk blow that split his skull.

In a short time, fifty of the regulars were slain, and amid the smoke and confusion, the other ten had escaped to the north where they were soon joined by McMillan's men who had given up their chase and started back toward the sounds of the battle in the cornfield. Along with the remains of the cavalry, they now outnumbered the Indians, who began moving back toward the St. Joseph behind them. By this time, Hall's troops were coming in from the west, and the Indians appeared to be trapped.

The warriors moved down into the shallow waters of the St. Joseph, caught between the two militia detachments. Blue Jacket, who was among them on horseback, gave a shout and led the braves in a desperate charge up the riverbank and right through the surprised left flank of Hall's line and into the trees and underbrush beyond. The Indians had taken five militiamen prisoner in their mad dash, and then they were gone.

The battle was over, and the white soldiers looked out upon the slaughter that had taken place in the cornfield. There were a number of slain warriors, but 50 of the regulars were dead as well as many of the militia. A final count showed that 63 of the Kentuckians had been killed in the various battles of the day. Hardin, greatly discouraged, organized a retreat of the remaining men back to Harmar's camp. The army marched out the next day, intent on returning to Fort Washington as quickly as possible.

"We have won a great battle," proclaimed Blue Jacket to Little Turtle. "You are a very great general. Tomorrow we can attack them as they retreat, which I believe they will."

"No," said the chief. "The white general may come back with his whole force, and we may still need to flee."

"He will not." Blue Jacket was sure that General Harmar had no fight left in him. "Besides, we have been joined by 150 Sac and Fox warriors. The five captives we took have told us how discouraged the soldiers are, and that we have killed the best of their soldiers. Also, they are short of provisions."

"And where are these captives? Can I speak with them?"

"I'm afraid not now," admitted Blue Jacket, suddenly feeling a bit sheepish. "We have put them to death."

"It would have been better had you not done that."

"I am sorry, Chief," said Blue Jacket, his voice revealing his sincerity. "But the white soldiers will fight no more, and we should follow them and attack again."

"It does not matter," insisted Little Turtle. "We have won a great victory. It is enough."

When it was clear on the next day that the white army was in full retreat, Blue Jacket gathered a force of more than 250 braves, a mixture of Miami, Shawnee, Ottawa, Sac and Fox, and other tribes, and began a pursuit. As they camped for the night, a full moon graced the sky, but as they watched, the braves saw a shadow cross the face of the moon until it was completely dark. This was quickly interpreted as an indication of possible disaster, and the warriors began to slip away until only Blue Jacket and a few of his Shawnees remained. The defeated American army returned to Fort Washington without further trouble from the Indians.

March 1, 1791

The little war party came up the west bank of the Ohio, and hearing noises, moved into a heavy stand of maple trees more than a quarter mile in from the river's edge. They watched as a man and woman toiled in a sugar camp located in a small clearing just next to the maple grove. The Indians were in a good mood, still filled with pride and confidence as a result of their convincing victory over Harmar just six months earlier.

The news of that triumph spread among the Indian settlements like wildfire, and there was renewed hope that holding the white man back beyond the Ohio River was now possible. As a result, strikes against the border settlers became even more numerous, and many of the tribes that had essentially given up were now back in the fray.

Little Fox and Red Storm were overjoyed that many of their Delaware brethren had taken up the fight again. This particular war party consisted of seven Delaware warriors and only two Shawnees. Little Fox smiled to himself as he made this count in his head, for he realized he thought of himself as Delaware instead of Chippewa. Fire Heart was along, as was their old friend Bald Rock, a frequent companion on their raids. Also with them were the young Delaware warriors Black Buffalo, Red Beaver, and Young Deer, who had been with them two years earlier at the time Red Storm received his wrist injury. The other two Delawares were Yellow Moon, the seventeen-year-old brother-in-law of Little Fox, and his older cousin, Cold Rain.

Little Fox had endured some harsh words from his wife, Bright Moon, when she discovered that her husband intended to take her young brother along on a raid against the whites. "He is too young," she shouted. "He cannot go."

"Are you his chief?" Little Fox answered with a laugh, hoping to blunt her opposition with humor.

Bright Moon was having none of that. "I am not his chief, but I am his sister and his only relative. I do not want him killed."

"And neither do I. But he is a man now and old enough for this raid. Besides, I do not intend for him to be killed, or me either."

The argument went on for most of the day and into the next one. Little Fox held his ground, and Yellow Moon refused to listen to his sister. Little Fox could only hope that her anger would have subsided by the time of his return. The boy's mother had died in childbirth, and his father had not survived an attack of smallpox. Little Fox could understand his wife's worry, but he wanted the boy to come along and learn how to be a warrior.

The name of the woman they were watching was Mary Riley who lived, with her husband Francis and six children, in a cabin a few hundred yards from the sugar camp. Francis and the oldest boy, John, had gone upriver to help with the building of a settlement on the Virginia side just above the mouth of Buffalo Creek. The man working with Mrs. Riley was her son-in-law, John Schemmerhorn, who was married to her twenty-year-old daughter, Ruth. They had an infant daughter, Claudia, which made a total of ten people living together in the cramped cabin.

As they watched, Little Fox and Red Storm took special notice as Schemmerhorn dumped a supply of wood next to the fire and said something to the woman. He picked up an ax and walked back into the woods a short distance where he began to chop down a small sapling. Signaling to Fire Heart and Bald Rock and pointing to the spot from which emanated the sound of the ax, Little Fox led them silently through the trees until they had surrounded Schemmerhorn, who was completely unaware of their presence.

A swift movement by Bald Rock, accompanied by a crushing tomahawk blow, ended the woodcutter's life. Bald Rock took the scalp and grinned as he held high an Indian belt that he had removed from around the dead man's waist. "We have avenged the owner of this belt," he hissed, examining its features. "It is a Shawnee belt."

"It is good," proclaimed Little Fox. "Now let us take the woman."

They moved back toward the sugar camp, gathering their companions as they went and descended upon Mrs. Riley as she stood next to a kettle of boiling maple water. She was too startled to offer any resistance, and they took her captive. She noticed the fresh scalp hanging on the belt of Bald Rock, and she knew that her son-in-law was dead. Fearing for her own life, she spoke up, offering to go with them if they would not kill her. Little Fox understood what she was asking even though he did not understand the words.

"We will not kill her," he said. "She might be useful in our village or as someone to trade. She is your prisoner, Bald Rock. The rest of us will visit her lodge and see what is there."

Bald Rock was unhappy with his assignment, and as soon as the others had left, he tied her to a beech tree limb using the belt he had taken from Schemmerhorn. He then set off after the others, hoping to get in on the plunder that was sure to come. By the time he reached the scene, the action was over. Little Fox and Red Storm were standing with two young women held as captives. These girls were twenty-year-old Ruth, who saw that it was her husband's scalp hanging from the belt of Bald Rock as he came up, and Abigail, who was sixteen.

Black Buffalo and Red Beaver were walking back toward the cabin, carrying the scalps of the Riley brothers William and Tom. William, nineteen, was outside when the warriors attacked, went back for his four-year-old brother who had cried out to him. With little Tom on his back, William made a run for it but was brought down by a shot from Black Buffalo, and Red Beaver killed Tom with his tomahawk.

Bald Rock motioned to Yellow Moon and Cold Rain to follow him into the cabin, searching for anything useful to take with them. Inside, they discovered the baby in her cradle. Hoisting the child to his shoulder, Bald Rock rushed outside, shouting with delight. "This must be the woman's daughter," he yelled to Little Fox. "We will see now what she says about this." He began to run back down the trail toward the maple syrup camp.

When he reached the spot where he had tied Mrs. Riley, he cried out in anger. The woman was gone, having freed herself from the sloppy job of binding that Bald Rock had done in his haste. "You should not have done this!" cried Bald Rock. In his fury, he took the child and dashed her head against the same tree to which he had tied the woman, then flung the body toward the fire. He sat down in despair and waited for his companions. Little Fox watched as his friends ransacked the cabin and set fire to it. He led them back to where Bald Rock was sitting.

"Where is the woman?" asked Red Storm.

"She is gone," admitted Bald Rock. "I don't know how she could have done so."

"You didn't tie her properly," observed Fire Heart.

"Maybe someone came and rescued her," argued Bald Rock, embarrassed at his mistake.

"No one has been here," said Little Fox. "But they will be soon for they will see the fire."

"We can track the woman," insisted Bald Rock. "She cannot have gone far."

"It does not matter. We have two captives. Let us go." Little Fox moved off in a direction away from the river, and the others fell into line behind him. In fact, Mrs. Riley was well on her way to safety at Carpenter's station, two miles to the north. Unknown to the Indians, another member of the family, eight-year-old Moses, escaped unseen to the south and made it to Waxler's station, five miles away.

The braves had traveled no more than a mile when Abigail, walking just ahead of Red Storm, became the subject of a dispute between Red Storm and Young Deer, who had taken a fancy to her and wanted her to walk with him. Little Fox, when he became aware of the noisy distraction, came back to find out what was happening.

"We cannot delay. The Long Knives are sure to come after us. Put an end to this trouble."

"I'll take care of it," answered Red Storm.

He led Abigail off into the woods behind them and soon returned without her. Young Deer, who had been prevented from following, met Red Storm on his return.

"Where is she?" Young Deer demanded.

"She is no longer with us," said Red Storm.

Abigail's sister, Ruth, watched all this unfold, filled with fear and anger. She wanted to cry out, but fearing what they might do to her, she remained quiet.

"Did you kill her?" Young Deer asked angrily, grabbing Red Storm's arm.

Pulling his arm free, Red Storm turned to face the young brave and pushed him in the chest with the index finger of his crippled right hand. He said nothing, then turned back and walked away. Young Deer stifled the desire to strike and stepped back. The rest of the warriors were moving on with some haste, and the angry brave realized that the woman was surely dead. Although he wanted to go back and find her, he knew it was useless. After a short time, he began to follow along, thinking of some way to make Red Storm sorry for what he had done.

March 8, 1791

Sam Brady was a natural leader. Nearly everyone agreed with that, even Lew Wetzel, who had long realized that he didn't ever regard anyone as his leader. Wetzel stood, admiring Brady now as he directed the men to make camp on a high ridge not far north of the site of the former Fort McIntosh. The presence of these men at this location was a result of the Indian raid a week earlier that resulted in the attack on the Riley family.

Word came to the settlements on Buffalo Creek on the Virginia side of the Ohio shortly after Mrs. Riley showed up at Carpenter's station. An early attempt to rescue the captured Riley sisters failed, and word was sent to David Shepherd, the Ohio County lieutenant. Shepherd ordered militia and scouts to take to the trail across the Ohio. A large group was put together, including some men under Captain Thomas Patterson from Pennsylvania, but most were Virginians led by Thomas Wells, Francis McGuire, and Sam Brady.

The initial gathering was held along Indian Cross Creek, after the river crossing made at Mingo Bottom. As the leaders discussed their plans, Captain Patterson became concerned with what he felt was a lack of enough provisions, but more than that, he was getting cold feet about pursuing Indians in violation of recent governmental orders forbidding such activity. Patterson counseled returning to their homes, but McGuire grew angry and insisted that they go on with the original plan.

After some heated talk, Brady offered to lead a party to go after the "murderin' Injuns" as he put it, and twenty-five others, including Wetzel, Wells, and McGuire agreed to go along.

"I think you, men, are making a mistake," said Captain Patterson, "but I wish you well."

With that he led the remainder of the would-be soldiers back across the Ohio and to their homes. After going to the Riley place to attempt to pick up on the cold trail, the Brady party moved north, striking Indian Cross Creek again, and following it to its headwaters. Near there on the evening of the fourth of March, they discovered a cold Indian camp. A number of discarded items were found.

"By God, look at this," shouted Tom Wells suddenly, holding up a silver watch. "This watch belonged to Francis Riley, sure as anything."

"How do you know?" asked Henry Darnell, who was beginning to think they were on a fool's errand.

"I think I've seen him carryin' it," replied Wells.

"I wish Francis had come along hisself," said Darnell. "Then we might know something."

Francis Riley and his son John had both wanted to accompany the expedition, anxious to avenge the terrible deaths of their family members. Mary Riley, however, had cried and insisted that they stay with her.

"I can't bear to lose nobody else," she had sobbed. In the end, she won out, and her men stayed home with her.

"Well, I'm sure enough," insisted Wells. "Let's find them damned red murderers."

"We'll go on in the morning," said Brady, ending the argument.

Wetzel had examined the ground before dark and found some old tracks. This was fortunate since a cold rain came during the night and washed away any part of a trail that may have existed.

"From what I saw, they was headed to the northwest on the way to the Tuscarawas, I reckon," Lew told Brady in the morning. "There's some old Injun towns up that way."

As they moved north, someone found some tracks that led away toward the north and east.

"What do you think, Lew?" asked Brady in light of this new information.

"Well, the old Tuscarawas trail leads back that way toward Fort McIntosh."

"Hell, I bet that's where they're headed, sure enough," put in Francis McGuire. "I bet they're goin' to the blockhouse over on the Beaver."

"I reckon you're right," exclaimed Joe Edgington. "That damned traitor Wilson runs a tradin' post there, and I'd guess them bastards is goin' there to trade in some of the stuff they took at Riley's."

There was a good deal of agreement among the men, and Brady finally made a decision. "All right," he said at last. "We'll go to the Beaver."

"Wait a minute," protested Darnell, who did not like the sound of that at all. "What about the Riley girls? I thought we were trying to get them back."

"I reckon they aren't with the bunch that made these tracks," reasoned Wetzel. "Likely, they split up."

"But why would they go all the way back to Pennsylvania?" Darnell was ready to recommend they all go home.

"Probably to trade with Wilson," answered Brady, who was now determined to visit the Beaver blockhouse. It seemed very likely to him that there would be Indians there, although whether they would be the ones guilty of the Riley killings was questionable. "No more arguments. We'll see who's at Wilson's."

An Indian trail had been discovered as they reached the ridge where they were now making camp along the bank of a small run, which would eventually be called Brady's Run. Darkness was falling when Joseph Biggs came to Brady.

"Sam, I'm smellin' smoke comin' from off to the east."

"The blockhouse ain't far, I think," said Brady. "Could be comin' from there."

"Could be," agreed Biggs. "But it could be an Injun camp too."

"Well, you're right. It could be. We'd better be quiet as we can. Tell the men we can't have no fires."

"Mebbe we should send out some spies," suggested Biggs.

Brady nodded his agreement and sent for Wetzel and Wells.

"Tom and Lew, we need you to take a look on down this run. It must go into the Beaver. Joe Biggs claims he smells smoke."

"I smell it too, Sam," asserted Wetzel. "I'll take a look."

"Good, and take Tom along too."

After a few minutes, the two men stopped and talked a minute.

"I'll go down this run, Tom," said Lew. "Why don't you go across that little valley and take a look on the top of that big hill over there?"

"Yeah, give me the tough job, eh, Lew?" laughed Wells. The terrain ahead of him did not look friendly.

"I ain't no fool, Tom," answered Lew with a grin. "But I'll trade with you if you like."

"No," declared Wells. "You're more apt to run into Injuns than I am."

"Just what I was thinkin'," said Lew to himself. He figured he was less likely to be discovered by the Indians than Wells. He nodded to Wells, and the two men separated. An hour later, Wetzel returned to the camp, which was noisier than he thought was prudent. He found Brady and made his report. "There's an Indian camp there all right just across the Beaver from the blockhouse. They are in a flat spot between the toe of a big hill and the creek. About a dozen of them, I'd guess, although I couldn't get a good count."

"Are they all warriors?" Brady wondered.

"No, there's a couple of squaws and some kids," replied Wetzel. "We can take 'em easy in the morning."

"Where's Tom?" asked Brady, suddenly realizing that he had sent out two spies.

"Tom took a different route. He should be back afore long."

Wells returned a half hour later. He had viewed the Indian camp from the top of the big hill, and his information confirmed what Wetzel had said.

"By the way, Sam," said Wetzel. "If these men get any louder, we may have them Injuns up here for supper."

"Well, it'd be just like you to invite 'em, you son of a bitch," chuckled Brady.

However, he passed the word for the men to quiet down and mentioned that the Indian camp would be attacked early in the morning.

March 9, 1791

The plan called for one group of twelve men, including Brady, Wetzel, and McGuire, to descend along Brady's Run and come upon the Indians from the south. The other detachment of twelve men led by Thomas Wells and Joe Edgington was to go over the big hill and come down on the Indian camp from the west. William Griffith and Thomas Madden were left to take care of the three horses that had been brought along.

Brady's party came to the mouth of the run and turned to the north, holding back while Wells and his men got into position on the big hill. They could see the camp ahead of them, several tents pitched along the riverbank and guarded on the north by a dense laurel thicket with heavy woods behind. Several men could be seen among the tents, and they appeared to be drinking heavily. There were three women there as well, and two young boys who were playing among the branches of a young sugar tree on the southern edge of the camp.

The boys, who were laughing and blowing on wooden whistles, caught sight of the white men huddled by the creek and immediately scrambled down, shouting as they ran.

"White men, white men," they called in unison.

"Damn it," yelled Brady. "We've lost our surprise."

Wetzel knelt immediately and fired into the camp, and this was followed by other shots from Brady's team. The Indians were scrambling to reach the thicket, and already one had fallen. Now shots came from above, and another brave along with one of the women, went down. Brady, who had given strict orders against killing any of the women and children, was angry when he saw the woman go down.

"Goddamn it," he growled and then shouted. "Don't shoot at the squaws or the kids neither."

Thomas Wells, coming down the hill next to Edgington, grabbed his partner.

"Joe, you shot that squaw. Why did you do that?"

"Didn't know it was a squaw when I fired. Hell, I couldn't help it."

Meanwhile, Wetzel had reloaded and fired again at one of the warriors trying to disappear behind one of the tents. By this time, the men were among the tents, but the remainder of the Indians had escaped into the thicket and woods beyond. Wetzel found the man he had shot and finished the job with a blow from his tomahawk. He gave his trademark yell and then took the scalp. The action had brought him into a frenzy of emotion, and he bent down and removed the warrior's bloody shirt, pulling it up and down over his own buckskin blouse.

"By God, you're a bloody devil, Lew," remarked McGuire, who had come up behind.

Wetzel, who began to feel a bit sheepish, tried to explain. "I get my dander up some fightin' these devils." He didn't remove the shirt, however.

The battle was over already. All twenty-four of the white men were in the camp, milling around and looking for plunder. Two men, along with young Solomon Hedges who was only sixteen, discovered a bloody trail heading into the bushes and started to follow.

"Hold it, men," called Brady. "It ain't worth it, and you're most likely to fall into an ambush yourself."

"He's right," agreed Wetzel. "It's an old trick of theirs. They'll be waitin' to shoot whoever comes along."

There was disappointment at the failure to obtain captives who could be traded for the Riley sisters.

"Who shot the squaw?'" asked Brady. "That's not what we wanted."

No one spoke up at first, but Thomas Wells felt the need to say something.

"I don't know who did it, Sam, but it was an accident anyway. Them savages was runnin' all over the place."

"I suppose we'll have to accept that explanation, but this ain't goin' to set well with some of our government authorities."

"How are they goin' to know what happened here?" asked McGuire. "We're the only ones who know what happened, and we ain't likely to talk too much." There was a murmur of agreement from the others.

"I hate them Injuns, and I ain't sorry about killing that damned squaw," whispered Joe Edgington to Caleb Wells. "I'll kill an Injun of any size and shape and any age every chance I get."

When Wells remained silent, Edgington continued, "And I don't take too kindly to any damned fool who disagrees with me."

Brady pointed across the Beaver to the blockhouse standing on the north side of the run now called Blockhouse Run. "I'm afraid we may have some witnesses right over there."

In fact, there were five men at the blockhouse, one of them a young Indian brave, and they had seen the entire action. William Wilson, who operated the trading post, and his friend John Hillman, had watched with dismay, and both would later testify against Sam Brady. Also present were Henry Baker, Lew Wetzel's old friend, and a man named Shane. As soon as the shooting had started, Wilson had gone to the shore of the Beaver and called out to the men to stop shooting, that these were innocent Indians. His voice had gone unheard in the din of the battle.

Now, with the fighting over, Wilson called across again, hoping to be heard. "Who is your commander?"

Francis McGuire, who was nearest to the spot where Wilson was standing, hollered back, "Each man is his own commander. Why don't you come over here if you want to talk."

Wilson did not feel it would be safe to go across the river. He knew what many of the frontiersmen thought of him, and the fact that some of them had seen the young Indian with him made him hesitant.

"Is Sam Brady with your party?" he asked finally.

"What if he is?" growled McGuire.

"I'd like to talk to him," answered Wilson.

When Brady appeared, Wilson came down to the river's edge, but he made no attempt to cross.

"Who was them Injuns anyway?" asked McGuire. "We tracked them from down below old Fort Steuben where some Delawares murdered a white family."

"Well, they are Delawares, but they can't be the ones who killed the family. I know them well. Some of them work for me."

"Well, we don't think much of your workers, then," snarled McGuire.

"Some of them are Moravians," Wilson pointed out. "They wouldn't kill nobody. I hired some of these men to bring some pelts from the salt licks north of the Beaver. It may be those tracks that you found."

"Well, we've been followin' their tracks from over near the Tuscarawas." insisted McGuire, although he knew that there was little evidence that the tracks led all the way back here. "Injuns is Injuns, and we caught up with 'em here."

Wilson finally gave up and went back to the blockhouse, muttering to himself. "I'll make them bastards sorry they did this."

May 31, 1791

Lew Wetzel had come to the new little town being called Charlestown nestled along the Ohio just above the mouth of Buffalo Creek. The reason for his visit was to confer with Sam Brady, who lived near the town. Rumors were flying through the settlements of the pending arrest of Brady and others for the recent killing of supposedly friendly Indians at the Beaver blockhouse. Wetzel thought it best to find out from Brady himself if these rumors were true, and if he might be in danger from the authorities also. Drusilla Brady was especially gracious when Wetzel knocked on the door of the big house.

"Oh, you are Lew Wetzel, aren't you?" she asked with a smile. "Sam will want to talk with you, but he isn't here just now. Could I get you a cup of tea?"

It was an uncomfortable moment for him; he was not used to someone offering him a cup of tea. Still he felt a flow of warmth wash over him, and he wanted to be polite. "Why, that is nice of you, but you don't have to do that for me."

"But I would very much like to, Lewis. You have always been such a good friend to my Sam. Please come in."

"Oh, I couldn't do that, ma'am," protested Lew. "My clothes and boots ain't clean enough to come into such a fine house. I'll just stay out here on the porch." He sat down on the top step.

Drusilla laughed. "Well, Sam don't let that bother him too much. But suit yourself. I will bring you some tea."

In a few minutes, Mrs. Brady returned with a small cup and saucer, the cup filled with steaming hot tea. Wetzel was unsure what to do with it. He had drunk tea before, but never from such instruments. His hand was shaking as he grasped the edge of the saucer and nearly dumped the tea before he caught the tipping cup in his other hand.

Drusilla was well aware that the rough borderman had probably never seen such a thing before, and she smiled. "It's all right, Lew. You're just like Sam. He hates what he calls my fancy dishes."

"I'm sorry, ma'am," apologized Lew, feeling the blush he knew was rising on his dark face.

"I hope you like the tea, anyway," she said.

Lew carefully took a sip and was surprised at how good it tasted. He felt awkward. "When do you expect Sam will be back?" he managed to stammer.

"Oh, it won't be long. It's almost dinnertime, and Sam's not likely to miss that." She watched for a moment and then decided to end her amusement at Wetzel's discomfort. "I'll leave you then," she said and went back in the house.

Wetzel watched her go, admiring her beauty, and feeling a bit envious of Brady, who he now saw riding up along the trail that led from the river. His thoughts went back to the day, more than two months earlier, when they had killed the Delawares at Beaver blockhouse.

The men had gathered up nine horses plus some guns, tomahawks, knives, kettles, bags, flour, and three gallons of old bear's oil, which they assumed came from trading with Wilson. They headed down the creek to where it emptied into the Ohio. The river was high, following some recent rains and snowmelt.

"How are we goin' to get across here with all this stuff," wondered McGuire.

"Here's a nice flatboat," Wetzel had pointed out.

"Lot of good that will do," said McGuire. "It's chained to that tree."

"Well," observed Wetzel, breaking into a wide grin. "It's agin the law to break a lock, but I don't reckon there's no law about choppin' down a tree."

They located an axe, and Lew proceeded to cut down the tree, after which they lifted the chain off the stump, freeing the boat.

"By God, Lew," noted Brady. "You're a master thief."

"I ain't no thief," protested Wetzel. "But it wouldn't be safe to leave a fine boat here like this without it bein' locked up. We'll take it for safekeepin'."

In good spirits now, the party crossed the river with the horses and the other goods. They found an unoccupied cabin and camped there. Realizing how hungry they were, and with their original provisions exhausted, they stirred the stolen flour into the rancid bear oil and ate heartily in spite of the bad taste. The next morning, they decided to break up and go home. The horses and goods were sold for more than $700, and days later, they came together and divided the money equally.

Lew waited now as Brady rode in.

"Well, welcome, Lew," declared Brady as he dismounted, fastening the reins to the porch rail. "What brings you here?"

"I guess I came for this here tea," said Lew with a laugh. "Your wife has treated me very nice."

"She's a peach for sure, but I doubt you came here just for that."

"I been hearing some bad stuff, Sam. I'm hopin' you kin set me straight."

"Maybe you're wantin' to get that reward they got on me, six hundred dollars, so I hear?"

Wetzel placed the cup and saucer on the porch floor and stood up. "Then it's true? The governor's put out a reward for you?"

"That's what I hear. The Injuns is stirred up, and I'm told that President Washington and Henry Knox are mighty upset with us. They're claimin' them redskins was innocent, and we just murdered 'em."

"How do they know it was you?"

"I guess that damned Wilson and his partner Hillman have named me and McGuire. They went to some judge over in

Pennsylvania." Brady dropped down, sitting on the top step. "It ain't good, Lew."

"Do they have all our names?" asked Wetzel, wondering how to react. "And how do you know this stuff?"

"David Shepherd told me all about it. Governor Mifflin is asking Governor Randolph to send us, that is, me and McGuire, to Pennsylvania for trial."

"Will he do it?"

"David says he might not. Shepherd has written to both governors telling them that we was trailing Injuns that had murdered a white family and taken captives. He did offer that reward though, and some bastard may decide to claim that."

"Well, surely one state can't be forced to send its citizens to another state." Knowing nothing of the law, this seemed only common sense to Lew.

"I guess they can. It's in our new constitution. It's called extradition." Brady sighed and stared at his feet. "At least that's what David tells me. He knows somethin' about that stuff."

"I reckon he does. I've always figured David was a man to be trusted."

"He is that," agreed Brady. "Now, why don't you come in with me? Drusilla has dinner ready, and I'm sure there's enough for you."

"Oh no, Sam. I ain't fit to be doin' that. But what do you plan to do. Will they arrest you?"

"Not if David Shepherd has anything to do with it," exclaimed Brady. "I ain't about to give myself up, and I don't think there's too many men can take me if I don't want to be taken."

"That's the God's truth if anythin' is. But what about me? Surely somebody's told 'em I was there too."

"I don't think so, Lew. David didn't mention you, and I sure ain't about to mention anybody." Brady put his hand on Wetzel's arm in a gesture of reassurance. "If I was you, I'd find someplace else to go for awhile 'til this dies down, which it surely will."

"I ain't one to run away from a fight, Sam, you know that."

"I know that, and so does everybody else."

"I have been thinkin' about joinin' my brother Jacob. He's livin' down in Kentucky these days."

Brady shook his head vigorously. "That's a great idea, Lew. Go and see your brother."

Mrs. Brady appeared on the porch. "Dinner's ready," she announced. "You're both welcome."

Wetzel immediately descended the steps. "Thank you, Mrs. Brady. Thank you for your kindness, but I must be off. Good-bye to you both. I'm on my way to Kentucky."

18

New Orleans

October 15, 1792

"By God, I need another whiskey. What's keepin' you, man?" The speaker was a man named Michael Forshay, who lived in a cabin on the Ohio side of the river, just below a fort that had been built in what came to be called Dillies Bottom. It was across the Ohio from the mouth of Grave Creek.

Forshay fancied himself an excellent hunter, woodsman, and Indian fighter and had spent the last several minutes expounding on these matters to the men gathered in Jones's tavern that evening. Jacob Miller sat at one of the tables near the door along with Alex Mitchell and Josh Davis.

"Think he'll ever shut up?" asked Mitchell, nodding toward Forshay.

"Doubt it," growled Miller, obviously annoyed with the man's behavior.

"He thinks he's better'n Wetzel or Zane or anybody."

"Well, Lew'll prob'ly be in here pretty soon anyway," said Mitchell. "We'll see what Mr. Braggart has to say then."

"I don't think he knows Lew at all," offered Davis.

"So much the better," laughed Miller. "Let's not let on that we know him either. It ought to be fun."

"Isn't Lew still down in Kentucky?" wondered Davis. "How can he be comin' in here?"

"He's been in Kentucky but came back a few days ago," said Mitchell. "I saw him earlier today, and he knows some of us were goin' to be here tonight. He'll be here."

Just then, Wetzel came through the door, shaking the water from his shoulders and arms as a heavy shower had come up just moments earlier. He spied his friends right away.

"Well, I might of known you damned loafers 'ud be in here," he said.

"Takes one loafer to know another, I guess," answered Miller, avoiding the use of Wetzel's name. "You ain't done nothin' useful in ages, I reckon."

"That's not what your woman says," remarked Wetzel with a laugh.

"Hell, you wouldn't know what to do with a woman if you found one."

"He'd know how to scalp her," chimed in Mitchell with a loud guffaw.

"I ain't scalped no woman nor no white man neither," said Wetzel, glaring at Mitchell. "At least not 'til now, but I may be about to start."

"By God, you're scarin' the hell outta me," laughed Mitchell.

"I'm goin' to get me a drink and find some better company'n this," grinned Wetzel, and he shuffled off toward the bar.

Forshay, who had downed the drink he was given, had taken special interest in the conversation between Wetzel and the men at the table although he couldn't hear much of it. He asked for another drink and then watched as Wetzel walked away. As soon as the bartender, Israel Jones the bar owner, had brought the second drink, Forshay ambled unsteadily over to the table where Wetzel's friends were sitting. He pulled up another chair and sat down.

"Who is that you was talkin' to?" he asked, wondering to himself if this might be the famous Lewis Wetzel.

"He just came from Kentucky," explained Miller. "Thinks he's a mountain man, but I think he's really just a damned old farmer."

"So you really think you're the best in the woods of anybody around here?" asked Mitchell, glancing at his friends with a knowing smile.

Forshay, well under the influence of the liquor he had consumed, stood up and began pointing his finger at Mitchell. "You'd better damn well believe that, my friend." He continued to talk while Miller and Mitchell egged him on. He regaled them with several stories of his prowess, his voice getting louder and louder until everyone in the room was paying attention. After a few minutes of this, Wetzel could take no more, and he walked slowly over to where Forshay was standing.

"See here, mister," said Wetzel quietly, standing close to Forshay and looking down on the shorter man, his black eyes flashing. "I ain't much on a hunt, but I'll bet you the liquor for the crowd that I can come in on you in spite of you, and you won't see or hear me until I strike you on the shoulder. You can pick your ground and name which shoulder I'm to hit into the bargain."

Forshay was taken aback at first, but he looked Wetzel up and down and figured he couldn't be bested by no Kentucky farmer.

"Why, I'll gladly take that bet," he said, breaking into a loud laugh and offering his hand to Wetzel. "You'd better have plenty of cash cause this looks like a mighty thirsty crowd."

Wetzel shook Forshay's hand and quickly dropped it. "Josh Davis here can serve as a judge. You can pick somebody yourself to be a second judge."

Forshay nodded and looked around the room, searching for someone he knew and could trust. His eyes fell on a man named Dan Carpenter whom he had done business with and who had heard the discussion.

"Dan Carpenter there, he's my choice," he said, looking to Carpenter and pleading for his assent with the look on his face.

"Will you do it, Dan?" asked Wetzel.

"I guess I can do that. When will it be?"

"Tomorrow," answered Wetzel immediately. "We'll meet here and make the plans a couple of hours before noon."

Forshay agreed and began to move toward the door. Carpenter joined him, and taking him by the arm, led him out into the night. The rain had stopped as they stepped into the street.

"Do you know who that was you just made that bet with?" Carpenter inquired.

"Some farmer, they said," Forshay replied.

"Hell, man, you just made a bet with Lewis Wetzel!"

October 16, 1792

The contest was to be held across the river. Forshay was entitled to make the choice, and he chose a spot just west of Kirkwood's blockhouse in what was to become the town of Bridgeport, Ohio.

The area chosen was open, spotted with a few scattered trees, and surrounded on three sides by a heavy thicket. On the fourth side, the north, there was a steep embankment, and Forshay sat down on the grass near that north bank. This would make it impossible for Wetzel to approach from the rear. The rains of the night before had blown through, and the sun shining brightly all morning had dried the ground. The trees had attained their autumn color, and many leaves were already on the ground.

"God, Lew," said Davis. "He picked a tough spot. I don't see how you'll ever get up to him here."

"It won't be easy," agreed Lew. "But that makes it even better when I win."

"But the ground is covered with leaves all around where he is sitting. They're dry and will give you away."

"Just watch and see, Josh. Let me know when all is ready."

Wetzel moved off to the south and up the hill that rose on that side. Davis waved to Carpenter, and the two judges moved over to take up a spot by a big tree near the steep bank about a dozen feet away from where Forshay was sitting. There were no others present as Wetzel had forbidden an audience, saying he didn't want anything distracting Forshay's attention.

"Well, you've picked a fine spot, Michael," observed Carpenter. "I don't see anyway he can sneak up on you here."

"That's the idea," laughed Forshay. "I can already taste them free drinks."

"Don't be too sure," Davis spoke up, feeling he needed to defend his hero. "Lew Wetzel is damned good in the woods."

"Are you ready, Mike?" asked Carpenter.

"Ready as I'll ever be."

Carpenter nodded at Davis and then called out as loud as he could. "All ready, Lew."

It was quiet for a short time, and then came Wetzel's reply from the hillside opposite them. "Better keep a sharp lookout there, Forshay, or I'll take your scalp for you."

After a few seconds, Wetzel shouted again, drawing out the word, "Ready."

Now came a long period of complete silence. Forshay searched the thickets on either side of him, never relaxing. Davis could not remember such a time of quiet. He thought he could hear his own heart beating. He knew better than to say anything for he wanted Forshay to have no excuses. Still he held no hope that Wetzel could fulfill his promise. Forshay nearly jumped to his feet once when he thought he heard something on his left. Of course, the rules worked out earlier that morning required him to remain seated, and he remembered in time to avoid controversy.

Davis was watching closely as well, but he could detect nothing. Where could Wetzel be, he wondered. At least fifteen minutes had passed with no discernible action. Suddenly Wetzel sprang from the far side of a tree behind and between the judges and Forshay, who had just turned his head away from where Wetzel struck. When he felt Wetzel's hand touch his shoulder,

Forshay fell forward and then jumped to his feet. He turned and looked at Wetzel with a look of surprise and dismay.

"Damn you, you beat me this time, but you can't do it again."

Wetzel grinned and said nothing, turning to walk away back toward the southern hillside.

Forshay watched him go and sat down again, saying nothing, keeping his eyes straight ahead. Davis stifled the urge to comment, as did Carpenter, and both judges sat down again as before, waiting for the signal from Wetzel.

Once again, the signal came from the hillside, and Forshay kept an even sharper lookout than the first time. It seemed likely to him that Wetzel might come in from the other direction on the second try, and he favored that side as he watched. In a much shorter time than any of them thought possible, Wetzel once again appeared and touched Forshay's shoulder without being detected.

"Well, you've won the bet," admitted Forshay, shaking his head in disbelief.

"Congratulations, Lew," offered Josh, and Wetzel smiled but said nothing. He turned to lead them all back to the big river where they had stowed the canoe. All four men climbed in, afraid to speak, and with Wetzel and Davis rowing, the big canoe glided upstream and around the north end of Zane's Island. They headed straight toward the landing just above the mouth of Wheeling Creek.

By the time the four men had landed and made their way up to Jones's tavern, a sizable crowd had gathered. Jacob Miller was there and the first to speak. "Well, who's buyin'? I'm sure lookin' forward to my free drink."

He could tell by the look on Forshay's face who had won the contest. He was not surprised. Forshay, to his credit, stepped boldly forward and announced the results loudly and with a laugh. "Well, I opened my big mouth at the wrong time, and it's goin' to cost me plenty, I can see that. Come on men, drink up. Wetzel beat me fair and square. I ain't never seen nobody better."

A loud cheer went up for Wetzel, and he held up his hand. "Mostly luck, I reckon, but I'll sure enjoy the results. Forshay here is a mighty good loser, so let's all have a good drink."

As they walked toward the tavern, a tall man edged up next to Wetzel.

"Lew," he said quietly. "My name's Abraham Parker, and I've got a proposition for you."

December 5, 1792

They eased the big flatboat into the landing at Natchez just past midafternoon. Several other boats were tied up there, and a surprising number of people were milling around in the flat area under the high bluffs. There were several commercial establishments, some that had a quite temporary look, including a few tents. As soon as the boat was secured, the owner, Abraham Parker, and three crew members scrambled ashore and headed for one of the taverns housed in a ramshackle hut not far from the landing.

The remaining member of the crew, Lewis Wetzel, was left to guard the boat. Parker had been promising the men for more than a week that as soon as they reached Natchez, they could get as drunk as they wanted.

"We need you to guard things, Lew," directed Parker as he stepped ashore. "Keep alert 'cause Natchez is full of thieves and pirates."

Wetzel wasn't surprised that he was to be left on board, for he knew that Parker had hired him chiefly because of his fighting abilities. Still he could not keep a look of disappointment from his face.

"Don't worry, Lew," said Parker with a smile. "I'll be back and relieve you. It don't take me very long to get good and drunk."

Wetzel watched the four men as they hurried away and then sat down on one of the short barrels filled with flour. It had been a long, hard trip begun over forty days earlier at Wheeling. Parker had offered a place on his flatboat for a trip to New Orleans with a load of flour.

"They're payin' big money for a barrel of flour in New Orleans," Parker had explained to Wetzel. "I'll pay you twenty dollars plus ten cents for each barrel we sell if you'll go along. You've worked on flatboats before, I'm thinkin'."

"Some," answered Wetzel. "That's a long trip, though. How many barrels of flour are you taking?"

"You're right, it's a long trip, but I think my pay is fair. I'm hoping we can get a hundred barrels on that boat."

Wetzel had agreed, and the trip had begun a few days later. Wetzel had first gone to see his mother, still living at the old place with Martin and his family. It occurred to him that he might not see her again, but worrying about such things was not his way, and he began to look forward to the adventure.

As it turned out, there were no major disasters during the voyage. They stopped each evening, Parker not wanting to risk losing any of his valuable cargo by running at night. The biggest problem was to avoid the numerous sunken trees—called sawyers by the rivermen—tangled branches, eddies, and occasional hang-ups on the sandbars. There were no attacks by Indians, which was the major concern of Parker and his principal reason for employing Lew Wetzel. Also, they avoided trouble from river pirates who were beginning to prey on the many flatboats on the Ohio and Mississippi.

The sun was getting low, and Wetzel was dozing lightly when he was awakened by a tall man calling to him in a quiet voice.

"Halloo there on the boat. Are you awake?"

Wetzel sat up, reaching instinctively for his rifle, standing against another barrel near him. "I reckon I'm awake enough. And who is askin'?"

"Just a friend," was the answer. "My name is Payette."

The man was slender and tall but looked strong and powerful. He appeared to be an American.

"Didn't know I had a friend by that name."

As he spoke, Wetzel was aware of movement on the boat behind him. He quickly raised his gun, pointed it at Payette, and stepped to his right, his back against a stack of barrels.

"Whoa, friend," protested Payette. "I don't much like where you're pointin' that weapon."

"Tell your partner behind me to get off this boat, or you'll soon find I'll do more'n just aim at you."

Payette was close enough to see Wetzel's face, and he quickly realized that he'd made a bad choice.

"Stand down, men," he shouted. "Our friend here don't seem to welcome us much."

Wetzel heard two splashes as Payette's accomplices jumped from the boat. Wetzel had not heard the second man earlier.

"Tell 'em to git around front where I kin see 'em," barked Wetzel. "And be quick about it."

The two men appeared on the shore off to his right. They were small men, Spaniards, thought Wetzel. He motioned for them to join Payette who carefully moved back a couple of steps.

"Now do you want to tell me what you're up to?" Wetzel had not lowered the gun.

"Just checkin' to see what you'd do, friend," said Payette, feeling more comfortable now.

"You ain't much of a friend, and I don't like you callin' me friend neither."

"There's three of us you know," Payette pointed out, "and I reckon that gun only fires one shot at a time."

Wetzel looked closely at each of the three men, his black eyes flashing. "You want'a try me? I ain't never killed a white man, but there's a first time for everything."

Payette began to smile. "Hey, there's no harm done here. We'll leave you be, for sure. Come on men, this here's a good and honest man, and we'll let him go back to his nap."

The three men turned and began to walk away when Payette stopped and spoke again to Wetzel. "I'd like to know the name of a man who bested me," he said. "You're the kind of man I'd like to have as a friend."

"The name's Lew Wetzel, and I don't need friends like you." He lowered the gun and sat down again on the barrel.

Payette waved and walked away.

"Damned fools," Wetzel said aloud. "I prob'ly should have killed 'em all." He decided that he'd better stay awake.

It was nearly dark when Wetzel took notice of a young woman walking toward the door of a tavern located in a more substantial building nestled against the side of the high bluff. She was the most beautiful woman he thought he'd ever seen, much prettier than Lydia Boggs or even Betty Zane. He wondered what she was doing going into such a place at this hour. He figured she was too beautiful to be a common whore. For sure, he intended to go into the place as soon as Parker came to relieve him. His impatience grew as he waited.

Within an hour Wetzel saw Abraham Parker walking unsteadily toward the boat.

"Damn it all, the man's drunk."

Parker managed to get on board, where he hollered to Wetzel. "Lew, I'm here."

He broke into a loud laugh. "I'm pretty drunk though," he admitted.

"I can see that, Abe," answered Wetzel. "I had some visitors who were up to no good. I don't know if I should leave you here by yourself."

These words seemed to straighten Parker up a bit. "The hell you say. What happened?"

"Nothin' much. I scared 'em off, but I suppose they could be back."

"Well, I need to let you go anyway. Give me your rifle. I'll shoot the first person who comes around here."

"Don't shoot none of our crew now, Abe." Wetzel wanted to go very much, but he didn't think Parker was in much condition to defend the boat.

"Where are they anyway?"

"Oh, they're drunk as skunks. Besides, they found a couple of women, and they won't be back 'til mornin'."

"Are you sure about me goin'?" asked Wetzel, half-afraid of the answer.

"You go, Lew, and have a good time. I just want everybody back here by dawn tomorrow."

As Wetzel began to walk away, Parker fished in his pockets and came up with three Spanish dollars. "Here," he said to Wetzel. "Take these along, should be enough for the night."

"Thank you," replied Wetzel, grateful to have coins he knew would be acceptable in any of the establishments. He hadn't expected such generosity, but Parker often surprised them with his liberality. The Spanish dollars, also called pesos or pieces of eight, were used as legal tender everywhere in North America. He stood for a moment, eyeing the saloon that the lady had entered. A dim light shone through the one window to the right of the door. He could see shadowy figures but could not see the woman. Raising a hand to his face, he felt the coarse stubble and knew that he must shave that off.

It was his custom to be clean-shaven whenever possible, for he didn't think he looked very good wearing a beard. Pulling his hunting knife from his belt, he ducked inside the covered living quarters on the boat. Going to his personal sleeping space, he searched his pouch, lifting out a small whetstone that he kept in order to keep his knife sharpened. He drew the knife blade across the stone several times, and then ran his finger across the blade. Not satisfied, he repeated the process twice more until the sharpness of the blade suited him.

On one of the poles in the center of the room, a small mirror had been attached and a round metal basin stood on a box below it. Parker was a fastidious man and had provided a washing and shaving station in the boat. Wetzel was thankful for that now, especially for the bars of soap that Parker had brought along and were stored in the box. Most pioneer families made their own soap, but it was usually in a gelatin form because the bars were expensive and difficult to make. Parker had purchased the bars from a merchant in Wheeling, thinking they would be easier to store. Wetzel took the bowl outside, dipped it into the river, and carried it half full back to the washing station. Working the soap until some lather formed, he slapped it on his face and began scraping the whiskers with his knife.

"Damn," he said after a short while, feeling the blade cut into his cheek. He had been determined not to cut himself, but it nearly always happened. He finished the job and dabbed at the bleeding cut with his finger. "Hell, Lew," he said to himself. "She ain't goin' to think you look good anyway."

After retrieving the scarves he sometimes wore in his ears, he tied them together and then around his neck, thinking this would help hide the cut from which the blood was still oozing. Now he strode out to the front of the boat where he could easily jump to the ground. Waving at Parker, he walked with purpose toward the tavern door. The room was dark and smoky, but it didn't take Wetzel long to locate the woman he had seen earlier and about whom he had been thinking ever since. She was behind the bar, talking with one of the patrons. After taking a quick look to both sides, noting that there were only three tables and a half-dozen men drinking, Wetzel moved straight to the bar where the woman was standing. Wetzel was not a man to be ignored, and the woman took immediate notice.

"Hello, sailor," was her greeting. She spoke English with a slight accent, which Wetzel recognized as French.

A lantern hung from the ceiling just to her right, and the shimmering light on her hair and face revealed her beauty, which almost left him speechless.

"I ain't no sailor," he finally managed to say.

"Well, you came on a boat, so I say you're a sailor." Her eyes sparkled, and from her wide lips came a throaty laugh. Wetzel had always found himself tongue-tied in the presence of a beautiful woman, and this time was no different.

He tried to think of something witty. "You're beautiful," he blurted eventually.

She laughed. "I'm glad you think so. Now what can I do for you?"

"I came in to see you," offered Lew.

The smile left her face, and she became very stern. "I'm not for sale!"

Embarrassed at what she clearly thought he was asking for, Wetzel did not know what to do. This was not at all what he had anticipated.

"I never meant that," he replied.

"Then what do you want?" she snapped.

"A whiskey, I guess."

"All right. I will get you a whiskey." She smiled at the man she had been talking to earlier, who was clearly annoyed with Wetzel. He said nothing, however, and turned away.

The woman, whose name was Marie, returned with the drink, but she held it back. "Do you have any money?"

Reaching into his pocket, Wetzel produced one of the coins Parker had given him and placed it on the counter.

"Ah," sighed Marie. "So you are a paying customer." She placed the glass on the bar and pushed it toward him. Lew took a drink, never taking his eyes off of Marie who continued to watch him.

"I'm sorry we got into a spat," said Wetzel.

"Well, most of the damned fools around here think any woman they see is a whore. I am not."

"I never thought you were. I thought you were much too beautiful for that."

"I guess you're different at that," she responded. "That is a very nice thing to say. What's your name?"

"My name's Lew. What's yours?"

They settled into a pleasant conversation. Wetzel learned that Marie's father owned the tavern, and her mother was dead.

She and her father ran the business together. Her presence affected Wetzel in ways he could not have described, and when she accidentally touched his arm with her fingers, the effect was immediate. He was dismayed when she had to go and serve other patrons but giddy with delight when she returned to talk with him. He admitted to being a hunter, but he avoided telling her about his reputation as an Indian killer. During their long conversation, Wetzel detected nothing to inform him about whether she was married or engaged. Finally he just asked her.

"I have no man yet, Lew," was her answer, "although I think my father has some plans for me."

After the fourth drink, Wetzel felt himself losing control, which he did not want to do in front of this wonderful lady.

"I'm afraid I must be goin'," he said to her sorrowfully, half hoping that she would stop him and ask him to go home with her. "We must go on to New Orleans in the mornin'."

"You have been a very nice customer," was all she said.

"I am sorry to say good-bye. Mebbe I'll come back to see you when our business is done."

She smiled at him, flirting in a way that gave him hope. "That would be nice."

He forced himself to turn and walk out the door, thinking he hadn't felt this way since before Lydia's wedding.

December 11, 1792

The flatboat and its precious cargo were tied snugly at the landing on the left bank of the Mississippi River just below the high levee built to protect the buildings of New Orleans. Wetzel stepped out of the covered quarters to discover a drizzling rain descending. They had arrived just after dark the previous evening, and he was disappointed to find that it was difficult to see much of the surroundings on this hazy morning.

He could see some people walking on top of the levee, and he thought he could detect the upper part of a building that might be a church. The twisting and turning of the river during their journey down from Natchez had disturbed his usually keen sense of direction. The rising sun, whose light was somewhat blocked by the clouds, seemed to be directly across the river from where he stood, which meant the river was flowing mostly north. This struck him as strange, since everybody knew that the Mississippi went from north to south.

Wetzel and his three companions had been left to guard the boat while Abraham Parker went in search of someone who could negotiate the sale of the flour. It had taken them five days to travel the more than 250 river miles from Natchez to New Orleans, their progress slowed by some heavy showers that forced them to take refuge on the shore. Parker learned upon their arrival that sales had to be arranged through government officials. His mission that morning led him to go to the Government House, located near the intersection of Toulouse and Decatur streets not far from where the boat was tied.

Wetzel knew none of this, but he was anxious to explore this city he had heard so much about. The only other city he'd ever been to was Pittsburgh, and his feelings about that were definitely mixed. It seemed to him that it would be all right if he got off the boat and went up to the walkway on the top of the levee. He could still keep his eye on the boat from there, but maybe he could see some of the town as well. The drizzle had reduced to something like a mist or heavy fog, but he decided to wait a bit longer to see if it stopped altogether. When he went back inside, he was met by John Kyle, another man whom Parker had signed on at Wheeling. Wetzel knew the family for they had some land in Ohio County.

"Good mornin', John," he said.

"Not much good about it, far as I kin see," answered Kyle, somewhat gruffly.

Kyle and the other two men had been angry with Parker the night before when he refused to let them leave the boat for the night.

"You got no right to keep us here," Kyle had insisted.

"Don't guess I'd need to pay you then either," was Parker's reply, and that had ended the argument.

"I'm goin' up on the levee and take a look around, John. I'll be close by in case there's any trouble."

"Hell, what trouble could there be right here in plain sight? It's still mornin', ain't it?"

"Trouble came up in Natchez, so I s'pose it could here too. Anyway, I'll keep the boat in sight."

Wetzel hopped off onto the riverbank and made his way up to the levee. He climbed up and found a gravel path maybe eight feet wide. Several people, some in military uniforms, were walking along the path, but they paid no attention to Wetzel. He could see an open, grassy plaza in front of him, and on the far side was what he had guessed was a church. It was under construction, he could see now, but still a way from being completed. Far down to his left, he could see a strange-looking square building with a high-pitched roof and many narrow columns on each side. This, he found out later, was the government building where Parker had gone that very morning.

There were buildings and houses in both directions formed into a kind of square. This was called the Vieux Carré, the old square, by the French, although Wetzel knew nothing of that. Off to his right there was a busy market with its open side facing the muddy street. A wide diversity of patrons scoured the offerings, and the varieties of food reminded Wetzel that he was hungry. Even though it was a gloomy day, there were people of obvious wealth; the women dressed in colorful finery with flashy hats, accompanied by slaves, both male and female. There were men who wore highly colored coats and short breeches with stockings, and many in military attire.

Wetzel was surprised at the number of blacks who mingled with the crowd. There were some slaves, of course, in Wheeling, but the Wetzel family owned none, and Lew had never really thought much about the institution. Here, though, many of the blacks shopping at the market seemed to have no connection with any of the whites. Parker explained to him later that there was a large population of free blacks in New Orleans. The white population was a generous mix of French, Spanish, and Americans.

A frown came to Wetzel's face when he recognized that there were also Indians present. He guessed there were Indians everywhere in the country, but it surprised him to find them here in the middle of the city.

As he looked around, Wetzel saw that Abraham Parker was making his way up the street from the direction of the government house, and he hurried back down to the boat before Parker could see that he had disobeyed the man's orders. He and John Kyle were standing at the bow as the boat owner made his way aboard. His manner was downcast, and they could immediately see that negotiations had not gone well.

"Hello, men," was Parker's greeting.

"Hello, Abe," said Wetzel. "You don't look too happy."

"Well, I ain't, and that's for sure."

"Nobody buyin' flour?" asked Lew.

"Oh, they're buyin' all right. Just ain't payin', that's the problem."

"So you didn't sell?" questioned Lew, suddenly concerned about the promised pay and the plans he was making for spending it.

"I sold," Parker admitted with a sigh. "There was no choice. The damned government controls the trade, and they do the buying. The problem is they're only payin' ten pesos a barrel, which ain't even a third of what I was told by people up north."

"How much is a peso?" John Kyle wanted to know.

"Same as a Spanish dollar or a US dollar for that matter. Don't worry, I sold 'em eighty barrels. I'll be able to pay you men what I owe."

"That don't sound too bad to me," remarked Wetzel.

"Well, it ain't what I expected. I paid too much for that flour on the front end." Parker didn't offer to share what he had paid.

There would still be some profit, he knew, and he could get something for the boat. "What's done is done."

Arrangements were made for the boat to be unloaded, which included help from Parker and his men. While they were unloading, a man came and offered to buy the boat. It was afternoon when they finished, and after this, Parker took Wetzel with him to pick up the money from the city agent.

The founding of the city of New Orleans by the French went all the way back to 1718, and within three years, a settlement was laid out in the shape of a large square, the Vieux Carré. There were to be eleven streets running basically parallel to the river, and another six intersecting them at right angles, giving the city sixty-six blocks. However, for many years, only the streets and blocks closest to the river had structures on them.

A levee was built in the 1720s to help protect from the yearly floods. The capital of Louisiana was moved to New Orleans in 1722. The French had paid little attention to the operation of the city of New Orleans. In 1762, Louisiana was ceded to Spain, and Alejandro O'Reilly, who succeeded Antonio de Ulloa as the governor of Louisiana in 1769, put Spanish law into practice. At the same time, he arranged for the construction of a building to house the Cabildo, the city government. The building was officially called the *casa capitular*, although sometimes the building itself was called the Cabildo.

The first casa capitular was burned in the great 1788 fire, which destroyed over eight hundred buildings, including St. Louis Church. These edifices on Chartres Street faced the Plaza De Armas, the block-sized open area between Chartres and Decatur, the street that ran just below and parallel to the levee. Reconstruction of the church began in 1789 and would be completed by December of 1794. Rebuilding of the casa capitular would wait until 1795. Three governors followed O'Reilly's short term, and in December of 1791, the current governor, Francisco Luis Hector, Baron de Carondelet, took office.

Parker explained some of these things to Wetzel as they walked to the Government House, which had served as the home for the Cabildo since the big fire. As they crossed St. Peter's Street, which formed the southwestern boundary of the plaza, a woman opened the door of one of the shanties on the far side of the street and emptied a pale of slop. It was then that Wetzel realized the source of the terrible stench that surrounded them. The gutters along the street were full of putrefying refuse of every kind.

"It's a shame that these city people don't care nothin' about what they do with their stinkin' waste," said Parker, who noticed Wetzel's revulsion at the woman's action.

"That fire must've been real bad, I reckon," said Lew, wanting to change the subject. "I saw where they was rebuildin' that church."

"Yeah, I was down here a couple of years ago not long after it happened. It was some mess."

By now the two men had reached Toulouse Street and stepped up on the porch of the Government House. Wetzel recognized it as the strange-looking building he had seen from the levee earlier. They went inside and down a dark hallway, pausing in front of a heavy wooden door. The sign on the door said Sindico Procurador General.

Parker pushed it open and entered the room with Wetzel close behind. There were several stations scattered around the large chamber with men seated at each one. In the rear was a large mahogany desk, one that had no doubt been imported from Spain. Behind it sat an important-looking man, shuffling some papers but looking immensely bored. His name was Juan Bautista Poeyfarré.

"Good afternoon, Señor Poeyfarré," said Parker. He continued to talk to the official, but it was mostly in Spanish, and Wetzel could understand none of it.

After a time, the man arose from behind the desk and walked over to one of his assistants. Although not a tall man, Poeyfarré was strongly built, and he exuded an air of command and authority. The aide got up quickly and strode out of the room while his boss turned to Wetzel and Parker with a broad smile. He indicated that they should take a seat and wait, then returned to his own desk.

"He's gone to get the money," Parker explained to Wetzel. "He will bring enough to pay you and the other men."

"What about the rest?" asked Lew.

He had been wondering how much there would be. Parker had told him that he intended to book passage on a ship to take him to Philadelphia. "It will be packed and placed onboard the ship. I intend to travel with it."

Parker had spent some time trying to talk Lew into going with him. John Kyle had agreed, but the other two intended to return to Kentucky by land. Wetzel had made no commitments. In a few minutes, the aide returned with a very large bag, which he placed on Poeyfarré's desk. Parker placed a saddle bag on the desk, and the men began transferring the coins, counting as they did so.

Wetzel was feeling somewhat helpless, particularly since he felt himself to be unarmed. His knife was in its usual place at his side, but his rifle, tomahawk, and other possessions had been left in Parker's hotel room above the Cafe de Aguila at the corner of Chartres and St. Ann.

Parker had insisted that the weapons would not be allowed in the Government House, but he wanted Wetzel to accompany him anyway. He promised that Wetzel and the other three men would be paid after the money was brought back to the room. The counting was finished, and Parker seemed satisfied. Throwing the bag over his shoulder, he said good-bye to the procurador general and his assistant, motioned for Wetzel to follow, and walked out the door.

"We'll look like easy marks to some robber," whispered Wetzel as he came up beside Parker.

"That's why you're along, Lew," said Parker with a smile.

"You should let me bring the 'hawk at least," grumbled Lew. "I'm feelin' undressed."

December 22, 1792

As Wetzel approached the door of the tavern in Natchez, he could feel the increase in his own heartbeat. He had no trouble recognizing the place, although he could not read the rough board sign hanging above, announcing that this was the Under the Hill Inn. This moment had been on his mind for more than two weeks.

In spite of his apprehension, no one had interfered with Wetzel and Parker as they returned to his hotel room in New Orleans. The wages were distributed, and the men had been left to find their own lodging for the evening. John Kyle told them of a place called Maison Coquet, with a reputation of being the hottest place in New Orleans, a city with a bawdy reputation of its own. The place had rooms for rent, along with just about anything else one might want.

Wetzel decided to check it out and went looking for it on Royal Street. He had no trouble finding the Maison, and the entrance led to a barroom filled with patrons drinking, gambling, and flirting with the women who floated around the premises. Thinking that this might be an interesting night, Wetzel first sought out a manager, wanting to secure a room for sleeping. He felt confident with the bag of coins he had just received from Parker stored safely out of sight inside his jacket. The manager was on station at one end of the bar nearest a rickety staircase that led to the second story. He stared nervously at the rifle Wetzel was carrying, loosely crooked in his left arm.

After Lew assured him that he meant no harm but just wanted a place to stay, the transaction was completed, and Wetzel made his way upstairs to his assigned room. He paid extra so that he would not have to share with some other man, although Lew was thinking it might be nice to share with one of the pretty women he had seen below. After eating and having several drinks, Wetzel went back to his room, still anticipating that he might take advantage of some of the vices clearly available downstairs. Yet his mind kept returning to Marie, the young woman he had met in Natchez. He realized that he wanted to see her again very much, and it diminished his earlier thoughts. To dally with another woman would be unfaithful to his feelings for Marie. He went to bed and slept soundly.

The next day, Wetzel paid a man to row him across the Mississippi, and he began a long trek through the woods and bogs that led to Natchez. It took ten days, which he enjoyed in spite of some heavy rains and cold weather. A couple of days were spent in hunting, which was only moderately successful, but helped supply him with food for his journey.

Although it felt good to him to be by himself in the woods, he was constantly drawn toward the little tavern in Natchez. When he arrived in the vicinity, he found a safe hiding place under a pile of fallen branches in a dense stand of loblolly pines. Here he stashed his rifle and his other belongings, including part of the money he was carrying. Now he was at the door of the inn, and he walked in, his gaze swinging naturally from side to side, as was his cautionary custom when in unfamiliar surroundings.

It was nearly dark outside, but Wetzel was surprised at the small number of customers present in the room. There was no sign of Marie, but he remembered that it had been late in the afternoon when he first saw her before. He went to the bar and asked for whiskey, which was quickly served by a short, stocky man with dark hair but blue eyes. Lew wanted to ask immediately about Marie but thought better of it. There was no speaking between the two, but Lew kept his eyes on the bartender, thinking that there was something familiar about him.

The time passed, and Wetzel, becoming impatient and beginning to feel the liquor after a pair of refills, realized he was hungry.

"You got anythin' to eat in this place?" he asked as the bartender walked by.

"We might have," answered the man, sensing the annoyance in Wetzel's voice.

"What might you have then?" queried Lew, his tone lacking his usual good humor.

"We've got some salt pork and some bread, I reckon."

"Well, bring me that then," ordered Wetzel.

"It'll cost one of them Spanish dollars you're sportin'."

"By God," exploded Lew louder than he intended. "That's damned high, I'd say."

Others in the room were staring at them. There were quite a few more men present than when he had come in, Lew now noticed. One of the patrons in particular smiled when he saw who was at the bar, and when Wetzel turned back to the bartender to order the food, the big man stood and approached the bar.

"Hello there, friend," was his greeting as he stepped in beside Wetzel. "Lew is the name, I believe."

"Hell, not you again," said Wetzel.

"Yes it is. The name is Payette."

"I know that," snapped Wetzel. "I'm surprised you've got the gall to talk to me."

"I just want to be friends, you know," laughed Payette. "Besides, you ain't carryin' that damned big rifle right now."

Wetzel's right hand dropped to his side, grasping the head of his tomahawk. "There's other weapons."

"Let me buy you a drink," offered Payette. "I'd like to talk you into workin' for me."

As they talked, Wetzel began to relax his feelings toward Payette, learning that he was from Kentucky. When the food came, they retired to one of the tables. Another hour passed, and they were joined by a young Spanish man named Pedro Hermoso.

Payette noticed how Wetzel kept eyeing the door and looking up to the bar. "You expectin' somebody, Lew?"

"Not really, I guess," stammered Wetzel, not wanting to share his feelings with these men. "There was a girl the last time I was here. Said her pa owned this place."

"You mean Marie," chuckled Payette. "Were you sweet on her?"

"No, I ain't sweet on her," protested Wetzel. "But I had hoped to see her again."

"Hell, Lew," said Payette, unable to keep from laughing. "Nobody in Natchez wasn't sweet on her. But you're way too late. She married a man named John Bailey 'bout a week ago. He's got some land up north."

She lied to me, thought Lew. He couldn't keep himself from blurting it out. "She said she didn't have no man."

"I reckon her pa had some say in that. His name is Richard King. He owns land on both sides of the river, as well as this tavern. Has a big herd o' cattle too." The gleam in Payette's eye let Wetzel know that Payette had a strong interest in the cattle, and this interest was not likely to be in Richard King's favor.

"That's her little brother, Henry," said Hermoso, speaking up for the first time and pointing to the bartender. "You could ask him about Marie."

Hermoso's English was good, although spoken with a strong Spanish accent. It dawned on Wetzel why he thought there was something familiar about young King. He resembled his sister—especially the blue eyes. The impact of what Payette said now came to him, and disappointment surged over him. What he had been thinking about for more than two weeks was all gone. What a fool he'd been. He called for another drink. By the time another hour passed, Wetzel was drunk. Usually he was a happy drunk, but now he was in the depths of despair.

"Where you stayin' tonight?" asked Hermoso, not so sober himself.

"In the woods, I guess," answered Wetzel, his words definitely slurred.

"Why not stay with me and my wife instead?" suggested Hermoso. "I just live a little way downriver from here. I got a couple daughters, but they won't bother you."

"That's a good idea," agreed Payette. "Stay with Pedro a few days and think about my offer. You'd be a big help to me."

"That's mighty nice o' you, Pedro," said Lew. "But I need to git my stuff."

"It's settled then," said Pedro, helping Wetzel to his feet. "I'm a hunter too, and we'll have lots of stories to tell."

"I'll see you two later," promised Payette. "Remember, Lew. I've got a real good job for you."

March 21, 1793

Wetzel had stayed at the Hermoso place much longer than he intended. It was comfortable enough, but there were tensions in the house that made Lew uneasy. Little had been asked of him, although he tried to help out as much as he could. What bothered him was the way Hermoso treated his wife, Ana Sofia, and his two young daughters, Gabriela and Rosita. There was frequent loud yelling, but it was the beatings that Pedro administered, often when drunk, that upset Wetzel.

Twice he had intervened, and Hermoso had threatened to throw him out, only to come apologetically the next day and beg Wetzel to stay. The wife, Ana Sofia, had become a problem herself. On the very first night at the house, Wetzel had caught her staring at him and then smiling coquettishly. He felt drawn to her because of this attention, but he was determined not to give into that.

He was there for only two weeks when one day she approached him and asked him straight out if he would like to sleep with her. Pedro and the girls were not there at the time, but Wetzel refused with great intensity, protesting that he could not inflict such a great wrong against his friend. At least two other times she had made the same proposal, once even in the presence of the two little girls. She was a pretty woman with dark hair and eyes, and there was an air about her that exuded her sexuality.

Wetzel determined that he must keep his distance. Hermoso had some pretty strange habits of his own. He was often gone, even at night, and when he returned, he sometimes brought a message to Wetzel from Payette, who continued to recruit Lew to work for him. On other days, Hermoso would head into the woods where he would remain all day. Wetzel had discovered a small shed deep in the woods, and he knew that Hermoso spent much time there. In spite of his curiosity, Wetzel had not tried to go inside. The man claimed to Wetzel that he was a skilled hunter and woodsman and that he had been a fierce Indian fighter.

Wetzel did not see these things in him, but the two often swapped stories of exploits against the red men. Yesterday, Wetzel watched Hermoso go into the woods and began to follow until he thought better of it. Instead, he retrieved a much-used fishing pole and walked the half mile down to the riverbank. He caught three large catfish, which he thought would do good for the noon meal.

On his return to the house, he saw Pedro coming up the trail toward him carrying a small bag. As he was about to hail the man, Hermoso suddenly pitched forward, having caught his foot on a protruding tree root. Wetzel rushed to him to offer assistance, but Pedro had regained his feet, issuing a chorus of curses. The bag had split open and silvery coins were strewn everywhere on the path. Wetzel picked up several of them, noting that they were Spanish dollars. On closer inspection, he could see that they were not real, although very good imitations.

"Give me those," demanded Hermoso quite angrily.

"But what are they?" asked Wetzel, realizing as he did so that it might have been better to say nothing.

"What do you think they are?" Hermoso's face was twisted into a scowl.

"Well, they look a lot like real Spanish dollars," said Lew with a smile, trying to make light of the situation. He didn't want Hermoso thinking he was accusing him of anything.

"They are toys for my girls," Pedro said now emphatically. "They like to play with them."

"I rcckon they do," agreed Wetzel. "Are you all right?"

"I'm just fine," answered Hermoso, getting himself under control. "What were you doing?"

"Just doin' a bit of fishin'. Caught some too. You're just in time to eat 'em for dinner."

Nothing more was said; but this morning, Hermoso had left shortly after breakfast, telling Lew to chop some wood and stack it near the door of the house. There had been an animated conversation with Ana Sofia in Spanish, accompanied by several gestures toward Lew, which left Wetzel wondering. The man's good-bye wave seemed friendly enough, and Lew thought nothing more about it. Wetzel was happy to complete the wood cutting chore, which was finished by midmorning.

The two girls provided an audience for much of the time but now had gone off to play in the backyard. There was still a chill in the air, although the morning sun was sending its warmth. Lew had removed his shirt while washing up after the job. Ana Sofia called out from the kitchen, announcing that she had some hot coffee for him when he came in. After emptying the wash pan, Wetzel threw the shirt over his shoulder and strode through the door. He had acquired a keen taste for southern coffee during his stay here.

Ana Sofia was wearing a light linen shirt, a garment that she used for sleeping. It was cut low in front, showing the cleavage and soft curves of her breasts. Wetzel was taken aback, although the sight had an immediate effect. He could see the outline of her nipples under the soft fabric. Her smile and her flashing eyes were a further lure, and he felt himself giving in to her obvious invitation. She did not speak often in English, and her manner now did not require words. Still she spoke to him in a soft inviting tone.

"Lie with me, Lewis."

"But the girls," stammered Wetzel.

She shook her head. "They outside."

She came to where he stood, putting one hand on his face while the other slid down his front, caressing him. His resistance began to wane, and he thought to himself, *Why not? Her husband is not good to her, he's not a good man.* He argued with himself as she drew him against her. How could he do this to a man who had befriended him and offered him a place to stay? It became too much, and he pulled away. An angry glare immediately clouded her face, and screaming a Spanish vulgarity, she grabbed his shirt with one hand and tore open her shift with the other, exposing her breasts.

Wetzel turned to leave and was startled to see the wide-eyed girls standing between him and the door. "I'm gittin' outta here right now," he shouted, turning aside to the room where he stayed, intent on gathering his few belongings. He continued to hear Ana Sofia screaming, and when he came out, he saw that Pedro had returned and was slapping his wife in a fit of rage. The little girls were huddled together near the fireplace, crying. The adults both saw Wetzel at the same time, and Ana Sofia pulled away from her husband, pointing at Wetzel and shouting "Pig, Pig," in English before yelling another torrent of Spanish words.

"I didn't do nothin' to her," Wetzel began to explain to Hermoso, who had drawn his knife and was waving it menacingly. "I didn't do nothin'."

"The hell you didn't," hissed Hermoso. "What do ya think she's screamin' about? Who tore her dress?"

"She did that herself," explained Lew. "I don't know what she's screamin' about. I don't speak Spanish."

"I ought to kill you right now, you son of a bitch," declared Hermoso, but he was afraid of Wetzel, and he stayed where he was.

"I guess you think you should, but I don't think you can. I don't want to hurt you. Just let me pass, and I'll be gone from your house forever."

The clatter of a band of horsemen outside interrupted the dangerous scene in the house. "What the hell?" exclaimed Hermoso as he moved to the door, keeping his eye on Wetzel at the same time. "Damn, it's old man King. What could he want?"

"Pedro, Pedro Hermoso, are you in there?" came the call from Richard King, the leader of the posse of thirty men who had ridden up to the front door.

"I'm here all right," acknowledged Hermoso as he stepped out onto the small porch. "What can I do for you?"

A jolt of fear went through him as he saw his friend Payette astride a horse, closely guarded by two men. Payette's hands were tied in front of him, although he was able to hold the reins.

"Where were you last night?" demanded King. "Were you with your friend here?" he continued, pointing to Payette.

"No, I was right here all day and all night," asserted Pedro, stopping himself from indicating they could ask his wife.

"And how do we know that?" asked King. "Will your wife vouch for you?"

"Uh, well, she's not feelin' too good right now, I'd rather you not bother her."

"What about him then?" said King, nodding toward Wetzel, who had just appeared. "What's your name, man?" asked King, addressing Lew directly.

"My name's Wetzel," answered Lew.

Before he could continue, Hermoso broke in. "Don't ask him nothin', Mr. King. He's a lyin', rapin' criminal."

Startled by the venom in Hermoso's voice, King turned to Wetzel. "What is he talkin' about?"

"This is what I'm talkin' about," shouted Hermoso, raising his left palm to reveal two counterfeit Spanish coins. "He gave these to my daughters."

King took the coins and examined them closely. "By God, they're fakes all right. Where did you get these?" he asked Hermoso.

"I told you, he gave them to my little girls."

As Wetzel began to protest, Hermoso went inside, returning with his two daughters, one on each hand. "Ask them, Mr. King. They'll tell you."

"Hello, girls," said King softly. "What are your names?"

The girls were both sobbing, but after a stern look from their father, the older of the two spoke up, "I'm Gabriela, and my sister's name is Rosita."

"Very nice names," was King's kindly reply. He held out his hand, displaying the two coins. "Tell me, have you seen these before?"

The girls looked at each other and at their father before nodding almost imperceptibly.

"Can you speak up for me?" asked King.

"Yes," said Gabriela.

"Where did you see them?"

Gabriela looked down, then at her father, then at Wetzel. "He gave them to us," she said, speaking more loudly and pointing at Lew.

"I think he may have more back in his room," offered Hermoso, pointing back inside the house.

King and another man, Luis Riano, slipped off their mounts and stepped up onto the porch. "Don't anybody move," barked King.

"We'll take a look." The two men went inside, then King came out again, grabbing Hermoso by the arm.

"Show us!" he commanded. They walked by Wetzel's belongings stashed in the middle of the room.

"What's that?" asked King.

"That's his stuff," answered Pedro. "He was ready to fly when you came up."

Hermoso led the two men back to Wetzel's room. He was glad to see that his wife had gone into their bedroom and closed the curtain at the opening.

Outside, Wetzel was considering his options. Three of the riders had moved their horses up closer and held their guns ready to react to any movement they regarded as threatening. Wetzel wondered if they would shoot if he were to suddenly break for the woods. The fact that he was completely unarmed made him hesitate. Surely this Richard King would not believe such flimsy evidence, he thought. An attempt to run would insure that they believed him guilty, and the likelihood of escaping unharmed was very small.

He decided to depend on the fairness of King, even though he resented the man for marrying off his beautiful daughter. It was a decision Wetzel would regret for the rest of his life. It was not long before King and Riano returned. King held several more of the counterfeit coins in his hand while Riano held up two small dies suitable for producing the fake dollars. Hermoso followed with a smug look on his face.

"Counterfeiting is a very serious crime in Spanish America," said King, directing his remarks at Wetzel.

The horsemen spread out in a half circle around the porch, and three others dismounted, one carrying a piece of rope.

"Tie him up, men," ordered King. "We'll have two men to deliver to Senor Gayoso."

As the men approached him, Wetzel tried to protest. "Those coins are not mine, they are Pedro's. I've done nothing wrong." Once again, Wetzel thought of trying to resist. He was sure he could get a knife off one of the men and do some serious damage. The punishment for that, however, would be quite severe., *Surely,* he thought, *they won't do much to me because of a few false dollars.* In the end, he submitted quietly as the men tied his hands and led him to an extra horse that had been brought along.

King had originally intended to arrest Hermoso, whom he still suspected was in on Payette's crime. However, a man guilty of counterfeiting would be of much greater interest to the Spanish authorities than a sidekick of a cattle rustler.

Hermoso managed to get in a few words as they led Wetzel away. "Good-bye, Mr. Lew Wetzel," he growled. "We ain't likely to see you again for a long, long time. You son of a bitch!"

Wetzel was placed on the horse and put next to Payette in the middle of the pack.

"Hello again, friend," laughed Payette. "We're both in a bit of a mess now, ain't we?"

"The difference is you're probably guilty, but I ain't," said Lew.

"Don't matter none. That bastard, Gayoso de Lemos will send us both to New Orleans. I've seen the prison there. It won't be much fun."

Wetzel said nothing more.

19

Prison

February 25, 1794

The Indians were in a festive and confident mood throughout the frontiers in both the south and the northwest. The resounding victories over Harmar and St. Clair had left them feeling they had finally turned the tide against the encroachment of the American settlers. The raiding of these settlements continued, as did unity conferences among the tribes.

In the late summer and early fall of 1792, an assembly of delegates from twenty-eight Indian nations was held at the confluence of the Auglaize and Maumee Rivers. Eventually an official message was sent to the US government announcing that the boundary between the Indians and the Americans was to be fixed as the Ohio River. The Americans had been making offers of peace negotiations, the latest of which was carried to this conference by a delegation from the Iroquois. The Americans were directed to attend a conference the next spring at Lower Sandusky.

The American president, George Washington, had pushed Congress to beef up the American army, and he appointed General Anthony Wayne to be its new commander. At the same time, wanting to avoid trouble with Britain and Spain, he and secretary of war, Henry Knox, made strong efforts to advance the peace process and prevent American retaliation against the

Indians. Several of his peace commissioners had been killed by the hostile tribes.

Wayne was ordered to prepare his army for war in case the efforts for peace were failures. Wayne was authorized to raise an army of five thousand men, and he began to gather them at Pittsburgh in June of 1792. The problems were great, for the quality of men who answered the call was low, and they were completely untrained. To further complicate the situation, Wayne's second-in-command was James Wilkinson, a shady character who had been involved in a secret scheme with the Spanish government in Louisiana. The intention was to make an independent nation in the west to include Kentucky, and which would be a close ally of Spain.

Wilkinson had even taken an oath of allegiance to the king of Spain, although this was unknown to the Americans. Wilkinson was still on the Spanish payroll, earning more than $2000 per year. He also took every opportunity to criticize General Wayne and create difficulties for him whenever possible. Kentucky had become a state in June of 1792, so the earlier conspiracies had cooled, but there were still strong feelings in the west against the national government. Wayne took advantage of the time being created by the peace negotiations and began to whip his men into fighting shape. He took them a few miles downriver from Pittsburgh to the old village of Logstown, a place that began to be called Legionville, the home of the American Legion.

In late April of 1793, Wayne moved his troops to Fort Washington. Both England and Spain were encouraged by the increased militancy of the Indians, providing support with supplies and promises of more direct help when needed. Carondelet, the new governor in Louisiana, envisioned forming an Indian army to guard Spanish possessions against the new American nation. The British, still holding posts in the north that were supposed to have gone over to the United States, used their agents to keep the Indians stirred up and expecting help, even from British troops.

Little Fox, living with his family in the town of Buckongehelas on the Auglaize just below its intersection with the Maumee, was well aware of what was happening with respect to the hated Americans. He had attended several of the councils and was determined to be a part of any organized Indian action against them. He knew of the movements of Wayne's army as it had left Fort Washington on October 7, although Little Fox would not have known the date.

In less than a week, the army had made it to Fort Jefferson. About that time, a band of Ottawas came through the village on a raiding party intent on stealing horses from the white army. The Ottawas were closely related to Little Fox's Chippewa tribe, and he enjoyed talking with them. The chief, Little Otter, invited Little Fox to join them, which he did. In four days, the Ottawas made their way toward the location of Fort Jefferson, easing down on the far side of Mud Creek past the fort and toward Fort St. Clair.

They were in just the right place to intercept a supply convoy a few miles north of Fort St. Clair on its way to bring needed provisions to General Wayne, who had been forced to wait at Fort Jefferson. The convoy consisted of twenty wagons and a ninety-man infantry escort under the command of Lieutenant John Lowry. The wagons and men were strung out on the trail, and Little Otter did not hesitate to attack at a place called the Forty-Foot Pitch.

Little Fox was amazed at its success. Fifteen of the soldiers were killed, including the commander, and ten were taken captive. Seventy horses were unhitched from the wagons, many of which were simply turned loose to roam the woods. There had been a grand celebration when the raiding party returned to the Indian villages on the Auglaize.

As winter approached, Bright Moon had talked Little Fox into going with a small group to a winter camp on a tiny lake at the end of a tributary of the Auglaize. There were eight warriors, along with thirteen women and children in the party, including Red Storm and his family. The journey was miserable, for the weather was cold and wet, with intermittent rain and sleet.

The birchbark canoe that served as their conveyance was nearly forty feet long and four feet wide. it took four of the men to carry it when necessary, and Little Fox was surprised at what took place when they reached their destination. The men carried it up from the water, inverted it, propping it up with some long branches where it served as a temporary shelter from the rain that continued to fall. A fire was built underneath, and the entire party was able to gain some comfort.

After a couple of days, Bright Moon insisted that Little Fox accompany her and the three children on a search for chestnuts. Little Fox argued that this was not something fit for a warrior to do, but Bright Moon noted that he was not doing any warrior-like things anyway. He was annoyed at his lovely wife's headstrong ways, but he loved her dearly, and in the end, he went along. When they returned, they found that a winter cabin was under construction. Logs, at least fifteen feet in length, had been piled on each other to a height of four feet. Posts were driven at each end to hold the logs together. The posts were tied together with bark. Another wall was raised opposite this one about twelve feet away. Forks were driven into the ground in the center of each end, and a long pole laid end-to-end on the forks. Poles were laid from the walls to the log running down the center, and small branches laid crossways on top of them. A final covering of linden bark was placed over the top.

Little Fox had usually managed to avoid such labor, but this time he joined in to help enclose the ends with split timber. A door was left at each end, and at the top, an open space was left to allow for smoke to exit. For bedding, the women used linden bark covered with bearskins. Fires were built from end-to-end down the middle of the structure, and bearskins were hung over the door openings.

This work was completed in December, and the little band settled in for the winter. The big canoe had been buried to preserve it for use in the spring. The eight warriors took turns going out in groups of four to hunt for meat while the women and boys went out looking for nuts of various kinds. When the hunters had a big success, the entire party would go out to carry in the meat.

Little Fox continued to worry about his friend Red Storm, whose sour mood never seemed to abate. His injured arm kept him from being a keen hunter, although Little Fox usually took him along and tried to give him the credit when they killed a deer or a bear. Red Storm could only think about the war that he was sure was coming against Wayne's army. They had been isolated from any news while in the winter camp, and Red Storm kept insisting that he and Little Fox should go back to the villages on the Auglaize.

"There will be no war until the spring," Little Fox assured his friend. "By then, we will be back with the others."

The winter dragged on, and the snow made the hunting more difficult. It was finally decided that horses were needed, and four warriors were sent out as a war party to obtain them. In mid-February, this little war party returned, having gone all the way to the frontiers of Pennsylvania. They brought back six horses and two scalps, as well as a good quantity of venison. There was great joy in the camp. The next day, the women went out to begin the process of making sugar.

Little Fox and Red Storm were sent along as protection. A large stand of sugar maples was soon found, and also an elm tree that was suitable for stripping of its bark. From this bark, the women made vessels for holding sap, each capable of holding about two gallons. In each sugar tree, they cut a notch sloping down, and at the end of the notch, stuck in a tomahawk. In this place, they drove a long chip whose purpose was to carry the sap out of the tree. Under this, they set a vessel. Larger bark vessels were made to carry the sap, and several brass kettles, obtained from traders, were brought along for the boiling process. Once enough sap was gathered, fires were built and the sap boiled in the kettles. The end result of the long process was the sweet maple sugar, and when brought back to camp, it was mixed with bear fat until the fat was very sweet.

The feast that followed was one of the best that Little Fox could remember. The taste of the roasted venison dipped in the sweetened fat was a delight that he did not think could ever be improved.

On this morning, clear but cold, Red Storm's wife, White Flower, came running to Bright Moon with tears falling down her cheeks.

"What is it, White Flower?" asked Bright Moon as the woman fell into her arms. "Why do you cry?"

"It is Red Storm," sobbed White Flower. "He is very angry, and he hit me." She turned her face so Bright Moon could see the swelling next to her eye where she had been struck.

"Why is he so angry?" Bright Moon was gently swabbing the sore spot with her fingers.

"I don't know, I don't know." White Flower sank to her knees, her loud wailing attracting the attention of others.

"I know," interjected Little Fox, who had been watching and listening. "Red Storm is angry with everything and everyone."

"It is not like him to hit his wife, is it?" Bright Moon turned to her husband, her eyes and facial expression pleading with him to do something.

"I will take him on a scouting trip this very morning," Little Fox announced with finality. "That will please him."

"That is good, husband," said Bright Moon. "But then I will have to worry."

"There is nothing to worry about. We will be gone a few days, and I think that will help everyone," said Little Fox, nodding toward White Flower. "Put some food together for us and some blankets."

Little Fox found his friend outside the lodge, hacking at some branches with his tomahawk. "Let us go on a scout," said Little Fox. "I want to see what the soldiers are doing. Get your gun and your things. We will leave right now."

Red Storm looked at Little Fox with surprise, then shook his head in agreement. He said nothing but went to retrieve his weapons and his pouch. In less than an hour, they were on their way out of the camp. Nothing was said between them, but Red Storm knew that this sudden action had something to do with what had happened with his wife. He would not apologize, even though deep down he was sorry for what he had done.

Little Fox knew where the soldiers had been a few months ago, and he reasoned that they would not likely have moved during the winter. There was a snow covering on the ground, crusted in places, which made the going a bit rough and left a clear sign of their passing. In three days, they angled down to the Wabash River, and Little Fox led them downstream, looking for the trail to Fort Jefferson. It was a great surprise to the two warriors when they discovered that a new fort had been built on the Wabash at the site of the great victory by the Indians over the American general, St. Clair.

General Wayne had sent troops to the area just before Christmas, and after clearing the battle site of the skeletons of the dead soldiers, they had built what Wayne called Fort Recovery. Red Storm immediately suggested that they take up positions from which they might be able to kill any of the white men who wandered too far from the fort. This was not at all in the mind of Little Fox, who explained that it was much more important to gather as much information as they could and report to the chiefs at the Auglaize villages. They skirted the fort, although not without noticing three cannon installed on an embrasure in the wall of the fort.

"They have cannon at that fort," noted Red Storm.

"Yes, we buried several of the guns after the victory over the white chief, St. Clair. The soldiers must have found them." Little

Fox had provided some of the physical labor at that event. "Come, let us go farther toward the other fort."

After a day's travel, the two braves discovered another bigger fort, the one General Wayne called Fort Greeneville, in honor of his friend in the Revolutionary War, Nathaniel Greene. This post was some six miles north of Fort Jefferson and built along the south side of what came to be called Greeneville Creek. There was considerable activity in the neighborhood of the fort, and as they watched from a thick stand of trees not far from the main gate, Red Storm and Little Fox saw a small party of men come out with a wagon, intent on cutting and gathering wood.

A bridge had been built across the creek just outside the gate. A few men spread out from each side of the wagon, and Little Fox could see that their duty was to scout for any signs of an attack on the woodcutters. Although the weather had warmed and the snow was melting, he knew that the soldiers would have little trouble trailing him and Red Storm if they discovered their tracks.

"We must go quickly, Red Storm," whispered Little Fox. "Before the white men discover our trail."

Red Storm started to argue, then thought better of it, and the two warriors moved quickly to the east, following the creek bed that meandered off in that direction. The stream was not frozen, and Red Storm suggested they enter the stream to hide their tracks.

"The water is too cold," said Little Fox. "We must hope they do not follow us."

"I hope they do," answered Red Storm. "Then we can kill them."

"You never change, my friend," chuckled Little Fox. "But that is much too dangerous. It is more important that we report what we have seen to Little Turtle. Now we must get back to our families and take them onto the main villages."

After following along the creek bank for several miles, the two friends turned to the north. The soldiers did not come after them.

July 10, 1794

The cell door swung open with a loud squeak, and the tall young Creole guard, whom Wetzel knew as Francois, set down a bowl of watery broth and a small piece of bread. Wetzel, still lying on his filthy pallet against the back wall, stirred and eyed the man, who gave him a toothless grin, nodded and closed the door, emitting a scraping noise and then a clank as the key secured the bolt.

The air was already stifling hot, and Wetzel was bathed in sweat. It was an effort to sit up, but the prisoner did so, straightening his twisted shirt. He could barely stand the smell, his own body the chief offender, for it had been many days since he had been given a chance to wash himself. He eyed the waste bucket sitting in the corner but decided to put off that necessity for a while, knowing the guards had neglected to empty it recently.

Once on his feet, he shuffled over and slumped against the wall near the door and picked up the bowl. Francois had not bothered to include a spoon, so Wetzel tipped it to his lips and drank greedily. His constant hunger had overcome the tastelessness of the food, and he drained the bowl quickly. The bread was good, and he ate it more slowly. He reflected again, as he had countless times before, on the run of luck that had brought him to this terrible low point in his life. When Richard King's posse took him in, he was confident that his innocence would come out; and if not that, then for an offense so petty surely the punishment would be light.

He had not reckoned with the intransigence of Manuel Gayoso de Lemos, who seemed delighted to have a counterfeiter in his grasp. He and Payette were sent off to Governor Carondelet at New Orleans with great enthusiasm. There had been no trial of any kind, and the two men were quickly incarcerated in the royal jail. After a few days of gloom, Wetzel's natural cheerful spirit arose again, and he undertook a serious effort to make friends with his keepers. His favorite was Francois, whom he called

Frank. Eventually he talked Frank into getting him an audience with the warden, a man named Francisco Pavaña. He came to Wetzel's cell one morning and entered the room along with a guard, not Frank, but a small Spanish man whom Wetzel knew as Juan.

"What is it you want?" asked Pavaña in Spanish.

Wetzel stared at the man intently as Juan translated his words. Frank had reported that Pavaña was fairly new on the job, as the previous warden had resigned because he was unhappy with his pay and the money provided by the city to keep up the jail.

"I'm innocent, and I think I deserve a trial," was the reply.

The warden shook his head vigorously and spoke quickly and angrily.

"He says that you are a bad criminal. Counterfeiting will not be tolerated. The governor saw the evidence, and there will be no trial." Juan struggled a bit with this translation.

"So how long am I in for?" was Wetzel's next question.

The warden shrugged and uttered a few words, turning then and leaving the cell.

"He says you will be here a long time," said Juan with a sad look, for he had taken a liking to Wetzel also.

Wetzel's loud protest was of no avail, and Juan had left quickly, locking the door behind him. After this, Lew began to think about escape, although it seemed impossible. He continued to cultivate his friendship with the guards, hoping they might provide him with the opportunity he sought. He lost all track of time and settled into the routine. Occasionally another man was put in with him, which helped a bit, and one day he had a visitor.

"By God, it's John Kyle," exclaimed Wetzel as Kyle came through the door held open by Frank. "Ain't you a sight fer sore eyes."

"Hello, Lew," said Kyle. "Lord, you don't look so good."

"Yeah, I don't much recommend the place," answered Lew. "The food sure ain't fattenin'."

The two men shook hands.

"How'd you end up in here?" asked Kyle.

"They claimed I was makin' fake money," replied Wetzel. "How the hell did you find me?"

"I heard some men talkin' in a bar. They said there was some American down in the jail, and since you had disappeared, I thought it might be you. 'Pears I was right."

"I'm mighty glad," said Lew. "But I thought you'd gone back with Parker."

"Well, I was, but then somethin' came up, and I decided to stay." Kyle broke into a wide grin. "'Twas a woman, but then it didn't turn out too good."

"That's always been my way with women," laughed Wetzel.

The two men talked for a long time until Frank came and told Kyle it was time to go. Before he left, Kyle pressed some coins into Wetzel's hand.

"These might come in handy sometime, Lew."

Wetzel kept his hand closed, not wanting Frank to see the coins.

"Thank you, John," stated Wetzel with great feeling. "Come and see me again."

"Sorry, Lew, but I'm headed back to Kentucky."

"Tell my friends hello there and not to forget me."

Kyle nodded and left without another word.

Wetzel watched him go sad, but with his spirits highly lifted by this unexpected visit.

The next day, Frank showed up with a deck of cards. "I know you've got some money there," he announced, pointing to the corner of the cell where Wetzel kept his few possessions. "I'd like to win some of it for myself."

"I don't know much about card playin'," protested Wetzel. "Besides, how do you know I've got some money?"

"I saw your friend give it to you," grinned Frank. "I'll teach you to play a good game my papa taught me."

Wetzel knew a little about poker and whist and some other card games, but he had never played much.

"What game is that?" he asked finally.

"Why, it's called brusquembille," answered Frank. "It's a good game for two people."

"Hell, I can't play a game called by a word that big," snorted Wetzel.

"We don't need to call it nothin'," said Frank. "We just play."

"What if I don't want to play?"

"I don't reckon the warden would approve of you havin' no money," Frank pointed out, still grinning.

"Frank, you're my friend, you wouldn't tell on me, would you?"

"I'll be a lot better friend if you let me have a chance at some of that money."

Frank taught Wetzel the rules of the game, and they played a few hands without betting. It was a simple game played with a thirty-two-card deck consisting of ace through seven in each of the four suits. Each player got three cards, and the top card on the remaining deck is turned up and determines trump. The leader plays any card, and the others need not follow suit, but the trick is taken by the highest trump, or if no trump, the highest card in the suit that was led. After a trick is taken, the players draw from the deck and play continues until all the cards are gone. The five highest cards in each suit have point totals, and each player counts the card points in the tricks won. The highest total wins the deal.

When they finally played with bets, each man put one Spanish real in the pot, and they began to play. Frank easily won the first three deals, but finally, realizing he might kill the golden goose, he let Wetzel win two straight times. The prisoner was greatly pleased by that, and playing cards with Frank, and sometimes Juan and another guard—a black man called Buck—became a regular pastime.

On this day, Wetzel was not feeling much like playing cards, and his small stash of coins was almost depleted. He intended to plead with Frank to bring him some water for bathing, although this was usually not an easy thing for the guards to do unless the warden had directed it. An hour or more passed before Wetzel heard footsteps in the hall outside his door. He could hear the noise of a door opening in the room next to him and detected the sounds of a man being shoved into the room. When his own door was opened, Frank stepped in and retrieved the empty soup bowl.

"You've got a neighbor, Lew. New inmate."

"Frank," implored Lew, ignoring the information. "Would you empty the damned bucket? It smells like hell."

"Buck'll be here after bit. I'll send him down to get it."

"Why can't you do it?"

"You know it ain't my job now, Lew," laughed Frank. "Enjoy your new neighbor."

Since he had been brought into the jail blindfolded, Lew had no knowledge of its layout. He had discovered a small gouge in one of the walls, and he at first thought it might be an outside wall. Having persuaded Frank to let him keep an old spoon that had come once with his meal, he used the spoon to dig at the hole for several days, finally breaking all the way through.

He was disappointed to discover it only opened into another cell just like the one he was in. Now he could hear the man on the other side making the rounds of the room, as he had done himself countless times, looking for some way to break out. After a while, there came a shout from next door. Several words in Spanish were spoken, then some English.

"Hello, Hello. Is anyone over there?"

Wetzel nearly jumped when he heard the voice. It sounded familiar to him, but at first he could not place it. He began to walk over to where he kept his things, and speaking softly, he said, "Yes."

"What? Did you say something?" came the voice again.

"Yes, yes," spoke Wetzel, trying to disguise the sound. "I am here."

Wetzel reached down and picked up the spoon, which he kept under his pallet. He could tell that the man next door had discovered the hole in the wall and was pressed against it, trying to see who was talking to him. Wetzel crept along the wall keeping out of sight.

"My name's Pedro," came the voice. "What are you in for?"

The hole in the wall was about chest high, and Wetzel, grasping the spoon, shoved the handle through the hole with all of his might. "You know what I'm in for, you son of a bitch, Pedro Hermoso. My name's Lew Wetzel."

Hermoso, whose face was pressed against the wall, screamed in agony as the spoon handle, just missing his eye, jammed into his face, bouncing off the jaw bone, and tearing into his cheek. Blood spurted, some even coming through the hole and landing on Wetzel's arm.

"I'm killed, I'm killed," screeched the wounded man.

"I don't reckon you're killed, but you ought to be, you bastard." Wetzel was peering through the hole himself, glad to see that it was indeed Hermoso he had injured.

The door was flung open, and Wetzel could see it was Frank and a soldier he didn't know. They took hold of Hermoso on either side and carried him out, trying to soothe him and promising medical attention. Wetzel slumped to the floor, his back against the wall. At the moment, all he felt was a deep satisfaction. It was not to last long. Within a few minutes, he was visited by Warden Pavaña and two soldiers.

"Put this man in chains," shouted the warden. "And take him to solitary!"

Although Wetzel could not understand all the Spanish words, he well understood the meaning, especially the Spanish word for *solitary*.

August 20, 1794

The light drizzle that ushered in the new day had become a driving rain, but Little Fox did not mind. He was huddled behind a fallen tree trunk and some twisted branches, awaiting an expected attack by the hated Americans. His mood was much improved these days, and he felt a surge of pride as he gazed around, noting his fellow warriors poised among the labyrinth of fallen trees and limbs. It seemed a perfect place to defend against the anticipated assault.

He was among his colleagues, the Delawares, who were in the center of the Indian defense, along with the Shawnees and the Miamis. Red Storm was just a few feet to his right, and the two friends exchanged a smile, shaking the water from their hair. It was rumored that as many as eight hundred Chippewas were on their way to join them, but they had not yet appeared, much to the disappointment of Little Fox. There was a small contingent of his blood brothers present, but they were on the Indian left, closer to the river.

Although feeling much better now, the last few weeks had been a time of disillusionment for Little Fox. Not more than two months earlier, at least two thousand warriors were gathered at the juncture of the Auglaize and Maumee, ready to fight the advance of Anthony Wayne's army, the bulk of which was still at Fort Greeneville, where Little Fox and Red Storm had observed it in the winter. Little Fox was still proud of the report he had brought back to Blue Jacket and Little Turtle, although the facts weren't completely new to the Indian leaders.

It was decided to take the fight to the Americans, but the chiefs warned that it would not be wise to attack the forts directly, but rather to try to intercept the frequent transport of provisions between the forts. As they began to move south along the banks of the Auglaize, Little Fox was greatly impressed by the huge cornfields along each side of the river. *This will supply our needs for the next two years*, he thought.

The Indian force was difficult to keep together, and it became widely scattered. A large number of the lake Indians were along, and they led in a swing down toward Fort Recovery, contrary to the plan Little Turtle had envisaged. A scout had brought word of a large convoy moving toward that fort, and the younger braves were determined. The old chief could do nothing but approve. The leading contingent had passed on the far side of the Wabash from the fort, and when it swung back to the wide prairie to the south, the braves encountered three hundred packhorses returning from the fort escorted by Major William McMahon with ninety riflemen and fifty dragoons. McMahon was soon killed with a number of his men, and the horses scattered.

Little Fox was part of this early attack along with several Chippewas, and they managed to capture one of the drovers. When his companions moved to kill the man, Little Fox intervened, arguing that the chiefs might want to question him. They tied him to a stump not more than a half mile from the fort. A contingent of men had emerged from the gates of the fort, intent on rescuing their comrades, but they were caught up in the wild melee of retreat and the screaming braves who were close behind. The stockade stood on a low hill just above the river, and most of the soldiers succeeded in reaching safety.

Little Fox, who had been running to catch up, stopped when he saw that the fight was over. He took the scalp of one of the dragoons who had fallen near the riverbank. He went back to find the captive, who was still sitting on the stump where they had left him. Although Little Fox had intended to take the prisoner back to talk with Chief Little Turtle, his plans were thwarted by his fellow Indians who now undertook a siege of the fort. There was heavy rifle fire in both directions, but the Indians had not reckoned with cannon fire from the fort, which now began to take its toll. Little Fox remembered seeing the cannon when he and Red Storm were here in the winter.

Although the shooting went on well into the night and for much of the next day, it soon became evident that the Indians would be unable to take the post. Many of the warriors regarded what they had done as a great victory, and well-satisfied, they began a return to the big camp on the Auglaize. Little Turtle tried to keep them to the original plan but soon saw that it was hopeless. When Little Fox brought in his prisoner, the chief was no longer interested and directed that the man be taken back with them to the Maumee.

After the warriors reached the main village, it was a further disappointment to find that many of the lake Indians were determined to return home, feeling they had done enough. Little Turtle went to Detroit, trying to find out what help could be expected from the British. The high spirits, which had been with the braves when they began the campaign, were gone. Word came that General Wayne had left his Greeneville fortifications and was moving north, and the original plan to meet him in battle in the wilderness was scrapped. Instead, the Indians abandoned their towns and began a move down the Maumee toward the new fort built by the British below the rapids of the Maumee called Fort Miamis.

These developments were extremely discouraging to Little Fox and Red Storm. At least, Little Turtle had kept a contingent of scouts observing the progress of the American army. The chiefs were informed when the army reached the St. Mary's River and constructed a small fort. Later when Wayne led his men down the Auglaize and stopped at its intersection with the Maumee, it was a surprise to the tribes, for Wayne was expected to advance on the Miami portage, where Harmar had been defeated. Of particular pain to the fleeing Indians was the news that their wonderful cornfields had been completely destroyed.

Little Turtle continued to hold some hope that he might be able to turn and catch the soldiers by surprise, as had been the signature nature of previous Indian victories. The scouts, however, reported that Wayne was careful to fortify each of his camps with trenches and breastworks and left no opportunity for the Indians to take advantage. While his men built another fort at the Maumee-Auglaize juncture, the one he named Fort Defiance, Wayne sent a note to the Indian chiefs, offering to negotiate a peaceful settlement.

A grand council was held at the place called Roche de Boeuf, where Little Turtle and Blue Jacket waited with over six hundred warriors. Buckongehelas, the primary Delaware chief, was also there. Little Fox and Red Storm sat where they could hear the speakers as various tribal leaders gave their opinions. The two friends were overjoyed when they were joined by Fire Heart, whom they had not seen for a while. Little Turtle advised that peace be sought: "This new white chief is not like the others. He never sleeps."

Buckongehelas joined in that sentiment, a development that angered both Little Fox and Red Storm. They weren't surprised at this because a year or two earlier, the Delaware chief had reprimanded his braves and sent an apology to the American officer, General Wilkinson, after the killing of three peace messengers sent by Wilkinson. The majority of voices, however, was militant. The Shawnee chief, Blue Jacket, took the opposite view from his long time coleader and became the recognized war leader.

Little Turtle proposed that the offer of negotiations be accepted, if only to gain time. The British agent, Alexander McKee agreed, and a message was sent back to General Wayne proposing that there be a ten-day suspension of operations. Indian hopes had been raised by the news that Colonel England, in Detroit, had dispatched strong reinforcements of men and artillery to the new Fort Miamis.

It soon became clear that the American general did not intend to abide by a suspension of action, for he began a determined march down the Maumee. By August 18, Wayne's troops had reached Roche de Boeuf, where he stopped to build a fortified camp to store his provisions and equipment. It was called Fort Deposit. The Indians had captured one of Wayne's scouts, a man named William May. Little Fox watched him brought into the Indian camp, which was now located a mile or so in front of the British fort. The Indians learned that Wayne would attack probably the next morning.

After the interrogation was complete, May was tied to a tree and used as target practice. Little Fox did not particularly approve of this behavior, and he went to say his good-byes to his family, for the women and children were being hustled off to some villages downriver from Fort Miamis. It was customary for the warriors to fast just prior to an engagement, for they believed that recovery from a belly wound was much better if the stomach was empty.

Little Fox and Red Storm had helped their wives and children to their new camp, then made their way to a posting along the edge of the fallen timbers, several miles upstream from the fort. The soldiers failed to come on the expected day, and with the rain this morning, many of the braves assumed that the attack would be delayed again. Suffering from the weather and the fact that they had not eaten since two days earlier, some four hundred warriors had returned to the area of the fort to obtain food. Little Fox watched this exodus with dismay, although his empty belly was beckoning him to join them.

"Our young men do not know how to prepare for a fight," growled Fire Heart, who had left his position to their left and stood behind where Little Fox was waiting.

"They are hungry," said Little Fox. "But I wish they had not gone."

"I think the soldiers are too cowardly to attack us here," offered Red Storm, coming over to talk with his friends. "Our position is very strong."

"They will come."

The others were surprised with the assurance in the voice of Little Fox.

"What makes you so sure, my friend?" asked Fire Heart.

"The rain is ending," noted Little Fox. "They will come."

It wasn't long until Little Fox's prediction was verified. A scout appeared with the message that the American army had begun its march.

A well-used Indian portage trail made its way from the area of Roche de Boeuf, the beginning of the rapids of the Maumee, all the way to the foot of the rapids where the British had built their fort. It was expected that the soldiers would follow this trail.

Little Fox was posted with the Delaware contingent in the center of the Indian line, a little way above the Indian trail. The Delaware chief, Buckongehelas, was walking behind the Delaware position, for he was in charge of their part in the action, even though he had been in favor of peace negotiations. Captain Pipe was also there, for which Little Fox was glad. Of course, that chief had dallied with peaceful overtures to the whites for several years, which cost him respect among the more militant warriors. Pipe had been a major player in the talks that resulted in the treaty of Fort Harmar several years earlier. Little Fox and Red Storm were proud that as many as two hundred Delaware warriors were present on this day.

The Miami contingent was just to the right of the Delawares, with the chief, Little Turtle, in command. The Shawnees, led by Blue Jacket, were on the left of the Delawares. Although some regarded Blue Jacket as the overall leader of the Indians for this battle, taking over from Little Turtle, the individual Indian units fought pretty much on their own under their own chiefs. Little Fox had high regard for Little Turtle, for it was his strategic planning that had led to many Indian victories. That the Miami chief seemed to have lost his desire for this upcoming battle was a cause for concern, but Blue Jacket was a fierce fighter, and his position with the Shawnees, thought Little Fox, would serve them all quite well.

The Indians had pushed hard for the British to put their regular troops in line with them, but the British commander, Major William Campbell put them off, promising to help when the time came. He did allow Captain William Caldwell, in charge of two companies of Canadian volunteers, to dress his men as Indians and place them on the far right of the Indian line. Between them and Little Turtle's Miamis, about 250 Wyandots commanded by Tarhe and Roundhead were ready for battle, along with a small mixture of Mingos and Mohawks.

General Wayne gave the order for his troops to begin their march a little after 7:00 a.m., more than two hours later than he had intended. He was frustrated by the fact that the drums used to convey orders had been disabled by the rain. His staff officers would have to be used to carry commands to the various units. He had about 3,300 men at his disposal, including 1,800 regulars and another 1,500 who were mounted volunteers from Kentucky.

It was roughly five miles to the area where the Indians waited, the location discovered the day before by Major William Price's advanced scouting battalion consisting of 150 mounted Kentuckians. That same group led today's action, divided into small units of twenty men or so, riding parallel and spread out over more than a half mile. A scout company of sixty-five under Captain William Kibbey crossed the Maumee and advanced along the southeast side as a cover for the army's right flank. Arrayed behind the lead units, and in accord with Wayne's precise planning, were more than a dozen different lines of troops, keeping a distance of one hundred yards or more from the unit just ahead. The width of the advance was more than a mile.

Most of the soldiers were having to make their way through trees and bushes and across steep ravines, except for the one part of Price's frontline closest to the river, which was down on the floodplain that featured prairie grass as tall as a man. The Indian portage trail that defined the route came near the Indian line on a high ridge. The ground was relatively open for more than two hundred yards from the edge of the ridge, covered with a few large oaks before changing into a densely wooded section.

Ahead of Price's advancing troops, who were walking their mounts, was the tangled woods and the Indian line. Two men walked a hundred yards ahead of each of Price's units. William Steele and Thomas Moore were the two scouts in front of Lieutenant William Suddath's unit. When a volley of shots came from the woods in front of them, both men fell dead. The battle was on!

Little Fox heard the firing far to his left and knew that it might be his brother Chippewas who were doing the shooting. There were about 25 Chippewas on the left, along with another 25 Potawatomis and over 200 Ottawas. The number of Chippewas was a great disappointment to him, for one report had said more than 800 were on the way from the Saginaw area. Still he hoped the ones who were here would acquit themselves well. There was an increase in the firing on the left, and in a few minutes, a runner came to inform them that the soldiers were now on the run. Immediately, a good portion of the Shawnees, including Fire Heart, moved out toward the sounds of the guns, and it wasn't long before they engaged a company of infantry. Red Storm had come to where Little Fox remained behind a huge log.

"Let us go, they are on the run." Red Storm had cast his gun aside and was brandishing his tomahawk in his left hand.

"We should wait until our chief tells us to go," cautioned Little Fox. He nodded toward the gun Red Storm had cast onto the ground. "You may need that, my friend."

"It is of no use to me anyway," said Red Storm, holding up his right arm, which had remained in a disabled state.

Shooting erupted not far in front of them, and at the same time, both Buckongehelas and Pipe appeared in front of the Delaware line, encouraging the warriors to move ahead and to their right. The idea was to get around the American left. The tangled logs and branches offered comforting shelter from the musket balls and cannon shells that were beginning to shower them, but it also made for a difficult passage.

Little Fox was sure of ultimate victory. How could the hated Long Knives resist the power of so many elite fighters as existed in the body of Shawnees, Delawares, and Miamis all around him. As time passed, however, there seemed to be no end to the American line. At least twice, the Indian advance stopped for a furious interchange of shots, with a resulting retreat by the American soldiers, but each time, there seemed to be another line right behind that put up a stiff defense.

At times, the American artillery found the range with balls and canister, and the woods seemed to Little Fox to be full of flying branches, bark, and pieces of metal. The sounds of battle far to the left appeared to indicate that the Indians had pushed the soldiers back some distance, but Little Fox could see no indication of much advance in the center or the right. In all the confusion, there was really no way to know how the battle was going except in his own immediate area. It was frustrating, and he found himself becoming fearful, especially when two Delaware braves fell dead just in front of him.

The great movement by the Indian center came to a halt. Captain Pipe appeared and appealed to his warriors to hold the line where they were. Wayne's troops led by dragoons, light infantry, and rifle battalions were attacking on both wings while a great column of regular infantry awaited the order for a bayonet charge. Bugles could be heard from both ends of the battle line.

"We are in danger here," said Little Fox quietly. "We may be surrounded, although we still have the Wyandots and Canadiens on our right," he continued. "Surely they will stop the advance there."

"Yes," pronounced Red Storm. "Then we will drive them back and kill them all, just like we've done before."

"This army is not fighting like the other white armies," noted Little Fox. "We may need to go back toward the British fort."

"Don't talk that way," shouted Red Storm. "We are sure to win this battle."

The American left, however, was much too strong for the Wyandots and Canadiens to handle, and beyond that, the eight hundred Kentuckians under General Thomas Barbee had been sent by Wayne to go around the Indian right and come in behind to trap them. Suddenly the center of the Indian line became aware of the advancing infantry in a determined bayonet charge. When their concerted volley failed to slow the advancing troops, the Shawnees, Delawares, and Miamis retreated to a new line.

A second volley had no effect, and the ordered Indian retreat began to disintegrate into a rout. Little Fox and several others tried to make one more stand, but the sight of the glistening bayonets advancing toward them with such resolve was more than could be withstood. Fire Heart had somehow found them in the midst of all the chaos, and the three longtime companions tried to stay together.

"We must go now," said Fire Heart, grabbing the arms of both his friends. Red Storm jerked away.

"I'm not afraid," he said. "Let us charge them with our tomahawks."

"Who will go with us?" asked Little Fox. "You are brave my friend, but there is no one to go with us."

A well-known young Shawnee warrior appeared in front of them, clearly in full retreat. "Tecumseh," exclaimed Little Fox. "You are retreating?"

"This battle is lost," he answered. "We must not be captured. We will make a stand with the British at the fort."

"Maybe we should try to cross the river," argued Red Storm.

"No, no," cried Fire Heart emphatically. "There are soldiers across the river. I was all the way down there, and I saw several of our men killed in the river as they crossed."

This was enough to convince even Red Storm, who began running back through the woods with Little Fox and Fire Heart right behind him. The bulk of the Indian defenders managed to escape the trap that was rapidly closing on them. Another huge surprise awaited, however.

The British fort, Fort Miamis, was built with one side on the edge of the river bluff and surrounded by ditches and mounds. The stockade was twenty feet high, and the British commander had nearly two hundred troops and fourteen cannon at his disposal. A large area around the fort had been cleared of trees so there was an open field of fire for the guns. When Little Fox broke through the trees at the edge of the clearing, a frightening sight assaulted him. Beyond the crowd of warriors milling about the field, he could see the Shawnee chief, Blue Jacket, arguing with a British officer on the wall near the gate. The gate was closed and the front wall was fortified with an abatis made of sharpened poles slanted upward at an angle.

The argument continued with Blue Jacket becoming angrier and angrier while clearly losing the argument. Finally he turned and in a loud voice announced to the crowd that the British were not going to honor their promises. "The English will not let us in. We must go on down the river and join our families. If necessary, we will fight again there to protect them."

The British troops on the wall watched as the dejected braves began to move on down the stream toward the camp where their families had been sent several days earlier. Many of the braves waved their fists angrily toward the British soldiers, who watched with dismay but did not reply.

"How could the British do this?" asked Red Storm. "They promised to fight with us."

"They are white men after all," said Little Fox. "We should know by now that no white man can be trusted."

"It is very true," agreed Fire Heart, sadness descending on him like a heavy blanket.

"I'm afraid our lives will never be the same again after this," said Little Fox. "Our raiding days will be at an end."

"Never!" exclaimed Red Storm. "Not until we have killed Wetzel!"

Little Fox shook his head. "We will never see Wetzel again."

December 9, 1794

Lewis Wetzel was dreaming. He was on a forest path with sunlight streaming in patches through the leafy branches. He was running, and the unhindered freedom sent his spirits soaring. It was as if he were flying through the air. But then everything twisted as they often do in dreams, and abruptly he was surrounded by unrecognizable pursuers. He tripped on an unseen root and pitched forward, face down. Covered by a pile of bodies, he felt smothered, unable to breathe. Expending every effort he could muster, he turned over on his back and the bodies were gone. He felt only something tickling his face, and he came suddenly awake. The first thing he saw was the backside of a solitary rat, perched now in the middle of his chest. He made a feeble effort to raise his arm and sweep the intruder away, but the rodent scurried off to the floor just ahead of the blow.

Wetzel watched in a semistupor as the animal wandered over and began to chew at a patch of dried vomit. Wetzel had been ill for two days, his misery brought on by a piece of spoiled meat brought as his only meal three days earlier. The freedom enjoyed briefly in the dream lingered for a while in his mind, but as he watched the rat, he thought of its ability to come and go through the small hole in the corner of his room.

"That damned rat is free, and I ain't," he muttered aloud.

There were days he had tried to catch the animal, thinking it would be better to eat than much of what he was given. He pulled the dirty blanket up to his chin, shivering in the cold that he realized had made his sleep fitful for most of the night. A dark mood descended over him, and he began to think again, as he often did, that he should find a way to end his own life. Solitary confinement was a horror unlike anything Lewis Wetzel could have imagined. The cell was tiny with no windows, and the prisoner was chained to a large hook embedded in the back wall.

There was room to stand up and shuffle around and to lie down on the dirty pallet, which was all Wetzel had been allowed to take from the previous cell. They had taken his money and an extra shirt he had possessed in the old room. As the weather had cooled, he had been given a tattered blanket, but it was not always enough to keep him warm. His friends among the guards—Frank, Juan, and Buck—were no longer allowed to spend time with him; the card playing days were over. A gloom and depression had descended upon him beyond anything he had ever known.

He felt his strength slipping away every day, his long hair, once a source of pride, now a homeland for lice and other insects. The beard he had long eschewed was thick and long. His thoughts became more and more centered on a desire for death. He tried to cheer himself by thinking about his family, especially his sisters whom he loved so dearly, but it became more and more difficult to even picture them in his mind. Once in a while, Frank would be allowed to release him from the chains, but always in the presence of one or two military guards.

Occasionally Frank managed to smuggle something in that was good to eat, but these times were rare, and recently when given a small loaf of fresh French bread, Wetzel found it difficult to even tear it apart. He had lost all track of time and season, although he was aware of the chill in the air. His cell was buried deep inside the jail, but he could sometimes hear things that were happening outside. The only window was a small barred opening in the door from which he could see enough light during daylight hours to usually distinguish night from day. One day after he'd been there awhile, he could hear the sound of the wind outside and loud banging noises. He surmised that it might be a hurricane. Not too long after he had been brought to New Orleans, he had experienced the first of the big storms. At that time, he feared the jail itself might be blown away. Frank told him about hurricanes and that they were not an uncommon event. After that, he began hoping for one bad enough to enable him to escape. When the latest one came, however, he could tell it was not strong enough to be of any help to him.

He had managed to fall asleep again, and when he awoke, the rat was gone. The smell in the room was overwhelming, although his stomach seemed to be returning to some normalcy.

He saw that his breakfast, such as it was, had been placed on the floor near the door, and he suspected even the rat had rejected it. He guessed the day was well along, and he could hear loud sounds outside. It was not wind that he heard, but men shouting. He was unable to make out what was being shouted, but it seemed to becoming more frantic. Struggling to his feet, he moved as close to the door as the chain would allow. It wasn't long before he could hear footsteps coming toward his door, and then he heard the key inserted and watched as the door was flung open.

Buck was there along with two soldiers, heavily armed. The soldiers aimed their guns at him as Buck came with keys to unlock his chains. "It's a big fire!" shouted Buck. "We must get you out."

Wetzel's heart jumped as he thought his chance had finally come. He was too weak, however, and could not resist as Buck tied his hands behind him with strong rope. The soldiers were uneasy, and he realized that they would rather shoot him and get out of there as quickly as possible. The fire must be really close, he thought. The idea of resisting and provoking the soldiers to kill him came to him, but in the end, he allowed them to hurry him out. It was not long before they were all at the front door of the jail and out onto the wide porch.

In spite of his condition, and the pain that the sudden bright light was bringing to his eyes, Wetzel was thrilled at being outside. It had been a very long time. The smoke-filled air almost choked them all, and they moved quickly into the street and across into the open green of the plaza. A fire wagon was in front of the church, and the men were frantically trying to pump enough water to douse small flames beginning to lick at the edges of the building. Behind them, the flames were leaping toward the sky, and the jailhouse was quickly becoming swallowed up.

The guards hustled Wetzel across the grassy plaza, and as his eyes became accustomed to the scene, Lew could see that other prisoners were around them. He thought he saw Payette, a man not easy to forget. He towered above his guards, and when he saw Wetzel, he shouted something and waved, then was out of sight. Wetzel had no idea about how many prisoners there might have been in the royal jail, but he knew that the authorities had a major problem on their hands.

He would try to stay alert for his chance to escape might still arrive. There were many people gathered in the open plaza, including a large contingent of soldiers. The prison warden was there, conversing with an officer of high rank, no doubt trying to decide what to do with the prisoners. The fire and smoke could still be seen back in the direction of the old jail, but a change in wind direction seemed to be slowing the spread of the fire and reversing it back on itself.

Wetzel was surprised to find himself standing next to Payette.

"Quite a fire, friend, would you agree?"

Wetzel did not feel strong enough and well enough to engage this man in conversation. He mumbled a simple "yes."

Payette, who always seemed to know all that was happening, explained that it was thought the fire was started by some boys playing in the yard of a house on Royal Street. It quickly spread north and east until it reached the royal jail. As they watched, it appeared that the church, nearing its complete rebuilding after the earlier fire, would be mostly spared this time.

Wetzel thought briefly of approaching Payette with the idea of trying to break away from the guards and getting lost in the confusion that was all around them. He knew that he would be of little help himself, but Payette was clearly capable of drastic action. Before he could broach the subject, the guards, supplemented by a squad of soldiers, herded the prisoners off to the north, following behind the warden and the officer.

"I bet they're taking us to the convent," said Payette.

The Ursuline convent was located three blocks to the north of the church and on Chartres Street. It was built of stucco-covered brick and was the second building to house the nuns on the same site. It was a symmetrical building with little ornamentation, although it did contain a beautiful circular staircase to the second floor, this staircase having been part of the original structure. It was up this staircase that the prisoners were marched and placed in rooms that normally housed the library and storehouse.

"This ain't bad," was Payette's comment after the prisoners had been settled in and fed with some fresh bread and water.

Wetzel was sure this was the chance to escape he had been awaiting, but in his muddled state, he could not focus on what needed to be done, and he found himself drifting into an acceptance of his fate and a relief at being out of solitary. The relatively plush accommodations of the convent lasted only two days, after which the convicts were led out to the river and placed on board a schooner called the Nuestra Señora del Carmen, anchored in midstream. The quarters in the hold were dark and damp, and had it been summer rather than winter, the place would have been unbearable.

Payette was angry. "Hell, the sons of bitches are treating us like dogs."

"There are worse things," muttered Wetzel.

At least he had some company.

March 10, 1798

In a little more than two months, the prisoners were removed from the prison ship and eventually placed in the new royal jail, hastily rebuilt near its old spot on St. Peter's between Chartres and Royal. It was a two-story building constructed this time of brick and stucco with a tiled roof.

Wetzel was placed in a cell on the second floor and though still in chains, it was no longer solitary. There was a barred window high on the back wall, which allowed some sunlight in the late afternoon. The visits from the guards resumed, along with some card playing, although Wetzel never had money again. Frank and Juan were not around after awhile, and he made friends with the new guards along with the soldiers who also performed guard duty.

Buck continued in his old job for several months but then received a promotion to the role of public executioner, which afforded him room and board at the jail, along with a small salary of about six pesos per month. He still found time to visit Wetzel occasionally.

Gradually Wetzel's old robust inner nature began to reassert itself, and he grew out of the depression that had held him in its grip since the days of solitary confinement. A new warden had been appointed, and shortly after that, conditions began to improve, especially the meals. The restoration of his bodily strength added to Wetzel's recovery.

Unknown to him, friends in western Virginia and Pennsylvania, having learned of his fate, were endeavoring to effect his release. The first attempt was a petition drafted by the editor of the newspaper in Washington, Pennsylvania, a man named Colerick. It was signed by many of the residents of the region and sent to New Orleans with Daniel Moore. Governor Carondelet would not even allow the petition to be delivered, sending it back unread to the disillusioned Moore. A second attempt was made by Richard Brown of Hollidays Cove and Philip Doddridge of Wellsburg, who had come down to New Orleans with a boat load of flour. Before leaving home and after hearing of the failure of the petition drive, the two men had gathered more than $ 1,000 from neighbors and friends with the hopes of bribing the Spanish authorities to release Lewis Wetzel.

Upon their arrival, the two men went straight to the Government House. "Who do you think we should go to with our offer?" Brown had asked.

"To the governor himself," answered Doddridge with confidence.

His confidence was disappointed, for the governor refused to see them. After considerable effort, they managed to obtain an audience with the Spanish intendant, a man named Juan Ventura Morales. The intendant was primarily involved with financial affairs, in charge of the royal treasury. Morales insisted that he had no power with respect to prisoners, and even if he did, he was insulted at the idea of accepting a bribe. The two Virginians were convinced that the main objection to the idea of bribery was that the amount was too small. In any case, their efforts were of no avail, and Wetzel remained in prison.

The next person to take an interest in Wetzel's plight was an old friend from Buffalo Creek who had been his companion on the Beaver blockhouse expedition. Francis McGuire determined to go to New Orleans with a bigger pot of money. His idea was to attempt the bribery at a lower level and managed to get in to the warden's office at the jail. The warden was newly appointed and determined to do his job well. He was a good friend of Governor Carondelet and shared the governor's dislike of Americans. He knew some English but refused to use it with this visitor, whose presence he regarded as an insult.

"I don't know what you desire of me, but it must be quick for I am a busy man," he rattled off in Spanish and waited for the translation to be given to McGuire.

"I know that you are busy, Señor Antonio, I just—"

McGuire was cut off in midsentence as the warden jumped to his feet, clearly upset by what the American had said.

"My name is José Antonio Ruby, and I will not talk with imbeciles who do not even know my name," he shouted, his eyes flashing as he glared at both McGuire and the interpreter.

When he understood what was happening, McGuire apologized profusely, bowing and pleading. "Please excuse me, señor, I did not hear correctly when your name was told to me. Please let me explain myself to you."

It took several moments, but finally, Ruby relented and sat down again.

McGuire remained standing and stated his business. He realized that it would be touchy to offer an obvious bribe under the circumstances. "Mr. Lewis Wetzel is a highly favored man in our part of the country, Señor José Antonio Ruby," he began carefully. "The people there would be very grateful if a way was found to set him free. They have sent some money along to help pay any expenses involved in providing his release."

Ruby's eyebrows rose at the mention of the English word *money*. He looked anxiously toward the interpreter as he translated.

"How much money?" was his immediate question.

"We have 2,000 in Spanish pesos," replied McGuire, suddenly feeling more confident.

"And just what did you think this money would be used for?" asked Ruby, a heavy frown on his face. "Did you think I would betray my responsibilities for such a small sum?"

"Oh no, sir," exclaimed McGuire. "This is not a bribe. We believe Mr. Wetzel to be innocent, and we would welcome an investigation of the case. We know such things cost money."

"This man Wetzel is guilty of a very serious crime against Spain and its government here," said Ruby. "His accuser, the honorable governor of Natchez, Manuel Gayoso de Lemos, had ironclad evidence, and the man was given the appropriate sentence of imprisonment for life. I will hear no more from you now. Please leave."

Ruby stood and turned his back to his American visitor as the translation was given. His momentary hopes dashed, McGuire made one last try. "Then, sir, might I be at least given the liberty to see Mr. Wetzel?"

"Absolutely not!" was the answer.

The warden turned and motioned to one of the military guards at the door. "Escort this man out of my sight at once."

Francis McGuire was an old frontiersman and not someone to be pushed around. He stood on the street outside the Warden's office where the soldier had left him, fighting to get control of his anger. "By God, I'm goin' to see Lewis Wetzel if it's the last thing I ever do," he muttered to himself. He had looked over the jail before asking to see the warden, and he knew there was a back entrance and that the public executioner had a room there. One of the friendlier guards told him that the executioner was a black man named Buck.

It was late in the afternoon as he made his way around to the back, staying out of sight as much as possible. The door was open, and once inside, he saw a door on the left that looked promising. He knocked and stood back, not quite sure what might transpire. When no one came, he knocked again, louder this time. In a moment, he heard some sound behind the door and suddenly it flew open, and a very large black man faced him, towering above him and with a hard look on his face. "Who are you, and why do you come to my door?" The words were in English, which surprised McGuire.

"I was hoping to see Lewis Wetzel," McGuire managed to utter. "Do you know him?"

The look on Buck's face softened. "I know him well. He beats me at cards," said the executioner with a soft laugh.

"Can I see him then?" McGuire was beginning to sense that he had found just the right man to help him.

Buck had not received any order from the warden about forbidding this American from visiting Wetzel and could think of no reason to deny the request. He called to a pair of soldiers sitting in the hallway.

"Come here," he commanded. "Take this man to the cell of the prisoner Wctzel."

To McGuire he said, "You will be searched and then taken to Wetzel's cell. I cannot let you stay very long, and you will not be admitted."

"Yes, yes, I understand," replied McGuire, highly pleased at this success.

He was amazed at the high-quality English spoken by the black executioner. At first sight, he had assumed Buck was a slave assigned to the office, not expecting a free black man who would hold such a position. He followed the two soldiers up a back stairway and halfway down the hall. They pointed to the door on the right and backed away. There was a small barred window in the door, and McGuire could see Wetzel sitting on the floor, slumped against the back wall, apparently asleep.

"Hey, Lew," he called. "Is that any way to greet an old friend?"

Wetzel was not in a sound sleep, and the voice registered quickly. It was familiar, but he couldn't see clearly enough to know who it was. He rose to his feet, squinting, then rubbing his eyes. "Who is it?" was the response.

"Why, Lew, you don't recognize an old neighbor?"

"By God," exclaimed Wetzel when he realized who it was. "If it ain't Francis McGuire. I figured them Pennsylvanians had hung you by now."

"They never did git around to it. Jesus, you look bad, Lew."

"It's what everybody says," admitted Wetzel. "Man, it's good to see you."

Wetzel was hungry for news from home, and McGuire obliged him. Far too soon, they were interrupted by the sudden appearance of Buck and two more soldiers, each holding a rifle in ready position.

"Arrest that man," shouted Buck, pointing at McGuire.

"What the hell?" was all McGuire could say before he was in the grasp of the two men who had first brought him to the cell.

"The warden has ordered your arrest," explained Buck. "You have lied to me."

"I didn't lie," protested McGuire, but he was well aware of what had happened. He did not struggle as he was hustled down the stair at the other end of the hall and straight to the warden's office.

Wetzel was left alone, wondering what had gone wrong. At least he now knew that his predicament was known back home. It was several days before he learned that McGuire had managed to talk the warden into letting him go. Buck reckoned that some money may have changed hands in the deal.

Today, another acquaintance from the upper Ohio valley showed up at Wetzel's cell.

"David Bradford!" said Lew, sticking his fingers through the bars to touch Bradford's extended hand. "How in hell did you find me?"

"Francis McGuire told me where you was." Bradford had been in New Orleans for many months, having been in trouble at home for his revolt against the government, beginning with his role in the Whiskey Rebellion. He was known to the Spanish authorities for his part in some of the shady negotiations with General Wilkinson and others to establish a new nation in the west friendly to Spain.

Bradford carefully cultivated his friendships, especially the one with Manuel Gayoso de Lemos, who was the new governor of Louisiana. The new governor had taken over in August of 1797 when Carondelet was assigned a new role as a governor of Equador in South America. Eventually Bradford began to talk with de Lemos about the fate of Lewis Wetzel. He was careful not to push too hard, and the governor seemed to become more and more ready to listen to a solid proposal to obtain the prisoner's freedom.

Unknown to Bradford, de Lemos had remembered Wetzel's case, and that the evidence against him was a bit shaky. At the time, of course, it was to Manuel's advantage to court Governor Carondelet's favor, and Wetzel had been sacrificed to the cause.

When Bradford ran into another Ohio valley pioneer, James Morrison, who had arranged passage on a cargo ship bound for Philadelphia, the two men hatched a plan that seemed workable. It would require some help on the inside, and Bradford convinced the governor to make that happen.

After some small talk, which encouraged the soldier escort for Bradford to stop listening, Bradford began to explain to Wetzel, in a low voice barely above a whisper, the plan for his release. "We're gonna' get you outta here, Lew."

"That's mighty good news, David. But how and when will that be possible?"

"Tonight, Lew. Here's how we'll do it."

When Bradford left, Wetzel sat down again, feeling dizzy. He was thrilled to know that he had friends willing to take such chances to get him out of jail, but he was not confident that it would come off as planned. He could only wait, now, for some time to pass. It was well past midnight when Wetzel, who had been dozing, came wide awake at the sound of a key opening his cell door.

It was very dark, although a bit of the moonlit night was entering the single window. He could see that it was David Bradford and James Morrison, along with Buck, entering his cell and pushing in a wooden box, which Lewis knew was a coffin. He stood and watched in the dim light as Morrison lifted the lid of the dreaded box.

"We have to get you in this thing, Lew," whispered Bradford. "And be damned quiet about it."

Wetzel knew that the escape plan involved faking his death, but Bradford hadn't revealed all the details. Obviously Buck was in on the plot, not entirely surprising to him, but he knew that Buck could easily lose his job and end up in the prison himself. He could not have imagined that the governor would be a part of the plan as well.

Climbing into the coffin, Wetzel found it difficult to get comfortable, the length being just slightly less than his height.

As they placed the top back in place, he noticed that they had provided a small notch just under it so that he could get some air.

"Don't worry, Lew, you won't be in there very long," promised Bradford.

Buck had left the room, going down the stairs, and entering the guardroom where two of the night guards were sleeping. He roused them roughly, then cautioned them to be quiet. "One of the prisoners has died, and we must get him out," explained Buck in Spanish. "We have him in a coffin, but I need you two to help carry it out back."

The guards, thankful that they had not been scolded for being asleep, went quickly up the stairs and into the open door where they found Bradford and Morrison standing above the closed coffin. They had no idea who these men were, but it was of no matter. At a nod from Bradford, the four men hoisted the heavy box and carried it out and carefully down the stairs. Although they tried hard to keep the noise down, one of the inmates at the end of the hall appeared at his cell door window.

"What's goin' on?" the man asked.

Neither Bradford nor Morrison spoke enough Spanish to be sure of what the man said, so they said nothing.

Finally one of the guards answered. "One of your mates died."

Just outside the back door, there was a small two-wheeled wagon hitched to a tall sad-faced mule. The men slid the coffin into the wagon as Buck watched without comment. Bradford and Morrison climbed up to the seat of the wagon. Morrison took the reins and spoke to the mule, who moved ahead with a jerk. They eased slowly up St. Peter's toward Royal, and passing that street, turned into an open shed. Once inside, they pulled the door closed and unhitched the mule. Climbing into the wagon, they quickly pried off the lid of the coffin.

Wetzel arose with a sigh, wiping the sweat from his forehead. "Man, I'm glad to be outta there and outta that damned jail."

"So are we, Lew," said Bradford. "Now we got to get you cleaned up."

Morrison produced a lantern, which he managed to light, and they showed Wetzel to a bowl of water on a stand with a shaving kit that Morrison had supplied.

"We ain't got no mirror, Lew, so try not to butcher yourself too much," laughed Bradford. "There's some nice clothes for you too."

Just after dawn, the three men emerged from the shed, the newly released prisoner sporting a clean-shaven face and fresh clothes. They strode down Royal to St. Ann, where they turned toward the river.

Wetzel had been told by Bradford that his escape would involve a sea voyage, but he knew nothing beyond that. By the time the men reached Decatur Street, which paralleled the river, the establishments on the shoreline were coming to life. No one paid them any attention, and they climbed onto the levee where they could survey the scene.

"It's down there," said Morrison, pointing to a ship standing out in the river, pointed mostly downstream.

Making their way to the riverbank, they walked down to a point opposite the ship, which was equipped with two square-rigged masts.

"It's a brig called the *Molly*," said Morrison. "I've arranged passage for us both, Lew."

"Where to?" Wetzel wanted to know.

"Philadelphia," answered Morrison.

"That's it, Lew. You're off to Philadelphia." Bradford took Lew's right hand and shook it vigorously. "You should be safe now. They think you're dead."

"I don't know what to say, David. You've saved my life. Both of you."

"Thank you is enough, Lew. You've done plenty for all us folks back home. I'm glad I could help."

"I won't forget, David." He took Bradford's hand again, squeezing it tight.

"It's time for me to get out of here," said Bradford. "Good-bye, Lew. Take good care of my boy here, won't you James?"

"I will for sure," declared Morrison.

Wetzel and Morrison stood watching as Bradford walked away.

"Come on now, Lew," insisted Morrison. "I want you to meet Captain Tepper."

20

ONLY IN HEAVEN

March 20, 1798

THE NIGHT JUST a few days earlier was still fresh in Lewis Wetzel's mind as he walked the deck of the sailing ship, a brig called *Molly*. It was hard to believe that his friends would go to so much trouble to get him out of that Spanish prison. David Bradford had even given him some money, saying he would need that once he got to Philadelphia. And James Morrison, whom he barely knew, had arranged for his passage on this ship.

It almost seemed like a dream that morning on the New Orleans waterfront when he and Morrison were rowed out to the big ship. Wetzel had never seen a ship that big, sitting quietly in a kind of haughtiness and grandeur as they approached its side. The two large masts seemed to reach almost to the sky, with the long yards attached squarely, and sails furled tightly against them. Of course he had spent time on a schooner out in the river just after the big fire, but he was in no condition to notice the beauty of a ship at anchor in those days. Besides, this one was much larger. Its length seemed to Wetzel to be well over one hundred feet.

"By God, that's a big boat," he exclaimed.

"You're right, and you'll wish it was even bigger when we get out in the ocean," observed Morrison. "I guess you've never been on a ship like this one before."

"Hell, no," laughed Lew. "Biggest one I've been on is one of them river flatboats."

"Ninety man crew on this brig," proudly announced the man doing the rowing, a member of the *Molly*'s crew. "Plus the damned officers."

Morrison and Wetzel, each carrying a personal pack, climbed up a rope ladder to reach the deck, and the rowboat returned to shore.

The ship's second mate, Mr. Sweeney, met them at the rail. "And who might you two gentlemen be?" he asked, although the tone was not friendly.

Morrison extended his hand. "I'm James Morrison, and this here is John Smith," he explained, deciding at the last minute that it might be safer to not mention Wetzel's real name. "Captain Tepper is expecting us."

"We'll see about that," said the mate. "You two stay right here." He quickly descended through a hatch near the center of the deck and was out of sight.

"John Smith?" chuckled Lew. "Didn't know they'd changed my name."

"Thought it best 'til we get out to sea," said Morrison. "Them Spaniards might change their mind and come lookin' for you."

Wetzel walked over and put his hand on a three-inch swivel gun mounted on a square stanchion that extended a foot or so above the deck railing. "They got guns on this boat. Is it a government boat?"

"No, just a cargo ship," answered Morrison. "I think they all carry some guns. There are probably some carriage guns on the bow and the stern as well. I guess they hope to ward off any halfhearted pirate attack, but I doubt they're very effective."

Just then, Mr. Sweeney emerged again and motioned for Morrison and Wetzel to follow him. "The Captain says to bring you down." The man seemed terribly disappointed that the captain was willing to see them.

"I think he wanted to throw us off," Wetzel whispered as they followed Sweeney down to the captain's cabin.

"Come in," came the call from inside the cabin as the second mate knocked on the door.

The three men entered to find the captain hunched over a small desk, writing something in a tattered logbook. He closed the book and stood up, facing his visitors. "Welcome, gentlemen," he said pleasantly. "It is nice to see you again, Mr. Morrison."

"Good day to you, Captain Tepper," replied Morrison. Nodding at Wetzel, he said, "This is my friend, John Smith."

The captain raised his eyebrows in surprise. "John Smith? I don't recall you mentioning that name."

"Well, Captain, under the circumstances, I think it best we use that name."

"Very well," responded Tepper. "Welcome aboard, Mr. Smith."

"Thank you," was all Wetzel could muster, feeling very strange at being called Mr. Smith.

The captain continued to eye Wetzel quizzically, a smile growing on his lips. "I must say, Morrison, he doesn't look much like a John Smith to me. But I am glad you both made it aboard. We will be sailing soon."

"Are there other passengers, Captain Tepper?" asked Morrison.

"Yes, a couple of flatboat men returning home. Mr. Sweeney will show you to your quarters. Not a very large room, I'm afraid, but much better than steerage. I will see you both tonight at supper. If all goes well, we should be on our way downriver by then."

The captain waved to the mate, who led them out and to their tiny room. It contained a chest, a small table, and two beds, one built on top the other.

"Well, this'll be our home for a couple of months, I suppose," observed Morrison. "It ain't much."

"Lots better than that damned jail," snorted Wetzel. "I ain't about to complain about nothin' now, I reckon."

Two days later, they were in the open gulf, and Wetzel was deathly sick. He soon discovered it was much better in the open air on deck, but he spent a good deal of time bent over the rail "heavin' up his insides," as he put it to Morrison. His illness lasted until on the fourth day he was able to keep down a large slab of salt beef and a piece of bread.

Wetzel was amazed at the work of the crew members, glad that he wasn't asked to climb the masts and rigging, furling, and unfurling the sails. He became well acquainted with some of the crew, in particular, Albert Scott, who was the ship's carpenter, and Sam Calder, a regular crewman who had the title of yeoman of the sheets.

Wetzel thought this an amusing title and was surprised to find that the word *sheets* referred to lines attached to the corners of the sails rather than meaning the sails themselves. He had also learned about the watches observed by the sailors. There were two divisions, one commanded by the chief mate, Mr. Waters, and the second by the second mate, Mr. Sweeney.

There were three night watches, the first, middle, and morning, each four hours in length. The first went from eight o'clock to midnight. During the daylight hours, the entire crew was up and about, although the division coming off the morning watch would go below during the forenoon watch. The four to eight afternoon watch was split into two dogwatches of two hours each so that no division stood watch during the same hours each day. The cook and the surgeon, as well as the carpenter and the sailmaker, stood no watch, usually being employed all day and on call at any time. No one was allowed to be idle during the day, except maybe on Sundays.

Wetzel was glad he was a passenger when he saw all the things the crewmen were asked to do. Already within the first few days, there had been a beating of a crew member who had sassed an officer. Scott told him that such beatings were very common on both merchant and naval vessels. He stood now at the rail on the starboard side of the ship, having spent some time watching his friend Scott, working on a socket for a piece of the fixed rigging that had torn loose.

The wind that had been coming in off the starboard bow suddenly changed and was coming directly from the west. Although it was dusk, it had become noticeably darker, and Wetzel saw for the first time the very black clouds on the western horizon. The wind had changed in velocity as well as direction, and the swells were suddenly higher and breaking with visible white caps. The boat began pitching with increased intensity. There was a call for all hands, and the men quickly ascended the masts, reefing in the sails.

Wetzel felt the return of the insufferable nausea in the pit of his stomach. He held tight to the rail, trying to stay out of the way of the hardworking crew. It wasn't long before it was clear to everyone that a violent storm was upon them. The boat had heeled over sharply to starboard until Wetzel thought the yardarms on the main mast might actually dip into the sea. It was then that a huge black wave broke over the side, Wetzel's grip was torn loose from the railing, and he was hurtling into the water.

He was stretched out almost flat as he hit, and though the wind was nearly knocked out of him, he did not go deeply under. Still he did go under, the saltwater stinging his eyes, rising up his nose and into his mouth. Though he was a strong swimmer, this was unlike anything he'd ever known, and there was a moment of panic and despair. He managed to get his head above the water, but when he tried to cry out, no sound emerged. He was helpless. *They won't even know I'm gone*, he thought. He knew that the ship was supposedly somewhere off the coast of Florida on the gulf side, but there was no land in sight.

"I'm a goner," he sputtered.

A wave broke over him and spun him around, the saltwater stinging his eyes. When he rose up on the next swell, he could not see the ship. The panic returned, and he struggled to keep his head above the next high surge. He turned a bit to his right and was elated to see the winking lantern through the spray, although it was unexpectedly far away. He began trying to swim in the direction of the light, but he knew the ship was moving away much faster than he could swim. Even so, he kept swimming with all the strength he could muster.

On board the *Molly*, Wetzel's disappearance had not gone unnoticed. Albert Scott, though busy with his work, had kept an eye on his friend as he stood at the railing. Before he could shout a warning that Wetzel should move to the center of the boat, he saw that the man was no longer there. Immediately he shouted the alarm.

"Man overboard! Man overboard!"

"Who was it?" came the cry from the first mate, Waters, who had just appeared from below.

"One of the passengers," was an answer from one of the men partway up the rigging on the foremast.

"It was John Smith," said Scott, who had left his post and was at the side, searching the waters off the starboard stern.

"Get the boat," shouted the mate, meaning one of the small rowboats stowed near the bow. "I need three volunteers."

Sam Calder appeared from his post near the main mast. "I'll go," he said. "The man's my friend."

"Me too," offered Scott.

"Take a lantern with you," advised Mr. Waters.

A third sailor, named Mills, quickly joined them, and the three men lowered the boat into the water—not an easy job with the pitching ship and the breaking waves. Calder and Mills grabbed oars and began rowing the boat out and to the rear of the *Molly*'s position.

Scott held the lantern high and began calling out, "Smith, Smith, where are you?"

"Man, it's gittin' too dark," said Calder. "We'll never find him."

"We've got to try," argued Scott, yelling the name Smith as loud as he could.

They continued for several minutes in complete silence, their fears growing as they distanced themselves from the ship.

"Turn a bit more into the wind," said Scott after a while. "The damned ship is goin' more sideways than forward. He may be more out that way."

Wetzel was tiring badly, but knew he must keep moving his legs and arms, or he would be gone. Just before he had decided he could keep it up no longer, he saw a flicker of light. It seemed much closer than the last time he had seen it. Had the ship turned toward him? The sight gave him some new energy, and he began again trying to swim toward the light. When he saw it the next time, it seemed even closer, but he could see now that it was not the ship. What could it be? He pushed even harder, and when he pulled himself above the swell flowing away from him, he again saw the flicker and then realized it was a small boat.

"By God," he tried to shout, "They're lookin' for me."

This discovery brought to him a new rush of energy. Again, he tried to shout. To his surprise, a sound came out louder than before.

"Help!" he cried once more as loud as he could.

"Wait," shouted Scott. "I thought I heard somethin'."

The two men stopped rowing, and they all began to yell. "Hello! John Smith! Hello!"

Wetzel was able to hear the sounds of men yelling, even made out the word *hello*. He paddled hard toward the sound.

"By God," hollered Albert Scott. "There he is." He pointed to splashing just a few feet ahead of them. In seconds, they were alongside the struggling Wetzel, and they pulled him quickly into the little boat.

"I don't know how in hell we ever found him out here in the dark," said Calder. "It's a miracle."

Wetzel was unable to talk for sometime, but he listened as the three men continued to gush about the unlikeliness of such a successful rescue. As they approached the big ship, Wetzel managed to raise himself just a little.

"Well," he murmured, his lips curling into a tiny smile, "reckon the devil ain't ready for me just yet."

May 17, 1798

The remainder of the trip by sea was without a major incident. Wetzel was fully recovered within a few days, and he sought out his two friends Calder and Scott to express his gratitude for their astounding rescue effort.

"I owe you, men, my life, that's sure," he said. "I think it only right that you know my real name."

"You mean it ain't Smith?" asked Scott with a smirk. "Can you believe that Calder?"

"Sure is hard to believe," agreed Calder.

Wetzel was puzzled. "Well, I don't know what you're goin' on about, but my name is Lew Wetzel."

The two men had quit laughing after that.

"Son of a bitch," exclaimed Calder. "I've heard tell of Lew Wetzel. You really him?"

"How in hell could you've heard of me?"

"Some flatboat man on my boat a few years ago," answered Calder. "He used to tell us stories about fightin' Injuns. Claimed Lew Wetzel was the greatest fighter of 'em all."

"That's a pretty tall story," protested Lew. "I can't think who'd 'uv told you that."

"Don't matter, I'm just glad to know you," claimed Calder.

"Me too," said Scott. "And to know your real name."

Wetzel tried to think of who Calder might be talking about.

"Parker! Was his name Parker?"

"Could be," agreed Calder. "Yeah, that sounds right."

"I'll be damned," exclaimed Wetzel. "Never knew Parker thought I was anything special."

They had endured a couple of storms, which provided some excitement, but Wetzel had become extremely bored. The food was the same every day, and although he liked the salted beef, Wetzel began to long for some variety, thinking of the potatoes, turnips, and other vegetables he enjoyed at home. The bouts with seasickness never completely left him either, and he was happy when the ship turned into Delaware Bay and moved up into the Delaware River. He began to look forward to finally getting back on dry land.

"How far do you reckon it is to Philadelphia from here," he asked Scott when they had entered the river.

"Oh. Eighty to one hundred miles, I suppose," offered the carpenter. "It'll be slow goin' though 'gainst that current."

The arrival at the port of Philadelphia finally came, and Wetzel was overjoyed as he stepped ashore in the famous city. His first few steps were unsteady after so many days aboard a rolling ship.

"Careful there, Lew," laughed Morrison, who was having the same problem. "You've got to trade them sea legs for land legs now."

Although he paid little attention to politics and government, Lew was aware that the country's capital was located here. He said a sad farewell to his friends Calder and Scott, the three men knowing they were not likely to ever see each other again.

"I'd be dead if it weren't for you," Wetzel said, aware that tears were forming and trying hard to suppress them.

"We're glad we could help such a famous man," remarked Calder with a big grin.

Wetzel embraced both men, something very unusual for him. Nothing more was said. He went then with James Morrison, leaving the riverside and moving along the street to the city center.

"Maybe we should stop in to see George Washington," he said to Morrison with a laugh.

"I doubt George is here, Lew. He's not the president now, you know."

"Guess I didn't know that, James. Who is the president then?"

"It is John Adams. He's been president for about a year now, I guess."

'Never heard o' him," said Wetzel. "Where's he from?"

"Massachusetts, I believe." Morrison was amused at this conversation, not what he expected from Lew Wetzel.

"Well, I don't reckon we need to see no Massachusetts man," laughed Lew. "I'm ready to go home."

Although they spent three days in the city, Morrrison was busy searching out some horses to carry them and their possessions on the long trek to Pittsburgh. Wetzel bought a rifle and knife, allowing that he had felt undressed all the time without any weapons.

When they reached Brownsville on the Monongahela, Wetzel took his leave from Morrison. "I'll leave you here, James," he told his benefactor. "And go cross-country to home. Reckon I ought to look in on my ma."

"I understand, Lew," said Morrison. "But I kind of need the horse to carry all my things."

"Of course you do, and that's all right. I can make it from here by foot just fine."

"Are you sure?" asked Morrison, who suddenly felt bad about leaving Wetzel without a horse. "Maybe we can buy one cheap right here in Brownsville."

"No need for that," Lew assured him. "I've spent more time walkin' the woods than I ever have ridin'."

"You've been a good companion," said Morrison.

"Don't know how I can ever thank you enough, James, You saved my life for sure, you and David Bradford."

"It was our pleasure, Lew. Good luck to you."

After all this, he had finally made it back to the Wetzel farm on Wheeling Creek. He stopped along the bank a short way above the cabin occupied by Martin Wetzel and his large family. Across the creek was the home cabin where he knew his appearance would be quite a shock.

It was late afternoon, and he assumed that his mother would be busy putting supper on the table. There was no one in sight at either location as he began his slow walk toward the creek and a crossing to the old homestead. He had decided against making his arrival known first at Martin's place. There were too many kids there, he thought, although he actually liked kids just fine. He knew of at least five who had been born to Martin and Mary, no, it was six, for there was a new one born a few months before he had gone to New Orleans.

He smiled at the thought, then waded through the creek and headed toward his mother's place. When he reached the door, Wetzel could hear the quiet conversation inside. He pushed the door open.

"Anybody here?" He could see his mother sitting at the far end of the table and a woman that he recognized as Ruhama Shepherd on the near side.

Opposite her was his brother Jacob, who jumped to his feet at the sight of Lew.

"By God, Ma, it's Lew. It's Lew!"

"You got that right little brother," announced Lew. "Hello, Ma."

Mary Wetzel tried to get up but slumped back into her chair, shaking her head. Jacob jumped around the table and embraced Lew. Ruhama stood where she was, watching the brothers' happy reunion.

"We thought you was dead," exclaimed Jacob. "Then we heard you was in some jail in New Orleans."

"Well, I ain't dead yet, but you heard right about the jail."

"Francis McGuire came to see us and told us about the jail," explained Jacob. "He didn't think you was ever gonna git out though."

By this time, Mary was in control of herself, and she came around to where her sons were standing.

"Let me hug you, Lewis. I never thought I would get that chance again."

The tears were flowing generously as she fell into the arms of her long-lost son. "Oh, son, I'm so glad to see you alive."

The tearful reunion went on for several minutes, and Ruhama felt awkward as she watched. After a while, Jacob noticed the look on her face.

"Lew," he said finally. "I want you to meet my wife, Ruhama."

"Well, I reckon I know Ruhama all right," smiled Lew as he gently pulled himself from his mother's embrace. "But you was a Shepherd the last I knowed."

Ruhama came around the table and stood next to her husband. She smiled at Lew. "You have a new niece just three months old."

"Well, now, that's happy news," said Lew with a grin. "I'm real partial to nieces. What's her name?"

"Her name is Sabra," answered Ruhama.

Just then a cry erupted from the other room. When Ruhama moved to attend to the child, Lew stopped her.

"Let me," he said. Soon he returned with the child in his arms.

"Hey there, little Saby. Say hello to your old uncle."

Ruhama looked worried, but the child had stopped crying. "He's good with the little ones," explained Mary Wetzel, smiling at the unlikely sight of her rugged son dropping into a rocking chair with the little girl nestled against his breast.

"Tell us what happened to you, Lew," enjoined Jacob. "It's been a hell of a long time since we saw you."

As he rocked the child, Lew recounted the long story of his adventures in the south. He left out any mention of the girl who had been the real cause of his troubles. By the time he was finished, Ruhama had taken the child, fed her, and put her to bed.

"Now, son, I hope you will stay with us for awhile," was the plea of Mary Wetzel. "You don't look like your old self. We need to fatten you up a bit."

"Sorry, Ma, I can't stay long. I've got unfinished business in Natchez."

When his mother shook her head and sighed, he embraced her. "Don't be sad, I'll stay for a few days. Long enough to eat some of your good cookin'. I've been dreamin' of that fer a long, long time."

September 20, 1799

The few days to be spent in the neighborhood that Wetzel had promised his mother stretched into several weeks. When he began to receive hints from his brothers of the need to spend some time in the hayfield, Lew discovered an urgent need to go to Kentucky. He signed on to help guide a family down the river to their new home in Mason County, Kentucky.

When they arrived at Limestone, Wetzel went looking for Simon Kenton and was chagrined to learn that Simon had moved on with his family to the Ohio country. There were many acquaintances there, however, and Lew found one of his favorite members of Kenton's boys, a rugged, fun-loving man named Andrew Grove. The two friends got drunk together the first night, and when John Young learned that Wetzel was back in town, he insisted that Lew stay at his house. It was there, of course, that McCurdy's troops had taken Wetzel prisoner nearly ten years earlier.

The time passed quickly and pleasantly for Wetzel, and he had lost some of the zeal that had driven him to go south again. It returned again when a boat arrived from Wheeling, commanded by a New Orleans trader, Jeremiah Kindall, from Brownsville on the Monongahela River. He had employed Captain Samuel Davis and four other men to hunt and kill wild meat to be sold in New Orleans.

When they landed in Limestone and found that Lew Wetzel was there, Kindall sent Davis to find Wetzel and hire him to go along. It took no argument, for Lew saw the opportunity as exactly what he needed to get back to his original mission. After several more days, the Kindall party left Limestone and moved off downriver. They made occasional stops and spent days hunting, then took time for smoking and jerking the meat. They passed by Fort Washington and the growing community around it, which had been named Cincinnati by General St. Clair in 1790.

The next point of interest was the Falls of the Ohio, the major obstacle to shipping on the Ohio River. The falls extended for about two miles, and the level of the river dropped by over twenty feet over that stretch. The growing town of Louisville, so named for King Louis XVI of France by George Rogers Clark, was situated on the south side. Just past Louisville there was a series of islands, which formed channels called chutes. Whether boats could pass depended on the water levels.

The north chute, which came to be called the Indian chute, was the easiest to navigate and could be passed successfully with great care and enough water flow. When the water was low, a portage was necessary. Fearful of losing his supplies and the small amount of cured meat they had already obtained, Kindall directed his men to unload the boat. The contents would be carried down to the town of Clarksville which was on the north bank at the foot of the rapids. Four of the men, including Kindall and Wetzel, floated the boat over the rapids, which they managed with no great difficulties.

"That was quite a ride," Lew informed Davis when they met on the shore at Clarksville.

"Glad it was you and not me," chuckled Davis.

Days later they came past the famous Cave-in-Rock, a known lair of bandits and river pirates. Many rivermen had lost their cargoes—and some, their lives—in trying to get past this spot.

"Sam Mason's been operatin' out of there," noted Sam Davis. "You remember him, don't ya, Lew?"

"I know a Sam Mason," agreed Lew. "But I didn't think he was no robber."

"Well, he is, and there ain't no doubt about it, so I hear."

"I guess Pa did think he was a horse thief now that I think on it." Lew remembered Mason as a soldier at Fort Henry. "He was runnin' a tavern in Wheelin' last time I seed him."

When they reached the mouth of the Ohio and spilled out into the Mississippi, Kindall ordered them to land the boat across on the Spanish side. There was good open land there, he thought, that would be a good place to find buffalo. After securing the boat, they made camp and planned to spend several days hunting in the area. All this led Wetzel to a new predicament.

He had chosen to hunt by himself, moving up the shoreline past where the Ohio entered on the opposite shore. A densely wooded area rose up in front of him and across the base of a peninsula that extended northward into a big loop in the Mississippi. It was late in the day when he spotted a small buck stepping out of the edge of the woods into an open glade covered with tall grass.

Finding a clear path for his shot, Wetzel quickly raised his rifle and fired. The deer was hit but not dropped, and he bounded back into the woods at least twenty yards ahead of where the hunter was standing. For maybe the first time in his life, Wetzel made the mistake of not reloading his gun. He plunged in after the retreating animal, intending to finish him off with his knife.

Wetzel hadn't gone far when he realized he had company. Ahead of him three stalwart and dark figures emerged from the trees. As he instinctively raised his rifle, he remembered that it was empty. Turning back, he began to run when a long stick was pushed in front of his legs, and he tumbled to the ground.

Immediately two Indians jumped on his back, and powerful arms pinned his own against his sides. In spite of his efforts, he was overpowered, and his wrists were bound behind his back. His adversaries pulled him to his feet. A tall brave stood in front of him.

"No kill," said the warrior, pointing at Wetzel. "White man pay."

There were seven braves in all, and from their appearance, Wetzel thought they might be Shawnees. *But what were Shawnees doing here?* he wondered. He did not know that a large contingent of the Shawnee tribe had moved many years ago to land not far from this very spot. Now he could only berate himself for his carelessness. "Guess all those days in jail has ruined me for huntin' Injuns," he muttered under his breath.

The tall Indian seemed to be in charge, and he led them back a couple of miles to their permanent camp. There were a half dozen more warriors at the camp, and an hour later, two more came in carrying the carcass of the buck Wetzel had shot. There was a white man at the camp, or at least half-white Wetzel guessed, dressed like a French trader. The leader spoke with the man and pointed at Lew, who could hear him say again, "White man pay."

"I guess that's all the English he knows," Wetzel said to himself.

He watched as the trader came over to him. "Hello. My name's Joe Lorimer," the man announced in English with a slight French accent. "I live among the Cape Girardeau Shawnees. My father brought them to this country almost twenty years ago."

"I'm Lew Wetzel."

"By God, I've heard of you," said Lorimer with some excitement.

"How could that be?" wondered Wetzel. "I ain't never been around here before."

"Do you know a trader named Pierre Le Clerk? He told me about you."

"I know Le Clerk. Didn't know he came way over here."

"It's probably best for you if these braves don't know who you are. They might want to avenge their brothers." Lorimer had lowered his voice to something just above a whisper. "Le Clerk told me you're famous for killing red men."

"I've killed a few," admitted Wetzel. "The tall one there said 'No kill'."

"Yes they want to ransom you. They know all about your hunting party and have been watching for just such a chance."

"Hell, they may be out o' luck on that. I doubt Kindall would pay much fer me. What do they want?"

"Gunpowder mostly, I think," answered Lorimer.

"But Kindall has no idea where I am."

"I'm going to see him now, and we'll be back in the morning if he chooses to come. You'll be kept here. It may not be too comfortable for you, but there's nothing I can do about that."

Lorimer was soon gone, and Wetzel was tied to a tree at the edge of the camp. He was not mistreated, and after it was dark and the Indians had finished their supper, one of them brought Wetzel some water and a piece of the venison they had cooked. The meat tasted good, and Lew thought it only right that they give him some of what he had shot in the first place. He had trouble sleeping, for his position was cramped and the deer hide strips tied to his arms were cutting into his wrists. He was resolved not to complain, and he endured the pain, falling into a restless sleep sometime in the early hours.

Wetzel was not at all sure that Kindall would try to rescue him, especially since he would be required to come to the Indian camp where he might fear for his own safety. He was quite relieved in midmorning when Lorimer showed up and Kindall was with him.

"What happened to you?" was Kindall's greeting. "I didn't expect you to be captured by no Injuns."

"Don't reckon I know," answered Lew. "Careless, I guess."

Their conversation was interrupted by Lorimer and the Indian chief, whom Lorimer called Big Tree. Big Tree spoke a flurry of words in his native tongue and ended with his oft-repeated phrase in English, "White man pay."

Wetzel was taken back to his tree and tied up as before. Negotiations between Big Tree and Kindall went on for sometime, but Lew could not hear what was being said. After an hour, Lorimer and Kindall came over to where Wetzel was held.

"You've cost me a cask of powder, Wetzel," grinned Kindall. "I hope to God you're worth it."

"It'll take another day to make the exchange," explained Lorimer. "In the meantime, you'll have to stay here."

"I'm much obliged to you both for helpin' me outta this mess," said Lew. "Especially you, Jeremiah. Reckon I'll be right here when you get back."

The two men nodded and walked away.

"Damn," exclaimed Wetzel. "It's all the fault of that damned Pedro!"

October 25, 1799

The freeing of Lewis Wetzel from captivity among the Cape Girardeau Shawnees had taken two full days. When the exchange was complete, Jeremiah Kindall had decided to move his hunting camp further down the Mississippi, although he wanted to stay close to the region where a number of buffalo had been seen.

"We'd better be extra careful," he warned his men. "Them damned Injuns may want more of our powder."

Hunters were directed now to go out in teams. Wetzel, still embarrassed that he had been captured, was paired with James Fulton, and they had been successful in several excursions. Today, having ventured more than three miles from camp, they had killed a large buffalo cow and were facing the problem of getting the meat transported. There were two horses at the camp brought along for just this purpose.

"You go back and get us a horse," Lew said to Fulton. "I'll stay here and guard the kill."

"I told you we shoulda brought one with us in the first place," protested Fulton. "Why don't you go back for the horse?"

"I'd be glad to," said Wetzel. "But I saw a passel of Injuns behind that tree line over there and thought maybe you'd rather I stay here."

That ended the argument, and Fulton hurried away, thinking he'd best bring some others with him.

Wetzel left the carcass lying in the trough of a large buffalo wallow that led up into a stand of cottonwoods, going in among the trees himself. He had seen some Indians, although not sure how many, and he thought it might be best to get out of the open and keep watch. He expected that the Indians might come and get the meat for themselves, thinking the white men had gone off and left it.

As he waited, Wetzel surveyed the terrain, amazed at how level the land was on this side of the Mississippi. For a man who grew up in the hill country of western Virginia, it was difficult to imagine such flatness. More than two hours passed when Wetzel saw Fulton and two others leading a horse toward where the dead buffalo was located. They stopped some twenty yards short and surveyed the scene.

"Wetzel ain't here," said Fulton. "God, you don't suppose the damned red men carried him off again."

"Not this time," shouted Lew, descending from his hiding place.

"God, you scared the hell outta me," exclaimed Fulton. "Did ya see them Injuns again?"

"Not a one," said Wetzel. "Let's get this meat loaded up and git outta here."

They quickly carved up the carcass choosing the best cuts, which they stuffed into pouches and tied to the horse's back. They wasted no time and arrived at the camp on the shore of the river in less than an hour.

"We need to move on," Fulton remarked to Kindall. "Wetzel saw a big party of Injuns."

"Is that right, Lew?" asked Kindall, who had been nervous about this very thing ever since Wetzel's capture.

"Well, I saw a party of Injuns all right, but I can't say how many for sure."

"Are we in danger, do you think?"

Wetzel, who was very much in favor of moving on down the river, for he was anxious to get on with the errand that had brought him along in the first place, thought carefully before giving his answer.

"I reckon we could be. If what I saw was a scoutin' party, there could be a hundred or more of the varmints. In that case, we're in big danger."

"I guess we should move on down the river a ways, but we have to wait for Davis. Him and Brown are still out somewhere."

"I think we should go on anyway," offered Fulton, whose fears were growing by the minute.

"Do you agree with that, Lew?" asked Kindall once more. "Should we leave right now?"

"I can't say, Jeremiah," answered Wetzel. "It could be just a small party, and if so, they would never chance hittin' us."

He watched and noted the expressions on the faces of Kindall and the other three men. He knew that if he pressed a bit, Kindall would order everything loaded on the boat, and they would push on down the river. He favored this, but he did feel bad about Davis.

"Lew, you know Injuns better'n any of us," said Kindall. "Do you think they'll come?"

"I'm surprised they didn't come in on me when James left. It could mean they was waitin' for the rest of their party."

"I think we'd better go," said Kindall. "Pack her up, boys, and git everything on the boat."

"You want me to wait here for Davis and Brown?" asked Wetzel.

"No, it wouldn't be fair. They'll figure it out and come after us." Kindall felt bad, but what else could he do?

It was getting dark, and a chilly wind had blown up by the time they pushed the big flatboat off and into the current. After they had travelled several hours, Kindall began to feel guilty about Davis and ordered them to put ashore.

"We'll make camp here, it's a good spot," ordered Kindall. The ground was flat and surrounded by heavy undergrowth. "We'll wait here for Davis and Brown."

Wetzel, having informed Kindall that he wanted to scout the area, slipped away in the night.

Davis and Brown returned to the original camp just after dark, after an unsuccessful hunt.

"They went off and left us," exclaimed Davis. "Them sons of bitches."

"What'll we do?" wondered Brown. "We ain't got no food nor nothin'."

"We'll make us a raft and go after 'em. I'm ready to kill somebody. That's fer sure."

The two men constructed a raft the next morning and got it out into the river. Things went well for a while, but then the raft hit a half-submerged log and fell apart. Davis was swept away but righted himself and was able to climb out onto a small cottonwood-covered island. He thought he saw Brown scramble onto the shore, but he wasn't sure. He never saw Brown again.

Though safe on the island, Davis had nothing to eat, and he spent two days there, surviving on a few scrawny berries he discovered. On the morning of the third day, having scoured the entire island, he was overjoyed to find a canoe stuffed under some heavy bushes, left there no doubt by an Indian hoping to use it again some day.

The canoe seemed okay, and Davis, breaking off a dead limb to serve as a paddle, got the craft into the water and was soon making his way downstream. In a couple of hours, he spied Kindall's camp on the western shore and managed to guide the little canoe to the bank. He began screaming as soon as he was ashore.

"Kindall, you son of a bitch, where are you?"

Wetzel, who had returned that very day, was resting against a tree some distance away and out of sight of the men in the camp, when he heard Davis shouting. He was glad Davis was all right, but he sensed that big trouble was coming.

Kindall emerged from his shelter on the boat and jumped ashore, striding directly to where Davis stood, continuing his rant. When Davis saw him, he shook his fist and began to berate Kindall directly.

"You damned fool, why did you leave me?"

Kindall listened until Davis ended his diatribe.

"Sam," he began quietly. "I don't blame you for being mad, but I felt we had to get away from that camp because of the Indian threat."

"Indian threat? What Indian threat? I never saw no damned Indians."

"Lew Wetzel saw them. Said there could be hundreds of them, and they was real close. I feared we'd all be lost if they came after us."

"Hell, I think Wetzel was just lyin' to you. He's been wantin us to move on anyway."

"I don't think so, Sam. Fulton was with him when he made that report."

"Well, I think he's a rascal, and I aim to settle this with him. Where is he?"

Wetzel heard this conversation, and he had no desire to tangle with Davis.

He didn't really blame Davis, anyway, and clearly Kindall had left him to take the blame. Since he had his few possessions with him, having taken them along on his scout, he decided to take his leave.

"I'll go on to New Madrid," he muttered. "And then on to Natchez."

By the time Davis came looking for him, Lew Wetzel was long gone.

August 20, 1800

Lew Wetzel finally received some good news. It was a long time coming, he thought. After leaving Kindall's party, he had made his way to New Madrid where he found work on another flatboat headed for New Orleans. Although his real destination was Natchez, he thought it only fair to complete his promise to go all the way to the Crescent City. Shortly after that, he had returned up the river to Natchez.

Wetzel's first visit was to Pedro Hermoso's old home, which he found in disarray. The cabin was partly burned, although the fireplace and its chimney were intact. The old shed in the woods had been demolished. There was no sign of the former occupants. It was no big surprise to Lew, for he knew that Pedro had been in jail for awhile, and there was no way to know what had happened to his family. The girls would be grown-up by now, he figured, and probably married.

He had immediately left for Natchez, hoping that someone there might know what had happened to the Hermosos. His first target in Natchez was the Under-the-Hill Inn, and as he approached the tavern, he could not help but think of the beautiful Maria whom he had loved at first sight. He was amazed to find her brother Henry still working as a bartender, although he learned later that Henry now owned the establishment. Henry King did not remember Lewis Wetzel, nor did he have any idea concerning the whereabouts of Pedro Hermoso. He did recall that his father had arrested Pedro for stealing horses, but he hadn't been seen again in Natchez after being sent off to jail.

Wetzel approached every man in the room and asked the same question. Only one man even knew of Hermoso, but he knew nothing more than anyone else. Thinking that Richard King might know something, Wetzel thought about going to him but decided against it. He couldn't be sure that King might want him returned to the authorities, and it was too risky. His efforts led to one after another disappointment. Twice he found people who had known Pedro and thought they knew where to find him. Neither was correct. Eventually Lew went back to the vicinity of New Orleans, where he began a systematic search in the outlying regions. He also visited every inn and every tavern, hoping to find someone who might have seen Hermoso. The months had passed, and Wetzel began to think it was time to give up this fruitless search.

Then his luck changed. He had left New Orleans and spent three days in the woods working around the west side of Lake Pontchartrain. A decision to move on around to the west and north past the end of Lake Maurepas turned out to be a wise one. He had followed on old trail across the Amite River and up to the Tickfaw, where he discovered a tavern in an old shack along the riverbank. He was surprised to find it, but he had never come this far around the lake before. Inside the tavern, Wetzel found a grizzled old man, short and stocky with white hair and only one arm. "Hello, stranger," was the greeting. "My name's Jeremiah Woods. What's yours?"

My God, thought Lew, *This man's an American*. Aloud, he started to say his name, then thought better of it. "Jacob Martin" is what he said, thinking it quite clever to combine the names of his two brothers.

"I'm mighty glad to meet you, Jacob," replied Jeremiah with a wide smile. "Don't git too many strangers around here. What can I git ya'?"

"A whiskey, I guess," said Lew. "If it ain't too early."

"Hell, never too early for whiskey," laughed Woods. "Do ya want boughten or my home brew?"

"What's the difference?" asked Lew.

"Well, one costs fifty cents and is likely to put you on your ass," cackled Woods. "The other'n costs a dollar."

"Well, I ain't much for bein' on my ass, but the fifty cents sounds good."

Wetzel was excited to learn that Jeremiah was from Kentucky. "How'd you lose that arm?" he asked after several minutes of conversation. "Injuns?"

"Naw, nothin' that excitin," laughed Woods. "Damned tree limb fell on me. They had to cut the arm off."

Wetzel wondered how the man had ended up all the way down here, but he changed the subject.

"Ever hear of a man named Pedro Hermoso?" he asked.

Woods, who had bent down behind his short bar to retrieve a glass, straightened up quickly at Wetzel's question. His face betrayed his shock at hearing that name. "What if I do?" replied Woods, who normally would not be so quick to give up the name of one of his customers. "Why do you ask?"

"I have some unfinished business with him," answered Lew, delighted at this turn of events.

"As a matter of fact, so do I. That son of a bitch owes me money."

"Well, I owe him something," said Wetzel. "Can you tell me where to find him?" Lew tried to keep his voice calm and nonthreatening.

"I can, though I don't suppose I should." Woods stood looking at Wetzel for a long moment. "Him and his woman live on a place down this river about a mile from the lake. I ain't sure what he does down there."

"I'm much obliged," said Lew, trying to keep the exultation out of his voice.

The two men chatted for a while longer, and Wetzel bought another drink. Woods asked to see his rifle, noting that it had been sometime since he'd seen a good Kentucky rifle.

It was early afternoon when Wetzel walked out and moved swiftly along the right bank of the river. He glided among the trees and bushes that lined the riverbank, staying out of sight as much as possible.

After an hour or so, he came to a clearing that paralleled a bend in the river and noted that a small cabin stood at the back. The clearing was surrounded by woods, and Wetzel moved stealthily around one side in order to get a better look at the cabin. A dog began to bark, and Wetzel shrank back farther into the forest. He was able to see, however, that a man had emerged from the log house holding a rifle and surveying the scene, trying to locate what had upset his hound.

"That ain't Pedro," Wetzel muttered to himself. "I'd best git on outta here."

As he pushed far away from the river before turning again to follow its path, the sound of the barking dog faded and was gone. He found himself in a swampy area, and he looked for higher, drier ground.

He had been around enough to know there was danger from poisonous snakes and even alligators. His mind, however, was firmly focused on his mission, and he knew that its culmination might well be near. He swung back toward the river, sure from what old man Woods had told him that he was bound to find Hermoso's place before too much longer. He was able to put out of his mind the stifling heat, which had his clothes soaked in sweat. He passed by a second homestead, but it seemed to be completely deserted. He took a chance and entered the little shack, trying to find some clue that it belonged to Pedro. A short search convinced him otherwise, and he moved on.

It was beginning to get dark when Wetzel saw a small stream entering the Tickfaw on the far side. A bit further on, he could see another clearing near a sharp bend in the river, which would take it finally into its destination at Lake Maurepas. A rough-built house stood in the center of the open area along with a small shed at the back. Smoke was curling from the chimney.

"By God, I reckon that's Pedro's place all right," he said aloud quietly. "Looks like somebody's at home. I bet I know what he does in that shed too."

After completing a circle of the entire clearing, Wetzel waited behind a clump of bushes near the river's edge. This very moment had been on his mind since he'd left the prison, but now he was undecided about his next move. He checked to make sure his rifle was loaded, and he rested his hand on the head of the tomahawk whose handle was stuffed under his belt. He wanted Pedro to know who was confronting him, but he wanted the rifle ready in case that was his only choice.

He dropped his pouch under a tree and prepared to make his dash across the grassy field to the front door. He moved along the edge in order to minimize the distance he would be in the open. He judged that the shortest distance would be at least fifty yards, and then decided it would be best to wait until darkness fell. His blood was up, and emotions were high, but Wetzel had learned at an early age that a hunter must be very patient. He settled in to wait, his only concern being that Hermoso would leave the house on some nightly mission. There was a back door, and it would be hard to see him leave if Pedro took that option.

An hour had passed before Wetzel was satisfied that he could reach the door to the house without being seen. The moon was still low in the east and had not cleared the trees on the far side, when Wetzel emerged from the bushes and trotted toward the little shack. The grass was tall in places, and there were enough dips and irregularities in the terrain to cause him to be wary of falling. His old abilities had not deserted him, and he made it to his objective with no problems. There was to be no more waiting, and he pushed the door open and charged through, holding his rifle in his left hand. The fireplace was on the wall to his right, and Ana Sophia stood in front of it. When she saw Wetzel, she began screaming.

"It is you!" she yelled and began to sob.

Wetzel was at her side in two quick bounds, grabbing her left arm and pulling her in toward himself.

"Where is that son of a bitch husband of yours?" he cried.

"Not here, not here!" She tried to pull away, but his grip was hard and tight. "No hurt me."

Wetzel heard the door slam, and he could see there was another room at the back, and that Hermoso had exited through the back door he'd observed earlier.

"The hell he ain't," shouted Wetzel, who threw Ana Sophia to the floor and ran for the back door. As he ran out, he could see very little in the darkness, although he could hear the rustling of leaves and branches near the river.

"Damn," he exclaimed. "I bet the bastard has a boat out there. If he gets down the river and into that lake I might never find him again." Wetzel ran as fast as he could, rushing toward the river. He tripped once on a heavy clump of grass but was unhurt and renewed his efforts to catch up with Hermoso before he could get away on the water. He pushed through the thicket that lined the riverbank, and when he found an opening at the edge, looked in vain for Pedro. He could hear sounds of splashing water, and though it was quite dark, he could see the dim outline of a boat and a man frantically paddling it down the stream.

He raised his rifle and tried to aim when suddenly a high-flying cloud cleared the moon, which had risen well above the tree line. The moonbeams were bright enough for him to see his target, and he quickly steadied the gun and squeezed the trigger. Almost instantly, another cloud had obscured the moonlight, and he could not tell if his shot had hit home. It seemed that he might have heard a scream of a man in pain, but he couldn't be sure. For all he could see, there seemed to have been no change in the direction of the boat. He started to move along the bank in that direction, but a combination of overhanging limbs and a stout bush impeded him.

By the time Wetzel could see downstream again, there was nothing to see. *He's gone round the curve, I suppose*, he thought. For a moment he thought about how to angle across the land and try to intercept the boat farther down before it reached Lake Maurepas. Then a peaceful calm overtook him, and he sat down against a fallen log.

"I reckon he's got away," Wetzel said aloud. "I s'pose I might uv hit him. Anyway, he knows who was after him, and if he's still alive, he'll have to keep lookin' fer me as long as he lives."

July 8, 1801

Sam Mason's life had changed considerably since serving as a captain of militia at Fort Henry more than twenty years earlier. His name was quite well-known now along the lower Ohio and Mississippi river valleys. He was probably the most famous outlaw in the area, and his name brought fear as well as loathing. Only the Harpe brothers had a bloodier reputation, and they were diminished somewhat since Big Harpe had been captured and hung, his head displayed on a fence post.

Mason regarded himself in an entirely different way, often protesting that he never killed anyone unless it was necessary. "I only want their money," he explained. He led a small band of cutthroats to carry out his thefts but had put together a wider system of associates to help him fence his items and avoid the authorities. At first, he had spent his time waylaying boats coming down the Ohio, with headquarters near Henderson, Kentucky, and later at Cave-in-Rock. The problem was that the stolen goods had to be delivered to markets in Natchez and New Orleans, and often his henchmen did not return with the money but kept it for themselves.

Mason had moved his enterprise down the Mississippi, and lived on the Spanish side of the river. The Spanish authorities did not bother to try to apprehend him since he mostly committed his crimes on the American side. Still he maintained hideouts in various places. Mason had established himself in New Madrid, holding a Spanish passport.

A bit later, he created a new headquarters at a place called Little Prairie, about thirty miles below New Madrid. Though safe from the prospect of arrest, these locations were a long way from the Natchez Trace. Mason had shifted his tactics to robbing travelers on the Trace, which was a common route for flatboat traders returning north with the money earned from the products sold in New Orleans or Natchez. One secret lair was established at Rocky Springs, and another a bit further south on Bayou Pierre.

Today Mason's little band was on the Bayou Pierre, the camp nestled in a thick stand of trees lying in a big loop in the creek that lay on the very edge of the Trace. Mason was anticipating the arrival of some travelers coming up from Natchez, carrying bulging purses he hoped. Seven people were with him, including his two oldest sons and one woman, the wife of his son John. Her name was Marguerite, and she often assisted in the planned robberies by posing as a prostitute, an enticement that was usually successful in luring the unwary traveler into the waiting trap. Also along was John Setton, who had joined them earlier when they were up the Arkansas River. His real name was Wiley Harpe, the younger of the famous Harpe brothers.

Although Mason did not know who Setton was, he had his suspicions. The younger Harpe had disappeared after his brother's death, and Mason had never seen the Harpes, but he had heard them described. Wiley Harpe was known for his red hair and his treacherous look. It was better, Mason thought, not to pursue those suspicions, for though he did not trust Setton, he found him to be quite useful. When killing was necessary, John Setton was quite willing to do the job.

Yesterday, the mail carrier, John Swaney had passed by, and Mason had intercepted him.

Swaney carried mail along the Trace between Nashville and Natchez, a distance of 550 miles. He rode a fine horse and averaged about fifty-five miles a day, completing the round trip every three weeks. He was well-known to travelers and was left unmolested by both white outlaws and renegade Indians. Sam Mason and his gang also observed this unwritten rule. He often assured Swaney that no mail carrier need fear him or his men.

"Hello, John," Mason said on this occasion. "On your way up to Nashville, I reckon."

"That I am," answered Swaney.

"Well, I don't want to slow you down. Just wonderin' if you might've passed any travelers along the way." Mason knew that the mail carrier traveled at a much more rapid rate than most other parties.

Swaney smiled. "Now Sam, I ought not to be tellin' about other men's business."

"Oh, surely not," agreed Mason. "But if there was, we could be ready to welcome them to our camp and treat 'em real nice."

"Oh, yes, I know pretty much how it is you welcome travelers, Sam."

Swaney well knew what gangs like Sam Mason's were up to, but he knew that his own safety depended on his discretion. He did not report their activities, and he did sometimes alert them about people he saw on the trail. He knew that some people in Natchez suspected him of helping the outlaws, but Swaney had his own standards, and he tried not to betray them. More than once, his appearance on the scene of a robbery had prevented bloodshed.

"There was a party, about a day back," he admitted finally. "Four men and a couple of extra packhorses. Now, if you don't mind, I'll be on my way."

"Farewell to you, John," shouted Mason after the departing horseman. He was quite satisfied with the information he had obtained, and he hurried back to his camp.

The party expected by Sam Mason was not far away. They had stopped to eat and then took their time, resting awhile before undertaking the journey again. Abraham Parker was the leader, and he had brought three rugged frontiersmen along to help him on the return trip. He was well aware of the dangers, especially since they were carrying a large amount of money with them. Some of the cash was in paper money, which had been carefully sewed into pockets inside the men's clothing. There was a significant amount, however, stowed in saddlebags on the packhorses.

Lewis Wetzel was anxious to get moving. After his episode on the Tickfaw River, Lew had rejected any thought of going back to Hermoso's cabin and dealing with Ana Sophia. Harming a woman was reprehensible to Wetzel, so he decided to go back north to Natchez. There was always the possibility that one of the Hermosos might have the authorities after him, but he doubted that there would be any danger in Natchez. He stayed in the area through the winter, enjoying some hunting trips up the Black River. He began to fall in love with the countryside, and it occurred to him that he might enjoy settling in that region.

Wetzel had experienced a calmness in his life that was unusual for him. The nagging lust for revenge that had haunted him after his escape from the prison in New Orleans was gone now. It surprised him in a way, for he had not finished dealing with Hermoso in quite the way he expected. It no longer seemed to matter to him now. He enjoyed the days around Natchez. There was plenty going on, including every kind of vice that man could imagine. He visited some of the houses of ill repute, and it was in one of them that he saw Jim Girty, one of the famous renegades of the Ohio Valley.

Wetzel had never seen Girty, at least that he knew about; but when told who the man was, Wetzel had put down an urge to attack him. Girty lived much of his life among the Shawnees and was often with them during attacks on the Americans. Girty's lover, Marie Dufour, was the madam in one of the houses, and Wetzel made sure he avoided that one.

In the spring, Lew returned to New Orleans. It was there that he ran into Abraham Parker. Parker had delivered a flatboat packed with goods to New Orleans and was ready to return with the earnings. Instead of going by ship, Parker intended to go up the Natchez Trace. He had two men ready to go with him, and when he saw Wetzel, he quickly hired him to go along as well.

Parker bought horses for all four men, plus two others to serve as packhorses.

Once they had begun the journey home, Wetzel found himself anxious to get there. He was feeling particularly sorry about what he knew had been neglect of his mother. He wanted to see her now, when so often in the past he had desired to get away.

Parker was still sitting with his back against a tree when Wetzel approached. The other two men were sleeping.

"Ain't it time to be goin'?"

"Now, Lew, I suppose it is, but I don't mind the men getting some extra rest. This trip won't be easy."

"I reckon not," agreed Wetzel. "How about I do a bit of scoutin' ahead of us? We've heard plenty about the dangers of robbers along here."

"That's a good idea, Lew. We'll wait here a bit longer, then come on."

"It'll be best if I go on foot," said Lew. "Bring my horse on for me then."

Glad to be alone for a while, Wetzel moved out along the trace, which mostly followed an old Indian path, called by some old-timers the Devil's Backbone. It passed through woods, where the trees were laced with grapevines and Spanish moss, and in other places through heavy canebrakes, with cane that grew thick and tall. The path itself was narrow and difficult for a horse to pass through. In some places there were depressions and also caves. There were numerous spots where a traveler could easily be ambushed.

Wetzel swung away from the trail and ventured far from one side, then crossed and did the same on the other. In one of his treks far to the left side, he came to the creek, the Bayou Pierre, although he did not know the name. As he moved up the creek, it turned down toward the trace, and after a short distance, he could hear someone talking. Wetzel moved back a ways, then crossed the path moving up the other side, well hidden in the heavy underbrush. He caught sight of what looked to him like a rough lean-to, with its opening toward the trace. He took a prone position and wiggled carefully forward until he had a clear view.

A woman was sitting on a small stool in front of the lean-to. No one else was in sight, and Wetzel wondered who she was talking with earlier. Although he realized the possibility of a deceptive trap, Wetzel found his body responding to the sight, for the woman had struck a very provocative pose, wearing a loose fitting blouse that left her exposed. A rough-hewn signboard was propped up next to her on which was written, Liquor and Entertainment. Although Lew could not read the writing, he had a very good idea of what was being proposed.

"Well, Lew," he muttered to himself, "you'd better not sample any o' this honey." There was at least one other person present, he figured, and it wouldn't be long before Parker and the other two men came along the trail. "I think I'll see for myself just what's goin' on here," he said quietly, and then he rose to his feet and made his way across the narrow road.

"Well, well, hello handsome stranger," called out Marguerite Mason as Wetzel appeared in front of her.

"Don't reckon I'm too handsome," replied Wetzel, self-consciously rubbing the pockmarks on his cheek. "What are you doin' way out here?"

"Why, this is where the good business is," answered Marguerite with a broad smile and fluttering eyelids. "We figure you travelers are needin' some fun about now."

Still cradling his rifle in front of him, Wetzel let his eyes sweep from side to side, searching for the woman's partner.

"What are you lookin' for, honey?" asked Marguerite. "I like a man to look me right in the eye when he's askin' for somethin'."

"I heard you talkin' to somebody," said Wetzel. "I think he ought to make himself known about now."

"Why, honey, I was just talkin' to myself. Why don't you come and sit next to me?"

Wetzel was sorely tempted and wanted to more than sit with her. But it was very clear to him what would happen once he agreed to go into the lean-to with this desirable woman. His duty was to get back to Parker and warn him that there were robbers about.

"I reckon that'd be a mighty big mistake," he finally said to her.

"Are you by yourself, honey?" she asked.

"I am, and I'd better be movin' on," said Lew. "Besides," he said with a grin, "I ain't got no money."

Before she could say more, Wetzel moved on up the trace, continuing until he was out of her sight. Moving far into the woods on his right, he made a wide circle back to the trail, expecting to intercept Parker and the others before they reached the ambush site. He did not have long to wait. He stood in the middle of the path, watching Parker and his men ride toward him single file.

"Hello, Lew," greeted Parker, stopping his horse just short of where Wetzel was standing. "Find anything?"

"I did," stated Wetzel. "There's a band of robbers not far ahead, settin' up an ambush. They're usin a woman to git us to stop."

"How many?" asked John Wood, who had pulled up just behind Parker.

"Don't know," was Wetzel's reply. "But it wouldn't take many to pick us off on this narrow trail. I've found a way around, and I think that's what we should do. It'll be hard goin', but it'll be best."

"Tell me 'bout that woman," said the last man, Mose Thomas. "Were she good lookin'?"

"She was a looker all right, Mose," laughed Lew. "She'd turn you every way but loose, I'm thinkin'."

Parker directed them to follow Lew's lead, and they turned away into the woods.

Back at the lean-to, Sam Mason emerged from near the creek, just as a rider came in from down the trace.

"There's three men ridin' up here leadin' three more horses. They'll be here pretty soon," reported John Setton. "Those packhorses are loaded. Reckon they're carryin' lots o' coin."

"Well, we're goin' to let 'em go this time," said Mason.

"What?" cried Setton. "Are you crazy?"

"I'm not crazy and that's the point!" answered Mason with emphasis. "The man who was talkin' to Maggie there was Lew Wetzel."

"So who the hell is Lew Wetzel, and why does it matter?"

"Because Lew Wetzel ain't a man to be messin' with," replied Mason. "He's killed more Injuns than any ten men. He's scoutin' for the ones you saw, and he'd be sure to kill a bunch of us if we try to rob him and the others."

"Hell, I ain't afraid of him or nobody else," declared Setton, jumping down from his horse. "Let's set up and hit 'em just like we planned."

"It ain't worth it, I said," exclaimed Mason with some heat. "Let's go back to camp and wait for the next bunch to come along."

August 8, 1801

The rest of the trip north brought few unexpected difficulties for Abraham Parker and his men. At Colbert's Ferry on the Tennessee River, they had arrived in late afternoon, and the Chickasaw Indians who manned the ferry refused to take them across until the next day.

"We need to get across tonight," argued Parker, "so we can get an early start tomorrow."

He noticed several of the Indians eyeing Lew Wetzel, and he spoke to Lew about it.

"Stay in the back, behind the horses, Lew. These Indians may know the name of Lew Wetzel, and we don't need any extra trouble from them."

The mailman, Swaney, had warned Parker that the Indians at this ferry could prove to be quite contrary. Parker offered them double their usual fare, and finally the Indians agreed to a crossing even as the darkness was falling. It was ten days now since they had arrived at Nashville, the northern terminal of the Natchez Trace. Parker had been anxious to push on, and they spent only one night in Nashville. This morning they had set out from the town of Lexington in Kentucky on the last portion of the trip, heading up the well-used road to Washington and Maysville.

Parker now lived in Washington, and so that was the end of his journey. These were old stomping grounds for Wetzel, and he looked forward to seeing friends there. The road came along the Elkhorn River, and as they passed the remains of the buildings of old Bryan's Station, Wetzel asked that they stop for a moment.

"My brother Martin told me about this place," he said to Parker. "I think this was the fort called Bryan's Station. Martin came here and escaped from the Shawnees."

"I didn't know your brother had been a captive of the Indians," remarked Parker. "When was that?"

"I ain't much good at dates," replied Lew. "But I think it was before we went out with Brodhead."

As they moved up the road, they became aware of an unusually large amount of traffic headed in the same direction toward Maysville. There were wagons and carts carrying what appeared to be entire families, as well as men on horses, and some just walking. Occasionally a song would break out from one of the wagons, and others would join in.

"They're singing hymns," said Parker. "That's surprising. I wonder what is happening."

As they neared the little town of Paris, Parker could contain himself no longer, and he sought out one of the men on horseback riding just a few yards in front of him. He hailed the man who stopped and waited for Parker to reach his side.

"What can I do for you?" asked the man in a friendly tone. "My name is John Rankin."

"Pleased to meet you," answered Parker. "I am Abraham Parker now of Washington, Kentucky, and I am wondering what is going on with so many people on this road."

"They're going for the meeting of the sacrament over at Cane Ridge," said Rankin. "I am a Presbyterian minister, and I'm on my way there myself. I've come all the way from Logan County."

Parker, a very religious man in his own right, was intrigued. "Is this meeting just for Presbyterians? I'm a Methodist myself."

"You would be quite welcome, my friend," replied Rankin with great enthusiasm. "There will be Methodists and Baptists there, I'm sure. I've heard that William Burke, a fine Methodist preacher will be speaking."

"Really?" questioned Parker. "I've heard of him, but I'm a bit surprised at the mixing of the sects."

"There's a revival going on, my man, a feeling of love and friendship all over this land. These sacrament meetings have been happening all summer. Please come and join us."

"I don't know," said Parker. "I've got some men with me."

"Bring them along," exclaimed Parker. "There'll be lots of preaching and singing, and tomorrow, a celebration of the sacrament, the Lord's Supper."

"These men are kind of rough," explained Parker. "Not sure they would fit in too well."

"It takes all kinds," answered Rankin. "They might be converted. It happens all the time."

"Where is this Cane Ridge?"

"Just a few miles to the east of Paris. You can follow the crowd."

Parker shook his head and turned away. "Thank you Mr. Rankin," he shouted back as he made his way to where his men were standing, holding the horses.

"So what is it, Abe?" asked John Wood.

"It's a camp meeting, a religious one with lots of singing and preaching," explained Parker. "I wouldn't mind lookin' in on it."

"Well, count me out," said Wood. "I ain't interested in listenin' to no preacher."

"Me neither," chimed in Mose Thomas. "Fact is, I'd much rather spend some time in this place we is just passin'."

They were just inside the little town of Paris, Kentucky, and on their immediate left was a large building called the Duncan Tavern. Parker stopped and motioned them to the side out of the rest of the traffic where he dismounted. They were in front of the Duncan Tavern. Wetzel was in sympathy with both Wood and Thomas, yet he felt that he owed something to Parker. He kept quiet and waited to see what Parker would say. Wood and Thomas got down from their horses, but Wetzel remained on his mount.

"I'm disappointed a little," admitted Parker, "for I'd really like to see what is going on at this meeting in Cane Ridge. Still I can't go on by myself, not with these packhorses loaded with treasure."

"Shouldn't be no danger at a religious meetin'," said Mose. "Them folks'll be too busy prayin' to be thinkin' about stealing."

"I'd like to think that," replied Abraham. "But there could be all kinds there. Besides, it's still forty to fifty miles up to Washington and Maysville."

"I'll stay with you," announced Lew quietly. "I can keep an eye on things whilst you attend the preachin'."

"I appreciate that, Lew. Are you sure you don't mind?"

"Well, I kind of deserted you the first time, and I reckon I ought to make that up to you."

"Hell, Abe," exclaimed Wood. "You'll be plenty safe with Lew. Mose and me'll get on up to Washington and wait fer you there."

Parker stood quietly for a moment, wondering if he should agree to this. Finally he said, "All right, Lew and me will go on to Cane Ridge. John, you and Mose already have half of your pay, and I'll give you the rest in Washington when we've reached there in two or three days."

"Sounds good to me," said John quickly.

Mose nodded his agreement.

"Take good care o' things now, Lew," laughed Mose. "We want to make sure we get the rest of what's comin' to us."

Wetzel nodded and picked up the reins of one of the packhorses, ready to move on. Parker shook hands with both

Wood and Thomas. He took the reins of the second packhorse from Thomas and climbed aboard his own mount. With a wave, he and Wetzel rejoined the people moving up the street while Wood and Thomas made their way to the door of the tavern.

Within a couple of hours, Parker and Wetzel reached the edge of the site of the meeting. The road had passed through a heavy canebrake, and now they could see a multitude of wagons and buggies parked among the trees.

Not far from them was a covered wooden lecture platform, which was being called the Tent, and beyond it some one hundred yards was the log building that housed the Cane Ridge Presbyterians. A man was standing on the platform, preaching in a loud voice to a large audience surrounding it. They could see that people were going in and out of the log church, indicating that there was preaching going on there as well.

"That looks like the state's governor, James Garrard," exclaimed Parker, pointing with excitement at the man on the platform. "This must be some very important meeting."

"You know the governor of Kentucky?" asked Wetzel.

"Can't say I know him," admitted Parker, "but I did meet him one time."

There had been heavy rains the day before so that the road, and the grounds as well, were in bad shape, filled with ruts and puddles.

"Let's go around to the far side," suggested Parker, "and see if we can find a good place to tie up the horses and make our own camp."

The large crowd made this a difficult task, but they found a spot several hundred yards past the meeting house. Wetzel made sure the horses were securely bound to some trees, yet with room to move around. He fed them with some grain carried in bags and used when no grass or other food was available. Parker made his way to the church building, and Wetzel sat down against a fallen log, planning to sleep a bit if he could.

Parker was met at the door of the church by Barton W. Stone, who was the minister at Cane Ridge.

"Hello, friend," was his greeting. "You're welcome to come in, but there are no seats left just now. I am Barton Stone, the minister here."

"I'm pleased to meet you, Mr. Stone. My name is Abraham Parker, and I am curious about the meetings here and what all is planned."

"As you can see, there is preaching here and out at the tent. This will go on for the rest of the day and early evening."

"We met a man named Rankin on the road out of Lexington," explained Abraham. "He said something about the sacrament."

"Oh yes," said Stone with a smile. "John Rankin arrived not long ago. He is inside. The Supper will be served tomorrow morning, which is Sunday, you know."

"Yes, I know, and I would like to attend. But I am a Methodist."

"Fine, fine," responded Stone with excitement. "Methodists are welcome. Brother Burke and I have worked that out." Stone was determined that there be no trouble between the denominations. He was destined to leave the Presbyterians himself not many years hence. "We'll have to do several sessions," added Stone, "since there will only be room for a hundred or so at a time."

"When will you begin?" asked Parker.

"Around eight in the morning I believe," replied Stone. "Be sure to join us later. Mr. Lyle and Mr. McNemur will be preaching this evening, and also Mr. Houston."

Parker enjoyed a meal with Wetzel and returned for the preaching, which moved outdoors because of the intense heat in the log church building. Wetzel chose to stay in their camp near the horses. As darkness fell, the numerous campfires reminded him of his days with Brodhead and with Logan. Yet this was much different. These people were intent on peace and love, not killing.

"I ain't never seen nothin' like this," he mused. He could hear the sounds of the preachers, but not what they were saying. He decided to put up a lean-to using a tent that Parker had brought with them. It had rained the previous day, and Wetzel thought the showers might return in the night. When he returned, Parker was beaming.

"You ought to have heard that preaching, Lew. It was awe-inspiring."

Wetzel laughed. "Your notion of pleasure is mighty strange, Abe. As fer me, I'm goin' to bed."

August 9, 1801

Lew Wetzel stood near the back of the crowd, but he could see and hear what was transpiring in front of him. A preacher had set up on the trunk of a fallen tree that had lodged against another tree, and he was preaching under an umbrella attached to a long pole held over him by one of his fellow Methodists. A steady rain was falling, having begun early in the morning. A large audience had gathered at the spot, more than one hundred yards east of the Cane Ridge meeting house, where others were still celebrating the Lord's Supper.

Parker had participated in the observance of the sacrament, as he described it, and had returned to their camp to inform Wetzel about his plans for the day. "I want to hear Burke preach," he said, "and some of the others. We'll leave tomorrow morning and go on to Washington."

"That's good," said Lew, who was wishing they were already on the way.

"Burke is a bit unhappy," Parker explained. "He wasn't asked to preach this morning by Mr. Stone, even though he thought he'd been promised. Anyway, he is ready now, and I want to get closer so I can hear him better."

Parker went on his way, and Lew moved up toward the gathering crowd. As he stood listening, Wetzel noticed a man standing next to him who had joined in the hymn singing with great enthusiasm and now was punctuating every sentence of the speaker with a loud "amen!".

The speaker stopped for a moment and asked the people to join him in a song.

Wetzel took the opportunity to question his neighbor.

"Who is the preacher?" he asked, tugging at the man's elbow.

"Why that's William Burke," came the answer. "He's mighty powerful, ain't he."

"Well, I ain't much of an expert on preachin'," said Wetzel with a chuckle.

"Are you saved yet, brother?" was the question. "I got saved yesterday. My name's Stephen Ruddell."

"Pleased to meet you," said Lew, glad to get the subject away from a question of salvation. "I'm Lew Wetzel."

"The hell you say," exclaimed Ruddell. "I've heard of you. You ain't exactly a friend to our red brothers."

As always, Wetzel was surprised to hear that some stranger knew who he was.

"How do you know anything about me?" Wetzel asked.

"I spent about fourteen years among the Shawnee," explained Ruddell. "I was a companion of the great warrior, Tecumseh. They called me Sinnantha, which means 'big fish'."

"How did that happen?"

"I was taken captive when the Indians and British under Bird captured my father's fort. They let me go after Wayne's victory in '94. Been livin' in Kentucky since."

"That don't tell me nothin' about how you heard of me."

"There was a French trader, Le Clerk was his name, I think," replied Ruddell.

"Damn, that Frenchman gits all over. You ain't the first he's told about me."

"Well, there's a Shawnee called Fire Heart, who knew about you too, and a brother of yours."

"My brother Martin spent three years with them bastards, then he got away."

"I don't think of them as bastards, Wetzel. I got to know 'em well, and they've got some real grievances against us white men."

This remark by Ruddell brought a dark look to Wetzel's face.

At this point, the preaching resumed, and Ruddell pointed ahead, indicating that he wanted to listen. Burke was preaching with fire and animation. "You sinners," he shouted. "You've got no hope except for Jesus. Change your filthy lives and accept salvation through Jesus Christ!"

At these words from the preacher, several people standing near him fell to the ground, lying perfectly still. On the other side of the half circle around the make-shift pulpit, a man began shaking and jerking, jumping around before falling. Next to him, a man began barking like a dog.

"What is this?" asked Wetzel. "Are these people crazy?"

"It's called the bodily exercises. The work of the Holy Spirit."

As they talked, several people went to pick up one of the listeners who had fallen. It was a woman, and she fell in such a way that her face was in a puddle of water. They laid her under a tree, and another umbrella was produced to shield her from the rain. She did not move.

"They'll be all right," said Ruddell. "God will protect them."

Wetzel shook his head and began to walk away. He neared a two-wheeled cart pushed off between two trees. A young girl was held up by a friend standing in the cart, and she was addressing a small crowd huddled around it in the rain. She wore a little hat, and the water dripped off the brim, but she was unaffected, the gleam in her eye accompanying a torrent of words. "Come and inherit the kingdom," cried the girl. "Become rich in the blood of the Lamb!"

How could a girl so young be talking like that, Wetzel wondered. "There are strange things happenin' here," he uttered aloud. He headed back to the lean-to at the camp he shared with Parker, determined to get out of the rain, and shut out the sounds that were making his stomach churn. He had been reflecting on his own life much more than usual, and all this preaching was not helping. He had never regarded his actions as being inappropriate, did not think of himself as a killer. Yet he was having trouble clearing his mind.

"To hell with this," he said as he settled in, hoping to sleep. "I'm ready to go home."

October 10, 1801

Wetzel had been home now for several weeks, and he was making the rounds visiting old acquaintances. Parker had agreed to leave for Washington on the next day, and once they reached there, Wetzel was free to go on his way. He was grateful to Parker, but the man could not stop talking about the events at Cane Ridge. He paid Wetzel the remainder of his wage and told him to keep the horse. Wetzel left immediately for home, choosing to follow along the Kentucky and Virginia side of the Ohio. His mother continued to beg him to stay on the homeplace, but Lew realized he would never be satisfied with that. He had made no plans, but he kept thinking about how much he liked the area on the Black River in Mississippi Territory.

One of his planned visits had been to the woman he had once loved, Lydia Boggs, now Lydia Shepherd. Lew had barely seen her since the day of the wedding, but he was seized one day with the thought that he really wanted to tell her for once how he had felt about her. He rode from the Wetzel cabin to the forks of the Wheeling, where he knew Lydia lived with her husband, Moses Shepherd. His mother had told him of the big mansion that Moses had built for Lydia, but Wetzel could not have imagined its magnificence until he saw it. His resolve at visiting Lydia began to melt away.

"By God, that's a big house," he exclaimed aloud. "I don't have any business here." He changed his mind, however, and tied his horse at the end of the hitching rail next to the walkway to the front door. He stood at the door for a moment, then finally reached up and engaged the knocker against its plate. It was not long before a black servant opened the door and asked who was calling.

"I came to see Lydia," replied Wetzel in a voice stronger than he felt.

The servant looked Wetzel up and down, clearly doubting that he was someone who should be allowed to see the lady of the house. Still he was polite and asked again for the caller's name.

"Tell Lydia it is Lewis Wetzel who has come to see her."

The look on the servant's face showed that the name was one he had heard before.

"I will see if she is available," he said finally.

As he waited, Lew noticed several black men working near the stone barn, slaves he figured. Wetzel had never much pondered the institution of slavery.

His own family owned no slaves, but nothing was ever said about it, a way of life that surrounded them but they ignored. Some people spoke against it, but Lew did not see it as a problem, only that he wouldn't want to be a slave himself.

His thoughts were interrupted by the appearance of Lydia. He was taken back by her look for she had aged more than he would have expected.

"Hello, Lewis," she said politely but not warmly. "I heard you were back."

"Hello to you, Lydia," said Lew, stammering a bit in spite of his best intentions. "You are looking nice as always."

"Won't you come in?" she asked, looking with care at his boots as if they might be ready to track on her clean carpet. "We call it Shepherd Hall."

Lew stepped in but stopped in the hallway, sure now that he should never have come. He could see into the reception parlor, its floor covered with a rich, colorful carpet. A decorative mantel stood on the far end, and the room was filled with expensive furniture.

"This is far enough," he said. "I just wanted to see you one last time. This is some house you have, Lydia."

"Thank you, Lewis. What do you mean one last time?"

"I'm thinkin' of goin' back to the south country again."

"Why would you do that? We heard you had been in prison down there in New Orleans."

"I was for a long time."

"They say New Orleans is an exciting place."

"I reckon it is if you like whiskey and whores." Noting the dark look that came across Lydia's face, Wetzel apologized. "Sorry about the bad language."

"It's all right," Lydia said after a moment. "What did you do to get thrown in jail?"

"Well, you know, I'm always doin' somethin', Lydia," answered Lew with a laugh. "But this time I was innocent. They claimed I was makin' false money, but you know I ain't smart enough to do that."

"I'm glad you're out now, anyway," said Lydia with a warmer tone. "Moses is not here today, but he would have been glad to see you."

"I didn't come to see Moses," replied Lew.

He couldn't bring himself to say what he had come to say.

Lydia, with the natural sense that women have about such things, was well aware that Lew Wetzel had been sweet on her and on her one-time rival Betty Zane as well. Of course, he was just not the type of man that the belles of the border would find attractive. Still she could feel his pain, and she had never forgotten the time he had come between her and disaster.

"Been shootin' any rabbits lately?'" she asked, a broad smile filling her face.

Wetzel grinned, happy that she had not forgotten that incident. His memory often returned to the sight of her bathing herself along the riverbank while he and a red foe had watched.

"Not lately, I reckon," he answered.

They stood quietly for a moment, remembering that day, nearly twenty years in the past.

"You saw me naked that day, didn't you?" Lydia asked suddenly, with a look of accusation.

Wetzel could feel the blush rising on his face. He looked down, then forced himself to issue a denial. "No, I didn't."

"I think you did," she insisted. "But it's all right, you're forgiven."

Wetzel seized the chance to change the subject. "How is your pa?"

"He moved to the Ohio country a few years back. We've not seen him, but he's doing well as far as I know."

"I heard that Moses's folks have both passed on."

"Yes, in 1795," said Lydia with a trace of sadness. "She died just a month after he did."

"I'm sorry," replied Lew. "I'd best be goin' now, Lydia, but it was awful nice to see you."

"Oh, you needn't go yet, Lewis." Lydia regretted her earlier lack of hospitality. "Why don't you come in and have something to drink."

"No, Lyddy," said Wetzel, relapsing into his youthful name for her. "I don't belong here. You and Moses have done really well, and I wish you the best. But I must go."

He looked up and down at her, then squarely eye to eye, his facial expression softening, revealing the feelings for her that had never completely died. Without another word, he turned and retreated down the walkway.

"Good-bye, Lew," she called softly after him.

Wetzel was staying just now at the home of George Cooksis who lived in Wheeling. Cooksis was a relative, although Wetzel could never remember just how the relationship worked. He guessed that George was a cousin of some kind of his mother. It didn't matter because Lew felt comfortable and welcome in his house.

He was especially fond of George's wife, Martha. It didn't hurt that she was an excellent cook. She had made a pumpkin pie, and she had placed a piece of it, still warm from the oven, in front of him as he sat at the small kitchen table.

"Here's some hot tea to drink with the pie," said Martha, placing a cup and saucer to the side of the pie plate. "It's so nice to have you stay with us, Lewis."

"There's no place I like much better," remarked Wetzel, slicing off a bite of the pie.

"You're a good man, Lewis," noted Mrs. Cooksis. "And you'd make some woman a fine husband. Do you intend to marry some day?"

"No," replied Lew. "There is no woman in this world for me, but I expect there is one in heaven."

Epilogue

May 10, 1804

Pierre Le Clerk had finally found the village where Little Fox and Red Storm were living.

They had returned to the site of Pipe's old town on the Upper Sandusky. It was ten years since the defeat at Fallen Timbers, and these Indians had ceased all hostilities with the whites. There was a different feeling in the camp, as if the time of peace had taken away the old sharpness and readiness for action that prevailed in Indian towns of the past.

Little Fox was very glad to see his old friend. "Bright Moon," he called to his wife who was still inside the lodge. "My friend Le Clerk is here. He will stay with us."

"That is very kind of you, Little Fox," said Le Clerk, knowing it would be considered an affront to refuse the offered hospitality.

"What brings you to our village?" asked Little Fox.

"I have news of an old enemy," was the reply.

"Don't you know we have enemies no longer since the British deserted us at the Fallen Timbers?" Little Fox refused to consider the loss to the Americans under Wayne to have been a defeat. He would forever blame the British.

"Yes, I know the tribes are now at peace. Still I supposed that you and Red Storm remain at war with Lewis Wetzel."

A look of surprise filled the Chippewa's face. "You know something of the man?"

"I know where he is living right now," answered Le Clerk.

Little Fox had lost his zeal for revenge against this one white man, yet the thought of an adventure, as in the old days, brought immediate excitement. For Red Storm, who seemed to be in perpetual depression, this might be just the news he needed.

"Let us go and see Red Storm," proposed Little Fox. "His lodge is on the other side of the village."

The news brought a light into the eyes of Red Storm that had been absent for many months.

"Where does he live?" asked Red Storm immediately.

"He lives in a cabin on the Black River in what the Americans call Mississippi Territory," explained the French trader.

"Is it far?" Red Storm wanted to know.

"Yes, it is very far, down the Father of Waters."

"But you said it was another river, one called the Black," argued Little Fox. "Now you say the Father of Waters."

"The Black River flows into the great river. His cabin is some distance up from the mouth of the Black."

Le Clerk spent several minutes trying to explain to the two warriors how they could find Wetzel's cabin. "The key is to go to the Chickasaw agency on the Tennessee River. I will show you how to get there. The Chickasaws will be happy to direct you to the source of the Black River. Once there, you can take a canoe down that stream until you find Wetzel's cabin."

The two Indian friends encountered unexpected resistance from their wives.

"You cannot do this," said Bright Moon. "You have a family that depends on you. This is silly."

"It is not wise, I agree," replied Little Fox to the woman he loved above all else. "But it is of great importance to Red Storm, don't you see? It will restore him to life."

"Not for long," said Bright Moon.

In the end, the two braves could not be dissuaded. Le Clerk was gone now, realizing the conflict he had brought to the two families.

As Little Fox and Red Storm prepared to begin their journey, Bright Moon held tight to her husband's hand.

"Please change your mind," she pleaded. "If you go, I will never see you again."

"Nonsense," replied Little Fox. "This is our destiny, and we will return in triumph."

APPENDIX

UNDERBOOK

Prologue

IN HIS WONDERFUL book *Freedom*, William Safire refers to the section entitled "Commentary and Sources" as an "underbook." I am borrowing that term as a title to this appendix to the preceding novel in which I hope to accomplish the same end as did Safire.

In reading any historical novel, I am always uncomfortable when I feel the author is tinkering with the facts. It is natural to wonder what is true and what isn't, and not knowing can leave one dissatisfied. This underbook is my attempt to help the interested reader who wants to know the truth. Lewis Wetzel was a real character who came of age during the American revolutionary period and was an important actor along the western Virginia border during the Indian wars that occurred there.

It has been pointed out by more than one author that Wetzel was as famous in his own time as Daniel Boone. Yet Boone's name has endured through the years while Wetzel's faded until he is unknown in the present age to all but a rabid few. He was never a regular soldier nor appointed to any official government agency, and as a result, he is rarely mentioned in any official record. What we know of him has come down from early amateur historians and biographers, legends, stories handed down orally through family members, and recollections by actual witnesses recounted many years later. The result is that nearly every incident in his life that has been reported comes to us in several versions, many of which differ drastically.

Most of the incidents in Wetzel's life that I have presented in the novel I believe to have really happened in some similarity to what I have described. The details and conversations are my ideas, and though I will try to explain why I chose them, I am the first to admit that I may have it wrong. Also, in the chapter accounts that follow, I will tell you what is pure fiction. Although the story told in the prologue was related by Allan Eckert [24], I have never found an independent confirmation. Therefore, I regard it as part of the fictional side of the book.

The story did inspire me to add the fictional Indian pursuit of Wetzel that occurs intermittently throughout. I should say that the book *That Dark and Bloody River* by Allan Eckert [24] is a very interesting historical narrative describing the settlements in western Pennsylvania, western Virginia, and Kentucky. Reading it rekindled my own interest in Lewis Wetzel.

Incidentally, the numbers in brackets, such as the [24] given above, refer to the identically coded items in the bibliography given at the end of this underbook. I will comment here that the epilogue is entirely fictional and nothing else will be said about it.

Chapter 1: Captivity

The story of the capture and escape of the Wetzel brothers is told in all the accounts of the border wars that touch at all on the Wetzel family. It surely happened, and it happened in some way similar to what is told in this chapter. The various accounts do differ in some ways, and in some cases there are significant differences. The most glaring error, made in a few of the early descriptions of the incident, has the father John Wetzel and some other members of the family killed by the raiders. A follow-up to this error included the supposedly famous oath by Lewis Wetzel to kill every Indian he met after that. Whether Lewis ever uttered such an oath is not clear to me, but there is no doubt that his father lived another nine years. He was killed by the Indians; but that took place in 1786.

My account follows closely the story told by Cyrus Wetzel to Lyman Draper many years later. Cyrus Wetzel was the son of Jacob Wetzel, and I am certain that he had heard this story from his father many times. His story rings true to me, and certain of the details that he tells seem to me to be just the type of details that his father would have told and that he would have remembered. One can find this statement from Cyrus Wetzel in the Draper manuscripts [74] and it has been reprinted in *The True Wetzelian*, [40, XIII5-6, XIV1-3].

There are several items, however, that deserve some attention. Let me list them with some brief comments:

(1) Dates. Although the date of the Wetzel boys' capture is disputed, most accounts indicate that the event occurred in August of 1777. My choice of August 8 is simply a guess. Some writers think it was more likely to have been in April and that the weather was cold. Cyrus Wetzel (CW), however, specifically says that the weather was hot and that his father was just a month away from his twelfth birthday (which is known to have been in September). The incident with the maggots is also told by CW and is the kind of thing that would be remembered. The one argument against the date is the insistence by CW that the four Wetzels had gone back to the farm to plant turnips. They had taken the plow horses to break up the ground. August would be awfully late to plant something. Perhaps my explanation in the story would suffice, perhaps not. I have been told by residents of the Wheeling area that it is not uncommon for a late crop of turnips to be planted in late summer. Many accounts say the boys were working in the cornfield, but CW clearly states that the crop was turnips.

(2) Fort Henry or Shepherd's Fort. Some accounts have said that the Wetzel family had taken refuge at Fort Henry rather than Shepherd's. Both CW and Lewis Bonnet [50, p. 11], a first cousin of the Wetzel boys, are less than clear on this subject. I chose Shepherd's Fort simply because it was closer

to the farm. Others think that there was no forting in early August. It is thought by some experts that the boys might have been sent to the farm alone, or that they had been left there for the night while their father and brother George returned to Shepherd's Fort as part of their militia duty. I see no compelling reason to not accept the story as told by Cyrus.

(3) The landing. Some accounts have the boys landing farther to the south than at Zanes Island and having to negotiate a much wider channel. CW is clear that they crossed to the island and were met there by the boys picking grapes. He names James Ryan as one of the boys.

(4) There have been questions about the lack of a rescue party sent out to find the Wetzel boys. It may have been thought to be too late by the time such a party could be organized. Also, there had been enough warnings about a possible large-scale attack that it was thought to be unwise to send anyone after them. That is how I have portrayed it, as did Eckert [24]. However, there is no real evidence known to me.

(5) David Shepherd was the Lieutenant of Ohio County and so its top military officer. He had been ordered to go to Fort Henry by General Hand sometime in the middle of August [47, p. 55]. Captain Mason had written to General Hand from Fort Henry on August 12 [47, p. 39], so I assume, was in temporary command there on that date while Shepherd was still with his family at Shepherd's Fort. Adam Grandstaff was the husband of Maria Catherine Wetzel, a niece of John Wetzel. Lewis Grandstaff was their son.

(6) There is some question about the route of the Indians after they had crossed the Ohio. Many experts think that the crossing may have been near Bellaire, Ohio, and that McMahon's Creek was followed until they reached the vicinity of Indian or Wetzel's Springs near St. Clairesville, Ohio. This could well be correct, but it is not a very long

distance for two days of travel. Cyrus Wetzel says that it was not clear where the Ohio was crossed, but they went a ways beyond that on the first day. "The second day was quite a hard days travel" said Cyrus, and they camped for the night "probably on Wills Creek, some ten or twelve miles from Coshocton." He mentions that the Indians had indicated, by pointing to the sky, that they would reach the village of Coshocton before noon on the next day. I do not see why Cyrus would have made up that story if it had not been told to him by his father [74, p. 74].

(7) Fort Henry. This fort was named for Virginia governor Patrick Henry, although its original name was Fort Fincastle. It was an important fort on the frontier and maintained that importance for more than ten years after it was built. It endured two major sieges, one in 1777 and the other in 1782. Some people argue that the second siege was the last real battle of the Revolutionary War. The fort stood on the bank of the Ohio, and its location can be seen today in an empty lot (an invitation for a reconstruction?) between tenth and eleventh streets on the west side of Main Street in modern-day Wheeling, West Virginia.

We list here some references with page numbers pertinent to this chapter:

[1, pp. 25–32], [17, pp. 229–230], [14, pp. 346–347], [24, pp. 112–117], [34, pp. 21–26], [39, pp. 82–84], [41, pp. 78–79], [47, pp. 38–55], [50, pp. 10–15], [51, pp. 8–9, 95], [57, pp. 38–64], [61, p. 135], [67, pp. 259–261], [40, I5, p. 1; II1, p. 4], [74, pp. 71–78], [81, pp. 161–163].

One last remark. I have included the reference [57] here, but will not include it again. It is mostly fictional. For a note about it, see [40, II4, p. 9]. Note that in a reference to the Draper Manuscripts, the expression 20S63 refers to volume 20 of series (S), page 63. For the references to *The True Wetzelian*, I5, p.1] means volume I, number 5, page 1.

Chapter 2: The Siege

The Indian attack on Fort Henry on September 1, 1777, did occur and somewhat in the manner in which I have related it. There was a second siege in 1782, and accounts of the first siege often contain events that were part of the second. In a footnote on page 224 of a special edition of Withers's *Chronicles of Border Warfare*, which Reuben G. Thwaites edited, he said the following: "Perhaps no events in Western history have been so badly mutilated by tradition, as these two sieges." [81]. The pure fiction in this chapter is limited to the conversations and to the activities involving the Wetzel family. The other details can be challenged, as I have made choices from among alternate accounts and descriptions, but they have been given in accordance with at least one historical account.

None of the accounts that I have consulted place the Wetzels at Fort Henry, except the book of Alan Eckert *That Dark and Bloody River* [24]. I do not know what source Eckert might have used in putting together his account, but I found it useful for my own purposes to make them part of the story. It is true that Cyrus Wetzel [74] and Lewis Bonnett Jr. [50] each said in at least one place that they thought the Wetzels were at Fort Henry, but none of the eyewitness accounts mention them.

Martin Wetzel was probably there since he was in the militia, and one historian does include his name as a survivor from Mason's and Ogle's men who went out off the fort that day [14, p. 226]. The correspondence between David Shepherd and General Hand that is mentioned is accurate and can be found in [47]. It might be useful to talk about a few details that have caused the most controversy:

(1) The dispatch by Shepherd of the two men to scout the suspected burning of the Grave Creek blockhouse is given by only one source. This was a testimony by a participant in the battle, Abraham Rogers, given over fifty years after

the action and recorded in the *History of the Panhandle* by Newton, Nichols, and Sprankle [61, p. 114]. No names of the two men who went on this scouting mission were ever given, nor do they seem to have been counted among the losses in the battle. It may be that this never happened, although Rogers rode in with Captain Ogle and would have been part of the conversation about observing smoke coming from downriver. Eckert also includes this incident.

(2) A wide variety of names have been given for the men who went out to get Dr. McMechen's horses. Two sources mention the rescue party, and only one—the account given by Mrs. Joseph Stagg (the former Mrs. Jacob Drennon) in the Draper manuscripts and recorded [47, p. 63]—reports that the body of Boyd was actually brought in. A Greathouse is named as being present, but the first name was not recorded. I chose to make it Jacob although it could have been one of two other Greathouse brothers, Daniel or Harmon. Not all accounts mention Andrew Zane, and some have him making it back to Fort Henry rather than Shepherd's Fort.

(3) The ambush set up by the Indians at Fort Henry had been planned well in advance and was their intended strategy in a number of attacks. In a letter to Colonel William Fleming at Fort Randolph on July 26, 1777 (and a similar letter to General Hand), Matthew Arbuckle talks about Indian plans to destroy garrisons at both Fort Randolph and Fort Henry, and the methods described were pretty much followed at Fort Henry on September 1. The information had come from Nonhelema, the "Grenadier Squaw," the sister of the famous Shawnee chief, Cornstalk, whose murder at Fort Randolph was one of the major causes of trouble between the Shawnees and the whites. She became a Christian and was baptized under the name Catherine. This information is found in [47, p. 26].

(4) There is some confusion about names of people who were killed, injured, and escaped. In a letter to General Hand dated September 15, 1777, David Shepherd wrote that one lieutenant and fourteen privates were killed, one captain and four privates wounded, and five privates escaped [47, p. 83]. The lieutenant would have been Sam Tomlinson, and the captain was Sam Mason. It is likely that these numbers included only members of the militia. We know that John Caldwell was one of the escapees. This story was told by Caldwell's daughter Nancy to a man named Meshach Browning and recorded in a draft of an autobiography written by Browning called *Forty-four Years of the Life of a Hunter*. Excerpts from Browning's book were published in vol. 12, no. 4 of [40]. Another name mentioned by several writers as having escaped is John Harkness.

(5) One of the most enduring stories in accounts of the first siege of Fort Henry is the presence of a white man who delivered an ultimatum to the inmates of the fort. Most of the early histories said that the Indians were led by the infamous renegade Simon Girty, but it was realized by later historians that Girty was still at Fort Pitt in September of 1777 and had not yet defected to the British. In some accounts, the proclamation from Hamilton was read aloud by someone who accompanied the Indian raiders. It is true that Hamilton had provided the Indians with copies of the proclamation, and they often left a copy on the doorstep of a cabin they had raided. Hamilton's proclamation [47, p. 14] reads as follows:

Detroit, June 24, 1777

By virtue of the power & authority to me given by his Excellency Sir Guy Carleton, Knight of the Bath, Governor of the province of Quebec, General and Commandant in Chief, etc. I do assure all such as are inclined to withdraw

> themselves from the Tyranny and Oppression of the rebel committees & take refuge in the Settlement or any of the posts commanded by his Majesty's Officers, shall be humanely treated, shall be lodged, and victualled, and such as come off in arms & shall use them in defense of his Majesty against Rebels and Traytors, till the extinction of this rebellion, shall receive pay adequate to their former station in the rebel service, and all common men who shall serve during that period should receive his Majesty's bounty of 200 acres of land. Given under my hand & seal. God save the King.
>
> Henry Hamilton Lieutenant Gov. and Superintendent

In my opinion, there was probably no white man present with the Indians at this battle and no ultimatums were given. It is thought that the proclamation of Hamilton did have its effect on the frontier. The letters flowing between various commanders to Fort Pitt often speak of suspected Tory conspiracies. That Half-King was the Indian leader is my assumption since he was a principal Wyandot leader, was mentioned by the Moravian missionaries as coming to the Moravian villages with a large party of Wyandots, and was the acknowledged Indian leader at the Foreman massacre, which occurred three weeks later on ground between Wheeling and the Grave Creek Settlement.

(6) The story of Captain Ogle and the wounded man in the weeds at the fence is told by Lydia Boggs Shepherd Cruger many years later to Lyman Draper. This account may be found, among other places, in [52, pp. 105–107]. She does not give the name of the wounded man nor does she mention the snake. Lydia was not at the fort since her father, John Boggs, was at Catfish Camp (present-day Washington, Pennsylvania) and led the relief party that came on the next day. Her first husband, however, was Moses Shepherd, a son of David Shepherd, who was at the fort that day. Another witness, Rachel Johnson [51, p. 104],

when asked about it by Draper, says she had no recollection about a snake, yet someone must have told Draper about the snake. Rachel was the slave known as Aunt Rachel and owned by a man named Yates Conwell and was inside the walls of Fort Henry during the battle.

(7) McColloch's leap is one of the famous legends that has come down to us from those frontier times. Some historians doubt that it ever happened; others say it was John McColloch rather than Sam. I am of the opinion that the incident did actually happen somewhat as it is described in the story. A man named Archibald Woods, who was probably in the fort, names the two men with Sam McColloch [40, XI 2, p. 9]. Some of the early histories claim that McColloch came with forty-five men. There is a difference of opinion about whether the two men, John McColloch and Peter Hanks, actually got into the fort.

(8) It was common for the frontiersmen to overestimate the number of Indians killed in a battle, and the 1777 siege of Fort Henry was no exception. Many early accounts estimate Indian losses at somewhere between twenty and one hundred. The Indians were known to remove their casualties from the field if at all possible. In a letter dated September 22, 1777 from the Moravian missionary David Zeisberger to General Hand at Fort Pitt, Zeisberger reports that the Wyandots and Mingoes were now gone, although some forty braves had returned to the Wheeling area. The Indians had reported that they had killed fourteen men at Wheeling while one Wyandot was killed and six or seven others were wounded. Two or three of those may have died a short time later. One of the wounded who died was the son of the famous Delaware chief, Wingenund [47, p. 95]. Wingenund had at one time been somewhat friendly to the whites and in particular to Colonel William Crawford, who was captured and burned at the stake in Ohio in 1782. Wingenund was one of the chiefs present at that famous incident.

(9) No one seems to know just how many people were in Fort Henry during this attack. There were at least forty-five to fifty men in the two militia companies and with the others who were in the area and had taken refuge at the fort; it is likely that more than one hundred people were there. An excellent discussion of this question may be found in [40, XI2, pp. 6–15].

References pertinent to this chapter are [1, pp. 54–56], [14, pp. 223–230], [24, pp. 120–149], [39, pp. 85–92], [41, pp. 45–65], [47, pp. 1–85], [51, pp. 5–6, 94, 104–105], [52, pp. 101, 105–107], [61, pp. 102–105, 114], [40, XI2, pp. 6–15; XII4, pp. 10–13], [81, pp. 219–230].

Chapter 3: Transition

The withdrawal of the settlers from Wheeling and its environs to points farther east seems to have happened after the events of September 1777, but the details are almost nonexistent. Both Lydia Cruger and Lewis Bonnett Jr. mentioned it in their remarks to Lyman Draper. The Wetzel family may have come back in the summer of the next year, although it was not clear. Some of the specific incidents given in the chapter did happen, but most of the details are fictional. Many families left Shepherd's Fort a few days after receiving word of the Foreman massacre, which occurred and was well-documented in most all the accounts of border warfare. The action of Lewis Wetzel as a guard on the flank of the caravan is purely fictional.

The route of the families and their destinations was not clear from the accounts. My choice for the families going to Dunkard Creek is a guess on my part, but I think it is credible. Some sources say they went to Catfish Camp, others to Redstone. Lewis Bonnett Jr. said they were camped on Meadow Run when Syckes found them. Meadow Run is located in southern Greene County, Pennsylvania and just a bit east of where Interstate 79 passes through the area today.

The Indian attacks on the Grice and Spicer families did occur, and I will say more about those incidents below. The capture of Martin Wetzel and John Wolf happened in April of 1778, and Wolf was burned at the stake after Wetzel was originally designated for that fate. Wetzel escaped after more than two years in captivity, and this will show up in a later chapter.

(1) John Collins. The account of his rescue by Captain Linn is true, although there is a variation in the details given by various sources. The name is given as John Cullins by some (the first name is also given as William), although I chose to use Collins since it seems to be the more common name. I have mostly followed the account given by Kellogg and Thwaites in *Frontier Defense* pp. 105–112 [47]. This includes the wording of an 1834 petition of John Collins to Congress for a pension (which was granted) and a fascinating account related by the son of a William Linn, whom Collins had visited, mistakenly thought was the man who had saved him. Collins then related the story to this William Linn, whose son reported it to Lyman Draper. Collins claimed in this story that his thigh had been broken by the rifle ball, and that Linn had in fact carried him to Shepherd's Fort on his back. Other accounts say that Linn had taken him on horseback, and this seemed more reasonable to me.

(2) Jacob Grandstaff. Most lists of those killed in the Foreman massacre include a Jacob Greathouse, a well-known name on the frontier. However, his death was well-documented and occurred in 1791. William Hintzen and Clark Wullenweber, the latter a descendent of the Grandstaffs, argue that it was the young Jacob Grandstaff who was killed and not Greathouse. It was a matter of misreading one name for another (see [40, XII3, p. 10]). Jacob Grandstaff's mother, Catherine Wetzel Grandstaff, was a niece of John Wetzel and first cousin of Lewis Wetzel.

(3) Jacob Drennon. Drennon was an experienced frontiersman and had spent time in Kentucky with Simon Kenton and Daniel Boone. In a footnote, Kellogg and Thwaites [47, p. 63], quoting from one of his descendants as given to Draper, said that Drennon would take no part either for or against the colonies. He was certainly no coward. He did sign the oath to Virginia and is on the list of signees given by Wingerter [79, pp. 61–71]. The words put in the mouth of Captain Linn were borrowed from a letter written by Captain Matthew Arbuckle from Fort Randolph on August 15, 1776 [46, pp. 185–186]. This is the same Captain Arbuckle who later imprisoned the Shawnee chief Cornstalk in November of 1777.

(4) The Grice family. The massacre of the Grice family is a fact and was mentioned by Lydia Boggs Shepherd Cruger in her statement to Lyman Draper. It is also recorded by De Hass. Rachel Grice did live after having a trepanning performed on her by Dr. Moore at Catfish Camp. She later became the wife of Henry Jolly, a well-known frontiersman, perhaps as early as 1781, bore him three (five?) children and eventually died (of her wounds, Cruger says) at age forty [52, pp. 108–109]. One account, by William Darby, says that Henry Jolly was one of the men who found her, but that is not likely, since he was fighting with the Continental Army in the east in 1777. Of course, it is possible that the attack on the Grice family occurred much later as some accounts have it. De Hass reports that the married daughter was pregnant and that the son John was taken prisoner and remained with the Indians for eleven years. He escaped while in Kentucky. De Hass also writes that Rachel Grice said that the man who scalped her had blue eyes and light hair, in other words, a white man [14, pp. 311–312]. It was not uncommon for whites who had been captured and adopted by a tribe to participate in these raids. Lewis Bonnett Jr. says that young Grice was a

prisoner for six years and then went to Detroit and other places, returning to Wheeling about 1788. Lewis Bonnett Jr. says that the skin never grew over the bone on the crown of Rachel's head, and this led ultimately to her death [50, pp. 31–32]. Elizabeth Jolly, a daughter-in-law of Henry Jolly, said in 1874 that Henry himself went to Kentucky to bring John Grice back to Wheeling [61, p. 247]. Sometimes the name Grice is written as Grist, but I believe Grice is correct.

(5) The Spicer family. Lewis Bonnett Jr. tells of the incident with the Spicers. He tells of John Syckes, another brother-in-law to John Wetzel, coming to Meadow Run and insisting that they all go with him to the mouth of Dunkard Creek. Eckert also gives a version of this story. Lewis Bonnett Jr. says that his father stayed back as a kind of rear guard. William (or Peter) Spicer, who was taken by the Indians, stayed with them and was often suspected as participating with them against the whites. He is, in particular, accused of being with the Indian party that massacred the Tush family on Wheeling Creek in 1794. Lewis Bonnett Jr. says that some time after the Wayne treaty was signed, Spicer came back and tried to reclaim his father's farm, but the other settlers threatened to kill him. He probably died still living among the Indians in 1815 or 1816 [50, p. 17].

(6) The capture of Wetzel and Wolf. My account here mostly follows the story as told by Cyrus Wetzel to Lyman Draper [74, pp. 66–67]. Cyrus Wetzel thought that Wolf may have been a relative, but I have found no clear explanation of that. Christiana Wetzel (a sister of Lewis Wetzel) married a Jacob Wolf, and Eva Wolf, a daughter of a John Wolf (but not the John Wolf who was burned), married John Bonnett in 1805. I have made the John Wolf of this chapter a brother of the Jacob Wolf who married into the Wetzel family, but this is only a guess with no evidence at all to support it. Cyrus Wetzel remarked about the Indian custom

of burning the first captive of the year. He must have heard this from his father, Jacob Wetzel, or from others in the family. The reason for Wetzel and Wolf to be on the way to Dunkard was not without controversy. Eckert says they were out searching for horses on the Wetzel farm. John Wetzel (Martin's son) said, in a narrative given to Draper [19, 2E8ff] that they were going east of the mountains with a load of furs. Others say they were acting as messengers. The place of capture is somewhere near the place indicated in the story. Cyrus Wetzel says that Martin was painted black and then directed to wash it off when they decided to burn Wolf instead. The account given of the killing of Cornstalk is accurate. Martin Wetzel was adopted by Cornstalk's widow. More on this in a later chapter.

(7) Chalahgawtha. In English, this Shawnee word becomes Chillicothe. The principal chief came from the Chalahgawtha sept of the Shawnee tribe, and the village of the principal chief was given this name. At the time of Martin Wetzel's capture, this village was on the Little Miami River, not too far from the current town of Xenia, Ohio, and some fifteen miles from modern Dayton, Ohio. It was not where today's Chillicothe, Ohio is located. It was to this town that Daniel Boone was taken after his capture in February of 1778. Whether Boone was there when Wetzel and Wolf were brought in, no one seems to mention. The timing was right for that to have happened, however. Martin Wetzel was known to Boone, as Daniel did vouch for him a couple of years later in Kentucky. A description of Black Fish is given in Eckert's *The Frontiersmen*, [21, p. 71].

References pertinent to this chapter are [1, pp. 49–50, 92–93], [14, pp. 223–234, 311–312], [24, pp. lxii, 148, 160–163, 167–169], [21, p. 71], [34, pp. 31–33], [39, pp. 97, 115–118], [41, pp. 53–58, 79], [46, pp. 144–145, 226–228], [47, pp. 106–112, 248–249,

252–296], [50, pp. 15–16, 31–32, 42–43, 52–53, 93–94], [52, pp. 16, 101, 108–109, 126], [61, pp. 141, 206, 247], [64, pp. 62–63, 80–81], [40, VII3, p. 15; XII3, p. 10], [74, pp. 65–66], [79, pp. 61–71].

Chapter 4: Inauguration

In this chapter, we introduce Lewis Wetzel's first action as an Indian fighter. Mostly I have followed the account as given in Powell's *History of Marshall County* [64]. Basically the same story is given by Newton in *History of the Panhandle* [61] and by Allman in *The Life and Times of Lewis Wetzel* [1]. Some experts question whether this incident ever happened, but the main source seems as reliable as any others, so I am not sure that there is any more reason to question this story than any other. The description of Martin Wetzel's captivity and escape is based on the statement of Cyrus Wetzel to Lyman Draper [74]. As usual, all conversations and many interactions (but not all) with the Indians are fictional though reasonable. The section concerning the Chippewa Indian, Little Fox, is entirely fictional.

The summaries of historical events are accurate.

(1) The incident that begins the chapter is usually dated in June of 1780 when Lewis Wetzel was two months short of his seventeenth birthday. He had been left at home to cultivate corn when the men came along trying to recapture the stolen horses, and although he did want to go with them, he resisted at first. The names of the other men were never given and so I have made them up from among names of people who lived in the area. Jacob Link had a blockhouse on Middle Wheeling Creek in Pennsylvania near the state line. He will appear again in a later chapter. Jacob Rigger had come to the Wheeling Creek area along with John Wetzel and Lewis Bonnett.

(2) Lewis Wetzel was famous for the ability to reload his rifle while on the run. This incident would be the first (but definitely not the last) time that he performed this feat. The writers indicate that he did receive much attention on the border because of this accomplishment and was sought after for scouting jobs. Josh Davis, a young acquaintance of Lew Wetzel and who accompanied him on a few of his escapades, said of Wetzel that "he could load his gun as well running as standing still, but to prime it he always stopped still." [7, pp. 103–106].

(3) Martin Wetzel's trips to Vincennes with his adoptive mother were described by Cyrus Wetzel. More than forty years later, when visiting his brother Jacob, who by then was living in Indiana along the White River, Martin "recognized the country and the stream." The words in quotes were as appeared in Draper's recording of Cyrus Wetzel's statement. Recall that Cyrus Wetzel was the son of Jacob Wetzel and Martin's nephew. The name of Cornstalk's widow has never appeared as far as I know, so I gave her the name of Wandering Bird. Cyrus says that the Indians referred to Martin as young Captain Cornstalk. The alcoholic binges of Wandering Bird were mentioned by CW [74, pp. 66–67].

(4) George Rogers Clark sent a platoon of soldiers to occupy the fort at Vincennes in July of 1778. Hamilton came out of Detroit with an army of British and Indians and recaptured the post on December 17, 1778. Daniel Boone had escaped and returned to Kentucky in June of 1778. Simon Kenton (a.k.a. Butler) was captured on September 13, 1778 after spying on Chillicothe and while Black Fish was at Boonesborough with his Shawnee warriors. Kenton is one of the most famous of all the frontiersmen (see Eckert's novel [21]). Kenton was using the name Butler

(and this is the name by which the Indians knew him) because he thought he had killed a man back in his home in Prince William County, Virginia. In fact, the man had not died, and when Kenton went missing, the man had been accused of killing Kenton. After learning of this around 1780, Kenton resumed using his real name.

(5) George Rogers Clark recaptured the post at Vincennes on February 25, 1779, overcoming incredible odds and extreme flood conditions. The British governor Hamilton was taken captive. On May 29, a force of Kentuckians under Colonel John Bowman attacked the Chillicothe village. By that time, the Shawnee nation had split apart with a large portion going across the Mississippi River and into Missouri, near the current Cape Girardeau. They were led there by Louis Lorimer, a French trader who had made arrangements with the Spanish authorities. Louis Lorimer is sometimes called Peter Lorimier or Peter Lorimie. Eckert [21, p. 232] says that four thousand Shawnees were on this journey while Hintzen says four hundred warriors were included [39, p. 134]. This left only one hundred warriors under Blackfish to defend the village. Shortly after the attack began, in which a section of the army under Logan was poised for success, Bowman lost his nerve and ordered a retreat, which was effectively harassed by the Indians. Black Fish was wounded and later died. In the next year, a three-pronged attack was planned by the British. One force under Captain Emmanuel Hesse left Mackinac and eventually went down the Mississippi. A second force under Charles Langlade advanced down the Illinois. The third force was under the command of Henry Bird and included one thousand Indians, mostly Shawnee, Wyandot, and Mingo, a detachment of British regulars, and two companies of veteran rangers from Niagara. He also had two cannon with him, which were powerful enough

to reduce any Kentucky fort. Bird came from Detroit, down the Maumee, the Miami, and finally the Licking in Kentucky, arriving at Ruddell's Station, which held some three hundred inhabitants on June 20, 1780.

The post surrendered after two cannon shots, and in spite of Bird's personal guarantee to the prisoners, a number of the captives were put to death by the warriors. Next they marched to Martin's Station where another fifty people were captured. In spite of this great success, trouble with controlling his Indian allies and supply problems forced Bird to return back across the Ohio. By the first of August, a force of nearly one thousand Kentuckians, determined to retaliate, had gathered at the mouth of the Licking, across from modern-day Cincinnati, Ohio, and prepared to avenge the attack by Bird. The indomitable George Rogers Clark led this force, which included such pioneers as Benjamin Logan, Daniel Boone, James Harrod, Levi Todd, William Linn (of Foreman massacre fame), and Hugh McGary. Clark had a cannon of his own, and the force quickly marched up the Little Miami, arriving at the abandoned Shawnee town of Chillicothe. A member of Clark's party, a Tory sympathizer, had sneaked away to warn the Shawnees, who had left the town, setting it afire as they pulled out. Leaving a part of the men to destroy the crops, the remainder went on to the Piqua town on the Mad River, where the Shawnee tried to resist. In the end, Clark won a clear victory, destroying the town and its crops. At least seventy-three Indians were killed while Clark lost about twenty. The death of Joseph Rogers occurred as described in the text. He was a cousin of George Rogers Clark [71].

(6) The placing of the tomahawk in the war post by Martin Wetzel is described by Cyrus Wetzel. It seems odd that Martin would be the leader of such a raid, although CW

implies that he was. They did go to Bryan's Station to steal horses, having crossed the Ohio at modern-day Cincinnati, and Wetzel made his escape to the stockade at the station. He was roughly treated and, according to CW, had almost decided to go back to the Indians. Daniel Boone did intervene and vouch for him. Bryan's Station was very near modern-day Lexington, Kentucky. In the summary of a letter to Colonel Brodhead at Fort Pitt from Harrodsburgh, Kentucky on January 21, 1781, Colonel Levin Powell writes that "seven with a white prisoner came to steal horses. The white man escaped to a station." In a footnote to this entry, Kellogg, in *Frontier Retreat on the Upper Ohio* [45, p. 319], in speaking of Martin Wetzel, notes that "he escaped from a band of Indians by pretending a desire to go to Kentucky to steal horses." Some of the more fanciful accounts of Martin's escape have him stealthily killing three or four of his captors, but this did not happen. It is perhaps worth noting that Kentucky at this time was still a part of the state of Virginia.

(7) Although Little Fox and the section involving him and the Chippewa Indians is fictional, it is true that some Chippewas did take part in the various battles against both the English and the Americans later. Long Knives is the name that the Indians used for the American soldiers and settlers. It had been given very early to the militia of Virginia and may have come from the knives they carried or from the swords worn by the officers [81, pp. 79–80].

References pertinent to this chapter are [1, pp. 33–37], [4], [7, pp. 103–106], [24, pp. 226–228, 236, 244–248], [21], [34, pp. 33–36], [39, pp. 115–118, 125–127, 133–147], [45, p. 319], [49], [61, p. 136], [64], [67], [71, pp. 184–198, 245–247], [74], [81, pp. 79–80].

Chapter 5: Militia

This chapter is devoted to the campaign of Colonel Brodhead against the Delaware village at Coshocton on the Muskingum in east central Ohio. This is the location of the present Ohio city of Coshocton. The Indian name for the village is often given as Goschachgunk, but I will stick with the anglicized version of Coshocton. Brodhead came with 150 regular army troops from Fort Pitt to Fort Henry in Wheeling where he was joined by 134 militia under Colonel David Shepherd. The militia were enrolled on April 10, 1781 and mustered out on April 28. Accounts of this campaign are given in nearly every one of the usual references on the border wars. The first such account (and one frequently copied by subsequent authors) was given by Doddridge in his *Notes on the Settlement and Indian Wars* [17].

The general account given in the text is as accurate as I could make it. The conversations and interactions among the men, although I have used real names, are my own inventions. The section concerning Little Fox and White Eagle is fictional, although a party of twenty Wyandots did make the trip to Coschocton to ascertain what had happened there. This is the first of only two times that Lewis Wetzel ever participated as an official member of an organized army marching against the Indians. The second and last was thought to be the campaign of Colonel Benjamin Logan out of Kentucky in 1786 against the Shawnees, although concrete evidence of this is not known (to me). [Note: At the time the words in the previous sentence were written, it is all I knew. Subsequently, I discovered indisputable evidence that Lewis Wetzel was with Logan in 1786. This campaign is discussed in detail in chapter 13.]

(1) Complete rolls of the militia involved in the Coshocton campaign are given in the book of Louise Kellogg, *Frontier Retreat on the Upper Ohio, 1779–1781* [45, pp. 461–469]. These rolls give the number of days served, the monthly pay, and the actual pay based on nineteen days of service. The pay amounts ranged from $575 per month for Colonel

Shepherd, $240 per month for Captain Ogle, to $16 Dollars and 60 90ths for the lowest private. The actual pay was prorated based on nineteen days. There is also an account of the cost for horses used by the soldiers and officers.

(2) John Heckewelder, the Moravian missionary at the town of Salem, tells of being summoned by Brodhead, and his language implies that this interview was held prior to the destruction of Coshocton [37]. Other authors indicate that this interview occurred on Brodhead's return from Coshocton. Brodhead, in his own account recorded in [61, p. 109] says that on the way back up the Tuscarawas, he stopped at Newcomerstown and there experienced great kindness by the Moravian Indians and those at Newcomerstown. (The location of this Ohio town on the north side of the Tuscarawas can be found on current Ohio maps.) C. W. Butterfield, whose account is given in *Frontier Retreat* [45, pp. 376–382], tells of Captain Killbuck's interactions as given in the text.

(3) Sam Mason, the same person who played a major role in the 1777 siege of Fort Henry, operated a tavern at Wheeling for several years, although the incidents recounted in the text are purely fictional.

(4) Brodhead's official report says that fifteen warriors were killed and upward of twenty old men, women, and children were taken. He closes the report by saying: "The troops behaved with great spirit and although there was considerable firing between them and the Indians, I had not a man killed or wounded, and only one horse shot." He does not mention the council at which it was decided to put the captive warriors to death. Doddridge [17, pp. 224–226]—whose account was used by most of the later writers about this event)—says that there were sixteen captives and that a council of war was held after dark to decide their fate. He also mentions that it was the Delaware chief Pekillon

who had pointed out these warriors. Eckert [24, p. 254] says that fifteen warriors were killed in the fighting, and sixteen were captured and later put to death.

Simon Girty, in a report to the English commander at Detroit, A. S. DePeyster, says that fifteen were killed and four were released beside the women and children who were also released (after being taken to Fort Pitt, we assume). This report was based on the dispatch of the twenty Wyandots to find out what had happened [8, p. 128]. Hassler [35, pp. 123–130] gives a fairly complete account of the expedition, and he says that the fifteen warriors were killed during the capture of the town. He says that Doddridge's account was totally unreliable. Another good report of this campaign is given by Fitzpatrick [25, pp. 405–406]. Fitzpatrick's book often reflects the Indian and British point of view. I am convinced that only fifteen Indians were killed, and that they were warriors. What remains in doubt is whether the warriors were killed resisting the attack, or were captured and killed afterward. I lean in this direction because of the report of Girty to DePeyster in which he states that Brodhead apologized for the killings of the captives he released, saying that he could not control the militia. Another factor is the later response of some of the Indians as explained in number 5 below. This is also mentioned by Booth in his book *The Tuscarawas Valley in Indian Days* [6, p. 197]. The account of the council, however, including the role of the Indian, Pekillon, is based on Doddridge's original report, which Hassler, in his book *Old Westmoreland*, says is unreliable.

(5) Most accounts do not mention that the slain captives had been tied to trees, but there is indirect evidence that this is what was done. At an attack later that summer by Indians at Link's blockhouse, three white captives of the Indians were tied to trees and tomahawked, with the Indians remarking, "Now we be militia!" [52, p. 74], [40, VII1, p. 4]. Dale Van

Every, in his book *A Company of Heroes*, says that in response to Brodhead's campaign, the Delawares burned nine Kentucky prisoners, one on each of nine successive days [71, p. 257]. Butterfield also mentions this burning [8, p. 127].

(6) Billy Boggs was a real person, although the words and actions I have given him are my inventions. He was once captured by the Indians and, according to his sister, Lydia Cruger, was concerned lest they hold him responsible for some act against them [52, p. 110]. In fact, some authors have said that Billy Boggs, along with Lewis Wetzel, killed the Indian Killbuck while held in confinement at Wheeling. Lydia Cruger said this happened just prior to the Coshocton campaign, and Allen Eckert, in an extensive account, has the killing done after the return to Wheeling and says that Brodhead questioned Lew Wetzel for several hours, even subjecting him to torture by using thumbscrews [24, p. 255–256]. It is a fact, however, that Killbuck lived until 1811 and was baptized by the Moravians in 1788 [46, p. 38]. Of course, there may have been more than one Indian by that name.

(7) Another incident that is mentioned first by Doddridge and copied by many later authors involves the killing of a Delaware chief who came over the river near Coshocton and was negotiating with Colonel Brodhead. According to Doddridge [17, p. 225], while this chief was speaking with Brodhead, a man by the name of Wetzel came up behind him and, taking a tomahawk from inside his hunting shirt, struck him dead. Through the years, the Wetzel involved was identified as Martin Wetzel who was not along John Wetzel and, eventually, Lewis Wetzel. Butterfield does not mention this in his account, nor does Simon Girty in his message to the British commander in Detroit about the Coshocton campaign. Of course, Brodhead does not mention it in his official report, but then he might

be inclined to omit mention of such an act for his own reasons. There is an excellent discussion of this incident, as well as the one mentioned in number 6 above, by William Hintzen in his book *Border Wars* [39, p. 148–161]. Hintzen makes a strong case that these two murders did not happen, but were confused in memories years later with similar incidents that are well-documented, such as the killing of the Shawnee chief Cornstalk at Point Pleasant in 1777 and the killing of the Shawnee chief Moluntha by Kentucky militiaman Hugh McGary during Logan's raid in 1786.

(8) Heckewelder, Edwards, and Zeisberger were missionaries in the Moravian towns as described. Later in the summer of 1781, the Moravian Indians were forced by the hostile tribes to move to the Upper Sandusky towns, and the missionaries, after being threatened with death, were sent to the British in Detroit.

(9) The story of the Delaware, White Eagle making a trip to obtain cranberries for his pregnant wife was based on a real incident described by John Heckewelder in [36, p. 159].

(10) Wingenund's town was some twenty miles distant from Half-King's town and was on the Sandusky near the present-day Ohio town of Leesville in Crawford County. It is thought that Colonel Crawford was captured near the site and taken to Wingenund's camp in June of 1782 after his failed campaign against the Sandusky towns. His burning at the stake a short time later on Tymochtee Creek was one of the most famous incidents of the time.

Pertinent references for this chapter: [1, pp. 46–47], [8, pp. 126–129], [14, pp. 179–181], [17, pp. 224–226], [18, pp. 265–266], [24, pp. 252–256], [25, pp. 405–406], [34, pp. 31–33], [35, pp. 123–130], [36, p. 159], [37, pp. 214–216], [39, pp. 115–118, 148–161], [45, pp. 376–382, 461–469], [50, pp. 16, 31–32], [61, p. 109], [40, VII1, pp. 4–11], [71, p. 257], [81, pp. 301–304].

Chapter 6: Waging War

IN THIS CHAPTER, we give an account of the attacks by the Delaware and some Wyandots on the settlements in western Virginia and Pennsylvania. The original attack led by the Delaware chief, Pekillon was intended to take Fort Henry but was prevented by the warnings the settlers had received based on information sent to Fort Pitt by the missionaries at the Moravian villages. This was another insult to the hostile tribes who regarded the Christian Indians as dangerous traitors. It led to the forced removal of the Moravians to a new home in the Upper Sandusky region, a move encouraged by the British and carried out by the Wyandot chief Half-King and the Delawares Pipe and Wingenund. They were urged on by the British agent Matthew Elliott as indicated in the text.

When their attack on Fort Henry was not successful, a part of Pekillon's band carried out the raids on the farms as indicated in the story. The scouting trip of Wetzel is purely fictional, including, of course, White Eagle, Little Fox, and the one-eared Red Storm. It is often stated that Wetzel had performed such scouting services, as did Jonathan Zane, but there are no specific accounts of it. The rest of the story is based on recorded accounts, although, as always, specific facts are debated and differ from one to another. There was a Wetzel who went with the snake-bit man, but it is never stated precisely which Wetzel it was.

I have taken the liberty to put Lewis there, and if it was he, it is natural to make him the winner of the shooting contest.

(1) Accounts of the forced removal of the Christian Indians from the Tuscarawas to the Upper Sandusky appear in many places. Perhaps the best are David Zeisberger's account, given in Russell Booth's *The Tuscarawas Valley in Indian Days, 1750–1797* [6, pp. 199–206], John Heckewelder's *Narrative* [37, pp. 215–281], and Alan Fitzpatrick's *Wilderness War on the Ohio* [25, pp. 232–233], which relates more of the British point of view.

(2) Heckewelder records some of the speeches given by the Indians, and I have made use of some of them in the scene at the Indian camp near Gnadenhutten. Although there was some sympathy for the Moravians, some of the language and threats were very severe, according to Heckewelder. Heckewelder, of course, was one of the missionaries present, and he was often fearful for his life and that of his family.

(3) The Moravians were in a no-win situation. The Pennsylvania and Virginia settlers thought they provided a haven from which the hostile Indians could launch their raids on the settlements. The hostile Indians accused them, and in particular, the missionaries, of providing warnings to the whites of impending raids (and this was true). It resulted in mistreatment from both sides and eventual tragedy in the next spring.

(4) There are many references to, but very few details about, the second attack on Fort Henry. It occurred in the morning of September 3, 1781. The fullest account is given by Hintzen in *Border Wars* [39, pp. 172–173], who includes a run for powder from Zane's blockhouse to the fort and back by Molly Scott. This episode is included in the text. This is partly speculation, motivated by a need to explain the late-life declaration by Lydia Boggs Shepherd Cruger that it was Molly Scott and not Elizabeth Zane who was the real heroine of the famous "gunpowder exploit" that took place in the 1782 attack on Fort Henry. Lydia was present at both attacks, and Hintzen believes she may have remembered a run by Molly Scott in 1781 and confused it with the one by Betty Zane in 1782. Betty Zane, the youngest sister of Ebenezer Zane, was not at Fort Henry in 1781. To make this controversy even more interesting, the descendants of Betty Zane accused Lydia of hard feelings toward Betty, arising from jealousy over Moses Shepherd, who eventually married Lydia.

(5) The attacks on Link's blockhouse and the cabins of Peak, Gaither, and Hawkins happened pretty much as described in the text. The best account is given in three successive issues of *The True Wetzelian* volume 7, issues 37, 38, and 39 [40]. Here are collected accounts from Lydia Cruger, Dr. John Hupp, and Henry Jolly. All three of these may also be found in Lobdell's *Indian Warfare in Western Pennsylvania* [52].

(6) The character of George Blackburn is not included by all of the writers. Only Lydia Cruger mentions him by name, and only she mentions the snake-bit man and that he was killed at Hawkins' cabin trying to run away with Elizabeth Hawkins, who was captured. I have made Blackburn the snake-bit man because Lydia mentions both, and I thought perhaps they were the same person. It is generally thought that the snake-bit man was Burnett, but that doesn't fit what Lydia Cruger says.

(7) There is no question that the three men tied to trees and killed were Link, Hawkins, and Burnett. Hawkins had red hair, and Burnett was also quite hairy. Some think that this interested the Indians and led to their being put to death. Another reason may have to do with Brodhead's expedition to Coshocton. Hawkins was definitely along, and possibly Burnett as well. The tying of the men to trees and the statement "now we be militia" are most surely related to what happened at Coshocton. This information was given by Henry Jolly, who claimed to be with the men from Washington, Pennsylvania (Catfish Camp) who had made two excursions into Virginia to help against the Indian attacks [52, pp. 74–77]. Jolly received his information from Jacob Miller, an eyewitness. There is no evidence that Lew Wetzel was with those men, although whichever Wetzel who was with Mrs. Link and Moses Shepherd must have met these riders coming from Catfish Camp.

(8) Presley Peak was taken to Detroit and eventually released by the British. Elizabeth Hawkins married a Frenchman while in captivity and, according to Lydia Cruger, had some children. She returned to the white world for a short time after her husband died but eventually returned to her life among the Indians. Hupp says that she was married to a Shawnee chief, but this seems unusual since the Shawnees were not involved. Nothing is known of the fate of Miss Walker. Heckewelder speaks of a prisoner brought to Gnadenhutten on September 4, 1781, taken by a party raiding across the Ohio. This could have been the boy David Glenn, but Heckewelder never refers to him as a boy. He tells of an unpleasant meeting with this prisoner in Pittsburgh in 1789, where the person told lies about his treatment by the Moravians [37, pp. 262–267].

(9) The episode with Mrs. Hawkins is told by Henry Jolly, although he does not claim to have been one of the men to go to her aid. Here is part of what he had to say about that many years later.

> 'My God, Indians here about two hours ago!' and the whole party appeared panic struck in a moment, and off they went, the fastest horse I believe foremost. I think there was not less than twenty-five of the party, and only two remained to assist the distressed woman. Such were the heroes of Washington County; such were the men who murdered the Moravians; such were the men that Colonel Williamson mostly commanded [52, p. 77].

(10) The escape by Jacob Miller is given mostly as described by Dr. John Hupp as indicated in number 5 above. Hupp's account implies that Miller returned to his home, but Henry Jolly says Miller that night made his escape and came to them next morning and gave a full account of what the Indians had done. When Miller came to them, it had to be somewhere along the route from Fort Henry to Washington, Pennsylvania.

Pertinent references for this chapter: [6, pp. 199–209], [8, pp. 131–134], [14, pp. 257–260], [18, pp. 270–271], [24, pp. 261–275], [25, pp. 431–433], [34, pp. 39–49], [35, pp. 148–152], [37, pp. 215–281], [39, pp. 169–178], [41, pp. 85–96], [52, pp. 74–77, 109–112, 134–143], [61, p. 110ff],[40, V4, pp. 9–15; VII1, pp. 4–11; VII2, pp. 2–11; VII3, pp. 2–13], [71, p. 264], [81, pp. 313–317].

Chapter 7: A Bloody Year

THE YEAR 1782 was most certainly a bloody year on the border. The bloodiest affairs, the Moravian massacre and Crawford's expedition, were described indirectly and incompletely in the text. Neither one involved Lewis Wetzel nor any of the Wetzels. The Moravian massacre seems so hideous that it is hard to believe it could have happened. It did come to be roundly condemned by many Americans, although the perpetrators mostly defended the action as justified. They had been outraged by the Indian treatment of Mrs. Wallace and her children and were convinced that those behind that atrocity were among the Moravians, or at least aided by them. Atrocities were commonplace in the Indian wars, and both sides were responsible. The Moravian massacre was the worst ever carried out by the Americans. Crawford's ill-fated campaign was an embarrassment to the Americans, and one (but certainly not the only one) of the great triumphs enjoyed by the Indians.

Most remembered is the fate of Crawford himself, whose burning at the stake was a gruesome affair. The Indians spoke a great deal about the need for revenge for the terrible killing of the Moravian Indians. In fact, this motive was used for many of their actions in the summer of 1782. It is true, however, that the Wyandots and hostile Delawares had mistreated the Moravians themselves, forcing them to leave their homes and relocate in the upper Sandusky region. The Moravians suffered greatly in the winter of 1781–82 and did not have enough to eat. It is why a number of them were allowed to return to their villages on the Tuscarawas in order to collect some of the corn still standing and not gathered in the previous fall. These were the Christian Indians who were killed in March of 1782 by the militia from western Virginia and western Pennsylvania under Colonel David Williamson. It is true that the hostile warriors did use the Moravian villages as a place to rest and eat and to use as a launching pad for attacks against the Virginia and Pennsylvania settlements. Probably even some of the Moravian villagers occasionally joined these forays. Some good references for all of this include [6, pp. 199–209], [8, pp. 154–189], [25, pp. 431–433, 445–458], [35, pp. 153–161], [37, pp. 215–281].

(1) Some historians have said that George Wetzel was killed in 1786, but 1782 is the correct date. There is an official document, which lists the death of George as in 1782. This remarkable document, held in the Virginia archives, is a petition submitted to the Virginia legislature in 1803 asking for pensions for the Wetzel brothers Martin, Lewis, Jacob, and John. It states the various services to the community by the Wetzels with respect to protection from the Indians and the injuries they received as a result. It shows the respect held toward them and was signed by several of the most prominent men in the region. Here is a brief statement extracted from this petition: "Your petitioners further state, that it is well-known to the whole country where they live, that their father and his sons during the period of Indian warfare aforesaid, rendered more service and protection of the frontier than any family that ever lived on it and more to their private detriment." [41, p. 77–83], [40, III2, pp.1–6].

(2) My description of the events surrounding George Wetzel's death is as accurate as I could make it, using accounts from Lewis Bonnett Jr., George Edgington, and Henry Jolly. These accounts may be found in one place in [40, III2, pp. 6–9]. It is hard to say which of the many islands in the part of the Ohio River called the Long Reach were involved. Jolly says George was buried on Pursell Island, the first island

below Sisterville. Bonnett says he was buried at the head of Captina Island, and Edgington says it was a "small island known as Wetzel's Island, one of the Long Reach Islands." The part about Parkinson's boat was given by Edgington. Of course, the conversations are entirely my inventions.

(3) Colonel William Crawford and Dr. John Knight were captured by Wingenund's warriors and brought into his camp on June 7 or 8 of 1782. Crawford and his army arrived near the Upper Sandusky Indian villages on June 3, and the battle was fought on the fourth and fifth. The retreat began in the wee hours of June 6. Crawford became separated from his command, and David Williamson led a large body of more than three hundred of the troops in the retreat, fighting off the Indians as he went. A decisive battle was fought on the Olentangy River on June 6, more than twenty miles from the original battle site. This battle, though not large in scope, was decisive in that the Indians mostly gave up their pursuit after that. Williamson and his men reached the safety of Mingo Bottom on the Ohio River on June 12. Crawford was taken from Wingenund's camp back to the towns on the Upper Sandusky on June 10. After a horrible ordeal of torture, he was burned at the stake on June 11 at a site a short distance west of Pipe's town on Tymochtee Creek. A sign on US HW 23, north of the town of Upper Sandusky, Ohio, gives directions to a monument for Crawford just a short distance east of the highway. Wingenund's camp was roughly twenty miles east of the Upper Sandusky villages and near the current Ohio town of Leesville, Ohio (see note 10 for chapter 5). Fitzpatrick [25, pp. 458–493] has a fairly thorough account of Crawford's campaign. The story of the eight Chippewas and their captives is given by Eckert [24, pp. 378–379]. I have no other verification of this, but it fit my purposes very well. I remind the reader that Little Fox, White Eagle, and Red Storm are fictional characters.

(4) An account of the attempted recovery of the horse by Thomas Mills and Lew Wetzel at Indian Springs is told in nearly every history that covers Lew Wetzel to any extent. I have based my story on the one told by Josh Davis himself, who was with Mills and Wetzel on this mission. Josh Davis was a cousin of Thomas Mills, and he told the story to R. H. Taneyhill in 1845, at which time it was published in the *Barnesville Enterprise*. It was recorded in Newton's *History of the Panhandle* [61, p. 196ff] and can also be found in [40, VI4, pp. 4–6]. Some accounts say that Mills found Wetzel at Fort Van Meter, but Davis says it was at Fort Henry. Davis talked about Wetzel's ability to load his rifle on the run but says that he always stopped to prime it. Many of the accounts of this incident (including the one by Davis) say that the last Indian (sometimes named as Long Pine) said "No catch dat man. Gun loaded all the time." But this seems unlikely, for why would he have spoken in broken English when there was no one to hear it, and if he spoke in his native dialect, Davis could not have understood it. Indian Springs eventually came to be called Wetzel's Springs. It is located about four miles east of the present town of St. Clairsville, Ohio [39, p. 396, footnote 84], [40, VI4, pp. 5–6].

(5) The story of Lewis Wetzel saving Lydia Boggs from an Indian along the Ohio shore is given by G. Cranmer in his *History of Wheeling* [12, pp. 308–309]. A slightly different version is told by Allman [1, p. 105]. I have enhanced the story and changed it up a bit. It is not a story included by very many authors, and I suspect that many experts doubt that it is true. Allman has a lot to say about Wetzel and Lydia Boggs, making them out to be lovers. This is hinted at by others, but as far as I have been able to determine, there is no real evidence that Lydia ever thought of Lew Wetzel in a romantic way. She eventually married Moses Shepherd after his engagement to Betty Zane (if such there was) was broken off.

(6) The information about the 1782 siege of Fort Henry is as true as I could make it, excluding any role played by the fictional Little Fox. Fitzpatrick [25, pp. 497–541] is a good resource, especially giving information from the Indian and British side. The attack commenced in the afternoon of September 11, 1782. As remarked before, accounts of this affair often have the facts mixed up with those from the 1777 siege. The John Linn who had observed the advance of the Indians from the crotch of a tree and escaped to bring a warning to Fort Henry is not, as far as I know, related to the more famous William Linn who appeared in chapter 3. There was only one casualty among the defenders of the fort, the injured foot of Daniel Sullivan, who was, in fact, taking the cannonballs to George Rogers Clark, at the time camped near modern-day Louisville, Kentucky. The run for powder by Betty Zane is a famous incident and accompanied by controversy. A few writers have put the event at the 1777 siege, but the biggest controversy came after Lydia Boggs Shepherd Cruger claimed in an affidavit signed in 1849 [52, appendix IV, pp. 153–155] that it was Molly Scott who made the run while Elizabeth Zane was still in Philadelphia. This cannot be taken lightly because Lydia was definitely at Fort Henry during this attack. However, Molly Scott never claimed to have performed this deed, and most of the evidence indicates that Betty Zane made the run. A good account with many quotes may be found in Newton's *History of the Panhandle* [61, pp. 124–131]. It is stated there that Betty Zane was once engaged to Moses Shepherd, who later married Lydia Boggs; and one of Betty's descendants ascribed Lydia's later remarks to a long-held jealousy. Bill Hintzen conjectures that Lydia may have been remembering the 1781 Indian attack where, perhaps, Molly Scott did perform a similar run for powder. A very thorough discussion of this affair can be

found in [39, appendix G, pp. 345–358]. I have not seen names of Indian leaders for this attack. Because of that, I have guessed that the major figures, such as Pipe, Half-King, and Wingenund, were not there. The names I used were real names, but I have no knowledge of whether those Indians actually participated.

(7) The exploding wooden cannon is also an oft-told tale, which sometimes appears in accounts of actions in other attacks or other sites. It sounds like one of those legends that turns out to be a myth, but enough writers tell this story that I believe it is true. The Indians, finding the cannonballs in Sullivan's boat and desperate for some way to knock down the walls of the fort, fashioned a wooden cannon and had it explode when they tried to fire it. Lydia Boggs Cruger is an eyewitness, and she tells the story [52, pp. 124].

(8) A road sign on US Highway 250 in Marshall County, West Virginia, tells of the 1782 attack on Fort Beeler and that Lewis and Martin Wetzel were defenders [67, pp. 296]. There is not much evidence concerning this event, most of it coming from Newton's *History of the Panhandle* [61, pp. 363–364] and from Allman's writings [40, VIII6, pp. 6–13]. The usual account says that the Indians "tunneled under the wall" and as they came up inside the stockade, Lewis and Martin Wetzel killed them with a tomahawk, six in all. That seems a bit much to me, so I lowered the count to two. I doubt that there was a real "tunnel" but something more like described in the text. There is no direct evidence to say that the Indians made this attack as a spin-off of the one made at Fort Henry. No exact date has been given for this attack on Fort Beeler, but it seems reasonable that it was around the same time as the September 11 attack on Fort Henry. It is stated in one place [61, p. 409] that Fort Beeler was not built before 1784, in which case an attack on it may not have happened at all.

Pertinent references for this chapter: [1, pp. 95–97, 105, 114], [8, pp. 136–137, 154–189, 208–209, 353–354], [12, pp. 308–309], [14, pp. 348–349], [18, pp. 270–274], [24, pp. 331–401, 412–426], [25, pp. 501, 522–541], [26, pp. 125–129], [28, pp. 217–222], [34, pp. 39–40, 50–66], [35, pp. 153–169, 184–185], [39, pp. 169–191, 199–202, 213–217], [41, pp. 77–83, 142–144], [50, pp. 9, 17–19, 45–46], [51, pp. 4, 7–8, 14–15, 92–97], [52, pp. 70–72, 113–125], [61, pp. 115–131, 196ff], [67], [69, pp. 259–261], [40, I5; III2; IV5; IX1, pp. 3, 5–6; XI5], [81, pp. 327–339, 356–360].

Chapter 8: The Wedding

The principal events of this chapter are depicted somewhat accurately, and they did occur. There are two turkey-gobbler incidents that are told involving Lewis Wetzel, and I have chosen to tell about one of them. The story, as I have told it, comes from Josh Davis who claims that Wetzel told him the story himself. My account of the wedding of Lydia Boggs and Moses Shepherd was partly based on a biography of Lydia Boggs Shepherd Cruger called *Time Steals Softly* written by Virginia Jones Harper. Lydia went on to become one of the great ladies of the region and figured prominently in its history. My description of the wedding, and perhaps some of Harper's, is drawn from the book of Joseph Doddridge [17], which describes customs of the early settlers.

(1) The story of the killing of the Gobbler Indian by Lew Wetzel comes from a newspaper article in the *Barnesville Enterprise* written by R. H. Taneyhill in 1845. Taneyhill based his article on an interview with Josh Davis, the former companion of Wetzel who was then living in Belmont County, Ohio. The article was reprinted in Newton's *History of the Panhandle* [61, p. 137]. Davis described the annual celebration at Fort Henry of "Old Christmas." He says that his description of Wetzel's tactics in killing the Indian are told as "he told me." Granted, this was more

than sixty years later, but it is as close as we will ever come to having something in Wetzel's own words. An excellent account of all this, including maps, can be found in [40, VI3, pp. 11–12; VI5, pp. 13–17].

(2) The actions of Lewis Wetzel at the Old Christmas celebration at Fort Henry are my inventions. It is true that Wetzel was known to be a friendly, sociable companion when among friends. Judge Foster, one of the territorial judges in the Ohio country, was quoted in August of 1789 as saying, among other things in speaking of Wetzel, "He was taciturn in mixed company, although the fiddle of the party among his social friends and acquaintances. His morals and habits, compared with those of his general associates and the tone of society in the West of that day, were quite exemplary" [67, p. 279]. Wetzel did, however, take the turkey legs and wings, and fashioned a turkey call as described. This information is given by Josh Davis.

(3) The information given in the discussion about the death of Sam McColloch is as factual as I could make it. Girty's Point can be reached by car today; a sign along the road that leads up from the mouth of Short Creek (HW2) points to the site. Just when it actually came to be called Girty's Point is not clear to me. Simon Girty was perhaps the most famous of all the renegades on the border. Sam McColloch, you will recall, is the frontiersman that made the great leap off Wheeling Hill during the 1777 siege of Fort Henry.

(4) There was a second turkey-gobbler incident that appears in the various histories, much more often than the one we described in the text. This incident occurred at a cave on the hillside above Wheeling Creek and to the south of the old railroad tunnel. There is a second cave on this hillside, closer to the tunnel, which is called Wetzel's cave. Some think that Wetzel may have stayed there at times, but this

is speculation. A good account of this gobbler incident as well as pictures of the caves may be found in [40, XII5, pp. 2–11]. Of course, it is possible that the two events were confused and that only one of them was real. In that case, I would side with the tale told by Josh Davis, a known companion of Lew Wetzel.

(5) As I pointed out in the notes for chapter 7, there is no solid evidence of any romantic feelings between Lydia Boggs and Lew Wetzel. That is certainly true about Lydia's romantic interests. Nothing I've ever read from her indicates any such feelings. It does seem possible that Lew might have been interested in her. He certainly knew her; she was the sister of his friend, Billy, and her father was the commandant at Fort Henry for a time. The event in which he killed the Indian who was stalking her (see chapter 7 and its notes) is related by two authors, but its authenticity is questionable.

(6) I am not sure of the exact location of the original Boggs cabin along Boggs Run. My description of the location is based on speculation on my part.

(7) The information about the capture and imprisonment of Billy Boggs is factual. Lydia was quoted as saying that Billy was afraid the Indians would take revenge on him for his part in the killing of Killbuck. However, since I am skeptical about the truth of that supposed incident, I instead mentioned the fact that the Indians were riled about Brodhead's expedition, which is true. Billy Boggs was on that campaign, although not necessarily involved as described in chapter 5.

(8) The information about the Boggs family and events surrounding the wedding was borrowed from *Time Steals Softly* by Virginia Jones Harper [33, pp. 47–58]. The description of a frontier wedding, I took (as did Harper, I suspect) from Joseph Doddridge's *Notes on the Settlement and*

Indian Wars [17, pp. 102–108]. Doddridge, who was born in 1769 and lived in Washington County, Pennsylvania, near the Virginia state line, included much about frontier customs of both reds and whites in his book published in 1824. Many later historians and biographers of those times used his descriptions in their own work. The toast to the bride and groom included in the text is taken directly from Doddridge (p. 105). That Lydia wore a black silk dress at her wedding is told by Harper and also by G. Cranmer in *History of Wheeling City* [12, p. 309].

Pertinent references for this chapter: [1, pp. 123–125], [12, p. 309], [14, pp. 341–343, 352–353], [17, pp. 102–108], [24, pp. 426–427], [28, pp. 233–237], [33, pp. 47–58], [41, pp. 144–145], [61, p. 137], [67, pp. 279–283], [40, VI3, pp. 11–12; VI5, pp. 13–17; X2, p. 12], [74, p. 82].

Chapter 9: Rescue

The story of Wetzel's visit to Pittsburgh is entirely fictional. I know of no evidence that ever puts Wetzel in Pittsburgh, although it seems quite possible that he might have visited because of its importance in those days. The rescue of Rose is one of the stories often found when Wetzel is being discussed. There are two or three versions of this story, and one version comes from a novel called *The Forest Rose* by Emerson Bennett. This novel was actually based on a different incident, the rescue of a woman named Washburn by two men named McClelland and White. Bennett admitted in the preface to a revised edition that he had changed the names to Wetzel, Maywood, and Forrest [40, I2, p. 2]. The version I have given comes from Cyrus Wetzel as told to Draper. One of the most popular versions has Wetzel accompanying a young man (sometimes a relative) to a home on Dunkard Creek, which is in ruins. The young man's girlfriend has been taken by four Indians (some stories say one is a white man), and Wetzel finds them and kills them after they have crossed the Ohio River near Captina. The first version of this story seems to have been published in 1852 in the *Weekly Review* or *Washington Review*. According to the editor of *The True Wetzelian*, this was a review of a fictional short story by William Darby.

A good discussion of this story can be found in [40, IX3, pp. 9–12] under the title, "Lewis Wetzel Rescues a White Girl." The reader should also consult [39, pp. 235–237].

(1) The descriptions of Pittsburgh streets and surroundings are taken from the book, *Pittsburgh, the Story of an American City* edited by Stefan Lorant [53]. I made particular use of a 1795 map of Pittsburgh on pages 62–63 of that book. The names of establishments are genuine and may (or may not) have been where I placed them in 1784. Any illegal, immoral, or illegitimate acts that took place in connection with those establishments are purely fictional. The name Pittsburgh was in use by 1784, I believe, and the role of Fort Pitt, from which the name was taken, had begun to diminish. To the best of my knowledge, Lieutenant David Luckett was the commander of Fort Pitt in July of 1784, but of course, he does not figure into the story.

(2) Of all the versions of the rescue of a white girl by Wetzel, I have chosen the one given by Cyrus Wetzel, who told Draper that he had heard his father tell this story in substance. You will recall that Cyrus's father was Jacob Wetzel, Lew's younger brother and a famous frontiersman in his own right. Cyrus's account of the Rose Forrest rescue can be found in the Draper Manuscripts [74, pp. 82–85] and also as reprinted in [40, XIV1, pp. 2–3].

(3) Lewis Bonnett Jr. also told Lyman Draper the story of the rescue of a girl at Short Creek, although he differs somewhat in a few details and gives the names as Rode

Kennedy and Raynolds (he could not recall the first name). He says that some thought the name was Rose, but he had seen it written as Rode. It is likely that there was a misprint in what he had read. Lewis Bonnett Jr. is a valuable witness, for Lewis Wetzel lived with the Bonnett family for a time. However, Lewis Bonnett Jr. was a six-year-old boy at the time of this incident, and his answers to Draper's questions were often based on things he had read long after the fact, which somewhat diminishes their value. His recollections about this rescue can be found in [50, pp. 33–36, 85–88, 95–96.]

(4) I do not know Frazier's first name, so I called him John. Cyrus Wetzel says that he and Rose were married and went to Kentucky shortly after this incident. Also, I only know that Frazier came from old Virginia, but I don't know where. Williamsburg is a guess. Lewis Bonnett Jr. says that Rose's parents were living on Buffalo Creek and that she was staying at Fort Henry. Cyrus Wetzel says she was going to visit friends on Short Creek.

(5) Old Crossfire was so-called because he was left-handed, which, when shooting a rifle, caused the lock and pan (with flashing powder) to be right in front of the shooter's eye. This could be very dangerous (see [39, p. 236]). Lewis Bonnett Jr. gave his name as the Great Canopsico, a Mingo chief who had killed many whites [50, p. 88].

(6) The descriptions imply that Fort Henry was still being used in 1784, although Lydia Cruger says that after 1786, it was replaced by the new Fort Randolph, which stood at the mouth of Wheeling Creek [40, II4, pp. 1–3]. I do not know that Silas Zane's wife was living at the fort, but Silas had gone on a trading mission with a man named George Green and was killed by the Indians near the Scioto River in Ohio on the return, perhaps early in 1785 [47, p. 59].

(7) Lewis Wetzel had discovered the Indians' canoe at the mouth of Short Creek and did warn Frazier and Rose about avoiding the river trail. There is no evidence that he might have sabotaged the boat, which was my invention. The trader Le Clerk is fictional.

Pertinent references for this chapter: [1, pp. 168–172], [14, pp. 359–361], [24, pp. 165–167], [28, pp. 233–237], [39, pp. 235–237], [41, pp. 147–148], [50, pp. 33–36, 85–86, 95–96], [53, pp. 1–70], [61, p. 137], [40, I2, pp. 1–2; IX3, pp. 9–12; XIV1, pp. 2–3], [74, pp. 82–85].

Chapter 10: Hunted

Much of the material in this chapter is fictional, although the adventure of Lewis Wetzel in the abandoned cabin and the capture of young John Wetzel are based on accounts in the literature. The first incident is usually referred to by Wetzel aficionados as "the hut in the storm" story. It is in fact this story that kindled my own lifelong interest in Lewis Wetzel. Zane Grey weaved this incident into his book, *The Spirit of the Border*, although he altered the facts a bit. In Grey's version, Wetzel jumped among the braves (eleven in all) and in a fierce struggle wrenched the shoulder of one and broke the arm of the other, before being captured and bound. He was later freed in the night at Wingenund's camp by Whispering Winds, Wingenund's own lovely daughter. Grey's thrilling words describing this action were gripping to a young boy of six or seven years when read to him by his brother. The capture of John Wetzel Jr. and the killing of Fred Earlywine, along with the subsequent rescue by Hamilton Kerr, Isaac Williams, and a Dutchman named Jacob, is a well-known story and believed to be true.

Most accounts indicate that four Indians were involved and three were killed. I made use of this incident to involve my fictional Indian party led by Little Fox and Red Storm.

(1) John Leith was a real person and one whose life was very interesting. The tracing of his life as given in the text is true, although I doubt that he ever met Lewis Wetzel. A fascinating little book *A Short Biography of John Leith: With a Brief Account of His Life Among the Indians* by John Leith, Consul Willshire Butterfield, and Ewel Jeffries first published in 1883, provides an excellent account of Leith's life, along with extensive notes by Butterfield [9]. This work was based on an 1831 publication called by essentially the same name and written by Ewel Jeffries, a self-proclaimed relative of Leith, who spelled the name incorrectly as Leeth. This part is given in the first person, coming from Leith himself.

(2) Leith was captured by the Delawares in Ohio in 1772 when he was about seventeen years old, having hired himself to an Indian trader. The incidents concerning him and mentioned in the text are true. Of course, his interactions with Red Storm, Little Fox, Fire Heart, and Lewis Wetzel are fictional.

(3) The account of the "hut in the storm" episode seems to have first appeared in the book by De Hass [14, p. 354] and was copied by later authors. Allman, a descendent of the Wetzel family, includes the story and even a photograph of a cabin, which he identifies as the very one in which Wetzel had taken refuge [1, pp. 147–150]. But Allman had given this same photo in an earlier publication, a 1928 *History of Limestone Community*, in which he identified the cabin as a "pioneer log cabin on Waymans Ridge, built about 1875." Whether this famous incident ever really happened is an open question among many Wetzel scholars. The location of the hut has never been clear and varies in the different accounts. Although I selected the time as in the spring of 1785, that is also a guess and not based on any real evidence. Good discussions of this incident can be found, as usual, in [40, XI1, pp. 2–5; XII4, pp. 6–9].

(4) The capture of young John Wetzel and Fred Earlywine is accurate and given by De Hass [14, pp. 286–289], although I have put in fictional discourse. It probably happened a year later than I have indicated, since it is said in most accounts that John Wetzel was sixteen years old at the time. I wanted to couple it with the hut-in-the-storm episode, since the fictional Indian party was used in both places. Most accounts say that there only four Indians involved, and all but one of them were killed by the rescue party. One brave who had been swimming the horse (sometimes the colt is not mentioned) did return to get the canoe and the rifles. After crossing the river, he set it loose, and according to Allman [1, p. 62], it came to rest some three hundred miles down the Ohio River at Maysville, Kentucky, with the dead hog still in it.

(5) The rescue party, consisting of Hamilton Kerr, Isaac Williams, and the Dutchman named Jacob, just happened to be in the area. Eckert [24, p. 471] gives the last name of Jacob as Hindemann, but none of the other writers gives him a name.

(6) A reasonable question often asked about the John Wetzel-Fred Earlywine capture concerns any mention of an attempt to rescue the boys. I have tried to address that in the text, although a better reason may be that there were no Wetzel men at home that day other than young John. I am not sure where the Earlywines lived; it is only said that they were neighbors of the Wetzels. Nor am I sure of where the Indians were hiding. I have assumed it was downstream from the Wetzel cabin.

(7) The discussion of the Indian treaties and the names of the chiefs at the Treaty of Fort McIntosh are accurate. The book by Downes has a good discussion [18, pp. 286–309].

Pertinent references for this chapter: [1, pp. 60–62, 147–150], [9], [14, pp. 286–289, 354], [18, pp. 286–309], [24, pp. 445, 468–472], [34, pp. 88–89], [39, pp. 224–225], [41, p. 80], [50, pp. 50–51], [54, pp. 450–451], [61, pp. 140–141], [40, V2, pp. 8–9; XI1, pp. 2–5; XII4, pp. 6–9].

Chapter 11: Father

Many of the details in this chapter are fictional, although the shooting contest with Gibson's troops and the death of John Wetzel are taken from accounts given in the historical literature. Also the events associated with John Leith are as accurate as I could make them. More than a year in time passes from the beginning to the end of this chapter. I do not know when the contest was actually held; it may have been several years earlier than in 1785 where I have placed it. I will say more about that below. The date of John Wetzel's death is now given as June 11, 1786.

For many years, it was supposed to have been in 1787, for that was the date given on a marker, which for a long time stood near the grave site along Graveyard Run in Marshall, County, West Virginia.

(1) Jones Tavern is a fictional establishment, although there must have existed such places in Wheeling by that time along the riverfront. Wheeling had become a jumping off place for people planning to find land in Kentucky in those days. There are references in army records of details going to Wheeling to obtain provisions, so there must have been several commercial establishments in the town. The early histories of Wheeling that I am aware of are not clear on this question.

(2) The notion of a manito or personal divinity as a tradition among the Ottawas and Chippewas is described by Kinietz in his book *Indians of the Western Great Lakes* [49, pp. 288–289, 326–328].

(3) My description of the burial ceremony and of an Indian widow taking a new husband is based on such an account given by Galloway in the book *Old Chillicothe, Shawnee and Pioneer History* [29, pp. 198–200].

(4) The rifleman's contest with the men of Gibson's company is based on a short paragraph in a letter from Isaac Leffler to Lyman Draper [19, 6E82.1–82.3] recorded in both Hintzen's *Border Wars*, [39, pp. 232–233] and [40, I4, p. 6; IX5, p. 11]. Leffler says that Alexander Mitchell and Wetzel had been out spying, came into Wheeling Fort where they met Captain Gibson and his company of regulars. No date is given, and I have put it into the summer of 1785. There is some question in my mind about who this Captain Gibson was. Most of the experts believe that it was John Gibson, who had commanded troops at Fort Laurens and at Fort Pitt. If it is he who Leffler is referring to, the date would have been much earlier, some think maybe 1782. However, Gibson was a colonel in 1781 and surely would not have been referred to as a captain in 1782 or later. In fact, he held the rank of colonel as early as July of 1777 when Lewis Wetzel was barely fourteen years old (see letter to General Hand [47, p. 35]). Hence, I have treated this Gibson, whom I called Tom, as another man who was a captain in the (regular) army as it existed in 1785. Construction on Fort Harmar at the mouth of the Muskingum River, at present-day Marietta, Ohio, began in the fall of 1785, so a company of soldiers could have been heading that way in the summer of that year. Of course, Leffler might have meant to say colonel instead of captain. If it was the famous John Gibson, then the date of this incident could have been no later than 1782. A discussion of the First American Regiment commanded by Harmar can be found in [72, p. 14].

(5) The events involving John Leith in section 11.4 are accurate and based on John Leith's own narrative and notes in [9,

pp. 59–64]. The Delaware Indian Que-shaw-sey, who called himself George Washington, is real and will appear again in a later chapter. Leith gave a sworn statement to Major John Doughty at Fort McIntosh on October 17 of 1785, which is recorded in the notes of the abovementioned document pages 61–64. Of course, the parts involving the fictional Indians Little Fox, Red Storm, and Fire Heart are purely fictional, as is any contact between Leith and Wetzel. A good discussion of the various treaty negotiations and how the Indians reacted to them can be found in [18, pp. 286–309].

(6) The death of Captain John Wetzel happened somewhat in the way that I have described it. My description is based primarily on the account given by Henry Jolly, which is recorded in [52, pp. 81–82]. He says that Moore was killed, Andrews escaped, and Lewis Wetzel was sick with the ague and had gone ashore. He did swim the river in pursuit, came back to Baker's Station, and walked to Henry Jolly's place that day. There are many other accounts, most with small (and sometimes great) differences in detail. For many years, the date was given as 1787. De Hass, who made a great effort in 1849 to find the grave site, claimed to have found a stone marker on which the date of 1787 was chiseled. However, C. B. Allman, a descendent of the Wetzel family, published in the appendix of his biography of Lewis Wetzel, [1, pp. 214–216], a copy of the "Appraisement of John Wetzel's Personal Property," dated August 19, 1786. This puts to rest any argument that he died later than 1786.

(7) Details about the burial of John Wetzel are sketchy. It does not seem likely that Lewis did it by himself, so I have provided Henry Baker to help him. It is possible that there were others present at Baker's Station, but it seems to me that if so, they would have heard the fighting and been involved. Some accounts say that he was buried the next day, and that is possible. Henry Jolly tells that a party of

nine or ten men went back the next day, but they went across to resume the tracking of the Indian party. Jolly says nothing about the burial. The grave site along Graveyard Run was marked for many years, but the original stone marker has been lost. A road sign entitled Baker's Station mentioned that John Wetzel had been killed nearby. This sign was located at Americana Park, seven miles below Moundsville, West Virginia. On July 21, 1940, a grave stone marking John Wetzel's death was placed at the grave site at a special dedication ceremony. That marker has since been moved to the McCreary cemetery, not far from the old Wetzel homestead in Marshall County, West Virginia [40, XIII3, pp. 9–12]. The date of death on the marker was June 19, 1786, although Hintzen says the correct date is June 11, 1786 [39, p. 226]. Also near the grave site was a beech tree, on which had been carved "J.W., 1787." [40, XII1, p. 9].

(8) It is not known what Indians were responsible for the attack on John Wetzel. There was an entry in the "Journal of Joseph Buell" (printed in Hildreth's *Pioneer History* [38, p. 144]) on June 19, 1786, saying that news had arrived that Indians had killed four or five women and children on Fish Creek. Thus the attack by my fictional Indian party on the cabin on Fish Creek, prior to their attack on Wetzel, was based on facts. No names of the women or children were given.

(9) The five white men on horseback, whom the Indians were trailing, and whose tracks Lewis Wetzel followed included, according to Henry Jolly, two of Lewis's brothers. How Lew would have known that, as Jolly indicated he did, seems problematic.

(10) The Wetzel claim may have been near the current town of Middlebourne, Tyler County, West Virginia. The mouth of Middle Island Creek is on the Ohio River near the modern

town of St. Marys, West Virginia, about forty-two miles from the site of Baker's Station and roughly sixty miles from Wheeling, West Virginia.

(11) In 1915, a West Virginia historian Sylvester Myers, along with another local resident, located the John Wetzel grave site, leaving a map of the area. He wrote that ten years earlier, some hunters digging in a muskrat hole, which penetrated the Wetzel grave, unearthed what was assumed to be the remains of a coffin and a crudely constructed handmade axe, supposed to have been the property of Wetzel. This axe was at one time exhibited at the Moundsville Echo, at least according to this story [40, XIII1, pp. 8–9]. It seems doubtful to me that there would have been a coffin available in which to bury John Wetzel, although sometimes families did keep a coffin around for use if necessary, and maybe there was one at Baker's. Indeed, it is said that Daniel Boone, in his home near St. Charles, Missouri, had built a coffin that he stored in his bedroom. At one point, an old Indian died when visiting there and was buried in the family plot in Boone's coffin. The claim is made that when the Kentuckians came to move Boone's remains to Kentucky, they took this coffin with the bones of the Indian instead.

(12) The names of John Wetzel's companions, Andrews and Moore, were given by Henry Jolly. I know nothing of them other than that, and my portrayal of them is purely fictional. Jolly said that Andrews did swim across the river and escaped. George Edgington says that Miller was with John and Lewis [51, pp. 15–16.]. Both agree that Lewis was ill and had gone ashore. Edgington says that Miller swam across the river and escaped to Wheeling. This might have been Jacob Miller who, Edgington says, was often with the Wetzels. Jolly claims that Lewis walked to his place that day, and that he returned with nine or ten men the next day. Lewis surely told Jolly who was along, but Jolly could have confused the names many years later.

Pertinent references for this chapter: [1, pp. 114–116, 214–216], [8, pp. 221–229], [9, pp. 58–64], [14, pp. 345–346], [18, pp. 286–309], [24, pp. 454–466], [29, pp. 198–200], [34, pp. 22–25], [38, p. 144], [39, pp. 225–226, 232–233], [41, pp. 80–83], [46, p. 213], [47, pp. 35, 296], [49, pp. 288–289, 326–328], [50, pp. 5–6, 52, 88], [51, pp. 15–16, 95], [52, pp. 81–82], [54, p. 449], [61, p. 135], [64, pp. 48–50], [69, pp. 262–263], [40, I3, pp. 1–5; I4, pp. 1–6; VI6, pp. 2–5; XIII1, pp. 6–9; XIII3, pp. 9–12], [72, p. 14].

Chapter 12: Kentucky

Very little is known about Lew Wetzel's life in Kentucky, although we know he was there in August of 1786. His name appears on the two petitions filed with the Virginia legislature, the first to establish the town of Washington, and the second to form a new county called Mason County, which included the towns of Limestone and Washington. The current Kentucky town of Maysville includes both of these. The great frontiersman Simon Kenton was one of the founders in this area and had built his own fort called Kenton's Station. Most of the incidents in the chapter are fictional, although built around events that were common to the time. The report of the death of John Wetzel and the pursuit of the Indians by Lewis Wetzel and the other men is real, but the Wetzel trip down the river is from my imagination. The petitions to the legislature were real, but I don't know how the signatures were obtained.

The Wetzel-Kenton trip into Ohio was invented, although I expect the two of them must have had similar adventures. Some of the names of Indian victims in Kentucky are actual.

(1) Lewis Bonnett Jr. says that he well remembered the day when the "express arrived of the death of my uncle Wetzel. My Father was a-raising a horse stable at the time the news was announced." He thinks Martin was there and that Lewis came in a few days later with two scalps. I believe this was

in error for it completely contradicts Henry Jolly's account. Bonnett's remarks are from the Draper Manuscripts and are recorded in *Recollections of Lewis Bonnett, Jr.* edited by Jared Lobdell and published by Heritage Books Inc. [50, p. 5]. Henry Jolly's account is given in [52, pp. 81–82]. Jolly tells of the return across the river, and that eventually the search was ended because of the illness of Lewis Wetzel. He also mentions the five-man hunting party, which included the two Wetzel brothers (not named).

(2) Portions of the Bonnett frame house mentioned in the story remain as part of the remodeled home, still standing on the old Bonnett property in Marshall County, West Virginia. The half-finished stone house was eventually made into a barn, which is also standing today. Clark Wullenweber and Bill Hintzen, experts in Wetzel lore, believed the stone foundation was originally intended as a house because of built-in fireplaces. An excellent discussion of this, including photographs, may be found in *The True Wetzelian* [40, XI3, pp. 2–19].

(3) The material about John Leith is taken from his own accounts found in [9, pp. 64–69]. The town called Tapacon was really the Moravian town of New Schonbrunn, Tapacon (or Tuppakin) being the Indian name. Of course, the interactions of Leith with Little Fox are fictional.

(4) The appraisement of John Wetzel's personal property was carried out on June 19, 1786 and signed by James McConnell, Lewis Bonnett, Lewis Lindhoff, and Martin Collons. The list of items and their values may be found in the appendix of the book by C. B. Allman [1, pp. 214–217]. Bonnett, of course, was John Wetzel's brother-in-law. McConnell was a man of some importance in the region. According to Gibson Cranmer in his *History of Wheeling City* [12], McConnell was appointed in 1777, along with

Sam Mason, Ebenezer Zane, and Conrad Wheat to "view the best and most direct way for the laying out of a road from Fort Henry to the first fork of Wheeling, and due return make to the next county court." He may have been related to Hugh McConnell, who participated in the 1777 siege of Fort Henry and whose sister Rebecca was the wife of young William Shepherd, a casualty of that battle and son of county lieutenant David Shepherd. I know nothing of Lindhoff or Collons. Lewis Wetzel's reactions are purely fictional. It is true that Lewis later took up residence at his uncle Lewis Bonnett's home.

(5) Thomas Nichols and James Gridler are real characters who were signers of the petition to make Washington a town in Kentucky, but everything else about them is fictional. There was an Austin Nichols who had land on Wheeling Creek, but whether he was related to Thomas Nichols, I do not know. How Lew Wetzel traveled to Kentucky is unknown, but it seems reasonable that he went by flatboat. Attacks on flatboats by the Indians were common in the 1780s, but there is no direct evidence that Lewis Wetzel was involved in one.

(6) Two biographies of Simon Kenton, *The Violent Years* by Patricia Jahns [44, pp. 174–196] and *Simon Kenton, His Life and Period, 1755–1836* by Edna Kenton [48, pp. 165–185], describe the dwellings and events in the Limestone, Kenton's Station, Washington area in Kentucky at the time of Wetzel's visit. William Wood was a Baptist preacher, who with the surveyor Arthur Fox, had purchased land from Kenton on which they planned to establish a town. The title for 320 acres was officially transferred in 1785, but this deed only covered part of the acreage, with as many as 700 acres eventually purchased. This information is found in a book published in 1987 by Nancy O'Malley entitled *A New Village Called Washington* [63, p. 7]. This

book is available at the Visitor's Center in the historic town of Washington. Edward and John Waller had built a cabin near the Limestone Landing, which was used as temporary shelter for new arrivals. The Wallers lived mostly at Kenton's Station. There was also the blockhouse that Kenton and others had built near the landing. Daniel Boone did operate a tavern for a time, located either in the blockhouse or Wallers' old place. Jahns [44, p. 188] says it was in "Waller's old blockhouse (on Front Street, halfway between Market and Limestone Streets)." Whether by this is meant the blockhouse that had been built near the landing and was mostly unoccupied, or the cabin that the Wallers often loaned out to new arrivals, especially single men, is unclear. The timing on this is uncertain, although it was probably in 1785 or 1786. It suited my purpose to make it 1786.

(7) The petitions. The first official petition asking the Virginia legislature to establish the town of Washington was dated August 22, 1786 and included 101 names, of which the 101st was one Lewis Whitsel. The list was published in *The History of Maysville and Mason County* by G. G. Clift [11, pp. 56–59]. Clift attributes the list to J. R. Robertson, *Petitions of the Early Inhabitants of Kentucky*. The petition states that over seven hundred acres have been set apart, upward of fifty families have settled there, "among whom are Mechanicks of divers kinds." This may have been a bit of an exaggeration, as other observers note that there were very few dwellings of a permanent nature, even a year or two later. The petition was granted officially on October 27, 1786 with the stipulation (among others) "that Edmund Lyne, Edward Waller, Henry Lee, Miles W. Conway, Arthur Fox, Daniel Boone, Robert Rankins, John Gutridge, and William Lamb, gentlemen, be trustees of the same." On August 25, a second petition was addressed to the Virginia legislature asking for the naming

of a new county called Mason County, formed out of the present county of Bourbon. There were 152 names on this petition, but it was not granted by the legislature until the following year. In fact, several petitions were filed and opposed by other sections of Bourbon County. In September 1787, the division of Bourbon County was approved, and the new Mason County was to be established on May 1, 1788. The town of Limestone was officially established as a town on December 11, 1787, and its name was changed to Maysville. Washington was the second largest town in Kentucky in the 1790s, and when Kentucky was admitted as a state in 1792, many westerners wanted Washington named as the capital of the United States.

(8) The capture of John Kinsaulla by the Shawnee chief Black Snake is based on real events described in both [44, pp. 191–192] and [48, p. 180]. Captain Snake, as he was sometimes called, did drag Kinsaulla to the wall of Taylor's cabin and observed the men praying. He refused then to kill him because "the Great Spirit would be angry." The location of Taylor's cabin, which was often used for preaching, is unclear. One account has it close to Kenton's station while another says it was near the town spring in the village of Washington. Kenton's Station was located on the west bank of Lawrence Creek, about one mile northwest of Washington.

(9) The killing of the two sons of Moses Phillips, who was a signer of the petition asking for a new county, is described in [44, p. 192], which says that Kenton's Boys gave chase but lost the trail. I chose to have the pursuit carried out by just Kenton and Wetzel. It is likely that Wetzel was one of Kenton's Boys during his stay in Kentucky at this time. Jahns [44, p. 210] writes that Lewis Wetzel was remembered by some of Kenton's Boys as being "friendly, hard-living, full of jokes and pranks, a huge man, a little like having a bolt of lightning around."

(10) The conversation between Wetzel and Kenton about Daniel Boone was based on a statement in [44, p. 188] that Daniel Boone was disliked, even hated, in Kentucky at this time.

(11) Simon Kenton married the girl Martha Dowden in February of 1787. She was seventeen at the time and was the niece of the wife of Simon's brother William. Another girl at Kenton's Station had a child by Simon before the year was out [44, p. 198]. This apparently did not cause any permanent rift between Simon and his new wife, Martha.

Pertinent references for this chapter: [8, pp. 115–116, 214–217], [9, pp. 64–69], [11, pp. 56–59], [24, p. 445], [21, pp. 323–324, 329–332], [44, pp. 174–198, 210], [48, pp. 165–185], [50, pp. 5–6], [52, p. 81], [63, pp. 6–8], [40, XIII2, pp. 2–5; XIII4, pp. 9–11].

Chapter 13: Logan

THE MATERIAL IN this chapter is based on an actual event, the expedition of Benjamin Logan against the Shawnee towns on the Mad River. There are numerous references to this campaign in the literature, but our information was supplemented by the discovery of a little-known reference to Lewis Wetzel in volume 2 of a work by Erminie Wheeler-Voegelin called *Indians of Ohio and Indiana Prior to 1795* [75]. The reference was to the Josiah Harmar Papers, held in the Clements Library of the University of Michigan [32]. Harmar notes that Lewis Wetzel, having been with Logan, brought him a report of the expedition.

The notes from this report, in Harmar's own handwriting, are included, as well as a number of letters Harmar wrote to others, including secretary of war Henry Knox, in which Harmar writes what Wetzel had told him. This is as close to an original source record of Lewis Wetzel that we will ever have. Of course, we have introduced fictional details, and the conversations are entirely from my own imagination.

(1) The rank of Benjamin Logan during this time is not clear. In his book *Historic Families of Kentucky*, Thomas Marshall Green says that Logan had been appointed a brigadier general in 1786, prior to going with George Rogers Clark at the beginning of his Wabash expedition [30, p. 136]. All other references to Logan, including those by Josiah Harmar, call him Colonel Logan. I have chosen to accept Green's statement, although it is on flimsy evidence. Perhaps the Virginia state authorities had conferred this rank, but it was unknown to many of his contemporaries.

(2) George Rogers Clark had assembled a force of 1,200 men at what is now Clarksville, Indiana, in September of 1786. He had originally asked for 2,500, but the Kentuckians were reluctant to volunteer, and Clark was disappointed. Clarksville is on the north side of the Ohio River opposite Louisville, Kentucky, the location of which, in those days, was referred to as the Falls of the Ohio. On about September 14, Clark decided it would be best for Logan, who was with him and in command of the men from Lincoln County, Kentucky, to go back and raise troops to attack the Shawnee towns on the Mad River. The idea was to prevent the Shawnees from joining forces with the other tribes to oppose Clark on the Wabash. It was around September 14 that Logan returned to gather troops, which he did rather rapidly [5, pp. 284–286]. The Kentuckians, who had suffered many raids by the Shawnees, were quite ready to strike a return blow.

(3) Logan's army crossed the Ohio River at Limestone on September 29 and 30 and moved west through what is now called Logan's Gap and then north along the present-day route of US Highway 68. In his deposition to Harmar [32], Wetzel says they left Limestone on October 6, but he must have been thinking of the day the attack began. Somewhere close to the old Shawnee town of Chillicothe, near present-day Xenia, Ohio, a man left the army and went ahead to

warn the Indians. Several of the accounts say the man was a Frenchman, although Eckert, in his book *The Frontiersman* [21] gives the man's name as Willis Chadley. No one else gives a name, and the name I have used is fictional. I have not been able to find the source that Eckert had for this incident. Some of the accounts say that the Indians killed this informant, but that seemed doubtful to me. Patricia Jahns, in *The Violent Years* [44, p. 197], says that the informant was sent on to Detroit. The Mackachack towns were a mile or so east of the current town of West Liberty, Ohio, which was itself the location of the village called Pickaway on the west bank of the Mad River. Wapakoneta was on the east bank of the Mad, two miles south of West Liberty, and Pigeon Town was on the east bank about three miles northwest of West Liberty. Wapatomica was a large and important Shawnee town on the west bank of the upper Mad River, about two miles below Zanesfield, Ohio, which was the site of Mingo Town. Blue Jacket's Town was at the present city of Bellefontaine, Ohio. It was bracketed by New Coshocton or Buckongehelas's Town, three miles to the north, and McKee's Town, two-and-a-half miles southeast on McKee's Creek.

(4) Many of the details about the attack on Mackachack come from the writing of young William Lytle and recorded in the history of Logan County, Ohio, as given in Howe's *Historical Collections of Ohio*, [42, vol. 2, pp. 98–100]. Writing at a later time, it is possible that Lytle attributed a bit more to himself than was actually true, but his accounts are important. The shooting of Curner by High Horn with an arrow, and the death of Captain Irwin are as described by Lytle. The actions of Lewis Wetzel are entirely fictional.

(5) High Horn or Spemica Lawba is a real and interesting character. There is controversy about his parents. Eckert says that his mother was Tecumpanese, the sister of the great Shawnee leader, Tecumseh [22, p. 288]. I doubt the

truth of this. It may be that his father was a white man named Joshua Renick. The mother was likely a Shawnee woman whose name is unknown. Some experts say that it is possible that Tecumpanese was the mother. It is likely that Spemica Lawba was being looked after by Moluntha and Nonhelema, and some people have speculated that Joshua Renick and Moluntha were the same person, but that is very doubtful. If one investigates Spemica Lawba online, there is considerable discussion of this subject. General Logan took a special interest in the boy, helping him learn to speak and read English. Later on, the boy referred to himself as Johnny Logan and served as an interpreter and aid to the whites in later affairs with the Indians. Several sources indicate that Moluntha was ninety-four years old at this time, but I am skeptical of that and suspect that he was much younger. However, there is no really solid evidence of which I am aware that would settle the question of the old chief's age.

(6) The killing of Moluntha by Colonel Hugh McGary was a hideous act and resulted in a court-martial for McGary in Kentucky on March 21, 1787. He was found guilty on two of the four counts and suspended for one year [29, p. 92]. (One can find a good discussion of this in the "Calendar of Virginia State Papers and Other Manuscripts," which can be accessed online.) It is doubtful that Moluntha was present at the Blue Licks battle, since the Shawnees had not participated there in any great numbers. (Recall the discussion in chapter 7 prior to the 1782 attack on Fort Henry.) Again, there is disagreement about McGary's rank. Some sources say he was a major, one says he was a captain, but the record in the Virginia State papers refers to him as Colonel Hugh McGary. I assume that is correct. McGary filed charges against Colonel Robert Patterson and Lieutenant Colonel James Trotter for taking rum and killing beeves at Limestone. Patterson was reprimanded, and Trotter found innocent. It is true that many

had blamed McGary for the defeat of the Kentuckians at the hands of the Shawnees at the Blue Licks in August of 1782, and he was very sensitive about it [71, pp. 298–299].

(7) Colonel Harmar was quite upset about this killing of Moluntha and mentioned it in letters to Captain Hamtramck, General Knox, and several others. These letters may be found among the Harmar papers [32]. Wetzel reported that Moluntha was flying the Stars and Stripes and holding up some papers, which were those signed by him at the treaty negotiations at Fort Finney (near present-day Cincinnati) in January of 1786. Moluntha did consider himself a friend to the Americans, although he also had written to Detroit in April saying that he had been deceived by the Americans asking for assistance and assuring the British "father" that he was his steady friend [75, p. 569].

(8) Isaac Zane lived at Mingo Town with his wife, Myeerah, and was present during Logan's attack. His cabin was not destroyed [75, p. 580] although there is no evidence that Lew Wetzel had any hand in that. Whether Wetzel would have known Isaac Zane at this time is unknown, although he certainly knew Isaac's brothers. Zane was an interpreter at the Fort Finney negotiations and lived with his family in the general area for many years. Mingo Town was at the site of the current Ohio town of Zanesfield, where the gravestones of Isaac and Myeerah may be seen today. Myeerah was the daughter of Tarhe, The Crane, an important Wyandot chief.

(9) According to an account by Solomon Clark in the Draper Manuscripts, Logan did post notices, asking for an exchange of prisoners in order to recover Robert Clark, who had been captured by the Shawnees sometime earlier near Limestone. Solomon and Robert were the sons of George Clark (not George Rogers Clark), who was a friend of Logan and also of Simon Kenton. In this testimony,

Solomon says that the Indians became convinced that Logan's expedition was intended to rescue Clark, whom they assumed to be the son of George Rogers Clark. This made them angry, and they shipped Clark off to Detroit. He was exchanged a year later at a special meeting between the Shawnees and Kentuckians held across the Ohio River opposite Limestone (currently the town of Maysville, Kentucky) [10]. George Clark was the brother-in-law of Colonel William Whitley, who was a friend of Logan and was along on Logan's campaign [10]. I placed Whitley at the site of Moluntha's murder, but that is an invention on my part.

(10) The Shawnee warriors had left their Mad River towns to join the Indian confederation under the Miami chief, Little Turtle, gathered to oppose the Wabash campaign of George Rogers Clark. The number of such warriors is not clear, but it was likely between two hundred and four hundred. Very few were left to defend their homes. The discussion in the text is mostly accurate and is taken from the book of Temple Bodley [5, pp. 276–299]. Clark had significant difficulties, including a mutiny in which ultimately as many as four hundred men from Lincoln County, Kentucky, left him and went home. Having pushed north of Vincennes, Indiana—referred to then as Post St. Vincent—and to within thirty miles of the Indians, Clark thought it wise to go back to Vincennes. The leading citizen among the French population, Colonel LeGras, wrote to the Indians saying that he and his friends had persuaded Clark to retreat, promising that the Indians would lay down their war hatchet. This lie was intended to mask the fact that Clark's forces were weakened. The letter, along with one from Clark, was sent to the Indians on October 10. The Indians replied on October 23, agreeing to negotiate. The Shawnees were upset at this and began to return to

their towns, which by now were mostly destroyed. George Rogers Clark was the one American commander feared and respected by the Indians.

(11) Why Lewis Wetzel was the one to bring the news of the Logan campaign to Colonel Harmar is not known. It may be that he was returning to Wheeling to spend the winter and stopped at Fort Harmar. Perhaps he was sent by Logan or Kenton. According to Major Denny, Harmar's aide, three men came in from Limestone [15, p. 297], and one of them was Wetzel, although Denny gave no names. Harmar wrote out an account based on what he called "Information from Lewis Whetzel at Muskingum, 14th Nov. '86." In addition, he wrote letters to Hamtramck, Knox, and others. In his letter to Hamtramck, he mentions that a "person of the name of Wetzell" arrived and had been with Colonel Logan. This may be found in the Harmar papers held at the Clements Library at the University of Michigan [32]. Some of this material has been printed in *The True Wetzelian*, vol. XV, no. 6: 2–12 and vol. XVI, no. 2: 10–11 [40]. Denny went by boat north to Pittsburgh on November 15, and it seems likely that Wetzel went along, although there is no real evidence for that.

(12) In Wetzel's deposition, he names six towns that were destroyed and says there were some others, although "their number did not exceed seven" [32, vol. 4, Correspondence & Documents, 88], [40, XV6, p. 3]. This is a bit confusing. In his letters, Harmar says Logan's party destroyed seven towns [32, Letter Book B, 5: 9–11, 19–21], [40, XV6, pp. 10–11]. Other writers have a different count of towns that were burned. Wheeler-Voegelin names eight villages [75, pp. 564–582], saying specifically that Buckongehelas's town was not destroyed while Eckert lists thirteen [21, p. 351], including Buckongehelas's Town. In the deposition, it is stated that the towns were burned and much corn destroyed.

> Eleven scalps were taken, including that of Moluntha. The party "made prisoner of twenty-five Indian women, and two children—four whites, who had been taken from us at some former place, and one Frenchman." In his book *A Sorrow in our Heart*, Eckert mentions two white women, Margaret and Elizabeth McKinzie (called Kisathoi and Tebethto by the Shawnees), who were present and walked away from the fighting. The two girls had been captured at their home on the Great Kanawha, near where it intersected the Ohio some eight years earlier. They were later found, according to Eckert, by the trader John Kinzie, who took them to Detroit and later married Margaret. If this is true, then they were not part of the four white women mentioned by Wetzel. A full discussion of the adventures of these women is given by Eckert in his book, *Gateway to Empire* [23]. Kinzie was an early trader and store owner in what became the city of Chicago. The loss to Logan's party consisted of three killed and three wounded, and the raid was accomplished in fifteen days, according to Wetzel. In his letter to Knox, Harmar reports that Clark had left for the Wabash on September 17 with 1,200 men, but 400 had left him. He also talks about the killing of Moluntha [32, Letter Book B], [40, XV2, p. 11]. Wetzel must have reported these facts. William Galloway says that the "loot" taken from the destroyed Indian villages amounted to "about $2.50 per man for the 885 men entitled to participate." [29, pp. 90–94].

Pertinent references for this chapter: [5, pp. 276–299], [8, pp. 225–236], [10], [11, p. 60], [15, pp. 297–298], [21, pp. 346–352], [22, pp. 286–293], [23], [24, pp. 477–478], [26, pp. 329, 345], [28, p. 102], [29, pp. 90–94], [30, pp. 136–138], [32], [38, pp. 144–151], [39, pp. 223–227, 256–258], [44, pp. 192–197], [48, pp. 182–185], [52, p. 73], [42, vol. 2, pp. 98–100], [56, pp. 110, 117–119], [69], [40, XV6, pp. 2–12; XVI2, p. 10], [71, pp. 298–299], [72, pp. 56–57], [75, pp. 554–583].

Chapter 14: Rewards

This chapter builds toward what is usually called the McMahan reward expedition. It is mentioned in nearly every historical source which has any reference to Lewis Wetzel. Most accounts give the date as 1786, but I believe the correct date is August 5, 1787. This fits much better with the fact that we know Lewis Wetzel was in Kentucky in August of 1786. It is also the date mentioned in the journal of John Mathews, recorded in Hildreth's *Pioneer History* [38, p. 183]. Mathews writes,

> Aug. 5. Mr. McMahan, with a party of volunteers, about twenty in number, crossed the Ohio River, intending to come up with the Indians who killed the man. They are determined to range the Muskingum country, where they hope to fall in with some party of Indians, or come to their trail and follow them into their settlements.

The details of most of the incidents are fictional, although the incidents themselves were suggested by various historical references.

(1) The Indians living in the towns in the Mad River region destroyed by Logan had mostly scattered by the summer of 1787. Some sources say that over 1,200 Shawnees were displaced, some going as far as Missouri, some going to towns on the Auglaize River in northeastern Ohio, some farther west to the upper Maumee in modern-day Indiana, some to the lower White and Wabash Rivers in Indiana. The Mingoes and Cherokees had gone south near the mouth of the Scioto. Discussions of these movements can be found in [75, pp. 547–584].

(2) The movement of the Shawnees at Wapatomica to Detroit in the winter of 1786–1787 is recounted in [75, p. 566]. The story of James Moore and his family, including the capture of

his sister, Mary, is given in [8, pp. 233–237] and also in Howe's *Historical Collections of Virginia* where, on page 494, he says that Mary (also called Polly) was eight years old at the time of her capture [43, pp. 489–494]. The Moores lived in Abbs Valley, Virginia, located in Tazewell County. This shows how far from home the Indians sometimes traveled on their raids. The description of these incidents in the text are accurate. Baptiste Oriome was a real character, and the American Stockwell purchased young Mary Moore for a half gallon of rum. James Moore found her with Stockwell in Frenchtown (modern-day Monroe, Michigan) where she was in very bad shape. He engaged Simon Girty and Alexander McKee to help get her released but was unsuccessful. Stockwell was brought to trial for ill-treatment of the girl but not required to free her. By 1789, James Moore was able to obtain his own freedom as well as Mary's, and they returned to their friends in Virginia.

(3) John Mathews of New Braintree, Massachusetts, came west to be employed as part of the team that was to survey the so-called Seven Ranges, a region of land in eastern Ohio that included all of the modern counties of Monroe, Belmont, Harrison, and Jefferson in Ohio, along with parts of Washington, Noble, Guernsey, Tuscarawas, and Columbiana counties. The eastern boundary of the ranges was along the Ohio River. Mathews kept a journal, extracts of which are printed in Hildreth's *Pioneer History* mentioned above. This journal is invaluable in having some record of the events in the area at the time. Mathews writes on May 8, 1787, that the surveyors had been called in as a consequence of information from Esquire Zane, that the Indians had killed three persons and taken three prisoners on Fishing Creek on April 25 [38, p. 180]. This is the basis for the Indian raids that I have described. No details are known, and no names given. There is no evidence that Lewis Wetzel was the one who found the bodies, but it suited my story to tell it that way.

(4) In the *History of Preston County* [76, p. 44], the story is told of Jacob Wetzel visiting his sister Christiana Wolfe and presenting her with a gift of a fairly fresh scalp, the hair of which was interwoven with silk and silver beads. The writer thinks it was in 1787. It is not clear where the Wolfe home on Muddy Creek might have been. I assumed that it might have been near the mouth on the Cheat River, although it could have been higher up toward the source. There is no evidence that Lewis Wetzel was along at this time. The rest of the story is fictional anyway.

(5) The Indian Grey Bear, who gave up his scalp for the Jacob Wetzel gift is, of course, fictional, as are the incidents with the mad woman Esther Cale and Sam Johnson. The killing of three whites and capture of three others is fact, as mentioned above, although the details are fictional.

(6) John Mathews records on August 4, 1787 that a man was killed by Indians across the Ohio not far from where he was staying at Esquire McMahan's. The next day, he mentions that Mr. McMahan, with a party of volunteers, set out to avenge this killing [38, pp. 182–183]. As I mentioned at the beginning, most accounts of this McMahan expedition date it in 1786. It is stated that a reward of $100 was set. It is not always clear whether McMahan put up the money, or it was gathered from among many. The shortness of the time makes me think that McMahan put it up himself. Mason [54, pp. 447–449] says that each man was to get $4 and the scalp-taker would get an extra $20. This seemed reasonable to me, so I put it that way in the text. Most accounts simply say that Wetzel was given the money in the end. The name McMahan is sometimes spelled McMahon, but Mathews, who spent a lot of time with McMahan, uses the spelling with the *a* rather than the *o*.

(7) John McDonald, a twelve-year-old boy in 1787, became a noted soldier and writer, who in 1839 wrote a series of six

articles on the Wetzel family in the *Western Christian Advocate* (Cincinnati, Ohio). These articles were the likely sources for a number of writers of later years. Unfortunately, they were full of errors based on hearsay and oral tradition. John's family lived in the area of Mingo Bottom in 1787, and in his article on Lewis Wetzel (which can be found in [40, IX3, pp. 5–6]), McDonald said that he first recollected seeing Lewis Wetzel "when he attached himself to a scouting party about the year 1787 or 88. My father then lived on the bank of the Ohio in Virginia, at a place known as the Mingo Bottom, three miles below Steubenville." He then goes on to give the story of the Reward Expedition. His account, as well as all the others that exist about this event, are much the same as I have given in the text. McDonald later moved to Maysville, Kentucky.

(8) McDonald does not say anything about Wetzel's building of the fire pit. De Hass [14, p. 351] describes this thoroughly and quotes Wetzel himself as saying it was like a "stove room." Clark Wullenweber, writing in [40, X6, p. 3] attributes this language to Wetzel's German heritage. "A stove room, Stube in German, is the principal living room of every proper German historic house," says Wullenweber.

(9) Lewis Bonnett Jr. says that Wetzel discovered the smoking campfire on or near the Tuscarawas River above the junction with White Womans River. This is above the modern town of Coshocton, Ohio. Lewis Bonnett Jr. says that the scalp that Wetzel brought back "hung in my father's up chamber room for better than two years" [50, p. 63]. Recall that Lewis Wetzel lived with the Bonnetts in those years. Young Lewis Bonnett often mentioned scalps hanging in the house that Lew Wetzel had brought.

(10) Adam Grandstaff—whose wife, Maria Catherine Wetzel, was the niece of John Wetzel and first cousin to Lewis Wetzel—was killed in April of 1787. This information is

given by Clark Wullenweber in an article on the Grandstaff family found in [40, XII3, p. 10]. Cranmer [12, p. 24] records this death but does not give a date. He spells the name Grindstaff, a common error.

(11) Absalom Wells, John Bukey, James McDonald (I'm not sure about the name *James*), and Jeremiah Devore were real people and could well have been present and part of the Reward Expedition. Whether they were or not is unknown to me, and any actions attributed to them in the text are fictional. Wells did have a flour mill on Buffalo Creek and probably was a good friend of Wetzel. The Bukey family was well-known in the area as good Indian fighters. Jeremiah Devore lived somewhere in the general area. By 1788, he had moved to Mason County, Kentucky. His son Nicholas, as quoted in the Draper Manuscripts, 19S, attributes the following statement to his father, talking about Lew Wetzel: "The Indians might as well shoot at the edge of a knife blade as to shoot at him."

Pertinent references for this chapter: [1, pp. 106–111], [1, pp. 233–239], [12, p. 24], [14, pp. 349–352], [24, pp. 424, 475–476], [28, p. 229], [34, pp. 76–80], [38, pp. 169–192], [39, pp. 237–239], [41, pp. 148–149], [43, pp. 489–494], [50, pp. 30–31], [54, pp. 447–449], [61, p. 138], [64, pp. 53–54], [69, pp. 264–268], [40, IX3; XII1, p. 6; X6, pp. 2–4; IX3, pp. 5–6], [75, pp. 547–584], [76, p. 44].

Chapter 15: Adventures

The incidents of this chapter are all based on accounts that appear in the literature, although, as always, the details are mostly fictional. These events were less prominent, and the dates I have assigned are guesses. The killing of John Baker most likely did happen in 1787 somewhat as described, and the hiring of Lew Wetzel by John Madison is given by several writers. Most accounts say that Madison was the brother of James Madison, the fourth president of the United States, but I could find no indication that James ever had a brother named John. Bill Hintzen says that John was a first cousin of James, and this seems most likely. On the other hand, Hintzen says in his periodical, *The True Wetzelian*, XIV1, p. 5 that he absolutely cannot accept the idea that Wetzel would go on a friendly visit to a Wyandot town. The account on which we based our story is given by Wetzel's nephew, Cyrus Wetzel, in a statement given to Lyman Draper [74, pp. 86–87].

By now, I needn't remind you that the Indian friends Little Fox, Red Storm, and Fire Heart, along with the French trader Le Clerk, are fictional.

(1) Ebenezer Zane served in the Virginia House of Delegates from Ohio County in 1780–81 along with Samuel McColloch, with David Shepherd in 1783–85, and with Benjamin Biggs in 1799–1800. James Madison was in that House in 1784–85 and also in 1799–1800. Patrick Henry was a delegate in 1780–81 and also in 1783. He had been governor of Virginia in the earlier years. Zane served on the state ratifying convention of 1788 along with Archibald Woods from Ohio County, and James Madison was a delegate from Orange County. These facts were obtained from a document supplied by the Virginia Historical Society entitled "A Bicentennial Register of Members of the General Assembly of Virginia," published for the general assembly of Virginia by the Virginia State Library in 1978. According to Wikipedia, Ebenezer Zane voted in favor of the new US constitution. There was considerable opposition to the proposed constitution, partly because some thought it gave too much power to a national government, and others wanted a bill of rights included.

(2) In the text I referred to Gooding's place. According to Cranmer [12, p. 138], Gooding's Inn was the first brick

building built in Wheeling. Later (I think after 1797), it was taken over by a prominent man, Zachariah Sprigg, who had operated a hotel in West Liberty. The location must have been near the river between Eleventh and Twelfth Streets in modern-day Wheeling. I do not know if this hotel would have existed in 1787. Probably it did not, but it seems like there should have been some lodging accommodations by that time. Jones' tavern, which I have used in previous chapters, is entirely fictional.

(3) Lew's answer to the question from Hamilton Kerr about what kind of luck he had is based on accounts of such an incident. Many of them said that Lew had killed three, and one got away. In his account, Lewis Bonnett Jr. said it was two of three, and this seemed more likely to be accurate [50, pp. 22–23].

(4) The killing of John Baker is based on an account originally published in the *Wheeling Intelligencer* in May of 1866 by Colonel Samuel Baker, a son of Henry Baker and grandson of John Baker. This account has been given in [40,VI5, pp. 18–19]. The writer claims to have been at the funeral, which was well-attended. Of course, Samuel Baker was only one year old at the time. The Wetzels participated in the battle and brought Baker back to his house, but there is no reason to think that John Madison was there. Leonard Raigor was one of the people who was listed as having attended the funeral. I do not know that he was present in the house during the fighting.

(5) Many of the accounts of the Madison affair indicate that the Big Sandy River, which enters the Ohio right along the border between West Virginia and Kentucky, was the original destination. All accounts agree that Madison was killed and Wetzel escaped, but there is a variation as to where it happened and how many people were in Madison's

party. I have followed an account given by Isaac Leffler in June of 1862 and printed in [40, X2, p. 11]. Leffler says they had camped at the mouth of the Guyandotte, which enters the Ohio River at the site of the present city of Huntington, West Virginia. Other accounts say they had discovered an abandoned camp. The details of the attack are my inventions, although Leffler says that Wetzel killed one of the Indians. He mentions the dog who, he says, "had fought off the wolves for 4 or 5 days and was so poor he could scarcely walk." Leffler also says that Wetzel, "on the second or third day got into the fort, got Alexander Mitchell to go with him, and perhaps some others, to bury the dead." It is not clear what fort he means. He could have meant the old Fort Randolph at Point Pleasant, but then it is not very likely that Alexander Mitchell would have been there. I took him all the way back to Wheeling, where Mitchell would probably have been. I included Jacob on the return trip because Lewis Bonnett Jr., in his account of the affair, thought that Jacob had been along. Josh Martin and the slave, Zeke, are fictional characters.

(6) Judge John Cleves Symmes was a very important person in the history and settlement of the state of Ohio. He was appointed a judge for the Northwest Territory, along with S. H. Parsons and James M. Varnum. His daughter Anna married William Henry Harrison in 1795, so Symmes was the father-in-law of one president and the grandfather of another (Benjamin Harrison). His land purchase between the Great Miami and Little Miami rivers was originally for 1,000,000 acres but later reduced to 311,682, according to E. Wheeler-Voegelin [75, pp. 608–609]. It was called the Symmes Purchase or the Miami Purchase. Joseph Buell, in his journal [38, p. 168], states that on August 27, 1788, Symmes landed at Fort Harmar, and Buell purchased four hundred acres of land from him at fifty cents an acre. It is here that I have supposed that Lew Wetzel

may have joined him. Benjamin Stites was a friend of Symmes, who had seen the country between the branches of the Miami River in March of 1786 while with some Kentuckians from Limestone, who were pursuing Indian horse thieves. He had gone back to New Jersey and interested Symmes in making the purchase. In November of 1788, Stites, with four or five families from the Limestone area, began settlement a little ways below the mouth of the Little Miami, a town he called Columbia. This, of course, is in the area of the present city of Cincinnati, Ohio. In September of 1788, Symmes, along with a party of Kentuckians, including John Filson, explored the regions around the mouth of the Great Miami as far up as the present Montgomery County. Filson was a surveyor and early Kentucky historian. The Kentuckians were disturbed by Symmes's friendly demeanor toward the Indians and left him. Filson was killed by an Indian shortly after leaving [75, pp. 608–609].

(7) According to Wheeler-Voegelin, there was a camp of Indians, including Wyandots, in the area, and Black Fish, the Wyandots's chief, lodged in Stites's house for part of the winter of 1788–89. The story of Wetzel's visit to a Wyandot town is given by his nephew, Cyrus Wetzel, to Lyman Draper and included in his long statement recorded by Draper in the Draper Manuscripts, [Draper MSS 20S86-87]. As I mentioned above, this episode seems highly unlikely, but Cyrus says it happened. I added some details, such as the aborted night attack on Wetzel, which are my inventions. A very good discussion of these matters is given in [40, XIV, pp. 4–7]. It is not clear just when and where this incident took place. In the only other reference in the literature, George Edgington says it happened at the time of the treaty negotiations at Fort Harmar, and that Wetzel went and was gone for about a year [51, p. 11]. This seems very unlikely to me.

(8) According to Dr. Albert Bowser, who exhumed Wetzel's remains at Rosetta, Mississippi, in 1941, the remains of a suit of buckskin were found. Could this be the what was left of the gift Wetzel was given by the wife of the Wyandot chief? [40, XIV1, p. 7].

(9) Fort Finney was built in late 1785 as a place for the negotiations for what was called the Miami Treaty in January of 1786. The Indians had been promised it would be dismantled, but according to Eckert, it was garrisoned for sometime afterward but was destroyed mostly by a flood in April of 1786 [24, pp. 460, 467].

Pertinent references for this chapter: [1, p. 195], [3], [12, pp. 41, 138], [14, pp. 353–354, 363–364], [19, 2S74–75, 20S86–87], [24, pp. 457–458, 460, 467–468], [38, pp. 140–164], [41, p. 150], [50, pp. 19–20, 22–23], [51, pp. 11–12], [61, p. 139], [64, p. 55], [69, pp. 268–269, 293], [40, VI5, pp. 18–19; X2, p. 11; XIII6, pp. 6–7; XIV1, pp. 4–7], [75, pp. 608–611].

Chapter 16: George Washington

The shooting of the Indian George Washington is one of the most famous of all the incidents in the life of Lewis Wetzel, and the one for which all the written accounts are in error in some way or another. Most of the earliest accounts were based on the one given by John McDonald in his series of articles on the Wetzel family in the *Western Christian Advocate* in 1839. The usual story was that George Washington was a chief attending a peace conference, and Wetzel shot and killed him just outside the gates of Fort Harmar. Supposedly, General Harmar had Wetzel arrested and intended to hang him, but he escaped. Later he was taken by soldiers in a tavern in Limestone and transported to Fort Washington, where again Harmar, who was now at Fort Washington, put him in irons and intended to hang him. A large contingent of Kentuckians came there and threatened to attack unless Wetzel was released, which Harmar finally agreed to do.

Even respected authors of our present day continue to repeat this story, including Dale Van Every, who writes of this "assassination" by Lewis Wetzel in his 1963 book, *Ark of Empire*. William Hintzen has an excellent discussion of this episode in his *Border Wars of the Upper Ohio Valley* pages 241–58. Even Hintzen was unaware, at the time of his writing, that the shooting had actually taken place on the Tuscarawas branch of the Muskingum, some ninety miles from Fort Harmar, and that George Washington, who recovered from the shooting, probably never came to the fort at all. The story I have told is as accurate as I could make it. The attack on the Purdy family was real, although the details are purely speculation, and the Indians who made the attack unknown. I do not know that Lewis Wetzel was in pursuit of the Indians, although he had been serving as a Virginia ranger around that time, and it is not unreasonable to suppose that he might have responded. It gave me a reason to place him in the Tuscarawas region where he had the opportunity to shoot Que-shaw-sey, alias George Washington.

I have followed accounts given by Lewis Bonnett Jr., George Edgington, Henry Jolly, Major Ebenezer Denny, and official correspondence involving Harmar, Doughty, and Lee found in the *History of Maysville and Mason County* by G. Glenn Clift [11] and *Outpost on the Wabash* edited by Gayle Thornburgh [70].

(1) The attack on the Purdy family is described by Gibson Cranmer in his *History of Wheeling City and Ohio County* [12, p. 23]. He gives no exact date nor the location of the Purdy farm, although he says it was in the spring of 1789. He says that a band of five Indians broke into the house just after dark one evening, killed Mr. Purdy and the two boys, bashing out the brains of one and carrying off the two daughters. Mrs. Purdy did make it safely to Wheeling

the next morning and gave the alarm, but it was too late to catch the "murderers." The two girls remained among the Indians for ten or twelve years and were well-treated. The fight by Lew Wetzel and Veach Dickerson with Little Fox and the Indians is, of course, entirely fictional.

(2) There was an Indian town called Old Tuscarawas, located just above the point on the Tuscarawas River where it is joined by Sandy Creek today, just above the modern town of Bolivar, Ohio. In the 1780s, the Sandy actually entered the Tuscarawas a little ways below where it does now (see maps 18a, 18b in *The Tuscarawas Valley in Indian Days* by Russell Booth [6]). I do not know if Que-shaw-sey lived in the Old Town, but he lived in a village somewhere on the Tuscarawas.

(3) In his journal, Major Ebenezer Denny has this entry for June 28, 1789: "June 28, 1789, a young Delaware came in with information that George Washington was wounded by some person in ambush, on the Tuscarawas branch of the Muskingum. They are willing to lay it to Brant's people, but at the same time think the mischief done by militia from Wheeling." [15, p. 337]. This clearly contradicts the common report that the shooting was done near the gate to Fort Harmar as I mentioned above.

(4) It is not clear as to how it was learned that Lewis Wetzel was the person who shot George Washington. Lewis Bonnett Jr. says that soldiers were sent to Wheeling to apprehend him and visited both old John Wetzel's and Captain Bonnett's to find him. He says that Wetzel went downriver on a flat and when opposite Fort Harmar, he called out in defiance, much as I have described it in the text [50, pp. 21–22]. Henry Jolly says that Lewis Wetzel went to Marietta and announced his presence to General Harmar in order to "cut a high swell" [52, pp. 82–83]. George Edgington says that Wetzel went to visit his sister on the Virginia side of

the river opposite Marietta, where he made no secret of having shot an Indian [51, p. 11]. I have not found any other source which indicated that his sister was living there at that time. The sister in question would have had to be Lew's younger sister, Susannah, who married Nathaniel Goodrich in 1785, according to an entry in the vertical file in the Genealogy Section of the Shelby County Library in Shelbyville, Indiana. This same entry says that Nathaniel Goodrich enlisted in Harmar's command "to build forts at Marietta and Cincinnati, at which time he met Lewis Wetzel who took him home for a visit. He met and married Lewis's sister Susannah and stayed there after his service." If this is accurate, then the Goodrich's could have been living in the area. I have seen no evidence, however, that Lewis Wetzel was involved at Fort Harmar in 1785.

(5) Accounts vary as to how long Wetzel might have been imprisoned at Fort Harmar. In my story, he escaped the same day, which I think is probably likely. I have followed Lewis Bonnett's account in this, who claims that he is telling what Lewis Wetzel told him. He names Isaac Williams as the one who came across the river to rescue Wetzel. Other authors gave other names. Lewis Bonnett Jr. said that Wetzel showed himself again to some Indians who came across and were defeated by Wetzel. I think Lewis Bonnett Jr. was confused here because he recorded that an Indian said, "No catch that man—gun always loaded" [50, p. 24]. That phrase, which probably was never said, usually appears in the accounts of Wetzel's going to find the horse of Thomas Mills, which we covered in chapter 7 (see note 4 in this underbook on chapter 7). Henry Jolly says that Wetzel told him he was treated well by Major Doughty, and Jolly seems to be speaking of this happening at Fort Harmar. Of course, it could have been that Wetzel was speaking of Doughty's treatment of him at the Miami River location.

(6) The town of Limestone in Mason County, Kentucky (which in 1789 was still in the state of Virginia), had its name changed officially to Maysville in the summer of 1787. However, it was still often called Limestone, and Wetzel had many friends there, including Simon Kenton. Many of the accounts say that the soldiers found Wetzel in a saloon and captured him there. They may have first seen him in a tavern, as I have it in the text, but he was taken from a private home, that of John Young. This capture by soldiers of a private citizen in a private home created quite an uproar in Kentucky, to use the words of General Harmar himself in a letter to Major Hamtramck on January 13, 1790. In that letter, Harmar orders Hamtramck to place Captain McCurdy under arrest on charges brought by Mason County Lieutenant Henry Lee [70, p. 215].

(7) My account of the happenings in Limestone and later in the Cincinnati area with Major Doughty, Judge Symmes, and Henry Lee is based on the account written by Lee in a letter to David Bradford and published in the *Kentucky Gazette*, October 24, 1789 [11, pp. 86–91]. Lee says that the soldiers entered the houses of the inhabitants and insulted and abused their owners. A number of the soldiers entered the house of a certain baker, William Caldwell, where they continued behaving in a very indecent and disorderly manner until they got all the bread he had without offering any compensation. They plundered and ravaged the gardens, vine patches, and corn lots of the inhabitants and carried off a number of their farming utensils. The capture of Lewis Wetzel in the house of John Young happened much as I described it in the text. Once he had been informed of these incidents, Lee says that on August 25, accompanied by about twenty men to work the boat, he went down the Ohio to the post opposite to the mouth of the Licking River and informed Major Doughty,

who commanded the garrison, of the outrages committed at Limestone. Edna Kenton [48, p. 192] speaks of Wetzel's arrest and says that a party of two hundred men went with Lee, including Simon Kenton, but this is in error.

(8) Nathan Boone, the son of Daniel Boone, made the following statement to Dr. Draper concerning the arrest of Lewis Wetzel at Maysville (Limestone):

> I believe we went on down to Maysville, as I well recollect I was there and witnessed with my own eyes the dragging of Lewis Wetzel down the riverbank at Maysville. A party of soldiers dragged him by his long hair, tied or cued, and this was in the daytime. I also saw Lewis Wetzel at Point Pleasant, probably after this occurrence. [19, 6S173], [40, XV3, p. 11].

(9) It is often stated that Captain McCurdy took Wetzel to Fort Washington and delivered him to General Harmar, who had moved his headquarters to this new fort. In fact, Fort Washington was not yet constructed, and Harmar did not arrive there until January 1, 1790. In a letter from General Harmar to Henry Knox dated September 12, 1789, Harmar speaks of a letter from Major Doughty dated August 21, 1789. In this letter, Doughty indicates that he arrived at the Little Miami on the sixteenth, and after reconnoitering for three days from there to the Big Miami for an eligible situation to erect the works for headquarters, he had at length determined to fix upon a spot opposite the Licking River (see Alfred T. Goodman Papers, Western Reserve Historical Society History Library). Thus on August 25, there could have been no Fort Washington, although perhaps some construction might have been started by then. Cincinnati did not yet exist either, although there were some settlements near the Little Miami, and also near the Big Miami (where Judge Symmes was located). The town

that became Cincinnati was originally called Losantiville. The location of Fort Washington described above was in the downtown of modern-day Cincinnati. I suppose it is possible that soldiers were already referring to the post to be built as Fort Washington, but I have no evidence of that.

(10) McCurdy delivered Wetzel to Judge Symmes as ordered and went on to Post Vincent (modern-day Vincennes, Indiana). Following is the text of a document given by Judge Symmes to McCurdy according to a note in [70, p. 208].

Federal Territory Northwest of the Ohio River

L:S:

Whereas Lewis Weitsel charged with an assault upon and wounding and maiming of George Washington an Indian in Alliance and friendship with the United States, lately made his escape from the custody of the United States Guard at Fort Harmar, and being retaken into custody at Limestone in the District of Kentucky by Sergt John Lalor and Patrick Delany of the United States troops under the command of Capt. McCurdy, and by Capt. McCurdy this day rendered in custody to the subscriber one of the judges of the FeoderalTerritory. These are therefore to certify that the said Lewis Wietsel, charged as aforesaid at the suit of the United States, has been in due form of law and agreeable to the proclamation and process issued for his apprehension by the Honble Judge Parsons of the said Feoderal Territory delivered to the custody of the civil authority by Capt. McCurdy. Given under my hand at Northbend this 26th day of August 1789.

Signd John Cleves Symmes

The above is a true copy of the original.

John Elliot

(11) Lee's encounter with Judge Symmes happened much as I have described it. Lee says that he left at the desire of Judge Symmes so that Wetzel might be further examined as to the loss of his money. Lee says that Wetzel was afterward bailed and released. Patricia Johns [44, p. 211] says the bail amount was $500, but I have no other confirmation of that. As far as I know, nothing further was ever done in regard to this crime of Wetzel's. Henry Lee wrote to General Harmar about the conduct of Captain McCurdy's soldiers, for Harmar encloses the letter he had received from Lee in a letter to Hamtramck dated October 25. Hamtramck wrote back on December 3, 1789 saying he had looked into the matter, and that the charges of plunder against the soldiers were flatly denied. Having apparently not yet received this letter, Harmar writes on January 13, 1790 to tell Hamtramck to have Captain McCurdy arrested. He also notifies Lee in a letter dated January 23 that he had ordered the arrest of McCurdy. In another letter to Hamtramck on February 20, 1790, General Harmar acknowledges the report by Hamtramck on December 3 but says the evidence is one-sided and that McCurdy is ordered to report in the spring for a trial. He noted that Lee was determined to prosecute the matter. In a letter from Fort Washington on August 27, 1790, Harmar reports to Hamtramck that Captain McCurdy has been acquitted, and that an amount of $19 dollars and 90 cents taken from Whitzell was received and delivered to the court. It is unlikely that Wetzel ever recovered that money. These letters may be found in [70, pp. 215, 218–219, 250].

(12) The names of men involved at Fort Harmar, Limestone, and at Cincinnati are real, but in some cases, their involvement is fictional. At least three different officers have been identified as the officers who arrested Wetzel at Marietta.

> In some accounts, Lieutenant Kingsbury is asserted to have gone to Wheeling to arrest Wetzel, but that seems unlikely, although he may have gone to make the first investigation. Hartshorne (whose rank is sometimes given as sergeant or as lieutenant) was the officer who took Wetzel into Fort Harmar according to Henry Jolly [52, p. 83] while George Edgington says it was Colonel Strong who, he says, Wetzel swore to shoot if he got the chance [51, p. 11]. I chose Kingsbury since I could see no convincing evidence it was one of the others. The parts played by Sprague, Stockley, Gregg, and Burton were probably real, but I don't know that they were the players. The acts of Lawler (or Lollar), Delany, McCurdy, Doughty, and Symmes are pretty much as given in the official correspondence. The names of the sergeants sent by Doughty to Symmes are not known, so Cooper and Cain are fictional.

Pertinent references for this chapter: [1, pp. 98–104, 133–139], [6, maps 18a, 18b], [11, pp. 86–91], [12, p. 23], [14, pp. 354–359], [15, p. 337], [19, 6S173], [24, pp. 492–503, 509], [34, pp. 67–75, 82–85], [39, pp. 241–255, 359–360], [40, III3, pp. 1–12; XVI2, pp.10–11], [41, pp. 151–152], [44, pp. 203, 210–211, 219], [48, p. 192], [50, pp. 23–24], [51, p. 11], [52, pp. 82–83], [59, p. 134], [61, pp. 139–140], [64, pp. 55–58], [69, pp. 272–289], [70, pp. 207–209, 215, 250], [75, pp. 521, 608–609].

Chapter 17: Beaver Blockhouse

The events of this chapter are real. The expedition of General Harmar against the Indian villages at the confluence of the St. Mary's, St. Joseph, and Maumee Rivers at Kekionga (present-day Fort Wayne, Indiana) was a failure that revived the spirits of the Indians and made them believe they might ultimately be able to force the whites to stay on the other side of the Ohio. The attack on the Riley family took place as described, although not really much is known about the Indians who carried it out. There is almost no evidence, other than the claims made by some of the men with Brady, that any of the Indians present at Beaver blockhouse had anything at all to do with the Riley killings. There is some variation in the accounts of the Beaver incident, some saying that eight Indians were killed. I have relied on the numbers given in the court depositions by Wilson and Hillman.

There was a flurry of correspondence concerning the killing of the Indians on Beaver Creek, mostly involving secretary of war Henry Knox. Cornplanter, a Seneca chief, wrote to complain to President Washington as early as March 17, 1791, just eight days after it happened, and Knox returned a letter on March 28 with condolences, explaining that President Washington had nothing to do with it. On that same day Knox wrote to Governor Mifflin of Pennsylvania urging him to take action to punish those responsible. On the next day, he urged that the accused Virginians be extradited to Pennsylvania, an act that was called for in Article IV, Section 2 of the new US Constitution. Both the governors of Pennsylvania and Virginia were involved, charges were made against Sam Brady and others, but no arrests were made. On March 25, 1793, Brady was brought to trial in Pittsburgh after he had come in on his own accord. He was acquitted at that trial.

(1) The descriptions of the battles with Harmar's troops are mostly accurate. As with any such battles fought in that era, there are great variations in the accounts. Although Harmar claimed that his expedition had been a success, and St. Clair agreed, an unbiased view showed it was anything but a success. Official reports show a loss of 75 federal troops and 108 militia while Indian losses were 30 killed and 15 wounded [72, p. 225], [24, pp. 734–735]. Harmar had over 1,400 men with him while the Indian forces are thought to be no more than 150. There is no question that the Indians regarded the affair as a resounding victory, and their

response was to increase their raiding of white settlements and push again for an agreement, which would make the Ohio River the boundary between them and the whites. Harmar was relieved of his command, and Arthur St. Clair, the governor of the Northwest Territories, was promoted to major general and given command of the army. Eckert [24, p. 527] indicates that Harmar's fondness for alcoholic drink contributed heavily to his failure, but this does not seem to be mentioned in other accounts. Although the Indians involved with Little Fox are fictional, Little Turtle and Blue Jacket were real and very important leaders among the Indians. Allan Eckert, in his book *The Frontiersmen*, claims that Blue Jacket was a white man, named Marmaduke Van Swearingen, who was captured by the Shawnees in 1771 at age seventeen and given the name Blue Jacket [21]. This has been a controversial issue over the years and always strongly denied by the Van Swearingen family.

(2) The dates and names of army participants in the Harmar campaign are accurate. One interesting note concerns the man, George Adams, who had followed Captain Fontaine into the Maumee, was hit by five bullets [39, p. 273] and, according to Eckert [24, p. 733], carried the five balls in his body for the rest of his life.

(3) It is worth noting that St. Clair led a trouble-plagued army against the Indians in the fall of 1791, and it resulted in the greatest defeat ever suffered by an American army against the Indians. He left Fort Washington in September of 1791 with something close to two thousand men intending to build forts along the way. Thus Fort Hamilton and Fort Jefferson were built, and on November 3, the army reached the area of Fort Recovery, Ohio. (The fort was built in 1793 under orders from General Anthony Wayne). A large confederation of Indians under Little Turtle and Blue Jacket, more than one thousand strong, attacked St. Clair

the next morning and completely routed his troops. Because of desertions, troops left as garrisons, and detachments sent on other errands, St. Clair had only 1,300–1,400 men with him when attacked. Of those, 630 were killed and 283 were wounded [39, p. 284] against Indian losses of fewer than 100. Ultimately, this great defeat led to the appointment of Wayne who commanded the American army in the victory at Fallen Timbers in 1794, which essentially ended the twenty-year war between the Indians and the western settlers in Pennsylvania, Virginia, and Kentucky.

(4) The attack on the Riley family is told in the Draper Manuscripts, although I have used primarily the story as related in a master's thesis written by Scott G. Barrow at James Madison University in 2005 [2]. Eckert also gives a detailed account [24, pp. 545–546]. Ruth Riley Schemmerhorn survived her captivity and was married to a German in Canada later on. Mrs. Riley (whose first name was not given and to whom I gave the name Mary) was reunited with her husband and lived to be nearly one hundred years old. Ruth's sister Abigail (or perhaps Mary) was killed as given in the story, although the reason may have been different.

(5) The settlement where Francis Riley and his son John were working at the time the home was attacked became a town called Charleston on land owned by Charles Prather. He had named the town for himself, but in 1816, the name was changed to Wellsburg and today is the county seat of Brooke County, West Virginia.

(6) There are differences in the accounts of how Sam Brady and his rangers became involved. I have followed Barrow's account. David Shepherd implied, in a letter written to Governor Mifflin on April 21, 1791, that he had authorized the action by the rangers [19, 4E22–24]. George Edgington,

whose brother Joseph was in Brady's party, says that Brady had returned from a scout in which he had seen a large group of Indians on the Stillwater. He raised a party of men and went in pursuit but failed to find any Indians. Some proposed to return by way of Beaver blockhouse and a vote was taken whereby half of the men voted to return home with Captain Thomas Patterson. The others went with Brady to the blockhouse [51, pp. 26–27].

(7) The Beaver blockhouse was built by the US army in 1788–89 after Fort McIntosh, a prominent fort on the Ohio, a mile or two west of the mouth of the Beaver River, had been abandoned. The blockhouse stood on the north bank of a run, called Blockhouse Run, at its mouth on Beaver Creek. The location is in the present town of New Brighton, Pennsylvania, somewhere around Fifteenth Street and Route 18. There is a picture of a monument marking the site in [40, VI3, p. 10]. (I was unable to locate this monument in January of 2014.) Although it was garrisoned by army troops at various times, apparently in March of 1791, it was being used as a trading post by William Wilson.

(8) It is not completely clear whether the Brady party really believed they were still following some of the Indians who had attacked the Riley family. Eckert says that they did find some things from the Riley household at the cold camp near the headwaters of Indian Cross Creek. This would be near today's Cadiz Junction in Harrison County Ohio [24, p. 547]. In the end, they probably felt justified (and their friends and neighbors would mostly agree) in punishing whoever Indians they found at the end of their journey. All the accounts indicate that Brady had forbade the killing of any women and children. He may have hoped to capture some women in order that they might later be exchanged for the Riley girls. He was upset at the shooting of the woman by Joseph Edgington. Although it was explained as

an accident to Brady, Edgington had privately declared that it didn't matter to him, and this was reported by his own brother, George [51, p. 27].

(9) My description of the Beaver blockhouse attack and its aftermath is taken primarily from Barrow [2], although George Edgington [51, pp. 26–27] and Eckert [24, 547–553] also give many details. I believe that Barrow was following accounts given in the Draper Manuscript 12E. Also I have used information taken from the depositions of William Wilson and John Hillman given to Judge John Johnstone of Allegheney County, Pennsylvania, in April of 1791 [78] as well as a statement to Draper by Alex Wells [19, 20S124ff]. The presence of Henry Baker and the man named Shane is given in [40, VI5, p. 18]. They seem to have taken no part and are not mentioned in any other place. A discussion of the terrain and a sketch of the region is given in [40, VI3, pp. 6–10]. The names that are used in the text are names of men who were members of the Brady party. The date of March 9, 1791 is accurate, but the prior dates are guesses on my part.

(10) In his account, George Edgington stated that Lewis Wetzel had worn out his moccasins and borrowed some shoes from Francis McGuire that hindered him because they were too large [51, p. 27]. Alex Wells told a tale about an encounter with a bear and her cubs by Brady's men on their way. He said that Lew Wetzel climbed a tree and brought out three cubs that were taken to be pets. I included the story about Wetzel cutting down the tree and freeing up the flatboat. This was related by Barrow [2] and was new to me.

(11) As I mentioned at the beginning, the killing of the four Indians at the Beaver blockhouse brought a storm of protest from Indians and also whites who learned of it. The great Seneca chief, Cornplanter, along with some others, wrote a

letter on March 17, 1791 to President George Washington, complaining of the killing of good people. By March 28, Henry Knox wrote to Governor Mifflin telling him of the complaints and urging him to take action and punish those responsible. On the same day, he wrote a letter of condolence to the Seneca chiefs, explaining that President Washington was not responsible and that Brady and others would be punished. He wrote to St. Clair the next day, recommending an inquiry by the proper magistrates and calling for the extradition of the Virginians to Pennsylvania as authorized by the Constitution, Article IV, Section 2. On March 31, Knox wrote to President George Washington reporting on the actions taken and that compensation would be provided to the Indians for loss of life and property. He expressed worry about reactions from the hostile Indians [65]. William Wilson carried out his threat and reported the incident to authorities, which led to his deposition before the county judge on April 9, 1791. Hillman gave his deposition the same day [78].

(12) On April 23, 1791, Governor Mifflin wrote to Governor Beverly Randolph of Virginia asking that Sam Brady and Francis McGuire be delivered to Pennsylvania under the provisions made in the US Constitution. He included the depositions made by Wilson and Tillman. Governor Randolph replied on May 3 that he would issue a proclamation, offering a six-hundred-dollar reward for Brady and McGuire. According to Barrow, others were indicted, but these two names were the only ones mentioned in the principal correspondence. The men remained at large in Virginia. On May 19, Randolph wrote again to Mifflin, including a letter he had received from David Shepherd and indicated that the actions of the Brady party might have been justified. On January 3, 1792, Randolph rescinded his reward proclamation [2].

(13) In the spring of 1793, Brady decided that it would be good to clear his name, and he decided to give himself up. Trial was set for May 25, 1793 in Pittsburgh. According to Barrow, as many as four hundred people, some from as far away as Kentucky, accompanied Brady to Pittsburgh. Some reports indicated that the mob would have rescued Brady if he had been found guilty. One story says that a woman named Jenny Stupes, whom Brady had rescued from the Indians, was in the courtroom with a hatchet concealed under her dress. Her intention was to kill the judge if Brady were convicted. In any event, Brady had several witnesses who discredited Wilson and Hillman as traders who supplied guns to hostile Indians. An Indian chief named Guyasutha testified that the Delawares who had been killed were bad and in the habit of killing whites under the "guise of friendship." It was not surprising that Brady was found innocent [2].

Pertinent references for this chapter: [2, pp. 9–27], [19, 4E22–28, 20S124ff], [24, pp. 523–529, 545–553], [21], [40, VI3, pp.6–10, VI5, p. 18, VI6, pp. 9–11, VII3, p. 19], [65], [72, pp. 222–226], [78].

Chapter 18: New Orleans

THE CONTEST BETWEEN Wetzel and Forshay, and the travel to New Orleans followed by imprisonment of Wetzel are actual events. The account of the Forshay incident follows the description given by Josh Davis, who was an eyewitness. Although nearly everyone who has written about Wetzel agrees that he went to New Orleans and that he was imprisoned by the Spanish government, there is very little known about the details. What I have written is mostly my invention based on scraps of information from a variety of sources. The dates I have given are guesses.

(1) I have closely followed Josh Davis's account of the challenge between Michael Forshay and Lew Wetzel. This was one of three Wetzel adventures related to R. H. Taneyhill by Davis and published in 1845 in the Barnesville Enterprise. It can be found in several places, including Allman [1, pp. 182–183], Newton [61, pp. 137–138], and [40, VI5, pp. 2–3].

(2) Davis says this happened "a little before Wayne's victory," which was in August of 1794. I've put it two years earlier for my own reasons, partly because I think Wetzel went to New Orleans by 1792. (Some think that it was in 1791.) Davis also says that it was when he (Davis) made a visit to Fort Henry. This is interesting since the original Fort Henry surely did not exist at this time. A new fort, called Fort Randolph (which we have discussed earlier), had been built in a new location, but perhaps the locals continued to call it Fort Henry.

(3) Dillies Fort is not mentioned in most discussions of early forts in the region, although current maps do indicate an area called Dillies Bottom as I have described it. The ground where the contest was held is described by Davis as a place a little "west of Captain Kirkwood's old cabin." The Kirkwood blockhouse stood on the site of the present Masonic Temple at the corner of Whitley and South Lincoln in modern-day Bridgeport, Ohio [40, VI5, p. 3].

(4) Cyrus Wetzel [74, 20S98] says that "one Parker engaged Lewis Wetzel to accompany him to New Orleans on a boat load of flour—sold at the high price of $65 per barrel." This was "about the close of the old Indian war." Cyrus says that they went again in the next year, and this time he sold the flour for $45 a barrel. Note: this statement by Cyrus Wetzel to Lyman Draper has been reprinted in [40, XIV2, p. 6]. These prices seem much too high, and in the book *The New Orleans Cabildo* by Gilbert Din and John Harkins [16, p. 199], it is stated that in 1793, "clever merchants were

buying flour from royal officials at ten pesos per barrel and selling it to the bakers for twelve pesos per barrel."

(5) Lewis Wetzel made at least two trips to the New Orleans area and possibly three, as I have assumed in my story. Cyrus Wetzel has the imprisonment occur after the second trip. There is no consensus among experts about the dates or purposes of Lewis Wetzel's travels to the south. I will have more to say about this in the last chapter.

(6) The incidents in Natchez are purely fictional, although Payette may have been a real character. The same can be said about New Orleans, although the history given is accurate. The book [16] mentioned above is the source of that information.

(7) In an article in *The True Wetzelian*, Jed Fox says that according to an article written by Mike Beatty,

> [T]here are Spanish records that show that, in 1792, Manuel Gayoso de Lemos, district governor of the Spanish post in Natchez, proudly reported to Governor Carondelet, that the citizens' patrol of 30 men, headed by the Natchez tavern keeper Richard King, had apprehended one Payette (a cattle rustler) and a counterfeiter named Lewis Wetzel. [40, VI5, p. 4]

Fox goes on to say that an additional motive for the arrest may lie in Gayoso's boast that the militia had "stopped the excesses experienced from men of Kentucky who were returning to their country, stealing horses, and committing other disorders." This, of course, is a source far from primary since I have not seen the article by Beatty nor the Spanish records.

(8) Several sources agree that Wetzel spent some time with a Spanish family, although only one, the book of Allan Eckert [24], gives the name Pedro Hermoso, which I decided to

use. Although there is a hint or two in other accounts that Lewis had some kind of affair with a woman, the account in my story is my own invention. Cyrus Wetzel [74, pp. 98–99] says that Wetzel discovered the molds and ran off some dollars in pewter, which he gave to the Spaniard's daughters, not thinking there was any harm in it. When the man returned and saw this, he reported Lewis to the authorities in order to divert attention from himself.

Pertinent references for this chapter: [1, pp. 173–184], [16], [24, pp. 557–558], [39, pp. 239–240], [40, VI5, pp. 2–3; XIV2, p. 6], [41, pp. 145–146, 152–153], [50, pp. 37–38], [51, pp. 12–13], [52, p. 73], [61, pp. 137–140], [74, pp. 98–99], [77, pp. 97–98].

Chapter 19: Prison

The main subject of this chapter is the New Orleans imprisonment of Lewis Wetzel, which most likely took place in the 1790s. Once again, the information about this is very sketchy and has several variations. The main thrust of the story is based on accounts from Cyrus Wetzel, Lewis Bonnett Jr., Henry Jolly, and George Edgington. Also interspersed is the story of General Anthony Wayne's victory over the Indians at the Battle of Fallen Timbers. I have used the fictional Indians Little Fox and Red Storm to tell the story, but the descriptions concerning the build up to the battle and the battle itself are mostly accurate. A primary source for the history related to Fallen Timbers is a recent publication *Fallen Timbers, 1794* by John Winkler [80], although it is a topic in most histories of the era. This battle essentially ended the twenty-year war between the woodland Indians living in Ohio and the settlers in western Pennsylvania, western Virginia, and Kentucky. The raids and burning of settler's cabins died out after this, and except for the efforts led by Tecumseh just before and during the War of 1812, the Indian wars east of the Mississippi, and not in the deep South, were over.

The date for the battle of Fallen Timbers is accurate, as is the date for the big fire in December 1794 in New Orleans. The other dates are inventions of mine.

(1) The events involved with the fictional Indian families of Little Fox and Red Storm set in the winter of 1793–94 are inspired by an account by James Smith on his experiences as a prisoner of the Caughnawaga recorded in the book *Captured by the Indians* edited by Frederick Drimmer [20, pp. 36–40].

(2) The attack by Little Otter against the convoy of Lieutenant Lowry on August 17, 1793 is well described by Hintzen in [39, p. 291]. Wayne's movements are recorded in Hintzen's account [39, pp. 285–298] and also by Van Every [72, pp. 314–330], who includes the information about James Wilkinson.

(3) The details about the jail environment for Lewis Wetzel are my inventions. There were prison wardens named Pavano and Ruby [16, p. 110], but whether they had any interaction with Wetzel is pure speculation. The stabbing of Pedro Hermoso, which led to solitary confinement, is mentioned by Lewis Bonnett Jr. [50, p. 38] and also by Eckert [24, p. 594].

(4) The attack by the Indians on Fort Recovery occurred on June 30, 1794. The packhorseman who was captured and tied to the stump was named James Neill. He gave an account related in [59] in which he states that he saw at least twenty dead Indians plus many wounded, who were carried off by their comrades. Neill said that when they reached the Maumee, the Indians said that no men ever fought better than the men at Fort Recovery. Jonathan Alder, who was with the Indians, says that Little Turtle and Buckongehelas were for peace after this [59].

(5) As mentioned above, there are many accounts of the Battle of Fallen Timbers. Though a battle of great significance, it lasted no more than an hour, and the casualties were not terribly high. Casualty figures are often in doubt. Some thirty to forty Americans were killed and ninety to one hundred were wounded; the numbers for the Indians is largely unknown, although it is probably similar to those of the whites. As mentioned above, the book by Winkler [80] is excellent for details.

(6) Although lots of words were exchanged between the Americans and the British after the battle, both commanders were careful to do nothing that might lead to war between the two nations. The fact that the British would not open their gates to the retreating Indians effectively closed the door on British influence and dominion in the region. A good discussion of these matters may be found in [72, pp. 326–330]. The American soldiers spent two or three days burning trading posts, villages, and cornfields in the region surrounding the fort [80, p. 83].

(7) There were two big fires in New Orleans, one in 1788, which destroyed more than 800 buildings, and the one in December of 1794, which burned 212 buildings, including the royal jail. A destructive hurricane hit New Orleans in August of 1793, and two smaller ones in August of 1794. A good source of information about New Orleans, including fires, hurricanes, and personnel for the jail and the government is the book of Din and Harkins [16]. The St. Louis Cathedral was destroyed in the 1788 fire, rebuilt and dedicated in late December of 1794. It escaped the second fire with minimal damage. It was rebuilt between 1849 and 1852 and stands on the spot today. The Ursuline convent was built in 1752 and still exists today, although additions and repairs have occurred over the years. There is no evidence known to me that it was used to house the

prisoners after the fire in 1794. There was a prison ship with the name as given in the text, but I do not know whether Wetzel was kept there, although it seems likely.

(8) The efforts to free Wetzel by citizens of the upper Ohio valley are mentioned by Henry Jolly [52, p. 73] and George Edgington [51, pp. 12–13]. Lewis Bonnett Jr. agrees with Edgington that it was Bradford who ultimately won the governor over and made it possible for Wetzel to be taken out of jail much as I have described it. Edgington agrees with Bonnett that the governor was persuaded to report that Wetzel was dead, but he says Wetzel came back to Wheeling on foot up the Natchez Trace. Bonnett says he was placed on a ship to New York. Henry Jolly claims that it was the petition that was successful, but Edgington says no notice was taken of the petition. Cyrus Wetzel says that Wetzel went on a vessel to Philadelphia, that the only way the governor could release him was to fake his death [74, p. 100], [40, XIV2, p. 6]. Allman says that the person who arranged for Wetzel's release was John Minor, and that Wetzel went on a ship to New York and then home through Philadelphia [1, p. 176]. No one ever said who the governor was, but in 1798, the governor was Manuel Gayoso de Lemos. I should mention again that the dates are a guess, as is the length of imprisonment, although most of the sources indicate that Wetzel was in jail for about five years.

(9) Olive Boone, the daughter-in-law of Daniel Boone, reported to Draper that in 1804, she heard James Morrison say that some previous years, he was down the river to New Orleans and thence by sea to Philadelphia, and Lewis Wetzel was on board. Off the Florida reefs in some gale he got thrown off into the sea, probably in the night. There he remained several hours but was picked up and saved. This can be found in the Draper Manuscripts 6S173, but it is also stated in [40, XIV3, p. 11]. No one ever said what the name of the ship might have been.

Pertinent references for this chapter: [1, pp. 173–184], [14, pp. 361–362], [16], [20, pp. 36–40], [24, pp. 557–558, 583–590, 594, 604–606, 632], [39, pp. 285–298], [40, XIV2, p. 6; XIV3, pp. 11–12]], [41, pp. 152–153], [50, pp. 37–40], [51, pp. 12–13], [52, p. 73], [59], [61, p. 140], [74, p. 100], [77, pp. 97–98], [80].

Chapter 20: Only in Heaven

The material in this chapter, although mostly fictional, is based on statements given in the literature about Lewis Wetzel. The trip by sea from New Orleans to Philadelphia was mentioned in a statement of Olive Boone, the daughter-in-law of Daniel Boone, recorded in the Draper Manuscripts. She says that James Morrison told her in 1804 that several years earlier, he had been on a ship with Lewis Wetzel from New Orleans to Philadelphia, and that Wetzel had fallen overboard off the coast of Florida. Several sources say that Wetzel had returned to the south in order to kill Pedro Hermoso. Lewis Bonnett Jr. recorded the account of Wetzel going with Sam Davis and Jeremiah Kindall down the Ohio and Mississippi. The story was told by Davis himself. The encounter of Wetzel with Sam Mason was told by Cyrus Wetzel in his report to Draper. Although the Cane Ridge Revival was a well-known historical event, and my descriptions of some of the happenings there are accurate, it was highly unlikely that Lewis Wetzel attended. The final statement by Lewis Wetzel about a wife in heaven was given by De Hass. The date given for the Cane Ridge Meetings is accurate. The other dates are fictional.

(1) Shipping between Philadelphia and New Orleans was common. Information is available at the Independence Seaport Museum, J. Welles Henderson Archives and Library at Penn's Landing in Philadelphia [60]. The brig *Molly* was one of many ships involved in that trade, although there is no evidence that would indicate it is the ship taken by Morrison and Wetzel. The names of the captain and other crew members are fictional. As mentioned above, this episode is

based on the statement of Olive Boone, which was also given in the notes on chapter 19. The reference is to the Draper Manuscripts, 6S173, but it is also stated in [40, XIV3, p. 11].

(2) The timing and the details of the sea voyage are my inventions. Some accounts say that Wetzel went to New York rather than Philadelphia, and one says that he came back to Wheeling by land. Researchers at the Seaport Museum in Philadelphia tried to find logs that would list passengers on ships arriving at Philadelphia from New Orleans in those early years but were unsuccessful. As is most common in these affairs, there is no convincing evidence. I see no reason for Olive Boone's statement other than she had heard it from Morrison.

(3) Several of the accounts indicated that Wetzel returned to Natchez in order to gain revenge against the man, Pedro Hermoso, who had betrayed him to the authorities and caused his imprisonment. In the Draper Manuscripts, 11E36 is an entry in which McDonald says that the last time he saw Lewis Wetzel was in 1797 at Manchester, twelve miles above Maysville. Wetzel said he was on the way downriver to kill or damage a rascal that had done him some injury. McDonald tells of a rumor that Lewis Wetzel had killed a Spaniard and was taken, tried, condemned, and hung. It should be noted that this is John McDonald, who was responsible for many incorrect statements concerning the Wetzels. There is no hard evidence that proves whether Wetzel killed Hermoso. Lewis Bonnett Jr. says that Wetzel told him that he could never rest until he killed that Spaniard [50, p. 38].

(4) The episode with Sam Davis and Jeremiah Kindall is based on the statement of Sam Davis given by Lewis Bonnett Jr. [50, pp. 37–40]. Bonnett says that Davis seemed very confused as he related this story. I have assumed that the Indians mentioned were the Cape Girardeau Shawnees, who had come to the area led by Louis Lorimer (or

Lorimie) in the early 1780s. A reference to this migration is given in the notes at the end of chapter 4. Of course, the timing and the details are my inventions.

(5) Information about Sam Mason and the Harpes can be found in the books by Otto Rothert [66], Paul Wellman [73], and Gary Williams [77]. My description of Mason and his activities are taken from those sources. The story that Mason decided against attacking the Wetzel party is given by Cyrus Wetzel [74, p. 98] in the Draper Manuscripts and is also printed in *The True Wetzelian* vol. XIV no. 2 p. 6. This account implies that Parker was along but has it happening at another time and place, namely the Kanawha region. I could find no evidence that Mason ever spent time there.

(6) The Cane Ridge Revival was a famous event in frontier Kentucky. My descriptions of the event and some of the speakers is accurate and taken from records of the events found in two principal sources: [62, pp. 26–54] and [27, pp. 163–166]. Stephen Ruddell was present and converted to Christianity while there. This information comes from the Draper Manuscripts, 22S55. Ruddell was with the Shawnees for fourteen years and fought on their side at the Battle of Fallen Timbers. He was captured as a young boy when the Shawnees and the English under Colonel Bird captured his father's fort in 1780. He became a preacher and went with Stone and others, spending much time in Missouri. The building housing the Duncan tavern still stands in Paris, Kentucky.

(7) The Cane Ridge Meeting House is still standing on the original site. A limestone superstructure was constructed around the old building to protect it. This was completed by the Cane Ridge Preservation Project in 1957.

(8) Barton W. Stone, who was the minister at the Presbyterian Church at Cane Ridge, later was one of the principal founders of the Stone-Campbell movement that became

the Disciples of Christ, the Christian Churches and Churches of Christ. After helping to author a document in 1807 called the *The Last Will and Testament of the Springfield Presbytery*, Stone gained a large following who called themselves Christians. In the 1830s, Stone and many of his followers combined with those of Alexander Campbell to form the Disciples of Christ [58].

(9) The reply of Lewis Wetzel to the query from Mrs. Cooksis was given by De Hass [14, p. 362]. It is not clear as to how the Cooksis family was related to Wetzel. The first name of Mrs. Cooksis is not known to me, and the name Martha is my invention.

(10) There is some evidence to suggest that Lewis did go south a last time and had a cabin on the Black River. Later, he went to live with his cousin Philip Sykes who had a place on the Homochitto River near the current town of Rosetta in Wilkinson County, Mississippi. There are a variety of stories that place Wetzel in Arkansas and Texas, and in some accounts he had a wife. The most reliable information indicates that he died, possibly of yellow fever, at his cousin's place in Mississippi in 1808 and was buried there. An article by Jed Fox in [40, VI5, pp. 4–12] tells of Fox's visit to the grave site. In 1942, a physician from Chicago, Dr. Albert Bowser located Wetzel's grave and had the remains taken to the McCreary Cemetery in Marshall County, West Virginia, a mountaintop grave site a mile above the old Wetzel home [41, pp. 181–182]. A nice gravestone marks the spot today, located next to the graves of Lew's mother and his brother Martin.

Pertinent references for this chapter: [13], [14, pp. 361–362], [27, pp. 163–166], [33, pp. 86, 91–94], [40, XIV2, p. 6, XIV3, pp. 11–12, VI5, pp. 4–12], [50, pp. 37–40, 119], [58, pp. 29–30, 83–96], [60], [62, pp. 26–54], [66, pp. 157–266], [73, pp. 95–128], [77, pp. 98–107].

Bibliography

[1] Allman, C. B. *The Life and Times of Lewis Wetzel.* 2nd ed. Nappannee, Indiana: E. V. Publishing House, 1931. Heritage Books Facsimile Reprint, 2003.

[2] Scott G. Barrows. "The Firing of Guns, the Shouts of the White Men, and the Screams of the Indians Was All That Could Be Heard: Samuel Brady and the Beaver Creek Blockhouse Incident." Master's thesis, James Madison University, 2005.

[3] A Bicentennial Register of Members of the General Assembly of Virginia, published for the General Assembly of Virginia by the Virginia State Library in 1978.

[4] Blackbird, Andrew J. *History of the Ottawa and Chippewa Indians of Michigan.* Yspsilantian Job Printing House, 1887.

[5] Bodley, Temple. *George Rogers Clark, His Life and Public Services.* Boston and New York: Houghton Mifflin Company, 1926.

[6] Booth, Russell. *The Tuscarawas Valley in Indian Days, 1750–1797.* Cambridge, Ohio: Gomber House Press, 1994.

[7] Boyd, Peter. *History of Northern West Virginia Panhandle.* Topeka-Indianapolis: Historical Publishing Company, 1927.

[8] Butterfield, C. W. *History of the Girtys.* Cincinnati: Clarke & Co., 1890. Reprinted, Columbus, OH: Longs College Book Co., 1950.

[9] ———. *A Short Biography of John Leith: With a Brief Account of His Life Among the Indians.* Cincinnati: Robert Clarke and Co., 1883. A reprint of an account by Ewel Jeffries first published in 1831 with notes by Butterfield.

[10] Clark, Solomon. "Deposition." Draper Manuscripts. Wisconsin Historical Society, Madison. 9CC1–4.

[11] Clift, G. Glenn. *History of Maysville and Mason County*. Lexington, Kentucky: Transylvania Printing Co., 1936.

[12] Cranmer, Gibson. *History of Wheeling City*. Chicago: Biographical Publishing Company, 1902. Reprint by Apollo, PA: Closson Press, 1994.

[13] Dana, Richard Henry. *Two Years Before the Mast*. Boston and New York: Houghton Mifflin Company, Cambridge: Riverside Press, 1911.

[14] De Hass, Will. *History of the Early Settlement and Indian Wars of Western Virginia*. Wheeling, West Virginia: Hoblitzell, 1851. Legacy Reprint, Kessinger Publishing.

[15] Denny, Major Ebenezer. *A Military Journal, 1781–95: Notes from the Memoirs of the Historical Society of Pennsylvania, Vol. VII*. Philadelphia: J. B. Lippincott & Co., 1860.

[16] Din, Gilbert and John Harkins. *The New Orleans Cabildo*. Baton Rouge and London: Louisiana State University Press, 1996.

[17] Doddridge, Joseph. *Notes on the Settlement and Indian Wars*. 3rd ed. Edited by J. S. Ritenour and W. T. Lindsey. Parsons, West Virginia: McClain Printing, 1989. First published 1824.

[18] Downes, Randolph C. *Council Fires on the Upper Ohio*. Pennsylvania: University of Pittsburgh Press, 1940, 1968.

[19] Draper, Lyman Copeland. Draper Manuscripts. Historical Society of Wisconsin, Madison.

[20] Drimmer, Frederick, ed. *Captured by the Indians*. New York: Coward-McCann Inc., 1961. Dover edition, 1985.

[21] Eckert, Alan. *The Frontiersmen*. New York: Bantam Books, 1970.

[22] ———. *A Sorrow in Our Heart*. New York: Bantam Books, 1982.

[23] ———. *Gateway to Empire*. New York: Bantam Books, 1983.

[24] ———. *That Dark and Bloody River*. New York: Bantam Books, 1995.

[25] Fitzpatrick, Alan. *Wilderness War on the Ohio*. West Virginia: Fort Henry Publications, 2003.

[26] Flint, Timothy. *Indian Wars of the West*. Cincinnati: E. H. Flint, 1833. Reprint, Kessinger.

[27] Foster, Douglas, Paul Blowers, Anthony Dunnavant, and D. Newell Williams. *The Encyclopedia of the Stone-Campbell Movement*. Grand Rapids, Michigan: William B. Eerdmans Publishing Company, 2004.

[28] Frost, John. *Border Wars of the West*. Cincinnati: Derby, Orton & Mulligan, 1854.

[29] Galloway, William Albert. *Old Chillicothe, Shawnee and Pioneer History*. Xenia, Ohio: Buckeye Press, 1934.

[30] Green, Thomas, M. *Historic Families of Kentucky*. Cincinnati: Clearfield Publishing, 1889. Reprinted, Baltimore: Genealogical Publishing Co. Inc., 1982.

[31] Grey, Zane. *The Spirit of the Border*. New York: A. L. Burt Company, 1906. Reprinted, Philadelphia, Blakiston Co., 1944.

[32] Harmar Papers, William L. Clements Library, University of Michigan, Ann Arbor.

[33] Harper, Virginia Jones. *Time Steals Softly*. Pittsburgh: Dorrance Publishing, 1992.

[34] Hartley, Cecil. *Life and Adventures of Lewis Wetzel, the Virginia Ranger*. Philadelphia: Evans Publishing, 1859. Michigan Historical Reprint Series.

[35] Hassler, Edgar. *Old Westmoreland, A History of Western Pennsylvania During the Revolution*. Maryland: Heritage Books, 2007. Facsimile reprint of the 1900 edition.

[36] Heckewelder, John. *History, Manners, and Customs of the Indian Nations Who Once Inhabited Pennsylvania and the Neighboring States*. New York: Arno Press & New York Times, 1971. Originally published in 1818 and revised in 1876.

[37] Heckewelder, John. *A Narrative of the Mission of the United Brethren Among the Deleware and Mohegan Indians*. New York: Arno Press & New York Times, 1971. Reprint edition.

[38] Hildreth, S. P. *Pioneer History: Ohio Valley and the Early Settlement of the Northwest Territory*. Cincinatti: H. W. Derby & Company, 1848. Reprinted by New York: A. S. Barnes & Co.

[39] Hintzen, William. *The Border Wars of the Upper Ohio Valley*. Connecticut: Precision Shooting Inc., 1999.

[40] *The True Wetzelian*, Edited by William Hintzen, published bimonthly, Freetown, Indiana.

[41] Hintzen, William and Joseph Roxby. *The Heroic Age. Expanded Version*. West Virginia: William Hintzen and Taylormade Printing, 2011. This is a revision of an earlier version, Pennsylvania: Closson Press, 2000.

[42] Howe, Henry. *Historical Collections of Ohio*. 3 vols. Columbus, Ohio: Henry Howe & Son, 1891.

[43] ———. *Historical Collections of Virginia*. Charleston, South Carolina: W. R. Babcock, 1852.

[44] Jahns, Patricia. *The Violent Years, Simon Kenton and the Ohio-Kentucky Frontier*. New York: Hastings House, 1962.

[45] Kellogg, Louise. *Frontier Retreat on the Upper Ohio, 1779–1781*. Madison: Wisconsin Historical Society, 1917.

[46] Kellogg, Louise and Reuben Thwaites. *Revolution on the Upper Ohio, 1775–1777*. Madison: Wisconsin Historical Society, 1916.

[47] ———. *Frontier Defense on the Upper Ohio, 1777–1778*. Madison: Wisconsin Historical Society, 1917.

[48] Kenton, Edna. *Simon Kenton, His Life and Period, 1755–1836*. Garden City, New York: Double, Doran & Company, Inc., 1930. This reprint is part of the First American Frontier Series. Advisory editor, Dale Van Every. New York: Arno Press & the New York Times, 1971.

[49] Kinietz, W. Vernon. *The Indians of the Western Great Lakes*. Michigan: University of Michigan Press, 1940.

[50] Lobdell, Jared, ed. *Recollections of Lewis Bonnett, Jr.* Bowie, Maryland: Heritage Books, 1991.

[51] ———. *Further Materials on Lewis Wetzel and the Upper Ohio Frontier*. Westminster, Maryland: Heritage Books, 2007.

[52] ———. *Indian Warfare in Western Pennsylvania and Northwest Virginia at the Time of the American Revolution*. Bowie, Maryland: Heritage Books, 2006.

[53] Lorant, Stefan, ed. *Pittsburgh, the Story of an American City*. Garden City, New York: Doubleday and Co., 1964.

[54] Mason, Augustus Lynch. *The Romance and Tragedy of Pioneer Life, V1*. Cincinnati: Jones Brothers, 1883. Reprint, Kessinger.

[55] May, John, "Journal," *The Pennsylvania Magazine of History and Biography*, 45 (1921).

[56] McClung, John A. *Sketches of Western Adventure*. Dayton, Ohio: L. F. Claflin & Co., 1854.

[57] Meyers, R. C. V. *Life and Adventures of Lewis Wetzel*. Philadelphia: Keystone Publishing, 1889.

[58] Murch, James DeForest. *Christians Only*. Cincinnati, Ohio: Standard Publishing, 1962.

[59] Murphy, John A. *Ft. Recovery and Fallen Timbers: Letters, Journals and Anecdotes*. Pataskala, Ohio: Brockston Pub. Co., 1997.

[60] J. Welles Henderson Archives and Library, Independence Seaport Museum, directed by Sarah Newhouse, Penns Landing, 211 South Columbus Blvd and Walnut Street, Philadelphia, Pa, 19106.

[61] Newton, J. H., G. C. Nichols, A. G. Sprankle. *History of the Panhandle*. Wheeling: Caldwell Publishing, 1879.

[62] Oliver, Lon D., *A Guide to the Cane Ridge Revival*. Lexington Theological Seminary Occasional Studies, Lexington Theological Seminary, Lexington, Kentucky, 1988.

[63] O'Malley, Nancy. *A New Village Called Washington*. Maysville, Kentucky: Old Washington Inc., Kentucky Heritage Council, 1987.

[64] Powell, F. Scott. *History of Marshall County*. West Virginia: Moundsville, 1925.

[65] Provisions at Beaver Blockhouse, Papers of the War Department, 1794–1800, wardepartmentpapers.org.

[66] Rothert, Otto A. *The Outlaws of Cave-in-Rock*. Illinois: Southern Illinois University Press, 1996. Originally published, Cleveland, Ohio: A. H. Clark Co., 1924.

[67] Roxby, Joseph. *Lewis Wetzel: Separating the Man from the Myth*. Manchester, Connecticut: Precision Shooting Inc., 1998.

[68] Spooner, Walter W. *The Backswoodsmen*. Cincinnati: W. E. Dibble Co., 1883.

[69] William Suddath, Draper Manuscripts, 12CC, 82–84.

[70] Thornbrough, Gayle. *Outpost on the Wabash, 1787–1791, Letters of Brigadier General Josiah Harmar*. Indianapolis: Indiana Historical Society, 1957.

[71] Van Every, Dale. *A Company of Heroes*. New York: William Morrow and Company, 1962.

[72] Van Every, Dale. *Ark of Empire*. New York: William Morrow and Company, 1963.

[73] Wellman, Paul I. *Spawn of Evil*. New York: Modern Literary Editions Publishing Company, 1964.

[74] Cyrus Wetzel, Draper Manuscripts, 20S, 63–105.

[75] Wheeler-Voegelin, Erminie. *Indians of Ohio and Indiana Prior to 1795, Vol. II*. New York: Garland Publishing, 1974.

[76] Wiley, S. T. *History of Preston County*. Knoogwood, West Virginia: Journal Printing House, 1882.

[77] Williams, Gary S. *Spies, Scoundrels, and Rogues of the Ohio Frontier*. Baltimore, Maryland: Gateway Press, 2005.

[78] William Wilson and John Hillman, "Statements of Deposition to Court, Allegheny County, Pa. April 9, 1791," Draper Manuscripts, 4E25–27.

[79] Wingerter, Charles. *History of Greater Wheeling and Vicinity, Vol. I*. Chicago, New York: Lewis Publishing Co., 1912.

[80] Winkler, John F. *Fallen Timbers 1794*. Oxford, UK: Osprey Publishing, 2013.

[81] Withers, Alexander S. *Chronicles of Border Warfare*. New Edition. Edited by R. G. Thwaites. Cincinnati: Robert Clarke Company, 1895. Reprinted, Parsons, West Virginia: McClain Printing, 2001. Original edition, 1831.

CPSIA information can be obtained
at www.ICGtesting.com
Printed in the USA
LVOW04s0218030816
498766LV00028B/899/P